2/03 9/0 LCD 11/03
12/05 5/13 LCD 8/05
09/06 3/18 LAD 06/06 unie

D0402745

THE
MUMMY'S
RANSOM

THE
MUMMY'S
RANSOM

Fred Hunter

St. Martin's Minotaur
New York

www.minotaur.com

Library of Congress Cataloging-in-Publication Data

Hunter, Fred.
    The mummy's Ransom / Fred Hunter.—1st ed.
        p.   cm.— (The Ransom/Charters series)
    ISBN 0-312-27123-9
    1. Ransom, Jeremy (Fictitious character)—Fiction.
    2. Charters, Emily (Fictitious character)—Fiction.
    3. Women detectives—Illinois—Chicago—Fiction.
    4. Police—Illinois—Chicago—Fiction.   5. Chicago
(Ill.)—Fiction.   6. Mummies—Fiction.   I. Title.

    PS3558.U476 M86   2002
    813'.54—dc21

                                      2001048658

First Edition: February 2002

10 9 8 7 6 5 4 3 2 1

For Jan Dunham,
in honor of her thirtieth anniversary

Prologue

There was a time when Chicago police detective Jeremy Ransom had worn his emotional detachment like a badge of honor, although he wasn't consciously aware of doing so. He had learned to rely on himself fairly early in life, having lost both of his parents while he was still in college. Though he'd been an adult by legal standards, he'd still been young enough to feel prematurely cut adrift in the world. When he'd entered the police force, it had not been difficult for him do what most detectives do: erect an invisible barrier to protect himself from being soiled by the depravity with which they come in contact on a daily basis. It may even have been easier for him to build that barrier than it was for most of his colleagues. But this emotional distance had not been something that Ransom found undesirable. In fact, he'd been proud of it.

The first real dent in his armor had come in the person of a frail, elderly woman named Emily Charters, who was a key witness in one of his cases. Over the years they had developed a keen sense of mutual understanding and respect, even affection, almost like that of a proud grandparent and an appreciative grandson. His relationship with her had so transformed his life that at times it seemed that that badge of honor would never be seen again. At least, not in her presence.

*　　*　　*

"The Chinchorro mummies lived from around 7000 B.C. to about 2000 B.C. along the desert coast of Chile—" the newscaster explained as pictures of the objects in question flashed across the screen.

Ransom was seated on the couch in Emily's living room, a mug of instant coffee in his right hand. Since her open-heart surgery a few years earlier, it had become his custom to stop by every evening after work to check on her. From this had developed the routine of sharing their evening meal, and his staying for a while before going home to the neglected apartment that now served as little more than a sleeping room. Emily sat in her favorite wing chair, a cup of hot tea on the side table, as they watched the evening news.

"Do you have any interest in that?" Ransom asked as the newscaster droned on.

"In mummies?" said Emily. "Oh, yes. At my age, it gets more and more difficult to find things that are older than I am. I suppose I have to be interested in them."

"Are you going to go to the exhibit?"

"Yes," she replied with a single nod. "Lynn and I have talked about it."

Ransom smiled. That was a friendship that had come as a surprise to him, as did many things with Emily. Lynn Francis was a young woman who had also come into their lives through one of his cases. When he'd hired her to clean house for Emily during her convalescence, he'd had no way of knowing that Lynn would become another member of their rather unusual family unit.

"You're not going to the opening, though, are you?"

Emily fiddled with the lace at the collar of her pale-blue dress. "I don't think so. I think it would be too crowded. Why do you ask?"

"I just like to be prepared. The exhibit's in my area. But if you're not going to the opening, I think we can safely assume there won't be a murder there."

"Jeremy!" she exclaimed with a twinkle in her eye. "You make me sound like the Angel of Death! Do you mean to imply that my mere presence at an event is a catalyst for murder?"

He gave her a sly smile. "Don't be coy with me, Emily."

"The exhibit opens this Friday, and it is expected to draw a record number of people to Dolores Tower," the newscaster said, concluding his report.

1

MONDAY

At the corner of Dearborn and Ontario, on what had once been a street-level parking lot, there had grown a giant glass wedge roughly the shape of a steam iron. This office tower soared to a height of fifty stories, rising from the center of a three-level square that covered an entire city block. The first two levels of the square were occupied by stores so exclusive and trendy that they served more as tourist attractions than as a marketplace. This generated a turnover that was unparalleled in area malls. A casual shopper stopping into the complex once a month was unlikely to encounter the same stores twice. The third level was designed as an exhibition hall that could house anything from the smaller conventions to larger art shows, and any other event that could be designed to bring potential shoppers through the first two levels.

This was Dolores Tower, named after Louie Dolores, who had designed it and executed its construction, along with many of the other newer buildings that dotted Chicago's most important neighborhoods. Many called the tower a monument to Dolores's ego, an impression that the man himself did nothing to deter. If one stood at the point of the building and looked straight up, the gleaming structure appeared to be cleaving the sky in two. That had been the expressed intention of its designer, according to quotes attributed to him in the local papers.

Critics had been evenly divided in their opinion of the building:

half were able to set aside their dislike for the man and praise the design on its own merits; the other half were not able to put aside their personal feelings enough to be fair to someone whom many believed was destroying the integrity of Chicago's landscape.

Louie Dolores had built an empire from humble beginnings. Blessed with an abundantly confident manner, he'd been able to secure the financing necessary to start the Louie Dolores Development Company—Dolores Development, for short—even if it was originally only an office in a trailer on a construction site. The company, which at the outset consisted only of Dolores himself, was responsible for everything from the initial design of buildings through to their completion, including the monumental tasks of wading through the mountains of obstacles to obtaining necessary permits, hiring the right companies to handle all aspects of the construction, and ensuring that the projects would be brought in on time and under budget. As his empire grew, Dolores starting taking over management of properties that his company had built.

As time went on, his work became somewhat easier. He found there were fewer obstacles to getting permits once he had enough money to smooth the way with an invisible trail of well-greased palms. And as his importance as a driving force in the changing face of the city increased, he found himself less troubled by accusations of failing to meet the city's standards in regard to hiring minority companies; and accusations of payoffs to local politicians to obtain land and rights that less important builders would never be allowed; and accusations that his building sites were not the safest.

But most troubling to his critics was Dolores's habit of running roughshod over Chicago's architectural history. Any historic structure that had the misfortune to have been built on prime real estate was in danger if that plat of land became important to Dolores. It didn't matter if it was a last vestige of the city's stunning art deco or buildings designed by the most significant and influential architects of the first half of the twentieth century. Dolores didn't hesitate to tear them down. Often these buildings were razed while the Chicago Commission for Historical Preservation was in the process of mounting a legal battle to protect them. Once the buildings were destroyed, no amount of criticism or protests could restore them, and the projects of Dolores Development went ahead.

However, it wasn't Dolores's building practices that had brought the current crop of protesters to the foot of his tower.

"I can't even see them," said Bill Braverman as he pressed his forehead against the massive window and peered down toward the street.

"Of course you can't," said Dolores. "The angle's too sharp. You saw them when you came in, didn't you?"

Braverman laughed. "Hard to miss a bunch of men in grass skirts and war paint. And the leader's perfect. His costume is the best! They were chanting something. I couldn't tell what."

"It's a chant for the dead. A funeral rite."

Dolores's tone was flat. Braverman had been with him for ten years now and still knew nothing of Chilean culture, although how he could've been expected to recognize a funeral rite is something Dolores himself couldn't have rationally explained. But it seemed to him that his personal assistant had successfully maintained a near-complete ignorance of his employer's heritage. Almost defiantly so. It was just another in what Dolores was beginning to view as his assistant's deficiencies.

"A chant for the dead?" said Braverman, turning away from the window. He pretended not to have noticed Dolores's tone, but it hadn't been lost on him. "That's fitting, isn't it?"

"Not in this case. It's for the recently departed."

The offices of the development company had relocated to the penthouse suite of Dolores Tower when the building had opened two years earlier. Dolores's office had windows facing north and east, giving him a panoramic view of the lake that was virtually unobstructed except for a few lesser towers. Far from the ultramodern furnishings one might have expected, the office was decorated like a den: the walls were Navajo white, the plush carpet a dark tan, and the furniture solid mahogany. A round coffee table and comfortable sling-back chairs were in the corner where the windows met. The west wall was taken up by a long credenza in which the blueprints for the company's many projects were stored, and over it hung several enlarged photos of Southwestern rock formations in deep reds and or-

5

anges. On the south wall, directly to the right of the door to the office, was a fully stocked wet bar, and next to it an entertainment center with a black-leather couch facing it. The office was even equipped with a full bath, complete with a glass-enclosed shower stall and gold-plated fixtures.

Louie Dolores sat behind the desk, his elbows resting on its top and his hands clasped together. His coarse black hair was cut short and parted on the left, his nails neatly manicured. In his dark Italian suit, he looked more like a lawyer than a builder.

"Do you want me to call the police?" Bill asked as he took a seat opposite his boss.

"Of course not. They're attracting enough attention without police intervention."

Bill sighed. "You know, you don't need the publicity."

Dolores's black eyes remained impassively leveled at him. "I didn't say I did. But the publicity will be good for the show. It doesn't matter how many ads I take out, or how may puff pieces they do on the news. There's nothing like a protest to get up public interest."

"They certainly look nutty enough to draw public notice."

Dolores smiled. "The nuttier the better. Makes it more likely we'll get camera crews out here. Especially after they hear about this."

He reached into the center drawer of his desk and pulled out a single sheet of soiled paper, which he tossed across the desk. Braverman picked it up and read it:

YOU DESECRATE, YOU DIE

The words "you" and "die" had been cut out whole from a magazine, and the word "desecrate" had been assembled letter by letter, apparently from the same source.

"Where did you get this?" Braverman asked, pushing the paper back across the desk.

"I found it on my windshield last night."

Braverman looked up. "Your windshield? Here? That means someone got into the garage."

"Yes."

"So you want me to call the police now, right?"

"No, Bill," Dolores said with the measured impatience of someone tired of repeating what his listener should already know, "I want you to call Channel 5."

"Everything's in place," said Ross Lipman, head of security for the tower. Lipman was a short, slender man with very white skin and a thin, black mustache. "We've been working on the space for weeks. We just finished it up this morning."

"This building . . . this hall . . . they are secure?" Hector Gonzalez asked doubtfully as they rode the escalator up to the third-floor exhibition hall.

"Christ, yeah! It's tight as a drum. I see to that. Christ himself couldn't get in here without passing through security. Not even for the Second Coming!"

"I see." Gonzalez didn't smile. In fact, he hadn't smiled once in the six months since the museum had agreed to put the bulk of its valuable collection out on loan. Actually, "on loan" wasn't exactly the term he would have used for this enterprise. What was happening was far from that.

At the top of the escalator there was a broad lobby with deep-red carpeting like one might find in a large, elegant theater. Across the lobby was a convex glass wall, behind which a heavy curtain masked the interior.

"As you can see," Lipman explained, "there are four doors, but only two'll be used for the exhibition: one for the entrance and one for the exit. Inside, visitors will follow their way through this long winding-like hallway, with bits of the exhibit set up here and there. You'll be really impressed, I think. Mr. Dolores designed it himself."

"Yes. I saw the plans."

"It looks just like one of those tombs."

"You mean an Egyptian tomb?" Gonzalez said with resigned disapproval. This was exactly what he'd been afraid of when he'd seen the designs. "They weren't found in tombs. They were in common graves."

Lipman stopped before reaching the center door. "Huh?"

"Common graves. Piled one on top of the other."

1

Lipman wrinkled his nose. "Well . . . well, we can't display 'em like that, now, can we? In a big heap!"

"No, we couldn't." Gonzalez realized it would be worthless to try to explain why they shouldn't be displayed as if they were in an Egyptian tomb, either.

"Hi, Al," Lipman said to the large man in a blue uniform who stood guarding the entrance.

"Mr. Lipman," Al returned, snapping a salute. He grabbed the handle and pulled the door open for them.

"This is Dr. Gonzalez," Lipman said. "From the Archaeological Museum of Chile. He should be allowed in and out without any problem, anytime he wants. Got it?"

"Got it. He got a badge?"

"Oh, yes, yes," Gonzalez said, patting his pockets. "I'm sorry. I stuck it in my pocket. I wasn't thinking."

"That's okay, sir," Al said jovially, "since you're here with Mr. Lipman. But you should wear it at all times, so none of the security people will stop you."

"Yes, yes, I'm sorry." He plunged his hand into his right pants pocket and his face relaxed when his fingers touched the smooth plastic cover. He scratched a finger slightly on the clothespin-like metal clip as he pulled the badge out, and turned a confused frown to Lipman. "Where should I wear it?"

Lipman patted his own tag, clipped to his breast pocket.

"Oh, of course." As Gonzalez affixed the badge, he turned to Al. "Thank you, young man."

"That's all right, sir. Just trying to save you some trouble."

"Let's go in," said Lipman. He led the way through the door and into a narrow, low-ceilinged hallway. The lighting, subdued to a predawn glow, was so well disguised it seemed to radiate from the arched ceiling, and music emanated eerily from hidden speakers. The music was a combination of rattles, drums, and wooden flutes, reverently muted. The walls and ceiling were a very light tan, and finely textured. Gonzalez reached out and touched the nearest wall.

"Sand?"

"Yes, sir," Lipman replied. "Mr. Dolores thought of everything."

"So it seems."

They continued down the hallway. At intervals on the walls there were plaques next to empty brackets on which the photos and artists' renderings would be hung. At farther intervals the walls opened into large chambers where the real attractions would be displayed.

Attractions, thought Gonzalez with a silent "humph." *That they would ever be thought of as attractions!*

"This is the first of the display areas," said Lipman as they came to a bend in the hallway. What had looked like a slight recess from a distance gave way to a chamber large enough for several display cases and the expected crowd.

"There seems to be room enough," Gonzalez said, "but the hallway is too narrow for the housings in which the mummies are being transported."

"Not to worry." Lipman went to the back wall. "This looks solid, but it's just latched shut on the back, you see. This whole wall pulls out and the cases will be brought right up into place and dropped."

"What?" Gonzalez exclaimed in horror.

Lipman was confused for a moment, then realized what had caused the older man's reaction. "Sorry. That's a figure of speech. 'Course, everybody's gonna be extra careful with them."

"Those mummies, young man, were here before the Christ, whose name you bandy about so freely! And once they were exposed to air and . . . everything else . . . they are deteriorating. Do you understand? The slightest trauma to them causes further deterioration."

Lipman's cheeks reddened, and he spoke as if surprised to discover he was dealing with some sort of fanatic who had to be placated. "I understand, Doc, I understand. Really, it was just a figure of speech."

After a long pause, Gonzalez sighed wearily. He'd been shocked into this outburst. Now that he'd made it, he didn't know why he'd bothered.

"Let's move on," he said.

Although the Egyptian influence of the tomblike hallway was unmistakable, Gonzalez couldn't deny that the plan for the exhibit was well-thought-out. The artifacts were going to be arranged along the time line that radiocarbon dating had proven, from the most recent

9

to the earliest. It would give even the most emotionally dead visitors the feeling of descending back in time.

Emotionally dead, Gonzalez thought with another humph.

"Beg pardon?" said Lipman.

"Nothing."

When they passed the last of the display areas, the hallway narrowed further before opening into the exit. It was something of a shock to come back into the bright light of the lobby. Gonzalez also found it disquieting when he realized they had come out of the door only twenty feet to the right of where Al stood guarding the entrance.

Gonzalez turned to Lipman. "It doesn't seem possible."

"What?"

"Even though I saw Mr. Dolores's design beforehand, and I knew it was circular, I wasn't aware of turning back so much that we would end up so close to the entrance."

Lipman smiled. "Oh! That! Yeah. There's a turn after each one of those little room things."

"Of course," Gonzalez said. Now that he thought back, he felt foolish for not noticing. It was like a series of boomerangs, sometimes arced, sometimes S-shaped, with the chambers at the center of the turns. From each chamber you could see back the way you'd come and forward into the next hall, but you couldn't see from one hall to the next.

"Very clever," he said without emotion.

"It meets with your approval, doesn't it?" Lipman asked.

As much as any of this could, he thought. "Yes. What are those?" He pointed to one of the long glass counters located at either end of the lobby.

"Those? Concession stands, of course."

Gonzalez turned his sad brown eyes on the head of security. "Faces of the dead on T-shirts?"

Lipman nodded happily. "And key chains. And little statues. Coloring books. Stuff like that. People love that sort of thing."

"Tell me, Mr. Lipman," Gonzalez said after a pause, "did you see those people protesting out on the street?"

"The nuts? Sure did!"

"It would seem not everyone loves that sort of thing."

Lipman's face went blank. "Huh? You're not worried about them pulling something, are you? Don't you worry about anything. They won't get in here!"

"They don't worry me. They interest me."

Across from the foot of Dolores Tower, on Dearborn Street, the protesters were carrying out their demonstration against Dolores Development's pending exhibition. They were a tiny band—six men and one woman—dwarfed into minuscule Davids by the gigantic Goliath looming over them. Each of them had dark caramel skin and were clad in grass skirts, or rather, panels of grass that hung down from their waists and the smalls of their backs, leaving their sides exposed. The woman had a pigment-dyed length of gauze wrapped across her breasts and tied behind her back. Each of them had long black hair hanging loosely to their shoulders, and their faces were hidden by masks. These masks had been cut from heavy cardboard and painted with a thick, dark gray paint. There were holes cut out for the eyes and mouths.

Two of the men kept a rhythmic beat on crude drums, while the woman rattled a bunch of shells that had been lashed together. The other three men stood stoically in the background holding long, thin harpoons with sharp stone points. The leader of the protesters was the tallest of the group, and the only one dressed differently. He wore the same gray mask, but his hair was somewhat wild and streamed up and out from behind the mask. His torso was wrapped in strips of gauze, with his legs and arms wrapped separately to allow him free movement. He stayed a few steps forward from the others, performing a slow dance while he chanted. It was an imposing, incongruous, and somewhat horrific sight.

This little band was a sharp contrast to the many passersby, most of whom were clad in proper business attire and paid the protesters as much notice as busy schedules would allow. But the protesters had the full attention of three camera crews from local television stations who filmed in silence, waiting until there was a break in the performance—or until their reporters got too bored to wait any longer before asking their questions. However, the protesters were savvy enough to avoid trying the patience of the media. Once they were fairly certain there were no more crews to come, the dance was brought to a close and the music faded out.

"Could I speak to you on-camera?" Robert Griswald asked quickly, edging out two colleagues. They would have to wait their turns.

The musicians fell back and the leader came forward.

"Can I have your name?" Griswald asked as his cameraman swept over to one side.

"Names are not important," said the leader, his voice a low rumble.

"Fine. I'm going to ask you a few questions. The shorter your answers, the more of them you'll get on the air. You understand?"

"I understand your words."

"Fine." He turned and gave a nod to the cameraman, who adjusted the camera on his shoulder and turned it on. "This'll be on tape, and it will be edited. Just so you know. Okay! That's a very interesting costume. What are you supposed to be?"

"I represent a bandage mummy, just one of the types of mummies that have been taken from our land and are being brought to this place to be exploited."

"You and your people are protesting the exhibition of the Chinchorro mummies that will be opening on Friday at Dolores Tower. You want to tell our viewers why?"

"The Chinchorro mummies are our ancient dead. Their graves were desecrated—"

"By your own people," Griswald interrupted.

"By building crews. Accidentally. But once they were discovered, they should've been allowed to remain at rest."

"But that happened back in the early eighties, didn't it? Why protest now?"

"It's bad enough that the remains were moved by archaeologists then, instead of being allowed to remain in their graves. And worse, that they were put on display in museums. But to transport them— to put them on display like a traveling sideshow—this is sacrilege. This never should've been allowed. They should be returned to their graves."

12

"Isn't there a city over their graves now?" Griswald hadn't really had to do much homework on this. He'd already done a report a week earlier on the coming exhibit, and the background had been conveniently provided by the Dolores Company.

"Yes. Arica."

"Is that where you're from?"

The large man hesitated. "I am Chilean."

Griswald smiled. "So, if there's a city built over their graves, it would be pretty hard to return the mummies to them, wouldn't it?"

"They still could be laid to rest. The dead should stay in their graves."

Hector Gonzalez stood waiting in the operator's booth of the underground loading dock. On his face was a sheen of perspiration despite the booth's comfortable air conditioning. Ralph Winters, the head of receiving, had offered him a seat when Ross Lipman brought him down, but Gonzalez preferred to stand. Not out of nervousness: he had, from the beginning, resigned himself to the belief that this enterprise would end in disaster, so he entertained no latent worries about it. If anything, he harbored a sense of anxiety for whatever was going to happen to be over, like someone who knows he is going to be buried alive and longs for the lid to be nailed down on the coffin so he can suffocate in peace.

He stood motionless in the booth for nearly three quarters of an hour, which did nothing for Winters's composure, before the first of the semitrailers arrived. The cab came into view on one of the monitors on Winters's panel. Gonzalez watched the screen as the door of the cab popped open and the driver climbed down, went to an intercom by the massive gate that protected the entrance to the dock, and held a brief conversation with Winters.

"All right," Winters concluded as he flipped a switch on the panel. "Come on down."

The driver walked back to his truck as the gate began to clatter upward. Winters sat back in his swivel chair and sighed, then looked over his shoulder at Gonzalez. "It's gonna take him a little bit to maneuver his truck down here. He has to back in."

"He's doing this himself?"

"Uh-uh. Mr. Dolores has some of our security people out there to direct him. There isn't any trouble with traffic this morning, 'cause Mr. Dolores got the city to shut down this block of Dearborn for the duration while the trucks arrive. That driver says they're all lined up behind him."

"Mr. Dolores must be a very powerful man," Gonzalez said colorlessly.

"Oh, yeah."

Gonzalez watched the monitor silently as the driver went through the laborious process of positioning the truck to be backed up onto the ramp to the loading dock, first pulling forward to the left, then reversing with a hard right. He repeated this several times before he was correctly in place. Although Gonzalez tried to remain impassive, he felt his heart skip as the truck made its final turn to the right, its rear end barely missing the wall of the entry as it swung onto the ramp. The perspiration on his forehead began to bead.

The attention of the two men was drawn away from the monitor to the ramp itself as the truck descended into view. Gonzalez grimaced as the rear wheels met the flat surface of the floor with a slight bounce that sent a noticeable vibration through the trailer.

"I was told you'll supervise," said Winters.

"That's correct."

They left the booth and went out onto the dock as a security guard in a tan uniform directed the driver in his approach. The guard waved him back, keeping his eyes on the lower back end of the truck, then whistled through his teeth and turned his palms up. The driver wasn't quite quick enough, though, and the truck didn't stop before coming into contact with the rubber bumper on the edge of the dock with a loud thud.

"God in heaven!" Gonzalez exclaimed toward the reflection in the driver's side-view mirror. "What is the matter with you? Don't you know the value of the treasures you're carrying?"

"Sorry," the driver called out dully.

"Sorry! And when our past has come to dust, I suppose you'll weep for us!"

The driver stared back at him in the mirror. Gonzalez checked himself. He was in the middle of a nightmare that could only be made worse by his resistance.

"Doctor! Please be calm. It should be all right!" The woman's voice echoed off the painted concrete walls in a way that made it sound as if it was originating from another dimension.

"Lisa?" Gonzalez called.

The passenger door of the cab opened, and the crew that had assembled to do the unloading craned their necks as a dark, shapely leg capped in a suede boot slid out onto the cab's high step. The rest of the woman was equally impressive as she emerged and jumped down to the floor. Her sleek black hair was pulled back tightly and tied at the nape of her neck, giving a severity to her flat, oval face. She wore a navy jumpsuit with a gold chain for a belt. She flung the door of the cab shut and then sauntered over to the dock.

"Really, Doctor, it should be all right." She raised her arms straight up, crooking a smile at two of the crew, who took their cue. They each grabbed an arm and hoisted her up to the dock.

"Thank you," she said over her shoulder as she went to Gonzalez.

"Mr. Winters, this is Lisa Rivera, my assistant," Gonzalez explained. "Lisa, this is Mr. Winters. He's in charge of . . ."

"Receiving," Winters said as he took the young woman's hand.

"Pleased to meet you," Rivera said, her amber eyes boring into him. She allowed her hand to be shaken for a moment, then withdrew it. She turned to Gonzalez. "As I explained, each of the displays is being held by an apparatus designed much on the order of the Steadycam, so that even if the truck is jolted, the cases themselves will suffer minimum, if any, movement."

"A minimum of movement can cause a maximum of damage!"

"Yes, I know, Doctor." She'd heard it all before, many times. She turned to Winters. "These are the men who will do the unloading?"

"Uh-huh."

"Good. Let's get underway. Carefully. Doctor?"

Gonzalez was staring at the back of the truck as if in a trance.

"Doctor?" Rivera said again.

"I was wondering, Lisa, if you would mind very much supervising the unloading yourself."

"Not at all," Rivera replied after a slight pause. "I'd be happy to. Gentlemen?"

She led the crew to the back of the truck. One of the men unlocked the door and rolled it up, revealing a mass of steel machinery in which carefully padded cases were suspended.

"If this stuff is as valuable as you say," Winters said to Gonzalez, "I'd think you'd want to oversee it. Matter of fact, I'm surprised you didn't ride with it from the airport."

Gonzalez shook his head slowly. "Every bump in the road would've been like tearing my flesh."

Winters gave him a confused frown. "Uh-huh."

"I cannot watch this. I'll be waiting upstairs. Up in the exhibit. Someone will show Miss Rivera the way?"

"Sure. Of course. This is gonna take a while, though."

Winters watched Gonzalez as he turned on his heel and quickly walked away, looking like a man who has suddenly discovered he's going to be ill. Gonzalez disappeared through a door in the east wall leading to a staircase up to the first level.

The process of backing each of the five trucks up to the loading dock one by one and emptying their contents took well over two hours, with all of the treasures remaining on the dock until the last truck was empty. Winters suggested that half of the crew could begin taking things up after the first truck had pulled away, but Lisa Rivera insisted that no items be moved unless she was present. Although Rivera was perfectly confident in the machinery that Dolores Development had provided for the safe transport of the treasures, she still felt that the actual movement of each item should be done under her watchful eye. Once all the trucks were empty, one by one the crew rolled the steel apparatuses, their dead cargoes suspended in eerie stillness in their centers, onto the freight elevator.

While the unloading was taking place, Louie Dolores was having a meeting in his office.

"So, Alderman Nathanson, there is a problem?" Dolores sat back in his leather chair, elbows on the arms, fingers pressed together.

The man sitting across from him was short and rather stout, and had adopted the unfortunate habit of trying to disguise his growing baldness with a comb-over, making his lack of hair all the more evident. "I thought we were on a first-name basis," the alderman said, shifting in his seat uncomfortably.

"All right then, Daniel," Dolores said with a smooth smile.

"Louie, the problem is the same as it's been from the start. I told you that when you first brought up the idea of razing the Stone Candy Factory. I've been floating the idea among the aldermen carefully, just asking around if anybody thinks the factory is a detriment to the district. Feeling people out to see what they think. There's a lot of resistance to it. In fact, there's nothing but resistance to it."

"It's not as if we haven't faced opposition before."

"This is different. I don't know that there would ordinarily be a lot of love lost over the Stone Candy Factory. Personally, I think it's an eyesore and I'd be glad to have it out of my district, but . . . people don't mention you by name, but they keep bringing up the Harrison project. There's still a lot of animosity toward you over that."

"That was almost four years ago."

"People don't have memories as short as you think they do. Especially when the Historical Commission is there to keep reminding them. You demolished that building before a decision was made about its historical-landmark status. Do you think the commission is going to let anyone forget that?"

"They don't mean shit to me," Dolores said, keeping his voice even.

"But they will. From what I've heard, they've been lying in wait for you, waiting for the next time you want to take down another building. It doesn't matter what it is, they're going to fight you with everything they have. And they might just win. There're enough bad feelings going around that the nature of the project might not matter, the whole thing will become an opportunity to take you down a peg."

"Which is why we should move as quickly as possible," Dolores said calmly, "so I can get that building down before anyone, especially the Historical Commission, knows what hit them."

"You have to *get* the building before you can raze it. And I . . . I don't know that I see that happening. Have you tried to buy it?"

Dolores nodded. "Through an intermediary, yes. Jeremiah Stone doesn't want to sell. He says they've been there fifty years and he doesn't want to move."

"Louie," Nathanson said with an exasperated sigh, "you see? This is what I mean! They don't want to move, so you want to leverage them out somehow, and that's just going to bring everybody down on you!"

"Not if they don't know that I'm doing it. And I'm already working to repair my image with that historical lot. Why do you think I brought this exhibit here? I could've just financed it being put up at the Field Museum, but I wanted it here, in my building, attached to my name, so all those people who say I have no respect for history would be forced to eat their words."

"You've had a regular band of protesters out there claiming that bringing the mummies here is just another example of your disrespect for history."

Dolores smiled. "No, what they've given me is the opportunity to voice my side of the story. To get my word out there. That's what usually happens with protests."

Nathanson looked down at his lap and sighed heavily, then looked up again. "I don't know how to tell you this, Louie, but those people who you're trying to get to eat their words, they're not stupid."

"We're getting off the track here," Dolores said with some impatience. "The Stone Candy Factory is sitting on a valuable tract of land. It's prime for development. In case you haven't kept up on what's been going on in your district, Alderman, west Grand Avenue has been redeveloped. There are luxury condominiums and lofts all around that factory. I would think you could see how valuable the land is that it's taking up. It's in everyone's best interest to get it out!"

"It's not going to be that easy," said Nathanson. He knew whose best interest the matter was really in, as well as who had built all of those luxury buildings. "Why do you need the city's support, anyway?"

"You know why. For one thing, once I get it, the block is going to have to be rezoned in order for me to build residences there. That'll take support."

18

"There is too much opposition," Nathanson said, shaking his head. "Maybe you should wait . . ."

"Wait? Wait for what? Wait until the Historical Commission gets wind of what I'm planning? Wait for them to start proceedings to declare the place an historic landmark? I suppose they could even try that with a factory. They've done it with everything else. Well, not on your life! There's too much money at stake! The time to move is now."

"Well . . . what do you expect me to do?"

"I expect you to do everything in your power to make it difficult if not impossible for that factory to remain where it is. Given the type of upscale buildings that have been erected around it, don't you think the property taxes of the factory should be reassessed? Drastically. After all, the property is worth far more than it was before."

"I don't have anything to do with—"

"And I understand there have been complaints about the stench coming from the factory."

"What? You mean the smell of chocolate? I don't think many people complain about that!"

"I've been in the area. It reeks. Perhaps the city should start fining them for noncompliance with city regulations . . . or something like that."

Nathanson's mouth dropped open, not in surprise, but in dismay. He had seen this coming, and he was afraid of what was about to happen. "I can't do that."

"Can't?" Dolores replied, manufacturing surprise.

Nathanson shook his head. "Louie, that factory may not be historic, but the Stone Candy Company has been a fixture in Chicago for half a century! People love it! Especially since Fields sent their candy manufacturing out of the city. If I made any move . . . if the city made any move to do the things you suggest, we'd most likely be driving them out of town. Do you have any idea what kind of furor that would cause? Especially since the real reason for it—even if nobody *knows* you're the one after that land—is going to be obvious to a blind man! People will know you're behind it. They know you built the condos. Nobody in the city council or anywhere else in the city government is going to swing to this!"

Dolores flexed his fingers together. "Hmm. How much do you think it would cost for you to be able to get them to 'swing to this'?" There was a tinge of disgust in his tone, as if he felt that loyalty that had already been paid for shouldn't require another installment.

Nathanson went red in the face. "It's not a matter of that!"

"It wouldn't be the first time."

"I'm not angling for money!" the alderman said angrily. "I just really don't think it can be done."

"I think it can."

Nathanson stared into that stoic face, reading what was there with a sinking feeling. "Why should I throw away my career supporting you in a plan that I think will fail?"

Dolores shrugged. "It is better, is it not, to risk facing rumors than it would be to lose everything facing the truth."

"Meaning what?" Nathanson said after a shocked pause.

"Meaning that if you refuse to help me, you give me no alternative but to go to the district attorney's office about the matter of your asking for payoffs."

Nathanson leaped off his chair. "What!"

"I'll simply inform the DA that you have just asked for a payoff . . . again."

"I've never asked you for a payoff! Never!"

Dolores stared at him without replying, willing him into backing down.

Nathanson continued haltingly. "I mean, you offered . . . money before . . . for my campaign . . . and God forgive me, I took it. But that was a campaign contribution!"

"I have been accused of bribing public officials in the past," Dolores said, his composure completely unshaken. "In the Harrison business you referred to earlier, for example. Along with Bill Braverman. I very successfully convinced the grand jury that I had only made an innocent contribution to your campaign. I was fully willing to go no farther, to not implicate anyone, as long as things were running smoothly. But I could very easily turn that case to my advantage. I could go to the DA and tell him that that was really a payoff."

"You'd be implicating yourself!"

Dolores shook his head slowly. "Not if I convince them that you gave me no choice. Not if I tell him that you demanded the contribution in return for your support . . . and your silence. I have Bill to back me up. Even if you don't go to jail, you certainly wouldn't—what's the saying? You wouldn't get elected dogcatcher in this town again."

"You couldn't do that!" Nathanson said with disbelief.

Dolores put his knuckles to the top of the desk and raised himself up so that he was eye level with the alderman. "You know better."

Hector Gonzalez waited for Lisa Rivera on one of the stone benches in the middle of the exhibit, his back against the wall and his eyes closed. He sat listening to the repeating loop of pseudo-Chinchorro funeral music.

At the age of sixty-one, Gonzalez had been through many crises of conscience as curator of the Archaeological Museum of Chile, some of them over difficult decisions it had been his lot to make, but more frequently over decisions that had been foisted upon him by the museum's board of directors that he had then been forced to carry out. But none had been more difficult for him to accept than the current one that had plagued his soul and brought him to this place. In the months since the decision had been made, a constant dialogue ran through his head: a one-sided argument that had many voices, all of them accusatory. It was as if the spirits of the dead were beleaguering him, urging him on to finally take action. His only answer to the cacophony was that he was too old. The vivid streaks of gray through his black hair should've told his accusers that much. But one of the voices invariably replied that perhaps the museum's directors would eventually look to replace him with someone who would not be so troublesome when it came to carrying out their commands. Even that had not been enough to spur him to action. But this—having to sit by as these precious icons of the past were shipped thousands of miles, an act that was sure to damage them further—could this be the last straw? The weariness in his bones was telling him that it was.

The music faded out as it came to the end of its loop. In a few seconds, it would begin again. The momentary silence was welcome and refreshing. He let his head rest back against the wall and sighed deeply.

Then his eyes opened. He had heard something: a noise in the distance from down the hallway, like the faint sound of rustling leaves. It was about two hundred feet to the next chamber and the turn that put the subsequent hallway out of sight. Out of the corner of his eye before he could turn his head, he thought he saw something disappearing around that far corner. It was just a hint of something approximately the color of wheat. The sound disappeared along with the impression.

Confused for a moment, Gonzalez considered what he should do. Nobody was supposed to be in the exhibit yet, and surely if that had been one of the crew or security team, they wouldn't have needed to flee, for that was indeed what the apparition seemed to be doing. Gonzalez considered going back down the hallway to the entrance to alert the guard to what he'd seen, but he knew that if the guard was there, he would've seen anyone entering or leaving the exhibit. Then again, whoever it was, had managed to get past without being noticed, presumably while Gonzalez had his eyes closed.

For a moment, Gonzalez had the disquieting feeling that he'd fallen asleep without realizing it. He shook himself, and decided that he would simply go down the hallway and see if anyone was there— and what they were up to—before going out and making a fool of himself in front of the guard.

He got up and absently brushed the back of his pants with his hand as he went down the hallway. He reached the chamber just in time to catch a fleeting glimpse of a gauze-covered hand and a flurry of shreds of fabric disappear around the corner at the far end of the next hallway. The music had resumed, underscoring the scene with a ghostly dirge.

Gonzalez hurried down the hall to the next chamber, and when he looked down the hallway, he saw nothing. It was not just as if the apparition had made it around the corner before Gonzalez could catch sight of it again, but as if it had completely vanished. Gonzalez could not sense movement ahead of him.

Despite his education, the belief in spirits that was his heritage was something he had not been entirely able to shake. Indeed, at the museum, he often felt as if the dead shells on display retained something of the spirit of their former lives. He stood for a moment staring blankly down the hallway, the invisible barrier of generations of superstition holding him in place. Finally, shaking his head with disgust at his own trepidation, he continued down the hall. After two more turns, he was in the long, narrowing passage. He went down it and out into the lobby. Al, the guard, was standing in front of the entrance to the left.

"Did someone just come out of here?" Gonzalez asked.

"Yeah. You," Al replied with a grin.

Gonzalez reddened. "Before me. Did someone come out just before me?"

"Nope. Nobody."

"Are you sure? You didn't let anyone else go into the exhibit?"

"Nobody but you. Something wrong, Doc?"

"And you've been here the whole time . . . you haven't gone away from the entrance for anything?"

"I took a break a while back, but my relief was on the door then. Door's always guarded," Al replied with increased concern. "What is it, Doc? Something wrong in there?"

For a second, Gonzalez debated with himself about whether or not to tell the guard what he'd seen. What he *thought* he'd seen. After all, this exhibit was priceless, and anything out of the ordinary should be reported. But then, what had he really seen? A hand out of the corner of his eye? A wisp of something?

"Doc?" Al repeated.

"No, no, nothing's wrong." He manufactured a sheepish smile. "I have been waiting a long time. I fell asleep. I think I had a bad dream."

Al smiled. "Doesn't surprise me. Sitting in that tomb thing, waiting for a bunch of mummies to get here. That'd spook anybody!"

"Yes, I suppose it would."

Gonzalez hesitated for a moment, then wandered back into the exhibit. Of course it had been a dream. Or his imagination, even though he'd never thought of himself as an imaginative person, despite his thoughts about spirits.

He kept coming back to spirits. Perhaps the spirits of the dead had been trying to play on his conscience, pressing him to finally take action.

By the time the first mummy was brought up in the freight elevator, Gonzalez had come to a decision.

2

Anna Braverman was the daughter of a strong-willed woman. Her mother, Barbara Tapley, had never been content to be what she termed a "corporate wife," defined as a woman whose usefulness ends at serving coffee. Barbara had been party to the first divorce in the unblemished marital line of the Tapley family, and thereafter was roundly snubbed by them for having committed this disgrace. However, since she had already been trying to devise a judicious way to sever all ties to the family, whose attitudes she believed were holding her back, she was more than happy to have those bonds cut for her. She had then done what she'd intended to do before becoming involved in a stifling marriage: she donned a sleek gray business suit and proceeded to scale the corporate ladder, puncturing the rungs with stiletto heels on the way.

The one product of Barbara's short-lived marriage that she didn't regret was her daughter, Anna, in whom she had tried to instill the same sense of ruthless independence. Barbara had beamed with pride when Anna achieved a master's degree in computer sciences, and watched with admiration as daughter gave every indication of super-seding mother: instead of becoming part of an already-established corporation, Anna had formed a consulting firm with two partners and developed it into a thriving business.

Barbara considered her daughter one of her great successes, an assessment with which Anna had readily agreed through most of her adult life. But as Anna had gotten older, she'd learned some of the pitfalls of the fierce independence into which she'd been raised, not the least of which was the difficulty of facing the fact that being independent meant that she didn't have to be like her mother.

The first deviation came when Anna had decided to marry Bill Braverman several years earlier, a decision that was more of a surprise to her mother than a disappointment. The second major difference had only begun to emerge recently, when Anna started to feel a growing sense of dissatisfaction with her life. It was something that was nearly impossible for her to express, though she was far from a shrinking violet by nature. No amount of strong will had enabled her to freely speak her mind when what was on it was in direct opposition to what she believed she should feel. To do so, she feared, would be a betrayal not only to herself and her mother, but to her sex in general.

"You look blue," Barbara said, lowering her water glass. "Is something bothering you?"

"No, not at all," Anna replied. She speared a bit of meat from her chicken Caesar salad and popped it into her mouth, her teeth lightly clicking on the tines of her fork.

"Don't lie to me, Anna. You're no good at it."

"All right. I should've said, nothing out of the ordinary."

"Bill is still working hard?"

"And long."

"You mean late."

Anna looked her in the eye. "He's always worked long hours."

"Hmm." Barbara raised her glass and took another sip. "You think there's another woman? It's always a possibility. I warned you before you got married—"

"We're not talking about you and Daddy."

Barbara ignored her. "Men resent career women. Even in this day and age. It must be something in their genetic makeup that makes them want to come home and find a woman waiting for them, no matter what they might say to the contrary."

Anna said nothing. She scooped some salad onto her fork and put it in her mouth.

"*Do* you think there's another woman?" Barbara repeated, her

high forehead creased, raising the crest of her unnaturally vivid auburn hair so sharply it might've been a wig.

"Yes. The same one there's always been. Her name is Dolores."

"This again!"

"With that exhibition coming in, he's been working even longer
hours than usual. He spends so much time slaving away for Dolores
Development that he hardly has any time for me."

"You sound like a bored housewife," her mother said disdain-
fully. "I would think you'd be glad he's staying out of your hair."

"Bill has always given me free rein. He's always let me do what
I want to do—"

"*Let* you?"

"Yes, let me. Before you start splitting hairs, I mean he's never
made a fuss about me pursuing my own goals at the expense of . . .
other things. We agreed on what our marriage would be before we
went into it: that we'd be two professionals, independent, living together. Bill's always given me complete and total freedom. But freedom works both ways, and I'm not sure I like it."

"Meaning what?"

Anna let her fork drop noiselessly on the thick white tablecloth.
"Meaning I'm forty years old and maybe I want more from life than
a roommate."

Barbara sat back in her chair and rested her palms on the table.
"Is there something the matter at your company?"

"There doesn't have to be anything wrong at work for me to be
unhappy."

Her mother raised an eyebrow.

"My partners and I are getting along perfectly well. And before
you ask it, we have more clients than we can deal with. I'm kept
running day and night."

"Then you should be satisfied."

Anna sighed deeply. "I know you were unhappy with Daddy, but
that doesn't mean you and I want the same things. I don't think
there's anything wrong with wanting to be the most important thing
to someone else."

"Oh, Christ, Anna, I didn't bring you up to be Sandra Dee! I
brought you up to be your own person, and to not make the same

mistakes I did. The minute you want to be the most important thing in someone else's life, you diminish yourself."

Anna's jaw was set. This was exactly the type of thing her mother was always saying without offering an explanation or a shred of proof. And Anna had had enough of it. "Tell me something, Mother . . . how do you figure that?"

"Allow yourself to be put on a pedestal and you're setting yourself up for a fall. It'll never work."

"It will if we both feel the same way about each other," Anna replied quietly after a pause. "The trouble is . . . I suppose . . . we don't feel the same way." She picked up her fork and resumed eating.

"Good," said Barbara with finality. "Then at least one of you is showing some sense."

Anna paused again before taking another bite. She eyed her mother across the table. "Oh, I intend to do something about it."

Although Martita Dolores shared Anna Braverman's independent spirit, or at least her belief that a woman had to be independent, she found it more difficult to exercise that spirit while being overshadowed by her husband's relentless spotlight. A highly competent contract attorney by profession, no amount of achievement on her part could eclipse the visible mark her husband was making on the city. If Marti experienced any bitterness or feelings of inadequacy over her lack of limelight, few if any ever knew about it. She was shielded by an innate mysteriousness that no one, including her husband, could penetrate.

Marti was an elegantly thin, statuesque woman with dark skin, high cheekbones, and long, wavy black hair. Always impeccably poised and impeccably dressed, her acceptance in the circles in which her husband's business and her own profession brought her was furthered by an aggressive sensuality that couldn't be hidden, even by a business suit.

"We will now move on to the Davidson matter," James Harker said as his secretary slid one set of papers out from in front of him and replaced it with another.

The partners of Harker and Associates, Attorneys at Law, which included Martita Dolores, were gathered around the long oval table in conference room A of their offices, located in one of the older office buildings on LaSalle Street. The late-afternoon sun was beating down on the windows, and the normally hyperactive air conditioning had gone slightly anemic, leaving the occupants of the room feeling damp and irritable. This was not helped by the fact that their daily meeting had now run on for over an hour.

"I have gone over the contract very thoroughly," said Marti, exuding her usual sultry confidence, "and discussed it with Mr. Davidson. He has decided to sue for breach of contract."

"And how do we feel about that?" Although Harker used the plural, he addressed this directly to Marti. All eyes turned to her.

"We feel it is advisable."

"But do we feel it's winnable?"

"Of course," she replied with a slight smile, "or we wouldn't think it was advisable."

"Good. Well, is there any other business we need to discuss?" Harker said as he pushed his chair back, belying his willingness to further prolong the meeting. The partners took the hint. "Okay. Then tomorrow, at the same time."

The rest of the partners rose a split second after their leader, then spilled out into the dark-blue carpeted hallway and disappeared into their various offices like so many pinballs falling into slots.

Once back in her office, Marti placed her black-leather briefcase on the windowsill next to a potted cactus that had achieved a height of nearly two feet. On the same side of the building as the conference room, sun streamed through the window, making the room hot and stuffy. Marti took off her jacket and hung it on the antique coatrack by the door. She shook the front of her pale-pink blouse to air it out and went back to the window. On the roof of a lower building across the street, several men, stripped to the waist and muscular from manual labor, were busy resurfacing the roof.

"I'll call the management directly about the air conditioning," James Harker said from the doorway.

Marti turned a dispassionate eye toward him over her shoulder. This was one of his favorite tricks, to come upon you quietly and break in on your thoughts. She wondered why he did it. Did he hope to catch his junior partners in the middle of something shady? Or did he hope to startle some sort of reaction out of them? Marti suspected it was a ploy to keep them off balance, merely to demonstrate that he could come upon them unawares. With her, it didn't work.

"There's no need," she replied. "I like the heat."

"Really?"

"I've never liked the feeling of cold air blowing across my skin. Did you want something, Jimmy?"

For a moment, he was distracted by the way her shoulder blades were showing through the back of her damp blouse. "I'm just wondering how everything is going."

"I reported on that in the meeting."

"I mean, everything."

"Everything is fine," Marti said blithely as she pulled out her chair and sat down.

"I was surprised you didn't say anything about the mummy exhibit."

She raised a surprised eyebrow. "What was there to say?"

"Oh, I don't know," he said, stepping into her office. "I thought maybe you'd do a little free advertising for your husband."

"He doesn't need it."

"And I guess I thought maybe there would be some sort of opening reception or something."

She smiled, using only the corners or her mouth. "You were expecting champagne and raw fish, no doubt. If there was going to be such a thing, you can be assured you would have been invited."

"No preview for the elite set?"

"You know that Louie is a man of the common people. He would never host an invitation-only affair like that. It would make him look like he was not common anymore. Even I will not get a preview of the exhibit."

Harker drew his lips to one side. "Come on, Marti."

"I suppose I could if I wanted to."

"You mean you don't?"

"I'm in no rush to see it, no. I have little interest in the dead. Only the living. It's Louie who's interested in dead things."

Harker swept the brown hair back off his forehead. Though nearing fifty, his face was surprisingly free of lines. "Yes. I read about that in the *Trib*."

"Louie will be glad to hear it."

"To hear what?"

"That you read about him in the paper."

He laughed. "Why, Marti! You sound as if you think your husband has brought this exhibit in for publicity instead of for the sake of its historical importance."

"My husband does what pleases him."

"So . . . the exhibit is being delivered today?"

"That's right."

"I take it Louie will be working late."

Marti sat back in her chair and absently fanned herself with an empty manilla folder. "Oh, yes. He will be in his tower very late. As usual."

"That's good," Harker said, taking a seat across from her. "That's good. So now we can get started."

It had already been an exhausting day for Hector Gonzalez, and it wasn't over yet. Once the mummies and the other artifacts were in place, he felt he could delegate to Lisa Rivera the responsibility for seeing to it that the reproductions of cave paintings and the illustrations of Chinchorro funeral and mummification practices were hung properly. But the responsibility for showing the illustrious Louie Dolores through the exhibition was one that Gonzalez couldn't shirk. So at four o'clock, while Rivera was still occupied with the installation, Gonzalez was waiting in the lobby for the Dolores party. The diminutive museum curator was seated on a hard bench of slatted wood, his brow damp from physical exertion, and a forlorn look in his eyes so deeply wrought that it looked like it would be there for the remainder of his life.

How long did it take me to work my way into my position? he asked himself inwardly. *And here I am preparing to be nothing more than a tour guide for a bunch of wealthy Americans. I am not listened to at the museum . . . no, I am listened to, but not heeded. And where am I now?*

His thoughts were interrupted when the door to one of the elevators opened and Dolores appeared. Gonzalez was relieved that the man wasn't accompanied by the entourage that he'd been expecting. Dolores's only companions were a man who looked to be about the same age as Dolores, and a woman about twenty years their junior. Gonzalez stood as they crossed the lobby to him.

"Dr. Gonzalez," Dolores said, offering a hand. "Nice to see you again. This is my assistant, Bill Braverman."

"Oh, yes," Gonzalez said as Braverman gave him his hand in turn. "We've spoken many times on the phone."

"It's great to finally meet you."

Dolores continued. "And my secretary, Paula Dryer."

"Miss Dryer," Gonzalez said, adding an abbreviated bow to the handshake.

With her free hand, Dryer adjusted her large round glasses as if for some reason she couldn't quite believe what she was seeing. "Pleased to meet you."

"Shall we proceed?" said Dolores.

"Yes."

Gonzalez led the way to the entrance, where Al had been replaced by the second-shift guard. The tiny nameplate on his breast pocket said "Nick." He stood to the right of the door, staring straight ahead and not acknowledging their presence. Gonzalez wondered if perhaps the staff had been instructed to treat Dolores like royalty, never looking directly at him and never, ever, making eye contact.

"My assistant is still in the process of hanging the artwork and diagrams," Gonzalez explained as they passed through the entrance, "but everything else is in place."

"I trust that the execution of my designs for the exhibit has met with your satisfaction," Dolores said.

As much as any could, Gonzalez thought. "Yes, of course. It is exactly as you showed us. It does graphically lay out the time line of the Chinchorro mummies."

They arrived at the first chamber, which now contained a handful of display cases. The most prominent one contained the remains of a Chinchorro male that looked like no more than a skeleton covered with grayish-tan, leathery skin. The emptiness of the eye sockets made it appear as if its eyes were wide open, and the lower jaw hung down, exposing a row of jagged teeth. It gave the haunting appearance of someone who had been frozen in mid scream.

"This is one of the natural mummies," Gonzalez explained to the small party. "Natural meaning that it was mummified by the desert climate in which it was buried. Natural mummies appear at the beginning and end of the Chinchorro culture. This particular one was radiocarbon dated as coming from around fifteen hundred B.C. The second case is a woman from around the same period, and the third is a child. A male child."

"Imagine that," said Paula, who felt the need to say something, since the others remained silent. But from her narrowed eyes and downturned mouth, her repulsion was evident.

"Along this wall is where we'll have photos of other early, natural mummies, correct?" Dolores said as they went down the hallway.

"Yes. Everything is being done to your specifications. Now here we have a mud-coated mummy."

The men stopped in front of the first display case in the second chamber and stared down at the contents thoughtfully. Paula suppressed a shudder. The case contained a footless body, its coloring also a grayish tan. However, this one showed no signs of the facial features that were so evident in the first. It looked almost as if it were fashioned by a child: a human-shaped mud pie. The body was dried and cracked, like earth that had been split by tremors.

"This one was dated at approximately eighteen hundred B.C. The mud mummies are exactly as they sound: the process consisted of coating the body with a pastelike substance made of clay and sand. Some were eviscerated, and some not. This one wasn't."

"Very interesting," said Bill. Although he'd seen photos of the mummies during the long negotiations and preparations for the exhibit, he'd never seen them in the flesh, so to speak. He made a mental note to return to review the exhibit at some point when Dolores wasn't in attendance so that he could give it his full attention.

Gonzalez led the three of them back through the ages, past the bandage mummies that looked like poor, rustic cousins of their Egyptian counterparts, with strips of skin rather than cloth used as wrappings.

Paula felt vaguely ill as Gonzalez described the complex process of eviscerating and stuffing the body, then stitching it back together. As he spoke, they reached the display of red mummies, so named for the coat of rust-colored paint they'd received. In fact, noticing her discomfiture, Gonzalez's description became a bit more detailed than it normally would have.

This time, Paula couldn't help but shudder. The red mummies had a coating over their heads and faces that looked much like the mud mummies, only these had features molded on: bare indentations for the eyes, pinched noses, and gaping mouths. As with the natural mummies, they looked like people who had been frozen at the moment of death: deaths that appeared to have been sudden and not very pleasant. The coverings on the faces were cracked like roughly handled porcelain.

"They all look like they're screaming," Paula said under her breath.

"Did you have a question?" Gonzalez asked.

She flushed slightly and pushed her glasses up the bridge of her nose. "No, I was just saying these are fantastic." She sounded anything but enthused.

Dolores gave her a patronizing glance, then turned to Gonzalez. "Shall we continue?"

Gonzalez led the way to the chamber that held the most precious treasures: three separate display cases containing black mummies, the oldest of the artificial mummification processes practiced by the Chinchorros.

Paula gasped when she saw the first one: a woman lying on her back, her perfectly flat body interrupted by two small, molded breasts and completely coated with black manganese. The outer layer of this was flaking off, which brought to Paula's mind stories she'd read of the flesh-eating disease. But that wasn't what had caused her reaction: this mummy had over its face—or rather, where its face had been—a flat, round manganese mask with a nose molded onto it and slits for the eyes and mouth.

"It looks like—" she started haltingly. "It looks like those people outside. The protesters. Their masks. Where would they have seen them?" She was unable to take her eyes off the thing in the case.

"For heaven's sake, Paula," Dolores said irritably. "Would you expect them to be protesting our having these things without knowing what they looked like?"

"Oh. No, of course not." Her cheeks reddened. She was not unintelligent, only caught off guard.

"And they could have seen them anywhere, from visiting Dr. Gonzalez's museum to watching PBS. These mummies are not exactly unknown."

"I know, I'm sorry," she said with a sheepish smile. "I don't know what I was thinking."

Dolores returned the smile. "They can be a bit startling when you see them for the first time."

Paula reached out and pressed the tips of her fingers against the display case. "They look . . . they look like very old statues . . . but they look alive."

"Yes, they do."

"That was the point," said Gonzalez. "We believe the Chinchorros preserved their dead like this to keep them as members of the family."

In the hallway between the black mummies and the next chamber, the party found Lisa Rivera directing a pair of workmen as they hung a large frame on the wall.

"Ah, there you are," said Gonzalez. "This is my assistant, Lisa Rivera. Lisa, this is Paula Dryer, Bill Braverman—"

"Yes, Mr. Braverman, we've spoken on the phone," Rivera said, ignoring Paula and offering him her hand. She seemed to instinctively know that Paula was unimportant.

"And this is Mr. Louie Dolores."

She held her hand out to him and smiled. "It is an honor."

"Why don't you show them what you're putting up here," Gonzalez suggested.

"Of course. This is an illustration of how the mummies were found at the Moro One site in northern Chile."

Dolores and his staff gazed thoughtfully at the drawing; it showed a hodgepodge of different kinds of Chinchorro mummies lying scattered separately and in small piles. To Paula, it looked like a garbage dump of human remains.

"It seems so disrespectful," she said, keeping her voice low.

Dolores looked at her quizzically. It was unlike his normally competent and composed secretary to show so much emotion.

Lisa Rivera eyed Paula coldly. "The Chinchorros had a deep and abiding respect for their dead, Miss Dryer. That much we know from the extraordinary amount of work they put into the mummification process."

"Oh . . . I . . . yes." Paula had been on the point of apologizing when she realized that the only ones she could've offended were the Chinchorros, and they were beyond caring. If only they didn't look so alive.

"We should get on," Dolores said to Gonzalez.

"Yes, of course. There are only two more chambers."

The three members of Dolores's party followed Gonzalez down the hallway to the next chamber, the smallest in the exhibition. It contained only one display case that held three figures. Each of these were between six and eleven inches long. They had round clay faces with the same open, wide-awake expressions of the large mummies. One even sported a long wig. But all three lacked limbs, their forms tapering off to a point at the bottom.

"These really should be displayed with the red mummies," Gonzalez explained, "since they date from the same period. But you wanted them set apart from the rest since they were so special, and I would agree."

"What are they?" Bill asked.

He shrugged. "Mummies."

"But they're so small."

"These are known as statuette mummies. Radiographs of them have revealed that each contains a human fetus."

Paula went noticeably pale.

"They mummified their fetuses?" Bill asked blankly, unable to take his eyes off the one with the wig.

"Yes. I suppose it was a way to immortalize something that died before—good heavens!"

Gonzalez cut himself off with this exclamation as Paula Dryer crumpled to the floor.

When Paula was sufficiently revived to be moved, the men escorted her out to the lobby and sent the guard to find her a glass of water. Although she vigorously assured him that there was no need, Dolores insisted on calling for an ambulance.

"Are you sure you want to do that?" Bill Braverman asked as Dolores got out his cell phone. "She says she's all right."

"I know that," Dolores said irritably as he dialed. "But there's no sense in taking any chances with her health. Besides, do you have any idea the kind of publicity this can get us when one of the first visitors to the exhibit faints at the sight of it?"

I should've known, thought Braverman. *Why did I even try?*

It was fifteen minutes before the ambulance arrived. Despite her protests to the contrary, Paula was glad to see it. She still felt woozy, and the fact that she'd passed out so unexpectedly had knocked her off balance in more ways than one.

"I'm sorry to be so much trouble," she said to Dolores as the paramedics secured her to a gurney. "I don't know what came over me."

"Don't be ridiculous. You couldn't help it. We just want you to be all right."

He patted her hand lightly as the paramedics wheeled her away. Then he turned to Bill. "Make sure the media hears about this."

"What was wrong with that silly woman?" Lisa Rivera asked as she and Hector crossed the lobby.

"She became unwell while we were looking at the statuette mummies."

"Fool. What is there about them to disturb anyone?"

"Actually, I believe she was unwell before that. She seemed a bit anxious even from the beginning of the exhibit."

"What is there to be anxious about?"

As they stepped onto the escalator, Hector gave his customary shrug, raising his shoulders with an apologetic frown. There was a sad-sack tinge to it that always made Lisa feel like laughing. "It is somewhat close inside the exhibit. It's possible that someone who is claustrophobic might find it difficult to manage."

"Do you think they should put up a warning sign?" Lisa replied with a hard smile. "People with claustrophobia should not enter?"

"I don't know that this is the case with her. I was only suggesting the possibility. She could be ill. Or she could have been overcome by the staleness of the air. I don't think the air is very well circulated in there."

"I worked inside the exhibit for several hours today without finding myself short of breath."

"As I say, I only offer it as a suggestion." His manner was stiff, just as it was when faced with one of those disagreeable and unchangeable decisions of the board of directors. "Lisa, is there somewhere we can talk?"

"If it doesn't take too long. Mr. Dolores told me there is a bar on the first level of this building."

"Did he?" Hector raised his eyebrows. "When did he do that?"

"While you were waiting for the ambulance to arrive."

"I see you are working with your usual speed."

She turned a quick, appraising eye on him as they reached the bottom of the escalator. It was unusual for him to be so personal with her. As they crossed the short distance to the next escalator, she said, "Mr. Dolores is a very dynamic man, and like most of his sort, has very little patience for waiting. He wandered into the exhibit and started up a conversation."

"And that conversation wandered to the subject of bars?"

Again she fixed her eye on him. She disliked this new directness, but she did still work for him and felt there was only just so far she could go by way of rebuff—even though she was fully aware of his present tenuous relationship with the museum's board. At last she said pointedly, "Conversations can wander in some very strange directions. Here we are."

They had reached the first level and paused at the foot of the escalator to locate the bar. Lisa spotted it at the far end of the hall to their right. They headed for it through the sparsely populated shopping area, past exclusive shops, including one apparently devoted solely to clothes in neon colors, and another offering fine chocolates that could be made to order in any shape or size. Its window displayed a three-foot-tall statue of a baseball player at bat, made entirely of chocolate.

The bar was called "O'Leary's," and was dark and bustling with activity. The huge, U-shaped bar was of a rich maple, polished to a shine and surrounded by soft, padded stools, as were the high, round tables that filled the rest of the room. There were five bartenders, each clad in black pants, vest, white shirt, and black bow tie. All of them appeared to have been hired for looks more than for expertise, although they certainly weren't lacking in the latter.

It was just after six o'clock when Hector and Lisa arrived, and the bar was filled with upscale businessmen and women, not a loosened tie among them, enjoying an after-work cocktail. Hector went to the bar to get two beers while Lisa appropriated a table that was just being vacated. When Hector rejoined her, he slid a small, square napkin in front of her and placed a tall glass of beer on it. Then he sat on a stool opposite her.

"Thank you," Lisa said perfunctorily. She raised her glass to her lips and took a healthy drink, then set it down. Hector sat with the tips of his fingers touching his own glass, but made no move to drink from it.

"This is very unlike you, Hector," said Lisa, breaking the silence. "What is so important?"

He sighed deeply. "You know how unhappy I've been with the decision of the museum to loan out this exhibit . . ."

"Ah! This again!" She smiled and lifted her glass, happy to be able to categorize their conversation. "You should be glad that so many seem to be interested in that bit of history you prize so much."

"History? The decision to 'loan' the Chinchorro artifacts to this . . . enterprise has nothing to do with history, it is commerce. Nothing but commerce." He was silent for a moment. He hadn't wanted to go over this again, and was sure that Lisa didn't either. "But that isn't what I wanted to say. I've made no secret of my feelings, I know. However, today, as I was waiting for you . . . when I saw them actually being . . . well, let us just say that now that we're here, now that there's a little distance between myself and the museum . . . and the board . . . I can see how foolish I've been."

"Really?" She was genuinely surprised.

"Yes. I suppose there really is no fool like an old fool. I suppose . . . maybe I'm just too old to continue to fight the rising tide—"

"You're not that old." She wasn't being kind, but rather, saying what she thought was proper.

"I'm old enough."

"We are in a business that values antiquity."

He looked up at her sharply. *A business.* "Yes, but I'm not quite that old."

Lisa straightened herself on her stool and took another drink. She didn't like where this was going. She had spent many years as Hector's assistant, a position that she considered an unnecessary apprenticeship. She felt she was forced to serve under a man who was as anachronistic as the objects over which he governed. Hector couldn't see the trend in antiquities: that far from being the mere museum pieces of a bygone era, they were becoming commodities in today's marketplace. Even if that marketplace was to museums. Hector couldn't see that the bones of the dead were now things to be bartered and sold, and in some cases, loaned out for a price. Or if he could see it, he refused to go along with it. But Lisa would, if only she had the chance.

"So, you are no longer going to fight the rising tide. That means that you intend to—as I think the Americans used to say—'go with the flow'?"

Hector's eyes widened slightly. "Oh, no, Lisa. When we get back to Santiago, I intend to resign my position with the museum."

"Really?"

He couldn't help but smile. "I congratulate you on your self-control."

"I don't know what you mean," she said coldly.

He let that go for the moment. "I will, of course, stay on until they have found a new curator."

"I shouldn't think that would take very long."

"As my assistant, I wanted you to be the first to know. I thought it was right to tell you first, since my leaving may very well alter your position with the museum."

"Yes. I would think so, too."

He studied her for a moment. "But not in the way you think."

"What do you mean?" she said, for the first time betraying a bit of uncertainty.

"Your position has been as my assistant. When I leave, there is no guarantee that you will remain in that position. It is customary for the new curator to select his own assistant."

Lisa's back stiffened. "I have every intention of pursuing the job of curator."

"Yes, I thought that you would. It has not escaped my notice that you've been earning the board's favor. I would go so far as to say *courting* it." He paused so that his meaning would not be lost on her. "But I would not be too sure that you will be the one to step into my place."

"I think I've proven myself to the board!"

"You have proven that you will not disagree with them, or at least that you will not openly disagree with them. But there are many things against you. Too many."

"Such as?"

"Your youth. Your relative inexperience."

She gave a derisive snort. "You think these things matter?"

"Perhaps. Perhaps not. And those things can change. One thing cannot."

"Yes?"

"You're a woman," he said matter-of-factly.

She laughed hollowly. "You old fool! This is the twenty-first century, not the Dark Ages! Such a thing does not matter!"

"The museum is not in America," he replied calmly. "Whether right or wrong, when it comes down to my replacement, I think it will be difficult to fight centuries of cultural tradition. Antiquated, perhaps, but a fact."

Lisa stared at him icily. "We'll see about that!"

"There is one other thing that doesn't change," said Hector. "My relationship with the board has been, over the years, rather like a marriage. And since time began, it has been true that a man may divorce his wife, but he never marries his mistress."

With this, he raised his glass and took a drink.

3

Bill and Anna Braverman lived on north State Street, three blocks away from Dolores Tower, in a luxury condominium built, of course, by Dolores Development. Their two-bedroom unit came with two full baths and a balcony that looked down on Holy Name Cathedral.

Anna arrived home first that evening, just as she'd expected to, around six o'clock. In an uncharacteristic burst of domesticity, she decided to prepare a full dinner. The assessment of her marriage that she'd made to her mother—that she and her husband lived like roommates—was nowhere more evident than when it came to meals, which they generally ate separately, whenever each of them got home. Grocery shopping was performed over the Internet, and their food delivered to the building's receiving room in their absence. Although Anna's business required her to work hours that were as unpredictable as Bill's, she'd found herself more and more responsible for the ordering and storing of their provisions. She tried to tell herself that she didn't mind, but she really was beginning to feel as if she lived alone, or as if her roommate had a much busier social life than she did. But she knew that Bill's neglect of formerly shared duties wasn't because of a packed calendar, but because he simply didn't care what was in the refrigerator, or whether anything was there at all. He didn't care.

Anna went into the kitchen, opened the cupboard over the sink and extracted a slim volume called *Simple Meals for Two*. It had been a gag wedding gift from one of her old school friends, but had ended up proving eminently practical, with its dozen or so recipes meant to be thrown together with ease by people normally too busy to cook. She leafed through the pages disconsolately, barely glancing at the photos of finished meals that looked much more elaborate than they really were. With a sigh, she closed the book and replaced it on the shelf. Simple or not, it was foolish to attempt any timed recipes without knowing exactly when Bill would be home. And she never knew.

She opened the refrigerator and surveyed the contents. There was a package containing two butterfly pork chops that she could easily broil, and the freezer held a pack of frozen mashed potatoes and a bag of mixed peas and carrots. Together, this could make a meal that could be prepared quickly.

And what then? she thought as she closed the freezer. *What will we talk about over dinner? How can I approach this? By telling my husband that I want to be married?*

Anna checked her watch. It was a quarter to seven. Once again the thought of Bill's busy social life came into her head, and she tried to put it out. It was her mother's fault. She never should've told her mother what was bothering her. She should've made up something about work. She knew what her mother would say about Bill: that she would jump to the conclusion that there was another woman. Anna knew it wasn't true, but her mother's questions nagged at her mind all afternoon, despite her better judgment.

Anna also tried to put out of her mind any thought that her sudden desire to demonstrate domesticity was a result of the seeds of doubt her mother had attempted to plant. No, she'd been honest with her mother about the dissatisfaction she was feeling in her marriage, made worse by the fact that this grew out of having successfully achieved the goals she and Bill had mutually agreed upon at the beginning of their marriage. And she knew that what she was contemplating now was a fundamental change in that agreement. But change to what? She certainly wouldn't be happy playing the role of a housewife, any more than she imagined Bill would accept that. Whatever it was she wanted to become, it seemed to be hiding just at the edge of her consciousness, fluttering away the moment she tried to focus on it.

Anna sat down at the kitchen table and rested her chin on her hands. The general ennui she'd been suffering the past few months was so unlike her that she was beginning to feel that she didn't even recognize herself. For the first time, she was coming to understand that this fundamental change, whatever it was meant to be, had already begun inside of her.

By seven-thirty, she'd grown too hungry and tired to wait any longer. With a frustrated sigh, she opened the package of chops, took one out, wrapped the other in plastic and put it back in the fridge. She broiled the chop while microwaving a small bowl of the peas and carrots. She then ate her meal while listening to the news on Public Radio. When she was finished, she washed her plate, the glass, and the pan, and left them in the drainer to dry.

Bill finally got home after eight-thirty, by which time Anna had settled onto the white couch in the living room, a glass of red wine in her hand and her feet propped up on the top of their glass coffee table. Although fully aware that she was being irrational, she'd grown angry while waiting for Bill to arrive: angry over the fact that he'd frustrated her plans for a meal together, which he neither knew about nor could've expected. And she'd tried to quell this anger with the wine and a sleeping pill.

"Hi," Bill said, bending to kiss her lightly on the forehead. "God, I'm beat!"

"Hello," she replied frostily. Had it been in her power, she would've made her skin go cold.

"Something wrong?" he asked lightly as he removed his suit coat.

"Of course not. I didn't expect you any earlier. Or expect to hear from you."

He looked at her with surprise. "You know that damned exhibit is opening tomorrow. You shouldn't have expected me any earlier."

"Yes, I know."

"You seem angry."

"No," she said, mentally kicking herself for betraying so much, as well as for the illogic of her feelings.

"Did I forget something? Did we have plans?"

Anna fought to remove the edge from her voice. "No! No, of course not." She took a sip of wine, then set the glass down so roughly that its stem broke, spilling the remaining contents onto the coffee table and the shag throw rug beneath it.

"My God, Anna! What's wrong?" Bill said with real concern. He dropped his jacket on a chair and sat beside her.

"Nothing," she said, her face becoming hot. "Nothing! I don't know why I thought you might be home earlier. It was stupid of me."

"I'm sorry," he replied, quite at a loss as to what was going on. "I would've been, except for the exhibit. And I had to stop at the hospital on my way home."

"The hospital?" Suddenly the redness faded from her face. It flashed through her mind that now that she wanted to change—to grow closer to him—that it would be just like cruel fate for something to be desperately wrong with him. "Why did you have to go there?"

"Oh, it wasn't for me. I had to check on Paula Dryer."

"Who?"

"You know, Louie's secretary. She went with us on a tour of the exhibit this afternoon and passed out. She was rushed to the hospital, and it fell to me to check on her."

"Why you?"

"Why do you think?" he said with a rueful smile. "I'm always the one delegated to do these things."

"Couldn't you have just called the hospital?"

He shook his head, still puzzled by her attitude. "I tried. Not enough time had gone by. She was taken to the emergency room. Their operator said she wasn't in the computer yet as having been admitted. And I couldn't get through to the emergency room. Louie thought it would be best for me to stop by."

"Oh. He did."

"As it turned out, it was a waste of time. She'd already been sent home."

"What a shame."

Bill's countenance hardened, less in reaction to her sarcasm than to the unaccustomed feeling of being at sea. "Why don't we just stop playing games and you tell me what's bothering you?"

"When you didn't come home, I decided to make an early night of it. I've taken a sleeping pill, just a few minutes ago. Maybe it's just making me irritable."

"With wine? Anna—"

"I need to wipe this up," she said with a nod toward the spilled wine. She started to get up, but he caught her hand and gently pulled her back. She didn't resist.

"No. Just tell me what's wrong."

She took a moment to collect herself, folding her hands in her lap and breathing deeply. Her head was slightly turned away from him so that her long auburn hair almost completely hid her face. "I don't know," she said at last.

"Come on, Anna, that's not fair!"

"Maybe not. But it's true. I'm sorry I was so cross when you came in."

He sat back on the couch and watched her. "Something is obviously on your mind."

"I don't know why I thought you might come home sooner," she continued, apparently not paying attention to him. "I didn't have any reason to. It was silly. I mean silly to get so upset about it. I just thought . . . I just thought . . . I wanted to talk to you."

Bill's concern had been growing as she said this. He was beginning to fear that something was seriously wrong. "About what?"

"I need a change," she said after a long silence. "I really, really need a change."

"Of what kind?" he asked with trepidation.

"I can't go on the way we've been going. It's just not . . . I mean, we're both in our forties now. Middle-aged, for God's sake! And what we have . . ." She shook her head slowly. "What we have, it shouldn't be enough. It isn't just you . . . it's my fault as much as yours."

"What exactly are you saying?"

Anna turned her face toward him and looked him square in the eye. "I want you to quit the Dolores Company."

She could barely believe that the words had come out of her mouth, almost before the thought had even fully formed in her mind. But once she'd said it, she realized that leaving his job would be just one of the stages in the changes she'd been contemplating.

"What?" Bill's jaw dropped when he heard this. He couldn't have been more astonished if she'd said she expected him to take wing and fly around the room.

Now that Anna had made a start, her customary confidence returned. "I said I want you to leave Louie Dolores."

He produced a half smile. "You make him sound like a mistress."

"There are similarities, if you count the sneaking around and the dishonesty."

The smile disappeared. "I don't know what you're talking about."

"For heaven's sake, Bill! You do all of his dirty work, and it's getting worse all the time! You almost went to jail for bribery."

"It was a campaign contribution," he said defensively. "The timing was just unfortunate."

Her lips curled. "This is me, Bill! You might have convinced the court about that, but not me. I want you to get out while you still can."

"And throw away everything I've achieved? You can't be serious!" He rose from the couch.

"I'm not just talking about you," she said quickly. "I know I need to change, too. I think . . . I think . . . I should sell my share of the business to Geoff and Andy, and move on. I want to get out of this place . . . maybe we could even move to a different city."

Bill's expression had fallen as open as a manhole. There was no way he could hide his shock. "Is this some sort of . . . sudden midlife crisis?"

"Not sudden."

"But I know you haven't thought it through. We're not just going to walk away from everything we've built."

Anna sat back. This wasn't the way she'd wanted this to go at all; she'd hoped for a nice dinner over which they could calmly discuss what she was feeling. But that had completely fallen through. She'd had to settle for tackling it when he got home, and it had turned into a disaster. And she knew she was partly, if not entirely, at fault.

"You and I have built our own little empires," she said wearily. "Separately. *You* and *I*. There is no *we*."

"What in the hell brought all this on?" Bill said helplessly.

"You don't see it, do you? You don't see how fast it can all fall apart?"

"What are you talking about?"

" 'Personal Assistant to Louie Dolores.' "

"Yeah? So? I'm indispensable to Louie. You know that. And I'm highly paid for it."

"There was a time when you wanted more than that. Remember? When we were younger? You wanted to be your own man. Not Louie's man."

"I *am* my own man!" he replied hotly, so stung by her words that he didn't hear the passion that was behind them.

"And what if something happens to him?" Anna said quietly.

"What do you mean?" Bill replied after a beat.

"What if he were to die suddenly? You'd be nowhere. Anybody would see you as just another high-paid flunky."

Bill bridled as if he'd received a hard slap in the face. "Is that the way you think of me?"

She shook her head slowly, letting it droop. "I don't want it to matter."

"Just what the hell is that supposed to mean?"

Anna rose from the couch unsteadily, like someone who has spent a long time on a boat and has just returned to land. Her eyes clouded over and she averted them from him as she headed for the kitchen. "I have to clean up this mess . . . or I'll never get the stain out."

Bill stood there for a moment in dumbfounded silence; then, before she came back into the room, he went out the front door, slamming it behind him.

It was after ten when Frieda Jablonski pushed the industrial-sized Hoover off the elevator and into the lobby of the exhibition hall. She then turned around and yanked the service cart off. It held her feather dusters, rags, and several different kinds of solvents. The dull ache in her meaty shoulder told her that her bursitis was starting to act up, and she raised her eyes to heaven in a brief, silent thank-you that she'd been assigned to clean the exhibit, since that meant she wouldn't have to haul the heavy equipment from floor to floor in her usual rounds.

Frieda was also pleased to have the assignment, because she believed it meant that her employers had recognized the quality of her work, as well as her honesty. She would've been much less flattered had she known the truth: a fairly recent immigrant, her limited command of the English language had led her superiors to the mistaken conclusion that she wasn't intelligent enough to steal anything.

Frieda crossed the lobby, pushing the vacuum before her and pulling the cart behind.

"Hallo, Nick," she said to the guard when she reached the door. "How are you?"

"Hi, Frieda," he replied tiredly from his perch on a high stool. There was not quite an hour left before he would go off duty. "Everything's quiet. Quiet as the grave."

Frieda stared at him with the barely masked confusion of someone who doesn't understand what's being said to her and doesn't want you to know it.

"I go to work now," she said.

"Go right on in!" He didn't bother hiding the superior smile. She hadn't fooled him.

"I leave my cart here?"

"Sure can."

She pulled the vacuum cleaner into the exhibit, left it by the entrance, and unraveled its lengthy cord as she made her way down the first hallway. The night before, when the exhibit was still empty, she had been taken through it by her supervisor and shown where everything would be located, and instructed in exactly what she should and should not do. Electrical outlets were hidden in each chamber.

The music had been turned off for the night, and the hollow stillness was broken only by the sound of her sensible shoes padding across the beige carpet. When she reached the first chamber, she stopped in her tracks with a loud gasp. She hadn't seen the displays before, and to come upon the mummies in their unexpectedly lifelike state of preservation while she was all alone was quite disarming. Like Paula, to Frieda, they looked as if they had been frozen at the moment of a death scream.

Although Frieda always worked at night, there was something about the eerie scene that brought the fact that it *was* night to the front of her mind, and it made her very uncomfortable. She averted her eyes from the display cases and went to the wall on the right, where the outlets were located. She slid back the small panel that hid them and plugged in the vacuum. Then she went back to the entrance, took hold of the vacuum's handle and roughly stamped the power button with her foot. The machine sprang to noisy action, and she began her work.

Frieda proceeded down the long hallway, humming to herself and wondering how the occasional snip of paper or lint could've found its way to the carpet when the exhibit wasn't even open yet. She gave no thought to the fact that several people, including those who had installed the displays, had been through the exhibition hall earlier in the day.

When she had nearly made her way back to the first chamber, she thought she heard something. She couldn't tell where the sound had come from, or even what kind of sound it was, over the roar of the vacuum. She stood still for a moment like a startled rabbit, listening, although she incongruously didn't turn off the machine for fear she might hear the sound again. Then she shrugged uncertainly and went on with her work. She pushed the vacuum into the chamber, trying to keep her eyes glued to the carpet as she cleaned around the cases.

Then she heard the sound again. It was something like a muffled scraping. This time she switched off the machine and pushed it to arm's length, but retained her grasp on it as if in need of its support. She strained her ears as hard as she could, listening for a repetition of the noise.

She had remained stock-still for quite some time before moving to turn the vacuum on again. But just before hitting the switch, she heard a noise once more, only this time it sounded like something rustling, rather than scraping.

With her hands trembling, she pushed the vacuum farther away, then crossed to the entrance of the chamber, where she could see down the hall. At the far end was part of the slanted opening to the next chamber, and the curve that took the subsequent hallway out of sight. As she watched, a dark face emerged from around the corner of the far chamber. It seemed to hang there, floating at the edge of the entrance: a charcoal-gray face, flat and dead.

Frieda's pulse raced and something rushed up into her throat. The dead face was looking straight at her. After a long moment, it started to move away into the next hall, seeming to pull along with it a body wrapped in tatters of cloth. It moved slowly, never taking its eyes— if that was what the tiny slits could be called—off of her.

When it had disappeared around the corner, Frieda found her voice.

Out in the lobby, Nick sprang off his stool when he heard the scream. He started into the exhibit, but stopped when he saw Frieda hurtling toward him, madly waving her arms. When she reached him, she flung her fists at his chest as if intending to pummel him, but he grabbed her wrists and held her off.

"What the hell is the matter?" he demanded. "What's wrong with you?"

Her eyes were wide with terror. "One of dem tings is alive!"

"What?"

"One of dem tings is alive in dere! Let me go!"

She wrested herself free from his grasp and fled for the escalator.

"Did you see anything?" one of the officers asked.

"No," said Nick, shaking his head. This little episode caused him to have to stay overtime, and he wasn't happy about it. "Nothing except Frieda when she came flying down the hall like she was crazy!"

"You were looking into the exhibit when that happened?" asked the other officer.

"No, no. I was just sittin' here. I heard her scream like a banshee from inside there, and I started to go in when she comes haulin' ass out of there! Looked like she'd seen a ghost. In fact, that's what she said she seen."

"So you did go into the exhibit."

Nick shook his head again. "Uh-uh. Not really. See, if I go in there, then whoever it was could've come out the exit without anybody seeing 'em. So I stayed at my post. I radioed for help, and my boss came down. Him and Mr. Dolores."

"Louie Dolores?" the first officer asked with raised eyebrows.

"Yeah. Took him a while to get down here. I'd never seen him in the flesh before."

"You called him?"

"Security did. They're supposed to report anything unusual to his office." He smirked. "This'd be it!"

"They went in and looked around? They find anything?" the second officer asked.

Nick shrugged. "Don't know yet. They told me to call you and then they went in. Haven't come out yet."

"They're still in there?"

"Uh-huh."

The officers looked at each other. Then the first one said, "Well, if we go in through the exit, we should meet up with them."

They were about to do this when two men emerged from the exit. The officers recognized the one in the expensive three-piece suit.

"Ah, good evening, Officers," he said. "I'm Louie Dolores."

He shook hands with them in turn. "Hello, sir, I'm Officer Nash, this is Officer Tully," said the first officer, with a glance at Dolores's dark hair.

"This is the night head of security," Dolores said with a nod toward his companion. "Chip Duggan."

"Mr. Duggan," said Nash with a nod.

Duggan returned the nod crisply. He was a squat man with red hair, a narrow face, and small, close-set eyes.

Nash turned to Dolores. "You're here very late."

"I run a multimillion-dollar business, Officer," he replied with a smile. "I have to work late."

"I understand you've had a disturbance here."

Dolores glanced at Duggan, who rolled his eyes. "Well, I don't think it's the kind you're expecting. Mr. Duggan and I have been through the exhibit. There's nothing out of place, and nothing is missing. We couldn't find any sign of anything wrong, or even of anyone having been in there—other than the people who were supposed to be."

"Uh-huh," said Nash.

"So it seems that the only disturbance has been from a highly imaginative cleaning lady."

Nash looked at his partner, then back to Dolores. "Your security guard here tells us that she claimed one of the mummies came to life."

Duggan chuckled, and Dolores produced the grin meant to show that despite his wealth and stature, he was still just one of the guys. "See what I mean?"

"Hmm. We'd liked to talk to her."

"She's in the security office right now," Duggan said. "You can talk to her, but I should warn you that she doesn't speak much English and she was pretty incoherent when I spoke with her."

"We'll still see her," said Nash.

"Fine," said Dolores. "Anyway, as I said, we've gone through the exhibit and found absolutely nothing amiss."

"I didn't see anyone come out," said Nick helpfully. "But you gotta understand, I didn't see anyone go in, either, and I would have. There was never anybody in there!"

"I think she was just frightened," said Dolores. "She'd never seen the exhibit before, and it can be daunting the first time. My own secretary fainted today when we went through it. I'm really rather embarrassed to have called you, but we didn't know what was happening at the time, and I thought it was better to be safe than sorry."

"Yeah," said Nash. He glanced at his partner again, then said, "I'm sure what you say is true, but since you did call us, maybe you wouldn't mind if we just made a pass through the place, just to make sure it's all right."

"I wouldn't mind at all," Dolores replied in a tone that conveyed his belief that they were wasting their time. "If you'll excuse me, I'll leave you to it. Chip can take you to the security office when you're done."

He strode across the lobby with his usual purposefulness and started down the escalator.

The officers headed for the entrance, but when Duggan moved

to accompany them, Nash said, "We're just going to have a quick look-see. You can wait here."

"Right," Duggan replied, reddening slightly.

The officers went into the exhibit, running a casual eye over the surroundings. When they reached the first chamber, Nash said, "You notice something funny about Dolores?"

"No. What?"

"His hair. It was wet."

"So?"

"So nothing. I was just wondering what he'd been doing that he got his hair wet."

Tully snorted. "Probably got a hot tub in his office."

Nash stared down at the first display case. "So, what do you think of this?"

"This stuff, or the 'incident'?"

"Either one."

Tully grinned. "Not much!"

4

TUESDAY

For one brief moment before opening his eyes, Hector Gonzalez had blissfully forgotten all of his troubles. He was back in his bed in Santiago, listening to the slow, comforting, rhythmic breathing of his wife as she slept. But then his eyelids fluttered open and he found himself staring at the ceiling of his room in the Reliance Hotel, and it all came back to him in a rush: the reason he'd been forced to come to Chicago, his newly formed resolve to leave his position with the museum, and worst of all, the further deterioration of his beloved mummies that he thought he could detect when he examined them after they'd been put in place—deterioration caused by their having been transported. The thought caused a sickening knot to form in the pit of his stomach.

Hector climbed reluctantly out of bed and straightened the neck of the white-cotton pajamas that had twisted into a stranglehold as he'd tossed and turned in the night. According to the travel alarm he'd placed on the nightstand, it was only five-thirty, much earlier than he needed to get up. He toyed with the idea of trying to get more sleep, but the certainty that he would now do nothing but lie awake and ponder his situation roused him to movement. He went into the bathroom and showered, then shaved. He noticed the deep, dark circles under his eyes and wondered if the sleep he'd just experienced had provided any rest at all.

When he was finished shaving, he dressed in the second of his brown suits and thought about whether or not he should call Lisa's room and invite her to breakfast. It was, after all, her first morning in Chicago and she was his assistant. It would be only polite to do so. But he decided against it. Their conversation of the previous evening had not gone well, and he had no desire to repeat the experience. Although Lisa adamantly disagreed with his assessment of her prospects, Hector could see in her eyes that she knew what he said was true, and more surprising was the realization that the idea was new to her. In the end, he had excused himself rather clumsily to escape the cold civility into which she had lapsed.

He combed his hair in the dresser mirror, patted his left-hand pocket to make sure he'd remembered the key to his room, then left. Just outside the door, he stooped to pick up the morning's *Tribune*, which the hotel thoughtfully provided to all visitors. He tucked it under his arm and headed for the elevator.

Just off the hotel's minuscule lobby there was a small café—more like a diner—open every day for breakfast and lunch. It had long since ceased to include dinner due to the fact that any businessmen who had been forced to cut corners by staying at the Reliance would be more apt to wine and dine their clients—if not themselves—someplace a little more fashionable.

Hector was greeted amiably by the young hostess who made it her business to recognize him, even though he'd been there only once before. She seated him in a small booth, away from the windows as he requested.

"Would you like to see a menu?" she asked as he slid into place.

"No. I know what I want."

"Good. I'll send the waitress over."

After he placed his order, he laid the newspaper on the table. The banner headline was something about the Middle East. He sighed and turned the paper over.

His eye was immediately caught by a smaller headline in the lower right-hand corner. His mouth dropped open as he read the story. When he'd finished, he raised his eyes and softly exclaimed, "Oh, my God!"

* * *

58

"Did you see this?" There was amusement in Detective Gerald White's voice as he addressed his partner. Gerald was clad in a dark-olive, off-the-rack suit and holding out a copy of the *Tribune*.

"What?" said Ransom, looking up from the mound of paperwork on his desk.

"This. Look what happened last night." Gerald dropped the paper in front of him and tapped his index finger on a story at the bottom of the page. The headline read:

THE MUMMY LIVES?

Ransom glanced up at his partner. "This is front-page news?"

"Only the first paragraph. The rest is on page seventeen."

Ransom quickly read the account of the terrified cleaning woman who swore that she'd seen one of the mummies get up and walk. Included in the story was a mention of the secretary who had fainted while viewing the exhibit and had been rushed to the hospital. After reading this, Ransom pushed the paper aside with a weary sigh. "This is Bram Stoker stuff, Gerald. If you remember, I'm a Dickens man."

"I thought you'd get a kick out of it," Gerald said as he picked the paper up and refolded it.

"A kick! Hardly. Everything going on around that exhibit is giving me the itch."

Gerald laughed. "Are you afraid we'll get assigned to it?"

"Assigned to what? The case of the roving mummy? There hasn't been a crime. As far as I know, resurrection isn't against the law." As he went back to work on the report he'd been writing, he added under his breath, "Even a well-timed resurrection."

Despite the fact that he had stayed at the tower very late, Dolores had risen early the next morning. The cook and housekeeper, Mrs. Dance, had set the automatic coffeemaker to begin brewing at 5:00 A.M., and Dolores found himself wakened by the alluring aroma before his alarm clock had a chance to break the peace.

He slipped his naked frame into his blue-silk robe and glanced down at his wife, who was lying on her back, perfectly still, with her hands folded across her stomach. Were it not for the slow, steady rise and fall of her chest, she might've been a beautifully appointed corpse. Dolores thought, not for the first time, that he probably had married her because he liked the way her black hair fanned out over white-satin pillows, forming a weblike halo around her head. He tied the sash at his waist and went to the kitchen.

Although Dolores was a chronic early riser, Mrs. Dance was not required to arrive early enough to fix his breakfast, a meal that he'd spent a lifetime ignoring in favor of liquid caffeine. And he preferred to have it in quiet and solitude, so much so that he tended to feel cheated if Marti rose at the same time as he did.

He poured a mug of coffee and stood over the sink drinking it as he looked out the window at the wooded area behind their Winnetka ranch house. A hazy morning sun was beginning to illuminate the line of trees, making them look like a washed-out photograph.

When he finished his coffee, he set the mug in the sink and went back to the bedroom and into the master bath. Once he'd cleaned up and dressed, he returned to the side of the bed and stood over his wife.

"Marti," he said softly but firmly. When she didn't stir right away, he repeated her name.

There was movement beneath her eyelids; then, keeping her eyes closed, she stretched dreamily, like a cat lounging on its back in the sun. "What is it?" she said sleepily.

"Where were you last night?"

Her face curved into a frown. "What?"

"Where were you last night?"

Her lids rose to half-mast. "I was here, of course. You were not."

"I was detained."

"You always are."

"And I called you. Several times. To let you know that I would be late."

She turned over on her side and propped her head up with her hand. "That was nice of you."

"There was no answer."

Marti didn't smile, but there was no hiding the amusement in her eyes. "There wouldn't be. I had dinner with my tiresome partners. I

60

came home with a terrible headache. I unplugged the phone and went to bed." She let one hand languidly dangle in the direction of the bedside phone. Dolores glanced down at it and saw the end of the cord protruding from behind the nightstand.

"It's only that I was worried when I couldn't reach you."

Now Marti allowed herself to smile. "There was no need." After a pause, she added, "I did hear you when you came in. You were very late."

"There was a disturbance at the tower."

"Hmm," she said, letting her eyes close.

"You remember that today is the opening of the exhibit, don't you?"

"Mm-hmm."

"And you will be there." It was a statement rather than a question.

"Of course I will, darling."

Dolores left the house feeling less than satisfied. There were times when he found himself hopelessly caught between his desires. He wanted his wife to be available to him whenever he called, and had his doubts about her when she wasn't; but at the same time, he would've held in contempt any woman who was at his beck and call.

He steered his black Audi out of the garage, flipping the switch for the automatic door as he peeled onto the street and headed for downtown Chicago.

It was barely seven when he reached Dolores Tower. As he circled the building to go to its underground garage, he noted that the protesters were already present on the corner opposite the front entrance, playing their drums and chanting as their leader danced before them.

Dolores normally liked the relative quiet of mornings at the tower, when the only thing open on the first level was the inevitable Starbucks. The sight of the occasional engineer or early office worker was a sign that the building was just waking up. But this morning, a steady stream of people was pouring in through the front door to the mall, and two camera crews were parked on the street outside.

Dolores reached the ramp that led down to the private garage. He rolled down his window, slipped his key card into the slot in the small, waist-high box on the left of the ramp, and the massive door clattered into action. He drove into the nearly empty lot, turning right and heading for the wall where his space was located; next to the private elevator for his penthouse suite.

After locking the car, he went to the elevator, inserted his card into the slot and pressed the button. The elevator door slid open quietly. Dolores got in, inserted the card into the slot at the base of the numbers, turned it and pushed the button for the top floor. He was quickly spirited up to his suite.

On the penthouse floor, both the private elevator and the public ones opened into a vestibule closed off by thick glass doors that were kept locked. These doors faced the blank wall of a hallway. A phone on the right wall was used to ring Dolores's secretary, who would then release the lock to admit welcome visitors. Dolores slipped his card into the slot of the small box beneath the phone. The door unlocked with a loud thud, and he pulled it open and went in.

He walked down the hallway to the right, then through the first doorway on the left, which opened into the reception area. A stack of mail nearly a foot high had been left on Paula's desk. He almost picked it up, but decided to leave it. There was more than enough work still left on his own desk.

He pulled his keys out of his pocket, unlocked the door to his office and went in. He laid his briefcase on the credenza, then crouched down, slid open the door on the far right, and withdrew a set of plans. He moved the blotter from atop his desk, leaned it against the side, and pushed away the pencil holder with its solid-gold contents. He then rolled out the plans and secured them at the right and left edges with a pair of matching paperweights.

Dolores sat in his desk chair, rested his elbows on the desk, and smiled down at the blueprints he had drawn up for the proposed condominium complex he planned to build at the soon-to-be-former site of the Stone Candy Factory.

At a quarter after eight there was a soft knock at the door, followed by the entrance of Paula Dryer. She was wearing a maroon dress and had her long brown hair pulled back and tied with a rubber band. She carried the now-sorted mail.

"Paula!" Dolores said. "I didn't expect you today."

"The exhibit opens today," she said distantly. "I knew how busy you'd be. I couldn't leave you alone." She placed the letters in the In box on his credenza. "These are the ones that need your personal attention."

He hadn't taken his eyes off of her. "But you had to go to the hospital yesterday."

"I told you there was no need for that. There's nothing wrong with me. They checked me over and said the same thing."

"Are you sure? You still look pale, and I don't want you to stay here if you should be at home."

"I'm fine."

Dolores's lips formed a half smile. "I understand. I'd seen the mummies before, but it never occurred to me that some people might find them—"

"It's all right," she said, crisply cutting him off. She didn't want to hear it. Although she'd been with Dolores for many years, she had a tendency to forget the kind of man he could be. Yesterday she had thought him overly concerned for her welfare, but she had appreciated the attention. Today she had seen the cause of that attention on the front page of the newspapers. She'd had an embarrassing episode that would've otherwise gone unnoticed, and he'd sent her to the hospital to exploit it.

On her way out of the office, she noticed the cushions on his couch were disarrayed. She straightened them in passing, then headed for the door. "Don't forget you have to be downstairs at ten to open the exhibit."

The atmosphere was far from icy in the Braverman household that morning. What had been sullen resignation on Anna's part the evening before had gestated into repressed anger that seemed to emanate like waves of heat from the general vicinity of her forehead. She and Bill maintained an air of civility, but not much more, as they breakfasted.

For his part, Bill had fallen into a state of perplexed unhappiness. He and Anna rarely quarreled from the simple expedient that the nature of their relationship precluded something so personal. But even at best, he found himself at a rather unfair disadvantage when it came to his wife. Anna was the only person in his life who could really throw his thought processes into turmoil. No matter how shrewd or competent he was in all other areas, he never quite felt sure of his footing with her during their rare disagreements. He had a secret suspicion that he knew the reason he found her so disarming: she was the only person in his life he could rely on to tell him the plain, unvarnished truth.

He looked at her across the table. Her head was bowed, and she was lifting spoonfuls of granola to her mouth at hypnotically even intervals. He looked back down at his own bowl and sighed.

Now that they were into middle-age—he couldn't deny it—the rules of everything seemed to be changing, including life with Anna. Over the past year, he'd sensed a growing dissatisfaction on her part: nothing overt, just a sort of vague distance as if something had shut down inside of her. There had been occasions when he'd considered asking her about it, but he didn't for fear of upsetting the status quo, or of violating the tacit terms of their marriage. And he knew that if it was something she wanted to talk about, she wouldn't hesitate to do so. If he were honest with himself, he suspected what the problem was—maybe even knew it—but in the past, he'd shied away from the awareness of it for no other reason than that he didn't know what to do about it.

And then had come that scene last night, when she'd spoken of change. Bill had thought he'd finally learn the reason for the semi-detachment she'd developed, even though it made him nervous. At first, he was relieved to find that the changes she wanted included him, because he'd worried that perhaps her ultimate plan was to leave him. But what she was proposing was so sweeping an upheaval of their lives that it had knocked him off his feet. He'd reacted badly. He'd accused instead of discussing. It should have been a moment in which they were further drawn together—a prospect so foreign to him that he found the idea disquieting as well—but instead, the gulf had grown wider.

Bill's face flushed again as he remembered what she'd said about the payoff he'd made on behalf of his boss. It was a payoff. He'd been a fool to characterize it in any other way to her. He'd even tried to fool himself by remembering his acceptance of something that

Anna did not: that in the matter of high-stakes real estate, that was the way things were done.

He thought back bitterly to the day Louie had put the money into his hand. Even though he'd agreed to it at the time, now he cursed himself for having done it. He'd never thought Anna would look back at the episode with disdain, as something that made him smaller in her eyes. And it didn't help that it had done nothing to improve his self-image. He'd been party to borderline corruption in the past, but had never before been involved in a directly criminal act. He shook his head. He was trying to fool himself again. It hadn't been the first time, only the most overt. He had wanted to refuse to do it but didn't, not because he was spineless, but because he wasn't going to throw away a high-paying career unless he was inextricably backed into a corner.

From there, his thoughts naturally progressed to what Anna had said of his career, that people looked at him as nothing more than a high-paid flunky.

And she always told him the truth.

He cleared his throat. "Anna?"

She looked up but said nothing. Her expression was neither hot nor cold. It was completely empty.

"Are you going to come to the ceremony this morning?"

"No," she said, going back to her cereal. "I have things I have to take care of."

"Did you see the mummy story?" Lynn asked as she placed the two full bags of groceries on Emily's kitchen counter.

Emily was seated at the table, the newspaper spread out in front of her. "Oh, yes. I did."

"That should certainly bring people in to see that exhibit. Louie Dolores thinks of everything! There's nothing he won't do for publicity."

"Yes . . . I hope that's all it is," Emily said vacantly.

Lynn paused in the process of unpacking the first bag and looked at her. "What do you mean? You don't believe a mummy got up and walked, do you?"

Emily smiled, her eyes twinkling. "Oh, no, of course not. I don't know what I meant, really, except that the story is very peculiar."

Lynn went back to unpacking. "It has to have been for publicity."

"Does it?"

The right corner of Lynn's lip curled. "All right, Emily, what are you thinking?"

Emily sighed deeply. "Only that . . . do you really think it was a publicity stunt?"

Lynn stopped. "What else could it be?"

"I suppose that's possible," Emily said, her voice growing rather faint as she lost herself in thought. "I suppose that's the most likely explanation. And even though there are probably very few who would actually believe that this could really happen, I suppose it would still excite the imaginations of a lot of people. . . ."

"You sound like you're arguing with yourself," Lynn said with amusement.

Emily came back to herself. "You're quite right, and it really doesn't matter."

"Does it make you want to see the exhibit earlier than we were thinking?"

Emily smiled. "Oh, no, my dear. I'm sure you're right about that, too. This little incident will bring in crowds. I can wait."

Lynn paused again as she pulled a head of lettuce from the second bag. "You really think that this is something more than a stunt, don't you?"

Emily sighed. "Let's just say I think it 'bodes some strange eruption in our state.' "

"Uh-huh," Lynn said with a wry smile.

The offices of Hamilton, Rogers and Braverman were located on the top floor of an old Huron Street three-flat that had been converted from residences many years earlier. Anna arrived at nine o'clock and fumbled her key into the lock on the front door. She had decided what she was going to do, but instead of gaining resolve, she had drifted into a sort of trancelike resignation that left her feeling as if she were carrying a pound of lead in her stomach.

She pulled open the door, but hesitated before going in. She turned and looked to the south. Across the street there was a line of two- and three-flats that had also been converted to businesses. Rising above them like a futuristic monolith was Dolores Tower. Anna had watched as it had been constructed, and bristled with anger along with her partners when they realized that the tower would block out the afternoon sun their offices had once enjoyed. Anna heaved a sigh. Maybe that was why the change had come upon her over the past year: the tower quite literally overshadowed her, just as she felt Dolores had done throughout her marriage to Bill. She entered the building, letting the door fall shut with a tired wheeze.

Anna climbed the stairs to the third floor, where a single door, heavy with varnish, held a brass nameplate bearing the name of her company. Even from outside, she could smell the cigarette smoke. She smiled to herself. She didn't approve of smoking, but somehow, it seemed right for a computer-consulting firm. She opened the door and went in.

Across the front windows of what had once been a living room, the partners had partitioned off three large cubicles for their individual work spaces. The remainder of the room was used as a lobby where they could meet with clients. The front bedroom had been turned into a workroom where the photocopy machine, shredders, and other equipment in common usage were kept. The back bedroom was used for storage. What once was a dining room was now a bull pen where the partners held their own meetings, most convenient because it was off the kitchen, the only room that had been kept to its original purpose.

Geoff Hamilton was the tall, lanky man with a predilection for brown sweater-vests and drinking Coke nonstop from morning till night; Andy Rogers was ruddy and blond, and had a ready laugh that covered a multitude of insecurities. They both called out good morning to her from the bull pen, and she went back to join them. As she entered the room, her heart began to sink. Anna had known both of these men since college, more years ago than she would like to think. Just as long as she'd known Bill. The passage of time was written on them. Geoff's dark-brown curls were now spiked with strands of white, and the lines on Andy's face were as deep as ruts.

"What's wrong with you?" Geoff said when he saw her. Andy looked up.

"What?" she asked blankly.

"You look like you were just at a funeral."

"Oh . . . oh, just tired, I guess. I took a sleeping pill last night. I don't think it's completely worn off yet."

"Want some coffee?" Geoff asked, noting her rather vague state. She hesitated before nodding. "Oh. Yes."

He jumped up. "I'll get it."

Anna pulled out one of the dark-green, padded chairs and sat down as he grabbed her mug from the rack on the side counter. "I wanted to have a talk with you guys."

"Oh-oh," said Geoff. "Sounds grim."

Andy laughed and tapped the ash from his cigarette into the glass ashtray on their round table.

"It is."

Geoff placed the mug in front of her and resumed his seat.

"Thank you." She wrapped her hands around the mug but didn't take a drink. She waited a long time before speaking again. The talk she'd tried to have with her husband the night before had gone very badly, and she didn't want to repeat that with them. "I know this will come as a surprise to you, but for a long time now, I've been unhappy . . ."

Her partners glanced at each other.

"It's not a surprise to me," said Geoff.

"Me neither," Andy added.

Anna looked up. "Really?"

"We're not blind, Anna," said Geoff with a smack of his lips. "It would be obvious to anyone who knows you well."

"We've been worried," Andy chimed in. "We've talked about it. We thought . . . well, we thought maybe there was trouble at home. But, you know, you don't really talk about that kind of stuff very much."

Geoff nodded in agreement.

"No, it's not that," Anna said slowly. "Not . . . it's me. I've decided to sell my third of the business and move on."

"You're kidding!" Andy exclaimed, his mouth falling open. "You don't mean that!"

"I'm sorry. I do."

"But you founded this place. With us, I mean. This has been your life!"

She looked at him, her eyes filled with sadness. "Yeah, it has. But you know, computers are just . . . I have other interests. I want to do other things."

"Like what?" Geoff asked.

"I don't know."

"It doesn't sound like you've given this a whole helluva lot of thought," said Andy.

"Yes, I have. I've been thinking about it for over a year. I might not know exactly what I want to do next, but I do know that I want out."

Now that she'd said this aloud for the second time, she could feel her resolve growing. It was as if putting it out there in the cosmos, or the universe, or whatever it was called, was what had been necessary for her to realize it was the right thing to do. She'd never before had time for those people she'd laughingly thought of as stargazers, but she wasn't so sure now that they were wrong: she'd sent the words into the cosmos, and they'd become concrete. She felt her spine go a little straighter.

"So, as per our original agreement, I'm going to give you two first chance to buy me out of my third before I go looking for someone else. But I want you to know that I intend to move quickly, so please let me know asap."

Geoff sensed something in her tone that made him curious, despite all the worries that were going through his head. "Anna, when you say you want out, are you just talking about from our partnership?"

"What do you mean?"

"Just that. Is that the only thing you're leaving?"

She looked down at her hands which were still wrapped around the mug of coffee. The warmth against her palms was comforting. "Actually, I'm thinking of moving out of Chicago . . . maybe West . . .

maybe to California. I'm tired of living here. I've been here all my life. It's time for a change."

Geoff glanced at Andy, who looked as perplexed as he felt. "Yes, but . . . how does Bill feel about all this? That'll mean . . . do you mean he's actually planning to leave Dolores Development after all these years?"

"He would have to," Anna replied enigmatically.

"And he's all right with that?" Andy asked.

"Of course he is," she said as she lifted the mug to her lips.

5

Hector and Lisa arrived together at the tower just after nine. The atmosphere between them was no more than civil. They passed through the first floor, which was alive with activity because the store owners had opened early to take advantage of the crowd expected for the opening of the exhibit. They took the escalator up and walked to the far end of the second floor.

A seemingly endless line of people snaked away from the box office, which was just to the right of the escalator leading up to the third floor. At the foot of the escalator stood a guard whose job it was to make sure everyone going up held a ticket.

Hector and Lisa could hear the steady, low roar of humanity from above even before reaching the escalator. To Hector, it sounded not unlike the chattering in the monkey house at the zoo. They showed their badges to the guard and he stepped aside, touching two fingers to the brim of his cap.

In the lobby, they found a sea of people, many of them surveying trinkets in the various vendors' counters, while others purchased soft drinks and snacks. Everyone seemed to be talking, or laughing, or eating. Red-velvet ropes strung between brass posts formed a mazelike aisle in which everyone who was not shopping stood in an orderly, curving line.

"Well," Lisa said as they made their way through the crowd,

"you should be pleased to see how popular our history is with these people."

"Our history? I don't think so," Gonzalez said grimly.

"What do you mean?"

"Good morning!" A cheery voice interrupted them. They'd arrived at the entrance to the exhibit and found Al guarding the door.

"Good morning," said Hector.

"I see you're wearing your badge right out in the open, just like I said. Good for you, Doc."

Hector smiled. "We're going to make one last check before the exhibit opens."

"Sure 'nuff. Here, let me get this." A wide red ribbon had been strung across the doorway. Al reached down and pulled it up as far as it would go. "You'll have to duck down a bit. This is here for the opening ceremony."

"Thank you," said Hector, stooping slightly as he passed beneath the ribbon. He was followed closely by Lisa.

"Just a minute," she said once they were out of the guard's hearing. "What did you mean when you said you didn't think they're here for history? Why do you say that?"

"Didn't you see the papers this morning?" Hector said as they proceeded down the hallway.

"Oh, that. That was nothing. Just the ravings of a half-witted cleaning woman, nothing more."

"Do you really believe that?"

Lisa smiled coldly. "So, perhaps you think Mr. Dolores has cooked this thing up for publicity? What of it? If he did, it was a very clever move. Look at the number of people wanting to see the exhibit."

"Publicity . . ." Hector said distantly, coming to a stop. "Publicity? That I don't know."

Lisa looked at him curiously.

"Is it publicity, or is it . . . something more." He appeared to be saying this to himself rather than to her.

"What are you talking about?" she asked sharply. They had work to do and needed to move on, and even at her best, she didn't like being held back by a foolish old man.

"Maybe it is not Dolores. Or publicity. Maybe it is not just a cleaning woman imagining things. Maybe it is something more . . ."

Lisa folded her arms across her chest. "Like what?"

He turned his eyes to her. "Maybe it is our ancestors. Maybe they are angry at this display. Maybe their spirit rises . . ."

The corner of Lisa's hard, flat mouth twitched and her brows raised uncertainly. For the first time, she thought it possible that her boss had passed foolishness and was approaching dementia. But this was not something she would allow to delay her. "Come on," she said. "We should do what we've come to do."

"I didn't see anything about the death threat in the paper this morning," Louie Dolores said when Bill Braverman came into his office. "Was it on the news?"

"No. After that business with Paula yesterday, I thought it would be better to wait for today."

"Did you?"

Bill recognized that tone. He wasn't supposed to think for himself. "Yes. We don't want to overload the media with information. You know what happens if a story gets too busy for them."

"Yes."

"And we don't want to seem like we're feeding them."

"It doesn't matter if we sound like that. You should know that. All of the local stations get a lot of advertising dollars from me. If I want to feed them, I will."

This is all I need, thought Bill. *Problems with Anna and now this.* "I suppose I should've talked it over with you, but I thought it would be all right. I also thought it would sound better coming from you."

"Hmm?"

"You'll be talking to the press in a few minutes, after you open the exhibit. I thought that would be a good time to work it in. I thought you could do it more naturally than I could."

Dolores kept his eyes leveled at his assistant as he thought about this. Finally, he sighed. "I suppose you're right. I hadn't thought about that."

B

"It can work in well with what you've prepared to say to the press."

"Yes . . . yes, that's true."

There came a single knock at the door. Marti Dolores entered without waiting for an invitation.

"Am I interrupting anything?" she said as they rose from their chairs.

"Not at all," her husband replied. "We were just waiting for you."

"I haven't kept you?" She didn't sound as if she cared one way or the other. "I had to stop at the office on my way, so I parked there and took a cab over here."

"No, we were having a little chat before going down."

"Ah. Hello, Bill."

"Marti," he replied with a slight nod.

"Shall we go, then?" Dolores said, extending an arm toward the door.

"All right."

Bill fell in behind them as they went out through the reception area. He paused by Paula's desk. "Are you coming?"

"No, thanks," she said flatly. "I had enough of it yesterday."

"Oh, yes," said Marti, looking down at the young woman. "Louie told me that you were very much affected by the exhibit."

"I . . . it was a little close in there," Paula said with a glance at her employer.

"Are you better now?"

"Much, thank you. But I'm sure it will seem even more close with a crowd down there."

"No doubt," said Marti with an indulgent smile. Then she turned to Dolores. "We'll be late."

They headed for the private elevator, but Bill hesitated for a moment. "Are you sure you're all right?"

"Honestly, Bill, I'm fine!" she said.

"Okay," he said, reddening and feeling more perplexed than ever.

Their ride to the third floor was a quick one. The elevator doors opened to reveal the lobby thoroughly packed with people anxious with waiting. When they saw Dolores, they broke into loud, spontaneous applause, like an audience first sighting the orchestra conductor.

Dolores made his way through the crowd, followed by Marti and Bill, and soon reached the entrance where Hector and Lisa stood waiting.

"Good morning, Dr. Gonzalez," Dolores said professionally. He shook the older man's hand as lightbulbs flashed, but he didn't even glance at Lisa.

"Good morning."

"Great crowd."

"Yes, it is," Gonzalez said.

A microphone had been set up for Dolores's use, and he stepped behind it and tapped it lightly. "Ladies and gentlemen . . ." He paused and waited until the tumult had died away and he was sure that all the cameras were trained on him. "Ladies and gentlemen, I thank you very much for coming out to the opening of this new exhibit, 'The Chinchorro Mummies.' These are treasures of the Chilean past that have never before been seen here in Chicago, and probably never will again. It is my pleasure and privilege to sponsor the exhibit, so that we here in the great city of Chicago may come to know this fascinating bit of history." Here he turned to Al, who handed him the long, sharply pointed scissors right on cue. "So, by cutting this ribbon, I hereby declare the exhibit open."

He followed through, deftly snipping the red ribbon dead center, letting it fall away to the sides. A loud cheer went up from the crowd, followed by another extended round of applause.

Al unhooked the velvet rope that held back the crowd and began to let them into the exhibit a handful at a time. Hector looked on with grave displeasure as the first group went through the entrance. Then he turned and without a word to Lisa, left the lobby.

"What now?" Marti asked her husband.

"Now, my darling wife, there are interviews to do."

"I'll start rounding them up," said Bill. "Channel Seven first, do you think?"

"Yes."

Bill disappeared into the crowd.

"You don't need me around for your interviews."

"It would look best."

"You don't have to have me on your arm. You're impressive enough on your own. And I do have cases to get to."

"It won't take long." His tone was firm enough to convey that this was something that was expected of her. She sighed with resignation, letting him know he was being tiresome.

"All right, Louie. I suppose you're right. It would be best to look like a family man for the cameras."

Far to their right, unnoticed by husband and wife, standing by a vendor selling a variety of T-shirts, was a woman in a faded floral dress and with a denim bag slung over her shoulder. She had short, dull red hair and a pale, round face spotted with a host of freckles. Rather than watching the crowd or perusing the merchandise, she appeared to be keenly interested in Dolores. When he sent Bill on his way, the woman divided her attention between Dolores and his assistant. Bill spoke to a reporter and another man who had a camera hoisted on his shoulder. After a few seconds, the threesome started to make their way around the perimeter of the crowd.

The woman took that as her cue. She started to move slowly toward Dolores and Marti, being careful not to draw attention to herself.

"You know Art Durant," said Bill when they reached Dolores.

"Of course. Art." Dolores shook the reporter's hand. The cameraman stood behind Durant, poised and ready.

Durant asked a series of brief questions whose sole purpose was to give Dolores an opportunity to advertise the exhibit. Once the preliminaries were out of the way, Durant said, "Not everyone is happy about the Chinchorro mummies being brought here."

"Yes. There has been an ongoing protest—a very colorful one, I might add—right outside the building. I've even received death threats."

"You have?" Durant said with interest.

"Oh, yes," Dolores said with an unconcerned smile. "I've been sent notes threatening my life for this 'desecration.' "

"You don't seem worried."

Dolores shrugged. "People who send anonymous threats are generally cowards. And I don't see this as desecration. Far from it. This is an important part of history, and it should be shared. As you know, history is very important to me, and I—"

"You're a liar!" a female voice boomed out.

With a catlike instinct, the cameraman immediately located the source of the disturbance and trained his lens on her. The other crews jockeyed for a position from where they could see the action. The stunned crowd fell silent.

"I beg your pardon, ma'am, we're filming here . . ." Bill said.

"You're a damn liar!" the woman yelled, not taking her eyes off Dolores. He was trying to look impassive, but there was fire behind his eyes. Marti stood by his side, her expression faintly amused.

"Madam, I don't know—" Dolores began.

"I know what you're trying to do! I'm Samantha Campbell. I'm with the Chicago Commission for Historical Preservation. This whole thing is a farce! You don't give a damn about history. You're just trying to divert attention from how you've raped the history of this city, destroying some of our most historically significant buildings!"

A pair of guards who'd been stationed on either side of the escalator started to cross the lobby toward the woman.

Bill tried again. "This is neither the time nor the place—"

"This is exactly the time and place! Right here at this farce! All the money in the world isn't going to buy you the goodwill of the people of this city. We know what you're doing! You've destroyed half the city, and now you're trying to get your greasy hands on the rest of it, starting with the Stone Candy Factory. And I'm telling you it's not going to happen. You are never, *never*, going to get your hands on that building!"

Despite his usual ability to control himself, Dolores did a double take at the mention of the factory. His face began to burn.

The guards approached the woman from behind and each grabbed an arm. She continued her tirade as they hauled her toward the escalator.

"It's not going to work, Dolores! People aren't stupid! We can see through you! *Right through you!* It's over! There's only one way to deal with people like you! I'm telling you, you'll *never* get the Stone Candy Factory!"

The moment the woman was out of sight, her fading voice was

drowned out as the crowd broke into an excited chatter, most of which sounded very amused.

Dolores stood glaring in the direction of Campbell's departure. Durant said, "So, Mr. Dolores, care to comment?"

"No," Bill interjected quickly.

Dolores turned a frigid stare at his assistant, then turned back to Durant. "Of course not. Such charges are unanswerable. To respond to them would only give them validity." He slipped an arm around Marti's waist, said "Come on," and steered her toward the elevator with Bill trailing behind. It was best for Durant that Dolores didn't notice the prominent smirk with which their retreat was greeted. Flashbulbs seemed to be going off from all directions.

"Well, if we're done, I'll be on my way," Marti said lightly.

"You will not leave right now," Dolores said through clenched teeth.

"It's not necessary for me to go all the way up with you and come back down."

"I think it is. It will be a show of solidarity."

Marti stared at her husband with a curious smile as Bill inserted his card in the lock of the private elevator. The doors opened at once.

"Louie, really, this is—" Marti began.

"Get on!"

She complied with a weary sigh. Dolores and Bill followed her in, the latter using his card and pressing the button for the top floor.

Once the doors had closed, Dolores turned to Bill, and measuring each word, said, "Get Alderman Daniel Nathanson in here! Right now!"

"I have no idea where he is," Bill replied.

"Get him here! I want to see him *today!*"

"What's the hurry?"

"You heard what that woman said. She used the name of the Stone Candy Factory!"

"Yes?"

"That can mean only one thing. The Historical Commission has been tipped off! I don't believe you or my wife would do that—"

"Thank you," Marti said with a wry twist of her lips.

He ignored her. "That leaves only one person. Nathanson!"

"You've had him floating the idea among some of the other aldermen," Bill said hesitantly. "Maybe one of them—"

"He hasn't been using my name!"

"I know, but people are bound to figure out what a trial balloon is all about."

"Are you going to do as I say?" Dolores snarled.

"I'll try. I don't even know if I can find him."

"Because if you're not going to do it, I can find someone who will!"

"Now wait a minute—"

"Just do it!"

"Nathanson is an alderman. He might not be able to get here today."

"He will if he knows what's good for him. He did this, and I know why. I'm going to break that bastard!"

The elevator came to a halt at the penthouse and the doors opened. Bill and Dolores stepped off, but Marti remained behind, propping the doors open with her left hand.

"Is my duty over?" she asked, looking her husband directly in the eye.

"Yes," he said curtly.

"Then if it's all the same, I'll leave now. Bill?"

He stepped back on, slipped his card in the lock and pressed the button for the lobby.

"Thank you," she said as he withdrew himself. She looked back at her husband. "It's been fun, as always."

The doors closed on her like the curtains at the end of a play.

"I'll get started trying to locate the alderman," said Bill as he headed for his office.

Dolores watched him go, his expression anything but satisfied. He went into his outer office, where Paula was busy sorting through a stack of papers.

"How did it go?" she said, looking up at him. The set of his features told her she shouldn't have asked.

"Paula, I want you to do something for me. I saw Lisa Rivera, Hector Gonzalez's assistant—you remember her?"

"Yes," Paula well remembered the woman who had ignored her the day before.

"I saw her at the exhibition hall. I want you to go down to the lobby, find her, and tell her I want to see her."

There was a beat before she responded. "Yes, sir."

It was after eleven when Marti arrived at her LaSalle Street office. Although compared to Dolores Tower, her office building looked like it was from the Stone Age, Marti felt more comfortable there. She passed through the heavy glass doors and gave an offhand greeting to the receptionist, who stopped her long enough to give her a handful of phone messages, all legibly scribbled on the firm's small pink forms. Marti leafed through them as she went down the hall to her office. Once there, she tossed the messages into her In box, laid her briefcase on the desk and flipped it open, extracting the papers on which she planned to work.

"You missed the morning meeting."

James Harker had materialized silently in her doorway, like a Cheshire cat, leaning against the jamb.

"You knew that I was going to," Marti replied, unfazed by his sudden appearance.

"How did it go?"

She looked up and flashed a crooked smile. "It went exceedingly well. I would say that Louie will have more publicity than he bargained for."

"Tell me about it."

He came into the room and sat in a chair on the opposite side of Marti's desk as she described the scene. She made no attempt to hide her amusement.

"You sound very pleased," Harker said when she'd finished.

"It sounds disloyal, I know. But it's so seldom that the king is caught off guard that I can't help myself. He was no match for an attack that he didn't know was coming."

"Hmm." Harker laid his hands on the armrests. "I wonder what will happen now."

She shrugged. "He will continue to move forward. He will get what he wants, no matter what the cost. And it will probably cost him now—now that people know what he's up to. He doesn't care what anyone thinks—"

"Not even you?"

"Not even me. He'll probably be more determined than ever now to move ahead, no matter who he steps on." She paused and her eyes narrowed. "And he will get what he wants in the end, you know. Unless someone stops him."

"He'll be there late again tonight, right?" ·

"Oh, yes."

For nearly two hours, Bill tried to locate Alderman Nathanson, but found his way obstructed by Denise Michaels, Nathanson's office manager. The alderman had a number of private meetings and public events scheduled that day, Michaels explained repeatedly, and this made him uncharacteristically difficult to reach. She assured Bill that if the alderman called in—the likelihood of which she expressed sincere doubts about—she would tell him that Mr. Dolores was trying to reach him.

This was the first time in many years that Bill found that invoking Dolores's name failed to get immediate results. He called several more times, pressing Michaels with the urgency of the matter, but no amount of friendly cajoling made a difference, even when that cajoling took on a decidedly acidic edge. Michaels continued to firmly but politely deny any knowledge of Nathanson's exact whereabouts, and repeated her intention of passing along the messages.

Bill wasn't surprised by this. If Nathanson really was the one who had leaked the information about the Stone Candy Factory, the next logical move would be for him to go incommunicado. But despite Dolores's certainty in the matter, Bill wasn't at all sure that Nathanson was the one. Bill was keenly aware that over the years, Dolores had grown to the position of believing just about anyone else to be a fool, but that was an attitude in which Bill didn't indulge. He thought it possible that Nathanson had been clumsy in his handling of the trial balloons, and even if he hadn't, those to whom he'd spoken could easily have put two and two together and realized who was interested in the property. But Bill also realized that suggesting that to Dolores would do no good. Unless Dolores came to that conclusion within himself, it was an idea he would never really consider.

Until that time—if it ever came—it was Bill's unfortunate duty to report his failure to locate the elusive alderman. He was just getting up from his desk when his phone rang. He snatched up the receiver before his secretary could get it, hoping that Nathanson was finally returning his calls.

"Hello?"

"Hiya, Bill!"

"Who is this?" he asked, his hopes collapsing.

"It's Geoff. Geoff Hamilton."

Bill's face melted into a puzzled frown. "Oh. Hello, Geoff. Is everything all right? There's nothing wrong with Anna, is there?"

"You tell me!" he replied with a laugh.

"What?"

"Just kidding, just kidding. No, she's gone out to lunch with a client. I just wanted to call and congratulate you."

"Congratulate me?" Bill said after a slight pause.

"Yes, and I wanted to tell you how surprised I was—both me and Andy, really—and happy for you."

"What are you talking about?"

"Anna told us this morning. Your big news."

Bill could feel the blood draining from his face, but he kept his composure. Years in his present job had taught him to never let on when he didn't know what was happening. "We've had lots of news lately. Which are you talking about?"

"About your big move! She came in this morning and told us you guys are planning to move out West. She told us she's selling her share."

Bill transferred the phone to his left hand and ran the fingers of his right hand through his dark-brown hair. "Oh. Sorry. I didn't re-alize she was going to do that so soon."

"We're really happy for you. And surprised, like I said. When did you guys come to this decision?"

"Only recently. Very recently."

"I can't believe you would leave Dolores Development! I mean, that was the really big surprise to me and Andy."

"I'm sure it was. Listen, Geoff, I'd love to talk, but I'm really busy right now, so I'll have to let you go."

"Oh, sure, sure. That's okay. I just wanted to let you know that we're pulling for you."

"Thank you," Bill said. He cupped the back of the mouthpiece with his right hand. "Oh. One thing: nobody knows about our decision yet. I haven't even told anyone here. So please, don't mention it to anyone, will you? I wouldn't want it to get out before I have a chance to talk to Louie about it. You can understand that."

"Oh, sure, yes," Geoff replied amiably. "Don't worry. Not a word from either of us!"

Bill hung up the phone and sank back into the chair behind his desk in a near stupor. His eyes stared into space.

Over in the offices of Hamilton, Rogers and Braverman, Geoff was smiling as he hung up the phone. Andy Rogers stared down at him over the wall of his cubicle.

"Well?" Andy asked.

Geoff looked up at him and nodded. "I told you so!"

When Bill was finally able to rouse himself, he pushed back his chair, laid his palms on the desk and slowly stood up. He still felt as if he were in a daze, but at least he was able to move. He remembered that he needed to report on Nathanson to Dolores, and headed for the door. But all he could really think about was Anna. Things she had mentioned to him only as possibilities, she had now turned into certainties, but she hadn't bothered to tell him about it. One thing was now clear: she was planning a big change, and it looked like that no longer included him. For the first time in his life, he found himself alone at a crossroads, not knowing what to do. He went down the hallway and turned left into the reception area.

"He's not alone," Paula said as he passed her desk.

He stopped and came back. "Who's in there?"

"Lisa Rivera."

"The woman from the museum?"

Paula nodded.

"What did she want with him?"

She looked up at him. "She didn't want anything. He sent for her."

"He did? I wonder what that's all about?"

"I don't know," she said evasively.

Bill leaned over, resting his knuckles on her desk. "You don't like Ms. Rivera, do you?"

"I don't have any opinion. Listen, Bill, I have to talk to you—"

They were interrupted by the opening of the door to Dolores's office. Dolores came into the doorway, standing aside to let Lisa through.

"We will talk about it more later, then?" he said.

Lisa smiled. "Yes. Over dinner."

They both noticed Bill at the same time, and although neither of their expressions changed, Bill thought he could sense a sudden reserve on their part. And they weren't alone. Paula seemed to instantly acquire a coat of frost at the sight of Rivera, but Bill chalked that up to simple jealousy.

"Good morning, Mr. Braverman," Lisa said, moving toward him. To Bill, she looked like an animated mannequin.

"Good morning," he replied, shaking her offered hand. "I saw you down at the ceremony. I'm sorry we didn't have a chance to speak."

"That's all right," she said with a faint smile. "The circumstances weren't the best." She turned back to Dolores. "Until this evening, then."

All eyes followed Lisa as she glided out of the room toward the elevator.

"Hard not to watch her, isn't it?" said Dolores.

"She makes an impression." Bill started for the door, but Dolores stopped him.

"Were you able to get Nathanson?"

"No. That's what I was coming to talk to you about."

"That pretty much answers the question, doesn't it?"

"The question?"

"Of who's responsible for the leak."

"Well . . . I'm not sure that's necessarily true," Bill said hesitantly. "I'm not convinced—"

"I am," Dolores said curtly. "You seem hard to convince of anything lately."

"Maybe we should talk about—"

"Not right now. Just keep trying to get him." He turned to his secretary. "Paula, I want you in here."

Dolores went into his office, leaving the door open for her. She grabbed a pad and pencil and got up from her desk.

"This isn't their first 'meeting,'" she said to Bill in a low voice. "What's going on?"

Paula exhaled sharply and glanced at the open door. "We have to talk. Not here. Later."

"All right. Sure."

"I'll come to your office if I can get away." She said this as she hurried into Dolores's office, closing the door behind her.

Bill stood in the center of the room for several seconds, looking toward the door and feeling very much as if his entire life had been shut away from him.

"I've been wondering about that myself," Alderman Nathanson said when he finally returned Bill's host of calls. "It was as much of a surprise to me as it was to Louie, I'm sure!"

"Then you knew about the incident before I told you," Bill said pointedly. "How is that? It's only four o'clock."

"Heard about it on the news on the car radio. About noon, I think. They had quite a bit to say about it."

Bill was having a difficult time holding his temper in the face of Nathanson's tardy call and his obvious amusement. He switched the receiver from one hand to the other. "I should tell you, Louie believes that you're the one who leaked the news about the factory to the Historical Commission."

Nathanson laughed. "That's rich! He told me what he'd do if I crossed him. Not likely I'd be the one to do it. It must've come from someplace else."

"Where would that be?"

"How the hell would I know? Anyplace! These things get 'round, you know. I can't be held responsible for that."

Oh, yes you can, thought Bill. It was increasingly hard for him to hide his irritation, since Nathanson was doing nothing to disguise his delight at the turn events had taken.

As if reading his mind, Nathanson said with the practiced sincerity of a politician, "Now, really, Bill, in all seriousness, I have everything to lose if I was to go about trying to foul Louie up. I can't say I'm not happy that it's happened, since it gets me out of the fire— at least for now. But I wasn't the one that did it."

"I wish I could believe that," said Bill.

"Well, you can. Now I'm sorry, but I've got to get going. I've got two more meetings to go to before I sleep."

"No, wait. Louie wants to talk to you."

"I don't have time right now."

"He wants to see you. He was very direct on that point."

"Out of the question," Nathanson said affably. "Too much on my calendar today. I'll tell you what, though. I'll have Denise call you and the two of you can work out a time."

"Dan, Louie's not going to like this."

"Can't be helped. Sorry. Bye now!"

The click on the other end came before Bill could respond. He laid the receiver back on its cradle. He rested his elbows on his desk, interlaced his fingers and rested his chin on them. He stayed like this for several minutes before he was interrupted by a soft rap at the door.

"Come in," he said, straightening himself in his chair.

Paula hurried into the room looking rather pale and more than a little anxious. "I'm sorry it's taken me so long. Louie has kept me busy all afternoon."

"I was just going to go see him."

"He's not there. He's run down to check on how the exhibit's doing."

"I just got off the phone with Nathanson. You heard about the leak?"

She nodded.

"Louie's not going to like this. Nathanson denies knowing anything about it. Of course he'd do that even if he were guilty. But I don't know what to think about it. He didn't want to talk to Louie, which is bad. Makes me think just maybe the alderman thought Louie would see through him. He sees through pretty much everything."

"Not everything," said Paula. "You need to forget about that for now. I have something more important to tell you. About Ms. Rivera, and . . . I don't think it's good."

Bill heaved an impatient sigh. "Oh, for Christ's sake, Paula! Louie has had women before. You know that better than anybody. It's none of our business."

"This is." She took a seat in front of his desk. "Bill, do you know what he had me doing this afternoon? He had me checking her background."

"What?"

"Her *professional* background."

"Why would he have you do that? He usually leaves that to me."

"I know."

"He hasn't said anything to me about wanting to hire her."

"I didn't think he had."

Bill stared across the desk at her. He felt as if he had had all of the unpleasant surprises he could handle for one week. "What would he be hiring her for? We don't have any positions open."

Paula raised her eyebrows significantly. "Maybe we will."

It took a few seconds for this to get through to him. "He's not going to replace me," he said with an uncertain laugh. "I've been with him since the beginning. Almost."

"And you know how he's changed over the years. And you of all people know what he's capable of, but—"

"Of course I do. But not me! Hell, we're like brothers." Even as he said this, a hundred pictures flashed through his mind: pictures of disapproving looks he'd noticed lately, and the growing sharpness in Dolores's attitude toward him over the past several months.

Paula sat back in her chair and curled her lips. "Have it your own way. I just thought I should let you know."

"The whole idea is ridiculous," he said with a lack of conviction. "He's only just met her."

"Are you sure about that? He went down to Santiago a couple of times about the exhibit. And . . . even if he did just meet her, he seems to have gotten to know her really fast."

Bill waved this off. "I'm sure there's nothing in it. Knowing Louie, he's just—I shouldn't say this, but if he is talking to her about a job, he's probably stringing her along to get what he wants."

"Could be." Paula didn't point out the obvious, because she didn't need to: Bill knew that if that were the case, Dolores certainly wouldn't have needed Paula to check into Rivera's background. She looked down at her hands and flexed her fingers together. "But I think he's already gotten what he wants."

Dolores didn't leave the office until seven, long after sending Bill home with a flea in his ear about his failure to produce Alderman Nathanson in the flesh. As Bill had expected, relaying the gist of his phone conversation hadn't been enough. Dolores took Nathanson's reluctance to appear as further proof of his guilt. And Bill's failure as further evidence of his decline. He was going to have to do something about both of them.

Dolores rang for his private elevator, and as he waited, he turned over in his mind just how to go about punishing the alderman for this betrayal. When the door opened, he got on, slipped his card into the slot and pressed the garage button. As the elevator ran smoothly and swiftly down the shaft, Dolores's mind turned to a more pleasant theme: the dinner he was about to have with Lisa Rivera and what would inevitably lie beyond it. He was intrigued by the strong, forceful woman and looking forward to an evening that would prove stimulating in more ways than one. In some respects, she reminded him of his early days with Marti, before their relationship had degenerated into an endless, complicated business arrangement in which everything, including sex, had to be negotiated. Of course, Lisa was quite a bit younger than Marti—almost as young as Marti had been when they met. Perhaps in time, Lisa would harden in the same way Marti had.

The elevator slowed to a stop at the garage level. The doors whisked open and Dolores stepped off, then stopped suddenly as the doors closed behind him. Given the late hour, the lot was empty, except for one other car parked on the far side. But Dolores thought he'd heard movement: a brief scuttling sound that came and went almost before it had time to register. He waited and listened, scanning the lot with narrowed eyes. Even though the place was fairly well-lit, the low ceiling and plentiful cement posts made it seem dark. When the sound wasn't repeated after an interval, he started to cross around the front of his car.

Just as he reached the door on the driver's side, a figure stepped out from behind one of the cement posts about thirty feet from him. The figure was clad head to toe in strips of cloth, and a coal-gray mask covered the face. Long black hair streamed out from above the mask. In its right hand it clutched one of the long harpoons of the type used by the Chinchorros, its tip made of stone and filed to a sharp point.

Dolores was startled at first by the sudden, bizarre appearance of this specter. It was as if the mummy that the cleaning woman had insisted she'd seen had come to life and gone into hiding, only to reappear now. But Dolores's surprise quickly evaporated, giving way to anger.

"What the hell are you doing down here?"

The specter didn't reply. The tiny, dead eyes remained pointed at him.

"You know you're not supposed to be down here!"

Again there was no answer. After a lengthy silence, the mummy began to move forward.

"What?" Dolores stammered, backing away. "What are you do-ing?"

The mummy continued to advance, slowly raising the harpoon as if about to spear a fish.

"What the hell do you think you're doing?"

The mummy lunged forward with a shriek.

Not realizing he'd already backed his way to within inches of the wall, Dolores turned and lurched away to escape the blow, and forcefully struck his head against the concrete as the stone point of the harpoon made contact with his neck.

6

WEDNESDAY

Y ou wanted to see us?"
said Ransom. He was framed in the doorway of Sergeant Mike Newman's office. Gerald White, Ransom's partner, stood directly behind
him, his face looming up over Ransom's shoulder like a full moon.

Newman sat at his desk drumming the sides of his thumbs against
its heavily scarred top. His salt-and-pepper hair looked a bit oilier
than usual, and there were heavy bags under his eyes. "Yes. I heard
from the mayor this morning—"

Ransom raised his right eyebrow as he interrupted. "The mayor
called you?"

"No, his message was passed on to me. What do you know about
Louie Dolores?"

Oh, Christ! Ransom thought with an inward sigh. *Here it comes.*
"I know what everybody else does."

"I mean recently. Did you happen to see the news last night?"

"Yes."

"Then you know he says he's received death threats."

"So he says."

"Well, we need to follow that up."

"We do? Did Dolores approach us about this?"

The drumming increased in intensity. "The mayor wants us to
follow it up."

"Nobody's been killed yet, have they?" said Ransom.

Newman sighed impatiently. "Dolores is a VIP, and the mayor wants to make sure we're doing everything necessary to ensure his safety."

"In other words, the mayor wants to make sure it looks like *he's* doing everything necessary. I wonder what that costs in terms of campaign contributions."

Newman ignored this. "He wants us to put our best man on it . . ." His voice trailed off as he added bitterly ". . . so I hear."

"And I'm the best man for this?" Ransom asked curiously. It was unlike Newman to so directly approach a compliment.

Newman had been looking down at his steadily moving thumbs. He raised his eyes to Ransom and grinned. "Yes, you are." After a beat, he remembered Gerald's presence. "You both are."

"Thanks," said Gerald.

Ransom eyed Newman for a moment. "Ah. I see." He turned to Gerald. "Let's go."

As they went down the back staircase to the parking lot behind area headquarters, Ransom said, "I had a premonition about this, you know, even though I thought I'd managed to stave off any trouble."

"How could you do that?" Gerald asked.

"I made sure Emily wasn't going to the opening of that damned exhibit."

Gerald laughed.

"She accused me of making it sound as if her presence at an event was a bad omen."

"Not seriously!"

"No, not seriously. I was teasing her about her past record. But it's like I told you before, this whole exhibit business has been giving me the itch. The building's too big, the exhibit's too big, and the man's too big. Too many people don't like him for too many reasons."

"And you're one of them."

Ransom stopped dead in his tracks and turned to look at his partner, who almost collided with him. "What makes you think that?"

"Oh, come on, Jer! In the zillion hours I've been stuck in the car with you, you've managed to mention a couple of times that you think this Dolores guy is destroying the city."

"Did I?" Ransom said. "I don't remember." Even after a decade with his partner, he still didn't relish the idea of anyone knowing him that well. Anyone besides Emily. They continued down the stairs. "At any rate, one of his detractors interrupted his little press conference yesterday."

"Yeah, I saw that," said Gerald. "So, I don't get it. The fact that you don't like him, is that what makes you the best person to talk to him?"

"Don't be silly, Gerald. Newman doesn't know what I think. But he does know that I don't care whether or not Dolores is a VIP."

He hit the bar that opened the back door and they both squinted as they went out into the bright sunlight.

"Well, it looks like keeping Miss Emily away from the opening did the trick," Gerald said, reverting to their earlier topic. "Nobody got killed."

"I don't know, Gerald. It's like that old joke." He came to a stop at the passenger door of the dark-blue Civic. "A man is walking through the woods and comes on another man who's sitting on a tree stump and knocking two sticks together. The first man says, 'Why are you doing that?' The second says, 'The noise keeps grizzlies away.' The first says, 'Why, there isn't a grizzly within fifty miles of here,' and the second says, 'See how well it works?' "

Gerald laughed. "What made you think of that?"

Ransom sighed. "Because right now I feel like the man with the sticks."

"Where's Braverman?" Dolores demanded of his secretary.

If Paula had been surprised by the tone of his voice and his use of his assistant's surname, that was nothing compared to the shock she received when she looked up. Dolores towered over her desk, his normally dark face reddened with anger. There was a large white bandage on the left side of his neck, and an ugly bruise, deep blue in its center and purple around the edges, on his right temple.

"My God!" Paula exclaimed. "What happened to you?"

"Answer the question! Is Braverman here yet?"

"Yes . . . yes, he was in at eight."

"Get him in my office! Now!"

Dolores marched into his office and slammed the door. Paula dialed a four-digit extension and when Bill came on the line, she relayed the message, urging him to hurry.

"I'll be right there," he said. He came out of his office quickly, pausing only to tell Alice, his own secretary, that he would be in with Dolores. Then he hurried down the hallway.

"Wait!" said Paula as he passed through the reception area.

He stopped. "What is it?"

"Just a warning. He's on the warpath. Something's wrong. I mean really wrong. He looks like he's been attacked!"

"What!" said Bill as he rushed for the door.

He found Dolores seated at his desk and staring in the direction of the door as if he'd been drawing Bill to his office through sheer force of will.

"Close it!" Dolores barked.

Bill complied. As he crossed to the desk, he said, "My God, what happened to you? Who did this?"

"Where the hell were you last night? I tried to get you for hours!"

"It didn't ring. I suppose Anna had the phone unplugged. We had . . . we had sort of a fight. She's been—"

Dolores slapped the top of his desk. "I don't want to hear the details of your personal life!"

"Why were you trying to get me?"

"Because of this, you idiot!" Dolores said, jabbing at the bandage on his neck with his index finger.

"Who did it?"

"That maniac! That goddamn maniac!"

"I . . . I don't . . ."

"That goddamn maniac who's down there doing his silly dance!"

"What? But he's—"

"Yes, I know! He's down there now, carrying on. Acting just like nothing happened!"

"I don't understand," Bill said helplessly. "What *did* happen?"

"He was waiting for me last night. Waiting in the garage."

94

"But how could he—"

"I don't know!" Dolores angrily cut him off again. "But he was there! He was waiting for me with one of those harpoon things. He grazed my neck with it."

"But . . . what happened? How did you get away?"

The redness in Dolores's face deepened. "I didn't. He had me backed against the wall. When he came at me with that thing, I slammed my head into the wall and knocked myself out. I must've been out for five minutes or more. When I came to, he was gone!"

"But this is crazy! Why would he do something like that?"

"Maybe he *really* objects to the exhibit!" Dolores said.

"Well . . . we should call the police."

"No, of course not," Dolores replied, with such utter disgust that Bill could see his career fading away.

"You don't want . . . not the media?"

"I swear to God, Bill, you really are losing it. No, I don't want to call the police or the media. There is another way to handle this—"

They were interrupted by a loud buzz from Dolores's phone. He snatched up the receiver and jabbed the intercom button. "What?"

Paula maintained a calm tone as her voice came through the receiver. "There are two police detectives here to see you."

"What?" Dolores said after a beat.

"Detective Ransom and Detective White."

Dolores's eyes flashed up at Bill. For an irrational moment, he thought his assistant had disobeyed him and called the police; then he remembered that he couldn't have done that yet.

"Show them in," he said. He replaced the receiver and rose. "The police are here."

Bill paled. "What? Why?"

"You're losing your nerve," Dolores said with quiet firmness. "You will not say anything."

"But shouldn't you—"

"Shut up! I'll do all the talking."

The door opened and Paula came in, holding the door aside as Ransom and Gerald passed through. She closed the door as she exited.

"Gentlemen," said Dolores, coming from behind the desk and offering his hand.

"Mr. Dolores," said Ransom, shaking it. "I'm Detective Ransom, this is my partner, Detective White."

"My assistant, Bill Braverman," Dolores said with a nod.

"Hello," said Bill.

Dolores took a deep breath. "I'm surprised to have a visit from the police. What can I do for you?"

"The question is, what can we do for you?" said Ransom. "We understand that you've been receiving death threats."

"I didn't call the police about that."

"No, but you should have. Death threats against someone of your . . ." He made a pretense of searching for the right word. ". . . stature aren't something to take lightly. That's why we were surprised when we learned about them. On the news."

"I didn't call the police because I'm sure the threats aren't serious."

Bill was staring at him with mute frustration. It was clear that he disagreed with Dolores and wanted to say something, but a mere glance from Dolores warned him to hold his tongue. Ransom didn't miss the silent exchange.

"The mayor seems to feel differently," Ransom said lightly.

"The mayor?"

"Yes. He's expressed concern about your safety."

"That was nice of him, but unnecessary."

"In light of his concerns and your high profile, perhaps you could let me decide whether or not these threats are serious." Ransom gestured toward the two chairs facing the desk. "May we?"

"Yes, of course."

Ransom and Gerald took their seats as Dolores crossed behind his desk and resumed his chair. Bill pulled a chair over from the table and sat beside the desk, where he could see both the detectives and his employer.

"I must say," Ransom began, "given the reason for our visit, that bandage is very provocative."

Dolores put a hand to it and smiled. "This? This is nothing. I just cut myself shaving."

"Really. Perhaps you should switch to a safety razor," Ransom said with a half smile. He allowed his eyes to fix on the bruise on Dolores's temple, but said nothing about it. "So, what form have these death threats taken?"

"The usual. Words cut out from newspapers or magazines." He reached into the center drawer of his desk, extracted a sheet and handed it to Ransom. "This is one I found the other day."

Ransom took it by the corners and read it. "Found it where?"

"Under my windshield wiper."

"When you car was . . ."

"I'm sorry, when it was parked in the garage here."

"I see. Is this a public garage?"

"No. There is a single-level private garage beneath the building. Public parking is in the multilevel lot across the street."

"So someone was able to get into your private garage to leave this note."

"Yes."

"You have security there, don't you?"

"Yes, of course," Dolores said, a slight edge to his voice. "You have to use a security card to get in."

Ransom elevated his right eyebrow. "Hmm. But someone was still able to get in. How many people have these security cards?"

"Everyone on my staff."

"No one else? This is an awfully big office building."

Dolores shook his head. "People who rent the other offices in this building do not have direct access to the secure areas. Building staff— by which I mean the engineers, security, and a few of the dock workers—are the only ones who do. The dock people are the ones that deliver things from receiving up to the various offices."

"Still a fair number of people with these cards."

"Yes, but I hardly think my staff . . . let me put it this way: my staff is thoroughly screened. I believe this note was left by an outsider. Obviously, there's a chink in our security."

"And you've had your security people look into it?"

For the first time, Dolores hesitated. "Well . . . I haven't yet. As I said before, I don't think this is serious."

"But even if the threat isn't serious, a breach of security would be, wouldn't it?" Though Ransom said this simply, there was a slight edge to his voice that implied he thought it curious that Dolores hadn't thought of this.

"No building can be completely secure, especially a garage," Dolores replied easily. "It does take a few seconds for the door to close once a car goes out. I imagine someone could've slipped in that way. Then all he'd have to do to get out is go up the stairs."

"The staircase isn't locked?"

He shook his head. "Not on the inside. You don't need a key card to get out through the staircase, only to get in."

"I see." Ransom looked back down at the note. " 'You desecrate, you die.' Have each of you handled this?"

Bill and Dolores both said yes.

"Do you have any idea who sent it?"

"None," said Dolores.

"Desecration. Do you know what that's referring to?"

"The exhibit!" Bill exclaimed.

Ransom and Gerald looked at him, Dolores didn't.

"Any particular reason you think that?"

Bill gave a cautious glance at his employer. "No. It's only that . . . I don't know, with this protest about the exhibit going on outside and everything . . . not that I have any reason to believe that he . . . any of them, really . . . have anything to do with this."

Ransom eyed him. "It's all right, Mr. Braverman. The leader of the protesters was on the news, and he used the word desecration. Perhaps that is what connected it for you."

"Yes, yes," Bill said with relief. "That's it. That and the fact that it just came the day before the exhibit opened."

"It was a logical connection. Any other candidates?"

"Who else could there be?"

"Oh, any number of people," said Ransom. He turned to Dolores. "There are people who believe that desecration is what you've done to some of our historic buildings."

"That's quite true," Dolores said without emotion.

"I believe someone expressed similar sentiments at the opening of your exhibit."

Dolores flushed slightly when reminded of this. He wasn't happy with the obvious fact that the incident was already common knowledge. "Yes, well, there will always be people who'll disrupt a happy occasion just to see themselves on television."

"Ah," Ransom said thoughtfully as he slid one leg over the other. "Is that what you think it was?"

"Of course. So, I'm afraid I don't have any leads for you."

"Have there been any other threats, besides this one?"

"There were a couple of others."

"With the same message?"

"More or less. I don't remember exactly. Like I said, I don't take them seriously."

There was a beat, then Ransom said, "So you didn't keep them?"

Dolores smiled apologetically. "No, I threw them away."

"I see."

Ransom stood up rather suddenly, leaving Gerald to scramble to his feet in an effort to not be left behind.

"Well, I don't think we need to take up any more of your time."

"I appreciate your concern, even if it is misplaced," Dolores said as he got to his feet. He was trying not to look surprised. Bill started to rise a split second after his employer.

"On the contrary, I think a man in your position should take a threat like this seriously, and we intend to look into it."

"Very well," said Dolores. "But I think you're wasting your time."

Ransom smiled. "The city pays me no matter what case I'm working on, Mr. Dolores."

"Point taken."

"May I?" Ransom said as he reached for the letter.

It was a rare moment of uncertainty for the self-assured developer. "Yes, of course."

Ransom picked up the sheet, folded it carefully and stuck it in the breast pocket of his jacket. "Thank you. We'll be in touch." He started for the door and said "Don't bother" when he noticed that Bill was advancing to show them out. Gerald said a quick good-bye and followed his partner.

They were silent as they stood waiting for the public elevator in the glass-enclosed vestibule. When the elevator arrived, they got on and Gerald pushed the button for the ground floor. Once the doors had closed, he said, "That was abrupt, even for you."

"Our departure? Hmm. I was getting tired of being stonewalled."

"Stonewalled?"

"Didn't their attitude strike you as a bit peculiar?"

Gerald shrugged. "A guy like that probably gets threats all the time. He's probably used to blowing them off."

"It's one thing to dismiss them, it's another thing to dismiss common sense."

"What? Oh, you mean the security stuff."

"Yes. I can halfway understand Dolores not being concerned about the threat, but it's difficult to believe he wouldn't be more disturbed that the person had broken into a security area."

"Yeah. You're right. But the way he explained it, it sounds like it would've been easy enough to do."

Ransom looked at him. "He should still be concerned."

The elevator stopped at the twenty-third floor to take on passengers, so the detectives suspended their conversation until they'd been deposited on the ground floor. As they walked through the mall to the Dearborn Street entrance, Gerald asked, "Do you think Dolores knows who put that thing on his windshield?"

"I don't know. What I found more peculiar is that Braverman seemed more worried about the whole thing than Dolores did. I got the feeling he knows something."

"How do you figure that?"

"Did you notice the tension when Braverman said he thought the note was referring to the exhibit? He said that without thinking, and he was sorry he did."

"Sorry? Why sorry?"

"I don't know that, either," Ransom said with a sigh. "There's only one reason I can think of."

They'd reached the revolving door. Gerald stopped and looked at his partner for a long moment. "Because Dolores didn't want him to say anything about it?"

"Exactly."

"That doesn't make any sense," Gerald said, shaking his head.

"If Dolores knows who's threatening him, why wouldn't he want to tell us?"

"That, to quote Hamlet, is the question. The one thing that's clear is that Dolores doesn't want the police involved."

Gerald started toward the door, but stopped when he realized that Ransom wasn't moving. He turned and found his partner staring into space, his eyebrows knit unhappily.

"What is it?" Gerald asked.

"Do you remember that article you showed me yesterday?"

"What? The one about the mummy? Yeah."

"Find out who answered that call, will you? I think we should talk to them."

"Why?"

Ransom sighed again. "Because it's another peculiar event."

"Why didn't you tell them about the attack on your life last night?" asked Bill once the detectives were gone.

Dolores sighed impatiently. "You know why. I already told you that we're going to take care of this some other way." He paused, laid his palms on the desk, and looked pointedly into Bill's eyes. "I would think that you would understand my reasons. However, if you don't . . ." He let his voice trail off suggestively.

"Of course I understand," Bill said after a beat. Dolores's tone wasn't lost on him. It carried the implication that this was just the latest in a long series of disappointments on the part of his assistant. "It's just, if your life really is in danger, I don't think we should take the risk."

Dolores produced a smile that didn't exactly inspire confidence. "I appreciate that. But as I said, we need to take care of this problem another way. I'm not going to let that fool or anyone else attack me and get away with it!"

"Are you sure it was him?"

"Of course I'm sure! I see him every damn day! Same costume! Same mask! He's out there in that same getup right now!"

"Yeah . . . I saw them when I came in. But I can't believe he'd attack you like that and . . . and then show up today as if nothing had happened. That would be crazy."

"It's happened. He's there."

"If you're not going to tell the police about it, what are you going to do?"

Dolores leaned forward, his smile growing malevolent and his eyes still fastened on Bill's. "It's not what *I'm* going to do, it's what *you're* going to do. . . ."

When the detectives got back to area headquarters, Ransom made a brief report to Sergeant Newman, while Gerald went off to perform his errands. When Ransom got back to his office, Gerald was waiting.

"I sent the letter to be fingerprinted, and I've got the other info," said Gerald. "Officers Nash and Tully at the Eighteenth answered the mummy call."

"The mummy call?" Ransom said as he crossed behind his desk. "I can see this going downhill very quickly."

He sat down and picked up the receiver, then dialed the number for the Eighteenth District. When the phone was answered, he asked for either Nash or Tully, and had a lengthy wait before someone came on the line.

"Nash here," said a youthful voice.

"Nash, this is Detective Ransom, Area Three. I understand you were called out to Dolores Tower the other night."

"Yeah, and I've taken a pretty good ribbing since then!" Nash replied. There was a smile in his tone.

"I can imagine. Can you tell me what happened?"

"Sure, but . . . you're not telling me something's come of this?"

"No, no, we're investigating something else that happened in that building, something that involved a break-in at their garage. I wanted to check out any other unexplained occurrence."

Nash snorted. "Unexplained occurrence! That's hot!"

Ransom cleared his throat. "Yes. Can you tell me what happened when you went there?"

Nash gave him a rundown of what Frieda Jablonski claimed to have seen.

"We went through the exhibit. Didn't find anything. And that Louie Dolores guy said nothing was missing."

Ransom's eyebrows went up. "Dolores was there?"

"Yeah. I mentioned that to him—that I was surprised he was there that late."

Ransom smiled into the receiver. "Did you, now? What did he say to that?"

"That he's running a million-dollar company and he has to work late. But I don't think he was working."

"Hmm?"

"Naw. He must have a gym in there or some workout equipment or something."

"Why do you say that?"

"His hair was wet, like he'd just stepped out of the shower before coming down."

"Hmm."

"Anyway, he kept telling us that he didn't think Jablonski had seen anything. He said she probably just got spooked in the exhibit. And that'd be easy enough to believe. You seen it?"

"Not yet."

"Well, it's kind of . . . I don't know, spooky."

"You sound doubtful," said Ransom, catching something unusual in the officer's tone.

"Well, there's one thing I really didn't like about the whole setup."

"Yes?"

"I don't believe in ghosts or spooks or mummies getting up and walking or anything like that. You ask me, the whole thing is stupid."

"Then you would be in agreement with Mr. Dolores. So what's the problem?"

Ransom heard Nash take a deep breath, then let it out slowly. "The problem is the Jablonski woman. I talked to her. She really was almost hysterical. We got her to quiet down a bit, and got the story out of her. But even then, she never stopped shaking. The way she was acting, it was too much."

"Too much?"

"You know, too much—too real for just being spooked."

"What are you saying?" Ransom asked.

Nash clucked his tongue. "I don't know what she saw, but I think she saw something."

Ransom was smiling when he hung up the phone.

"What is it?" asked Gerald, who had half-reclined on the old Naugahyde couch that was flush with the wall. "What are you smiling about?"

"I think Officer Nash is going to make a very good detective."

Things remained tense in the offices of Dolores Development for the rest of the day. After Dolores instructed Paula that he was not taking any calls, he emerged from his office only once. His mood seemed to have mellowed somewhat when he came over to her desk.

"I want you to do something for me. See if you can track down Lisa Rivera. She's staying at the Reliance Hotel. I'm afraid I stood her up last night. Smooth things over for me—you're good at that—and ask her to meet me at O'Leary's at seven, if she will." His lips crooked into a smile. It was evident that he was confident Rivera would show up. He went back into his office.

Paula did as she was instructed and reached Rivera with her first call to the Reliance. Then she called Bill and filled him in on the latest development.

For his part, Bill chose to keep to his office, feeling that under present circumstances, it was best to stay out of the line of fire. The specter of Lisa Rivera, and his boss's intention for his attacker, were bad enough without risking further direct confrontations. He didn't see Dolores again until stopping in to see him just before leaving that evening. Paula had already gone home, so he tapped on the door and poked his head in without being announced.

"Louie? Everything okay?"

Dolores looked up from the plans he'd been scanning. "Yes?"

"It's six-thirty. I'm on my way out now. Just wondered if you wanted me to wait and go down with you."

"Don't be ridiculous."

"Okay."

Bill started to retreat, but paused when Dolores called his name.

"Bill, you're going to take care of that matter this evening."

"Of course I am."

"Good." Dolores looked back down at the plans, and Bill left without another word.

Anna had been driven to leave work early by a debilitating headache occasioned, she believed, by the release of tension now that she'd put things in motion, as well as the first inklings of stress at the prospect of telling Bill what she'd done.

She swallowed a handful of aspirin, washing them down with a bottle of designer water. She then laid back on the sofa and drifted off into a clouded sleep in which she seemed to be wandering through billows of mist. She would slowly wave her hands in front of her, hoping to part the mist, but the prospect of its clearing always seemed to remain just out of reach.

When she woke, she checked her watch. She'd been asleep for over an hour, but her headache had abated. In its place was a drug-induced sense of euphoria. She felt that everything, somehow, would turn out for the best, that she no longer had to worry about anything. The impasse with Bill would be over. She didn't necessarily think the means were important. She and Bill might end in parting, but that would be all right, just as it would be all right if they stayed together. Everything seemed to have changed. It all seemed so clear, now that she was finally taking steps.

She cautiously rose from the couch, fearing that sudden movement might renew the pounding in her head, but once upright, she found herself still relatively pain-free. Since it was almost time for dinner, she went into the kitchen, but stopped in the center of the room, lost for a moment in indecision. It didn't seem important to eat now, and she couldn't think of anything she wanted to have anyway. Perhaps when Bill came home . . . which she was sure he would do very late. But tonight, that wouldn't bother her. Tonight, she would take everything in stride. She wrapped her arms around her chest, hugging herself tightly, eyes closed, and a broad smile spread across her face.

After Anna had spent several minute like this, swaying back and forth slowly and lightly humming a half-remembered tune, she let her arms fall to her sides.

Then she headed for the front door.

Hector Gonzalez came back to Dolores Tower at a quarter to seven. After a second day of endless heavy traffic through the exhibit, he wanted to walk through it and see how the artifacts were holding up. At least, that's what he told himself. In reality, he had been intrigued ever since reading the newspaper account of the cleaning woman's experience in the exhibit. Until he'd seen that, he'd almost been able to convince himself that his own experience had been the work of his tired imagination, or a dream. But the cleaning woman had seen something, too. It wasn't just him.

Maybe the spirits of the dead really did still live; or maybe they had been brought back by this . . . "desecration" was the only word he could think of for it, even though he found it inappropriate. He didn't feel it was a desecration to have the mummies on display; they'd done that much in his own museum. The desecration lay in moving them, risking damaging them for the sake of money. Would the spirits of the dead feel as he did about that? After so many centuries of lying dormant, would they rise to avenge themselves over this kind of slight?

If he calmed his mind and looked at it rationally, he thought it hardly probable. The Chinchorros were fisherpeople, quiet and peaceful by nature. They weren't warriors. *And goddammit*, Gonzalez thought as he entered the mall, *they weren't Egyptians! There are no curses! Dolores even has me thinking about them the wrong way!* But still, he wanted to go up and look through the exhibit now that it was closed for the day. Perhaps sit for a while. And wait.

Wait for what? he thought. *A reappearance of the ghost?* But he couldn't help himself. He was drawn back to it.

Hector had entered the building from the rear. He was crossing the mall toward the escalator, but when passing O'Leary's, he glanced in and suddenly came to a stop. Lisa Rivera was seated at the bar alone, sipping a clear drink in a short glass. She was wearing a black, form-fitting cocktail dress, her exposed knees crossed and turned slightly to one side.

Even with the strain there had been between them, Hector didn't like the idea of leaving her sitting alone in a bar without checking to make sure whether or not she wanted company. Fighting the pull of the exhibit, he went into the bar.

"Good evening," he said, coming up on her left.

"Hello, Hector."

"Are you alone?"

"I appear to be," she said somewhat ruefully, stirring the drink with a small plastic stick.

"Do you want company?"

"Thank you," she said, not unpleasantly. "Actually, I'm waiting for someone."

"Mr. Dolores?"

She smiled. "Don't sound so disapproving, Hector."

Part of the burden lifted from his heart at her tone. It was as if now that their positions were clear, and now that he was definitely leaving the museum they were meeting more as equals than they ever had. And perhaps she had resigned herself to the truth in what he'd said to her.

"I wasn't disapproving," he said kindly. "It is none of my business."

She took a drink, then put the glass down on the small, square napkin. "If you want to know the truth, I don't think I've made much of an impression on Mr. Dolores. I was supposed to have dinner with him last night, but he stood me up. His secretary called me today and said that something came up last night that was unavoidable, then asked me to meet him tonight."

"He's an important man," said Hector.

"I think he likes people to know that."

"Is he late now?"

"No, I ended up being ready too soon, so I thought I might as well come here early and have a couple of drinks."

"You're anxious?" he said with a surprised smile.

"No, bored."

"That would be closer to the truth, I think. Do you want me to stay with you?"

She shook her head. "I'm fine on my own."

"Very well," he said as he started to move away.

"By the way, Hector, what are you doing here so late?"

He performed one of his mournful shrugs. "I just wanted to check the exhibit."

"You can't leave it alone, can you?" she said, some of the usual hardness returning to her voice.

"I don't have much longer," he said.

He went out of the bar, leaving Lisa looking after him with a puzzled frown.

"They sent you to him because of the mummy?" said Emily, knitting her thin, gray eyebrows with incredulous amusement.

They had just finished dinner, and Lynn Francis was clearing the table after pouring out three cups of hot tea. Lynn's straight, tawny hair was tied back in a ponytail and she was wearing a tomboyish combination of black jeans and white shirt. Ransom and Emily were seated opposite each other at the kitchen table. Ransom had just told them a little about the errand he'd been sent on that morning—he couldn't bring himself to call it a case—and they continued the conversation over tea.

"No, not because of the mummy, because of the death threats," said Ransom. "I take it you read the article in the paper about the mummy."

"Yes. And I saw the poor woman on television." Emily paused, then her voice took on a disapproving edge. "I must say, the local news media has a lot to answer for. They shoved microphones in Miss Jablonski's face when she was clearly very distressed."

"I thought the woman was hired to say those things," said Lynn. "For publicity. But Emily doesn't think it was a publicity stunt—although I haven't been able to get out of her exactly what she does think it was."

"Mr. Dolores would have us believe that she was imagining

things because of being alone in the exhibit," said Ransom to Emily. "What was your impression of her?"

"Well . . . it's difficult to say with someone who doesn't speak the language well. You don't know how much of your impression is being formed by the simple fact that it's difficult for them to express themselves clearly. I don't want to sound unkind . . ."

"As if you could."

". . . but I thought her rather credulous."

"So you think she's an unreliable witness."

"Not at all! I would be inclined to believe that she saw something. Probably what she said she saw."

"What!" Lynn exclaimed, dropping a dish into the sink with a clatter. "You can't be serious!"

"Oh, but I am," Emily said simply. "Unless she's mentally defective, or taking some sort of mind-altering drug, the whole thing is just so much nonsense!"

Lynn's forehead creased attractively. "That's what I meant."

"No, dear, what I'm saying is I don't think the imagination of a healthy person would stretch to producing a mummy just because the surroundings are a bit . . . unusual."

"You think the woman actually saw a mummy?"

"Someone dressed as a mummy, certainly."

Lynn shook her head slowly. "But why would somebody dress up like that and go sneaking around the exhibit when there's nobody there?"

"Ah, but someone was there," Emily replied, her light-blue eyes twinkling.

"You think someone set out to scare the cleaning woman?"

"I can see no other purpose in it—and after all, that is what happened."

Lynn laughed and turned on the tap, sending hot water splashing into the sink full of dishes. "I wouldn't argue with you. As crazy as that sounds to me, knowing you, it will turn out to be true!"

Ransom smiled. "Well, you'll be glad to know that you agree with Officer Nash."

"Oh?" said Emily.

"Yes. At least as far as believing that Jablonski actually saw something. I don't think he's taken it any farther than that."

"The question is, what reason could there be for someone to do that?" Lynn said.

Emily absently took a sip of tea as she gazed into space. She said vacantly, "It's interesting, isn't it? People always seem to complicate matters more than they need to."

Lynn's forehead creased again. Not for the first time, she was finding it hard to understand how Emily had gotten from one point to the next. "Sorry, Emily, I don't follow."

Emily adjusted herself in her chair and gently cleared her throat. "I mean, people often say, 'Why was this done,' or 'Why did that happen,' because the obvious answer is so hard to believe. You quite naturally ask why someone would be dressed as a mummy in the exhibit when only a cleaning woman is there, because the obvious answer seems fantastic."

Emily arched her brows until they formed points in their centers.

Lynn released a throaty laugh. "But that brings us back to publicity, doesn't it?"

"I'll admit that's a possibility. I would think that a headline— even a small one—that read 'The Mummy Lives?' would be sufficient to bring in the masses." She shifted again in her seat. "But what I meant was, the object was to scare the cleaning woman . . . However, I think the real question is, what does one thing have to do with the other?"

After a beat, Ransom said, "Now I'm the one not following."

"I mean, what does the incident of the mummy have to do with the death threat sent to Mr. Dolores?"

"Oh. Probably nothing."

"And yet you looked into both."

"Only because they both were a little strange."

Lynn switched off the water. "I thought you said it wasn't strange for Dolores to get death threats."

"Yes, but it was unusual that he wasn't more concerned that security at his building had been breached—that someone broke into the garage to leave the threat."

"Perhaps no one did," said Emily, her cup poised at her lips.

"Huh?" said Lynn.

Emily shrugged and replaced her cup in its saucer. "If the mummy was a publicity stunt, perhaps the threat was, too."

"Emily, you're amazing!" Lynn exclaimed with obvious admiration.

Ransom looked at the young woman. "You know, that idea *had* crossed my mind as well."

Lynn returned a sly grin. "You're amazing, too, Mr. Detective." She turned back to the sink and started washing the dishes.

Ransom said to Emily, "It occurred to me that the most likely reason he didn't tell the police about the threat was because he put it there himself, another ploy for publicity. But there're two things about that that bother me. One is that the note itself wasn't really necessary."

"Maybe it was a preventive measure," Emily offered, "in case the police showed up, as you did. I've seen him interviewed now and then. He doesn't seem like the type of man who would do things by half."

"Maybe. But it seems like an awful lot of trouble to go to when he could've just said he threw it out like he did with the rest."

"What is the other thing?"

"The fact that his assistant, Bill Braverman, seemed so worried about Dolores's safety. Braverman is his right-hand man. I don't think Dolores would've hatched this kind of scheme for publicity without Braverman's aid. Then again, Dolores seemed unhappy that Braverman showed that concern to us."

"Hmm. That *is* puzzling."

"And there's also the fact that Dolores looked like he'd been struck, at least once."

"I would think he would've wanted to tell the police about that, if he actually had been attacked," said Emily.

"Exactly." Ransom heaved a frustrated sigh. "All we have are questions that I was forced to look at because the mayor stuck his nose in it, and we don't even have a body."

"Poor dear," Emily said chidingly. "To be so disappointed that nobody's been murdered!"

*   *   *

Louie Dolores couldn't have agreed with Emily more. It was seven o'clock when he finally rolled up the plans he'd been working on and put them back into the credenza. He switched off his lights, left his office, pausing to lock the door. He went through the reception area to the hallway, fishing in his pocket for his key card. Once at the elevators, he slipped the card into the slot and rang for the car.

As he waited, he thought scornfully of Bill's offer to accompany him to the garage, as if he were a frightened child. The only reason the attacker had bested him the night before was because he had been taken by surprise. That wouldn't happen again. Tonight he would be on his guard. Besides, he wasn't going down to the garage just yet. He was going to meet Lisa. A warmth came over him as he thought of her. It might be a long time before he actually left the building.

He heard the *whoosh* of the elevator as it approached, and the double bell signaled that it would be going down. Dolores took a step closer to the door.

The doors slid open, and there stood the mummy. It looked as it had before, the dead-gray mask with its staring, pinhole eyes, the hair streaming out behind its head, and its torso and limbs wrapped in gauze. But this time, its right arm was raised, and in its hand gleamed a long, sharp blade.

Before Dolores could cry out, with one swift movement the mummy swung the blade down, plunging it into his victim's chest.

Dolores's hands flew forward on impact and clamped the mummy's arm, but his entire body began to tremble violently and his grip loosened almost immediately. A soft gurgling emanated from his throat as his knees gave way. He slumped to the ground.

The mummy stood over him for a moment, staring down at the painfully contorted body. Then it reached down with its bandaged hands, grabbed Dolores by the ankles, and dragged him onto the elevator.

1

Bill cursed aloud as the cars slowed to a near halt on Lake Shore Drive, although he wasn't nearly as irritated by the stop-and-go traffic as he was by the job his employer expected him to perform. He gently beat the bottom of the steering wheel with his fists, resisting the urge to lay on the horn, which would do no good and probably only serve to agitate other drivers.

It took nearly forty minutes to reach his destination, which gave him ample time to contemplate what he was about to do.

The orders he'd received from Dolores preyed on his mind not shrinking from having involved him in bribery, Dolores was now perfectly willing to turn him into a borderline hoodlum. He was expected to hire thugs to beat Dolores's assailant to within an inch of his life. The relish with which Dolores had outlined everything he wanted done to the man had turned his stomach.

Oh, for Christ's sake! Bill said to himself with disgust. *In the long run, it really doesn't matter, does it? Let it go!*

He got off Lake Shore Drive at Hollywood, then turned on Kenmore and drove slowly down the street. Half of the buildings were missing their numbers, and he'd been here only once before, so he wanted to be sure of finding the right place. When he located it, he wedged his car between an ancient Plymouth and an even more ancient Impala and climbed out.

The building in question was a large, old, red-brick apartment, so dilapidated it looked as if the vibrations from the doorbell might cause it to shatter. Bill went into the vestibule and pressed the bell for the man he wanted to see. When there was no answer after a considerable wait, he rang again. A couple of minutes went by with still no answer.

Bill cursed under his breath as he headed back to his car. He could've called to see if the man was in before coming all the way up here, but the man never answered the phone, and Bill didn't want there to be any possible way that anyone could trace a connection between the two of them, anyway.

He got back into his car, switched on the motor, and carefully extricated the car from its tight spot.

As he headed back toward Lake Shore Drive, the fruitlessness of his journey, the distaste he felt toward the mission to begin with, and the fact that the uncompleted task would loom over him until it was accomplished, nagged at his mind until he thought he'd scream.

8

THURSDAY

Paula Dryer arrived at Dolores Tower just before eight in the morning. She drove her car into its place four spaces over from her boss's. She wasn't surprised that his car was already there—he often arrived long before she did—but she was a little disheartened. Still feeling the strain from Dolores's unexplained fury of the previous day, Paula had hoped to have a brief respite from the tension before he came to work. But it was not to be.

She switched off the ignition, took up her purse and opened the door of her car. After locking it, she went to the private elevator, inserted her card and pressed the button. She tapped her foot as she waited, already sensing a tightness in her stomach from the certainty that the rapidly decaying atmosphere around the office would be no better on this day, if not worse.

Paula heard the quiet *whoosh* as the elevator descended and came to a stop. When the door opened, she took a step forward, and froze in horror when she saw what was lying on the floor. She screamed as she fled toward the stairs.

"I hate to say I told you so—" said Ransom as he flicked the ash from his cigar out the window.

"No you don't," his partner interjected.

"—but I knew something would happen at this exhibit. I did say that."

Gerald laughed as he turned the car onto Dearborn. "Yes, you did."

When they reached Dolores Tower, they found a squad car pulled across the entrance to the parking level, and a uniformed officer standing by the key-card box. When he saw them, he tapped on the roof of the squad, signaling for his partner to pull out. As it moved away, the officer came over to the detective's car.

"Officer Hershey, Detectives," he said with a nod.

"White and Ransom," said Gerald, for once giving himself top billing. "The body is down there?"

"That's where it was found. Tully and Nash are keeping an eye on things."

"Really?" Ransom said.

"They took the call."

"This must be their lucky day."

"Huh?"

"Nothing," said Gerald. "Can you open the door?"

"Sure." He reached into his pocket and pulled out a plastic card. "They gave me one of these key-card things. We wanted to keep the door closed. Didn't want to attract attention."

"Good idea," said Gerald.

Hershey went over to the box and stuck the card in. The huge door shivered, then began to rise.

"Into the belly of the beast," said Ransom as they proceeded down the ramp.

The garage was empty except for two civilian cars near the elevators and another squad car parked several spaces away. An officer was leaning against it.

Gerald pulled up behind Paula's car and switched off the engine. As they got out, he said, "Are you Nash or Tully?"

"Nash," the officer replied, coming toward them.

As Ransom had imagined during their phone conversation, Nash was quite young and exuded the kind of confidence that was unmitigated by years of experience. He had flawless skin, bright brown eyes, and a smile that implied he was genuinely pleased to meet them.

"Ah! Officer Nash," said Ransom, offering his hand, "Ransom. We spoke on the phone yesterday. This is Detective White."

"I remember," said Nash.

"I thought you were second shift. You and your partner are on days now?"

"Yeah. Switched this morning, and this is the first call we get. Can you imagine? I guess I shouldn't be surprised, though."

"Why's that?"

Nash shrugged. "This place is big as a city. I suppose it would have it's own crime rate. 'Course, since this is a 'name,' our supervisor's been and gone."

"He didn't call for any more backup?" Ransom asked as they went toward the elevator.

"Didn't seem to be much point."

"Oh?"

"He's obviously been dead for more than a few hours. It's not like we have to stop everyone from leaving the building. Whoever did it is long gone. The evidence techs are on their way."

"Hmm."

"And it looks like it was done in the penthouse."

"Have you been up there?"

Nash shook his head. "No, Tully went up there. He called down and told me there was some blood by the elevator. I didn't go up—because there's an emergency door over there, and I didn't want to leave the area unsecured."

The three of them stopped at the open elevator. The body of Louie Dolores was in a sitting position on the floor, his legs stretched out in front of him. The dead, staring eyes had a look of wonder about them. Ransom thought that one could have mistakenly believed that the mogul had simply decided to sit on the floor on his way down, were it not for the knife protruding from his chest and the crusts of dried blood running from his nose and the corner of his mouth.

Ransom knelt down and cautiously examined the chest. "You're right, Officer, he's been dead for quite a while. I don't see any other wounds. It looks like he was stabbed just once, straight through the heart."

"That must've taken a lot of power," said Gerald.

"Or anger," Ransom said as he straightened up. "He must've been caught by surprise."

"How do you figure that?"

"Did Dolores strike you as the kind of man who couldn't defend himself? Only one wound and not much blood, and it doesn't look like there was a fight. My guess would be he was surprised and the killer got the knife in before Dolores even knew what was happening."

"At least we're not going to have to search for the murder weapon," said Gerald sardonically.

"Yeah, but why leave it?" Nash asked.

"It's an ordinary enough knife," Ransom explained, "so it would be almost impossible to trace. But if nothing else, leaving it stemmed the flow of blood. Who was it that found the body?'

"Girl named Paula Dryer."

"Oh. His secretary."

"You know her?"

"We met yesterday."

"She's up in the penthouse with Tully." They were silent for a moment, then Nash added, "You know, I was thinking, this is a private elevator—Dryer told us that. Only him and a few others have keys for it. Since he's been dead a while, and since he was found here, doesn't that mean—" He broke off when he noticed Ransom's raised eyebrow. His cheeks turned a slight pink at the thought that he'd been overstepping his bounds.

"Yes?" Ransom prompted.

Nash continued somewhat sheepishly. "I was thinking maybe he was killed last night when he went to leave."

"That sounds logical."

"So somebody could've surprised him upstairs, then tossed the body on the elevator to hide him for a while."

"Is this the only elevator up from here?"

"Yeah. You'll have to use the public ones. Go through the emergency door and up the stairs one flight, you come out all the way to the back of that mall thing, right by the elevators to the offices."

"That's one eager cop," Gerald said on their way up the staircase.

Ransom cocked an eye at him. "I don't mind eagerness when someone has the skill to back it up. I just wish I didn't feel quite so much like I'd just had my first face-to-face encounter with Eve Harrington."

Gerald smirked. "I'll bet he wishes he was the one who went upstairs and found the blood."

They got to the elevators and rode up to the penthouse. Officer Tully was waiting for them in the hallway. Tully was stockier than Nash, with heavy-lidded eyes and a slight scowl that hinted at an early onset of cynicism.

"You the detectives?" Tully said as they got off the elevator.

Ransom nodded. "Ransom and White."

"Nash radioed you were on your way up."

"Where's the secretary?"

"She's in the lounge, down the end of the hall." He jutted a thumb down the hallway to their right. "The blood's over here." He stepped across to the private elevator and pointed to the floor, then to the door frame. "Here, and here."

"Hmm," said Ransom, giving the stains a cursory glance. "Stay here and wait for the evidence techs."

"Sure thing," said Tully.

The glass doors had been propped open. The detectives passed through them and went down the hallway.

"That's interesting," said Ransom.

"What is?"

"Did you notice how close to the door the blood is?"

"So?"

His right eyebrow went up. "And there's a little blood splattered on the frame, but none on the door. So the door must've been open when he was killed. The position of the blood on the floor is consistent with where it would've fallen if he was facing the door when he was stabbed."

Gerald stopped as his paper-white forehead creased. "But that would mean . . . that would mean the killer came up in the private elevator."

Ransom nodded. "If I'm not mistaken, that would seriously limit our list of suspects."

"But that's . . . how would they know he'd be standing there waiting for the elevator?"

"That's something we're going to have to figure out."

Gerald shook his head. "That'd be an awfully stupid thing to do, wouldn't it? Kill him in a way that would limit the suspects."

Ransom smiled. "Yes, it would. And it makes it look like Officer Nash was right."

"About what?"

"If he was facing the elevator when he was killed, chances are it was when he was leaving."

They continued down the hall until they reached an open doorway on the left. It was a large room with windows taking up two walls and a full-service kitchen across the third. A small dining table with chairs stood in the corner of the windows, and to the right was a long, coffee-colored couch. Paula Dryer was stretched out on this. Her left hand was draped across her midriff, and she held her right wrist to her forehead. Her face was pale and streaked with red, and she was staring at the ceiling.

"Miss Dryer?" said Ransom.

"What!" she exclaimed, sitting bolt upright. Her glasses had been perched just above her hairline. She fished them down to her nose. "Oh!"

"You remember us from yesterday?"

"Yes."

"You're the one who found Mr. Dolores this morning?" Ransom said as they came into the room. He pulled a chair up beside the couch, while Gerald sat at the table and took the small spiral notebook and stub of a pencil from his inner jacket pocket.

Paula nodded in response.

"When was that?"

"About eight . . . I was running a little late."

"How did you find him?"

She stared at him blankly for a few seconds. "He was on the elevator."

"Yes, I know. What I meant was, was the elevator sitting down there when you arrived?"

"No, I had to ring for it. And I waited . . . and when it came . . .

the doors opened . . ." Her eyes teared up. "There he was!"

"And then you called the police?"

She nodded again. "I ran . . . I ran up the stairs, to the first floor . . ."

"What time did you leave here last night?"

"About five-thirty," she replied with a loud sniff.

"Who was still here then?"

"All of the staff was gone except me, and Bill—Bill Braverman—and Mr. Dolores." Her eyes suddenly opened wide. "You don't think Bill . . . ?"

Ransom smiled. "Right now I'm just trying to get the facts straight. Would you know what time Mr. Dolores intended to go home?"

"He wasn't going home. He had a d—" She broke off on the brink of an indiscretion. "He had a meeting last night at seven."

"With who?"

"Lisa Rivera," Paula replied, her voice becoming hollow. "She's from the Archaeological Museum of Chile."

Gerald jotted down the name.

"She was meeting him here?"

"No. They were going to meet at O'Leary's."

"I see."

"No, you don't," she said quickly. "They had business to discuss. Real business."

Ransom allowed a significant pause. "I took it that was what you meant when you referred to it as a meeting."

Some of the color came back into Paula's cheeks.

"Do you know what the meeting was about?"

She shook her head without looking up. He gazed at her thoughtfully for a moment without speaking.

"Did anyone else know he was meeting her?"

She started to shake her head, but stopped herself. "I told Bill. And Alice, his secretary. Most everybody probably ended up knowing."

"Do you know where Ms. Rivera is staying?"

"At the Reliance Hotel."

Ransom crossed his legs and rested his folded hands on his knee.

"Miss Dryer, about the private elevator . . . does it operate only between this floor and the garage?"

She raised her eyes. "Oh, no. With a key card, we can stop it at any floor, or call it from any floor. Of course, we don't usually have any reason to do that. Except, like the other day, they took it down to the third floor, to the exhibition hall. But ordinarily . . . I guess we do end up just using it to go from here to the garage, mostly."

"And all of the staff has key cards?"

"Yes, I do. Mr. Dolores . . . did. Bill. His secretary Alice, and the support staff."

"There are no other keys?"

"There's a few extras in my desk, in case anybody loses theirs."

"None are missing?"

She shook her head. "I don't remember how many there were. But . . . I don't see how anyone could've stolen one. The only people who know they're in my desk already have one."

"I see," said Ransom. "Do you all use the garage?"

"We're all allowed to park down there. Bill doesn't. He just lives three blocks from here."

"Hmm. Where is Mr. Braverman?"

"I don't know!" Paula burst forth with an unexpected sob. "He should be here! He should've been here by now, but he's not!"

"Have you tried to reach him?"

"No, the policeman said not to."

Score one for Tully, thought Ransom. "What's his number?"

She gave it and Gerald wrote it down.

"Mr. Dolores was married, wasn't he?"

"Yes. To Martita Dolores." Her eyes suddenly widened. "Oh, my God! She doesn't know! Someone will have to tell her!" From her panicked expression, it was clear she found the idea terrifying.

"We'll be the ones to do that," said Ransom.

Paula nearly collapsed with relief. "She . . . she won't be home now, I don't think. She's a lawyer with Harker and Associates. I think she'd be there."

"Thank you," Ransom said, rising from his chair. "Could you give that address and Mr. Braverman's to my partner? Then you can go."

She nodded gratefully. Ransom was almost out of the room when he remembered something and paused in the doorway. "Oh. One other thing, Ms. Dryer. Out of curiosity, have there been any repeat appearances of your mummy?"

"What?" she said with blank surprise.

"There was a commotion here the other night when a cleaning woman saw a mummy. I just wondered if there'd been any more occurrences."

"No. Not that I know of. I'm pretty sure I would have heard."

"Yes. Well, thank you."

He went down the hall to the reception area and dialed Braverman's phone number. Gerald caught up with him just as he was replacing the receiver.

"A machine?" Gerald asked.

"No. No answer at all."

"That doesn't look good. You want to run over there first?"

"No. First I want to find out why Mrs. Dolores doesn't seem concerned about the absence of her husband. But before we do that, let's have a quick look at his office." He tried the door, but found it locked.

Gerald went to the hallway, where Officer Tully was still waiting. "Tully? You know where there's a key to the office?"

"Yeah." He reached into his pocket and pulled out a small key ring. "I asked the secretary for hers. She keeps them in her desk."

"Good. Thanks," said Gerald as Tully tossed him the keys. He went back to Ransom and unlocked the door.

Everything in the office was as it had been the day before, except that the papers on the desk had been cleared away.

"The best of everything," Ransom said as he surveyed the bottles neatly arranged atop the bar. "But no sign he'd been entertaining."

"Look at this," said Gerald. He had opened the door to the left of the desk and switched on the light inside. Ransom came over and looked into the full-service bath. Plush towels hung on a rack beside the glass shower stall. The marble pedestal sink had elaborate gold-plated fixtures, and the floor and walls were tiled in the same color and pattern.

"I hate peach," said Ransom, wrinkling his nose. Then he tilted his head to one side. "Hmm."

"What?"

"I was just wondering . . . if you were in a mummy's costume, would you need to clean up once you got out of it?"

"I guess. Maybe. Why?"

"Officer Nash said that it took Dolores a while to come down to the exhibit after he was called when the mummy made its appearance, and when Dolores did arrive, his hair was wet. I wonder if it was possible for him to put in an appearance, run upstairs, do a quick cleanup and get back down there."

"You think Dolores might've been the mummy?"

"It's a possibility."

"Why would a millionaire want to do that?"

Ransom curled his lips. "Maybe he enjoys scaring up publicity for himself. Or maybe he just enjoys scaring women."

Gerald laughed, turned off the light and closed the door.

Ransom sighed. "Nothing out of the ordinary here. The techs will go over it, but I doubt if they'll find anything. Let's get going."

They locked the door and gave the keys back to Tully. They had to wait a few minutes for an elevator to arrive, and when it did, it was full of evidence technicians. Ransom made the introductions.

The youngest of the crew, a man with unruly black hair, said, "The rest of us are down in the garage working on the elevator."

"Good," said Ransom. He then showed them the bloodstains and instructed them to go over the entire penthouse. "And call the coroner's office and tell them there's a VIP on the way. They'll have to allow him to cut in line."

The detectives got on the elevator and started down.

"Why did you ask Dryer about the mummy?" Gerald asked.

"Because of something Emily said."

He laughed. "I should've known!"

Ransom shot him an irritated glance. He had the utmost respect for Emily and perfect faith in her prowess at deduction, but this was the second time in as many days that someone had intimated that she was perhaps more gifted than he was, and despite his feelings for her, it was beginning to nettle him.

When Gerald noticed the displeased expression on Ransom's face, he cleared his throat. "I mean, what did she say?"

"She suggested that the appearance of the mummy the other day may have something to do with the threats on Dolores's life." He pursed his lips. "She said that, by the way, because she thought I sensed a connection."

"Come on, Jer. The cleaning woman was probably just imagining things."

"Officer Nash believes she was too upset for it to have been imagination. He thinks Jablonski saw something. And for the record, Emily does, too. She thinks Jablonski probably saw a mummy."

"That's crazy."

"I'm glad to hear you say it," Ransom replied with a crooked smile. Although he wouldn't have admitted it even to himself, he was pleased to have shaken his partner's faith, however slightly, in Emily's omniscience. His pleasure was short-lived, though.

"The funny thing is," said Gerald, "she'll probably end up being right."

"I know," Ransom intoned.

Twenty minutes later, the detectives walked through a pair of glass doors and into the lush lobby of Harker and Associates. A trim young woman with long blond hair greeted them from behind a curved mahogany desk. "May I help you, gentlemen?"

"We're here to see Martita Dolores," said Ransom, showing her his badge. "Is she in?"

"Yes," the receptionist replied without blinking. She reached for the phone. "Let me see if she's available."

Ransom raised his right palm. "We'd like to surprise her."

"Oh." She replaced the receiver. "Ms. Dolores is down that hall, third door on the right."

"Thank you."

The receptionist's eyes followed them as they went down the hallway. When they reached the office, they found the door open. Marti was seated at her desk, twisting a pencil between two fingers as she intently scanned a brief. She didn't look up when they stopped in her doorway.

"Ms. Dolores?" said Ransom.

"Yes?" She raised her eyes at the unfamiliar voice, and the corners of her mouth curved downward.

"I'm Detective Ransom, this is Detective White. May we have a word with you?"

"I don't remember seeing you before. Do you have something to do with one of our cases?"

"No, this is a personal matter."

Her frowned deepened. "All right. Sit down." She straightened up and tossed the pencil onto the desk, then took the top button of her wilting white blouse and shook it, airing out the damp fabric.

The detectives took the seats facing the desk.

"What can I do for you?" she asked.

"We're here about your husband."

Her expression didn't change, but she pushed her chair back slightly. "My husband. Is he in some kind of trouble?"

"I'm afraid it's worse than that, Ms. Dolores. Your husband is dead."

There was a long pause, then without emotion Marti said, "I see."

"His body was found this morning at Dolores Tower. Apparently he's been dead for several hours."

"Hmm."

"Most likely since last evening. Of course we'll have to wait for the autopsy to know more about that."

"Mm-hmm."

Ransom could feel Gerald looking at him. He considered the astonishing woman for several seconds, then said, "Forgive me, Mrs. Dolores, but you don't seem upset by this news."

Marti's face seemed to tighten. "I'm not given to histrionics. My people prefer to grieve in private." A hint of a smile appeared. "I can produce tears if it will make you more comfortable."

Ransom cocked his head slightly to one side. "Grief is one thing, but I would think you'd be surprised."

126

"That is part of being a lawyer. No matter what happens, one is never to betray surprise."

Ransom resisted the urge to point out that they weren't in court. Instead, he smiled. "Much like being a detective. But even I can be surprised sometimes. For example, I'm surprised you haven't asked how he died."

She pushed her chair back farther and folded her arms. "I didn't need to. You introduced yourselves as detectives. That means he didn't die of natural causes, am I right?"

"That's right. He was murdered. Could you tell us when you last saw him?"

"Yesterday morning."

"Had he told you he would be out all night?" The tone in which this question was asked was designed to convey just how baffling he was finding Marti's attitude.

"No."

"Then I really am confused. Weren't you at all concerned when he didn't come home?"

She shook her head. "Not at all. It often happened."

"His business would keep him out all night, and he wouldn't call?"

The right corner of her mouth twisted upward. "Of course not. Only his mistresses would keep him out all night."

Ransom sat back in his chair. "You're very frank."

"I have no reason not to be. My husband was Chilean, Detective. South American men view mistresses as a sort of cultural imperative. South American women know this."

"And what do they do about it?"

"They accept it."

"Is that what you did?"

"I am part of my culture."

"But . . . you are an American, aren't you?"

"Yes."

Ransom waited for a moment, but when nothing more was forthcoming, he asked, "Did you know any of the women he had affairs with?"

She smiled. "Naturally he didn't discuss them with me. I assume any woman he came in contact with who would consent ended up in his bed."

"And that didn't bother you?"

"It was a matter of indifference to me."

Ransom's eyes shifted for a second to his partner. Ordinarily, Gerald wouldn't be taking notes when they broke the news of a death to a loved one—at least not until they got into questioning—and he hadn't started now. But it hardly mattered. Ransom didn't think he'd forget a word of this encounter.

"Do you know of anyone who would want to kill your husband?" he asked.

A faint sadness crossed Marti's face as she answered. "There are so many people, I hardly know where to begin. Old lovers, old rivals. Any number of people that he has crossed or climbed over, bureaucrats, other builders, historians . . . I believe one of them actually threatened him yesterday. Perhaps you heard?"

"Yes, I did. So you don't know of anyone in particular who had a grudge against him."

She shrugged, feigning helplessness. "They are legion. I don't envy you your job."

"When you say 'people he crossed or climbed over,' I assume you're talking about business. Has there been anyone lately who he's done that to?"

She shrugged again and shook her head.

"I would think it would be something recent," Ransom continued, his eyes narrowing. "Maybe connected to a recent . . . or even a future . . . project?"

"Perhaps his assistant could tell you—Bill Braverman. Have you spoken to him?"

"Not yet."

"He would know much better than I what was happening with Louie's various projects."

"Hmm. Your husband didn't discuss his work with you at all?"

"No," she replied simply.

"And he didn't tell you about anyone threatening him?"

"Louie did not consider other people to be a problem, and I don't believe he was ever threatened by anyone."

"He showed us a death threat he received."

"I didn't put that clearly. I meant that Louie never *felt* threatened by anyone."

Ransom narrowed his eyes. "So, Mrs. Dolores, would you mind telling me what you were doing last evening?"

She smiled coldly. "Do you think I might have killed my husband?"

He spread his palms. "It's been known to happen."

"Because he was unfaithful to me?"

"Murders have been committed for less reason than that."

"Huh! I suppose they have. Well, Detective, I spent last evening with James Harker, the senior partner in this firm."

"How late were you with him?"

"Until around midnight."

Ransom elevated one eyebrow. "This was business?"

"Some of it."

"I see. I assume Mr. Harker can verify this?"

The smile disappeared. "*Verify* it?"

"That would be standard procedure."

"Yes, I'm sure he can. Now, if you'll excuse me, there are people I should inform about Louie, and arrangements to be made."

"I think we're through with you for now," Ransom said after a pause. As he rose from his chair, he added, "Oh, by the way, your husband had a private elevator in his tower. Do you have a key to it?"

"One of those card things? Yes, I do," she replied. "Somewhere I don't carry it, of course. I have no need to. I was never there without Louie."

"I see."

Ransom started for the door, followed by Gerald, but Marti stopped them.

"Detective?" She turned her head slightly to one side. There was something sensual about the move. "You don't really think I killed Louie, do you?"

"I don't think anything in particular at the moment. But we have to consider it."

Her smile returned. "Perhaps I should see a lawyer."

The detectives stopped at the reception desk and asked for Harker. When the receptionist told them he was out for the day, they asked for his home address and phone number. She hesitated, more as a matter of form than anything else, then supplied it.

They didn't speak as they rode down to the lobby in the crowded elevator. Gerald spent the time jotting down a few notes on his pad, which he stuck back in his pocket when they reached the ground floor.

Once they were out on the street, Gerald said, "Geez, Mrs. Dolores certainly is . . ."

"I think the word you're looking for is 'formidable,' " Ransom offered.

"Yeah."

"That she is. What I found most interesting is how easily she adopted the past tense when referring to her husband."

"I don't care what she says, she should've been more surprised about his murder, even if she is a lawyer!"

"Really?" said Ransom as they reached their car. "I don't find that unusual at all."

"You wouldn't," Gerald said with a laugh as he opened the door. He climbed in behind the wheel.

Ransom got in on the passenger side. "When someone is able to maintain themselves that well, there's only one emotion I can imagine them letting get the best of them."

"What's that?"

"Anger."

Gerald laid his hands on the wheel and looked out the windshield thoughtfully. "You said that knife could've been driven in with anger. You think she could've done that?"

Ransom reached into his pocket and withdrew one of his plastic-tipped cigars. "I think she could've calmly sliced him into fillets and served him for dinner."

9

Gerald pulled into the No Parking zone in front of the building in which Bill Braverman lived. He switched off the motor and they got out of the car and went up the walk. Neatly trimmed hedges in concrete boxes lined each side of the high-arched entrance.

"He didn't do anything by half," Ransom muttered as they approached the front door.

"Who?"

"Dolores. He designed this place."

"This one, too?"

He nodded. "And look at it. It's a condominium, and this archway looks like the entrance to a palace!"

Twin panels of glass slid apart as the detectives neared them. Inside, a security guard was seated at a high desk facing a small bank of monitors.

"Can I help you?' the guard asked.

Gerald flashed his badge. "We're here to see Bill Braverman."

"Okay." He typed the name on the keyboard on his desk. "Thirty-five-o-one. The elevators are through the door to the right."

He pressed a red button and after a short, loud buzz, the door popped open.

"Thank you," said Gerald.

They went through the doorway into a brightly lit hall, arched to mirror the entrance but on a much smaller scale. The walls and ceiling were covered with pale-yellow fabric, and enormous pots of plastic mother-in-law's-tongues sat on the floor on opposite sides of the four elevators. Gerald pressed the button and they waited.

"Look at that," said Ransom.

"What?"

He cocked his head toward a corner of the ceiling, and Gerald looked up. The wall covering was peeling away, and there was no evidence of any attempt to mend it. He then directed Gerald's attention toward the opposite corner, where a large portion of the ceiling and walls were badly stained with water.

"Every building has some problems," said Gerald.

"This place isn't that old," said Ransom. "It's just indicative."

The door of the second elevator opened. The detectives got on and Gerald pressed Thirty-five. The doors closed with a clumsy clank and after a slight pause, the elevator shot upward. It shivered to a stop at the thirty-fifth floor.

A brass plate on the wall opposite the elevators pointed the way to Unit 3501, at the far end of the hallway to the left.

"The corner unit," said Ransom, "of course."

Gerald rang the bell. There was a lengthy pause before they heard sluggish footsteps approach on the other side of the door.

"Who is it?" asked a faint female voice.

"Mrs. Braverman?" said Gerald.

"Yes?"

"Detectives Ransom and White. We're here to see your husband."

There was a slight pause, then the sound of a bolt being snapped. The door was pulled open slowly. Anna Braverman stood with one hand on the door and the other on her stomach. Her cheeks were puffy and her eyes red. The temporary elation that had manifested itself the previous evening had been replaced by a more profound torpor than she'd displayed before.

"The police? You're here to see Bill?"

"Yes. Is he here?"

She shrugged dully and pushed open the door. Ransom glanced at Gerald; then they followed her into the living room.

"I'll get him," she said as she went through a doorway toward the back of the apartment, leaving them standing in the center of the room.

"Mrs. Braverman seems a bit under the weather," Ransom said quietly.

Gerald responded with a "Huh!"

Bill Braverman came into the room through the back doorway. He was dressed for the office in white shirt and dark-blue pants, and had a red tie hanging around his neck, knotted but not tightened. There was a slight flush to his face, and his jaw was clenched.

"Oh! It's you," he said when he recognized the detectives. "You wanted to see me?"

"Have we interrupted something?" Ransom asked.

"No. I was just getting ready for work."

"So I see. We were surprised that we didn't find you there this morning."

The redness deepened. "I wanted some time to myself. If you're here to talk to me about those death threats again, it could've waited until I got to the office. I don't see why—"

Ransom cut him off. "We're not here about the threats, Mr. Braverman."

"Then what?"

"Louie Dolores has been murdered."

There was a beat, then Bill said, "If this is a joke, it's not funny!"

"I think you know it's not a joke."

The blood drained from his face. "What? How would I—"

"We wouldn't be here for a joke."

"Louie's dead?" Bill said as he sank onto the couch.

"Yes."

"I don't believe it!"

Ransom took a seat in a chair right-angled to the end of the couch. Gerald took a seat on the opposite side, then took out his notebook and laid it on his leg.

Ransom said, "Mr. Dolores was found this morning by his secretary."

"Paula found him?"

"Yes. Of course she was very distraught. She was surprised that you weren't in to work yet."

"I didn't . . . I was just taking my time this morning. I sometimes do."

"Hmm. Any particular reason you chose this morning to take your time?"

Bill was silent for several seconds. "No."

"It appears that Mr. Dolores was killed sometime last night. We're trying to retrace his movements. Ms. Dryer told us that when she left last night, the only two people still in the office were you and Dolores. Can you tell me when you last saw him?"

"Yeah, sure. At about six-thirty, when I left. I stopped in to see if—" His eyes widened when he broke off.

"Yes?"

Bill took a deep breath. "I stopped in to see if he wanted me to ride down to the garage with him."

"You drove to work?"

"No. It was just as a precaution."

"Because of the threats?"

There was a longer pause this time. "Yes."

Ransom crossed his legs. "Mr. Braverman, when we talked to the two of you yesterday, I got the impression that you took the death threats more seriously than Dolores did. Why was that?"

"Well . . . you . . . you're wrong. I—"

"Mr. Braverman, please," Ransom said with a weary sigh. "Both my partner and I noticed your agitation when we were discussing the threats. It was obvious you wanted to say something, and equally obvious that Dolores was holding you back. Now, would you mind telling me what was on your mind?"

Bill's eyes had grown wider as Ransom said this, as if surprised to discover that he'd been so transparent. He cleared his throat. "You called it yourself. It was about his neck and the bruise on his forehead. He was attacked the night before. In the garage."

"Why didn't he want us to know that?"

"I don't know," Bill replied hesitantly, looking away.

Ransom sighed. "You've been running interference for him for a decade. It's hard to believe you wouldn't know his motives for hiding the truth."

"Well, I—" He broke off again, then exhaled sharply. "I suppose it doesn't matter now that he's dead. Louie could be a very vindictive man. He wanted to take care of it himself."

Ransom allowed a long silence. "So he knew who attacked him?"

Bill hesitated again. "Yes . . . no. He thought he did."

"Who was it?"

"I'm not sure. Louie said a lot, but I'm . . . I'm not sure."

"Mr. Braverman, I don't understand why you're hedging."

He sighed. "Louie also had a habit of going off half-cocked. I don't know—I mean, I had some doubts about whether or not he was right, and I don't want to get an innocent person in trouble."

"Your reservations are duly noted. However, Dolores was threatened, you tell me he was attacked, and now he's dead. Surely you can see why I need to know who it was he thought attacked him."

Bill looked down at the floor. "You're right."

Noting his continued discomfort, Ransom said, "Yesterday you seemed sure that the threats had something to do with the mummy exhibit. Is that because of who attacked him?"

He looked up. "Have you seen any of the news about the exhibit?"

"A little."

"Then you might know that there's been a small group of people outside the tower protesting it."

"Yes?"

Bill sighed again. "Well, Louie was sure that the person who attacked him was the guy that's leading the protest."

"I see. But you don't agree."

He shook his head. "Louie said the guy was dressed up in that getup—the mummy getup. Mask and all. Hell, it could've been anybody! I told him that. Everybody's seen that guy. Louie didn't see the man's face."

Ransom shrugged. "But it was a logical assumption."

"Except that the guy was back the next day, protesting outside the tower. I mean, he'd have to be crazy to attack Louie and then show up again the next day like nothing had happened, wouldn't he?"

"One would think," Ransom said with a faint smile. He couldn't remember whether or not he'd seen the protesters there that morning. "What happened?"

"What?"

"Obviously, Dolores wasn't killed during this attack. What happened? Did he manage to fight the person off?"

"No. He told me he hit his head against the wall and knocked himself out. When he came to, the guy was gone."

There was a long silence, broken only by the sound of Gerald's pencil scratching against his pad as he tried to keep up with the conversation.

At last, Ransom said, "That's very interesting."

"What is?" Bill asked blankly.

"This is the second sighting of a mummy I've heard of at Dolores Tower. Except this one didn't make it onto the news. Dolores knew about the first appearance . . . and then he was attacked by someone dressed as a mummy. I'm surprised he didn't make the connection."

"I told you—"

"I'm just surprised that after being attacked, knowing that this person was apparently wandering about so freely in a building that is supposed to have security, he wasn't much more concerned."

"I don't . . . I can't speak for what was going on in Louie's mind . . ."

"You can't?" Ransom said with very evident surprise.

The redness rushed back into Bill's cheeks. "But *I* was concerned! You noticed that yourself. I wanted him to tell you about it. I just didn't want him to accuse someone outright—without being sure."

"But he didn't tell us about it," Ransom said. "Now, you said something earlier about that being because he was . . ." He made a pretense of looking to Gerald to fill in the word.

"Vindictive," his partner said.

Ransom turned back to Bill. "And you said he wanted to take care of this himself. How did he plan to do that?"

A moment elapsed, then Bill said, "I have no idea."

"In order to do anything about it at all, he would have to know the identity of the person . . ."

"But I told you—"

Ransom smiled coyly. "No, I mean he would have to know the identity of the protester."

"Oh," Bill said after a beat. "I see what you're saying. That makes sense."

"Did he know his identity?"

He swallowed hard. "I'm sorry, I really don't know."

"I see," said Ransom after a long pause. "Is there anyone else?"

"Excuse me?" Bill said blankly.

"Anyone else Dolores had altercations with recently . . . verbal or otherwise?"

"Oh . . . well, there was that woman from the Historical Commission . . ."

Ransom narrowed his eyes when no more information was offered. "It's hard for me to believe that a magnate of Dolores's caliber didn't make more enemies than that. Even Mrs. Dolores concedes that much."

At the mention of Marti, Bill looked up sharply. There was something like fear in his eyes. "You talked to Marti?"

"Of course. She gave us several possibilities."

"I'll bet she did," he said with empty bitterness. He went on reluctantly. "Well, I suppose there was also . . . Daniel Nathanson."

"The alderman?"

"Uh-huh. On Monday, he was in the office. I think they argued."

"About what?"

"I wasn't at the meeting, but Louie said they argued," Bill replied evasively. "And I know Louie was mad at Nathanson yesterday. He tried . . . I mean he had me try to get him on the phone all day."

"Why?"

Bill sighed heavily. "You . . . I don't know if you saw the news, about the opening of the exhibit. Louie's been trying to get the land that the Stone Candy Factory is on. He's been trying to do it . . . privately."

"You mean secretly."

He ignored this. "But somehow word got out. That woman from the Historical Commission, she mentioned the factory by name."

"What does that have to do with Nathanson?"

"Well . . . Louie thought Nathanson leaked the information to the commission. On purpose."

"Why would he do that?"

Bill stared at him for a moment, the fear seeming to intensify. Then he relaxed slightly. "Well, that's just it! I don't know why. That's why I thought Louie might be wrong about him. And Nathanson—when I finally got him on the phone, he said he didn't know how the news had gotten out."

"You were disagreeing with your boss quite a bit, weren't you?" Ransom said lightly.

"Sometimes . . . when someone has worked his way up from nothing, when they get to the top, they can get hard to reason with."

"And that can make them more enemies."

"Yes."

"Hmm." After a pause, Ransom continued. "Getting back to the beginning of our conversation, you said you saw Dolores at six-thirty. Did he go with you?"

"What?"

"Did he ride down with you to the garage?'

"Oh. No, he . . . he acted like I was being silly."

"Well, you were, weren't you?"

"What?"

Ransom shrugged. "You knew he had a date."

"A date?"

"With Lisa Rivera."

"Oh. Yes. I wouldn't call that a date."

"Well, whatever you call it, it was for seven o'clock, in the building. He wouldn't have been leaving at six."

Bill stared at him confusedly for several seconds. Then his face cleared. "Oh, I see what you're saying. I guess I forgot about that. I was so worried about him being attacked."

"I see. So you left without him."

"Yes."

"And how did you spend the evening?"

Bill went pale. "What?"

"Just a matter of form. You left the building at six-thirty. Did you come here?"

"Yes . . . well, not exactly. I did come home to get my car. I spent . . . I just went for a drive."

"A drive?" Ransom echoed with a raised eyebrow.

"Yeah."

"At six-thirty?"

"That's right," Bill said defensively.

"When did you get back?"

"About seven-thirty . . . eight."

"Can your wife verify this?"

"No," Bill said, the color flooding back into his face. "She wasn't here when I got home."

"Hmm." Ransom got up from his chair, and Gerald did likewise, snapping his notebook shut and returning it to his pocket. "Well, I think that will be all for now. You'll keep yourself available?"

"What? Yes. Yes, of course," Bill said confusedly as he got to his feet. "I'll do whatever I can to help."

"Good."

"I should . . . I should get to the office. There'll be a lot to do."

"You might as well wait a while. At the moment, our tech crew is going through the offices."

"Oh. Okay. When will it be all right?"

"To go to *your* office? This afternoon it should be, although parts of the penthouse will be off-limits, and you won't be able to use the private elevator. One other thing: now that Dolores is dead, who will be responsible for the company?"

"I would think Marti would."

"You have no stake in the company?"

"No," Bill said after a lengthy pause. "I was Louie's personal assistant. I was . . . I don't know if . . ." He trailed off in frustration, then sighed. "I don't know."

"I see."

"Here we have a case where the right hand would have us believe that he didn't know what the head was doing," Ransom said as they rode down in the elevator.

"He sure didn't seem to know a lot for a personal assistant," Gerald agreed. "Did you buy any of that?"

Ransom sighed. "I know it's early days yet, but there is an awful lot about this whole setup that just doesn't make sense. Braverman obviously didn't want to tell us about Alderman Nathanson. He only did because he thought Marti Dolores had told us."

"I know. But why wouldn't he want to tell us that? It didn't have anything to do with him."

Ransom eyed his partner. "You have a very short memory. Braverman was implicated in a bribery scheme."

"Oh, that's right! I remember. Nathanson was supposed to be involved, wasn't he? But this still doesn't have anything to do with that . . . that we know of."

"True. But there were other things wrong with what he said. I don't know why Braverman would lie to us, but I'm sure he did. Dolores was a shrewd man. He might have jumped to the conclusion that that protester was the one who attacked him, but if he said he wanted to take care of it himself, then he must've known his identity."

"Unless he was just going to have someone run him down, or shoot him," Gerald offered offhandedly.

Ransom curled his lips. "Dolores was a ruthless businessman, but does hiring a drive-by strike you as his style?"

"No, but I don't get what you're saying. Why would he know that guy's identity?"

"Dolores was a powerful man. I would think he'd get some background on the people who are defying him. If not before, then certainly after he was attacked. Which is what makes Braverman's attitude so puzzling."

The elevator came to a stop at the lobby and they got off. As they headed for the door, Gerald said, "Because Braverman would've been the one who was told to get the information."

"Exactly. So why lie about it? If he knows who this guy is, then why not tell us? Dolores is dead. It doesn't matter if Braverman goes against his wishes. And we're talking about a murder here. But there's something even more curious about that attack on Dolores."

Gerald sighed inwardly. He probably should've been used to the way Ransom stopped in mid thought by now, but it almost always nettled him, even if only a little bit. Ransom could easily have finished his thought unprompted, but he enjoyed forcing Gerald into the role of Watson. *I suppose I should be grateful*, Gerald thought. *If he didn't do this, I'd probably never get to talk!*

"All right, I'll bite. What's more curious about the attack?"

"The fact that he survived it," Ransom intoned. "Once he was knocked out, why didn't our mummy finish him off? Why wait until the next day?"

"Who knows?" Gerald said vaguely. "Maybe he was interrupted."

"That's the most obvious answer. Of course, if that were the case, it's odd that whoever did the interrupting didn't find the unconscious Dolores."

"Of course," Gerald said wryly.

"There's another possibility."

"What's that?"

They came to a stop by the car. "That it didn't happen."

Gerald's jaw dropped. "We saw the bruises!"

"We saw bruises. We only have the story of what caused them secondhand, passed on from the 'victim' himself. Just as we only have Dolores's word that he found that death threat on his windshield."

"Well, Jer, I mean . . . I hate to point out the obvious, but he's dead! You don't think he was threatened?"

"I'm just saying I think this is all very odd. When he received a death threat, he went to the media instead of the police. When someone supposedly actually attacked him, he didn't go to either one. When we came on the scene, he readily produced the threatening letter, but he didn't tell us about the attack, even though he had the wounds to prove it. Why tell us about a vague threat but not a direct attack?"

"Well, then how do you account for those wounds?" Gerald asked skeptically. "If you don't think he was attacked, I mean."

"I'm only talking about possibilities," Ransom replied. "But it's easy enough to inflict wounds on yourself."

"Then why didn't he tell us about it?"

Ransom shrugged. "Maybe it was just something else he planned to tell the media instead of the police, and we warned him off."

Gerald considered this for some time, his hand resting on the handle of the driver's door. "You know, it also could be that whether or not the threats were real, someone grabbed at the opportunity to kill him."

Ransom smiled broadly. "Very good, Gerald."

He laughed. "You don't have to look so surprised. Where to now?"

"We should go back to Dolores Tower. Word may not be out yet that he's been killed. I want to see if the protesters are still over there."

As they got into the car, Gerald said, "You know, even if Dolores was making that stuff up, I mean about being threatened and everything, it still doesn't make sense that Braverman wasn't in on it.

"Yes, except for one thing: Braverman's anxiety yesterday when Dolores didn't want him to talk was real. I'd be willing to swear to that. But he's still trying to hide something."

"Yeah. I wonder why he was so angry when we got there."

Ransom grinned in the fashion that made him look like a wicked elf. "And his wife so sullen? I'm not surprised you wonder. You and Sherry are disgustingly harmonious."

"Huh?" Gerald said, pausing in the act of turning the key in the ignition. Then the light dawned and he laughed. "Oh! Sure! They were having a fight."

"Um-hmm."

Ransom was wrong in his assessment of the situation between the Bravermans. They hadn't been having an argument. Far from it. Her decision made and her elation past, Anna had retreated into a morose silence, speaking only when forced to by convention, and then rarely more than one or two words together. Despite the fact that she had planned to tell Bill of her decision to sell out, it had proven much harder to bring herself to do it than she'd thought it would be. She had so far refrained for fear of causing more unpleasantness, avoiding the whole matter as if it would somehow resolve itself.

The anger Ransom had noticed in Bill grew from the fact that he'd given Anna every opportunity to tell him herself about her decision to sell her part of her firm, and still she had said nothing. He'd made leading comments about the future, and asked carefully worded questions about her company, all designed to lead her to an admission, but Anna had sullenly refused to rise to the bait.

The game had ended when the detectives arrived to talk to Bill. By the time they left, Anna had dressed and was ready to leave for work. She'd come into the living room, shoulder bag in hand, and found Bill seated on the couch, staring off into space. She didn't really want to invite discussion, but even in her withdrawn state, her curiosity would not allow her to leave without finding out why the detectives had been there.

"What did they want?" Her voice sounded dull and flat.

Bill looked up. "Louie is dead."

The words sent a vibration through the protective shell Anna had erected around herself.

"He is?"

"He was murdered last night."

"Do they know who did it?"

"No. They think . . . well, I'm a suspect."

"Really."

"It's crazy! I didn't have any reason to kill him! Just the opposite. But I don't have an alibi. I was out last evening. Driving."

"They won't think anything of it," she said dispassionately as she slipped the strap of her bag over her shoulder. "Like you said, you didn't have any reason to kill him. You least of all."

She started for the door.

"Anna, when I got home, you weren't here. Where were you?"

She stopped and looked back over her shoulder at him. "I went for a walk. You were driving, I was walking. That's all."

The detectives covered the distance between the Braverman's apartment building and Dolores Tower very quickly. From half a block off, they could see that the protesters were in their usual place. Gerald brought the car to a stop beside a Volkswagen parked near the corner and switched off the motor, much to the vexation of the driver of the car directly behind them. The driver honked angrily, then pulled slightly to the left, craning his neck over his shoulder, waiting for an opening.

The protesters were going through their usual ritual, with the five costumed men and lone woman providing a dour musical background for the mummy as he went through his dance. They seemed oblivious to the arrival of the detectives. Ransom and Gerald got out of the car and watched them for a moment. The passing foot traffic paid them little attention, not because the public was so jaded that it didn't heed something strange happening in its midst, but because the protest had now been going on long enough that everyone had become inured to it.

Unlike the reporters earlier in the week, Ransom didn't wait for the dance to end before making his move. He reached into his pocket and pulled out his badge as he approached the mummy.

"Excuse me," he said, flashing the badge. "We'd like to have a word with you."

The mummy stopped his slow dance and pointed the flat, gray mask at the shield.

"You would interrupt the death ritual?" The voice rumbled from behind the mask.

"The dead won't mind," said Ransom.

The mummy kept his voice low and even. "This is outrageous. Does Dolores have so much money that he can buy policemen to harass us?"

"Of course he does," Ransom said blithely, replacing the badge in his pocket. "But that's not why we're here. I want to ask you a few questions, and you might want to step away from your friends so that we're not overheard."

The mummy hesitated for a moment, then reluctantly followed as Ransom led him a car length away from the others. Gerald brought up the rear.

"What is this?" the mummy asked.

"First, the mask, please," said Ransom.

The mask was held on by a thin, black-elastic band attached through tiny holes at each side. He reached up, took hold of it by the chin and swept it back over his head, revealing a strikingly handsome bronze face with straight black brows, dark-brown eyes, and a hard, flat mouth.

"Now what is it?" he said.

"Do you have some identification?"

There was another hesitation, during which the man stifled an angry sigh. He turned back to the group and called, "Carla! My wallet!"

The female protester came over to them, pulling the requested item from a cloth bag she kept strapped under her arm.

"Here," she said as she handed it to him. "What's wrong?"

"Nothing. Yet. Keep playing."

She rejoined the group with a timid glance over her shoulder at the detectives. The man flipped open his wallet and pulled out a driver's license, which he handed to Ransom.

"Juan Muñoz," Ransom read. He handed it to Gerald, who jotted down the name and address, then returned it to its owner.

"I ask you again, what is this all about?" said Muñoz. "I know Dolores sent you. But we have every right to protest, and we'll keep doing it until he has returned the Chinchorro mummies and their artifacts to my people."

"He didn't send us," Ransom said simply. "Louie Dolores is dead."

"What?" Muñoz said after a beat, his faintly exotic accent disappearing in a single word.

"He was found murdered this morning."

"But—" He stopped and tried to quickly draw himself back together. "I can't say that I'm surprised. To someone who has committed desecration, I would expect this to happen. But what does it have to do with me?"

"Desecration . . ." Ransom said slowly, savoring the word. "It's odd. Dolores received a death threat the other day that used that word."

"It's a common enough word."

"I never use it," Gerald said unexpectedly.

Ransom raised an eyebrow at him with a hint of a smile.

"Like my ancestors," Muñoz said, "I am a man of peace."

"Your ancestors being the Chinchorros?"

"Yes."

Ransom scrutinized the tall young man for several moments, and Muñoz tried not to flinch under the gaze. He was almost successful.

"Mr. Muñoz, it might interest you to know that Louie Dolores accused you of attacking him."

"What?" he blurted out, his accent once again failing him.

"The night before last. He said that when he was leaving for the evening, you attacked him in the tower's private garage."

"In the—" For the second time, he broke off and attempted to regain some of his stoicism. "How am I supposed to have gotten into Dolores's private garage?"

"By slipping in before the garage door closed."

"If he accused me of this, why didn't you come for me before?"

"We didn't know about it until this morning. If we had, we would've talked to you earlier. But you see the problem, don't you?"

"What?"

"Louie Dolores said you attacked him, and now he's dead."

"I did not attack him!"

"Why would he say you did?"

"To cause me trouble! To stop the protest!"

"I can't think that this protest worried Dolores very much, can you?"

"There's a tide turning against him. Keeping him in the public eye, people will—would—finally realize the damage he was doing. So yes, I think it worried him."

"Hmm. Well, let's say you were aware that Dolores was going to try to cause you trouble. That might've given you a reason to want to stop him. If this 'desecration' wasn't enough reason."

"But I'm a man of peace!" Muñoz said loudly, his apprehension growing as he realized the seriousness of the implication. "Peace! That's why I've been leading a peaceful demonstration out here this past week!"

"Yes," Ransom said, glancing over at the rest of the group. They continued their drumbeat and chanting, but their eyes were fixed on their leader. "This is quite a full-time job, isn't it?"

"A . . . It's important, yes."

"Tell me, what do you do for a living?"

Muñoz's jaw hardened noticeably. "I'm between jobs right now."

"I see. And the rest of your little band?"

"Some are like me, some have taken time off to be here because they believe in our cause."

"Mr. Muñoz, where were you last evening?"

146

"Me? Why?"

"Just give me an overview."

"I was out. All evening."

"Alone?"

"Part of the time. I had a few drinks. In a bar."

"Did you see anybody you knew?"

"No."

"And the night before last?"

"Same thing."

"So, there is no one who can vouch for your movements either last night or the night before."

"No," Muñoz replied after a long pause.

"Hmm. Well, that'll be all for now. We'll be talking to you again later."

Muñoz's breathing sped up a bit. "Look, Officer, Dolores was a—"

"Yes?" Ransom said with a raised eyebrow.

"He must've had a thousand enemies!"

"But only one he accused of attacking him. Stay in town."

He gave a nod toward Gerald, and the two of them went back to their car.

Muñoz stood staring after them as they rounded the corner; then he went back to the group.

"That's it!" he announced.

They stopped drumming and chanting, and the whole group faced him with their dead masks.

"What do you mean?" said one of the men holding a drum.

"Take off these stupid masks and get out of the costumes! It's over!"

"Juan!" said Carla, laying a hand gently on his arm. "What is it? What did those men say?"

"Don't come back down to this building," he said, ignoring her entreaty. "I'm getting out of here!"

10

"Where to now?" Gerald asked as they headed down Dearborn.

"The Reliance. I think we should talk to the other woman."

"You mean Lisa Rivera? Dolores's secretary said they were having a business meeting."

"I know, Gerald."

"You think it was something more?"

"He was meeting her after work in a bar. His wife said he would try it on with any woman who would have him."

"That doesn't mean he tried it with Rivera already."

"I know that, too." He pulled a cigar out of the pack in his jacket pocket and shoved the lighter into the dash.

Gerald shot him a glance. "The Reliance is only about four blocks from here."

"That's right," Ransom said after a pause. He replaced the cigar.

"With all the people who had a reason to kill Dolores, why do you want to talk to Rivera now?"

"If he was killed on his way out of his office, then he didn't make his date, which would mean he was killed between six-thirty and seven. If he did make his date, then Lisa Rivera saw him later than anyone else we know of."

"That would mean he went back to his office." Gerald thought for a moment as he turned the car onto Ontario. "But that wouldn't make sense."

"No. I could believe the killer knew when Dolores would be leaving the office, but not that he would go back there."

They hung a left at Wells, continued down half a block and pulled up in front of the Reliance Hotel. As they went in, a tired, middle-aged African-American man who appeared to be a combination doorman and bellhop told them they couldn't park there with the resignation of someone who knows he'll be ignored. Gerald showed him his badge, and the man shrugged and said, "Okay, Boss."

Any of the charm the cramped lobby of the Reliance might have exhibited stemmed from the fact that the cold, industrial decor had faded into the realm of nostalgia. The carpet was dark pink with tiny, widely spaced pale-yellow flowers, and was worn to within an inch of its life. A love seat and two matching chairs, their brocade a mere memory, were grouped around a pockmarked coffee table on which rested a stack of magazines whose mailing labels had been torn off.

Gerald had kept his badge out to show to the desk clerk. "Lisa Rivera?"

She glanced down at a printout on her desk, then looked up. "Five-oh-three. Should I call her?"

"Don't bother."

They went down the short hall to the single elevator.

"Hardly the type of place one would expect Louie Dolores to put his guests up in," Ransom said while they waited.

"I was just thinking that," said Gerald.

The sound of vibrating metal signaled the arrival of the elevator. A modestly dressed young couple with stringy hair and backpacks got off, then the detectives got on. Gerald pressed Five. It seemed to take longer for the noisy box to ascend the four stories than it had taken the elevator at Dolores Tower to reach the penthouse.

Room 503 was halfway down the hall. When they found it, Gerald rapped his knuckles lightly on the door.

"Yes?" came a voice from within.

"Ms. Rivera? We're Detectives Ransom and White. We'd like to speak to you."

The door opened abruptly. Lisa Rivera stood in the opening, her sharp features pinched with curiosity and her long black hair hanging loosely down her back. She wore a tan suit with a brown blouse.

Ransom was immediately struck by the resemblance between Rivera and Marti Dolores. Lisa appeared to be a newer model of the same brand.

"Detectives?" Lisa said.

They showed her their badges.

"Please. Come in."

She stepped aside, then closed the door after Ransom and Gerald had crossed the threshold.

The decor of the room was a continuation of the lobby and hallway: the same elderly carpet, contrasted by a lighter pink quilted sateen bedspread. White sheers fluttered in the breath of an asthmatic air conditioner.

"Have a seat over here," she said, pulling out the hard wooden chairs from the table by the window. A ceiling light hung from a long rubber cord over the table at about the level of Ransom's forehead.

"Sorry about the light," she said. "It's supposed to be adjustable, but it's not."

"That's all right," Ransom said once he was seated. Gerald sat in the lone padded chair pushed a couple of feet back from the table.

Lisa folded her hands as if ready to begin a meeting. "Now, what can I do for you?"

"I take it you haven't heard?" said Ransom.

"Heard what?"

"Louie Dolores has been murdered."

"He what?" she said after a split second. She might've been a fresh edition of Marti Dolores, but she was nowhere near as adept at hiding her feelings as her older counterpart: her eyes betrayed to Ransom a great deal of distress.

"He was murdered. His body was found this morning at Dolores Tower."

"At the tower."

"We understand he had a date with you last night . . ."

"Yes?"

She hadn't batted an eye at the word "date." In fact, her mind seemed to be on something else entirely.

"Did he keep it?" Ransom asked.

"No. I waited, and when he didn't show up, I left."

"When was that?"

"Oh . . . I don't know . . . about a quarter to eight, I suppose," she replied absently.

Ransom's right eyebrow ascended. "You waited a long time."

"What?" she said, a flicker of life returning to her eyes. "Yes, I did."

He gave her an ingratiating smile. "Forgive me, but you don't seem like the type of person who would wait that long for anyone."

She looked puzzled for a moment, then smiled. "Mr. Dolores was a very important person."

"You didn't think it was strange when he didn't show up and didn't call?"

She shook her head. "It was the second night in a row it happened."

"Really?"

"Yes. We were supposed to meet the night before. Same place. He didn't show up then, either. His secretary called yesterday morning and made his apologies. We rescheduled."

"What excuse did she give?"

"Just that something important had come up. A man in his position, it's to be expected. And not questioned. I was wondering what excuse she would give today. I suppose being dead is one I would have to accept."

Ransom pursed his lips. "It would be the gracious thing to do. How long had you known him?"

"Well, I—" She stopped cold and looked at him. "Oh, my God! I just realized . . . are you telling me that while I was waiting for him, he was lying dead somewhere in that building?"

"It would seem so."

"Hmm. Not a very nice thought. You asked when we met. It was about six months ago in Santiago, when they were completing arrangements for the exhibition."

"Did you get to know him well?"

Her eyes narrowed. "Not *too* well. I have been getting to know him better here."

152

"I see," said Ransom. "So this actually *was* a date you were supposed to be on."

"A date?" The distraction she'd shown earlier had now completely faded. Her spine stiffened. "No, it was not a date. It was to be a business meeting. Mr. Dolores was talking to me about coming to work with him."

"A job?"

She nodded. "Yes, as his personal assistant."

"I thought he already had one."

"Bill Braverman? Yes. Seems like a nice man. It's a shame."

Ransom was a bit taken aback, though he didn't show it. His surprise was more with himself than with her: he thought it possible he'd misjudged her at first, and that she really was closer to being like Marti Dolores than he'd given her credit for. He also realized that her earlier distress had not been over the murder, but over the loss of her potential job.

"So Dolores was planning to dump Braverman?"

"It seems like it."

"Did Braverman know about this?"

"I couldn't say," she replied with a sly smile. "Mr. Dolores was, I think, the kind of man who would let you know if he was displeased with you. Maybe Braverman did know."

"I see." Ransom leaned in toward her. "Ms. Rivera, if he was talking to you about a position somebody already had, he must've told you why he was thinking of replacing him."

She drew back, trying to appear reluctant to answer. "He said that Mr. Braverman was not doing a good job. That's all."

"Hmm," Ransom said thoughtfully. "Well, given the reason for this meeting, I assume that you didn't tell anyone about it."

"No, I didn't." There was a pause, then something occurred to her. "Oh, but Hector knew."

"Hector?"

"Hector Gonzalez. He is my boss at the Archaeological Museum of Chile. He stopped into the bar last night."

"When?"

"Sometime before seven. I don't know exactly. I told him I was waiting for Mr. Dolores. Of course I didn't tell him why."

"Seems to be a very popular spot."

"The bar?" She shook her head. "It's just convenient."

"Was Mr. Gonzalez meeting someone?"

"I think he just stopped in because he saw me. He was only there a minute. Not even I could keep him from his precious mummies."

"Hmm?"

"Hector is . . . the best word for it I guess is 'quaint' about his mummies. He thinks of them as his children. Or his private possessions. He was going up to check on them, to see how they were doing after their busy day."

She had said this dispassionately, but Ransom sensed something behind the words. He wondered if she was trying to cast some sort of suspicion on her employer, or if she was merely angry with him for some reason.

"You make him sound very interesting," said Ransom.

"Hector?" she replied with surprise. "No. He's really very dull when it comes to his mummies. He has spent nearly a year doing nothing but complaining about the exhibit and the museum's treasures being loaned out—as if a museum can be run on air."

Gerald looked up from his note-taking and glanced at his partner.

"I'm sorry," said Ransom, "I don't understand."

"Mr. Dolores offered, and has paid, a sizable donation to the museum in exchange for this exhibit."

"I see. I imagine that didn't sit well with Mr. Gonzalez."

"Of course not. He's complained very much about the arrangement. Nothing has been right in this business as far as he's concerned. Mr. Dolores spared no expense when it came to the preparations and transport of the mummies. He provided state-of-the-art equipment to ensure that they were disturbed as little as possible, but even that did not placate Hector. He—" She stopped when she noticed the faint smile on Ransom's face. "Of course Hector is quite right. Moving the mummies at all can . . . has the potential of causing more damage to them."

"That didn't bother you?"

"As an historian, yes. But I am also a realist, Mr. Ransom. Unlike Hector. These decisions are made outside of me, but I can see the reasons for them."

Ransom eyed her shrewdly. "If Mr. Gonzalez fanatically objected to the exhibit coming here, I'll bet the people in charge of your museum appreciated you a lot more."

Her eyes grew cold. "I think fanatical is too harsh, maybe."

Do you, thought Ransom. "Is Mr. Gonzalez staying at this hotel?"

"Yes. In Room four-oh-four."

"I must say, I would think that an organization like Dolores Development would put you up somewhere a little more . . ." He allowed his voice to trail off suggestively.

"Classy?" Lisa offered.

"Yes."

"I'm sure Mr. Dolores would have, but he is not putting us up. He didn't bring us here, the museum sent us."

"Really?"

She nodded. "Mr. Dolores thought our presence was unnecessary. Personally, I don't think he wanted to be bothered with Hector . . . or anyone from the museum."

"If that's true, he certainly changed his mind about you," Ransom said.

For a moment, Lisa looked as if she didn't know how to respond to this. Then she said, "I have been very fortunate."

"And how will you stand with Dolores Development now?"

"I don't understand," she said hesitantly.

"Well, I believe Mrs. Dolores will be in charge of the company now. Do you think she'll take you on?"

He could see the muscles working in her jaw. "I don't know."

"So, it would appear that Dolores was killed between six-thirty and seven, if Rivera and Braverman were honest about the times," said Ransom.

"Why did you do that?" Gerald asked as they walked back to the elevator.

"What?" Ransom said innocently.

He laughed. "You *know* what! Why did you bring up Dolores's wife?"

"I felt like reminding Ms. Rivera that he had one. Somehow I don't think she'll do as well with Mrs. Dolores as she did with Mr. Dolores."

"So you think she had something going with him?"

Ransom nodded. "Oh, yes. When I tried to pin her down about whether or not it was a date, she denied it, and then she tried to draw my attention to other people. She was fairly subtle about Braverman, until I forced her hand. She was less subtle about Gonzalez, which makes me wonder if there was some kind of rift there."

"You think Dolores was really offering her a job?" Gerald asked.

"Yes. Rivera doesn't strike me as a stupid woman, and it would've been stupid to lie to us about something that other people *might* know about. I think Dolores at least told her there was a job. Which is what makes it even stranger that she felt the need to implicate other people. The job was as Dolores's personal assistant. She wouldn't have wanted him dead. Why kill the goose who was going to lay the golden egg?"

"Unless there really wasn't a job."

They came to a stop at the elevator.

"But how would she know that for sure? She couldn't very well talk to his staff about it, and even if one of them said there wasn't a job, why believe them? Dolores himself told her there was one."

Gerald pressed the Down button. "You want to talk to Gonzalez?"

He nodded. "Yes, as long as we're here. But let's take the stairs."

The nearest staircase was in a doorless shaft beside the elevator. The wide steps were an iron mesh whose black paint had been worn away through years of use. The detectives went down one flight to the fourth floor and quickly located Gonzalez's room.

Hector answered the door clad in a dark-green suit, white shirt, and mustard-yellow tie. His skin glistened, and he wore the worried expression of a foreigner who fears he is about to be hauled away for a crime he didn't realize he'd committed.

"What do you want?" he asked, narrowing his eyes at their badges.

"We're here about Louie Dolores," said Ransom.

Some of Hector's apprehension faded with surprise. "Mr. Dolores? What about him?"

"He's been murdered."

His eyes became saucers. "Murdered?"

"Yes. May we come in?"

"But what does this have to do with me?"

Ransom smiled in an attempt to allay some of the older man's distress. "We don't necessarily think it has anything to do with you, but we were hoping you might be able to help us."

"Yes, yes," Hector said, animating after a hesitation. "Come in."

The room was a carbon copy of Rivera's, except that the adjustable lamp was raised halfway to the ceiling, and most of the decorative stitching on the bedspread had unraveled. Hector didn't offer them seats. They stood grouped in the center of the room.

"What has happened?" Hector asked, sticking his right hand into his trouser pocket.

"We believe Dolores was killed last night at the tower. Your assistant told us you were there last evening."

"Lisa? You've spoken with Lisa?"

"Um-hmm. Were you there?"

"Yes, but I didn't see Mr. Dolores," Hector said quickly.

"Ms. Rivera said you were on your way up to the exhibit."

"Last night?"

"Yes."

"And Mr. Dolores, he was killed?" Hector said blankly.

Ransom searched the curator's eyes, trying to put a finger on what he saw there. It wasn't fear or surprise, or sadness. If anything, it was awe. "Mr. Gonzalez, is something the matter?"

"This happened last night?" he said again, slowly lowering himself onto the foot of the bed.

"Would you like some water?" Ransom asked.

Gonzalez didn't reply. Ransom glanced at Gerald, who went into the bathroom and came back a moment later carrying a full glass of water. He handed it to Gonzalez, who took it but didn't drink. He held the glass in both his hands, resting them in his lap.

When Ransom felt the silence had gone on long enough, he said, "Mr. Gonzalez?"

Hector raised a pair of watery eyes to the detective. "Ever since the museum started talking with Mr. Dolores, I've felt them."

"I beg your pardon?"

"I have felt them."

"Who?"

"The dead. The Chinchorros. Gone for all these centuries. They honored their dead, the Chinchorros. But when the last one died away, who was there to honor him? All the past year, I have felt them."

Gerald had quietly taken out his notebook and was jotting this down. In the pause, he glanced at his partner.

"I'm afraid I still don't know what you're talking about," Ransom said.

"The body dies, but the spirit lives on. Do you believe that?"

"It's possible," Ransom replied enigmatically.

"Ever since this exhibit was proposed, I've felt their spirits stirring. But I didn't know why. I didn't know if they were upset or offended . . . or something else . . . but I didn't think it would come to this."

Ransom scrutinized him for a moment before asking his next question. Gonzalez sat placidly holding the glass and staring straight ahead, as if looking into another world.

"Are you saying you think this was some sort of vengeance?"

Gonzalez looked up. "The Chinchorros were simple fisherfolk. Superstitious, but not given to . . . things like curses; from everything we know about them, we at least know that much. But . . ." He looked pleadingly into Ransom's eyes. "But what can we really know about a dead civilization? Is it possible?"

"Mr. Dolores wasn't killed by a spirit," Ransom answered gently. "You might want to drink some of that."

Hector looked down at the glass as if surprised to find it in his hands. He raised it to his lips and took a sip.

"Mr. Gonzalez, Ms. Rivera told me that you were upset about the exhibit coming here."

He nodded sadly. "These mummies were buried before Christ walked the earth. Any movement of them causes further deterioration.

To move them for money . . . for commerce . . . seems almost . . . sacrilege."

Ransom stopped himself from registering surprise. He'd expected Hector to call it a desecration. "You're not the only person who feels that way."

"Really?"

"I'm sure you've seen the protesters outside the tower."

"Yes, I have," Hector said quietly. "That is very strange."

"What is?"

"That there is a protest."

"Why strange?" Ransom asked. "I would think you'd agree with them."

"What? No. What they are saying, it is . . . do you know what it's like when you have a dream, and it isn't a nightmare, but somehow nothing in it seems right?"

"Yes."

"That is what I feel when I see those people who are demonstrating. Just another thing that doesn't seem right."

"In what way?"

Given the opportunity to enlighten someone about the mummies, Hector came back to himself somewhat. "I didn't want the Chinchorros moved, because of the damage it would cause them. But until I came here, I'd never heard of anyone who wanted them returned to the ground. That is opposed to what we know of them. The Chinchorros honored their dead. That was the reason for the mummification. We believe it was so that they could keep the bodies of their loved ones aboveground, part of their family units. In fact, it is more surprising that they ever buried them at all. We don't know why that was done."

"I see," Ransom said with interest. "So there is no sort of movement in Chile to have the mummies returned to their graves?"

"I've never heard of such a thing."

"That is very interesting." He was silent for a time. "Tell me, since you were against the exhibit, how did you feel about Louie Dolores?"

"You don't think I killed him!" Hector said, dropping the glass. Some of the water splashed across his shoes.

Ransom shrugged. "I'm bound to ask it."

Hector picked up the glass, but seemed at a loss as to what to do with it. Gerald took it from him and carried it into the bathroom, returning right away.

"I didn't kill him. It is another thing we believe about the Chinchorros, that they believed the dead had power. You wouldn't want to kill anyone."

Ransom had furrowed his brow as he listened. He was finding Hector very perplexing, first by his vagueness and then by this identification with the Chinchorros. "Quaint" was the word Lisa Rivera had used in describing Gonzalez, but Ransom didn't agree. Nor would he have described the museum curator as a fanatic. What Ransom was thinking was quite different: Gonzalez was acting as if he'd suffered a shock, although as far as Ransom knew, the curator didn't know Dolores well enough to have been put into this condition by the news of his death. There had to be something else, but Ransom was at a loss as to how to discover what it was.

Finally, he said, "So you were not upset enough about Dolores bringing your mummies here to take action."

"Oh, yes, I did take action."

"What did you do?"

"I finally came to a decision. I have decided to resign my position at the museum."

"That's a very big step. I would think getting pushed into it would add to your resentment."

Hector heaved a world-weary sigh, shaking his head. "I have no resentment. My decision, it is not just because of this; it is many things. My problems are with the museum, not Mr. Dolores. If it hadn't been him, it would've been someone else."

"I see," said Ransom, though he still couldn't account for Hector's vagueness. He decided to try a different tack. "Mr. Gonzalez, did you know that Dolores was thinking of hiring your assistant?"

"What?" After a pause, he smiled. "So that was it."

"That was what?"

"She was trying to get a job. I knew she was . . . I don't know the proper words for it . . . playing at him?"

"Making a play for him?" Gerald suggested.

160

Hector nodded. "Yes."

"What made you think that?" Ransom asked.

"The evening before the exhibit opened, we went down to the bar to have a talk. Lisa suggested it as a place we could do that. But she had just gotten into town that day, so I asked her how she knew about it. She said Mr. Dolores had told her."

"Really?" said Ransom.

Hector smiled sheepishly. "I am ashamed to say I accused her of making very fast work."

"I would agree with you."

"That's what our talk was about, you see."

"I'm sorry, I don't see."

"I told her I was going to leave the museum. And I also told her—well, Lisa is a very forceful woman, and I knew she would be expecting to move up—that I didn't think she would be promoted into my position."

"Why is that?"

He shrugged. "There are many reasons."

"So, she would have every reason to want Dolores to stay alive . . ."

The worried expression reappeared on Hector's face. He looked as if he were afraid he'd inadvertently implicated Lisa in some way. "You can't think that she killed him."

"I don't know what to think as of yet. Right now I'm just trying to sort out the people we know were at the tower last night. Tell me, after you ran into Ms. Rivera, what did you do?"

"I went up to the exhibit. You'll think me . . . you will think I am a foolish old man, but I just wanted to sit there for a while."

"Did you see anyone?"

The vagueness returned like a shroud separating Hector from his surroundings. "Anyone . . ."

"Yes," Ransom said.

"There was Nick, yes. A nice young man, I think. He is the guard in the evening."

"Anyone else?"

There was a long pause during which a tremor went through Hector's lower lip. "Who would there be?"

"That's what I'm asking you," Ransom said.

Hector seemed unable to raise his eyes. He rested his forearms on his legs and twined his fingers together. His hands began to tremble. "There was a guard on the door. No one else could've gotten in."

Ransom narrowed his eyes. When he'd asked if Hector had seen anyone, he'd meant anywhere in the tower. He was finding the curator's focus on the exhibit very interesting. "But someone got in before without being seen by the guard. Isn't that right?"

Hector slowly shook his head. He gripped his left hand with his right in an effort to stop them from shaking. "That is not possible . . ."

"We suspect that someone has been moving pretty freely around Dolores Tower," Ransom said lightly. "We thought maybe it was the young man who's been leading the demonstration outside the building."

Hector finally looked up, his eyes wide. "It wasn't him."

"You saw someone?"

"It wasn't him. It was one of our ancestors. I saw him again!"

"Again?"

He spread his hands, and the moment his grip was loosed, they began to tremble worse than before. The tremor spread up his arms and through the rest of his body. "We were wrong. Their mummies were meant to last. We've hurried their deterioration. They are not quiet . . ."

"What did you see?" Ransom asked.

"I saw a mummy! I saw a mummy!" He buried his face in his hands and began to weep.

"You saw this last night?"

Hector gasped for breath between sobs, and turned his terrified eyes to Ransom. "There was blood on his hands!"

11

Ransom accompanied Gerald as far as the parking lot of area headquarters.

"Make the report to Newman," he said as they stood beside his car. "And I think we'd better put a tail on Muñoz for the time being."

"But Gonzalez said—"

"I don't know how much we can make of anything he said. But now we've been told that the mummy was seen on the premises the night of the murder. Dolores said it was Muñoz, dressed as a mummy, who attacked him. We'd better keep an eye on Muñoz while we get this sorted out. And we'd better get this sorted out fast." He stopped and withdrew the pack of cigars from his pocket.

Gerald said, "Well, while I'm doing this, what are you going to be doing?"

"I'm going to see Emily."

"Now?" Gerald said, smiling coyly. "Should you be smoking?"

Ransom paused in the act of lighting up. "She's not my mother, Gerald. And she's aware that I still smoke."

"Sorry."

As Gerald headed for the back door of headquarters, Ransom climbed into his own car. He rolled down the window to mitigate the effects of the smoke, then leaned back against the seat with his left palm pressed against the steering wheel. After taking a few relaxing puffs, allowing the smoke to stream across the inside of the windshield, he switched on the engine and started for Emily's house.

"He saw a mummy?" Emily said. Her bright, incisive eyes gazed at Ransom over the rim of the teacup she had poised to her lips when he'd made this announcement.

"That's what he says. A mummy with blood on its hands." Ransom took a sip from the Styrofoam cup of coffee he'd picked up on his way to her house. They were seated at her kitchen table. "I had a sort of flashback in that hotel room."

"Oh?"

"To my youth. *Creature Features.* Every Saturday night, me and every kid I knew would gather in front of our TV sets with a big bowl of popcorn and watch one of those old Universal horror pictures. That kind of thing is fun when you're a kid. It's a lot less amusing when someone starts spouting dialogue from one of those movies in real life."

"What happened to Mr. Gonzalez?"

"He's been hospitalized. I don't know for how long."

Emily finally took a sip of tea, then set the cup in its saucer. "Is he a creditable person, do you think?"

"When he's not in need of sedation? I would think so. We're not talking about a peasant here. He's the curator of a major museum. And he has a Ph.D."

"So it's not only Frieda Jablonski who has seen the mummy."

"No. And that's not all."

Ransom filled her in on the investigation thus far. She listened with great interest.

When he had finished, she said, "Well, this is all very mystifying, isn't it?"

"Is it?" he said with a half smile. "I would've thought that once I told you everything I know, you would be able to pull the solution out of the air."

Despite his light tone, Emily sensed something underlying his words. Her mind went back to the first discussion they'd had about the case, and Ransom's reaction when Lynn credited her for her astuteness. Emily knew that although Ransom's ego wasn't normally fragile, everyone needs recognition now and then, and his usual confidence was the very thing that would prevent ordinary accolades from being forthcoming: people wrongly assumed that he didn't need them.

"No. I couldn't quite do that," she said, clearing her throat. "You are the detective in this family."

Were it in Ransom's nature to blush, he would've done it then.

Emily continued. "You think Mr. Braverman was lying to you?"

"I think they were all lying to me, except Gonzalez, and he barely made sense. But as for Braverman—if Dolores thought it was Muñoz who had attacked him, and he said he was going to do something about it himself, I can't believe that Braverman didn't already know who Muñoz was."

"Maybe he simply hadn't found it out yet."

"That's possible. But why not just tell us that?"

Emily thought about this for a while. "Mr. Braverman was always being linked with Mr. Dolores in the newspapers. It's very difficult to believe that he didn't know everything his employer knew."

Ransom smiled. "Gerald will be glad to know you agree with him. And Braverman's initial reluctance to tell us about the argument with Nathanson is even more curious. Now, I think Lisa Rivera, Dolores's assistant-in-waiting, lied to us about the nature of their relationship."

Emily pursed her lips. "Perhaps not."

Ransom was surprised by this. "You don't think they were having an affair?"

"I don't think I would call it that," she replied, adjusting herself in her seat primly. "Mr. Gonzalez said it, didn't he? He said that Lisa was 'making a play' for Mr. Dolores. Did she strike you as the type of person who would use sex to get what she wants?"

"Yes. But I was including that under the category of having an affair."

"Hmm," Emily said wistfully. "To me, an affair always implied some sort of emotional attachment."

He produced an impish grin. "And you always accuse me of being Victorian."

"Was Ms. Rivera at all upset at the news of the murder?"

"To tell the truth, at first I thought she was. But later, I got the feeling that that was only because Dolores's death ruined her job prospects."

"She most likely regretted her efforts."

Surprise registered on Ransom's face. "Emily, that is probably the kindest way something like that has ever been put."

Emily's cheeks turned pink. "Did you also believe that Mrs. Dolores was lying?"

"Definitely. The same way Braverman did. She said that her husband never discussed business with her."

Emily nodded in agreement. "Mr. Dolores was quite vocal in the media about his conquests—the business ones, I mean. It's difficult to believe he didn't boast about everything to his wife. From what I've seen of him on the news these past few years, he's always seemed like a man of great ego. I think it would be in his nature to tell his wife what he was doing, if only to let her know how clever he was." Her mouth formed a slightly disapproving frown.

"Exactly," said Ransom. "Then there's Juan Muñoz."

"What did he lie about?"

Ransom sighed. "I don't know. There is something very wrong there, but I don't know what it is. It's the one area where I agree with Braverman. It would certainly be strange for Muñoz to attack Dolores, then show up the next day as if nothing had happened."

"I don't know about that . . ." Emily said absently.

"What are you thinking?"

"Just that . . . if Mr. Muñoz was the attacker . . . since he didn't kill Mr. Dolores at the time, perhaps his aim was to terrorize him."

"Um-hmm?"

"And wouldn't that do it?"

"I'm sorry, you've lost me."

"Showing up the next day outside of the building as if nothing had happened. Wouldn't that presumably have added to Mr. Dolores's terror?"

"Assuming he had any, it might. But I don't think Dolores was easily terrorized."

166

"But if this man, Mr. Muñoz, is new to the country, or new to Mr. Dolores, he might not know that."

"I don't think he's new to the country," Ransom said. "He has a local driver's license, and an indefinable accent that seems to slip a bit when he's caught off guard. But besides that, I think it would be stranger for him to show up the morning after having killed Dolores." Emily started to say something, but he filled it in instead. "I know— unless he thought that would make him look less suspicious."

"How did he react when you told him about the murder?"

"The same way he reacted to everything: surprised, then cagey. It was very strange."

They fell silent for a time. Ransom was lost in thought and Emily sipped her tea with an expression on her face that could best be described as that of an anthropomorphized calculator.

"It's like a Joshua tree . . ." Emily said at last.

"I beg your pardon?"

"A murder investigation. It's like a Joshua tree, isn't it? All the branches intertwined and twisting in every direction. Too many branches."

"And still more to come. We didn't get to talk to Alderman Nathanson yet because Gonzalez's little episode ended up taking up much of the afternoon. And then there's Samantha Campbell, the woman from the Historical Commission who disrupted the opening of the exhibit. We have to talk to her."

"And then there's the mummy."

"Yes," Ransom said, heaving a weary sigh. "Who may or may not be Juan Muñoz. It's an annoying little wrinkle."

"But an important one. It may not be that his appearance on the scene is as significant as the fact that he is actually *able* to appear."

Ransom smiled. "I'm afraid you've lost me again."

She straightened herself up. "Well, you said you were surprised that Mr. Dolores wasn't more worried about the breach of security."

He nodded. "Because of the death threat left on his car."

"Yes, initially. But that was before you knew of all the sightings of the mummy. Now, if these sightings were real, then as you said, someone is roaming around that building very freely." She paused, then added, "A security building."

Ransom's face lightened. "Which would mean the mummy has a key card."

"A most peculiar thing for a mummy to be carrying, don't you think?"

Ransom sighed again. "You know, I wasn't inclined to take that death threat against Dolores seriously because he took it to the press instead of to us. The whole thing looked like a publicity stunt. And even though he's been murdered, I still think there's something wrong with it. Despite his being attacked, he really didn't want us to investigate the threat."

Emily thought about this for quite some time. "Could it be that Mr. Dolores wanted to take care of the threat on his own, as well as the attack?"

"I suppose so. But if the threat and the attack were real, then why wasn't he concerned about security?" He took a drink from the Styrofoam cup.

"*If* they were real."

"If any of it's real. I'm sorry, Emily—I know you're inclined to believe Frieda Jablonski, but too much of what's going on is just too . . . odd. Particularly this mummy business. The attack on Dolores aside, why appear to other people? To Jablonski and Gonzalez? To establish the presence of the mummy before the murder? So whoever it is would get blamed for it? Why bother? Nobody witnessed the murder. And surely in this day and age, nobody would be expected to believe that an actual mummy is responsible. I had chalked Jablonski's sighting up as another publicity stunt."

"But then Mr. Dolores was attacked."

"So he said. And now Gonzalez says he saw the mummy. But quite frankly, Hector Gonzalez's behavior didn't inspire confidence. I don't know if I can take anything he said as true." He paused and took a deep breath. "Which brings me to the reason for my visit."

"Your reason?" Emily said, her thin eyebrows arching. She had assumed he had simply stopped by to commiserate, as was his custom.

"Yes. Before he completely broke down, Gonzalez said some very provocative things that we need to sort out as quickly as possible. We need to know when and where he saw the mummy last night. And he said he saw him 'again,' so we need to find out about the other

time . . . or times. But most important, when I told him that we suspected the mummy was Muñoz, he said, 'It wasn't him.' We need to
know why he thinks that."

"Yes?" Emily said quizzically.

"I can't think of ånyone better able to help do that than you."

"I'm sure you can do it," she replied self-effacingly.

He was silent for several moments. "I've been reminded a couple
of times recently of your talents," he said, looking down at his cup.
It was unlike him to look away from her when speaking. "Not that
I needed to be. It's been a sort of tweak to my ego."

"Nonsense!" Emily said kindly. She was surprised to hear him
being so frank about his feelings. "You know how good a detective
you are."

"I suppose I do. Maybe it's just that I'm getting older. When you
get into your forties, you go from believing that you're the best to
feeling the need to have everyone else believe it. When I was younger,
I didn't give a second thought to what anyone thought."

She bestowed her warmest grandmotherly smile on him. "I don't
believe for a minute that you care what everyone thinks of you."

He looked up at her. "Not everyone." After a pause, he said, "At
any rate, Gonzalez's condition—his mental condition—was very
shaky when he was taken to the hospital. He'll need to be handled
as gently as possible, and I think you could do that better than I can."

"Now, Jeremy—" Emily began to protest, but he raised a palm.

"Let me put it this way: I think you can get answers from him
sooner than I could. It's more expedient to enlist your aid than to
wait. Dolores is a VIP, and we'll have everyone from the mayor to
the media breathing down our necks until this is solved."

"So you want me to talk to Mr. Gonzalez." She couldn't bring
herself to say "question him."

"Yes. I'll take you to see him and have you do the talking."

"Well, I would be glad to help, of course. When will we do it?"

"As soon as possible. I'll check on his condition tomorrow morning. I'm hoping we'll be able to see him by the afternoon. Before that,
I have an alderman to track down."

* * *

It was an efficiency apartment, with a Pullman kitchen that at one time could be closed away by a wooden accordion panel. But the panel had jumped its track long ago and ever since had hung precariously by the bolt that held one end in place.

The walls were yellowed with cigarette smoke, and the brown carpet smelled of mildew. A card table and a single chair sat under the window, in which a cheap, oscillating fan tried in vain to bring in some air.

A small, old black-and-white television sat on a TV tray on one side of the room, and on the other side was a twin bed with threadbare green-and-white-striped sheets.

Juan Muñoz was lying on the bed, his face turned toward the TV. All afternoon the news had been full of Dolores's murder. The reporters said repeatedly that the police had no leads as yet, but then they invariably followed by recounting the story of the appearance of the mummy, complete with joking speculations—as joking as propriety would allow—about the possibility of a curse.

But having been accosted by the police, Muñoz couldn't find any humor in the story. In fact, as the day wore on, his peace of mind eroded.

If the police came to see me, he kept telling himself, *then they think there's some truth to the mummy thing! And they think it was me!*

At intervals, he would jump up from the bed and pace the room, as if the movement—any movement—would help calm him down. He would pace until he felt the squalid, claustrophobic room in his bones. Then he would collapse back onto the bed.

And then his agitation would start to build again. As it grew, he would snatch up the receiver of the phone that lay on the floor half under the bed and punch in a number on the pad. Each time, he got either a busy signal or a recorded message. He would then slam down the receiver and lie back on the bed for a while, letting his pent-up fear fester until it led to his pacing again.

It was after four o'clock when the phone was finally answered by a human being.

"It's about time!" Muñoz exclaimed.

"Are you crazy, calling me?" said the voice.

"I have to talk to you!"

"I can't talk now!"

"I've been trying to get you all day," Muñoz said angrily. "You do have to talk now!"

"I've been busy. Haven't you heard the news?'

"Heard it? The police have questioned me!"

"Questioned *you?*" the voice said slowly.

"Yes!" said Muñoz. "And they said they're going to question me again. They said Dolores said I attacked him."

"Yeah. I know."

"And now the guy's dead! You know how that makes me look?"

"What do you want?" There was no hiding the strain in the voice.

"I want money. I've got to get out of town!"

There was a long pause. "Well, we owe you money, anyway. It may be a little difficult, but I'll do what I can."

"You'd better!" Muñoz said, more panicked than threatening. "If I can't get out of town, if I'm questioned by them again, I'm telling them *everything!* Then they'll know that I didn't have anything to do with it."

"Are you at home?"

"Yeah."

"Stay there. I'll see what I can do."

12

The Braverman's home phone had been ringing when Bill plugged it back into the wall late in the morning that Dolores's body was found. He picked up the receiver and dropped it back in its cradle, then lifted it again. When he heard the tone, he dialed his secretary's home number. Alice was still in shock from having heard the news of Dolores's death when she was turned away from the office earlier, but he managed to calm her down enough to get her to understand that he wanted her at work at noon.

Bill arrived at Dolores Tower to a firestorm of media, impossible to avoid because the first level of the tower was open to the public. They shouted questions at him, following him as he made his way to the tower elevators, but his only reply was that he didn't have any information yet.

Up in the penthouse, he was stopped by the police when he got off the public elevators. They allowed him to go in after he identified himself. He glanced at the elevator around which three policemen were huddled, and his stomach clenched when he saw the bit of blood.

With the help of Alice, Bill spent the day fielding calls from reporters who wanted news, colleagues who wanted to express their condolences, and associates who called to cautiously inquire about how Dolores's death would affect their various projects. Although he did what he could to placate them, in actuality he didn't know.

As the afternoon had worn on, he'd become nagged by the feeling of working without a net. Louie Dolores was Dolores Development. Without him, the business was like a body with no head. He grew keenly aware that despite what Anna might think of him, his presence at the company was more essential than ever, at least for the time being. He began to wonder if Marti Dolores would view him the way Anna did, or if she would see him as the invaluable helpmeet he'd been to her husband. She probably wouldn't want to run the company herself. There was no reason to believe she would be interested in doing that. Perhaps his value would be recognized to the point of his being moved up to actually running the company. But as much as he tried to entertain thoughts of being promoted, his imagination couldn't stretch past his being integral only on an interim basis. What would happen after that was beyond him.

When he finally left the office that evening, he still had one matter to take care of, but he decided to run up to his apartment before going on. It was nearly seven o'clock, and he didn't know whether or not Anna would have come home yet. But if she had, he wanted to tell her that he was going out. In their present situation, he didn't think it would make matters any better to keep her in the dark about his whereabouts. He could've just called from the office, but since he had to go back to their building to pick up his car, he thought it would look better if he spoke to her in person.

He found Anna sitting in the living room, her feet propped up on the coffee table and a book resting on her knees. Her long, blond hair was pushed back behind her ears, and she wore a pair of black-rimmed glasses. Bill always liked it when she wore her glasses—something she seldom did anymore—because they somehow made her look younger. Maybe it was because it was a throwback to their college days, when she almost always studied in them.

She barely looked up when he entered the room, but she did say hello.

"It was a bitch of a day," he said lightly. "Nothing but calls, nonstop all day long."

"Uh-huh."

"There's going to be a lot of ends to tie up. Louie must've had a hundred projects going, and they all need to be sorted out."

"Hmm."

"I suppose I'll be an important part of whatever happens now, because I'm really the only one who knows the details of Louie's business. You should've been there! I must've heard from every goddamn person he knew. A lot of them are sweating about what's going to happen to their plans with Louie gone. It was pretty disgusting. Here the man is murdered, and all these people care about is what's going to become of them."

"That is terrible," Anna said without bothering to look up from her book.

He watched her for quite some time. So long, in fact, that he was surprised the scrutiny didn't disturb her. But she continued to read, slowly moving her eyes across the page, then turning it when she reached the bottom.

"Anna . . ." Bill said at last, swallowing hard, "Geoff told me that you plan to sell out."

"Did he?" she said after a beat.

"Yeah. Why didn't you tell me?"

"I thought I had."

"You . . . you mentioned it as a possibility. You didn't say . . . you didn't sound final about it."

She turned another page without reading it. "Nothing's final yet. They haven't made a decision about whether or not to buy me out."

There was a pause. "And if they do, what will you do then?"

"I haven't made a decision about that, either."

He came over to her and sat on the arm of the sofa. "Anna . . . now that Louie is dead, things will be different."

For the first time, she looked him directly in the eye. Behind the glasses, her eyes seemed to burn with an intimate knowledge of him. "Will they?"

"Yes." He said it, but he was unable to bear the intensity of her gaze. He looked down at his hands, which were resting on his knees. "I have to go back out. I just ran in to tell you I'd be out for a while . . . so you wouldn't wonder."

"All right," she replied, turning back to her book.

Bill stood up and headed for the door. Before closing it, he called back toward the living room, "I'll see you in a little while."

There was no answer.

"You should've gone home," James Harker said as he refilled the wine glasses.

"I didn't want to go home," Marti replied. She stood by the glass door that opened onto the balcony. Harker's apartment was on the river just north of the Loop. It faced northwest, so that from the balcony Marti could see the full expanse of the city, stretching all the way out to O'Hare. Streetlights were just beginning to burn through the late evening haze.

"Didn't want to face the empty house?" Harker asked.

"I didn't want to face the press. Or the telephone. If I answer the phone, I would have to listen to condolences; if I don't answer it, there are those who might actually come over unasked to make sure I'm all right. If I'm not there, they will say, "Oh, the poor widow, she has gone into seclusion, she is so broken up over the loss.' "

Harker would've laughed, but he didn't think it would be appropriate under the circumstances.

"You've thought that all out?"

She cast a glance his way. "Before you divorced, didn't you ever wonder what it would be like if your wife died?"

He pressed the cork back into the bottle. "Well, maybe, but not quite to that extent."

Marti gave a rueful laugh. She took hold of the handle and pulled the door open, then stepped out onto the balcony. She went to the railing and rested her hands on it. Harker followed her out, carrying two glasses of wine, one of which he handed to her.

"I've always liked the view from here," she said after taking a sip. "At night, it's like a Christmas tree that has fallen on its side. I always wanted to live in a high-rise."

"Why haven't you?"

"Louie. Louie didn't like them."

"What?" Harker sputtered into his glass.

"He loved to design them. He loved to build them. And he certainly loved the money that they poured into his bank account. But he didn't want to live in one."

"I can't believe that. I was surprised when you bought in Winnetka. I would've thought Louie would want the newest of everything."

She shook her head slowly. "For all his 'modern design,' he was strictly traditional. 'Families should live in a house' he said over and over. As if we were ever a family."

"Well, you'll be able to sell the house and buy anything you want now. Live wherever you want."

"Not just yet. It wouldn't look right."

"Huh?"

"I mean it would look suspicious to suddenly sell up and move. I shouldn't change anything for a while."

"If you sold the house, people would probably just think you couldn't go on living there without him."

She smiled. "Or that I couldn't wait to be set free."

Harker gently pushed aside the hair covering the nape of her neck, then leaned over and lightly kissed her there.

Marti didn't move. "Have you ever heard of a telephoto lens?" she asked.

He stopped. "Nobody will be looking for you here."

"We can't know that. And one picture of me being nuzzled on your balcony on the day of my husband's murder would certainly kill the image of a grieving widow."

This time, he let himself laugh. "I don't think anybody will ever think of you that way."

"No. Perhaps you're right. I made a mistake with those detectives today. I could tell they were suspicious of me because I didn't react badly at the news. At least the one asking the questions was. I didn't pay attention to the other one. But I just found I couldn't act like I felt anything for Louie."

"They're detectives," said Harker. "They're probably used to people reacting to bad news in ways that defy explanation."

"I wouldn't want to rely on that. The questioning one—Detective Ransom—he is no fool."

They stood for a while in silence, watching the city lights brighten as the sunlight evaporated and listening to the sounds of traffic below.

"So, what happens now?" asked Harker.

She sighed heavily. "Nothing right now. For the time being, things will go on as they have. But I will soon have to start looking into taking over Louie's company."

"Which will make you the most powerful woman in the city," he said as he slipped his arms around her.

"Yes," said Marti. "And we have at least one client that I know will be delighted!"

13

FRIDAY

The media circus had begun in earnest by Thursday nightfall, with television reporters speculating in lieu of facts, and the newspapers scrambling to uncover information in time to meet overnight deadlines.

Ransom and Gerald were thankful to find themselves overlooked by the media. Louie Dolores had been such an important factor in the current growth of the city that the upper-echelon of the department were falling over themselves to get on-camera to express their outrage about the murder and their certainty that the case would soon be solved. Ransom marveled at the verbal dexterity with which the police commissioner, the mayor, and anyone else who could get on-camera could answer direct questions without saying anything.

As long as these luminaries were busy with the media, they had little time to exert the pressure that would trickle down, however anemically, to the street level where the detectives worked. But Ransom knew that after a few days of seeking the limelight in the media, these luminaries would run out of ways to say they had nothing to report, and the pressure would increase. So that morning, the two detectives received a cursory admonition from Sergeant Newman to get results fast, then left for Alderman Daniel Nathanson's office.

"According to the report I got this morning," Ransom said once they were on their way, "there were two sets of fingerprints on the death threat, Dolores's and one other, which would be Braverman's, since he handled it."

"So it really could be a hoax," said Gerald.

"Or the person sending the threat was very careful." He pulled out his cell phone. "What's the number for Dolores's office?"

Gerald kept one hand on the steering wheel while he fished in his pocket for his notebook. He turned the pages back with his thumb until he found the number, then read it off.

Ransom dialed and waited.

"Dolores Development." It was Paula Dryer's voice.

"Ms. Dryer, this is Detective Ransom. I'm afraid I'm going to have to ask you to keep the mummy exhibit closed today."

"What? Why?" the young woman sputtered.

"We're going to have to go over it, and we have to do that without a crowd. I don't know how soon we'll be there, but I don't want anyone going into the exhibit in the meantime. Can you take care of this?"

"Yes . . . yes, I guess I can. Do you know when we'll be able to reopen?"

"Tomorrow, if all goes well."

He said good-bye and disconnected, then stuck the slender phone back in his pocket.

"Why did you do that?" Gerald asked.

Ransom sighed. "On a long shot. Jablonski and now Gonzalez both saw the mummy in there—Gonzalez, if he can be believed, saw it the night of the murder. We're going to have to take it seriously."

"But *can* he be believed?"

"Hopefully I'll find that out later."

Alderman Nathanson's office was located in one of the ancient buildings directly across the street from Marshall Field's on Wabash, where the elevated train tracks spanning the street for the length of the Loop leave the street itself in a state of perpetual semigloom.

They found a space by a fire hydrant a couple of doors down from the building that housed Nathanson's office. Gerald wedged the car in between the curb and one of the el's steel posts, then they went into the building. The directory listed Nathanson's office on the twelfth floor, and after a short wait for one of the antiquated elevators, they found themselves at his door. The top half of the door was a heavy, frosted pane of glass on which was painted DANIEL NA-THANSON, INSURANCE. Gerald opened the door and they went in.

The outer office in which they found themselves was far from roomy. The walls were a sickly shade of off-white, and the floor was covered with a dirty brown carpet. Directly across the room from the entrance was the door to an inner office. To the left of the entrance was a seating area that contained only two chairs and a small table supported by a single, slender pedestal. To the right was a gunmetal-gray desk behind which sat a round-faced woman of about forty. She wore a light-blue pantsuit and a white-knit blouse that had a small faint round stain on the left breast. She looked up as the entered and didn't appear to be pleased with the interruption.

"Can I help you?" she asked in an uninviting tone.

"We're here to see Alderman Nathanson," said Gerald as he reached into his pocket.

"Do you have an appointment?"

He pulled out his badge and showed it to her. "Is he here?"

"Yeah, he's here. Wait a minute." She picked up the receiver of her phone and pressed a button. They heard a muted buzz from the inner office. "Two men here to see you," she said without preamble. "Police." She hung up the phone and rolled her eyes up at them. "Go in."

"Thank you," said Ransom, who couldn't help smiling at the woman. She responded with a glare.

They went into the inner office, and Gerald closed the door behind them. This room was decorated in the same sorry colors as the outer one, but most of the wall space on the left was taken up by shelves crammed with books, and on the right, by file cabinets. On the far wall behind the desk there was a grimy window looking out into an alley.

Nathanson rose as they entered and came out from behind his desk, extending a hand. "Hello, gentlemen. Daniel Nathanson. My secretary didn't give me your names."

"I'm Detective Ransom," he said as he shook the hand. "This is Detective White."

Nathanson shook Gerald's hand. "Detectives?" he said with a

nod to show that he was impressed. "Have a seat, have a seat!" He gestured toward the old wooden chairs facing his desk as he crossed back behind it and resumed his seat. "And what brings you to me today?"

"We're investigating the murder of Louie Dolores."

There was a split-second blip in the alderman's affable demeanor. "Terrible thing. Terrible. Louie was a great boon to this city. He'll be a terrible loss."

"Yes," Ransom said lightly. "I believe I heard you say that on the news."

"But why would you come to me about that?"

"You understand that in a murder investigation, we have to follow up everything to determine whether or not it is pertinent to the case."

"Of course," Nathanson replied with a glance at the notebook Gerald had taken out of his pocket. "But I still don't see what that has to do with me. I knew Louie, of course, but . . . not well enough to kill him." He smiled, apparently pleased with his own wit.

"Yes, but we have to follow everything up nonetheless."

Nathanson shrugged broadly. "Okay. Shoot."

"I understand that Mr. Dolores was trying to reach you on the day he was murdered."

"Yes, but that was what I call one of my 'alderman days.' "

"Hmm?"

"Oh, just one of those days when I had a lot of personal appearances and things scheduled in my role as alderman for this district. So I didn't get to talk to Louie."

"I see," Ransom said slowly. "And you could, of course, provide a list of these events."

"What?" Nathanson exclaimed, all traces of his smile disappearing. "Just what do you mean?"

"As I said, we have to check out everything."

"I don't get your meaning. At least I hope I don't!"

Ransom was unfazed. "If you can't remember it, your secretary can provide us with your schedule for that day, can't she? If not, your appearances as alderman are a matter of public record."

Nathanson sputtered. "I don't . . . I don't believe . . ."

Ransom gave him a placating smile. "Mr. Nathanson, from what we heard, Dolores was furious with you. It would be perfectly natural for you to want to avoid him." *But not to lie about it.*

The corners of Nathanson's mouth turned down in a puzzled frown. To Ransom, it looked as if the alderman couldn't decide whether he should be angry or relieved. After a while, he produced a sheepish grin. "Well, all right then, I was avoiding him. I don't know why I shouldn't admit it."

Ransom raised an eyebrow. "Neither do I."

Nathanson added quickly, "Except that it doesn't look good for someone in my position to be avoiding someone in Louie's position. I didn't want to seem—" He broke off, not wanting to put it into words. "But you didn't know Louie, did you?"

"I never had the pleasure."

"Huh. Well, he could be unreasonable. Hell, he could be volatile. Sometimes."

"But I'm sure he could also be a good friend," Ransom said with an unreadable smile.

Nathanson hesitated again. He didn't know how to take that. "Yes, he could. I did talk to Bill—Bill Braverman—that day."

Ransom crossed his legs. "So he said. He told us that Dolores thought you leaked some information about the Stone Candy Factory . . . about his intention to acquire the land."

"That's right," Nathanson said, almost proudly. "But I didn't have anything to do with that. I don't know how the Historical Commission found out about it."

Ransom allowed a pause, then said, "Forgive me, but you sound glad that it happened."

"Well, no, I'm not glad," he said falteringly. "No, development is always good for my district, and Louie's work was always first rate, and . . . well, just look at how he's transformed the near north side . . ."

"I have," Ransom said flatly.

"I see you're one of those people who don't like progress, but I can tell you, the building that Louie has done, it's been great for the city. Pumped up revenue. Pumped up property values. I'm . . . I'm glad that the information was leaked, because to tell you the truth, there would've been a battle about the Stone Candy Factory. But I'm glad that I wasn't the one that leaked it."

"Because it made Dolores so furious."

"Yes, there's that. But like I said, I think the building-up around here has been a great thing for the city."

"Hmm." Ransom considered this for quite some time before continuing. Gerald sat lightly tapping the tip of his pencil against the page of his notebook.

Finally, Ransom uncrossed his legs and said, "There's one thing I don't understand. Given your unreserved support of Dolores's projects, why would he have accused you of leaking the information?"

Nathanson's eyes widened. "I . . . I . . . don't know. Like I said, Louie was volatile . . ."

Ransom nodded. "And unreasonable, yes. But would he be so unreasonable that he would've jumped to that conclusion with absolutely no reason?"

"I . . . maybe he thought I did it by accident."

"But if that were the case, or if you had nothing to do with it, as you said, then I don't see why you would avoid him. Couldn't you just tell him that?"

"You didn't know him!" Nathanson said loudly.

"I just thought that perhaps there was another reason Dolores might have jumped to the idea that you leaked the information."

"Like what?"

Ransom leaned forward. "I understand you had an argument with Dolores the day before the exhibit opened."

Nathanson's jaw clenched and his face turned red. He pushed himself back in his chair and folded his arms. "I suppose that weasel Braverman told you that?"

Ransom's right eyebrow went up again. "Weasel?"

"Oh, yeah, the guy that always does the dirty work. I suppose he told you about that argument, but he couldn't have told you everything!"

"Couldn't he?" Ransom said, playing a gambit that he hoped would pay off. "His close friend of many, many years has just been murdered. Do you think he would hold back?"

Gerald smiled inwardly.

Nathanson again appeared to be at a loss for how to proceed. He considered them for a long moment, then gave up with a heavy sigh.

"You're right. They're birds of a feather. So he told you about the blackmail."

Ransom cocked his head in a way that could've been construed as assent. "Why don't you tell us about it?"

Nathanson huffed. "I suppose Braverman figures that since he stayed out of the room and Louie did all the talking, he's free and clear."

"I suppose that's true."

"But don't you believe it for a minute! Braverman plays all innocent, but he always knew everything Louie was doing. Hell, he carried out most of it."

"I'm still waiting to hear your side of this."

He huffed again. "Did you ever hear of the Harrison project?"

"Yes."

"But you probably don't know the whole story. It was an entire block down there on Harrison Street, middle of an area that's been in the throes of redevelopment for years, and this old, three-level apartment building was taking up a whole block."

Ransom pursed his lips. "That would be the building that was occupied at the time by low-income people who had lived there all their lives."

Nathanson hesitated before continuing. "Yeah. There were a lot of people against that project because of that, and because the building was an example of . . . I can't remember what kind of architecture. All I know is the Historical people thought it was important. For me, I thought it was an eyesore."

Ransom sighed impatiently. "Yes, I know. It was the kind of project that could've been held up by the city, but you helped swing opinion in its favor."

Nathanson nodded ruefully. "And if that was all there was to it, nothing more would've been made of the whole thing. Everybody had been moved out of it, and the only holdup to going ahead was the Historical Commission, which was trying to save it. But Louie couldn't wait. He jumped the gun. He demolished the place while the historical designation was still pending, and claimed it was a mistake . . . claimed he thought he had the okay. Everybody was mad, even me! But the Historical Commission most of all, and they pressed the district attorney's office to investigate . . . both Louie and me, because of my support."

"This is old news," Ransom said. "You were accused of taking bribes for your support, but the grand jury found no evidence."

"It was a campaign contribution!" Nathanson said defensively. "And they had the word of Louie and Braverman."

"And this, I hope, brings us to the day before the exhibit opened. Why did Dolores think you leaked the information about the Stone Candy Factory?"

"Because . . . because I didn't want him to get it," Nathanson admitted reluctantly.

"Hmm?"

"It was too soon. And the situation was too much like the Harrison project. I didn't think it was . . . wise for him to go after it. But Louie wanted what Louie wanted."

Ransom sat back in his chair and gazed at the alderman, who looked rather beaten. "I see. And that is why you argued?" He made it sound as if he didn't believe this.

Nathanson heaved a sigh. "If you talked to Braverman, you know why. It wasn't much of an argument. It was a threat. Louie told me that if I didn't help him get that land, he would go to the DA and tell him I demanded a bribe in the Harrison project."

"They would've been admitting they'd lied to the grand jury."

"That's exactly what I said. But you know what he said? He said they'd claim I forced them into it. That they lied under duress. They would've come out looking like victims, and I would've come out looking like some sort of . . . some sort of . . ."

"Crooked politician?" Ransom offered.

"Yeah," he replied after a beat. But his face hardened as he went on. "Louie had money, and they would've lied, Detectives. They would've gotten away with it."

Ransom waited, letting the alderman's words hang in the air. "That would seem to give you one very good motive for murder."

Nathanson's mouth dropped open and his face turned noticeably white. "But don't you see? I didn't have any reason to kill him! I was off the hook because somebody spilled the beans about the candy factory. Don't you see that? He couldn't have gone ahead with the project. That's the only reason I was happy it was spilled!"

"Yes, but you knew that Dolores thought you were the one who leaked it. So one could argue that you were even more on the hook than ever. Now, can you tell me where you were early Wednesday evening, specifically between six and seven?"

"I don't believe this!" Nathanson said, rising from his chair. "You don't really believe I murdered him, do you?"

"You haven't answered the question," Ransom said calmly.

"Wednesday night? Wednesday night between six and seven? I was at home. Having dinner with my wife. She can tell you that!"

14

"You're being very quiet," said Ransom as they rode down in the elevator.

"That really bothers me," Gerald replied as he absently plucked a piece of lint from the sleeve of his jacket.

"What does? The idea of a crooked politician?"

"No. I don't know, when we first heard about Nathanson, he seemed outside this whole thing to me. Now he seems like the prime suspect."

"Does he?"

"You heard what he just said. I mean, everybody we've talked to was having some sort of problem with Dolores, but Nathanson's the only one with a flat-out motive."

Ransom shrugged. "Everyone has a motive, as far as I'm concerned. His wife because of his infidelity—no matter how much she denies letting it bother her; Braverman because he was being replaced, even though we don't know whether or not he knew that."

"Lisa Rivera?" Gerald asked as the elevator doors opened at the lobby.

Ransom nodded. "Maybe he didn't really have a job for her. Maybe he was playing her for a fool. She doesn't strike me as the type of woman who would appreciate that. And then there's her boss, Hector Gonzales. One does have to wonder if he is unhinged enough to have committed murder."

They went out through the revolving door and headed for the car.

"What about Juan Muñoz?" asked Gerald. "We don't know what he's up to yet, or what he was doing in that building—if it was him. So what motive could he have?"

"I hardly think he's sincere about his little protest," Ransom said wryly. "But let's suppose he is. Let's suppose he really objects to the mummies being on display here. A zealot is a dangerous thing."

Gerald came to a stop on the driver's side of the car and looked over the roof at his partner. "Yeah, but that still leaves Nathanson with the most solid motive. I mean, all the other stuff is just conjecture—"

"And not necessarily things that people would kill over," Ransom interjected. "Like infidelity. Divorce, maybe, but kill? I don't know."

"But Nathanson could've gone to jail."

Ransom smiled. "Cheer up, Gerald, he still might."

They climbed into their respective seats. Ransom automatically pulled out a cigar and jabbed the lighter into the dash.

"You know," said Gerald, "the way I see it, the trouble is that the least likely suspects are the ones with no alibis: Rivera and Gonzalez. The other ones have somebody to vouch for them."

"Braverman doesn't. He was out for a drive."

"Oh, that's right."

"But when it comes to the right-hand man, I have a problem with his motive. Do you really kill someone because you might lose your job? Especially when your job is as assistant to the person you're killing?"

Gerald smiled. "You're right."

"And you think Rivera and Gonzalez are unlikely?"

"Well, sure," Gerald said. "Isn't it most likely he was killed by somebody that knew him well?"

Ransom shook his head slowly. "I don't know about that. I do have one very big problem with Nathanson as the murderer, though."

"What's that?"

Ransom turned an incredulous gaze at him. "The mummy, Gerald."

"The mummy?"

"Yes. His appearances are somehow tied up in this. Can you see our distinguished alderman creeping around Dolores Tower in a mummy suit?"

Gerald laughed. "Nope." He suddenly stopped. "But I could see him paying someone to do it for him."

"I wonder who that would've been," Ransom said with a coy grin.

The lighter popped out. He lit the cigar, sending a cloud of smoke billowing around him.

"So you want to tackle Muñoz again?" Gerald asked as he rolled down his window.

"No. Not until we have more than speculation to go on. We have one more person to talk to before we try to sort all these people out. Did you get the address of the Historical Commission?"

"Yep. It's on Fullerton."

"Let's go there and see if we can talk to Samantha Campbell."

Gerald drove over to Lake Shore Drive and headed north. On the way, Ransom pulled out his cell phone again and called the McCormick Hospital for an update on Hector Gonzalez's condition. After a terse discussion with the operator, he was transferred to the nurses' station at Gonzalez's unit. He identified himself, and a nurse named Davis informed him that Mr. Gonzalez was doing all right, and that Ransom could probably speak to him a little later in the morning.

Traffic was heavy but moving at a good clip, so they made it to Fullerton in about ten minutes. They exited the Drive and headed west.

"It's been a long time since I've been in this neighborhood," said Ransom.

He leaned back in his seat, resting his arm on the windowsill and taking leisurely drags on his cigar as he watched the buildings go by. It took a while for them to get through the stoplight where Lincoln and Halsted cross Fullerton, but after that, they proceeded quickly.

A few blocks west of Lincoln, they went past a row of very old townhouses. In front of one was a slender, attractive woman who looked to be in her late fifties. Clad in a peasant dress and a broad sunhat, she was busy weeding the garden, assisted by two men about half her age who were engaged in a water fight with the hose.

"Now there's an unlikely trio," Ransom said, wrinkling his nose.

About five minutes later, they reached a block of stores and pulled up in front of the one in the center. On the left side of the front window, subdued Gothic lettering about three inches high announced "The Chicago Commission for Historical Preservation." The door was set back in a small alcove shaped like an inverted bay window.

As the detectives went through the door, a bell jangled overhead. A row of brightly colored plastic chairs was pushed up against the back wall of the room. The walls were covered with photos, old and new, of a selection of Chicago's landmark buildings. On the glass of several of the frames, a large red circle with a slash through it had been drawn. Ransom took these to be the ones for which the Historical Commission had lost its battles.

The doorbell had been an unnecessary touch, since the lone occupant of the fusty office was seated at a desk in the center of the room. Her dull red hair was bobbed, and her excessively pale skin made her plentiful freckles seem dark. She looked up from her work as the detectives came through the door.

"Can I help you with something?" she asked.

"Are you Samantha Campbell?" Ransom asked.

"Yes."

"I'm Detective Ransom, this is Detective White. We'd like to speak with you about Louie Dolores."

"Oh, God!" she said, dropping her pen on the desk and sitting back. "I knew you'd get to me eventually. It's because I made a scene at the opening of his mummy exhibit, isn't it?"

"To a certain extent," Ransom replied. Her smile made her look quite open, like one of Shakespeare's peasants. He also noted that Emily would've been proud of him for making the allusion.

"I was just joking with a friend of mine last night about that. When I heard the news, I said, 'Oh, God, this had to happen right after I made that scene! Now everybody's going to think I did it!' "

"We don't necessarily think that. May we sit down?"

"Sure. You mind pulling up chairs?"

Gerald grabbed a couple of the plastic chairs and moved them in front of the desk. Then he and Ransom sat down.

"But really, Mr. . . . Ransom, right? You don't really think I killed him, do you?"

He shrugged. "There was obviously no love lost between the two of you."

"That's for sure! You see those red circles?" She gestured toward the pictures on the wall. "Those are all historic buildings—important historic buildings—that have been torn down since the commission was formed five years ago. All that destruction in just five years. And guess what? Over half of those fell to Louie Dolores. And you know why? Because he had money, and he wanted more."

Ransom smiled. "Not for the sake of progress? Not for the good of the city?"

Her face clouded over. "You remember the Empress Theater? One of the finest examples of art deco in the city—not just the city, the country! And he was allowed to bulldoze it. The city made noise about declaring the facade an historic landmark—the facade, Mr. Ransom! But in the end, they decided that another faceless box of a high-rise was more important than preserving the history of this city!" She waved toward the pictures again. "Each and every one of those is another example of the travesties to history that Dolores and his ilk have perpetrated on this city in the name of their own bank accounts. Don't be fooled by any claims of altruism and 'the good of the city'—all of this destruction has been done in the name of the almighty buck!"

Ransom raised his hands. "You are preaching to the converted, Ms. Campbell."

Gerald rolled his eyes inwardly. This was something to which he could easily have attested, having spent hundreds of hours in the car with Ransom railing on about the city's history, geography, and more recently, the atrocities being done to them.

"I'm sorry," Samantha replied, her cheeks coloring. "I'm very passionate about history."

"I can see that. But you must see that your passion, coupled with the incident at the opening of the exhibit, does make you someone we need to talk to."

She stared at him for a few moments. "Yes, I suppose it does. But I would never kill anyone. Really. Not even a lowlife like Dolores. I can't say I'm sorry to see him go, though."

"It puts an end to your troubles."

She laughed pleasantly. "Not likely. There'll always be another Dolores. Our fight to preserve Chicago's history is never going to be over."

Ransom considered this. It echoed Hector Gonzalez's sentiments about Dolores: that if it hadn't been Dolores who had paid for the loan of the mummy exhibit, it eventually would've been someone else.

"Ms. Campbell, when you disrupted the opening, I believe you said something to the effect that there was only one way to deal with people like Dolores. What exactly did you mean by that?"

Her lips spread into a broad grin. "I'll have to watch what I say in the future. That's like one of those movies where someone says 'I could just kill you' and the person they say it to ends up getting murdered." She shook her head. "No, Mr. Ransom, I wasn't making that kind of threat against him. What I meant was that decent people like the ones that work for the commission, we like to behave . . . well, decently. But you can't do that with somebody like Dolores, because they don't play by the rules, and they'll do whatever they want to get what they want."

"Like with the Harrison project."

Samantha's cheeks colored again, this time with anger. "He was fined for his 'mistake.' Did you know that? As if a fine could ever hurt him! I'm sure he incorporated it into the price of the condos he built on the site."

"Someone found a way to hurt him," Ransom said without inflection.

Samantha folded her hands on the desk. Any sign of anger or amusement vanished from her face. "What I meant was that we would no longer play fair. We would do whatever was necessary—including disrupting the opening of his exhibit—in order to keep his . . . his . . . actions in the public eye. You keep blackening his image long enough and the public perception of him was bound to change."

Ransom mentally noted that this was the same strategy mentioned by Juan Muñoz. It crossed his mind that there might be a possibility that Muñoz was genuine.

Samantha continued, "And then it would've been harder for him to get city approval for his projects, because there would've been a *lot* of opposition. It couldn't have just been us and a few others being voices in the wilderness." She paused. "Please tell me that you don't really think I had anything to do with the murder."

"No, I don't."

Gerald glanced at him, surprised by this admission.

Samantha looked surprised as well. "Then . . . then why did you want to talk to me?"

"Partly because it was necessary in a thorough investigation. You made what sounded like a threat, in public, and the man is dead. That's not something we could ignore."

"But you could've—"

"And then there's the problem of the reason for your appearance at the opening."

"You know why I was there."

"No, I mean, you said that you knew he was trying to get his hands on the Stone Candy Factory."

"Yes?"

"How did you know that? It was supposed to be a secret."

The grin unexpectedly made a reappearance. "It was?"

Ransom raised his right eyebrow. "Yes. So how did you know about it?"

A stray strand of her hair had become dislodged. She swept it back behind her ear. "It doesn't have any bearing on the murder. I don't think I should tell you."

"I'll have to be the judge of whether or not it's relevant."

"I don't—Mr. Ransom, the person who told me really didn't have anything to do with this. I promise you that."

"I'm afraid that's not enough." Ransom leaned forward in his chair. "Ms. Campbell, you seem to be a woman of integrity. Let me tell you this: before he was murdered, Dolores told people that he was sure Alderman Nathanson was the one who leaked the information."

She sat back in her chair, folded her arms, and stared at him unhappily. "Nathanson. Dolores had Nathanson in his pocket. We've known that for years. As if *he* would've told me anything!"

"We've talked to the alderman. He told us that it was greatly to his benefit to have the information leaked. And I'm afraid that that, along with some other things he said, paints him in a very bad light."

Samantha's brow furrowed and her frown deepened. Clearly she was suffering an internal struggle. At last she said, "We would've lost against Dolores."

"I beg your pardon?"

She shook her head slowly, disgusted with herself. "We would've lost. In the end, he would've torn down every historic structure in this city and replaced them with vertical boxes filled with overpriced condos. The whole city would've ended up looking like a pile of glittering packing crates. It's on the way to that now."

Ransom sighed impatiently. "Ms. Campbell . . ."

"Because you're right. I have integrity. I couldn't even let a worm like Nathanson be suspected falsely." She paused and took a deep breath. "It was Jeremiah Stone."

"Hmm?"

"The one who told me that Dolores was after the candy factory. It was Jeremiah Stone himself."

"Jeremiah Stone!" Gerald exclaimed once they were back in the car.

"You sound impressed," said Ransom.

"I am. He's the guy that started Stone Candy, isn't he?"

"I believe so."

"I didn't know he was still alive. This changes everything."

"How so?"

"Well, if Stone told the Historical Commission about Dolores's plans, that means Nathanson's off the hook."

"No it doesn't," Ransom said as he pulled out a cigar.

Gerald rolled his eyes, though in this case it was hard to tell if it was a reaction to being contradicted or to the prospect of more smoke. "Why not?"

"It doesn't make any difference if Stone was the one who told Samantha Campbell about Dolores's designs on the property. What matters is that Dolores *believed* it was Nathanson. Braverman told Nathanson that, so Nathanson knew he was in jeopardy. Both Braverman and Nathanson told us how unreasonable Dolores could be. Do you think he would've ever taken Nathanson's word for it that he wasn't responsible for the leak?"

"I see what you mean," Gerald said with a sigh. He leaned forward, stuck the keys in the ignition and switched on the engine. "So we go talk to Stone now?"

Ransom glanced at his watch. "No. It's after eleven. Head back for headquarters."

"For what?"

"For my car. I'm going to go pick up Emily."

"Why?" Gerald asked with surprise.

"I'm going to take her to have a little talk with Hector Gonzalez."

"You don't want me along?"

"No. You saw the condition he was in yesterday. I think Emily will be able to get more out of him than we could. And the fewer people there, the better. But there's something I want you to do. See if you can scare up Frieda Jablonski—I don't mean that literally—and meet us at the exhibit at . . . I'd say two o'clock."

"What for?"

He sighed. "I want her to show us exactly what happened when she was there. I want to put this mummy to rest."

15

The McCormick Hospital was located on Twenty-second Street just west of Michigan Avenue. It was noon when Ransom approached the visitors' information desk with Emily on his arm. Dressed in a dark suit with a powder-blue silk blouse, she looked exactly like a grandmother who was being escorted by her grandson for a visit to an ailing relative. The woman at the desk looked Gonzalez up on her computer, then directed them to the seventh floor. After a short elevator ride, they arrived at the seventh-floor nurses' station.

"Is Nurse Davis here?" Ransom asked.

"Yes," said the young blond man who was seated behind the desk. He called over his shoulder, "Gerry?"

A woman in a white uniform closed a file drawer at the back of the station and came over to them. She had short black hair with premature strands of gray, and wore thick glasses with clear plastic frames that magnified the tiny crow's-feet around her eyes.

"Can I help you?" she asked perfunctorily.

"Yes. I'm Detective Ransom. I spoke with you earlier about Hector Gonzalez."

She nodded, then turned a questioning gaze at Emily.

"This is Emily Charters, who is assisting me," said Ransom.

Emily cleared her throat. "I'm pleased to meet you."

Davis turned back to Ransom. "Can I see some identification?"

"Certainly."

He drew his badge out of his inner pocket and held it up to her. She pulled her glasses forward slightly and peered at it, then looked him in the eye.

"Thank you."

"I was with Mr. Gonzalez when this episode occurred. How is he doing?"

She glanced at the young man behind the desk. He was unsuccessfully contriving to appear disinterested.

"Come with me," Davis said to Ransom and Emily.

She came around the back of the U-shaped station and joined them, then led them down the hallway. The hall was active with several nurses sorting through carts of medications, as well as a pair of heavyset women in pink uniforms and white aprons who were fussing over an unwieldy, multilevel cart packed with trays of food.

"About Mr. Gonzalez," Davis said crisply once they were out of general earshot. "The doctor who treated him is calling it exhaustion."

"I take it from your tone you don't agree?"

"Far be it from me to disagree with a doctor." Her voice was devoid of irony. "A doctor is a doctor. I'm just a nurse. And exhaustion can cause very serious problems."

Ransom smiled. "Nurse Davis, you are a very shrewd woman."

She stopped in her tracks and looked at him. He returned the gaze calmly, while Emily stood at his side observing them like a schoolteacher waiting to see how her pet pupil would perform.

"What do you mean by that?" said Davis.

"Just that I have the feeling you are choosing your words very carefully. And I have the feeling you want to tell me something that you need to be . . . circumspect about."

She continued to stare at him without speaking, though for all her stoicism, she appeared to want to say something.

"I have another feeling," said Ransom. "I have a feeling it's something you think is important for me to know about Mr. Gonzalez's condition. All I can tell you is that whatever you have to say will go no farther. I'm only interested in solving a murder."

Her eyes flexed behind her glasses. She looked to her left and right to make sure nobody was nearby, then leaned forward and lowered her voice.

"I probably shouldn't say anything . . . but I think the doctors are not erring on the side of caution when it comes to Mr. Gonzalez."

"What do you mean?"

"I used to work over at Northwestern, in their psychiatric-care unit. I've seen people who've had nervous breakdowns before."

"And you think that's what happened to Mr. Gonzalez?"

Her eyes slued to the right and left again. "I wouldn't go that far. But I'd say if it wasn't, it was damn close."

Emily's thin eyebrows knitted together. "If that is the case, why wouldn't the doctors, as you put it, err on the side of caution?"

Davis leaned closer to them. "Because he's from a foreign country. Getting payment from his insurance company is iffy at best, and they don't want to keep him here any longer than they have to."

"I see," said Emily.

"Why are you risking telling us this?" Ransom asked.

Davis pursed her lips. "I've been attending Mr. Gonzalez. He seems like a very sweet man who's . . . who's a little at sea right now. He's under light sedation, but I wanted you to know what I thought, because if he is that close to the edge, I wouldn't want anything to happen to push him over."

"Well, put your fears to rest," said Ransom as he patted Emily's hand. "That's what my assistant is here for."

"Oh?" Davis seemed quite perplexed for a moment. Then she looked at Emily as the light dawned. "Oh! Well, okay. I know you have to talk to him, and I wanted you to be prepared."

She led them to the last room on the left side of the hall. The beige curtains were closed against the noonday sun, but the blinds behind them were left open, bathing the room in a dusky haze. The walls were eggshell and unadorned, except for a watercolor of a farmhouse on the wall facing the bed. A television was suspended in the corner to the left of the painting.

Gonzalez lay in the lone bed, covered by a blanket the same shade as the curtains. His head had lolled to the left, slightly off his pillow, though his eyes were open and staring at the ceiling. He looked like he'd been suffering from insomnia for several months. His lunch was on a tray pushed carelessly aside.

"We'll take it from here," Ransom said when Davis started into the room.

She hesitated, looking from the bed to Ransom. "Well . . . okay." She left reluctantly, and Ransom quietly brought Emily into the room and stood by the foot of the bed.

"Mr. Gonzalez?" he said softly.

There was no response.

"Mr. Gonzalez? It's Detective Ransom. How are you feeling today?"

Gonzalez's eyes twinged.

"I was hoping you'd feel well enough to talk a little bit. Not to me. I've brought a friend to see you. I told her what happened with you yesterday, and she is very concerned about you. Her name is Emily Charters. Emily, this is Hector Gonzalez."

"Good afternoon, Mr. Gonzalez," said Emily, whose intent gaze had not moved from Gonzalez's face since they'd entered the room.

At the sound of her voice, Gonzalez's eyes moved in her direction. With an effort, he moved his head back onto the pillow, then closed his eyes.

"Forgive me . . ." he said, his voice dry with disuse.

Emily glanced up at Ransom, then said, "That's quite all right, Mr. Gonzalez . . ."

"Forgive me . . ."

"We understand."

Ransom turned to Emily and started to bend over in order to whisper something in her ear, but he was interrupted by Gonzalez.

"Forgive me . . . for not . . . being more presentable."

"As I said, that is quite all right. We do understand that this isn't the best time for you," said Emily.

Gonzalez inhaled deeply, his chest and stomach expanding; then he exhaled a deep, troubled sigh as he allowed his eyes to open. "I have been most tired. Most, most tired. I think that must be it. I can't think what has been going on in my head."

"What has been going on?" she asked.

He managed a faint smile. "You look like a very kind woman."

"Thank you. Jeremy has been telling me how concerned he was for you."

"Jeremy?"

"Me, Mr. Gonzalez," said Ransom.

A dark cloud quickly passed over his face. He didn't look at Ransom.

"He thought perhaps it might be easier for you to talk to me. Because, you see, it is so very important that we talk to you. We need your help."

"I don't know if anyone can help. Not with my head."

"Might I sit down, Mr. Gonzalez?"

"I'm sorry. Please."

Ransom pulled a chair over beside the bed for Emily and she sat down, adjusting the hem of her skirt. Then she folded her hands in her lap. She watched Gonzalez quietly, not wanting to prompt him for fear of appearing too eager and discouraging him from cooperating.

Ransom leaned against the windowsill on the opposite side of the bed and folded his arms. It was taking an effort not to drum his fingers on something as his patience waned.

"I don't know what is wrong with me," Gonzalez said after an interval so long that Ransom had despaired of his ever saying anything.

"What do you mean?" Emily asked softly.

"I'm . . . I'm not sure I should talk. They might think . . . the doctors . . . that I'm not right in my head." He said this with great effort, then paused and furrowed his brow. "But maybe they would be right. Maybe I am not well."

"We all get confused sometimes. When I was a girl, I used to think I always knew exactly what was what about everything. Now it seems a day is not complete unless I've been thoroughly confused at least once."

He smiled warmly. "But that is not what I mean."

"I know. What you're talking about is something deeper. Perhaps it would help to talk about it. That can sometimes make the mist disappear."

Gonzalez studied her face for a time. Apparently he liked what he saw there, because the muscles in his jaw began to slacken. His eyes shifted in Ransom's direction, then back to Emily.

"Can we not be alone?"

"I'm afraid Jeremy must stay with me," she replied matter-of-factly. "But it really is no matter. Jeremy's only sin is his impatience. I can tell you from my own experience that you will never find a gentleman who is more fair."

This assurance seemed to be enough for Gonzalez, though he still kept his eyes steadfastly averted from Ransom and trained on the old woman.

"I feel . . . I feel as if everything I knew has died away, and the whole world has become strange . . ."

"Well, it's no wonder," Emily said with unexpected vigor.

Despite his faded state, Gonzalez looked startled. "It is?"

"Of course. It's probably true. This world has changed at an astonishing rate, particularly in the last few years. It's completely different from when I was young. And as you get older, even the people in your life have a habit of dying away. It's very easy for the world to suddenly look completely new and very strange. But you are considerably younger than myself. You do have people in your life who have been constant, don't you?"

"Yes . . . yes, there is my wife. And the men of the board of directors at my museum. I have known many of them most of my life." A look of distress suddenly played about his face. "But even they have changed . . . they are different now than they once were. They do things that they would never have done before. And everything seems to be moving . . . more . . . faster and faster. I cannot take it all in anymore."

Emily smiled reflectively. "I know what you mean."

"You do?"

"Of course. That also is true: things are moving faster."

"You see it too?' he said eagerly.

"Most assuredly," she replied. "Did you think it was your imagination?"

"No, no." He sighed deeply, closing his eyes, then opening them again. "But I thought . . . maybe I was the only one who saw it."

"Ah!"

Ransom remained by the window, keeping perfectly still, looking on in admiration. He had been witness to Emily at work before, but never quite on this level. And as always, he found himself impressed with her. The minor irritation he'd felt at their acquaintances' observations about her in recent days disappeared entirely. In a rare moment of removal from his own ego, he had to admit to himself that there were things Emily could do that he could not.

"But may I ask you something?" Emily said, shifting in her seat.

"Yes."

"When you say the board of your museum does things now that they wouldn't have before, do you mean, for example, allowing this exhibit to be brought here?"

He let his eyes travel up to the ceiling. "I tell myself that they do not know what they are doing, that they don't understand the damage this will do, but in truth, they do know. They simply do not care. They do it for the money. And . . . and . . . I know that they must."

She leaned forward intently. "What do you mean?"

"I know they must do it," Gonzalez admitted sorrowfully. "The museum must have money to survive. The past must be sacrificed for the survival of the present . . . and the future."

Emily glanced over at Ransom, who held up an index finger, signaling for her to wait.

"Excuse me, Mr. Gonzalez," he said as gently as possible. "Does this mean that you did hold it against Dolores . . . the fact that the exhibit was brought here."

Tears pooled in the older man's eyes. His right hand went absently to his forehead. "No. It is as I said to you before. If it hadn't been him, it would've been someone else. And . . ." His voice became barely audible. ". . . it was necessary." The tears spilled over, running down the sides of his face and into his ears. "But I did not kill him. Mr. Dolores."

"No one believes you did," Emily said firmly, shooting an admonishing glance toward Ransom.

Gonzalez wiped the tears away with his wrist. "Then what can I do to help? You said you wanted my help."

"That's true. You see, Jeremy told me that you said some things yesterday that may help solve the murder, and we would like for you to clarify them, if you can."

"What is it I said?"

"It was about seeing a mummy."

At the mention of this, Gonzalez's eyes widened. His hands started to tremble as they had the day before, and he clasped them together. "I must not talk of this."

Emily reached out to him with her pale, thin fingers and laid her hand over his. The trembling subsided. "It is very important. What you saw may be the key to solving the murder."

"You will think I'm mad."

"I assure you that is not the case."

He turned away from her, but when his eyes lit on Ransom, he quickly turned them back to the ceiling.

"It started several months ago . . ."

"What did?"

"The feeling that these ancient ancestors . . . the Chinchorros . . . that they disliked being bartered and traded. I felt I could hear them speak. Not really speak, but whisper . . . softly . . . so I could not hear the words. But I knew what they were saying." He took a long pause, then turned his eyes back to Emily. "But it was not them, was it? It was me."

"Yes," she said with an understanding smile. "But the mummy?"

His face clouded over. "That was when I started to believe . . ."

His voice trailed off and he said no more. Emily thought of urging him to continue, but decided to ask a different question instead. "You said you saw the mummy the night of the murder. Where did you see it?"

"In the exhibit."

"Yes, but where exactly?"

"I had just gone into it . . ." he said slowly, picturing it in his mind. "I had just gotten to the first display. And I saw him . . ."

"Where?" Emily pressed.

Gonzalez's eyes widened. "He was coming out of the next chamber . . . far down the hall."

"You said there was blood on his hands."

"His hands were stained dark . . . dark red. Stains."

"You noticed these stains in particular?"

He nodded wearily. "They weren't there before . . . at least, I don't think they were."

"Ah," said Emily with interest. "That was the other thing we wanted to ask you about. You said you saw the mummy before. When was that?"

"The first day I was here. The day we installed the exhibit. In the morning. While I waited for the exhibits to be brought up. I was sitting in there, alone. I thought I had fallen asleep. On a stone bench. In the center of the exhibition. And I woke up. I thought I heard a noise. And there he was . . . just going around the corner and the end of the hall. And I followed." His eyes widened again and he lifted himself up slightly. "But when I came out . . . the guard, he told me he had not seen anyone."

"Do you think he was lying?"

"No, no," Gonzalez said, lowering his head back onto the pillow. "I think he was telling the truth . . . it was me . . . it was just me. That's when I thought perhaps the spirits of the dead had . . . so I came back the next evening, to see if I would see him again, and then the next evening . . . and that's when it happened. That's when I saw him again. And later, I heard about the murder." He sighed deeply. "The spirits of the dead . . ."

Emily laid her hand on his once again. "Mr. Gonzalez, you don't need to trouble yourself any longer on that account."

"No?"

"You really did see what you thought you saw," she said quite firmly.

"But that's not—"

"It was not your imagination. It was not a spirit. It was someone playing what I could best describe as a very nasty game."

"A game?" he said after a long pause. He was beginning to look relieved.

"A very dangerous game that ended in murder."

They left Gonzalez a far sight happier than he'd been at the onset of their interview. Emily's calm assurances that he hadn't been imagining things went a long way in allaying the fears he'd been entertaining about himself.

"I hope that met with your approval," Emily said when they were back in the car.

Ransom resisted the impulse to pull out a cigar. He still didn't smoke in her presence. "If you don't mind me quoting Lynn, Emily, you're amazing. I couldn't have done that."

"Nonsense," she replied. "Certainly you could have. You simply find it easier to be yourself."

"My dear Emily," he said as he turned the keys in the ignition, "that's the closest you've ever come to insulting me. Now, what was your assessment of Mr. Gonzalez? Is he crazy enough to have committed murder?"

Emily looked at him with surprise, scanning his face to see if he was serious. "I don't believe he's crazy at all."

It was Ransom's turn to look surprised. "At all? He seems to me a very troubled man."

"Troubled . . . yes, I would agree that he's troubled, but not unhinged. I think that he's come to a crossroad in his life."

She appeared to believe that this explained everything. When she didn't continue, Ransom for once found himself in the position of playing Watson. He tried not to sound irritated when he sighed.

"Do you want to explain that?"

"What? Yes! Oh, I'm sorry! He probably, for some time, has been approaching those crossroads, which often happens as you get older. And I think he finally arrived at them when the prospect of the exhibit came up. When his board of directors agreed to it, Mr. Gonzalez realized the extent to which life has changed: far beyond what he wanted it to. But you see, everyone comes to such a crossroads in their life eventually, sometimes many of them. It has happened to me. One can either decide to embrace changes, or one can be trodden down by them . . . or simply come to a stop, like your Miss Haversham."

Both of Ransom's eyebrows slid up. "Good Lord! Just this morning I was thinking of Shakespearean analogies, and now you're using Dickens. Maybe the whole world really has gone mad!"

Emily laughed. "But what I am trying to say is, I don't believe

Mr. Gonzalez is unhinged, I just think he's come to a crossroads and he's having a bit more difficulty getting past it than most."

"All right," Ransom conceded. "Accepting that, what was all that business about hearing voices? When he said 'It wasn't them, it was me,' you seemed to understand it perfectly."

"Yes, I think I did," Emily replied. "It was his guilt, his conscience."

"Guilt over what? He hasn't done anything that we know of."

"Guilt because no matter what he believes on a conscious level, deep in his heart he knows that the board of his museum made the right decision."

"Of course!" Ransom said, realizing that this made perfect sense. "You know he is planning to resign from the museum."

"No, I didn't know that," Emily said with a great deal of interest. "That's wonderful!"

Ransom couldn't help but laugh. "Why do you say that?"

"It means that whether he realizes it or not, he has accepted that things must change, and he's decided to take charge of his own part in that process. I take that as a very definite sign."

"I notice you don't say what it's a sign of."

"We shall see."

"Well," said Ransom, "if you really believe that Gonzalez wasn't involved in the murder, that leaves us with another interesting problem: the mummy appearing to him. Why do that, unless the person behind it knew about Gonzalez's delicate state of mind? And I think that would mean Lisa Rivera is involved, because I don't know who else would know about him." Another idea struck him. "Except . . ."

Emily nodded. "Except that even knowing his state of mind, how could anyone have known that he would be in the exhibit when he was?"

Ransom sighed. "Which brings us back to Lisa Rivera. She probably knew he was waiting there that morning when he first saw the mummy. And she knew he had gone there the night of the murder. Of course, she apparently didn't know ahead of time that he would do that."

Emily didn't seem to be paying attention. She was gazing off into the distance, lost in her thoughts. She said absently, "I see . . . I see . . . yes, I suppose that's possible."

"What is?"

Emily quickly came down to earth. "Well, I was just wondering: do you think it possible that Mr. Gonzalez wasn't really the target?"

"What do you mean?"

"I just thought of something. These sightings all happened at different times. He said the first time was in the morning . . . the second was in the evening."

"Yes?"

"The attack on Mr. Dolores in the garage?"

"That was in the evening. I don't remember if Braverman told us the exact time."

"And Frieda Jablonski saw the mummy quite late, didn't she?"

"Yes. After ten."

"Well . . . do you think perhaps there was no specific target?"

"Are you saying these were random attempts to scare people? That seems far-fetched."

Emily pursed her lips and tilted her head slightly to one side. "The more people who believed there was really a mummy, or could attest that someone dressed as a mummy was there . . ." She let her voice trail off suggestively. "Perhaps the person only chanced on Mr. Gonzalez. After all, at the other times—the ones later in the evening—whoever it is could've been relatively certain of happening upon someone else . . . such as a member of the cleaning crew, or a member of the security staff."

"That's true," said Ransom, glancing at his watch. "It's getting late. How would you like to see the Chinchorro mummy exhibit?"

"You mean now?"

He nodded. "I have arranged a private showing. The exhibit's closed, and we're going to see just where the mummy came from."

It took them twenty minutes to get to Dolores Tower from the hospital. Ransom pulled into the loading zone in front of the building and switched off the motor.

"Can you park here?" Emily asked doubtfully, eyeing the No Parking sign beside which they'd stopped.

"*I* can," Ransom said as he got out.

He went around the front of the car and opened the passenger door for her. After helping her out and closing the door, he escorted her into the building. Emily kept her hand lightly resting on his arm.

"Good heavens!" she exclaimed once they'd gone through the revolving door. She was taken aback by the block-long bustling within the mall. "Where do we go?"

"Up the escalator. Can you manage?"

"Oh, yes."

As usual, Ransom had to rein himself in to keep from rushing his elderly companion. When they reached the second level, he indicated the second set of escalators at the far end of the mall. They found the box office open, though it bore a hastily printed sign saying that the exhibit was closed for the day.

As they approached the foot of the escalator, the guard moved to stop them, but Ransom flipped out his badge. The guard said, "Okay, sir," with a quizzical glance at Emily, and stepped aside.

The lobby of the exhibition hall was in perfect silence, broken only by the muted sounds from the mall below. Al sat perched on a high stool by the entrance to the exhibit. He tried not to look overly interested in their arrival, although like any naturally gregarious person, he couldn't completely disguise his relief at the presence of another human being.

Much to Ransom's surprise, a woman was seated on one of the benches far to the left of the exhibit's exit. Her hands were resting on her thighs, and she was staring down at the floor.

"That's Bill Braverman's wife," said Ransom quietly to Emily.

"Yes?"

They went over to her. She was wearing a dark-brown dress with large buttons that ran from the knee-length hem to the collar. The top two buttons were undone and the wide lapels spread sideways. Her hair was combed, though not carefully, and a small clip with a gold butterfly was nestled to the right of the part. She gave no indication of noticing their approach.

"Mrs. Braverman, isn't it?" said Ransom.

"Yes?" she said as she raised her head. "Oh. It's you. Hello."

"What brings you here?"

"I wanted to see the exhibit. They say it's closed," she replied with a curious lack of expression.

"Then why did you stay?"

She shrugged. "I don't know. I was tired. I know the guards. They said I could sit here as long as I wanted. That's all right, isn't it? Do I have to leave?"

"No. I'm just surprised you didn't want to go up and see your husband."

Something seemed to shut off behind her eyes. "No. I just wanted to sit here. In the quiet."

Ransom was about to ask her another question when suddenly Emily looked up at him and spoke. "Jeremy, I'm wondering . . . I've been on my feet a very long time. I hate to be a bother, but would you mind if I sat down for a while?"

"Not at all," he replied after a beat. He tried to sound apologetic for not having thought of this himself.

"Would you mind if I joined you, my dear?" she said to Anna.

"No. That's fine. I should probably leave anyway . . ."

"No, please, don't go on my account."

Emily laid a hand on Anna's arm as if to steady herself as she took a seat beside her, which had the effect of temporarily staying the young woman's departure. She then looked up at Ransom. "Jeremy, perhaps you could see if you can find Gerald White, since you can't take me home until your business is done."

Ransom gave her a smile so indicative of believing her to be a crafty old woman that she nearly laughed. "I'll do that," he said. He was about to walk away when he decided to give her a little of her own. "Are you sure you'll be all right here? Maybe it would be better if I could find you a seat that had a back?"

"I'm sure I'll be quite all right here," she said primly.

He left them together and went across the lobby to the guard.

Emily sighed deeply. "It's such a difficult thing, getting older," she said, contriving to sound like a chatty old woman. "One seems to get tired so easily. When I was your age, I used to run from morning till night—going here, going there—always keeping busy. Now it seems if I do two errands on the same day, I'm completely exhausted."

"I suppose . . ." Anna said vaguely, not knowing what else to say but trying to be polite.

"I imagine you do that now."

She looked at Emily with some confusion. "What?"

"Keep busy."

"I try to."

"Do you work?" Emily asked breathily. "I know most woman do nowadays, don't they?"

"Yes. I do."

Much to Emily's surprise, Anna sounded unsure of her answer. "My name, by the way, is Emily Charters."

"I'm Anna Braverman."

"You are married to Mr. Dolores's assistant, aren't you?"

She nodded. Emily again noticed that she seemed uncertain.

"That must be very interesting. I can't imagine all the things you do and all the types of people you must meet on a daily basis."

"Yes, it is," Anna said dully.

Emily looked at her long and hard, trying to assess whether or not she'd laid enough groundwork that a bit of probing would seem innocent. She decided to give it a try. She leaned in toward Anna. "If you don't mind my saying so—I realize I don't know you at all and it's really not my place—but if you wouldn't mind my saying it, you seem to be . . . rather unhappy."

Anna looked up as if surprised that someone had noticed.

"I've heard about the dreadful murder," Emily said. Then she suddenly gasped. "Of course, you *knew* Mr. Dolores! How foolish of me. I'm so sorry!"

Anna was already shaking her head before Emily had finished her sentence. "No. It's not that."

"Oh?"

She looked away. "No."

Emily tried to draw her out. "I'm so sorry, I didn't mean to presume. I suppose it was because the murder just happened the other day, and then we find you sitting here alone. I thought perhaps that was the reason . . ."

"No, it wasn't that." She sounded as if Emily was beginning to wear her down. "I really did want to see the exhibit."

"I would think you could do that at any time with your husband, couldn't you?"

Anna looked down at her hands, which she'd folded in her lap. "I suppose I could. But I wanted to see it on my own. My husband has . . . spent a lot of time on it."

"I see. I imagine it's difficult when work takes someone away from you."

Anna again looked up. She suddenly had the feeling that the old woman could read her mind. After a lengthy silence, she said, "Miss Charters, have you ever done something really . . . really drastic, and then wondered if you did the right thing?"

"Yes," Emily said slowly, giving the word weight.

Anna's lower lip began to tremble. "I mean *really* drastic."

"What kind of thing are you talking about, exactly?"

"I moved too soon," Anna said vacantly. "And now it's too late to change it."

Emily's eyes had narrowed incisively. "I'm afraid I don't know what you mean."

If Anna noticed the alteration in Emily's demeanor, she didn't show it.

"I own a part of a business. I decided . . . I was so unhappy with my life, you see. I decided to change it. But the minute I did it, everything went even more sour."

"What did you do?"

"I decided to sell my part of the business and start over again somewhere else."

"With your husband?" Emily asked after a slight pause.

Anna sniffed. "I tried to talk to him about it, but it all fell apart. The things we wanted when we got married, they're just not the same anymore."

"What was it you wanted?"

"A partner. We wanted to be partners who didn't stand in each other's way. We wanted to be free to grow on our own. We've made a success of it, too. Bill has a good job. He works very hard at it.

214

Long hours. He has put his job first for as long as I can remember. But that's the way we wanted it."

"I see."

"Bill has worked very hard, and Louie . . . Louie did nothing but take advantage of him. He practically ate Bill alive. He worked Bill to the point where . . . the job was more important to him than our marriage. That's the way Louie wanted it. That's what he expected. He's probably the one who . . ." There was a long pause. "But Bill loved his work, and it was what we agreed to."

Anna looked into Emily's eyes and was surprised to find true understanding there. Her cheeks turned pink and she looked away. "I did something I'm not very proud of. I told my partners I was going to sell . . . but I didn't tell Bill—my husband."

"I see."

"And he found out about it from them."

"So he may have thought you were going to leave him." Anna kept her face averted. "Were you?"

"To tell you the truth . . . I hadn't decided. I think I thought it was inevitable."

"May I ask when this happened?"

"On Tuesday. The day this thing opened. So I don't know if—" She broke off anxiously.

"Yes?"

All of the energy seemed to drain out of Anna. Whatever she'd been about to say, she'd changed her mind. "If I'd only waited, things might have been different."

"Because now your husband is free, in a manner of speaking," Emily said pointedly.

"Yes." She looked back down at her hands. "It was my fault. Whatever happens. You can't change the rules in the middle of the game, can you? It's not fair."

"I don't know that fairness necessarily enters into it," Emily said kindly. "But one does have to remember in changing the rules that the other party might no longer know how to play. They need time to learn."

"But now he knows what I did. He knows I was moving ahead

without him." Tears welled in Anna's eyes. "I'm not supposed to feel this way."

"What way is that?"

"Miss Charters, is it wrong to *want* someone to stand in your way?"

Emily patted her hand. "No, my dear. It is not wrong to want to *matter*."

"Emily?" said Ransom.

She had been so intent on her conversation with Anna that she hadn't noticed his return. "Oh!" she said with a start. "I didn't hear you!"

"Sorry. I didn't mean to startle you. I got Gerald on his cell phone. He's on his way up now." He smiled. "Are you rested enough to come with me?"

She offered him her hand. "Yes, this has been most sufficient."

"Miss Charters?" said Anna.

With Ransom's aid, Emily had gotten to her feet. She turned and looked at the young woman's upraised face. "Yes?"

"Thank you."

"Not at all!"

She took Ransom's arm and the two of them headed for the entrance to the exhibit.

"What was that all about?" he asked.

"She is a very unhappy young woman."

She gave him a brief overview. When she'd finished, Ransom sighed. "So there was no love lost between Mrs. Braverman and Louie Dolores. Emily, I'll thank you not to dig up any more suspects. And if you find one more lost soul in this case, I'm going to start believing in the mummy." When they reached Al, Ransom said to him, "Would you call Ross Lipman now and ask him to come down?"

"Sure thing," he replied, immediately complying.

"Who is Ross Lipman?" Emily asked.

"The head of security."

It was then that Gerald appeared at the top of the escalator. He was followed by a clearly distressed and reluctant middle-aged woman. A drab gray-cotton dress covered her stocky figure like a tent, and a triangled scarf was tied over her hair. On her feet was the largest pair of shoes Emily had ever seen on a woman. She thought with an inner chuckle that they looked like large, black gravy boats.

"Hello, Miss Emily," Gerald said with a warm smile.

"Detective White," Emily replied, inclining her head. "How is Mrs. White?"

"Sherry is fine, so are the kids." He turned to Ransom and said in a low voice, "Jer, while I was at headquarters, I picked up the surveillance report on Muñoz from last night. There's something you need to see."

"Let's get through this first."

"All right. This is Frieda Jablonski."

The woman in question was standing half-hidden behind Gerald, like a child who is shy of introductions. Gerald glanced over his shoulder at her, then stepped aside and presented Ransom and Emily.

"Good afternoon, Ms. Jablonski," said Emily.

The cleaning woman stared at her like a startled deer. "Good afternoon." She turned to Ransom. "I have not been here since that night. I refuse to after that night. They have not made me come back." Her tone implied that he would be held responsible if there was a recurrence of her first unpleasant experience there.

"We greatly appreciate your cooperation," Ransom said amiably. "This won't take very long. All we want you to do is show us exactly where you saw the mummy."

She turned her head slightly to one side, never moving her eyes from his. It made her look comically skeptical. "You believe?"

"I believe you saw something, yes."

She looked doubtfully into the entrance.

"It will be perfectly all right. All of us will be with you."

"Okay," she said after a long pause.

She made no move to enter. Ransom realized that she was waiting for a guard to proceed her, so he offered his arm to Emily and they led the way inside.

"Send Lipman in when he gets here," he said to Al as they went by him.

"Sure thing!"

Frieda followed closed behind Ransom and Emily, and Gerald

brought up the rear. They proceeded at such a slow pace that they looked like an underdressed funeral procession.

"Where were you when it happened?" Ransom said over his shoulder.

"I was at the first ting."

"Hmm?"

"The first ting, the first ting!" She jabbed her index finger down the hallway.

After a pause, Ransom said, "Very good. Tell us when we get there."

They continued their sluggish pace down the hall. Just as they reached the turn where the chamber was located, Frieda unexpectedly slapped Ransom on the shoulder with her meaty palm.

"Here!" she exclaimed. "This is where I am!"

They came to a stop and peered into the chamber. It was the first time that Emily or the detectives had seen any of the exhibit firsthand, and they found themselves drawn toward the cases. Frieda kept uncomfortably close to Gerald.

"Fascinating," Emily said, gazing down at the "natural" mummies.

"Hmm." Ransom turned to Frieda. "So you were in here when you saw the mummy?"

She nodded vigorously. "Yes!"

"And where was he?"

Frieda very slowly went back to the opening of the chamber and pointed to the right. The three of them joined her. Directly in front of them was the curving wall. From that vantage point, they could see to the left the hallway toward the entrance, and to the right, the hallway to the next display area. They could just barely see the opening on the right side where the hall once again veered to the left and out of sight.

"Can you tell me what happened?" Ransom asked.

Her eyes widened considerably. "He come out of dere! He come out and look at me! He is all covered with . . . with . . ." She patted her arms and her chest.

"Bandages?"

"Yes! And his face is all like coal, and flat. And he has eyes! Little ones! He looks at me!"

"And what happened then?"

"He poof!"

"I beg your pardon?"

She put her hands up in front of her face, palms outward, and jutted them forward as she opened her fingers. "He poof!"

"I see," said Ransom. "Thank you very much, Ms. Jablonski. You've been a very big help to us. I don't think we'll be needing you anymore."

"I can go?"

"Yes."

She looked down the hallway toward the entrance. "Alone?"

Gerald almost laughed. "I'll escort you, Ms. Jablonski. Come with me."

"Thank you," she replied with a great sigh of relief.

Ransom and Emily went down the second hallway.

"I take it 'he poof' means that he disappeared," said Ransom.

"Now, Jeremy! All things considered, I think she was doing remarkably well."

"Hmm. Well, assuming that he didn't dissolve before her very eyes, he must've gone into the next hallway. According to the police report, the guard didn't see anyone enter or leave the exhibit except Jablonski. So the question is, how exactly does a mummy get in and out of here without being seen or heard."

"Still assuming, of course, that he didn't dissolve," Emily said with a twinkling eye.

They reached the second chamber and went inside. Like the first, this one had ceilings that sloped down toward the walls, giving the feeling of being inside a cave. Emily was once again very interested in the contents of the cases.

"Mud mummies," she said quietly. "The person that Ms. Jablonski and Mr. Gonzalez saw was made up as a bandage mummy. So people weren't necessarily meant to believe one of these got up out of their cases and went for a walk."

"Not with the body count remaining the same. And he was seen in different areas of the exhibit. This must be where Gonzalez saw him the second time, but the first time, he was farther into the place. My guess is that they were supposed to think it was a restless spirit—which they did." He glanced at Emily. "Are you getting tired?"

"Oh, no!" she replied brightly. "I'm finding this most interesting. There's something not quite . . . right about these mummies, isn't there?"

"What do you mean?"

She looked down into a case. "I'm not sure I know what I mean. It's only that . . . some of these mummies are from seven thousand years before Christ. Seven thousand years! It really does give one pause, doesn't it?"

Ransom nodded. "I know what you mean."

"I'm not sure you do. I mean that I'm not sure they should be here."

He raised his eyebrows. "You mean you're agreeing with the protesters?"

"What? Oh! No, that's not it at all. I mean they shouldn't still exist."

"I'm afraid you've really lost me, Emily."

She shook her head. "I'm putting this very badly." She thought for a moment, then lifted her head. " 'For dust thou art, and unto dust shalt thou return.' It may not be nice to think that one day we all must die and wither away to dust, but it's the natural order of things. I mean, these things are fascinating because they are so old, and because they show us a different culture . . . one that has died away. But the thing I find the most interesting about it is that these people who went to such lengths to preserve themselves are now extinct."

"Then what's all that talk from Muñoz and Gonzalez about being their ancestors?"

"I think that is because current Chileans may have some blood in them from the earlier cultures. I don't know—I really haven't read all that much about them. But I don't think they can establish a direct link."

"There you are," said Gerald as he came into the chamber leading another man. "This is Ross Lipman."

"Mr. Lipman," Ransom said with a nod. "I'm Detective Ransom, this is Emily Charters."

"Hello." Lipman squinted at Emily as if trying to fit her into the picture with the two detectives.

"Mr. Lipman," said Ransom, "the cleaning woman who saw the mummy said that it came out of this area."

"Oh, that," Lipman replied with a laugh. With his right hand, he smoothed back his hair. "That was more than we were able to get out of her."

"You were here?"

"No, Chip is on at night—Chip Duggan. He wrote up the report, and he told me all about it himself."

"She didn't give Mr. Duggan the details?"

"No. He said she was babbling. All Chip could get out of her was that she saw a mummy."

"So this area wasn't specifically checked out."

Lipman shook his head. "I don't think so. They didn't know about this, I don't think. But look, Chip and Mr. Dolores went through the place after it happened. There was absolutely nothing wrong in here. I tell you, the woman was seeing things!"

"Ms. Jablonski was seeing things, young man," Emily said firmly, "but they were things that were here."

Lipman shot her another glance, this time tinged with annoyance.

Ransom said, "Is there some way to get in here without going through the exhibit itself or the lobby?"

Lipman turned an incredulous eye on Ransom, clearly amazed that the detective was taking the old woman seriously. "Yes, there is."

"Why don't you show us?"

He hesitated a moment. "I have to open it from the other side. You want to come with me or you want to wait here?"

"I'll wait here with Emily. Detective White will go with you."

Lipman shrugged and left the room along with Gerald. Ransom and Emily perused the contents of the cases, but their wait wasn't very long. In less than two minutes, they heard a very muffled sound that was repeated twice, then the back wall of the chamber was quietly and effortlessly pulled away. There stood Gerald beside Lipman.

"There you go," said Lipman.

Ransom had to duck slightly as he and Emily went through the newly formed exit into the dark haze of the bowels of the exhibition hall. The floor was tiled, though the light was so low they couldn't see the pattern. The windows were tinted against the natural light, and piles of boxes and machinery added to the gloom.

"My, it's quite dark back here," said Emily.

"Nobody's supposed to be in here," said Lipman. "Not many lights. We keep it dark to keep any light from seeping in through the seams in the exhibit walls."

From the outside, the structure designed to house the artifacts looked like a long, snaking creature that was either sleeping or dead.

"How many of these outlets are there?" Ransom asked.

"One in every chamber. It's how they got those damn cases in there. You should've seen the way they were packed. They were in these big metal things that looked like something out of *Aliens*."

"But you can't open the displays from the inside?"

Lipman shook his head. "Nope. They got these latches on them, see?" He showed them the back of the movable wall, tapping each of the latches in turn. "Like those things you use to secure a window."

"That doesn't seem very secure to me."

"These aren't really for security, they're just to keep the public from leaning against the back walls of the exhibit and falling through."

Ransom peered at the latches. "I don't see any blood."

"Blood!" Lipman exclaimed.

". . . and his hands were covered, so there won't be any prints." He sighed and looked up at Gerald. "But we'd better have the lab out to check anyway. We don't want to miss anything." He turned back to Lipman. "So how does someone get back here?"

Lipman sighed, but he no longer seemed irritated. Apparently he was beginning to feel that if the police were giving so much credence to this, it might be in his best interest to do so as well.

"We came in through an access door at the far side of the lobby."

"Which you couldn't do without the guard seeing you," Gerald added.

Lipman said, "There are also two doors, one on each side of the exhibition hall, leading to staircases. And of course, there's the freight elevator."

Ransom sighed heavily. "So anyone can get in using a staircase."

"No, not on this floor."

"Oh?"

"No. Too many people rent the hall and want to leave things here securely. And we have a lot of shows here where expensive stuff is kept. You need a key card to get in the stairway doors on this floor, and you can't operate the freight elevator without it, either."

"So anyone with a key card can get back here."

Lipman shook his head again. "No. Your card has to be programmed to open the doors on this floor. The only people with access are the security staff and the staff of Dolores Development."

"Hmm," said Ransom. "Leave this open for now. Our people will be here to go over it. Let your guard know."

"Okay," Lipman said as he left them.

"Does that shorten your list of suspects?" Emily asked. "I mean since the only people with access to this floor work for Dolores Development."

"Not necessarily. It doesn't shorten the list for the murderer," Ransom replied, "only for the role of the mummy, unless they're one and the same. In order for him to pull his disappearing act, he had to go out this way. And come in this way as well."

"Jer, you've got to look at the surveillance report," Gerald said, reaching into the inner pocket of his jacket. He extracted a three-sheet report that had been stapled in the upper left-hand corner. He unfolded it and handed it to Ransom. "There're a lot of apartments in the building, so they really couldn't tell who was there to see Muñoz and who wasn't, and most of it was foot traffic. But look who owned one of the cars that stopped by there last night." He tapped the notation in question with his index finger.

"My God," Ransom said softly.

"What is it?" Emily asked.

"Last night Mr. Muñoz was visited by Bill Braverman."

"Oh, dear," Emily said after a pause.

"So there's a connection," said Gerald. "If Muñoz is in with Braverman, then that means he could get one of those key cards."

Ransom was slowly shaking his head. "Why would he wander around down here after killing Dolores? It doesn't make any sense. We need to find out what the connection actually is."

16

While Gerald called in for the evidence technicians, Ransom saw Emily to a cab. He disliked the idea of sending her home on her own, but she made light of his protests.

"I'm perfectly capable of seeing myself home," she said with the sly smile she reserved for the occasions when she felt he was being oversolicitous. "And you must do your job."

A cab squealed to a halt at the curb in front of them. As Emily got into the back, Ransom stepped over to the driver's window. He reached into his pocket and pulled out a small leather billfold and a twenty-dollar bill as he gave the driver Emily's address. The driver, a painfully thin East Indian with large, round eyes, reached up for the money. As he pulled it away, Ransom opened the billfold, revealing his badge. The driver goggled at him.

"I trust you'll take good care of my friend," said Ransom.

The driver nodded nervously. "Yes, sir! Yes, sir! I'll do that!"

"Thank you." Ransom stepped back and looked into the car. "I'll see you later on. Thank you for your help."

He closed the door and the cab pulled away so cautiously it looked as if the driver was afraid the street was mined.

Ransom went back into the building and met Gerald, as arranged, by the elevators to the office tower. When they reached the penthouse, they went through the glass doors, which were still propped open, and Gerald started toward the left to Braverman's office, but Ransom stopped him.

"I want to have a word with Paula Dryer first."

They went into the reception area and found Paula seated at her desk, her elbows resting on its top and her head in her hands. She didn't hear the detectives approach until they'd almost reached her. She looked up suddenly. Her face was streaked, but she had stopped crying.

"Oh! Hello. I was just . . . I forwarded my phone to voice mail. I couldn't take it any more. It's been call after call all morning without a stop."

"It must be very difficult. Why didn't you take the day off?" said Ransom.

"I couldn't. There's way too much to do. On top of everything else, there are business associates calling from all over who don't know what's happened yet. They have to be told." She glanced at the phone, then managed a weak smile. "I guess I'm not doing any good having my phone transferred."

"There's only so much one person can take. Everyone needs a break, especially with something like this going on."

Gerald shot him a curious glance. It wasn't like his partner, to commiserate in this fashion.

"Why don't you come and sit down over here for a few minutes," Ransom asked, indicating the grouping of chairs across the room from her desk.

"No, I really shouldn't."

"I have a couple of questions to ask you. We might be more comfortable over here."

Paula blinked. "All right."

She rose slowly, pushing up her glasses and giving a gentle tug to each side of her black dress, then came out from behind the desk and crossed to the guest chairs. Despite being harried and in mourning, she managed to look rather stylish. The dress was obviously new. She took a seat, then the detectives sat on either side of her.

"I really don't know what more help I can be," she said, shifting uncomfortably. "I don't know anything about the murder."

"I wanted to know about something else. Were you aware of

what was going on between your employer and Lisa Rivera?" Ransom asked.

"What was going on?" Paula echoed. She sounded disheartened, as if he'd just confirmed something for her. "I didn't know about it." When she saw his raised eyebrows, she looked down at the floor. "I didn't know for sure."

"But you suspected," he said carefully. He'd been referring to the fact that Dolores was planning to hire Lisa, but Paula's interesting reaction made it evident that there was more to the relationship.

Her glasses had slipped down her nose. She pushed them back up and sighed. "Maybe a little more than that. You don't know what it's like to be the secretary of a powerful man, do you?"

"Tell me."

"You have to arrange everything for him. You have to schedule all of his . . . meetings for him. You understand?"

Ransom nodded. "I believe so."

Paula looked him in the eye. "I really, really liked Mr. Dolores. You have to understand that. And he trusted me."

"Yes?"

"But there were things that I didn't like. I mean, I didn't really care for Mrs. Dolores—she's not exactly someone you can warm up to—but I had to see her at events here, and at office parties, and things like that. And it's hard to face someone when you know . . ."

"If it makes you feel any better," said Ransom, "Mrs. Dolores was aware of her husband's affairs."

"Well, it doesn't make me feel any better," Paula said sharply. "It's one thing to know about it, it's another to be the one ordering dinner for them."

"What do you mean?"

"Whenever he was 'entertaining,' I was the one who made all his reservations for him, and ordered his flowers or whatever else he wanted. I even ordered the dinner for them when he was entertaining in his office. I mean, I know it was none of my business what he did, and I'm not a prude. But it didn't sit right."

"Did he entertain Ms. Rivera in his office?"

"I don't know for sure."

"You think he did?"

She was silent for a few moments. "The sofa in his office is a pull-out. When I went in there Tuesday morning, the cushions weren't quite right. I fixed them. So I think he had company there Monday night. But I was . . . indisposed Monday afternoon, so if he did, I didn't make the arrangements."

"I see." Ransom considered this with the index finger of his right hand pressed to his lips. "Ms. Dryer, were you aware that Mr. Dolores was planning to hire Ms. Rivera?"

"Did she tell you that?" Paula replied sadly.

"Is it true?"

She nodded. "Yes, I think so. Mr. Dolores didn't say anything to me directly, but he had me check out her professional background."

"Did you know what position it was for?"

Paula looked down at the carpet and sighed. "I don't know that for sure either, but I think it was for Bill Braverman's job."

"Why did you think that?"

"Mr. Dolores hasn't been happy with him lately. Actually, he hadn't been happy with him for a while. Anyone who works up here could see that. And then . . . well, there was his asking me to check on Ms. Rivera's background. Normally, Mr. Dolores had Bill do that. Then the other day, Bill was here when Dolores and Ms. Rivera came out of his office and they acted . . . they acted too much like they weren't up to something. Do you know what I mean?"

"Yes, I do," said Ransom. "Do you know why Dolores was unhappy with Braverman?"

She shook her head and sighed. "Bill hasn't been himself. My grandfather—he owned a farm downstate—he would've called it 'being off his feed.' "

Ransom smiled. "How so?"

"For a while now, Bill's been off his feed. You know, not concentrating. Stuff like that. I think he's having problems at home."

"How long has this been going on?"

She shrugged. "At least . . . several months. Maybe a year or more."

"Hmm. Do you think Braverman knew he was going to be replaced?"

"Just because I was asked to check Ms. Rivera out? No. But I did tell him what I thought. I might seem like a traitor—to Mr. Dolores, I mean—but Bill is a nice guy, and I thought he had a right to know."

"I understand. Is he in his office?"

"Hmm-hmm."

Ransom got up from his chair, followed by Gerald. "Thank you, Ms. Dryer."

"Thank *you*, Detective," she said as she rose.

"For what?"

"For giving me a legitimate reason to ignore the phone for a little while."

He smiled. "My pleasure."

The detectives left the reception area and went down the hall to the right.

Alice was seated at her desk outside of Braverman's office. Her eyes were wide and blank. She held the phone to her ear and had the frazzled appearance of someone who is being given instructions from several people at once.

As they walked past her, she animated, slipping her hand over the mouthpiece. "Wait! He's on the phone!"

"That's all right," said Ransom. "And hold the rest of his calls until we're through."

"I . . . all right."

Gerald tapped on the office door and they went in. As Alice had said, Braverman was on the phone. His elbows were resting on the desk and his tie was askew. As they entered, he looked up and froze for a split second.

"Yes, I know you do," he said into the phone. "However, you know what has happened. Presumably Mrs. Dolores will be handling things as soon as she is able, but as of yet, we . . . she hasn't come in, which is understandable under the circumstances." As he listened to the caller, he reluctantly waved the detectives to the chairs facing his desk. Gerald took out his small spiral notebook and stub of a pencil as they waited, much to Braverman's dismay.

"No, I'm not going to try to reach her on your behalf, her husband was just killed. I'm not going to bother her with business just yet. I know it's holding you up, and I'm sorry about that, but there's nothing I can do about it. As I told you, I'm not in charge of the company, so it will have to . . . yes, I know how Louie felt about it, and as soon as Mrs. Dolores is here, I'll advise her accordingly." After a moment, Braverman smiled. "Good-bye." He replaced the receiver.

"The art of threatening without saying anything," said Ransom.

"What?" Braverman exclaimed.

"I take it from your smile that when you told your caller you'd advise Mrs. Dolores accordingly, he didn't know exactly how to take it."

He smiled again. "Old habits die hard. He was pissing me off. Louie's dead and all the guy cares about is what it means to him, just like all the rest."

"Hmm. Mr. Braverman, when I asked you if you knew who the leader of the protesters is—the one who dresses as the mummy—you said you didn't know. Would you care to try that one again?"

Braverman went pale. "What do you mean?"

"It might interest you to know that we've had Juan Muñoz under surveillance."

"Oh, God, oh, God!" Braverman moaned. All the rest of the color when out of his face.

"Last night you paid a call on someone whose identity you said you didn't know."

Braverman's breathing had quickened, and it was a while before he said anything. Apparently he was assessing the situation and trying to decide how to proceed. "It isn't what you think."

"Well, why don't I tell you what I do think. I think you knew you were going to lose your job, and you knew you were going to lose your wife—"

"What?" Braverman exclaimed again. He looked thoroughly astonished that Ransom knew about this, but no less so than Gerald, who nearly snapped the point off his pencil in surprise.

"From what I understand," Ransom continued, "your wife seems to feel that Dolores Development—which means Louie Dolores—was the cause of the current strife in your marriage."

"Did my wife tell you that?"

"No." Strictly speaking, Ransom was giving an honest answer; it was Emily who had given him the information. "But it's true, isn't it?"

When Bill didn't answer immediately, Ransom went on: "And it looks like you hired Muñoz to kill Dolores for you, or to help you do it, before either of those things could happen."

"No, no, no!" Braverman said, trying to pull himself together.

Ransom shrugged. "It would explain a lot: for instance, how Muñoz was able to gain access to secure areas of the building. You provided him with a key card. Perhaps it even explains why Dolores felt the matter of the attack on him in the garage could be handled privately. Perhaps he somehow found out about your plan? Maybe in investigating Muñoz, he found a connection to you. Or perhaps you were the one who was supposed to do the investigating—that's something you did for him, wasn't it?—and Dolores was suspicious when you failed to get results?"

"It's not that way at all!" Braverman said. "You've got to listen to me!"

Ransom leaned forward, his narrowed eyes leveled at Braverman. "I'm perfectly willing to listen to the truth, but you've lied to me already, and I wanted to impress upon you just how bad things look for you. Do you understand?"

"Yes! But please, you've got to see why I had to lie. I went through this before when Louie gave Nathanson—" He broke off, then rephrased what he'd been about to say. "—when Louie was accused of trying to bribe Alderman Nathanson. I've run enough risks working for him, and with your investigation and everything, I didn't want to get implicated in fraud."

Ransom sat back. "That would be much better than being implicated in murder."

Braverman looked down at the top of his desk for several seconds, marshaling his courage. Then he looked up. "I know Juan Muñoz. So did Louie." He took a deep breath. "He was working for us."

Gerald looked up. Ransom said, "Was he?"

"He's an out-of-work actor. Louie had me hire him to lead the protest. Juan came up with the other people."

"Why?"

"For publicity, what else?"

"He wanted to generate *negative* publicity?"

"It wasn't negative. Don't you see? Louie wasn't a fool! He knew that his image needed some repair. That was the reason for bringing in the Chinchorro mummy exhibit in the first place—so he could show that he had some respect for history."

Ransom's brow was deeply furrowed. "And the protest?"

Braverman sighed heavily. "It brought publicity, but it wasn't really negative. A protest like that is guaranteed to bring out the press, so not only was it free advertising for the exhibit, but with every interview Louie gave because of the protest, he got the chance to talk about his respect for history, and the importance of preserving it, and for people to get the chance to appreciate it."

"Why the elaborate charade? There must've been an easier way to show his respect for history . . . like preserving a historic building, for example."

Braverman shook his head. "Nobody would've believed that. Nobody! Everybody would've seen through that in a minute."

"Especially when he was trying to get his hands on another landmark," Ransom said wryly.

"Don't you see? The fact that it's so convoluted is what makes it so hard to argue with! People may have their doubts about his motives for bringing the exhibit here—they may think it's hype, or damage control, or whatever—but the connection is . . . is tenuous enough that they'll always have some doubt. And they get to see a bit of history that they probably wouldn't have gotten to see without him. So chances are they'd appreciate him, even if they still begrudged him for it."

"And the 'visitations?' " Ransom said after a short pause.

"The what?"

"The mummy appearing in the exhibit. Surely that wasn't part of Dolores's image adjustment."

Braverman heaved a disgusted sigh. "No, it was just more publicity. Louie wanted that. He thought rumors of one of the mummies coming to life would get a lot of press. He was right. It made the front pages."

Ransom pursed his lips. "I understand how it was possible for

Muñoz to move around the building, he had a card. But how could he get into the building without being noticed?"

"He could just walk in the front door," Braverman answered with a shrug. "He didn't come in in costume, and nobody knew what he looked like because he always wore that mask when he was protesting outside. All he had to do was go up one of the staircases, use his card to get to the back of the exhibit, and change there."

"I see."

Ransom was silent for quite some time, mulling all of this over. Then he said, "This is all very interesting, but it doesn't explain why Muñoz would attack Dolores."

"Well, that's just it! That's why I didn't want Louie to tell you about that."

Ransom glanced at Gerald. "But you *did* want him to tell us he was attacked, if I remember."

"Yes . . ." he replied, uncertain for a moment. "But I didn't want him to point the finger at anyone in particular. That's all I meant."

Ransom smiled. "You still haven't explained your need to see Muñoz last night."

Braverman didn't speak for several seconds, then sighed again. "He called me. He wanted money."

Ransom's right eyebrow slid upward. "Blackmail?"

He shook his head. "We owe him some money. He was working for us, you know. And that would've gone on for a while, but—" He broke off and smiled. "But you scared him, and now he refuses to go on with the protest."

"Did you give him any money?"

He shook his head. "Not yet. I went up and talked to him, to calm him down. But with Louie dead, everything's tied up for the time being. Juan doesn't have anything to worry about though. I'll be able to get him the rest of his pay eventually. He's just going to have to hold tight for a while."

Ransom sighed. "What about the death threats? The one left on Dolores's car?"

"I don't know anything about that. It might've been genuine. Louie might've done it himself. He wasn't above that sort of thing."

"I daresay," Ransom replied with a curled lip. "But without your knowledge?"

"Mr. Ransom, I know I lied before, but you see why now, don't you? What I'm telling you now is the absolute truth."

Ransom pressed the tips of his fingers together and considered this. The silence continued for so long that Braverman finally said, "Do you have anything else you want to ask me?"

"Only one thing. What did Dolores intend to do about Muñoz?"

"What?" Braverman said blankly.

"You said he was going to take care of the matter of the attack himself. What did he intend to do?"

Braverman thought long and hard before answering. "He was going to have him . . . attacked."

"That makes sense," said Gerald. "I mean, you asked me if I could see Dolores hiring a drive-by, and I couldn't—but I can see him hiring goons to beat up a guy that attacked him."

"An eye for an eye? I suppose so. Somehow I think Muñoz would've gotten the worst of the deal." Ransom sighed. "Why do I always find it so suspicious when someone says 'I'm telling you the absolute truth'?"

"Probably because it sounds like they're protesting too much," Gerald replied.

Ransom raised his brows. "Shakespeare, Gerald? I'm impressed."

"Actually, I heard that on a rerun of *The Mary Tyler Moore Show* last night. How did you know about Braverman's wife? That sure came out of left field!"

"Did you notice the woman sitting in the lobby of the exhibition hall when you got there?"

"Uh . . . yeah."

"That was Mrs. Braverman. Emily had a very illuminating conversation with her."

Gerald's face broke into a broad grin. "Oh."

When the elevators opened, they headed across the lobby. They were halfway to the entrance when they spotted Lisa Rivera coming through the revolving door. When she saw the detectives, she made straight for them.

"Mr. Ransom, I called your headquarters and they told me you might be here."

"You needed to talk to me?"

"Well, yes," Lisa said, placing her hands on her hips. "I was just wondering how long I'm going to have to stay in town. With the exhibit installed, and—without any disrespect for the dead, my job prospects are over, too—there really isn't any reason for me to stay here. You must know by now that I didn't have anything to do with Mr. Dolores's death."

"Must I?"

"Of course," she said after a slight hesitation. His reply had apparently unsettled her.

He decided to take a calculated risk. "If that's true, then I fail to see why you felt the need to lie about your relationship with him."

"What are you talking about?"

"Your 'date' in his office Monday night."

Lisa folded her arms across her chest. "How did you know about that?"

He smiled. "I'm a detective. You don't deny it, do you?"

"What's the point?"

"So you were having an affair with him."

She laughed derisively. "I'd hardly call it that! He expressed his interest during his visits to Santiago. I didn't give in to him then, but when he approached me Monday about a job, I thought what the hell? It might help me get it."

"You didn't think he might just be saying there was a job?"

"To get me into his bed?" she replied, eyeing him shrewdly. "It didn't matter. He was not unattractive. I wasn't busy. I would've slept with him anyway. If it helps me get a job, more the better. If not, at least I wasn't bored during my stay."

Ransom couldn't help smiling. "I don't think we need keep you any longer, Ms. Rivera."

Gerald shot him a surprised glance. Lisa also looked as if she'd been caught off guard. "You mean for now?"

"I mean at all," Ransom said as he started for the door. "You're free to go back to Chile."

"Are you sure about that?" Gerald asked once they were outside.

"Yes, I am," said Ransom. "I dearly love people who know what they want. They make things so much less complicated."

Gerald laughed. "So what do we do now? Go talk to Muñoz again?"

They stopped at the curb beside Ransom's car. He sighed deeply. "I don't know what we'd talk to him about right now. I still don't see why he would've killed Dolores."

"If he knew Dolores was out to get him . . ."

"Yes, but that was because of the attack. The attack itself is still unexplained. And if he's the killer, why show himself in the exhibit after the murder?"

"What if it's like you said to Braverman, maybe he hired Muñoz to kill Dolores."

"If that were the case, neither of them would want to implicate him by putting in an appearance after the murder. We'll have to talk to Muñoz again, but . . ." He thought for a moment. "All the way through this case, there have been two threads, the personal one and the historical one: the people who may have wanted to kill Dolores for a personal reason, or the ones who might've wanted to do it because they objected to what he was doing to the city's history. There is one more strand to that historical thread: Jeremiah Stone. The Stone Candy Factory isn't far from here. Let's see if Mr. Stone is in."

Anna Braverman had stayed seated in the lobby of the exhibition hall for quite some time. She watched the detectives leave, taking with them the old woman whom Anna had found so oddly comforting.

She had spent that time thinking about what Emily had said: about how when you changed the rules, the other person needed time to learn how to play the game anew. For the first time, she began to realize the full magnitude of what she'd done. She had changed the rules, something that she had felt was a necessity for her peace of mind, but she hadn't given Bill the credit that was his due. Sure, he had reacted badly when she broached the subject of change, but she'd blurted it all out so suddenly and so forcefully that what other response could she have expected?

She hadn't given Bill time to adjust to the idea; she hadn't given him an honest chance. That much was made clear to her in the brief exchange she'd had with Emily. Instead, she'd withdrawn, prematurely accepting defeat and retreating into depression rather than waiting him out to see if time would make him more comfortable with her ideas.

Despite this new understanding of the situation, Anna had remained sitting there, not yet ready to completely pull herself out of the mental lethargy into which she'd allowed herself to slip. But a while after the detectives had left with Emily, the peace was shattered by the arrival of a group of men, each carrying cases or cameras and noisily chatting with each other. Anna watched in puzzlement as the guard greeted them and took them into the exhibit.

The interruption finally shook her out of her torpor. She took the escalator back down to the first floor, then went to the tower elevators. She had now determined to tell Bill that she understood what he was going through, and that changes could be implemented more slowly, if that would help.

When she reached the penthouse, she went through the glass doors and down the hall to the left. Alice was on yet another phone call, and looked up in surprise when she saw Anna.

"Mrs. Braverman!" she exclaimed.

"Hello, Alice," Anna said as she went by the desk.

"But Mrs. Braverman! Mr. Braverman isn't here."

Anna stopped and turned a gaze of utter surprise at the secretary. "He's not?"

"No. He went home. About half an hour ago."

Anna started to say something else, but couldn't find the words. She headed back toward the elevators.

*   *   *

On the way to the Stone Candy Factory, Ransom took out his cell phone and dialed Emily's number. She picked it up on the fourth ring.

"Hello?"

"Emily, it's Jeremy."

Gerald smiled to himself. Ransom only used his first name when speaking to his adoptive grandmother.

"I just want to make sure you got home all right."

"I'm perfectly fine," she replied. "The taxi driver was most attentive. He even saw me up to the door, and he seemed quite anxious about my welfare . . . one would've thought you'd threatened him." There was amusement in her voice.

"Don't be silly."

"What will you do now?"

"We're on our way to the Stone Candy Factory to talk to Jeremiah Stone."

"I see. How did your interview with Mr. Braverman go?"

He hit the salient points of his conversations with Braverman, Paula Dryer, and Lisa Rivera.

"My word!" Emily exclaimed when he'd finished. "Ms. Rivera is very forthright, isn't she?"

"Very much so."

"It does, however, explain one thing: why Mr. Dolores's hair was wet when he was called down to the exhibit because of Frieda Jablonski."

"It does?"

"Presumably he cleaned up afterward."

"Yes . . ." Ransom said distantly.

"Jeremy, you sound very odd."

His eyes had clouded over and he slowly moved his head from side to side.

"Jeremy?" Emily said with concern. "What is it?"

"I don't know. There's something . . . not . . . right about that, and I can't quite put my finger on what it is."

"It will come to you the minute you distract yourself from it."

"Yes . . . Emily, I have to go now. We've reached the factory. I'll talk to you later."

"Very good."

The Stone Candy Factory stood on a slight hill on Grand Avenue, just west of the Chicago River, in an area that was once populated solely by industrial buildings and railroad tracks. It was now the last of the factories, dwarfed into obscurity by its new neighbors: a string of luxury high-rise condominiums that made the wedge-shaped building look like the last shanty in a formerly undeveloped slum.

Although Ransom had heard of the candy company all of his life, he had never seen it in anything but newspaper photos. As they parked at one of the meters in front of it, he could see that it would've been an uphill battle for the factory to survive had Dolores not been murdered. It probably would be even now. The building itself had no real historical significance. Built on an incline, the east end was two stories high, while the west end tapered off into a single floor. That and the fact that it was constructed of Chicago brick were its only outstanding features: design-wise it was basically a box with windows. It had been built for strictly utilitarian purposes rather than aesthetic value. The Historical Commission would've had trouble arguing in its defense.

But in the case of the Stone Candy Factory, the building was only a small part of the story. The Stone Candy Company was an old, established, family-owned business that was a beloved fixture in Chicago, a city that had been taken over by chains and developers.

Even before getting out of the car, the detectives were enjoying the enticing aroma of chocolate that filled the air.

"On a good day, you can smell it all the way over on Michigan Avenue," said Ransom.

Gerald was staring at the building. "They want to save this place? I don't get it."

Ransom curled his lip. "It's not a matter of preserving the building, Gerald, it's preserving a way of life—and the idea that the little guy shouldn't be run out of town by big business. Stone Candy has always been here, and if it had to move, it would probably be all the way. Do you remember the uproar when Marshall Field's moved its candy operation out of the city?"

Gerald rolled his eyes. "Yeah."

"No die-hard Chicagoan wants to see that happen to Stone Candy. It's an institution."

"Moving hasn't hurt Field's candy."

"That's a matter of opinion," Ransom said as he started for the entrance.

Gerald followed him through the double doors at the west corner of the building. They found themselves inside a small box of a room with bright, white walls and no furniture. Directly across the room was a door and to their right, a window shielded by a closed venetian blind. Beside the window was a doorbell. Gerald pressed it, and a loud buzzer sounded inside. After a wait of less than a minute, the blind shot upward, revealing a plump, pleasant-faced woman dressed in a white uniform, her gray hair topped with a nearly opaque white-mesh cap.

"Can I help you?" she asked.

"We'd like to see Jeremiah Stone," said Ransom. "Is he in?"

"Mr. Stone!" The woman could hardly have looked more dumbfounded had they asked her to explain nuclear fission.

"Yes. Is he here?"

"Well, yes . . . but . . ."

Ransom pulled out his badge. "I'm Detective Ransom, this is Detective White. We need to see him."

"Wait here," she said as she abruptly dropped the blind.

"I feel like I've just asked to see the Wizard," said Ransom.

It was a few minutes before the woman returned. She came out of the door and said, "Come on back. He'll see you."

She led them down a long, narrow hall with offices on either side, then came to a stop at the closed door at the end. She looked over her shoulder at them and said, "This is him," then opened the door and they went in.

The austerity they'd seen so far ended at the threshold to Stone's office. Inside was a deep-piled, immaculately clean carpet—chocolate-brown, Ransom noted with an inward smile—and the walls were covered floor to ceiling with shelves lined with musty tomes. The massive desk was a deeply stained mahogany, on top of which was an old-fashioned blotter, a cup holding several silver pens, and a large lead-crystal bowl filled to the brim with chocolates. Unlike Dolores's office, there was no entertainment center. Apparently Stone was serious about business. His only concession to the outside world was a reproduction antique radio—with a curved top and lighted dial—that sat at an angle on a shelf behind his chair.

Ransom had never even seen a photo of Stone. He had expected a jovial man, rotund enough to smooth out the sign of his advanced age. He was thoroughly surprised by the reality: Jeremiah Stone was seated on a comfortable leather chair behind the desk, and looked about as Dickensian as a modern man could. He was emaciated, with sunken cheeks and eyes, a thin, sharp nose, and white hair in which Ransom thought he could detect a hint of green. He was wearing an ill-fitting, dark-blue suit.

The woman introduced the detectives and motioned them into a pair of circular chairs with low backs that struck the two men uncomfortably in the area of their kidneys.

"Thank you, Susan," Stone said in a reedy voice. "You may go back to work now."

She left, closing the door behind her.

"Would you care for some candy?" Stone asked, waving a bony hand toward the crystal bowl.

"Not while I'm on duty," Ransom replied with a smile.

"Do you mind if I do?"

"Be my guest."

Stone dropped his hand into the bowl and rummaged for a moment. Ransom thought it looked rather like one of those old arcade games where you try to fish a prize out with a metal claw. Gerald averted his eyes and pulled out his notebook.

"Bridge mix," Stone said. "Don't know why I like it so much, 'cept that every bit is different." He pulled out a handful and popped a couple of pieces into his mouth. "What brings you fellas here? Don't think I've ever talked to police officially before."

"We're investigating the murder of Louie Dolores."

"Really? Why?"

"Because he was murdered," Ransom said after a beat.

Stone shook his head. "I didn't know anybody cared who did it, long as it was done."

"You think he was that unpopular?"

"I think he was a bastard!"

He punctuated this by tossing another bit of chocolate in his mouth and loudly crunching down on it. "Ah! Malted milk!"

"I'm afraid it's our business to care about who killed him."

"Prostitution's a business, too. Not something you should be proud of."

It took an effort for Ransom not to smile. He liked the old man. "Then let's just say that under the circumstances, it's a dirty job, but somebody has to do it."

"Just like prostitution," the old man snickered. "Fair enough. But why come to me?"

"Our investigation took us to Samantha Campbell."

Stone smiled, revealing a row of teeth that looked a bit gray. "Ah! Good girl. Has a good head on her shoulders, that girl."

"She said that you were the one who told her that Dolores was after your factory."

"Not the factory, the land it's sittin' on. I bought this land for a song over fifty years ago. Bastard wanted to get it from me."

"With all due respect, this isn't exactly a historical building. Why go to the commission?"

"Should've done your homework, son."

"I beg your pardon?"

"Should've done your homework." He popped a couple more chocolates into his mouth. "I'm one of the contributors to the commission."

"No, I mean I don't understand what you thought they could do for you."

"Just what they were startin' to do: make a stink! Like I say, I'm one of their contributors. I'm kept appraised of what they're doing. I know how they feel about Dolores, and how they wanted to stop him. They were waiting for something to make some noise about."

"And you gave it to them."

"Sure did!"

"But how did you know?"

The old man's bushy white eyebrows went up. "How'd I know what?"

"That Dolores was after your land. He was trying to keep that a secret."

"A man comes here—nobody I've never seen before—and offers

to buy my land at a very good price. When I say no, he offers me twice what the land is worth. A very good piece of change. When I say no again, he tells me that maybe someday I'll *want* to sell the land, and that I might regret that I hadn't taken his offer when I could."

"And what did you say to him?"

"I told him to go to hell!"

"Good for you," Ransom said. "But what made you think he was from Dolores?"

Stone smiled craftily. He spilled the rest of the candy he'd been palming onto the blotter. "You know what bridge mix is, son?"

Ransom shrugged. "A variety of different candies coated with chocolate."

Stone nodded once. "Malted milk, caramel, jellies, nuts, raisins. Look at them." He waved his hand over the candy. "Can you tell me which one is a caramel?"

Ransom looked at the bits of candy strewn on the blotter. Most of them were around the same size, with slight variations in shape, some of them dark and some light. The only readily identifiable ones were the Brazil nuts and the almonds, and that was because of their distinctive shapes.

"Sorry, I can't."

Stone reached out and plucked up one piece, bit it in half with his front teeth and showed the center to the detectives. "Caramel."

Ransom smiled. "So how could you tell?"

Stone leaned forward, his smile growing sharper. "I just *know*." He popped the other half into his mouth and sat back.

"That's all there was to it? You just knew the man was an agent for Dolores?"

"That, and I'm not an idiot! Didn't have to be a brain trust to figure that one out. You must've seen all those brand-spanking-new buildings gone up all over this neighborhood. Every one built by Dolores. He didn't bother me at first. I don't think he knew how successful they'd be. But they were. So now he wants the whole neighborhood, and he come after me."

"But you didn't have to sell."

Stone sighed. "Fannie May is a chain. Marshall Field's, they're a chain now, owned by a bigger chain. We're just one little family business. I'm comfortable, Mr. Ransom, but not rich."

"What does that have to do with it?"

"Feh! That man telling me someday I'd want to sell. It was a threat, pure and simple. Dolores was going to try to force me out!"

"How could he do that?"

"It's already started. Had the city here about the smell—said people over in the high-rises been complaining about the smell from the factory. Said 'smell' as if it was a bad thing. It's chocolate, for Chrissakes!"

Ransom couldn't help smiling.

"Had city inspectors over here. They said somebody going by the building reported they'd seen rats all over the place. Rats! You wouldn't find a rat anywhere near this building, and neither did the inspectors. But they held up production for a day, we went late with orders and we lost money. Hell, we even had the goddamn EPA out here! Somebody called them in. And that was only the beginning. I imagine all this building up around here is going to make my property taxes run sky-high! Trouble is, anyplace I try to move the factory in the city now is going to be too expensive."

"So it was very fortunate for you that Dolores was killed when he was."

Stone scrunched up his face and considered this while he chewed in silence. "Maybe, maybe not. The die's probably cast now. Eventually somebody'll probably force me out."

"So you do think it would've been possible for Dolores to do that?"

"Uh-huh."

"And you couldn't afford to fight?"

The sly smile returned. "'Course I was going to fight! But when you don't have a lot of money to spend on it, you have to be careful what you do."

"What did you do?"

"I hired a lawyer to start fighting anything that might come up, including the harassment from the city, 'cause where the harassment was really coming from, that would've ended up on the news. But I got a very special lawyer to do it."

"Who's that?"

Stone snatched the rest of the candy off the blotter. "Harker and Associates." He tossed the candy into his mouth.

"What?" Ransom said.

Gerald looked up sharply, at first surprised at the announcement, then surprised by his partner's slip.

Stone nodded. "That's right."

"Isn't that a conflict of interest?"

"Not for me. Not if they're going to do their job and do it well. I figured this way I'd have inside information going for me."

"Why would they agree to this?"

"That you'd have to ask them, but I was confident they'd do the job. They started by disrupting the opening of that exhibit, stealing some of old Louie's thunder, and our next move was going to be to expose what was going on over there."

"At the tower?" Ransom asked.

"Uh-huh."

"And what exactly would that be?"

"You know that protest going on out there? It's a fake! We were going to the press with that." He smiled. "He thought he could harass me, I could do the same right back."

Ransom was quite impressed with the old man. "Mr. Stone, what on earth made you think that Harker and Associates would even consider taking you on?"

Stone wrinkled his nose. "You ever seen man and wife together?"

"You mean Mr. and Mrs. Dolores? Yes, on the news."

"So have I." He reached over to the bowl and picked a piece of candy off the top and rolled it between his thumb and forefinger. "This one's a jelly." As before, he bit it in two and showed the center to the detectives. "See?" After a beat, he tossed the remainder in his mouth, a satisfied smile spreading across his face. "I love bridge mix."

17

"She lied to us," Gerald said on the way back to the car.

"Most of them lied in one way or the other. As blasé as Mrs. Dolores tried to make it sound, I didn't believe she didn't know anything about her husband's business."

"But this goes beyond that! She knew all about the fake protest, so she knew about the mummy. And she has a key card."

"She also has an alibi, if you'll remember," said Ransom.

Gerald shrugged. "Harker? He could be in it with her."

"But I don't think *she* could be the murderer," Ransom said as they reached the car. "Aside from the alibi, she has something else a little harder to shake: a recognizable face. Juan Muñoz could come into the building inconspicuously because nobody knew what he looked like; the employees could come and go as they pleased because they belonged there. But I don't think Martita Dolores could stroll into Dolores Tower without being noticed."

"Yeah. You're right," Gerald said with disappointment. "But . . . but . . ."

"We're just going around in circles," said Ransom. "We have to talk to Mrs. Dolores. Do you have the number at her office?"

"Yeah." He pulled out his notebook as they got into the car, then flipped through the pages until he found what he was looking for. Ransom typed the number into his cell phone as Gerald read it off.

"Harker and Associates," said the crisply efficient voice of the receptionist.

"This is Detective Ransom. Is Mrs. Dolores in?"

"Not officially."

"What does that mean?"

"She stopped in just a little while ago, and she's still here, but she's not taking calls."

"Tell her not to leave before we get there."

"Don't you want to—"

"No." He cut her off, then snapped the phone shut and put it away.

"You're kidding? She's there?"

"No doubt enjoying making everyone uncomfortable," Ransom said wryly.

Fifteen minutes later, they were at Marti's office. She was dressed in black jeans and a black knit top with a scooped neckline. Around her neck was a thin silver chain from which dangled a single pearl.

A man with sandy hair was seated facing her desk. When the detectives appeared in the doorway, Marti looked up with evident displeasure, and her companion rose and turned around.

"This must be the detectives," he said, extending a hand to Ransom. "I'm James Harker."

Ransom introduced himself and Gerald. The three men remained standing.

"I received your order to stay," Marti said, the right side of her upper lip arching. "I don't like being ordered around."

"Think of it as a firm request," said Ransom. "I'm rather surprised to find you here today . . . though nobody seems to be spending much time mourning the death of your husband."

She sat back in her chair and folded her arms. "I left work yesterday right after you gave me the news—as soon after as I could, to be perfectly accurate. And I didn't come back until this afternoon, to take care of things that couldn't wait. You should know, Detectives, that in the legal profession, some things cannot be put on hold, even for a death."

"I meant no disrespect," Ransom said with a smile that a lesser woman would have found alarming. He then added to Harker, "We'd like to speak with Mrs. Dolores."

"I'll stay, if you don't mind."

"Very well." He turned back to Marti. "Mrs. Dolores, you lied to me."

"Wait a minute!" Harker exclaimed. "That's pretty drastic, isn't it? If there's been some sort of misunderstanding—"

"Oh, there's no misunderstanding," Ransom said smoothly. "And unless you're here to represent Mrs. Dolores, I'd appreciate it if you didn't interrupt."

"*Represent* her? Do you mean you're going to arrest her?"

"Not yet."

"Jimmy, please!" Marti said sharply. "I can handle this." She turned back to Ransom. "You were saying?"

"You told me that your husband didn't discuss his business with you."

"Yes?"

He studied her for a moment. It had been a long time since he'd come across anyone quite this cool. "We've just had a chat with Jeremiah Stone."

Neither Marti nor Harker said anything right away, but Ransom noticed the electricity in the air.

"And?"

"Marti, I don't think you should—"

"Shut up, Jimmy!" she said irritably. She sounded as if she knew he was destined to make matters worse.

Ransom continued. "He told us of your plans, which, to put it as nicely as possible, could've been considered disloyal to your husband." He turned to Harker. "And quite frankly, I'm amazed you would even consider taking Stone on as a client."

"Nobody was more surprised than I was when he approached us."

"Approached me," Marti corrected.

"He came to you personally?" said Ransom.

Marti leaned forward and rested her forearms on the desk. "If nothing else, the old man has a sense of humor. He said he was under the impression that I didn't care much for my husband."

Harker started to caution her again, but she stopped him with a glance.

"This seems like an extraordinary move for him to make . . . and for you."

"If you've talked to Stone, you know he's an extraordinary man. And he's no fool. He knew that if he could enlist us to fight for him against my husband's company, the whole matter would be front-page news. He knew that . . ." She narrowed her eyes and added significantly, ". . . and so did I."

"I see," said Ransom after a lengthy pause. "According to Mr. Stone, your knowledge of your husband's business included the bogus demonstration going on outside his tower."

She rolled her eyes. "Something that Louie considered a particular stroke of genius. Maybe it was. He was nothing if not clever."

Ransom was silent for a moment. "Then you did know the intimate details of your husband's business."

"So?"

"So why lie about it? It's perfectly natural for a husband to discuss his work with his wife."

She didn't respond right away.

Harker cleared his throat. "I might've been responsible for that—at least partly."

"No you weren't," Marti said firmly. "I am responsible for the things I do. It was an . . . on-the-spot decision on my part. Jimmy and I discussed it later, but it was my decision."

"To lie?"

"I didn't know where your investigation would lead you. But I knew if this came out—our relationship with Stone—it would make me look bad. I suppose I just wasn't thinking clearly."

Ransom smiled. "That's difficult to believe of you."

Her expression hardened. "Believe it or not, Detective, I was surprised by the news of my husband's death. No matter what you may think of our relationship—for that matter, no matter what *I* might think of it—Louie was a large part of my life for a very long time."

Ransom considered this. She sounded genuine enough, but he couldn't shake the feeling that this was exactly the type of thing she would have calculated to be the best thing to say under the circumstances.

"The problem that I'm having," he said at last, "is that the person who murdered your husband had very intimate knowledge of his business. Like you."

"But the evening Louie was killed, Marti was with me," Harker said.

"So she told us." Ransom looked him pointedly in the eye. It took a few seconds, but Harker finally realized the implications of being her sole alibi.

"You're not . . . you're not thinking that I can be involved too?"

Ransom ignored him and turned back to Marti. "The murderer has a key card to the building, like you. The murderer knew about the bogus protest, and about Juan Muñoz."

"Who?" Marti said blankly.

The onset of understanding is often described as a light dawning, because understanding spreads from knowledge like morning sunlight spreading across an open field. But on this occasion, for Ransom, understanding came in a flood, like a damn bursting. In a flash, he knew.

"Juan Muñoz," he repeated. "The man your husband hired to play the mummy."

The side of Marti's upper lip arched, this time with distaste. "You mean one of those protesters? How would I know their names? Louie didn't bother discussing that with me."

Ransom was out of his chair before anyone knew what was happening. Although Gerald was used to his partner's habit of abruptly ending an interview, normally meant to discomfit the person being questioned, this time Ransom's departure was so precipitous that he was halfway down the hallway before Gerald caught up with him.

"What is it?" he asked.

"His hair was wet!" Ransom exclaimed, banging through the door to the law offices and out into the corridor.

"Yeah?"

He punched the button for the elevator. "His hair was wet, and I'm a complete and total idiot!"

"What? Why?"

"I suppose my only consolation is that Emily didn't see the significance either. She said it, but she didn't see it."

"What are you talking about?" Gerald asked with some irritation.

Ransom looked him in the eye. "Get on the phone, get hold of whoever the hell is watching Juan Muñoz's apartment right now and tell them to go in!"

"What!"

"Just do it!" Ransom barked, punching the button again. "I hope to God we're not too late to catch him!"

18

It was a long time before their knock was answered. Gerald had to rap his knuckles against the door a second time, louder. At last they heard slow, quiet footsteps approaching the door from the other side.

"Yes?" came the voice from within.

"It's Detectives Ransom and White," said Gerald. "Please open the door."

They heard the bolt snap, then the door slid back. Anna Braverman stood in the opening, her eyes bloodshot and her cheeks glistening with tears.

"Where's your husband, Mrs. Braverman?"

"Gone." Her lips trembled.

"Do you know where?"

She shook her head.

"May we come in?"

She nodded and stepped aside, then closed the door and followed them into the apartment.

"You have no idea where he's gone?" Ransom asked.

She shook her head slowly and lowered herself onto the couch. "I stayed at the tower for a very long time after I saw you . . . then I decided . . . to go up and talk to him. But he was gone. When I came home, I found . . . in the bedroom . . ."

Ransom went down the hall in the direction she was pointing and looked in at the first open door. It was the bedroom. The closet door was open, and some of the empty hangers were tangled on the rod, others strewn on the floor. Apparently he had torn the clothes off of them in a very big hurry.

Ransom came back into the living room. "He's made a run for it." He looked down at Anna. "Do you know if he took his car?"

"I don't know," she replied, her voice hollow. "The garage attendant might know."

Gerald pulled out his phone. "What's the number?"

She gave it to him and he dialed. When the attendant answered, Gerald asked if Braverman had driven out, then looked over at Ransom and nodded. "About an hour ago."

"Ask him if they have the plates on file."

Gerald complied, then took out his notebook. After a short wait, he jotted something down, thanked the attendant and disconnected. "Got it."

"Call it in," said Ransom. As Gerald did this, Ransom sat down beside Anna. "Are you sure you don't have any idea where he would go? Is there anyone he would go to?"

She stared at him blankly. "I don't even know him."

Although he wasn't consciously aware of having made the decision, Bill had chosen to head south on I-57. He believed they would probably think he would go west, and that's what he intended to do eventually. The quickest and most logical way to head west was on I-80, so he knew that was the first place they would look for him. Instead, he headed south, intending to go west later, using older roads. He was being careful to keep his speed within the posted limit, but would find himself involuntarily accelerating as he thought of all he'd lost and how unfair it all was. Each time, when he realized how fast he was going, he would immediately ease off the gas pedal and let the speed drop.

His fevered mind was plagued with thoughts of how he'd been losing his job, and losing his wife, and how he'd long since lost his honor. And all of this because of one man.

Anna was right! I was a flunky! A thug! She didn't even know the half of it . . .

His foot pressed down harder on the gas pedal.

What did I do for him? Risked going to prison for carrying out his bribes? All of his dirty work? And he was going to dump me! Just dump me!

With a start, he came to himself and looked at the speedometer. He was going seventy-five. He took his foot off the pedal and watched the needle drop back to fifty-five.

If only Anna had waited! Just for a few more days! If she'd waited, Louie would've been gone, my life would've been my own again . . . well, maybe not my own, but Marti would've had to keep me on, at least. But no, Anna couldn't wait! Goddamn her, if only she'd waited!

He'd brought the speed back up to seventy before realizing it, and let it drop again.

Braverman was so lost in his mental turmoil that he didn't notice the state trooper parked overhead as he approached a viaduct. After he'd sped through it, the trooper got into his car, swung it across the road and headed down the entrance ramp.

I should've stopped. I should've stopped the whole thing the minute I knew Anna was leaving. I should've known it was too late then. But I thought . . . I thought . . . I still might've . . .

His thoughts broke off when he saw the flashing yellow light in his rearview mirror. He immediately checked his speed, but the speedometer showed under sixty.

Bill had tensed markedly at the first sight of the state police car, but after the initial shock, the stress started to drain out of his body as if somehow a plug had been pulled. His limbs became flaccid and he sank back against the seat. His arms were stretched out to the steering wheel, but he was barely touching it with his fingertips. His right foot became like lead, growing heavier. His slack muscles could do nothing to restrain it as it slowly weighted down the gas pedal.

The rushing landscape became unreal to him, like a painting where the colors are not quite right. As the speed continued to mount, the scenery blurred and Bill could feel himself becoming drowsy. It was in this confused state that he noticed the next overpass, rapidly approaching in the distance. It was the one clear, fixed point in the increasingly dizzying scene, and he unconsciously focused on it. An overwhelming sense of weariness washed over him. He was only dimly aware of an intermittent yellow light sweeping across his face, a reflection from the rearview mirror of the flashing light atop the state police car that was managing to keep pace with him.

If only she'd waited . . . if only I'd acted sooner . . . if only . . .

The overpass came closer and closer, looming over the highway, its cement posts reaching down into the earth like the fingers on the hand of God.

Bill couldn't fight the weariness any longer. His eyelids became as heavy as the foot that was now pressing the gas pedal to the floor. He tried to keep his eyes open, but only halfheartedly, knowing that the fight was already lost.

The overpass was almost upon him. He was unaware of his own intent as his fingers moved the steering wheel to the left.

The state trooper slammed on his brakes as the car he'd been following drove directly into the center post of the overpass. The car took the impact at a point slightly to the left of its center, and the momentum sent it spinning into the viaduct, bouncing back and forth off the right and center walls like a scrap-metal pinball. The car continued its wild spin until it reached the other end of the viaduct. The last of its turns sent it onto its side, where it teetered precariously for a moment before the weight of the chassis brought the car down on its roof.

19

SATURDAY

It was his wet hair," said Ransom. He took a sip from his mug. "You reminded me of it."

He hadn't been able to get to Emily's house for dinner Friday night. There had been too many ends to clear up, and reports that needed to be made right away. He had called her and told her what happened, but didn't have time to offer her any explanation until they had dinner together the next evening. Lynn Francis had joined them. She was savoring an after-dinner cup of tea with Emily while Ransom had his coffee.

"You thought there was something wrong about that at the time," said Emily.

"Yes, but I couldn't figure out what it was. I should've known when we questioned Lisa Rivera. But if not then, I really should've known when you reminded me of it."

She made a noise that sounded like "tut!" "It didn't occur to me either. I suppose Ms. Rivera has confirmed it?"

He nodded.

"I don't get it," said Lynn. "What was so significant about Dolores's hair being wet?"

Ransom took a deep breath. "Officer Nash told me that when Dolores came down from his office after being called about the disturbance, he commented on the fact that Dolores was there that late. Dolores said something about having to work long hours. We assumed—wrongly—that Dolores had stayed at the building waiting for the call about the mummy's appearance, so he could be on hand to make sure there was publicity. But that wasn't it at all: he was there having a tryst with Lisa Rivera."

"A tryst?" Lynn said with a sly grin.

"That's a perfectly descriptive word," Emily said in a mildly rebuking tone.

"That was why his hair was wet," Ransom continued. "Because afterward, he'd taken a shower."

"Well, what did Lisa Rivera confirm for you?" Lynn asked.

"That he was surprised by the call, my dear," said Emily.

Ransom explained. "The security staff is under orders to report anything unusual to Dolores's office. They didn't really expect him to be there, they were going to leave a message. But he answered the phone, and when he heard what it was about, he came down."

"I'm missing something," said Lynn.

"You see," said Emily, "Louie Dolores didn't know anything about the mummy."

"What!"

Emily nodded, shaking the bun that was not quite carefully enough pinned at the back of her head. "Oh, it was his idea to hire people to stage a protest, and I'm sure he knew who Mr. Muñoz was, but Mr. Dolores knew nothing of the business of the mummy making appearances in the exhibit."

"You're kidding! But it was in the paper the next day!"

"To be sure, he seized the opportunity once it presented itself. The moment he heard that one of his cleaning staff claimed to have seen one of the mummies resurrected, he saw it for the opportunity it was. Mr. Dolores didn't achieve his success by letting such things slip by."

"Everyone had it backwards," Ransom said with a rueful smile. "People kept telling us that it was impossible to believe that Dolores would hatch a plot without Braverman being in on it. The possibility that Braverman could hatch a plot without Dolores knowing anything about it didn't even enter their minds."

"So it was Braverman who got Juan Muñoz to make those appearances in the exhibit?" Lynn asked.

Ransom shook his head. "Muñoz was never in the exhibit."

"What!" Lynn exclaimed again.

"I believe the reason he acted strangely when we talked to him was because he was afraid we'd find out the protest was a fraud."

"Oh!" Lynn sat back in her chair, her mouth hanging open. "Oh! I get it! Braverman was the mummy!"

"Exactly," said Emily.

"But what was the point of all that?"

"To establish the idea that Mr. Muñoz was coming into the building and . . . I don't know . . . I suppose 'acting peculiar' would be the best way to put it. That's also reason for the nonfatal attack on Mr. Dolores in the garage: so Dolores could report that Mr. Muñoz was after him."

"But he didn't report it."

Emily smiled. "No, he stubbornly refused to, much to Mr. Braverman's consternation, I'm sure."

"I think you'd be surprised," said Ransom.

Her thin, gray eyebrows arched. "Oh?"

"Braverman very well might've been distressed at first that Dolores didn't tell us, but he used it to his advantage. It was obvious to both Gerald and me that Braverman wanted to tell us something when we first met with Dolores, and Dolores was holding him back. By later telling us about that attack himself, Braverman managed to distance himself from Muñoz. But Braverman ended up doing himself in—no pun intended. His work at implicating Muñoz was so effective that we put Muñoz under surveillance. If we hadn't done that, we might never have put it together."

"He knew the game was up the moment you told him he was seen going into Mr. Muñoz's apartment, didn't he?" said Emily.

Ransom nodded again. "He would've said anything to get us out of his office."

"Why did he go there?" Lynn asked as she brushed a stray strand of hair back off her forehead.

"To kill Muñoz," Ransom replied.

"You're kidding!"

"When the police went in, they found Muñoz in his bathtub with his wrists cut. It'll be a while before we get the toxicology report back, but my guess is that Braverman slipped him a sleeping pill—after the body was found, we asked his wife about it, and she does have some sedatives. Anyway, most likely he slipped them into a drink, and once Muñoz was out, he did the rest."

Emily shuddered. "What a dreadful way to kill someone."

"Wait a minute, wait a minute, wait a minute!" Lynn said, holding up her hands. "If Braverman wanted to implicate Muñoz, why didn't he just give you his name when you asked him about the protester? That would've sent you right to him."

"Because he hadn't had a chance to kill him yet," said Ransom. "And Muñoz alive would've told us who'd hired him. You see, it didn't matter if *Dolores* told us that Muñoz attacked him—the attacker was wearing a mask, so he couldn't have positively identified him. We couldn't have arrested him. But then when Dolores was murdered, Muñoz would've been the prime suspect. Only, we would've found that he'd 'committed suicide,' presumably out of remorse or whatever for having killed Dolores."

"How do you know all of this?" Lynn asked.

"I don't, really. I'm just guessing. But it's an educated guess. I think Braverman intended to kill Muñoz on the same night that he killed Dolores—that was the real purpose of the 'drive' he said he was taking when Dolores was killed. But Muñoz told us he was out that night. If he'd been home, Braverman might very well have gotten away with the whole thing. It was very fortunate that Muñoz was out."

"Relatively speaking," Emily interjected with an impish grin.

"Yes, because Braverman didn't get the chance to kill Muñoz until we had him under surveillance."

Lynn sighed and shook her head. She took a sip of tea, then set the cup back on the saucer. "This sort of thing must be awfully frustrating to you."

"Why?"

"I mean because there are so many things you'll never have the answer to."

"For instance?"

"Well, Emily told me that you thought Dolores was killed while he was waiting for the elevator, by someone who rode up in it. How could Braverman have managed that?"

Ransom and Emily looked at each other and smiled.

"What?" Lynn said with mock irritation. "What do the two of you know that I don't?"

Emily chuckled. "It's only that once we knew who the murderer was, the solution to that aspect of it was simple. Mr. Braverman went to Mr. Dolores's office before leaving, ostensibly to see if Mr. Dolores wanted to be accompanied to the garage, for safety's sake. Of course Mr. Dolores was not the kind of person who would ever agree to that. It would've been an insult to his manhood. Mr. Braverman knew that. What he was really doing was checking to see if anyone else was in the penthouse."

"He already knew when and where Dolores was meeting Lisa Rivera," Ransom explained. "Paula Dryer was keeping him informed."

Emily continued, "Then all he had to do was go downstairs, change, and wait in the private elevator until Dolores called for it."

"There was nobody else there who *could* call for it," Ransom added. "Then Braverman put the body in the private elevator, took the freight elevator down to the second floor, and put in his appearance in the exhibit. Then he put on his street clothes, and took the stairs down to the garage."

"Why the garage?" Lynn asked.

"Because with his key card, he could get out that way without anybody seeing him."

"You see, it was plain from the way the blood was splattered that Dolores was killed while facing the elevator, apparently by someone who'd come up in it, but as it turned out, that looked more mysterious than it ended up being," said Emily. "And if by chance anyone had spotted Mr. Braverman in the act, they would've thought he was Mr. Muñoz."

"Did you ever find his mummy costume?" Lynn asked Ransom.

"There are a million garbage cans in the city of Chicago," he replied. "We probably never will."

"Well, I still have the biggest question for you," Lynn said. "Why did he do it?"

"Probably for the very reasons I gave when I confronted him: he was losing his job and his wife, and he thought Dolores was responsible for both."

"But didn't he just learn both those things?" Lynn asked. "Wouldn't it have taken him time to come up with this whole mummy plot?"

"Oh, I think the problem goes back quite a way," said Emily. Ransom's eyebrows went up. "Hmm?"

"You told me that Paula Dryer said Mr. Braverman had been 'off his feed' for over a year. It had probably been going on for a while before anyone had noticed the change in him—like with senility, you notice that a loved one is occasionally forgetting things, but it is a while before you notice a pattern."

"What are you saying, Emily?"

She shifted in her chair. "He had not been himself for over a year? And possibly longer? Wouldn't that take it back to the time of the unpleasantness over the Harrison project?"

"I see," Ransom said, nodding with understanding.

"What of it?" said Lynn.

"Well, nobody ever doubted that a bribe had been made, or that Mr. Braverman had carried it out. Everyone simply believed that they'd gotten away with it. I daresay, if Mr. Braverman had been an honorable person at one time, being called before a grand jury—being implicated in something like that, and very nearly going on trial—would've weighed heavily on his mind. I daresay that Mr. Braverman felt that Mr. Dolores had turned him into a criminal. Perhaps it wasn't a far step from that to actually becoming one."

They fell silent. Then, as if on cue, the three of them lifted their drinks to their lips. Emily and Lynn set down their cups, while Ransom kept his mug poised between his hands.

Emily clucked her tongue. "For all of his money, Mr. Dolores must've been a very unhappy man."

"Why do you say that?" Lynn asked.

"Look at all of the people around him with all their little plots against him. His wife, his right-hand man . . . not to mention the Historical Commission, the Stone Candy Company. It's hard to think that someone's death would make so many people happy."

262

"I don't think it did that," said Ransom. "His wife wanted him alive so she could make a name for herself fighting him in court. And Jeremiah Stone might be happy for the moment, but he knows his factory will eventually be swallowed up by a developer."

Emily pursed her lips and nodded thoughtfully. "That is most likely true."

Ransom took another drink, then put the mug down on the table. "Well, enough of that. Tomorrow is Sunday. What are you going to be doing?"

This time it was Emily and Lynn who shared knowledgeable smiles.

"What?" said Ransom.

"Our Emily has a date!" Lynn replied mirthfully.

Ransom raised his right eyebrow, which made Emily laugh. "Jeremy, you are not nearly so good at hiding your surprise as you think you are."

"Only with you," he replied, shaking his head. "Only with you."

"I didn't actually get much of a chance to see the exhibit," said Emily. She was clad in one of her best dresses, navy blue with tiny silver buttons that were fastened up to the collar. She wore a gold locket on a chain around her neck. It was nine-thirty the next morning, an hour before the Chinchorro mummy exhibit was set to reopen to the public. "It is very kind of you to give me a guided tour."

"Kind? No, Madam, it is not kind," said Hector Gonzalez. "It is the very least I can do for someone who has helped me the way you have."

"I did very little."

"You helped me find my way back out of my own mind. Without you, I think maybe I never would've found my way."

"We all get a little lost now and then."

"I doubt very much that that is true of you."

Gonzalez hesitated as they reached the second chamber. Emily stood with her arm through his.

"It was Mr. Braverman that did it?" he asked, not for the first time. She had explained the whole thing to him, but he was having some difficulty shaking the mental quagmire in which he had so recently been mired and accepting the truth.

"Yes," she assured him.

"You do not know, do you, why he chose to bedevil me in this way?"

"Mr. Gonzalez—"

"Hector, please."

She applied a gentle pressure to his arm. "Hector. We will, of course, never know for sure. We can only conjecture. But I believe it was quite by accident. When you saw him for the first time, it was late in the morning, wasn't it?"

He nodded, his sad brown eyes trained on her. "The day the exhibit was installed."

"During a period when the exhibit was supposed to be empty?"

His brow furrowed deeply. "Yes. They had, they told me, just completed construction that morning. The workmen were gone. And I . . . I was supposed to be downstairs, at the loading dock."

"Exactly. I think he decided to make a trial run, so to speak, expecting that nobody would be here. But you were. So, you saw him quite by accident. You said it was fleeting, didn't you?"

"Yes. It was as if he were running away."

"You see! That's probably exactly what he was doing. He was surprised to find you there, and he ran away."

Hector's eyes had widened. It seemed to finally be sinking in. "And he went out of the back of one of these chambers?"

"That's right. Having already opened the latches. When he appeared to Frieda Jablonski, he did it purposely, trying to establish that Juan Muñoz was 'haunting' the building, for lack of a better word. The second time you saw him, after he'd committed the murder, he was trying to be seen by one of the cleaning staff, and failing that, perhaps he would've made a little noise and drawn the guard in so he could be seen . . . again, just fleetingly. It was quite by mistake that you were the one to see him again."

"So it was not aimed at me."

"No," Emily said kindly. "It was just very, very unfortunate that he accidentally involved you." She didn't add what she was thinking:

that had Braverman known the delicate balance of Gonzalez's mind at the time, he would've exploited it.

"It was a terrible thing that he did."

She patted his hand. "Yes. But it's over now."

He led her into the chamber. She listened with great interest as he expounded on the various types of mummies on display, their history, and where they'd been discovered. Then he led her down the hallway toward the third display area.

"Tell me," said Emily, "have you finally reconciled yourself to all of this?"

"You mean to the mummies being loaned out?" He considered this for a moment. "I believe I have accepted that it was inevitable. I believe the museum did what it had to do to survive . . . as sad a choice as I may think it to be. But the Chinchorros, they are dead. And we must do what we must for the living, I suppose. In my day . . . I mean in earlier days, this would not have been done."

They had entered the chamber and came to a stop at the first of the cases.

"If you have reconciled yourself to this, will you be keeping your position at the museum?"

"No. I still intend to resign. The times have changed too much for me there." He smiled for the first time. "Lisa thinks I am incapable of change."

"Young people don't understand these things," Emily said wistfully. "She doesn't understand that you *are* changing."

"You are right. She doesn't." His left hand hovered over the case in which one of the bandage mummies was on display. "These things are my past."

Emily sighed. "But they are fascinating, aren't they!"

A YEAR IN THE

LIFE OF A

Rose

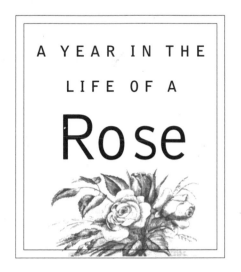

Other books by Rayford Clayton Reddell

Full Bloom

The Rose Bible

Growing Fragrant Plants

Growing Good Roses

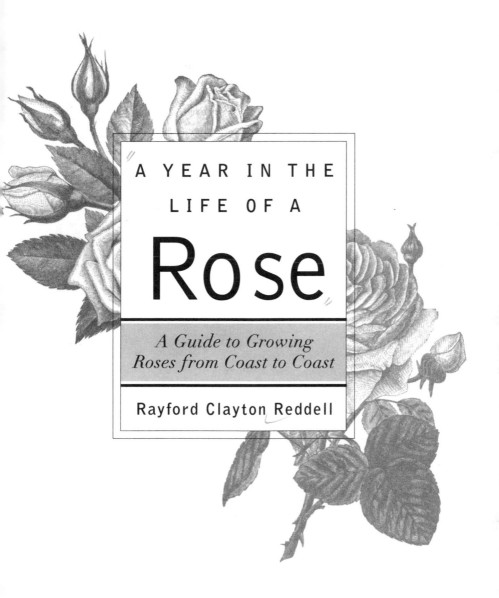

A YEAR IN THE
LIFE OF A
Rose

*A Guide to Growing
Roses from Coast to Coast*

Rayford Clayton Reddell

Harmony Books / New York

Published by Harmony Books, a division of Crown Publishers, Inc., 201 East 50th Street, New York, New York 10022. Member of the Crown Publishing Group

Random House, Inc. New York, Toronto, London, Sydney, Auckland

http://www.randomhouse.com/

HARMONY and colophon are trademarks of Crown Publishers, Inc.

Design by Nancy Kenmore

Printed in the United States of America

Library of Congress Cataloging-in-Publication Data
    A year in the life of a rose: a guide to growing roses from coast to coast / by Rayford Clayton Reddell. — 1st ed.
    Includes index.
    1. rose culture — United States.   2. Roses — United States.   I. Title.
SB411.R398   1996
635.9'33372 — dc20   96-22068

ISBN 0-517-70669-5

10   9   8   7   6   5   4   3   2

To Denise Minnelli Hale,
who sparked this book
into happening

Contents

Contents

Acknowledgments

Besides Denise Minnelli Hale, who coerced me into writing this book, I owe thanks to:

The extraordinary staff at Garden Valley Ranch, particularly Jayne Rosselli Hofer, my snappy managing partner, and Ned Wales, the Ranch's capable foreman.

My thirteen regional rose gurus for sharing the nitty-gritty on how to best grow roses in their USDA zones.

My many friends at Harmony Books, particularly editors Leslie Meredith and Sherri Rifkin, and especially Mark McCauslin and Robin Strashun, not only for being the only constants in my publishing association, but also for never wavering in their staunch support.

Preface

NOT LONG AFTER I CONSIDERED MYSELF SUFFICIENTLY experienced with roses to begin offering advice on how to grow them well, a friend turned to me for help.

"I have a special favor to ask," she began, then revealed what she had been hiding on her lap during lunch.

"This is a wall calendar for next year," she continued, "and I wonder if you could fill in the dates for proper watering and fertilizing of my roses. I've read *what* you say to do, but I'm never certain precisely *when* to do it."

I told my friend that I couldn't possibly grant her wish because, first, my roses and I lived more than 100 miles from her garden and in dissimilar weather. Second, I pointed out, I'm never sure what I'm going to feed my roses until mealtime. "Just call me when your roses look hungry," I offered, "and I'll tell you what to feed them." She took me up on my proposal— often.

A year later, with another year-at-a-glance calendar in tow, she began lunch with an apology. "I hate pestering you," she confessed, "but I'm a very scheduled person, and I really need detailed instructions."

I admitted to myself that I was tiring of the telephone calls. "Besides," I asked myself, "how hard would it be to map out a rose year, foodwise? Watering schedules will be a snap."

On request, I filled in the next year's calendar. My friend was overjoyed.

Shortly after coming to my friend's rescue, an editor from the *San Francisco Chronicle* called to ask if I'd be interested in writing a feature article on feeding roses in San Francisco.

"Not your biweekly column," he explained, "but a piece written specifically for the Bay Area, outlining what to do when."

"Yes," I answered immediately, chuckling to myself that I already had the bulk of the work done.

I wrote the piece, offering specifics for what the *Chronicle* called "A Gourmet Diet for Roses" (see chapter 3). In it, I divulged the precise fertilizers I intended to feed my own roses, including hefty shots of Epsom salts.

I was amazed at the results; so were nearby drugstores and garden centers. One pharmacy called the week after the diet was published to report that they had sold more Epsom salts in the last week than they had in the preceding five years.

"Why have Epsom salts been such a secret?" they asked. "If it's good for roses now, it always was, right?"

Now, of course, I bless my friend for motivating a book on a year in the life of a rose, because it has given me the opportunity to tell many timely "secrets" about good rose culture.

In order to avoid the obvious pitfall of speaking only about roses in my precise locale, I've solicited the help of rose experts across the United States — in southern California, where the climate is even more ideal than my own; in the Deep South, where winters are just chilly enough that roses must be protected; in deserts, where summers are scorchers and winters are biting; and in the Midwest, where winters are so severe that one wonders that roses grow at all.

Before understanding precisely how to feed and water your roses (depending on which USDA zone you garden in), it's essential to grasp the rose's life cycle, from leafless plant to well-foliated, free-flowering, billowing bush, then back to dormancy again. Once you realize the importance of each stage, how best to coax roses to the next is a breeze.

Chapter
One

WINTER

IT MAY AT FIRST SEEM ODD TO BEGIN A BOOK ON ROSE culture with winter, but this is when the rose cycle actually begins. Life for new rosebushes commences as soon as their roots are sunk into soil. For rosebushes in the ground longer than a year, winter also marks a new beginning—that of this year's cycle.

When winter occurs in your garden is, of course, determined by where you live; more specifically, by your precise USDA zone, which is discussed in chapter 7. How long winters last also varies among zones. No matter winter's length, however, late in the season is the proper time to address two key aspects of growing good roses: planting and pruning.

Proper times for planting roses in America may differ by as much as five months. For instance, I plant bushes as soon as they're available from suppliers (often as early as November). At the other extreme, gardeners in chilly USDA Zone 4b may have to defer planting until mid-April.

Winter temperatures may also determine whether rosebushes are planted as bareroots or from containers. Where climates are temperate, bareroots are generally preferable; where winters are severe, bushes potted up in containers may be the only option because there is a limit to how long bareroot plants can be kept in cold storage without drying out.

MAKING ROSES FEEL AT HOME

When most gardeners decide to plant roses, they give considerable thought to how much they're willing to pay for plants, instead of worrying about spending enough on materials for filling the holes created for their new bushes' homes. No matter what the quality of a rosebush, it can only live up to the hole in which it's planted.

Before getting out a shovel, choose sites carefully. Roses like at least five hours of full sun each day — the earlier, the better. Bushes also appreciate being sheltered from the wind and being placed beyond the bounds of competition from the roots of neighbors. Next, roses demand a nearby source of water plentiful enough for a weekly soak during summer. Finally, drainage should be as close to perfect as possible. If you worry that a hole you've prepared might not drain well enough to suit a rose, fill it with water. If the hole hasn't drained completely in an hour, dig 6 inches deeper and fill the extended depth with a layer of coarse gravel before preparing the hole for planting.

The Almighty Hole

After experimenting with an array of dimensions, I've decided that the ideal hole for a rose is 2 feet wide by

18 inches deep. This may seem shallow, but remember that roses don't have taproots.

Plan to find a new home for at least half of the dirt removed from your dig — all of it if your soil is poor. (Some of it can be recycled when you mound the newly planted bush; see page 20.) Instead of reusing soil that's already spent, buy packaged all-purpose gardening soil.

To half the soil needed to refill the hole for a bareroot bush mix equal parts of aged manure and organic materials. Most nurseries carry only cow and steer manures, but if you can get your garden spade on aged chicken, turkey, or rabbit manure, your roses will bless you. Any one or a combination of several organic materials will do — peat moss, "nitralized" sawdust (sawdust to which nitrogen has been added), or compost.

When planting bushes from containers, augment the soil in the container itself with the same organic materials used for bareroot plants.

Preparing the Bush
(or Getting the Bush Ready)

If you plant bareroot bushes soon after you get them home from a reliable nursery or shortly after you receive them from a shipper, they will be in good condition. If planting must be delayed because of bad weather, the bushes may dry out. To replenish moisture, submerge the bushes in water, covering all roots. Depending on how dried out the bushes have become, they can be soaked for up to 24 hours; the dried parts will plump and fill out nicely.

Some rosarians soak their rosebushes for two hours before they plant them no matter how quickly they arrived from the supplier. "Who knows how long ago they were dug up and left in cold storage?" they ask. These same clever gardeners suggest that you add some household bleach (about ⅛ cup per 5 gallons of water) to your soaking tub, thereby zapping whatever unwanted bacteria might be hanging around. They'll also mention that a shot of all-purpose liquid fertilizer or vitamin B1 wouldn't hurt either.

Next, all broken stems and roots must have their damaged sections cut out. Using sharp shears, make a clean cut into healthy growth ¼ inch from the break.

The final step is to fashion a cone of soil rising out of the hole to the height at which the rosebush is to be planted. Think of the cone as a tepee of soil rising out of the hole, and form it bit by bit from handfuls of the planting mixture patted down to eliminate air pockets. When the cone is at the right height, formed and compacted, the hole is ready for its bush. But first an anatomy lesson.

The Heart of the Bush

Bushes of modern roses are really a grafted combination of two separate rose varieties. "Rootstock" is the part underground. It comes from older varieties known not for their blooms, which are usually insignificant, even ugly, but rather for their capacity for massive root development. Onto this rootstock the desired variety is grafted to grow above the ground: the hybrid. Where the graft of the two varieties is made, a globular bulbous landmark — the bud union — develops, which forever bears testament to the marriage.

The bud union is the heart of the rosebush. It is from there that major new growth will develop when conditions are right. More important, for now, the bud union is the landmark for determining proper planting height. If you garden where winter temperatures regularly dip below 20°F, you must position the bud union at or just below the soil surface. If you live where winters are more temperate, place the bud union 2 inches above the soil and plan to add mulch level with the bud union's base. Check the right height for the bud union by laying a shovel handle or stick on the ground and across the hole.

Setting the Bush

Set the bush directly onto the tip of the cone, carefully spreading roots outward and downward. Then, holding the bush in place, begin filling in the rest of the hole, pressing down the soil mixture firmly enough to eliminate air pockets but being careful not to break any of the fragile roots. Use your hands, not your feet, to tamp down the soil. When half of the filling is completed, water to soak thoroughly.

If you plan to use dry fertilizers, this is the time to apply them. Dry fertilizers are either water-soluble granules or timed-release capsules. Both types are

rated on the package label by their content of nitrogen, phosphorus, and potassium (respectively, chemical symbols N, P, and K). If you decide on timed-release
fertilizers, remember that they may not go to work
until spring sufficiently warms the soil to break them
down. Whichever dry fertilizers you apply, choose a
formula with the highest number first, such as 20-10-
10, which has twice as much nitrogen (the growth
stimulant) as phosphorus or potassium.

Dry fertilizers should be applied and watered in
before the remaining soil is added to fill the hole.
Once water has drained, fill the hole with soil mix and
tamp everything down. Water thoroughly again.

Covering Bare Canes

If bushes aren't mounded after planting, all previous
efforts may prove to have been made in vain. Bareroot
rose canes left uncovered will dry out, and cold winter
winds will parch them.

Any of the materials you've just been working with
can be used for mounding; a combination of them
would be ideal. Mix the leftover soil from the hole you
dug with any of the suggested organic materials. Heap
the combination over the bush until at least half of the
plant is covered. Wet the mixture down, being careful
not to wash it away, and congratulate yourself on a
well-planted rosebush.

Once bushes are planted and mounded, they should
be left alone except for keeping them just on the wet

side of moist. If it doesn't rain periodically, water mounds yourself and get ready for a glorious eruption.

INEVITABLE PRUNING

Accomplished rosarians admit that when they were novices, pruning scared them more than any other aspect of successful rose culture.

"All decisions seemed so final," they remember. "I considered skipping pruning altogether."

Despite such grumblings, rosebushes must be pruned for two reasons: (1) to eliminate nonproductive (or damaged) growth, thereby encouraging new, and (2) to shape plants.

Dormant rosebushes aren't certain which way you want them to grow unless you prune to budding eyes pointed in the right direction. If not aimed correctly, Rambling and Climbing roses don't know whether to scramble this way or that. Without an annual thinning, shrub roses become thorny tangles of insignificant flowers on spindly stems. Face it—roses demand to be pruned.

When to Prune

Debates over the proper time to prune repeat-blooming roses focus on winter versus spring pruning. Those in favor of winter pruning point out that bushes cut back early have a chance to adjust to their new shape and size, without supporting wood that's going to come off anyway. Those advocating later pruning

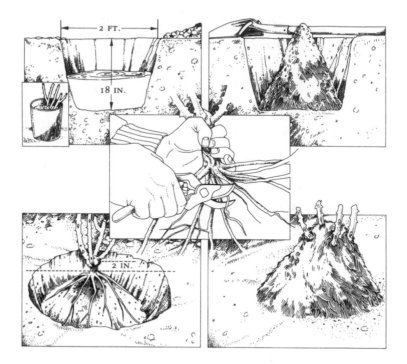

HOW TO PLANT A BAREROOT ROSE *Choose a site that gets shelter from the wind and at least five hours of full sun each day.* Dig a hole 2 *feet wide and 18 inches deep and fill it with water. If it takes the hole more than an hour to drain, improve drainage by digging deeper and adding gravel.*

While you work on the almighty hole, soak the bush *in enough water to cover its roots. Add a little household bleach to the water to kill any bacteria present, and a liquid fertilizer to give the bush a head start.* Form a cone *by patting handfuls of planting mixture until you've fashioned a tepee of soil rising from the hole.*

Just before you put the bush in place, trim off any damaged or broken roots. *Use sharp shears to make a clean cut into the healthy growth ¼ inch from a break. Some rosarians cut off ¼ inch of all root tips, claiming that it stimulates growth—probably a good practice.*

Place the bush *by draping its roots comfortably over the cone. Make sure the bud union is at the right height for the amount of mulch you plan to add. A shovel laid across the hole will help you gauge height.*

Holding the bush in place, begin to refill *the hole with soil, patting it down with your hands. When the hole is half filled, water to soak.* Dry fertilizers *should be sprinkled into the half-filled hole and watered in before the rest of the soil is added.*

Mounding *is the final step for a well-planted bush. No matter which mounding materials you use, heap them to cover at least half the plant. Water again.*

mention that tender new growth can be brutally affected by late frosts and unseasonable cold spells. Listen to what Vita Sackville-West, an ardent rose grower herself and an early-20th-century English garden trendsetter, had to say on the subject:

"Argument still rages in the horticultural world about the best time of year to prune roses. According to the old orthodox theory, the time to do it was the second half of March or in early April. Present-day opinion veers more and more strongly in favour of winter pruning. It seems to me common sense to cut the plant when it is dormant, rather than when the sap has begun to rise and must bleed the wound.

"I know there are objections. People say, 'Oh, but if you prune your roses in December or January, they may start to make fresh growth in the mild weather we sometimes get in February or early March, and then comes an iron frost and then what happens to those young tender shoots you have encouraged by your precipitate pruning?'

"All I can say in answer to that is that you will just have to go over your roses again and cut away all the frost-damaged shoots back to a new eye lower down the stem. You might have to do the same thing after a March pruning, so you will not have lost any time, and on the whole I am on the side of the winter pruners."

Of course, one must remember that Ms. Sackville-West was growing roses in England, where winters are severe. For many of us, controversial pruning methods occur further back in the calendar year. For instance,

where I live, near the coast in northern
(USDA Zone 9), there is argument whether t
December, January, or February, but all a
pruning should be well over before March. In colder
climates, pruning can be contemplated no sooner than
late March (maybe even later).

I've experimented with both approaches. I've
pruned half of the bushes of one variety early and the
remainder some weeks later. They bloomed at about
the same time. The only differences were the slightly
longer stems and somewhat larger blooms produced
by early pruning.

I now begin pruning the day after Christmas. One
reason is that I have some extra time then. The other is
that we never know how erratic the weather will be for
the next two months. If the sun is shining, we prune.
Besides, we have more than 8,000 bushes staring us in
the face and simply must begin as soon as we can.

My advice in sum: Prune as soon as possible once
dormancy is safely broken, that is, when you're sure
there won't be another hard freeze.

In addition to checking to see what my rose gurus in
chapter 7 have to say, ask your consulting rosarian for
ideal pruning dates for where you garden. County agricultural extension agents usually have a suggestion,
since all dormant plants, not just roses, need timely
cutting back. Also, find out if there are any pruning
demonstrations being given in your area. Many rose
societies prune roses in their local municipal gardens
and give informative lectures while they're doing it.

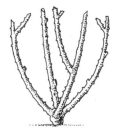

HOW TO PRUNE A ROSEBUSH Strip *the bush of all foliage two weeks before you approach it with shears. Bushes that are stripped of growth are given a signal to start over, resulting in swollen eyes where new growth will appear. These landmarks help eliminate pruning dilemmas.*

Remove all dead and twiggy growth. *Wood that has lived past its time won't rejuvenate, nor can growth develop that is thicker than the wood from which it grows. Since the goal of pruning is an urn-shaped rosebush with a free interior,* remove canes that cross over the center of the bush.

Cut remaining canes to the desired height, *depending on how severely you decide to prune. Make sure that each 45° cut is made ¼ inch above a swelling bud that points away from the center of the bush.*

Stripping the Bush

You'll be very happy if you take this advice: Strip the bushes of all foliage two weeks before you prune. When leaves are removed from rosebushes, the plant is given a signal to rejuvenate the foliar process immediately.

The first sign that the bush is bouncing back is when you spot swollen "eyes" where new growth is to appear — at the juncture of leaf formations and the stems on which they grow. When dormant, these eyes may not be easily visible to the human eye. Once their growth begins, however, accelerated by stripping, they swell, turn red, and become more obvious. When you arrive with pruning shears, you must find these landmarks in order to make cuts in the right places, so make it easy on yourself and give nature a chance to help you.

Foliage should be cut, not ripped, off. If you tear the leaves off, you may damage the bark just at the juncture where the dormant new bud eye is, stunting or preventing its development.

Dormant Spraying

Bushes stripped for pruning are ideal candidates for dormant sprays. These special spray materials are formulated to quash any diseases a bush may be sheltering and provide a healthy environment for the coming new growth. They're quite safe and easy to use. There are many on the market, most with a base of sulfur (the precise formulation doesn't seem to matter much), which is known for its effective disease eradication. If you plan to use a dormant spray, and I urge you to, please do it at this point. The spray is not meant for the new growth that will be appearing rapidly once you've stimulated the bush to produce it.

Downy mildew, a disease new to American gardeners, has become a mighty threat to rose growers. The most effective treatment for downy mildew is prevention, best achieved with applications of a zinc- or copper-based dormant spray material.

While you're at it, spray the soil around the bush as well. This area can harbor disease spores left from fallen leaves and cuttings, and dormant spray will safely knock them flat.

Tools

Pruning requires certain equipment without which you will injure the bush, yourself, or both. Shears head the list.

We rosarians will lend you any tool but our shears. We use them for everything—for pruning, clipping, harvesting. We can't walk through the garden without them because we never know when we're going to see something that has to come off right now, before it gets worse or before we forget where it is.

Shears must be kept sharp so that clean cuts can be made. Always buy shears that *can* be sharpened, not those that "never need sharpening," for they will. I hate admitting that for the first few years I grew roses,

I paid to have my shears sharpened and oiled. I knew that I should be doing it myself, but I'm generally so clumsy with my hands that I feared it was one of those tasks I couldn't master.

This time I was wrong. I'm proud to say that I now have the sharpest shears around, and keeping them that way myself is a piece of cake. All you need is a soft Arkansas sharpening stone, which you can get at any nursery or hardware store, and a can of all-purpose household oil. Drag the cutting edge of the shears lightly over the stone the way you would a knife over a honing steel. You'll work out the right motion for sharpening by following the contour of the blade as you rake it across the stone. Apply the oil to the sharpening stone as you go. The stone is porous and without the oil the cutting edge of the shears won't glide easily across it. By the time you finish, there will be a thin, even layer of oil over the shears' edges, facilitating cutting.

Give shears a thorough sharpening before you begin pruning, and again each time you feel them compromise a clean cut.

It's wise to have a single pair of shears with which you prune, harvest blossoms, and maintain bushes. Find one pair that will do all these things well, keep them sharp, and always store them in the same place so that you don't mislay them. Shears should be comfortable to hold and easy to work. The ones I prefer are on the heavy side of average weight. Anything lighter seems flimsy.

You'll be surprised and confused when you shop for shears; there are so many! Not only are there all sizes, but shears come in various shapes and for stated purposes. I finally settled on the one I like best—Felco No. 2. I'm fairly nationalistic and buy American products whenever I have a reasonable option, but I move camp to Switzerland when it comes to shears. These shears are not cheap (none of the good ones are), but they'll last a lifetime if properly cared for.

You can now buy shears that have a ratchet action. Progressive squeezes of the handle are made until the shears are tight enough to make an effortless cut. Pruning requires some hard squeezing, and ratchets may prove welcome after a short while.

Bushes more than a year old will develop canes that are too thick to cut with shears, even ratchet-action ones. For those, you will need loppers or a saw. Loppers are those cutting tools with relatively small blades and handles 20 inches long. The extension of the arms provides the leverage needed for hard cuts. If canes you need to cut are in the way of each other, the only entries to the bud union may be small, requiring a narrow saw blade with which cuts flush with the bud union can be made. I have found that even with older bushes, I'm able to make 70 percent of my cuts with shears and 20 percent with loppers. For the remaining 10 percent, where hands, even in gloves, can't reach, I must resort to a saw. Pruning saws designed specifically for these situations are ideal, and so are those saws called keyhole.

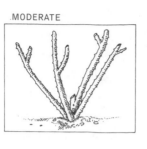

MODERATE

LIGHT

SEVERE

SEVERITY OF PRUNING *How severely you prune your bushes in winter will determine how many blooms you have in spring.* Severe *pruning (necessary in bitter winter climates) results in fewer blossoms but finer quality.* Light *pruning will yield lots of showy garden display, usually on flimsy stems.* Moderate *pruning is a compromise.*

that probably must be removed since these openings are breeding grounds and entry spots for diseases.

Learn to judge the vigor of rose wood by examining the pith (inside wood) within bark. Creamy white or green pith, with no brown spots, is healthy. Brown or blackened wood is very old or dead and won't produce blooms. Fresh wood is much easier to cut than dead wood, and you'll learn to feel the difference with your shears.

Multiple canes coming from a single bud union will vary in color by age. New canes are often either quite red or a clean, healthy-looking green; older wood is darker, typically scaly. Some rosebushes facilitate your pruning decisions by color-coding their canes; others produce wood of the same color, regardless of age, making pith examination mandatory.

Once only healthy wood is left, stand back to get an overall picture of the bush in order to decide how much more to take out. I like to leave at least four canes on any bush, and as many as ten on strong, proven growers and performers.

Severity of pruning is determined either by where you garden or by the general effect you seek. *Light* pruning requires a minimum of cutting, with bushes left tall, after only twiggy, wrong, or dead wood is removed. Next season's blooms will be short stemmed but profuse. *Moderate* pruning leaves five to ten, 1- to 4-foot canes per bush, depending on the vigor of the variety. Generally, half of each cane should be pruned

off. Moderate pruning produces not only a fine garden display but also some long-stemmed roses. *Severe* pruning, which often leaves only four canes per bush cut less than 1 foot tall, is either for gardeners who live in cruel winter climates where winter protection is mandatory or for those bloom fanciers in search of the longest-stemmed roses possible.

Ideal pruning height will vary by variety. Bushes don't grow the same or to a standard height, nor can they be pruned identically. Some grow tall, and nothing you do, including pruning them only inches from the ground, is going to make a difference in the end. In fact, if you try to change some of their natural habits, they'll get back at you during the growing season by spending all of their time growing to the height at which they are comfortable for blooming. Until they get there, they may not bloom at all. Other tall bushes have to be pruned severely, not because you would even consider changing their growth habits, but because if you don't, you won't be able to reach blooms without a ladder by summer's end.

Keep in mind also why you grow roses to begin with. If you value your roses mostly for their contribution to the landscape, prune lightly to moderately. If you grow roses to enjoy their blossoms indoors, prune moderately severely. If, as my chillier rose gurus admit in chapter 7, you prune with an eye toward a deep freeze, prune as severely as you must.

While there are no cardinal rules where pruning is concerned, certain generalities help. For instance, try

Finally, gloves. Rose thorns are vicious, particularly at pruning time when dormancy has allowed them to harden and winter has whittled them sharp. You won't be able to make the necessary cuts without holding onto canes and thorny areas, so gloves are a must.

Proper rose-pruning techniques depend on the type of rosebushes being pruned. Because modern varieties are the most demanding, let's begin with them.

Modern Roses

Before grabbing pruners and heading toward a modern rosebush, fix in your mind's eye what a properly pruned bush should look like. Ideally, modern rosebushes should form a classic urn shape, with canes radiating from the bud union, arching outward and upward around a free center. But the purpose of opening up a bush's center is not simply an aesthetic one. It's also crucial in enabling light to reach the interior growth, thereby aiding the metabolic process for chlorophyll production. Moreover, it greatly improves air circulation at the center of the bush, which helps prevent fungal diseases such as mildew. Blossoms appearing in the center of rosebushes are wasted anyway, because they inevitably tear from being rubbed against other unwanted growth.

What to Take—What to Leave

First, take out what you *know* must come out: all twiggy growth, unhealthy or dead wood, and canes that cross the center of the bush. Split bark is also a sign of wood

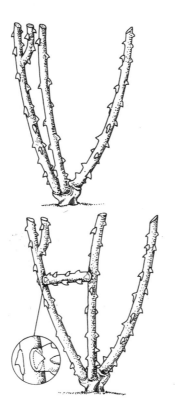

SPREADING CANES *The best canes on a rosebush are sometimes too close to each other. Rather than taking out one of them,* spread them apart *with a length of rose wood from a cane that you've already cut off another bush. Thorns on the canes you want to spread will help to secure the temporary stretcher.*

to leave no wood on a rosebush less thick than a pencil (unless, of course, you're pruning a Miniature rosebush or a diminutive Floribunda whose canes never reach such dimensions). Or, if a bush has proved itself a hardy grower and bloomer, leave more than the customary number of canes. In cases where the best wood comes right from the center and crosses the middle of the bush, leave it alone and prune around it. If you grow more than one bush of a variety, try pruning them differently to see for yourself what suits you best.

If you're a novice at pruning rosebushes, I recommend that you leave all wood on bushes that you're not sure should come out; it can always be taken out later when the growth it develops clarifies whether or not it should remain. But as you gain confidence in pruning techniques, I recommend the opposite — when you have doubts about certain wood's worth, cut it out.

Often the healthiest canes on a rosebush are growing too close to each other and you'll yearn to spread them apart. You can. Decide, within reason, how far apart you'd like to spread them, and cut a section that length from a cane you've already pruned (from that bush or any other). Insert the ends of your spreader into thorns on the two canes you're separating, and don't worry that you might not be able to find it again after foliage develops. No harm will come if the prop lingers until you prune again next year, by which time the canes will be permanently spread apart and it can be removed.

Where to Cut

If you've followed the advice at the beginning of this
section and stripped your rosebushes of all their
foliage at least two weeks before you intend to prune
them, you'll have no difficulty spotting dormant eyes
— they will have swollen and turned red. Look for dormant eyes facing *outward* from the center of the bush,
and make pruning cuts ¼ inch above them.

When I first grew roses, and for many years thereafter, I was assured that proper cuts should be made
precisely at 45° angles, with the downward slope
toward the bush's center. I've since learned that this is
nothing more than needless busywork. I'm still careful
not to make cuts so close to the budding eye that I
might damage it, and I generally avoid flat cuts where
water could collect, but I've long since abandoned the
45° angle requirement.

Frequently, the precise spot at which you yearn to
prune has no budding eye pointed in the right direction. You have two choices for how to treat this aggravat-
ing situation: cut higher than you'd like to, planning to
cut lower later after additional eyes swell; or make what
rosarians call "knobby" cuts, which leave ¼-inch stubs
on last year's stems. Dormant eyes abound just under
the junctures of stems and the canes on which they
grow. Knobby stubs aren't as attractive as clean cuts
above a budding eye, but they'll do the job and impend-
ing foliar growth will soon disguise them anyway.

When whole canes need to be removed from a bush,

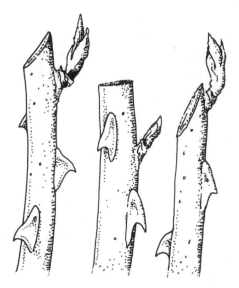

RIGHT AND WRONG CUTS *Before you approach your rosebushes with shears, memorize the perfect pruning cut — the one on the left. Make your cuts on a 45° slope, about ¼ inch above a swelling bud eye. The cut in the middle is too flat and too far removed from its new eye; the one on the right cuts too sharply into new growth.*

they must be cut off at the bud union. Here, too, rosarians quibble over precisely how these cuts should be made. Hard-nosers say that a cut should be made flush with the bud union to keep it looking respectable. Gardeners in search of as much bloom as possible recommend leaving a ¼-inch stub under which a surfeit of dormant eyes lie. Although I'm not a fence sitter in matters such as these, I find myself subscribing to both schools. When a bush is so vigorous that it produces more canes than I can keep up with anyway, I cut flush with the bud union. With less vigorous varieties, I leave that stub and hope my fellow greedy bloom seekers are correct (they are more often than not).

Post-Pruning

Should pruning cuts be sealed with orange shellac, rose paste, tree-wound paint, or aerosol sprays designed for such purposes? It depends on whether or not you live where caneborers exist. If local agricultural agents say not, don't bother.

As for sealing pruning "wounds," that shouldn't be necessary either if you prune at the right time. If, on the other hand, you learn that sealing is required for where you garden, seal only cuts larger than ½ inch in diameter; the rest will heal themselves without help.

Cleaups, however, are vital no matter where you garden. Cuttings, foliage, and twigs that inevitably fall to the ground during pruning are setups for disease. Remove them all and throw them away (never add them to mulch or a compost pile).

Species and Antique Roses

Species and once-blooming roses existed long before humans learned about the necessities for pruning or had tools for the job. Moreover, many of these rose-bushes mature into gargantuan shapes that won't respond to general rules for shaping anyway. Besides, gardeners often choose these house eaters because only such monsters fill large spaces, and pruning may lessen expectations.

Most experts say that if roses in these categories are pruned at all, cuts should be made right after plants flower, so that new growth will be encouraged on which next season's crop will blossom. I agree, but only to a point.

First, I don't prune these roses at all for the first three years I grow them; with some, not until they've been in the ground for five years. The only exception to this seemingly neglectful attitude involves cutting out dead or twiggy growth anytime I spot it, regardless of season.

Once these heirloom roses have grown to the approximate sizes I'm looking for, I begin pruning just after they finish flowering each season. Although I'm still not fixed on general shaping just yet, I remove all wood that either has proved itself unproductive or looks as though it's about to become so. Then I grant only general garden care for the balance of the season and strip foliage late in winter, two weeks before I intend to consider any further pruning.

I realize that this approach is unconventional, that

purists would say all pruning should be completed when flowering is over, but I've found that the abundance of foliage confuses me. Remember that just because these bushes quit flowering, they don't stop growing, and their mass of foliage camouflages those spots where judicious pruning cuts should be made.

Two weeks after foliage has been stripped, dormant eyes swell, turn red, and show me where to properly place my shears. Only then do I seriously prune for shape and size.

Climbing Roses

Climbers repeat their blossoms during each season and should be pruned late in winter. Climbers should also be stripped of foliage before getting pruned, not just to encourage dormant eyes to swell but also because naked canes are easier to shape into classic climbing form.

For their first several years of growth, Climbing roses require little pruning except for the removal of dead or spindly wood. Then, as vigorous varieties mature, more wood (including entire canes) must be sacrificed if plants are expected to remain within bounds.

The controversy over proper pruning for Climbers has nothing to do with main canes or strong laterals growing from them—those should simply be shaped into place with their tips pointed downward to ensure that sap flows throughout their lengths. Argument, however, exists over how to handle the stems that grow from these canes and laterals. They are, after all, the wood from which blossoms are produced. Many experts advocate cutting back all these side shoots to 3-inch lengths. Several rosarians devoted to Climbing roses, though, maintain that side shoots should be cut back to a mere stub on the heftier wood from which they sprout. The rationale behind this latter theory is that abundant dormant eyes exist where stems meet canes and laterals and that leaving short side stems will only encourage weak stems. Again, I side partially with both camps, depending on whether I grow certain Climbers for general garden display or in hopes of producing blossoms for cutting on strong stems — the stronger my quest for sturdy cut flowers, the harder I prune.

Rambling Roses

Rambling roses demand even less pruning than Climbers do, mainly because Ramblers blossom only once each season and their overall shape is generally informal. Because Ramblers are usually rampant growers, however, more of their basal growth must be cut out each season to make room for new. Ramblers that are *Rosa multiflora* hybrids, for instance, are so vigorous that new basal growth is often choked out unless older wood is first sacrificed.

On the opposite extreme, Banksian roses are generally left unpruned altogether, as are certain other specific varieties such as the voracious 'Kiftsgate' and the evergreen 'Félicité et Perpétue'. Just as with modern roses, it's important to know the pruning preferences of individual Rambling roses.

Standards

Roses grown as standards should be pruned when and how their bush counterparts are, except that they must never be allowed to grow as large, or else they become top-heavy. Pruning to outward-facing eyes is paramount since the head of the standard must always be kept in shape and plants must not become lopsided.

If you like weeping roses grown as standards, go easy on pruning, especially of long weeping stems; otherwise, plants become too bushy. With many weeping varieties, only thinning and nipping back of tips are necessary.

After growing roses for 26 years, I've decided that I may never stop experimenting with pruning techniques. Some summers, I decide that my pruning was too lax the previous winter because bushes grow too tall. If I reverse my pruning techniques the following years, I'm often just as annoyed with bushes that grow too close to the ground.

I've also learned that there are many more varieties of roses than I ever thought possible that demand special approaches to pruning. For instance, the most recent additions to rosedom, Landscape roses, require what I call shaping rather than pruning. With certain heirloom roses, only dead wood must be removed; healthy wood seems to know exactly how much to grow and spread. Similarly, I rarely take pruning shears to my China or Alba roses, probably because they grow in considerable shade, which seems to lessen their growth aspirations.

As for Miniature roses, I'm almost ready to prune them the way my British peers do: with hedge clippers. Where my modern rosebushes (especially Hybrid Teas) are concerned, however, I follow to the letter every guideline suggested in this chapter.

Chapter Two

SPRING

ONCE THEIR WINTER DORMANCY PERIOD IS OVER AND rosebushes are ready to grow, they literally have at it. To realize their full potential, they must be helped along and properly coaxed toward the kinds of blooms you're after.

PROMOTING GROWTH

When leaflet sets begin appearing on exposed wood and the danger of frost is past, it's time to unmound bushes. Lots has been going on under the mounds that cover newly planted bushes, and mounding materials must be removed carefully to avoid damage to tender new growth. Slow trickles from a water wand are perfect; clumps of mulch will fall from the canes, causing no damage. If you can't use water, remove the mulch gently with your fingers, not with your whole hand or a tool. New growth can be snapped off with a single false move.

Unmounding gives you the starting materials for mulching, which is simply layering organic material over the soil among the bushes. In all of rose culture, nothing is more practical or more beneficial for rosebushes and the beds in which they grow.

Depending on where you've placed the bud union (as discussed on page 19), you can pile mulch anywhere from 2 to 4 inches thick. I use at least 3 inches of mulch because I plant the bud unions that high above soil level, inasmuch as I grow roses in a mild climate and needn't worry about exposed bud unions being damaged in a hard winter freeze.

Mulching makes three important contributions to rose culture. First, water flows over and through mulch each time you irrigate, slowly releasing nutrients. Mulch is organic and contains valuable nutrients that aren't available all at once. They break down steadily during the growing season, usually reducing their bulk by half each year.

Second, mulch conserves water and provides a blanket of protection from the hard rays of the summer sun. Suggested irrigation schedules call for watering infrequently but deeply. Mulch keeps water under the soil surface.

Finally, mulching controls weeds. If mulch is thick enough, weeds can't easily grow through it. If they do, they're not difficult to remove because the soil under the mulch is friable and their roots haven't anchored themselves.

Feeder roots that develop along larger roots benefit greatly from mulch. They gobble up nutrients as soon as water leaches them from organic mulch materials.

Once you begin mulching, adding dry organic materials in the spring gets easier each year. Mulch becomes more friable, looser, and more amenable to additives.

It's easy to rake a circle around each bush, work in dry organic material, and cover the whole thing with fresh mulching materials for the coming season.

Manure is the single most important material, but remember that it must be aged to keep from burning the bud union and the delicate hairlike young feeder roots just beneath the soil surface. In addition to manure's nutritional value, an even bigger plus is the heat it generates as it decomposes. It warms the soil and boosts bacterial reactions that expedite mulch breakdown.

Chicken is the richest of fowl manures, with a nitrogen count of 1.5 percent. Turkey is a close second, especially if the manure hasn't been mixed with shavings or feathers.

Among animal manures, sheep is richest (1 percent nitrogen), followed by pig or horse (0.6 percent) and cow (0.5 percent). Accuracy compels me to mention that liquid sludge has a nitrogen count higher than all other sources of manure (2.5 percent), but I doubt if you want your garden to smell like a sewer.

Another mulch material I've become sold on is alfalfa. It's readily available, inexpensive, and easy to use. Alfalfa comes either as meal or pelleted. Both work, but make sure there are no additives. I use two 2-pound coffee cans full of it around each bush I either unmound (newly planted bushes) or remulch (existing bushes). After spreading alfalfa around the base of bushes, I cover it with other mulch material. The reason I cover it is that its khaki green color makes alfalfa look like foreign matter compared with other mulch materials, with are usually some shade of brown. If you don't find it unsightly until it, too, turns brown, don't cover it and watch how quickly it breaks down.

As it disintegrates, alfalfa yields an alcohol called tricontanol, to which roses take a particular shine. When it reaches their roots, roses act as though they've been aching for a stiff drink. Some rosarians claim it stimulates new basal breaks (growth from the bud union). I wouldn't care to guarantee such results, but neither would I want to deprive my bushes of an annual alfalfa feed.

Additional mulch materials can be anything organic that breaks down into humus: compost, aged bark, leaf mold, rice hulls, or peat moss. Sawdust and wood shavings are good sources for mulch bulk, but they require nitrogen to complete their own breakdown. If you have an ample supply of shredded wood materials, just add extra nitrogen to help them break down so they won't usurp what's meant for the bushes.

Lawn clippings and pine needles are also good mulch components, but they have a tendency to "mat" if they aren't mixed in well. Water simply runs off the surface of these mats, preventing effective irrigation.

Because I live near a mushroom farm, I use spent mushroom compost for mulch. If I gardened closer to the wine country, I'd use pomace. If I lived in the Midwest, I'd look for buckwheat hulls or ground corncobs. In Louisiana, I'd go after bagasse. All are perfectly wonderful sources of nutritional mulch, and one may be only marginally better than another — it's their availability that matters. Look around your local area for sources of nutritious, inexpensive mulch.

If you persist in not mulching, you must do something each spring to loosen soil before you apply dry fertilizers around the base of the bushes. Soil with no blanket of mulch becomes hard and compacted, and fertilizers can't be scratched in. Compressed soil also inhibits the development of feeder roots.

A NEED FOR DISCIPLINE

In the giddiness of spring, well-grown rosebushes of modern hybrids optimistically sprout more new growth than they can realistically support. The remedy, "nipping in the bud," requires no equipment other than your fingers. Finger pruning also assures that gardeners get the precise blooms they had in mind.

Tender rose growth is so supple that you won't need tools to remove it; just rub it off with your thumbs. Start at the tops of bushes by inspecting new growth on laterals (rose wood emanating from main canes). Laterals often require discipline because they're capable of sprouting buds along their entire lengths. Begin rubbing out new growth by sacrificing anything growing toward the center of the bush. Ultimately, owing to limited space and poor air circulation, interior growth produces shredded blossoms or diseased foliage.

Next, think carefully about how many sprouts you leave per lateral. If you worry that you're leaving too many and yearn for long-stemmed beauties, rub more

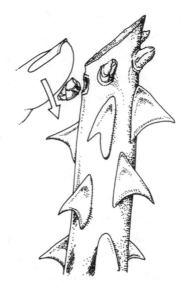

FINGER PRUNING *Your hands are all you need to tame spring's frisky rosebushes. Healthy plants become optimistic in their hopes of supporting growth. Remove excess growth by rubbing off some buds with your thumb.*

off. "You have to take to get," a teacher of mine used to say.

Apply identical thumb rubbing to the heart of the rosebush, the bud union — the base of rosebushes made globular from the graft of a modern hybrid onto vigorous rootstock. It is from this landmark that important new growth stems.

By spring, the average modern rosebush has been pruned of all but six or seven main canes (vigorous Grandifloras may be left with more and diminutive Floribundas with fewer). Then, warmed by spring sun, bud unions swell and sprout multiple red nubs that develop into new canes. If you're after long-stemmed, large flowers, you have no choice but to curtail exuberance.

Bud unions of healthy rosebushes may well sprout a dozen new canes during the first month of spring. That's too many; rub half of them off. First, rub off any budding eyes growing in the middle of the bush. Next, try to anticipate whether those you leave will interfere with others as they grow. If you think that everything won't be able to coexist, rub off more.

COMBATING DISEASES AND PESTS — BIOLOGICALLY OR CHEMICALLY?

In the late 19th century, southern California citrus growers were plagued with an infestation of cottony-cushion scale that jeopardized whole groves. Then, in 1989, when researchers found that the red-and-black vedalia beetle is this deadly scale's natural predator, the insects were imported in droves to graze on infested growing fields. Ever since this remarkable alliance, gardeners have split into two camps—those who insist on a strictly organic approach to their horticultural pursuits and those who allow chemicals to play a part.

Integrated Pest Management

Today biological approaches to pest control are commonly known as integrated pest management (IPM). At its simplest, IPM rests with hybridizers who modify plants genetically to increase their resistance to disease and insect attacks. The latest introductions to rosedom, Landscape roses, are markedly more disease resistant than their predecessors were, and hybridizers are taking note of the buying public's embrace of these relatively carefree plants.

At a more complex level, certain IPM programs utilize microbial insecticides to cause fatal diseases in specific pests. The very first microbial insecticide, *Bacillus thuringiensis* (Bt), for instance, was a boon for plants affected by caterpillar infestations. Bt is just as effective today as it was when it was developed in the 1940s.

Most fascinating of all are the IPM programs that employ insect sex pheromones to confuse and frustrate mating in crop-destroying moths (notably, whiteflies). These clever "semiochemicals" (a term coined by IPM'ers to denote chemicals that have no toxic side effects) met with unanimous approval when they were developed in the 1970s and 1980s.

Motivation runs high among researchers to discover new biological approaches to pest management that work, especially when existing chemical insecticides don't. Devastations of a wide range of hundreds of millions of southern California crops (mostly cotton and vegetables) by strain B of the sweet-potato whitefly, for instance, continue to this day despite widespread use of chemical insecticides. Does a natural predatory insect exist to combat the nasty whitefly? Can a semiochemical be developed that will scramble their sexual mating patterns? Researchers are hard at work seeking answers to these questions.

Another compelling reason for discovering biological control for pests is that almost every economically important insect and mite pest to horticulture has become resistant to at least one pesticide; many to several.

Chemicals

Despite the environmental impact of chemical sprays, gardeners have elected to use them for several reasons. First, the effect of the right chemical for the immediate job is often dramatic. Second, chemical pesticides are easily obtained and, for the most part, inexpensive. Third, chemical pesticides have not only allowed farmers to extend their growing seasons but have also made the cultivation of certain crops possible in less than ideal circumstances. Finally, because they kill surface bacteria, pesticides have been found beneficial after harvest, helping to maintain product quality and extend shelf life.

Because chemical pesticides have been such a heated subject among horticulturists for so long, it seems as though they've been with us forever; they haven't. Arsenic- and lead-based materials existed in the late 19th century, but synthetic insecticides weren't developed until World War II. Once these formulations caught on, new synthetic products were introduced at an alarming rate, including ones so potentially harmful to the environment that they've since been yanked from commerce. When naturalists put their feet down regarding the environmental impact of chemical pesticides, favor again turned toward IPM.

Although I'll soon explain my particular stand on this biological versus chemical debate, in fairness I must first address the actual hazardous implications of chemicals in the garden. Once you fully understand the warnings printed on the labels of chemical sprays and follow directions to the letter, you'll learn that many products aren't nearly as dangerous as you may imagine.

As part of their pesticide registration regulations, most states require manufacturers of chemical materials to clearly label their products in one of three toxicity categories, depending on their LD50 — a term you must be thoroughly familiar with if you have any intention of employing garden chemicals.

LD50, usually listed as oral (the amount that must be swallowed) but sometimes quoted as dermal (the amount that must be absorbed by the skin), is an expression of the lethal dose in milligrams per kilogram of body weight that kills 50 percent of laboratory test animals.

Chemicals with an LD50 between 0 and 49 constitute Toxicity Category I, with labels marked "danger" or "poison" (usually accompanied by a skull and crossbones). I believe these chemicals have no place in the garden, ever.

Toxic chemicals in Category II have an LD50 somewhere between 50 and 499 and are considered moderately toxic, hence the "warning" label. The probable lethal dose for a 150-pound man is between 1 teaspoon and 1 ounce.

Category III have "caution" printed on their labels because LD50 rates between 500 and 4,999 mean that the average man's oral lethal dose is between 1 ounce and 1 pint.

For perspective on the relative toxicity of common items, you should know some LD50 ratings (the lower the LD50, the more toxic the chemical). Nicotine is 53; caffeine, 192; aspirin, 1,240; and table salt, 3,320. Understand also that the probable lethal dosages of garden chemicals refer only to concentrations of the active ingredient of the product, not the commercially available diluted form—to croak, you'd have to drink even more of that. Still, you don't want even a headache, so if you decide to admit moderate- to low-toxicity chemicals into your garden, take precautions.

First, to avoid any possibility of irritation, cover all body parts and wear goggles and rubber gloves, including when mixing spray materials. Never use a solution stronger than the manufacturer suggests, don't remove chemicals from their labeled containers, and keep materials stored far from any child's reach.

When you must spray, use the safest material for the job. I used to rely on agricultural soaps, but I found that they were effective for only three to four days and left an unappealing soapy residue. Then I found a water-based miticide with an LD50 rating of 5,150 (almost nontoxic) that lays waste to diabrotica—those nasty gnawing insects that look like green ladybugs but are anything but beneficial.

I'd truly like to abandon chemicals altogether and would if I could. Recently, I attended a seminar where a rosarian spoke of his IPM program, mainly about how it pleased him. He cheerfully told about his swarms of beneficial ladybugs, praying mantises, and lacewings—a means of pest control that sounded ever so much more relaxing than the rigors of a regular spray program. I envied him. On the flight home, I actually considered another shot at IPM. I soon changed my mind.

A sudden heat spell, for which northern California is famous, seemingly summoned every thrip (a minute sucking insect) in Sonoma County. Thrips are like that. They give no evidence of mounting an army, but unexpected intense heat musters them in formidable swarms. Although they have a preference for white and pastel roses, in time thrips invade even deeply colored roses. Their presence is telltale — succulent immature petals disfigured with ugly brown splotches created by microscopic gnawers.

I realized that no number of ladybugs, praying mantises, lacewings, or whatever predator hungers for young thrips could have possibly kept this infestation in check. It was out of control and I sprayed (blossoms only) the next morning.

As a grower of garden roses for their cut blossoms, I've learned that the floral trade doesn't know the difference between mildew, blackspot, or rust. Similarly, they can't tell the difference between aphid, thrips, or spider mite damage to roses. But they do know when something is wrong and they steer clear of garden roses on those market days. So, I spray regularly, but always with the safest solution possible for the job. Even so, secretly, I still envy the IPM'ers. And, because my chemical program is modest (and as nontoxic as I can make it), ladybugs still frequent my garden. I'm certain they at least handle the aphids. For all I know, they (or my modest flock of praying mantises) keep the famous rose midge in check, too, since I've never (thank goodness) seen one.

Chapter
Three

SUMMER

SUMMER IS ALMOST EVERY GARDENER'S FAVORITE SEA-
son. Depending on how early it occurs, how long it
lasts, and which roses are cultivated, summer blossoms
seem nonstop.

HARVESTING BLOSSOMS

This chapter tells how to harvest rose blossoms properly, how to get the biggest bang for the buck from fertilizers, how to achieve the rose "look" you want, and
how to keep rose blossoms alive longer than you ever
thought possible. First, how to harvest roses properly.

When to Cut

Rosebushes begin drawing in moisture with the first
hint of approaching dusk, and they hold it until the
morning light gets strong. Since you want blooms with
as much moisture in them as possible, cut either
before midmorning or after midafternoon.

We cut all roses in the late afternoon at Garden
Valley Ranch simply because it's more convenient than
in the morning. When summer days are long, we begin
cutting after 5:00 P.M., even though we face thousands
of cuts each evening. As the days grow shorter, particu-

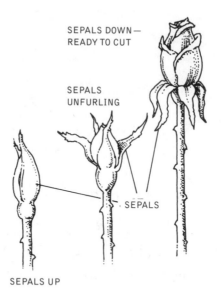

SEPALS DOWN —
READY TO CUT

SEPALS
UNFURLING

SEPALS

SEPALS UP

SEPALS *Sepals grow like leaves from just under the rosebud to cover its tip. Sepals unfurl and arch downward to signal that a bloom is ready to be cut. If the sepals aren't down, or if the bud isn't "cracked," the bloom won't open after it is cut from the bush.*

larly once daylight savings time ends, we start earlier. What you most want to avoid is cutting during midday, especially during hot weather, when blooms are limp. The hour of the day at which roses are cut from their bushes is actually far less important than the conditioning you give the roses after you cut them.

Stage to Cut

Blooms of each rose variety must reach a certain stage of openness before they can be cut if they're expected to open farther or fully. The safest general rule to follow is: Wait until the sepals are down.

Sepals are those leaflike coverings of rosebuds. They are easily as individual as foliage, and some are downright decorative. Most are the same color green as the foliage of the bush on which they grow, but some have red serrated edges. Sepals grow from just under the bud and join their tips over it, completely surrounding the swelling bloom. As buds develop, so do sepals, until they can contain the bloom no longer. They then begin to unfurl one by one. On some roses, this unfurling is dramatic, as the sepals arch gracefully backward in brackets that seem to lend architectural support to the coming bloom.

When the sepals are down and the bud has started to open ("cracked" in florist's lingo), the bloom can be cut. How far the bud must have opened before the cut is made varies from one kind of rose to another. Those varieties with fewer petals don't have to be open very far before they can be cut. As petalage increases, so

CUT AT 45° TO
CENTER OF BUSH

WHERE TO CUT   *What you take from a bush vitally affects what you leave behind.* **Properly cut blooms** *leave at least two sets of five leaflets on the stem from which they grew. The five-leaflet set above which the cut is made should point outward from the center of the bush — the direction in which your new rose will grow.*

does the necessary degree of bud openness. Heavily petaled roses must show a row of petals in addition to a well-defined center around which other rows of petals are developing. If you cut them before this stage, they won't finish opening. With certain other blooms, surprisingly, the sepals needn't be down at all before you cut.

Observe the sepals closely as you cut blooms, and you'll quickly become attuned to these variations.

Where to Cut

If you commit to memory only one fact regarding harvesting rose blossoms, make it this one: Where you cut a bloom is vital to the bush it is leaving. To cut blooms at the right place, you must familiarize yourself with patterns of rose foliage.

Rose leaves usually come in sets of three, five, and seven, increasing in number from the bloom downward to where its stem begins. Heirloom or particularly healthy modern varieties produce nine or more leaflet sets. For this lesson, remember only *five*.

Properly cut blooms leave at least two sets of five leaflets on the stem from which they're cut. More would be nice, especially if a newly planted bush can't yet afford to give up long stems.

Selecting the precise five-leaflet set above which to make the cut is equally important: it must point outward from the center of the bush. At the very base of leaflets and the stems from which they grow is an axil that reveals a swelling red bud. For modern hybrids, this dormant eye is the beginning of the rose that will bloom some six to eight weeks after you make the cut.

Once you've selected which five-leaflet set to cut above, make the cut ¼ inch above the axil at an angle (45° is model) with the downward slope toward the center of the bush.

Cut for the Bush or the Bloom?

If you cut with the bush in mind, stem length must sometimes be sacrificed. Ideally, the bush must keep a certain shape, growing outward so that the stems don't bang into each other and don't compete for light. If no convenient five-leaflet set is facing away from the bush, or if the stem is on the short side of average and what you really want would require taking everything, then you must cut shorter stems. If a bush is very young or acting poorly, then it is wise to cut shorter stems — these bushes need all the help they can get, including the food extra leaves may generate. You'll feel better about your short-stemmed roses if you dwell on the good that what you leave behind does for the rest of the bush.

If you must, you can cut for the bloom anyway if you want to enter a rose show and know you'll need all available stem length to have a prayer for a blue ribbon. Or you may have just purchased a new crystal bud vase that will show off the stem and foliage of your prize blooms. In those cases, I say go for it. Just acknowledge that you're being piggy and resolve not to do it more often than necessary, or bushes will wither from your greed.

If you've been told not to cut blooms from first-year bushes, pay no attention to such silly advice. Even though you dutifully leave a bloom on a bush because you've been warned that new bushes need all the foliage possible to generate food, you must cut it off anyway when it begins to drop its petals. Otherwise, the bush thinks it's time to "go to seed" and will expend energy developing the hip, a rose's seedpod. What can possibly be gained by leaving the bloom on the bush for these extra few days, a week at most? If you plant roses for garden display, that's one thing; leave the blooms and gain the few extra days' work from their foliage. But if you want blooms in the house, take them. Just be kind when you know you must.

Keep in mind that a nascent rose at the site just cut from can have a stem only as thick as that of the bloom just harvested. If you cut from twigs, you'll get more twigs. If you're going to be disappointed with the stem you're about to cut and see that only spindly growth will come from where the cut is made, cut back farther.

A GOURMET DIET FOR ROSES

In my 26 years of growing roses, not a summer has passed without gardening friends calling to report that something is terribly amiss with their roses.

"I can't imagine what's gone wrong," they lament.

"The first flowers were magnificent and there were armloads of them, but now there's not a handful of roses in the whole garden, and the bushes look exhausted."

When I ask when the plants were last fed, I'm regaled with the formula used in early spring, which often sounds delicious, horticulturally speaking—bonemeal, hoof and horn, and a generous blanket of organic mulch that includes aged manure.

As patiently as I can, I explain to my friends that the spring banquet was indeed grand and point out that the roses obviously appreciated it, as shown by that magnificent spring flush of bloom.

"If you want more blossoms," I assure, "you've got to feed again, and again after that—right through October. And you can't keep feeding them the same meals; roses appreciate certain food at precise times."

After serving as a rose dietitian for more than two decades, I'm ready to offer a feeding program for established rosebushes and shrubs, but *only* for where I garden—USDA Zone 9 (specifically, Zone 9a). For a program closer to where you garden, refer to chapter 7.

First, some caveats to my rose diet:

For new plants, sickly plants, and Miniatures, cut all fertilizer dosages in half.

Make sure rosebushes have been well mulched with organic materials such as compost, wood shavings, and aged manure (chicken and turkey are best, but steer will do); preferably, use a combination. Mulch is not only nutritious on its own, it also provides the perfect medium over which concentrated fertilizers should be applied.

Learn the significance of N,P,K—the three most essential elements in soil fertility (always expressed in three consecutive numbers on labels of all fertilizers, granular or liquid).

N is the chemical symbol for nitrogen, which not only is a growth stimulant but also is essential in the formation of chlorophyll and as a regulator in plants' uptake of other nutrients.

P stands for phosphorus, which stimulates root formation and flowering. Phosphorus also hastens plant maturation by converting starches to sugars.

K signifies potassium (potash), which is important for the development of stems and leaves; it also increases plants' disease resistance and hardiness.

Understand that I'm a pig when it comes to rose blossoms; I want as many as possible from as early in April as I can bring them to bloom until as late in November as feasible before rains and chilling temperatures take the upper hand. Consequently, I'm a heavy feeder.

As far as I'm concerned, winter is officially over on the last day of February, after which I'm free to put pressure on my roses to start performing. I begin the first week of March, in full knowledge that I'm rushing the season and that an unseasonal late frost (not unheard of in California's Sonoma County) may nip my efforts in the bud.

My suggested feeding schedule is for modern roses

only—those that repeat their bloom. I use the identical program for my once-blooming heirloom roses, but only through June.

Here is my diet for two feedings each month.

March and April

First week: Feed with a granular, water-soluble fertilizer concentrated in nitrogen—31-0-0 (a slow-release formula), 33.5-0-0 (ammonium nitrate), 21-0-0 (ammonium sulfate), or 15.5-0-0 (calcium nitrate).

Always apply granular fertilizers in accordance with their manufacturers' suggested rate and around the drip line of rosebushes—that imaginary circle that would exist if bushes were dripping from being soaking wet. Granular fertilizers can be spread directly on the ground (as opposed to being diluted first) as long as they're watered in well.

Third week: Feed with ¾ cup Epsom salts per bush (again, water in well). Epsom salts (properly, magnesium sulfate) activates plant enzymes essential to the growth process. In rosedom, that translates to vibrant red growth emanating from the base of rosebushes.

If you have only a few rosebushes, buy Epsom salts at the corner grocery or pharmacy; it's inexpensive. If you have more than a dozen roses, you might want to invest in a bag of industrial-grade magnesium sulfate—even cheaper. Although it doesn't meet the purification standards of pharmaceutical-quality Epsom salts, roses won't know the difference.

May and June

First week: Feed with a granular, water-soluble, balanced fertilizer such as 10-10-10, 15-15-15, or 20-20-20 (whichever is on sale). During the bulk of the rose season, rosebushes need equal amounts of nitrogen, phosphorus, and potassium.

Third week: Feed with ½ cup Epsom salts per bush.

July and August

First week: Feed with granular, water soluble, balanced fertilizers such as 10-10-10, 15-15-15, or 20-20-20 (more likely on sale now than earlier).

Third week: Feed with fish emulsion at the rate of 1 tablespoon per gallon. Dissolve the emulsion in water and pour 2 gallons of the mixture around the drip line of each bush.

September and October

First week: Feed with a granular water-soluble 0-10-10. This mixture is a favorite among garden plants—not just roses—because it encourages no new growth (the 0 signifies an absence of nitrogen), but the concentrations of phosphorus and potassium assure continued bloom and wood hardened in preparation for winter pruning.

Third week: Feed with fish emulsion at the same rate prescribed for July and August.

Don't apply fertilizers after Halloween. Even when seasons are extended, as they have been recently (I've been cutting knockout roses in December), the soil around properly fed rosebushes holds plenty of nutrients to bring those last rose blossoms to buxom maturity.

There are other foods that roses find tasty, of course. Chelated iron, for instance, is considered by many rosarians basic to a well-balanced diet. Not only is chelated iron a quick greener-upper, it's touted to be a fine soil penetrant. There are also certain trace elements such as zinc, boron, and manganese that sometimes get depleted from garden soil. (Only a soil test will tell for certain if this has happened, in which case soil should be punched up with the appropriate element.)

If your roses still seem hungry despite this hefty diet, you can fertilize to your heart's content with additional shots of fish emulsion, which is not only thoroughly organic but is also incapable of burning plants.

Still, I'm willing to bet that gardeners near me won't have to supplement the feeding schedule suggested here, no matter how piggy they or their roses are.

DISBUDDING FOR THE LOOK YOU SEEK

Next to pruning, disbudding roses frightens gardening neophytes more than any other aspect of good rose culture. Once the principles are grasped, however, disbudding is a snap — as mindless as weeding.

Disbudding is nothing more than deciding whether you want one-to-a-stem blooms or sprays of blossoms on a single stem, depending on your own preference

DISBUDDING   *Disbud for the bloom formation that suits both you and the varieties you grow. If blooms are prettiest one to a stem, pinch out the side buds as soon as you see them developing and direct all energy to the terminal (main) bud. If a bush likes to bloom in sprays, and you too like masses of blooms, pinch out the terminal bud, which otherwise will open before everything else.*

or on what is generally considered most beautiful for each rose variety you grow.

One-to-a-stem disbudding is meant mostly for modern Hybrid Teas, many of which produce only one bud per stem anyway, as if they already know that that's how they're prettiest. Others produce one large bud at the end of a stem and small buds, usually two, just beneath.

The large bud, properly called the terminal bud, is the one you want to leave. Side buds should be removed when they get to be about ¼ inch long, when they can be grasped at the base and snapped off close to the stem without leaving a stub. When making these snaps, be certain to hold onto the terminal bud so that you don't end up with it in the palm of your hand.

Side buds can be left, of course, to develop into blooms themselves. They'll always defer to the terminal bud, however, and open only after it has finished blooming. If you imagine that side buds will open in a vase after the terminal bud has finished blossoming, forget it; most won't. If you like the looks of side buds anyway, leave them.

Disbudding for sprays is the exact opposite of disbudding for one-to-a-stem blooms. For sprays of blossoms, terminal buds are removed and side buds are left to develop. Terminal buds left in sprays will develop fully and open before side buds have a chance at maturity. If varieties look better in sprays, remove terminal buds and channel energy into the spray formation. What's more, do it early so that no scar is left.

There's no problem deciding how to handle a stem

with three buds; simply remove the smaller two. Nor is there a problem with stems holding five buds; remove the largest one. The problem is when you encounter a stem with four buds. One-to-a-stem or spray? Your call.

Please don't imagine that disbudding is necessary; it isn't. Gardeners disbud only if they plan to exhibit their blossoms for competition or if they want to enjoy blooms as cut flowers without unsightly scars from bud removal. Otherwise, many rose varieties could drive you mad if you intend to keep up with their disbudding needs. Finally, if you decide to cut a spray of blossoms whose terminal bud should have been removed as soon as it was spotted, maturing side buds will eventually camouflage the scar of its removal.

If you spot a terminal bud in blossom and want to enjoy it indoors, cut it off and use a low-necked opaque container to hold it. Assuming you keep enough water in the diminutive vase, even blossoms with short stems will reach maturity and open fully.

Few gardeners, even adamant rosarians, disbud blossoms from dowager roses. Because the majority of rose varieties in this group blossom only once each year, when they bloom, they literally have at it.

The attitude you should take with heirloom roses is to enjoy all that their shrubs have to offer. Don't disbud them. Elect instead to delight in a smashing show in the landscape. Besides, antique roses are admired mostly for the form their mature blossoms assume. Cut early, maturity is never achieved; left on the bush, flowers age to perfection. Just before petals fall, blossoms should be deadheaded to prepare for the grander show yet to come.

BLEACH — THE TICKET TO EXTENDED VASE LIFE

It galls me to think of the money I've wasted on floral preservatives. At a recent convention of flower growers, I heard a presentation on proper conditioning of garden rose blossoms. The researcher had certainly done his homework. Using a clinical approach, he had divided ten dozen roses into buckets containing various amounts of bleach and floral preservatives — one bucket had neither, some had only bleach, some only preservatives, and some both (in varying strengths).

"Results are conclusive," he declared. "Freshly cut roses can't take up preservatives. Bleach is all they can handle."

For another week, I pretended I had heard wrong. Of course, preservatives help to make rose blossoms reach their finest stage of beauty! Where were nutrients to come from? Surely not bleach. Then I got a copy of the transcript of the meeting and saw those blasted words in print. I didn't rest until I had replicated his study.

My results were a carbon copy of those I had heard reported two weeks earlier. After pondering the results, I have a theory — not nearly so scientific as the study itself, but one that makes sense to me.

Flowers go into shock when they're amputated from

CUTTING STEMS UNDER WATER *Stems cut from bushes draw air that bubbles its way to the blooms, causing them to nod in premature death. To avoid air bubbles,* recut *stems—dip their tips into a bowl of water and cut off ¼ inch of stem. This process will ensure a longer life for all your blooms, not just your roses.*

their mother plant. Unless stems are submerged in water soon after they're cut, flowers wilt, shrivel, and soon die. Water alone, however, won't ensure that blossoms reach full maturity.

Roses, camellias, azaleas, and other woody-stemmed flowers take so long to mature on plants that their stems are coated with bacteria by the time they are harvested. Unless a biocide such as bleach is added to water, bacteria will collect around the tips of fresh cuts and prevent stems from taking a proper drink.

Further, freshly cut stems apparently can't be expected to absorb preservatives. My cut-flower guru and I proved that with our experiments; stems submerged in water that contained preservatives also clogged — not with bacteria, but with the preservatives themselves.

Lest you imagine that you should toss out all of the floral preservatives you have on hand, you should know about a second experiment.

Using roses identical to those in the first study, the original researcher and I tested again with preservatives, this time by adding them to a second solution of water. Results were once more conclusive — after soaking for 24 hours in water to which bleach alone has been added, roses benefit from preservatives.

Going back to my theoretical interpretation of these findings, I believe that while roses can't absorb preservatives when freshly cut, they can after they've recovered from shock. Not only that, without the nutrition supplied by preservatives (sugar is a fine substitute), cut roses won't mature properly. With the punch preservatives afford, blooms actually keep growing, even in a vase.

In practical terms for properly conditioning roses and other pithy-stemmed flowers, here's how these data translate to the longest possible vase life:

After you cut roses from the garden, under water recut ¼ inch off their stems and put them in a container with hot water (stems absorb hot water more quickly than cold) to which bleach (household bleach works perfectly well) has been added (½ ounce per 8 gallons, or $\frac{1}{64}$ ounce — two to three drops — per quart). In the darkest, coolest spot you can find, store the container until the water comes to room temperature (preferably, overnight).

Then recut stems under water again and arrange them in containers holding water fortified with ¾ teaspoon (per quart) of floral preservative.

Although the original research didn't address the issue of adding bleach to the second (or subsequent) batches of water and I haven't conducted a third study, I always use a couple of drops of it anyway.

In fact, I'm so sold on bleach that I use it with hollow-stemmed cut flowers, too. Can't hurt.

Chapter
Four

FALL

IN ROSEDOM, FALL IS THE EASIEST SEASON OF THE year. With plenty of time for armchair gardening, tempting catalogs get perused with an eye toward next season's roses. As for the roses themselves, work on the plants is virtually over the minute the possibility of low winter temperatures exists. If you've followed the advice of several of my zonal rose gurus (see chapter 7), you've probably given your roses a meal of 0-10-10, a fertilizer formulated, weather permitting, to bring to maturity all blossoms on bushes. That last meal just about spells the final work for the year. From here on, simply enjoy what Mother Nature doles your way.

As long as it doesn't rain, rose blossoms will withstand cold; some varieties even stand up to below freezing temperatures. Rain, however, is another matter and will discolor blossoms, maybe even induce botrytis (a fungal disease that rots petals from their bases upward). The final blow, of course, occurs when rain is accompanied by cold temperatures. Once that combination deadly to garden roses occurs, head indoors and plan for next season.

ARMCHAIR GARDENING: ORDERING NEXT YEAR'S CROP

You may as well begin with the right roses if you intend to give them the care they deserve and to reap for yourself the many pleasures of good rose culture. What you buy depends on where you garden, how much space you have, whether you want roses for the landscape or as cut flowers or both, and, of course, on what you like.

Unless you're an ardent pioneer, go with proven performers. There are two good ways to identify stellar roses. First, the American Rose Society (hereafter called simply ARS) identifies star performers in its annual publication, *Handbook for Selecting Roses*.

Here's how the system works. First, roses are classified as to type, in 57 categories ranging from the first roses known to humans (species roses) to the hottest new hybrids in commerce. Next, there is color classification, which divides roses into 18 categories, including blends and shadings of major colors. Finally, there is the national rating, representing the collective opinions of voting rosarians from all districts in the United States. Granted, certain varieties do better or poorer in various sections of the country, but those regional differences have a way of evening out in the final analysis, generally making the average score a safe one.

Each year participating ARS members rank new introductions and thereafter reconsider merit with periodic reviews called "Roses in Review." The final results, a numerical assignment on a scale of 1.0 to

10.0 for each variety, are published annually in the *Handbook for Selecting Roses*. The one score represents an average of values for garden bloom performance and for exhibition value. The national ratings are:

> 10.0 *Perfect*
> 9.9–9.0 *Outstanding*
> 8.9–8.0 *Excellent*
> 7.9–7.0 *Good*
> 6.9–6.0 *Fair*
> 5.9 and lower *Of questionable value*

The *Handbook* can be had by sending $5 (which includes postage) and a self-addressed, business-size envelope to the American Rose Society, Box 30000, Shreveport, LA 71130-0030.

The second way to discover which roses to grow is to join the ARS and your local ARS chapter. If you are even casually interested in roses, I strongly suggest that you consider doing so. Annual dues for ARS membership are $32 ($30 for senior citizens). Local membership dues vary greatly.

There is no substitute for getting a handle on local rose talent (both rose varieties themselves and the people who grow them well) and no easier way to do so than through the ARS. Anyone, member or not, can write to the society and ask for the names of consulting rosarians in his or her area. The roster is free. Advantages of ARS membership include receiving regional publications, a national monthly magazine, and the yearly *Rose Annual.*

If you decide to contact your locally appointed rosarians, have some specific questions in mind. You might be after strong rose fragrance, specific colors, high bloom yield, varieties with few thorns, blooms that close at night, or long-lasting cut blossoms. Seeking local advice also helps you avoid choosing varieties of roses that perform poorly in your region.

Bareroot or in a Container?

I bought no bareroot bushes the first year I grew roses. I started too late in the season to buy them, and I had an uneasy feeling about them besides. Handling fist-fuls of sticks just didn't feel comfortable, and I wasn't optimistic that they'd amount to much. I got over my worries, and so will you when you come to appreciate three advantages of bareroot plants.

First, aiming at your practical side, they're cheaper. Bushes in containers cost more than bareroot plants, not just because of the containers themselves but also because of the labor required to put the bushes in them. Second, container roses have to readjust to the soil in their new home after they either are removed from their cans or grow through their biodegradable containers. Bareroots, however, can be planted exactly as you want them to grow. Finally, and most important, at no time of the year are varieties as available as during bareroot season (the time when roses are naturally dormant). Be aware, though, that bareroot season varies widely by zone. The rule of thumb is that the higher the USDA zone number, the earlier the season may begin. In Hawaii and California, for instance, we request bareroots as soon as they're available — usually November. Few suppliers will ship bareroot bushes after early April, however, because dormancy can't be held any longer even with the best of cold storage facilities.

You should also bear in mind that new introductions to rosedom sell out quickly, as do proven performers. If you expect to delay ordering bareroot plants and rely on what nurserymen pot up, you're likely to plant only alternate choices.

Rose Suppliers and Their Catalogs

Nurseries and mail-order houses for roses have lots to recommend them — they offer wide selections of rose varieties and efficient shipping methods that assure healthy plants, timely in their arrival. If shipment is unduly delayed or stock is beneath your expectations, most suppliers will replace plants with no questions asked.

Catalogs (especially color ones), however, can be misleading. They sometimes suggest that certain varieties have highly desirable qualities (powerful fragrance, extreme vigor, disease resistance, bountiful bloom), which, if you grow them, you're apt to find they don't have at all. Color photos can make a variety look better than it looks in real life or lend a hue to which it can never truly aspire. Others are pitifully unjust and either rob the poorly depicted variety of its true color or fail to capture its exquisite form. Order catalogs anyway. Most are free, and you can compare them for varieties on which suppliers agree. Above all, learn catalog lingo. "Tender" means the variety is likely to freeze. "Disease prone" suggests rampant mildew. "Powerfully fragrant" describes roses from which you can safely count on scent. "Light fragrance" may very well mean no discernible aroma.

Visit your closest municipal rose garden. There you can see numerous varieties and decide for yourself which appeal to you and which obviously perform well. Also, you can usually preview new introductions not yet rated by the ARS.

Grading

Rosebushes being marketed by growers and suppliers must be graded according to specific standards. For the most part, you shouldn't consider buying anything but grade 1 — bushes that have been field grown for at least two years. More precisely, plants must have at least three vigorous canes (main stems), each of a specific length (longer for heirloom varieties and aggressive modern hybrids; shorter for Floribundas and Miniatures). Grade 1½ denotes fewer canes, but it may be acceptable if no grade 1's are available. Never buy grade 2. Most suppliers sell only grade 1 to the general public, so you'll never have to make the choice between 1 and 1½ unless you are notified that only grade 1½ is available, at a lower cost.

As for those wax-coated, packaged rose plants available in supermarkets, I can't honestly tell you never to buy them, but I'm tempted to. First, one rarely receives a guarantee as to variety or replacement (such assurances are routine from suppliers). More important, the waxing, while theoretically a sound procedure that permits prolonged and safe storage, is actually problem ridden. Plants that are wax coated tend to dry out, and later growth and root development can be inhibited. Finally, the sun is supposed to melt the wax, but you may very well be planting long before heat from sunlight is anywhere near intense enough to melt wax.

When to Order

When you place an order for bareroot rosebushes, you get to choose the delivery date. It can be ASAP or at the tag end of the shipping season, depending on when you think you'll feel like planting and when it's safe to do so where you garden.

There's a move afoot among rosarians for fall planting, based on the theory that roots put in the ground in November have a chance to settle in before they have to start growing in the spring. I march with this group, but I can afford to because I grow roses in USDA Zone 9, where winters are never severe enough to damage new, tender growth that's bound to appear soon after I stick a bush in the ground. If I lived where temperatures plummet regularly, I'd ask for rosebushes to be shipped after the danger of hard frosts is past.

Regardless of when you want plants to arrive, order them early to make sure you don't end up with substitutions, especially if a variety you like is "in short supply" or a catalog specifies "one per customer, please." If you dillydally, you'll either get your money refunded or, at best, be placed on next year's waiting list.

TESTING SOIL — MANDATORY, NOT OPTIONAL

I seriously considered omitting a section on soil tests, having been accused of haranguing gardeners over their importance, but after corresponding with my gurus whose experiences are shared in chapter 7, I was reminded that I'm not the only rosarian who swears by pH. If you're the least bit serious about growing stellar roses, testing soil is mandatory, and fall is the ideal time to collect soil samples and to set garden soil's pH straight.

The pH scale runs from 0 to 14 to distinguish the relative degrees of acidity or alkalinity of a soil. The lower the pH, the more acidic the soil; high numbers signify alkaline conditions. Soils with a pH of 7 are neutral, precisely where most agricultural crops like to grow. Plants that blossom, however, are finicky about the pH of the soil in which they're expected to flower.

Rhododendrons, for instance, like acidic soils, but only to a point. If the pH drops below 5, plants will vegetate beautifully but won't blossom. Rhododendrons in soils with a pH higher than 7 will bloom, but flowers will be stunted or aborted before maturity. On the other hand, lavender won't budge unless the soil is alkaline. Roses prefer soil with a pH slightly below neutral — 6.5 is considered ideal.

Fall

When I first decided to get acquainted with my soil's pH, I thought I should test it myself. I bought two kits—one with a tiny gauge and another with fibrous papers on which I spooned bits of moist soil, then watched for color clues. I got different gauge readings every time I sampled the same soil and my test papers never turned identical colors.

I turned to the Yellow Pages.

Experts who test soil samples are listed under Laboratories—Testing. They send foolproof instructions for collecting samples. To get an idea of a garden's overall pH, soil is gathered from several sites, then mixed inside a plastic storage bag and mailed for testing.

Reports from soil laboratories don't merely assign numerical pH values, they tell you what to do about them. If, for instance, that site you've set your eyes on for roses proves to be so acidic that only rhododendrons or azaleas would be happy growing there, you might be told to add limestone to make it more alkaline. Conversely, if the site of your rose dreams is too alkaline, you might be instructed to give it an acidic boost of soil sulfur.

Besides revealing pH, soil analyses tell about soil salinity (whether you're under- or overfertilizing) and soil fertility (whether nutrients are available) as well as how to correct for any deficiencies. If you fertilize with an irrigation system, a report on soils taken from several areas will reveal whether your garden is being watered evenly or only in pinpoint spots.

Once you've corrected the pH of the soil in which your roses grow (which you should do annually), fertilize accordingly. When you begin and end will, of course, vary with where you garden. In southern California, for instance, where roses blossom for ten months of the year, fertilizers are applied over a longer period than they are in, say, New England, where blossoming may not commence until June or July and may conclude before the end of October. If you request your local soil laboratory to suggest a feeding program for your roses, including when you should begin and end it, they will.

As discussed by my zonal rose gurus in chapter 7, all sorts of soil deficiencies exist. But they can all be corrected to make it possible for roses to perform at their peak.

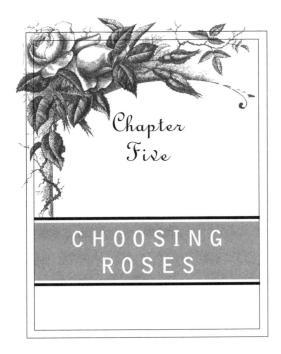

Chapter
Five

CHOOSING ROSES

IF YOU ALREADY GROW ROSES, YOU'VE PROBABLY DECIDED which kinds suit you. If you don't yet grow roses, I'd like to help you experience immediate success by suggesting varieties that are practically foolproof.

Before dealing with specific choices, however, there's a horticultural war afoot that you should know about.

THE WAR OF THE ROSES

Five separate friends sent me copies of a recent article written by a man so smitten with heirloom roses that his passionate prose was heavy with sexual overtones. He confessed being unprepared for the sensuous qualities of his Gallica rose 'Madame Hardy'. Instead of calling his Alba rose 'Maiden's Blush' (the way most English-speaking people would), he referred to her as the French do—'Cuisse de Nymphe'—and spoke of petals that resembled the thigh of an aroused nymph. No doubt about it, dowager roses turn this guy on.

"Doesn't it strike you as odd," a friend asked in the margin of her clipping, "that someone gets off so on antique roses but considers the ones you grow no more exciting than last year's models from Detroit? What's with you rose nuts?"

As a rosarian, it pains me to admit that my fellow rosebuddies are indeed split into two camps that rarely see eye to eye — those devoted to old garden roses and others who prefer modern hybrids. I believe this tempest in a teapot should be put to simmer.

What separates old roses from new? A year — 1867, when the French breeders Guillot Fils hybridized 'La France', the first Hybrid Tea rose. Nineteenth-century hybridizers craved roses with high-pointed centers, and 'La France' was precisely what they had in mind, although its supply of pollen was stretched thin as breeders scrambled to parent crosses in pursuit of bold new colors.

By the beginning of the 20th century, there were enough new roses around to warrant a new name to separate old from new. Those who preferred the older kind began calling them "garden" roses, labeling their offspring "modern." Soon after, the rose world split asunder.

Garden roses have their modern offspring beat hands down as far as lineage is concerned. How can any man-made hybrid compete with ancestors that grew long before we humans existed? Even a modern rose such as 'Peace', whose budwood was stowed onto the last airplane to leave France just before it was occupied in World War II and which then went on to become the floral symbol of the United Nations and the All-America Rose Selection for 1946, can't compare with the legendary apothecary rose, *Rosa gallica officinalis.* No one is sure how old the latter is, but we know that it was planted all over the Roman Empire and was probably the first rose imported into the American colonies.

Old roses have names that set them a class apart from modern hybrids — 'Gloire de Dijon', the heirloom Climber, sounds ever so much more alluring than 'Holy Toledo', the modern Miniature; the famous Bourbon rose 'Souvenir de la Malmaison' seems infinitely classier than the hybrid Floribunda 'City of Belfast'. By name alone, how could a Hybrid Tea such as 'John F. Kennedy' hope to compete with the Centifolia rose 'Chapeau de Napoléon' or 'Barbara Bush' with the Gallica rose 'Empress Josephine'?

But do you grow roses for their names? If not, there are certain legitimate differences between heirloom varieties and modern upstarts that you should know.

First, heritage roses mature into shrubs, whereas hybrids form bushes, which means that old garden roses are considerably more graceful in the landscape than their descendants are. Second, with certain notable exceptions, old garden roses have but one flush of bloom each year — not such a drawback as it first seems. If you bother to count the annual blooms from an antique garden shrub, you'll find that they equal those from the most generous modern rosebush; they simply occur over one extended bloom rather than piecemeal over a summer.

Next, the heated dispute over fragrance. I suppose if

you bothered to sniff every antique garden rose known, then every modern variety, you'd find a higher percentage of perfumed varieties among heritage roses. That is not to say, however, that modern roses aren't scented. Personally, I believe God (and Germany's hybridizer Tantau) created 'Fragrant Cloud' in 1963 to put an end to bellyachers who lament the loss of fragrance in modern roses. The delicious scent of 'Fragrant Cloud' is enough to satisfy the piggiest of perfume fanciers.

Modern roses have a range of scents, too — citrus, honey, raspberry, musk, apricot, vanilla, clove — no two alike. To my nose, 'Angel Face' smells nothing like 'Granada', which doesn't remind me of 'Color Magic', whose aroma doesn't favor that of 'Double Delight', even though each of these modern hybrids has a ravishing fragrance.

Of course, I have to admit that far too many modern roses have little or no fragrance. 'Touch of Class', an All-America Rose Selection for 1986, is a smashing rose, but it smells of nothing at all. There are others — 'Olympiad', 'Olé', and 'National Trust', to name some reds (I happen to think that scentless red roses are inexcusable). Keep in mind, however, that not all old roses are fragrant either; simply a higher percentage of them are perfume blessed.

Disease resistance is a close call. True, many heirloom varieties are tough old birds, but others are not — the famous Hybrid Perpetual 'Baroness Rothschild', for example, is so susceptible to powdery mildew that, each August, my bushes look as though I shook sacks of flour over their heads. Oddly enough, the modern bushes most adamantly resistive to disease are the ones hottest off the hybridizing bench. Landscape roses (as they're getting to be known) such as 'Bonica', 'Carefree Delight', and 'All That Jazz' demand no spraying and little pruning.

Above all else, antique roses are revered for the majestic forms of their mature blooms. Although the buds of many of these fine old roses are charming, they more often look cuppy rather than elegant. During bud development, petals appear curiously twisted or trapped against their neighbors, causing one to fret that nothing spectacular will ever occur. Blooms may, of course, remain cupped, but more often blossoms flatten into complex patterns as they swirl or quarter their petals. Some continue to grow by reflexing into a dome. Others conclude by revealing clusters of stamens or button eyes in their centers. However they finish their outrageous show, blossoms of antique roses are delightful to watch mature.

Take members of the Damask rose family, for instance. Varieties such as 'La Ville de Bruxelles', 'Madame Zöetmans', and 'Marie Louise' stage a show that's a sight to behold. Cupped blooms turn lavish as they reveal petals so numerous that they quarter and segment mature blossoms. Finally, petals reflex and lift their centers around button eyes.

"Modern roses are too prissy," purists complain, "a little too perfect. We want decadence, not symmetry." I say wait a while. In a couple of days, the most perfectly formed of hybrid buds will mature into a buxom, irresistibly informal bloom.

The old-rose diehards that I love to collar are those whose minds aren't yet irrevocably closed to the merits of some modern hybrids. When I find one who's willing to listen, I talk about "decorative" hybrids. That term has always amused me, for it's as condescending as it can be — used to describe roses that don't have a lot of show potential. Yet, for sheer beauty, decorative roses are as lovely as the best of the trophy winners. 'Duet', for instance, is rarely seen on the show table because its center usually doesn't rise above the rest of the bloom. But when it's three-quarters to fully open, who cares? Mature blooms of 'Duet' are majestic in their form and in the arrangement of their two-tone pink petals.

'Just Joey' is another decorative modern hybrid. Buds are globular and not particularly interesting. As the bloom begins to open, however, it's "Katie, bar the door." Blossoms reach immense proportions, with frilly, apricot petals that are drenched with fragrance at all stages.

Although I've never been ambivalent about roses, after listening carefully to arguments from both factions of the war, I decided not to surrender to either side but to fight for both. Still, while drafting my treaty, the battle raged.

Each Halloween, when I've told my bushes of the black-red, intensely fragrant Hybrid Tea 'Mister Lincoln' that I blessed the day I planted him, was I being disloyal to my crimson-purple Gallica rose 'Charles de Mills' that gave me the shivers on Mother's Day? Was praising the ever-blossoming, sassy mid-pink Floribunda 'Sexy Rexy' tantamount to disloyalty to the once-blooming, pastel pink, irresistible Centifolia 'Fantin-Latour'?

During those years, I suffered a recurring dream that always turned into a nightmare. It started well, with my arrival at heaven's gates, but matters took a sharp turn when a surly archangel appeared to inform me that my allotted celestial land would hold only 12 rosebushes and that I must declare which they were to be, within an hour.

The first night these nagging images appeared to me, I awoke from deep slumber and couldn't go back to sleep until I had completed the first draft of my list. The next day, obvious substitutions occurred to me, so, of course, I had the dream again and bettered my selections.

That dream ended after several years of delicious agony, when I finally honed my immortal selection to four heirloom roses staging majestic six-week floral extravaganzas each year and eight modern varieties blooming their heads off all season long.

My rose war on earth is over, too — 8 to 4 in favor of the kids.

ROSES FOR FAIR-WEATHER GARDENERS

As I mentioned in chapter 4, the American Rose Society, with their annual *Handbook for Selecting Roses,* offers a dandy solution for locating stellar roses. There are, however, certain facts to keep in mind when you consult this fine guide.

First, modern roses are heavily favored among those rosarians who vote on these matters. Although heirloom roses are listed and rated, their numbers pale in comparison to the roster of modern hybrids.

Second, a large number of voting rosarians are more interested in the exhibition potential of the roses they cultivate than they are of general landscape contributions. If you, too, grow roses to enjoy the perfection of their blooms, you share an interest with those who want to exhibit. But if you, like me, don't give a hoot about rose competitions, relying on this guide alone will keep you from planting varieties that produce armloads of long-stemmed roses for enjoying indoors. Scores for such varieties have been marked down because they don't perform well at the show table.

Realize also that while color may be important to you, it's not to hard-core exhibitors who have their sights set on ribbons and trophies.

Exhibitors don't care about fragrance either; therefore perfume plays no part in rose ratings. The most recent edition of the *Handbook for Selecting Roses,* which has a special listing of "High-Rated Roses," includes two Hybrid Teas without a whiff of fragrance — 'Touch of Class' and 'Olympiad', both of which are firebreathers at the show table.

That said, if you do use the ARS shopping handbook as your sole shopping companion, in most cases you'll be headed for fine roses. Among Floribundas, for instance, 'Europeana', 'Iceberg', and 'Sexy Rexy', are all recommended. They're fine choices, as are the Grandifloras 'Gold Medal' and 'Queen Elizabeth', surely the best pair of Grandifloras in the world. Similarly, the guide will lead you to good Miniatures, heirloom roses, Climbers, Ramblers, and Shrubs — not necessarily your ultimate choices, but fine beginnings.

Rather than take the score listed in the handbook for gospel, ask local gardeners with a keen interest in roses which varieties best suit your needs. Or visit a local rose garden and take notes.

Finally, keep in mind that the scores listed in the handbook are averages taken from rosarians across the United States. Averages, of course, don't alert you to local talent. Some roses, for example, flourish in Portland, Oregon, but merely piddle around in Portland, Maine. Or vice versa.

The most direct route to the skinny on local talent is to learn if your nearest chapter of the ARS publishes a list of ratings obtained strictly locally. If so, get a copy and learn which roses shine nearby. The San Francisco Rose Society, for instance, publishes such a list in each edition of their *Growing Roses in San Francisco*. The Bay Area is a superb example of why local advice is so important. San Francisco and certain nearby coastal areas have a climate all their own. No matter how hot days become, nights are cool. Although such climates have their pluses (namely, they foster deeply colored roses that develop extra-large blossoms because of the temperate climate in which they slowly mature), there are also drawbacks (namely, they offer a welcome mat for powdery mildew because of inevitable fog). With these factors in mind, consulting rosarians in San Francisco will go on to explain specific attributes of roses that perform well in the city. For instance, because of the chilly conditions, roses with 30 or fewer petals behave best. More heavily petaled varieties require more heat than San Francisco usually affords. Using white Hybrid Teas as an example, 'Honor', with its meager 23 petals, is a better choice than 'White Masterpiece', which has more than 50 petals per blossom and performs better in USDA zones higher than 7.

Even with countrywide averaging of rosarians' scores, truly great roses transcend locale and outdo themselves almost without regard for where they're planted. In *The Rose Bible,* I took a deep breath before even contemplating the 50 roses to highlight in a section called "Immortal Roses"—varieties that either have remained in favor since they were discovered or show all likelihood of doing so. I agonized over many varieties before reluctantly omitting them from the list of immortals.

That great heirloom roses also transcend locale is proved also by a survey taken by Steve Jones of

Valencia, California, and published in the October 1995 issue of *The American Rose*. Votes for favorite "OGRs" (old garden roses) were tallied from respected American OGR aficionados and from new rosarians interested enough to complete a questionnaire published in an earlier edition of *The American Rose*.

Results were predictable, with age-old favorites scrambling to the top of their category — the sumptuous 'Souvenir de la Malmaison' among Bourbon roses, the irresistible Centifolia 'Fantin-Latour', the caressable Damask rose 'Madame Hardy', and the ever charming 'Madame Alfred Carrière' (my vote also for the best of the Noisette roses). Other families were well represented by varieties long considered to be the best of their group.

Favoritism among roses is due to more than personal appeal. How easy they are to cultivate and bring to good bloom is just as important — as it should be.

The same is true for modern hybrids, except, of course, that there are far more of them. With new varieties introduced into commerce yearly in hefty numbers, modern roses swing in and out of vogue — particularly when it comes to color trends. Classic hybrids persist, however. I'm not certain, for instance, that a pink Grandiflora rose finer than 'Queen Elizabeth' will ever be hybridized or that the Hybrid Tea 'Pristine' will ever be surpassed in its color class. There's no shortage of fine, easily cultivated roses in commerce.

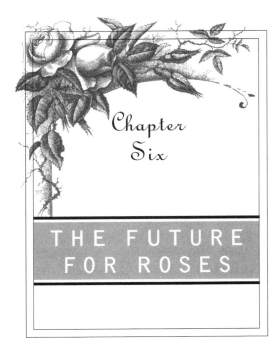

Chapter
Six

THE FUTURE
FOR ROSES

I GREW UP WITH A MOTHER WHO REFUSED TO ADMIT roses to her garden.

"Why should I grow something with more diseases named for it than any other plant?" I can still hear her asking.

Consequently, when, as an adult, I decided to grow roses seriously, I prepared myself for pampering plants in need of considerable care, which was just as well since the roses I grew then needed constant coddling.

Inasmuch as I didn't know any better, I grew 'Sterling Silver' because I had been told that no mauve rose could top it for form and fragrance. As it happened, that wasn't true. 'Angel Face', a sassy Floribunda, was every bit as fragrant and almost identically colored. And mauve roses such as 'Paradise' were even more beautifully formed than the notorious "Sterling Rose."

Similarly, I cultivated 'Chrysler Imperial' because of its reputation for being the most fragrant dark red rose in commerce. It wasn't, of course; it was simply more well known at the time than 'Mister Lincoln', a rose of equal depth and coloring as well as perfume.

After growing roses seriously for more than 25

years, not only have I learned things on my own (for example, to avoid duds such as 'Sterling Silver' and 'Chrysler Imperial', simply ignoring their notorious reputation), other rose lovers have steered me toward simplified rose culture. Best of all, I have become one of 25 official judges in the All-America Rose Selection process and maintain a garden at my ranch devoted to roses being considered for the prestigious award. The combination of passionately growing roses for 25 years and observing firsthand what's coming down the rose pike in an AARS test garden has made me ready to predict certain aspects of roses of the future.

Above all else, they'll be easier to grow—a trend irrevocably established with the introduction of "Landscape roses," a classification first used to describe 'Bonica'. This carefree rose from the legendary hybridizing clan of France's Meilland family was the first Landscape rose to cop the crown of an All-America Rose Selection, which it did in 1987.

Swept away with prospects of armloads of lightly scented, pale pink flowers in clusters on gracefully arching stems, I couldn't wait to get my hands on plants of 'Bonica'. I planted 20 bushes.

Because I was intent on growing roses that sold well as cut blossoms, in those days I had tunnel vision for varieties that grew only on upright bushes and produced roses on long cutting stems. 'Bonica' isn't that sort of rose, and instead of becoming an upright bloom factory, it turned into a billowing shrub that arched its

languid floral limbs into pathways and generally inter-
fered with order.

I yanked my plot of 'Bonica' out of the growing field.
One bush, however, looked particularly healthy and
gave a convincing appearance of yearning to grow in
my garden. Just as I was taking it to the pile of other
bushes I intended to give away (I never trash rosebushes just because they've fallen out of my picky
favor), I noticed a large hollow stump with nothing
growing in it and planted this lone 'Bonica' there. That
was seven years ago. Since then, I've never sprayed the
bush, nor have I taken my loppers to it at pruning
time. Today it's a mighty sight to behold, and all summer long, visitors skid to a halt as they approach it. I've
learned, of course, that there's more to a rosebush
than the roses themselves and that landscape contributions are equal in importance to bouquets.

Four years after the debut of 'Bonica', another
Landscape rose won the coveted All-America title—
'Carefree Wonder', a carefree bush indeed that's more
rounded than 'Bonica', decidedly disease resistant,
and blessed with shocking pink blossoms whose petals
have a creamy reverse. Some diehard enthusiasts of
modern roses complain that the blooms of 'Carefree
Wonder' don't display the high-pointed centers associated with prissy Hybrid Teas, but most gardeners
consider this a small price to pay for such a, trouble-
free rosebush. In 1992, another Landscape rose made
the All-America Selections list—'All That Jazz', a

5-foot by 5-foot plant that produces single, fully petaled, coral blossoms with golden yellow stamens.

In case I've led you to believe that I'm automatically swept away with a rose simply because it wins an All-America award, let me assure you that I'm not. Several of the most famous Landscape winners have never claimed my garden home, mostly because I find their coloring garish, even when they've ideally placed in the landscape.

A winner for 1996, however, is another matter. 'Carefree Delight', the latest member of the "Carefree" series from France's House of Meilland, has won my heart, although I *do* wish it had another name. I hate "series" names. First, after a while, you can't remember one from another. Mostly, though, naming a rose another in a series is vaguely condescending. In the specific case of 'Carefree Delight', it's downright insulting.

'Carefree Delight' is the quintessential Landscape rose, not only because it fits so well into the landscape but also because, as advertised, it's fuss free. Foliage is small, but dark glossy green and seemingly impervious to disease. Above all else, 'Carefree Delight' is a happy rose, and although shrubs begin flowering later than most varieties, once they start, they don't stop. Also, as good Landscape roses should, blossoms look best when left in the garden. Tight little carmine-pink rose-buds open their five petals into lightish mid-pink, five-petaled blossoms that can reach up to 3 inches each. Golden yellow stamens are smack-dab in the middle of a bright white eye. As if all this weren't enough, wood on 'Carefree Delight' turns a handsome shade of mahogany brown in winter—the same time it produces a smashing crop of hips. As you can tell, I'm besotted by this rose.

My affection for 'Carefree Delight', however, seems casual in comparison to what I think of one of the winning All-America Roses for 1997. As far as I'm concerned, 'Scentimental' is the most exciting rose of the current decade. I do wish it had been blessed with a more fitting name (one not so cutely spelled), but I don't think the appellation will stand in the way of its success. What's more, I predict that 'Scentimental' will serve as a great arbiter for the ongoing feud between rosarians devoted to old-fashioned garden roses and those fond of modern hybrids. That's because it possesses attributes dear to both camps: it looks like an old rose but blossoms like a voracious modern upstart.

Besides all that, this hotshot Floribunda is uniquely colored. Petals are deep hot pink, shaded rose, splashed with creamy to pure white random striations. To cap off the entire affair, fragrance is strong and the handsome deep green foliage is impervious to disease.

There lies another clear wave of the future—disease resistance. The reason, naturally, is public demand. Gardeners (to say nothing of rosarians) are sick and tired of combating the many diseases familiar to roses. Even with the use of the safest-possible chemicals, spraying is a drag.

People laugh at me when I claim that it should be illegal to propagate 'Sterling Silver', the first modern mauve rose. When it was introduced in 1957, rose lovers were willing to go to certain extremes (namely, spraying with fungicides at least once a week) to grow the lovely fragrant beauty. After all, there was no alternative (assuming one wanted more than one flush of mauve blossoms per year). Now, of course, there are modern mauve roses that put the dowager 'Sterling Silver' to shame and people should stop laughing at my suggestion.

My prediction that we may someday not have to spray roses at all isn't as far-fetched as it seems. Gardeners averse to chemicals have already discovered the merits of tough roses such as those of the Rugosa family, many of which demand no special treatment whatsoever. The mere fact that these attributes are being passed on to the roses hottest off the hybridizing bench is testament to the certain trend for the creation of carefree rose varieties.

Beyond resistance to disease, other aspects of general rose culture are being simplified, too, including pruning. British rosarians have already been experimenting with pruning rosebushes with hedge clippers. And it's working. True, the more easily cultivated types of roses are responding best, such as Miniatures, Ground Covers, and aggressive Shrub cultivars, but in time even prissy Hybrid Teas and Floribundas may not need tedious attention at pruning time.

Hybridizers have likewise been paying attention to other wishes from the public, including the desire for a return of fragrance to roses. Once upon a time, nearly all roses were fragrant. Then, as new varieties began appearing that would win ribbons and trophies at rose shows, fragrance was put on a back burner (perfume carries no weight in the judging of exhibition roses). Now, because the buying public has put its foot down, fragrance is practically a prerequisite for the success of new rose varieties. Furthermore, perfume is becoming expected in color groups that previously had been relatively scentless — white, for instance. Although there were once few fragrant modern white roses, now they abound, such as 'White Lightnin'', 'Sheer Bliss', 'Margaret Merril', and a host of others. The time may come when roses without a trace of fragrance may not even be introduced into commerce.

Personally, I have always blamed the intense interest in exhibiting roses as a cause for certain basic problems with roses at large, especially tendencies toward disease and lack of fragrance. It all began in the mid-19th century when hybridizers were frantic to develop new roses. Not only was gardening in its heyday, floral exhibitions had become the rage, and no flower was more popular than the rose. Exhibitors didn't care about the appearance of the bushes on which their prizes grew; the flower, specifically its bud, was what they were after.

Determined to breed roses that would win ribbons at rose shows, it seems that hybridizers decided to interbreed every rose family they could get their hands on. New roses emerged that produced flowers similar to their ancestors but that grew on plants that could no longer be called shrubs. In fact, the bushes were downright clumsy and too tall for most gardens. Still, there *were* those lovely blossoms in exciting new forms and, of course, aspirations of trophies. Before the pollen scrambling was over, more than 3,000 new varieties had been introduced under the family name of Hybrid Perpetual.

When Hybrid Tea roses came along, matters only worsened. The Hybrid Tea, with its tall pointed center and prissy form, was precisely what it took to win at rose shows, and rose exhibitions grew by leaps and bounds — again at the expense of the average gardener interested in disease resistance and fragrance.

The color range in which roses are available is constantly widening. The American Rose Society presently lists 16 separate color classifications. That number may well reach 20 before the end of this century, since new color combinations are regularly being introduced into commerce.

As for the elusive blue rose, I'm beginning to doubt if it will ever truly exist. A few years ago, researchers excited the rose world by announcing that they were getting considerably closer to discovering an inarguably blue rose, but I now believe that was simply publicity hype to generate new funds for research. Besides, I'm convinced that researchers are fiddling with extracting blue pigments from the wrong flowers — petunias, which to my eyes aren't truly blue (more like deep lavender or bluish purple). For my money, delphiniums, irises, morning glories, or lobelias would be a far better bet.

My opinion about a "black" rose is essentially the same. New varieties appear now and then that are said to be black but are actually that dark only while in bud. As petals mature, they inevitably turn some shade of dark red. Besides, I'm not certain we'd truly like a black rose if one *is* ever actually hybridized.

Regardless of what the future holds in store for the colors of new rose varieties, overall appearance is bound to change. This has already been clearly demonstrated with the immense popularity of David Austin's "English roses."

Shortly after 1950, Austin, a hybridizer from Albrighton, England, launched a rose-breeding program that worked wonders in reuniting two rose camps: those who craved old-fashioned roses and those devoted to modern hybrids. The line of roses Austin eventually developed was so different from anything else in commerce that they qualified as a whole new race — the English rose.

When Austin began hybridizing his new beauties, he knew precisely what he was after — sturdy shrubs, remontant (repeat blooming) with delicate, pastel, fragrant, old-fashioned blossoms. In order to achieve his dream, he crossed modern Climbers, Floribundas, and Hybrid Teas with two of the oldest rose families known — Gallicas and Damasks.

The very first results were somewhat disappointing,

for although the overall "look" was right, the varieties blossomed only once each season. Subsequent crosses, however, brought Austin his dream, and there are now more than 100 separate varieties in commerce.

At first, of course, they were available only in England. In no time, however, American rosarians changed that, and the English rose has increased in popularity in America ever since.

It's no surprise that other rose breeders are following Austin's lead. The famous French firm of Guillot (they introduced 'La France', the first Hybrid Tea rose), for instance, is about to introduce a line they have been developing. Other breeders, including Americans, are bound to follow, and soon.

Not only is the appearance of roses likely to change, so is the way they grow, more specifically what they grow *from*.

Currently, more than 95 percent of roses in commerce are grafted onto rootstock (that portion of a rosebush that remains underground). Rootstock comes from older rose varieties that, although their blooms are usually insignificant and sometimes unattractive, are known for their capacity for rapid, extensive root development.

The alternative to growing rose varieties budded onto rootstock is to grow them on their own roots. Roses on their own roots grow from cuttings. Although it takes longer to grow rosebushes from cuttings, advocates of own-root roses believe such rosebushes are worth the wait. First, roses growing on their own roots are virus free. Rose propagators have been plagued for years with rootstock infected with virus impossible to eradicate except with heat so intense that entire plants are sacrificed. If present, virus in the rootstock is eventually transmitted to the hybrid, rendering it unsightly. Second, because they grow on their own roots, roses taken from cuttings don't develop suckers. Third, own-root roses are said to be more winter hardy and to enjoy a longer life than budded roses.

With all these pluses going for own-root roses, you may very well wonder why all roses aren't grown that way. There are several reasons.

First, not all roses (particularly, modern hybrids) grow well on their own roots. The general rule of thumb is that the stronger the hybrid (in this case, strength equals vigor), the more likely it is to grow well when rooted from cuttings. 'Queen Elizabeth', for instance, performs well on its own roots—no surprise since it is a decidedly vigorous variety. 'Angel Face', on the other hand, performs poorly when rooted from cuttings. Although it's a fine rose, 'Angel Face' is low on vigor.

Second, some rose varieties (especially, vigorous heirloom varieties) grow out of bounds when grown on their own roots. For these hell-bent-for-survival varieties, rootstock seems to keep them within bounds.

Finally, and perhaps most important, there is a question of money—the bottom line, even with roses.

Newly introduced varieties of roses are patented for

17 years, during which time the hybridizer receives a portion of the proceeds of plants sold. Sales are easily tracked with rosebushes that have been budded onto rootstock, and each bareroot plant is accompanied by a tag that guarantees the variety as to type. So many tags, so much royalty.

Although theoretically possible, financial management is not so simple with own-root roses grown from cuttings. A system is in operation whereby rose propagators are instructed to report the number of plants they have cultivated from cuttings, but it's basically an honor system and difficult to track.

Difficult or not, own-root roses are going to increase in numbers in garden centers, and commerce will have to work out a monitoring system to ensure that hybridizers receive the portion of sales rightfully due them. Among other reasons for the inevitable trend, budding has become something of an art form and fewer nurserymen are able to do it themselves. Sheer economics will someday make budding roses onto rootstock a technique of the past.

On a final note, I believe that the future of roses is severely affected by nomenclature. *Modern Roses 10,* the current bible on rose varieties, lists more than 16,000 separately named cultivars. Not only is that number more than any human can keep track of, the vast majority are no longer in commerce, either being a dud to begin with, proving to be a flop later, or being surpassed in performance by more recent introductions.

Imagine, for instance, that some clever person

finally hybridizes a truly blue rose and wants to name it, say, 'Blue Boy' (or 'Blue Girl'), 'Blue Chip', 'Blue Diamond', 'Blue Glow', 'Blue Heaven', 'Blue Mist', 'Blue Moon', 'Blue Nile', 'Blue Perfume' (assuming it's fragrant), 'Blue Ribbon', 'Blue River', 'Blue Skies', 'Blueblood', or 'Blusette'. No can do; all these names have already been taken (although only a couple are still in limited commerce).

The identical fate would befall a hybridizer who came up with a truly black rose. 'Black Beauty', 'Black Garnet', 'Black Ice', 'Black Jack', 'Black Jade', 'Black Night', 'Black Pearl', 'Black Prince', 'Black Ruby', 'Black Tea', 'Black Velvet', and 'Blackberry' are already taken, even though 'Black Jade' is the only one of these roses I've actually ever seen.

The naming of roses falls under the jurisdiction of a horticultural International Code of Nomenclature, which, at present, states that no name already listed as having been in commerce may be used even if the rose variety is no longer being propagated. The mere fact that the variety might exist in a gene bank (having once been used as a parent of a current rose) is enough to keep the name in perpetuity. Nonsense; the name pool must be purged. Otherwise, we'll keep getting roses with terminally cute names because so many perfectly good names have already been taken.

Chapter
Seven

ROSES BY ZONES

ALTHOUGH ROSES ARE CONSIDERED TO BE AMONG THE most adaptable of all flowers in America, they, too, vary widely in their growth habits from coast to coast. In Hawaii, rosebushes never go dormant and can literally bloom themselves to death. At the opposite end of the continuum, in areas of deep winter freeze, many gardeners treat roses like annuals and replant bushes each year rather than going to the trouble of affording them adequate winter protection.

Those who garden where winters are especially chilly may have to content themselves with varieties such as Rugosa roses known to stand up to freezing winters, whereas West Coast rosarians can grow any variety they please. To give garden newcomers a hint of what to expect from roses in their area, the United States Department of Agriculture has lent a mighty hand.

USDA PLANT HARDINESS ZONES

Of the multitude of factors that affect the hardiness of garden plants, none is more important than cold. In recognition of winter's preeminence, the USDA pub-

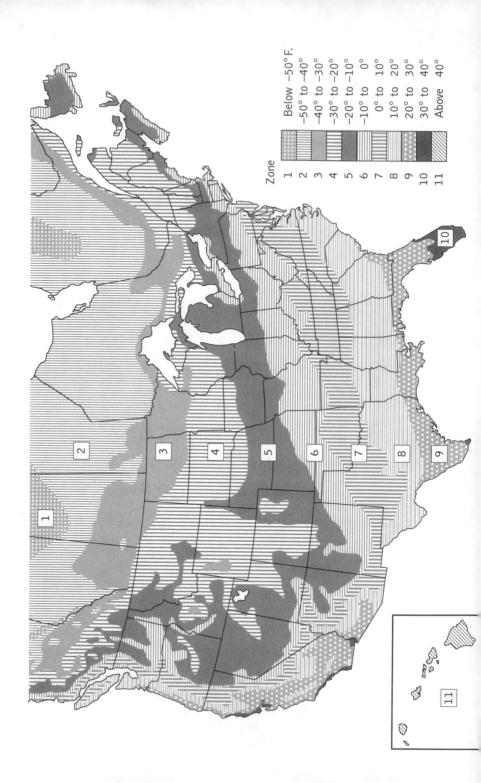

Zone	
1	Below −50°F.
2	−50° to −40°
3	−40° to −30°
4	−30° to −20°
5	−20° to −10°
6	−10° to 0°
7	0° to 10°
8	10° to 20°
9	20° to 30°
10	30° to 40°
11	Above 40°

lished a Plant Hardiness Zone Map in 1960. With average annual minimum temperature measured in Fahrenheit as the sole criterion, the United States was divided into 10 zones increasing in 10-degree increments from $-50°$ to $40°$F.

Then, in 1990, Zones 2 through 10 were further subdivided by 5-degree increments into a and b subzones. Also, Zone 11 was added for those areas in the United States where average minimum temperatures are above $40°$F. Finally, temperatures are now listed in both centigrade and Fahrenheit.

The USDA Plant Hardiness Zone Map is not the only system in use, of course. There are also the Arnold Arboretum (Harvard University) map and, for western gardeners, the vastly superior map found in the *Sunset Western Garden Book*, which divides the western United States into 24 climate zones, taking not only average winter temperatures into consideration but also quantity and seasonal frequency of rainfall, wind patterns, and even fog.

Keep in mind that no zonal map, not even the sophisticated *Sunset*, should be taken as gospel where gardens are concerned. Climates are inconsistent, making rigid lines impossible.

To get a basic idea of your garden's USDA zone, first locate it on a USDA map, noting whether or not you're near a dividing line. If you are, bear in mind that your garden's hardiness may occasionally resemble that of gardens across the line. Remember, too, that your garden may harbor microclimates up to 200 feet wide. Dense evergreens planted at the foot of a garden's slope, for instance, often trap cold air and make that portion of the garden colder than the rest. At the other extreme, south-facing walls accumulate and reflect heat, creating a warm microclimate.

Although certain roses are sufficiently hardy to withstand winters as cruel as those in USDA Zone 4a, where average minimum temperatures hover between $-30°$ and $-25°$F, selections are limited to ironclad varieties such as Rugosa roses. Gardeners in these areas of deep freeze will attest that Rugosa hybrids are hardly a compromise, but admit that a wider array of roses would be preferable.

In order to become familiar with the growing conditions for roses across the United States, I established rose gurus in 13 USDA zones (4b through 11). In each case, our eventual goal was to devise a feeding program for roses in these subzones similar to the "Gourmet Diet" I propose for where I grow roses (USDA Zone 9a), discussed in chapter 3.

As you'll see, the yearly lives of roses vary widely for these rosarians, as do their feeding programs and bloom cycles. Even though you'll be most interested in advice for your precise USDA zone (and the immediately adjacent ones), I encourage you to read what all these fine horticulturists have to say. Here are their stories.

USDA ZONE 4B: GREENFIELD, WISCONSIN (−20° TO −25°F)

Although the mercury has been known to plummet to −28°F near where Bill Radler grows roses, the lowest winter temperature is more usually −20°F, which is still plenty cold. Snowfalls are typical, but they can't be relied on for insulation, and those growing roses in this or similar climates listed as USDA Zone 4b have no choice but to provide rosebushes with protection from winter.

In a booklet entitled *Rose Growing Simplified,* published by Friends of the Boerner Botanical Gardens in Hales Corners, Wisconsin, Radler describes methods of winter protection in detail.

Taking the easiest first, Radler refers to the "do nothing" approach—the one preferred by those who hope that rosebushes will do nothing more dramatic in winter than die back to ground level.

Next easiest is the "soil mound" method, in which canes of rosebushes are tied together with soft cord (to prevent cane abrasion) to accommodate a 10-inch-high, 12-inch-diameter cylinder of ¼-inch mesh hardware cloth. After Thanksgiving (earlier if night temperatures drop into the low teens), cylinders are filled with soil. When the soil in the cylinders is frozen solid, canes can be cut back to the tip of the mound, then covered with an insulating layer of weed-free hay or evergreen boughs.

Cylinders aren't removed until the frost is out of the

ground—usually in early April. Leaving them on longer increases the risk of damaging soft new shoots during the removal process.

Radler admits that the soil-mound method is the traditional approach to winter protection, but he hastily points out that it is, perhaps, the least dependable.

Next is the "Styrofoam rose-cone" method, in which commercially available cones are placed over plants that have had their canes tied together, then shortened as necessary to fit under the cones. Cones are left in place as long as temperatures are below 25°F; Radler cautions, however, that gardeners never try to remove them if they are frozen to the soil.

Four 2½-inch-square holes cut into the top sides of the cones provide ventilation. Bricks laid on top not only hold the cones in place, they also provide a means for adjusting the size of the vent holes in accordance with temperatures. When temperatures drop below 0°F, Radler suggests placing unventilated rose cones over the ventilated ones. If canes get moldy, either the holes in the cones are too small or the cones were put in place too early.

The "tipping" method calls for burying rosebushes without actually digging them up. Soil around the bushes is loosened to the point that the bushes will bend to soil level and into trenches dug to accommodate them. Plants are tied into compact cylinders, then pegged to the ground. After Thanksgiving (earlier if required), tipped plants are covered with mounds of soil or leaves.

Dry, compacted leaves also provide what Radler calls the easiest and most foolproof of winter-protection schemes. The bed of rosebushes is first encircled with 2-foot-high ¼-inch hardware cloth. In late November, bushes are pruned to 12-inch heights and covered with dry leaves compacted by repeated thumps with the back of a bamboo leaf rake. Finally, the mound of leaves is covered with a tarp or sheeting to keep leaves dry.

Radler suggests waiting until the middle of April before removing winter-protection materials, pointing out that disastrous results may occur if bushes are uncovered when cold weather is still in the forecast.

Spring pruning is begun as soon as protection has been removed and is completed by the first week of May. Similarly, planting commences in mid-April (unless frost leaves early, in which case bushes can be planted as soon as danger of frost is past).

Blooming commences around the middle of June and persists until late October. In between, the usual rose plagues occur—blackspot, powdery mildew, leaf rust—and familiar pests pay a visit—aphids, spider mites, caterpillars, sawflies, leafhoppers. Although Radler says that most gardeners in his area use chemical sprays, he doesn't, in part because he's interested in breeding roses resistant to disease. He also follows an integrated pest management program for control of insects and spider mites.

An advocate of controlled-release fertilizers, Radler uses a three-year formula called Eeesy Grow Root-contact that's specially formulated for roses. He also relies on mulch and compost for nutrient supply. Further, he's a firm believer in soil tests, having dealt with soil high in phosphorus.

If soil tests indicate that all-purpose fertilizers are appropriate, Radler recommends soluble ones such as Stern's Miracid 30-10-10 (or Kmart's equivalent). Although he fertilizes infrequently, he states that those who want to really "push" their roses may fertilize at two-week intervals throughout the growing season until mid-August.

Unless gardeners in USDA Zone 4b have suitable walls on well-heated buildings or are willing to tip plants into the ground each winter, few Climbing roses can be grown there. Two specific varieties of Climbers introduced from Canada have, however, been found to be winter hardy without protection. 'Henry Kesey' (red) and 'William Baffin' (pink) are the names to remember.

USDA ZONE 5A: INDIANAPOLIS, INDIANA (−15° TO −20°F)

Jan Shivers says that in 1991 a record low was set in her garden, −29°F. More typically, winter lows are as the USDA says they should be and daily temperatures are rarely above 0°F. Consequently, as in all USDA zones below 6, Shivers and fellow Indiana rosarians pray for early (Thanksgiving) and regular snowfalls, to insulate rosebushes from winter's parching winds. Snow alone won't do the job, however. Without some protection, canes on even mature rosebushes will freeze to ground level.

The favored methods for protecting bushes in the ground include individual rose cones designed to protect a single rosebush and shelter boxes fashioned from lumber and Styrofoam that, depending on their size, can cover entire beds of rosebushes.

When individual rose cones are used, holes are punched in the top to allow for air circulation. Bricks placed on top hold the cones in place and can be moved to cover holes during sudden dips in temperature. If shelter boxes are employed, their lids are designed to be removable to avoid heat buildup, a known cause of rose fungal disease.

Local rosarians have found ways to avoid cones and shelters, including growing roses in containers that can be moved to garages or insulated buildings and generously mounding and collaring oak leaves (foliage from oak trees doesn't pack tightly and cause fungal disease) over plants. Also, the "tipping" method described earlier is used, in which entire bushes are gently uprooted and leaned into a trench large enough to contain them (mandatory if tree roses are cultivated), then mounded.

Finally, preferring to forgo the bother of storing cones and shelters or the tedious work of tipping, many rosarians dig up all their roses each year and put them in large, deep pits that can be heavily mounded with soil.

Shivers says that if spring is mild, she begins pruning as early as mid-March but stays on the alert for a cold snap by keeping her winter-protection kit (cones and mulch) on standby. Pruning is always completed by April 15.

Similarly, she orders bareroot rose deliveries for the last week of March or first week of April and plants no later than three days after delivery. Again, cones are kept nearby.

Although some years she has cut her first roses as early as May 15 and as late as June 10, May 30 is more the norm. Similarly, though they may be doused in snow, rosebushes in Indianapolis have been known to bloom as late as Thanksgiving. On average, however, Indiana roses call it a year in late October.

Because Shivers is highly sensitive to chemicals, she uses integrated pest management tricks such as using the spray from a water wand to control spider mites. Since pests (including inchworms and cucumber beetles) and fungal diseases are well represented in USDA Zone 5a, most rosarians resort to chemical sprays when necessary.

Shivers suggests a regular feeding program. Her roses get liquid fertilizer (balanced formulas, applied at the manufacturers' suggested rates) every two weeks throughout summer in addition to a boost supplied by soluble spikes. Because she grows most of her roses in containers, when it doesn't rain, Shivers waters every day; when temperatures rise above 90°F, she may water twice a day.

USDA ZONE 5B: CHICAGO, ILLINOIS (−10° TO −15°F)

Steve Rulo, an avid rosarian in Palos Park, Illinois, reports that although the thermometer in his garden has been known to nosedive to −29°F, the customary low is −10°F. In any case, winter protection is a must, not an option.

Rulo's personal approach to protection requires constructing boxes (designed with ¾-inch plywood sides and 2-inch Styrofoam tops) to cover entire beds. Before being put to rest, bushes are pruned to 20 inches and bud unions are covered with soil.

Pruning (below pre-pruning 20-inch heights) begins when the ground thaws (usually during the first week of April) and should be completed by April 25.

Planting is also usually scheduled for the first week of April, but recent mild winters in the Chicago area have permitted planting bareroot bushes as early as mid-March.

Although mulch is favored by many gardeners, Rulo shies from it, preferring to keep the soil around rosebushes well aerated and accessible for raking in granular fertilizers.

Roses typically bloom for four and a half months — from June 1 until mid-October. In order to get as many blossoms as possible, Rulo suggests the following program for fertilizing:

After plants have been pruned and all winter protection has been removed (usually the last week of

April), feed on a per plant basis with ½ cup nitroform (38-0-0), a source of slow-release nitrogen; 1 teaspoon urea (46-0-0), a fast-release nitrogen; 1 teaspoon chelated iron; and ½ cup Epsom salts.

Because all of these food sources are granular and easily mixed, Rulo first calculates the number of bushes he intends to feed, mixes granules proportionately in a wheelbarrow, cultivates into the soil 1 cup of the mixture around the drip line of each bush, then waters in well.

After spring's feed, he reapplies urea, chelated iron, and Epsom salts (at the same rate) every three weeks until mid-August, when all feeding stops.

Twice in the blooming season — immediately after the June flush and again one month later — Rulo recommends feeding each bush ½ cup of an organic product such as Milorganite (6-2-2) or Sustance (5-2-4). Between these granular feedings, fish emulsion is applied at the manufacturer's suggested rate.

If foliage appears chlorotic, dosages of chelated iron are increased to 2 teaspoons. Similarly, and because he exhibits, in midsummer Rulo increases urea dosages to 2 teaspoons per plant (never more than 1 tablespoon, for fear of burning foliage).

A firm believer in soil analysis, Rulo recently found that his soil had a buildup of both potassium and phosphorus. Because these elements are known to leach slowly, the only phosphorus and potassium he uses now is that contained in the organic fertilizers applied during June and July. Nitrogen, on the other hand, which is known to leach quickly, is featured in granular feedings.

The soil tests Rulo conducted revealed another problem with his soil: acidic conditions, with pH values of 5 and below — a situation probably caused by the high content of peat moss in the soil. To correct for the acidity, three times each year he adds dolomitic limestone at the rate of ½ cup for each established rosebush.

Willing to admit chemicals to his garden, during summer Rulo sprays at least every other week, for the usual fungal problems (blackspot and both downy and powdery mildew) and pests (spider mites, midges, leafhoppers, and cucumber beetles).

USDA ZONE 6A: WICHITA, KANSAS (−5° TO −10°F)

Like other USDA zones, Zone 6a has had its share of record-breaking winters. Where Louie Chestnut gardens, a record −35°F was set in 1992. But typically, −5°F is as cold as it gets — cold enough for winter protection but not the valiant efforts necessary in lower USDA zones. Chestnut makes do with newspaper collars. Using three double sheets folded in thirds, she staples enough papers together to form a collar for the base of each plant, which she then fills with leaves or straw.

The recommended date for beginning pruning is March 20, with an eye toward completion by April 20. Planting may commence even sooner, as early as the first week of March, weather permitting. Both to afford protection from unexpected frosts and to keep plants from drying, after planting, bareroot bushes should be well mounded.

An advocate of organic rather than chemical fertilizers, for spring's feed (after the first week of April), Chestnut suggests a meal of 1 cup Veldona (5-5-5), 1 cup alfalfa pellets, and 1 cup Epsom salts per bush. Every other week during summer, per bush, she uses 1 gallon of liquid fertilizer (either Miracle-Gro or Rapid Gro) mixed at the rate of 1 tablespoon per 3 gallons of water.

Chestnut usually cuts her first rose each season on Mother's Day and expects to continue harvesting until the latter part of October.

USDA ZONE 6B: NASHVILLE, TENNESSEE (0° TO −5°F)

Zone 6b represents a crucial dividing line where roses are concerned, specifically in the matter of winter protection. Although the temperature in Nashville dipped to −17°F during the winter of 1985, average minimum temperatures are closer to 0°F. While winters in this zone are not harmful to the majority of heirloom varieties of roses, tender modern hybrids demand modest winter protection—either protective cones or a mound of mulch materials. Many varieties of Climbing and Rambling roses survive Nashville's winters, but most gardeners aren't willing to risk planting standards (tree roses).

Robert L. Whitaker, president of the American Rose

Society from 1991 to 1994 and an avid rosarian, prunes roses each spring from mid-March, intending to complete pruning by the first of April.

Bareroot rosebushes may be planted as early as the last week in November as long as they remain well mounded until April 1. Most planting is conducted during early March; even so, bushes are kept mounded until early April.

If bushes are pruned high (for garden display), the season's first blossoms are expected in mid-May; if pruning is low (for exhibition quality), blossoming reaches its peak in late May. October 15 is the customary date of the last blossoms each year.

Because precipitation is high in Nashville (an average of just under 4 feet of rain each year, plus a foot and a half of snow), fungi are problems. First, blackspot; then, powdery mildew. Pests are strictly seasonal—aphids in the spring, thrips and spider mites later, when temperatures increase.

The fertilization schedule suggested by Whitaker is as follows:

April 1, per mature rosebush (plant)—3 cups Mills Magic Organic Mix, 1 cup dolomitic limestone, and 2 tablespoons calcium nitrate.

April 15, per plant—½ cup Epsom salts plus Mills Easy Feed Soluble (fish meal and seaweed), mixed at the rate of 1 tablespoon concentrate per 1 gallon water.

May 1, per plant—a combination of Mills Easy Feed Soluble (1 tablespoon per gallon) and Sequestrine (1 teaspoon per gallon).

May 15, per plant — 1 tablespoon Mills Easy Feed per gallon.

June 1, per plant — 1 tablespoon Mills Easy Feed per gallon.

June 15, per plant — ½ cup Epsom salts plus Mills Easy Feed Soluble, mixed at the rate of 1 tablespoon concentrate per 1 gallon water.

July 1, per plant — 3 cups Mills Magic Organic Mix, 1 cup dolomitic limestone, and 2 tablespoons calcium nitrate.

August 15, per plant — ½ cup Epsom salts plus Mills Easy Feed Soluble, mixed at the rate of 1 tablespoon concentrate per 1 gallon water.

September 1, per plant — 1 tablespoon Mills Easy Feed per gallon.

Extreme summer heat accounts for the lull in fertilization from July 1 until August 15. Although temperatures usually hover just under 90°F, they often soar well over 100°F. During such scorches, water is as much sustenance as roses can handle. Whitaker claims, however, that roses benefit from a summer mulch of dehydrated manure and pine needles.

For potted roses, Whitaker suggests the following regimen:

April 1 — 2 cups Mills Magic Organic Mix.

April 15 — ½ cup dolomitic limestone.

May 1 — ⅓ cup Osmocote (9-month formula).

Because weather and temperatures vary so widely during the growing season, Whitaker and other consulting rosarians in Nashville have observed that certain roses perform best in spring, others in fall, and some are outstanding all season long.

Among Hybrid Teas, for instance, 'Olympiad', 'Double Delight', 'Gold Medal', and 'Sheer Bliss' perform best in spring, while 'Pristine', 'Bride's Dream', 'Uncle Joe', and 'Crystalline' are rated better in fall.

'Touch of Class', 'Color Magic', 'Paradise', and 'First Prize' are better bets for season-long performance.

USDA ZONE 7A: WASHINGTON, D.C. (5° TO 0°F)

Although it recently dipped to −10°F in our nation's capital, winter lows more customarily hover near 5°F, as the USDA says they should. Consequently, Hubert Jessell and other esteemed rosarians make short work of winter protection — they plant bud unions 2 to 3 inches below soil level. Using this technique, Jessell says the only roses he's lost in 12 years were in poor condition when they were planted bareroot.

Still, winters can be extended, meaning that pruning shouldn't commence before the middle of March. After moderate winters, pruning should be completed within two weeks, no later than immediately after budding eyes show signs of growth.

The preferred arrival date for bareroot bushes is early March. Planting is done right away unless there's frost, in which case plants are kept moist and cool. Jessell uses mounds of soil; others recommend plastic bags with ventilating holes.

Jessell says his first rose to bloom is 'Canary Bird',

sometime in late April, but that the majority of his roses blossom during the second half of May. Because winter often begins late, blooms may be cut into November, sometimes December.

A firm believer in mulching, Jessell says he swears by mulch for four reasons: to stabilize ground temperatures throughout the year, to conserve moisture in summer, to discourage weeds, and to cover any traces of diseased leaves remaining after cleanup. Preferring pine bark, Jessell maintains a 2-inch carpet throughout the year, replenishing as the mulch breaks down.

In April, Jessell's feeding program calls for a blend of one 2-pound coffee can of aged cow manure, one 2-pound coffee can of compost, 1 tablespoon Epsom salts, and ¾ cup alfalfa meal.

Despite the fact that it won't begin breaking down until the soil warms in May, he also includes ¾ cup Osmocote 18-6-12 at this time; it's convenient and incapable of harm.

In June, after the first flush of flowers, Jessell feeds with a blend of 20-20-20 (1 gallon per bush, diluted at 1 tablespoon per gallon of water) that includes trace elements. Although the same feeding can be repeated for successive bloom cycles, he does not recommend fertilizers after mid-August.

Jessell swings both ways in his program for disease and pest control — he sprays with chemicals for disease and uses integrated pest management techniques (horticultural soaps and oils) for pest control.

The Potomac Rose Society publishes annually a list

of rose varieties recommended for the Washington, D.C., metropolitan area. Perusing it is like reviewing a roster of roses highly rated by the American Rose Society at large — all varieties can be grown here, some better than others.

USDA ZONE 7B: FORT WORTH, TEXAS (10° TO 5°F)

James R. McCarty of Fort Worth, Texas, knows his roses. Besides growing them for many years, he's now the newsletter editor for his American Rose Society chapter, and thoroughly in the know on what's happening with roses in his zone of Texas.

Wide swings in temperature are not uncommon in McCarty's Fort Worth garden. One year, the minimum average temperature was −8°F; during the summer of the same year, the thermometer reached 112°F. On average, however, minimum temperatures are rarely below 20°F, but summers almost always include intense heat waves.

McCarty recommends that pruning take place as close to Washington's Birthday (February 22) as possible and that it be completed by March 1.

Bareroot bushes are planted over a one-month period, beginning in late January, after which local nurseries pot them up. Although some rose mail-order houses will ship bareroot plants as late as the first week in May, McCarty shies from these late arrivals because plants have dried out and must be soaked for at least six to ten hours before planting. Bud unions of bushes planted early are covered with mulch, but no other steps are necessary for winter protection.

In an average year, roses begin to flower during the first week of April, peaking during the last week and during the first two weeks of May. The final flush of the year occurs during the last week of September and the first two weeks of October.

In between these periods of splendor, heat is a major problem, with transpiration so rapid that many gardeners are forced to water daily (container plants, sometimes twice a day). Extraordinary needs for water create a problem all its own — rapid leaching of nutrients.

McCarty says that he knows of no successful rosarian interested in modern varieties in his areas who doesn't employ a chemical fungicide. Blackspot seems to be unrelenting and powdery mildew always a threat. During heat spells, spider mites thrive in numbers.

Gardeners who grow old garden roses, assuming they choose varieties known to perform well locally, may avoid chemicals altogether.

Realizing that gardeners have different goals for their roses, McCarty has two suggested feeding schedules. For those interested in reasonable bloom for minimum cost and labor, his "conservative" feeding plan is as follows:

After pruning, completed by March 1, mulch rosebushes well with compost or pine bark and feed each bush 1 cup meal (cottonseed, alfalfa, blood, fish, or a blend of all).

In mid-March, on July 1, and again in September, feed each bush ½ cup 12-24-12, making certain that the manufacturer specifies that the formula is "slow release."

For those who exhibit or who are in search of perfection, McCarty suggests a "fast track" program, as follows:

March 1, per plant — 1 cup meal (blood, cottonseed, alfalfa, fish, or a combination of all) and 2 to 3 tablespoons Epsom salts.

March 15, per plant — ⅓ cup granular 12-24-12 (or 10-20-10).

April 1, per plant — 1 gallon diluted Miracle-Gro, Carl Pool Instant Rose Food, Peters Soluble Rose Food, or K-Gro.

Every two weeks from April 15 to June 15 — 1 gallon per plant of any of the fertilizers suggested for April 1.

July 1, August 1, and September 1 and 15 — 1 gallon per plant of any of the fertilizers suggested for April 1.

McCarty cautions followers of his fast-track regimen that they must plan to use plenty of water, both before and after fertilizer applications. Also, he mentions, they should resign themselves to working more and spending more money than those following the conservative approach.

Still, if gardeners seek larger blooms, more of them, greener and more luxuriant bushes, and "traffic-stopping rose beds," the fast-track approach is the ticket.

USDA ZONE 8A: SHREVEPORT, LOUISIANA (15 TO 10°F)

Leonard Veazey is no ordinary rosarian. As grounds supervisor for the national headquarters of the American Rose Society in Shreveport, Louisiana, he is in charge of more than 20,000 rose plants. Consequently, he's deeply appreciative that winter protection of roses isn't required in his USDA zone.

Although it got as cold as 5°F in 1989, many years it gets no colder than the mid- to upper 20s; some years it's barely below freezing.

Veazey's target date for pruning is February 20. Because rosarians from Louisiana, Mississippi, Alabama, Arkansas, Oklahoma, and Texas come to the ARS headquarters to help prune the massive collection of roses, the exact date is set for the weekend closest to February 20. With the mighty assist from his pruning armada, Veazey usually finishes pruning in two days; stragglers, within the week.

Bareroot bushes may be planted before pruning even begins — as early as mid-January, if plants are available.

Depending on weather, blossoming commences about mid-April and continues until the end of October or early November (occasionally, until Christmas).

Again because of the formidable number of roses under his care and a shortage of staff, Veazey approaches fertilizing with an eye toward saving time. A firm believer in soil analysis (twice a year on ten randomly chosen gardens on the grounds), he follows test results to the letter, which surely is why pH at the ARS gardens is so stable that the same granular fertilizer has been used for the last two years — Carl Pool's 15-5-10. Besides the major benefits of this blend, trace elements are included at the following rates: calcium (Ca), 5.1 percent; magnesium (Mg), 2.5 percent; sulfur (S), 5.5 percent; boron (B), 0.026 percent; cobalt (Co), 0.00065 percent; copper (Cu), 0.065 percent; iron (Fe), 0.60 percent; manganese (Mn), 0.065 percent; molybdenum (Mo), 0.00065 percent; zinc (Zn), 0.17 percent.

The blend is applied around the drip lines of bushes at the rate of ⅓ cup per plant every four to six weeks from two weeks after pruning through the first week of September. The only other fertilizer applied during the growing season is fish emulsion, which is added to the spray formula being used to control diseases.

Because of Louisiana's unusually high humidity, blackspot is a mean enemy throughout the year, as is powdery mildew in spring and fall. Consequently, Veazey and staff spray every seven days from the first signs of budding growth through the end of October. They have found, however, that when the temperature remains above 95°F for an extended period of time, spraying does more harm than good, so they abandon fungicides during extreme heat waves.

Although spider mites, thrips, aphids, and cucumber beetles are prevalent, Veazey restricts spraying with miticides to early spring (again, only if necessary). Insecticides are employed when pests are actually present, not as a preventive measure.

USDA ZONE 8B: ST. GABRIEL, LOUISIANA (20° TO 15°F)

When I was growing up in Louisiana, people referred to "north" and "south" Louisiana as though the state were cut right in half, which indeed it almost is according to the USDA (New Orleans and other cities on the Gulf of Mexico actually form a third zone, 9a).

Carolyn De Rouen gardens in St. Gabriel, Louisiana, just outside Baton Rouge. Although she grows roses of all ages, she specializes in modern hybrids, especially Hybrid Teas.

Recent winter temperatures in south Louisiana dipped to 12°F. Customarily, lows hover in the upper 20s—never low enough to require winter protection.

As might be expected from the mere 5-degree difference between Zones 8a and 8b, pruning near Baton Rouge is recommended near the same time as that in Shreveport—during the last week of February. De Rouen points out, however, that Louisiana is no stranger to moderate heat spells in February that encourage rosebushes to quickly sprout new growth. At such times, she encourages that pruning commence soon after sprouting.

Also because of those unexpected heat spells, bareroot bushes are planted as soon as they're available, as early as November and through December and January. Otherwise, a sudden heat flash can burn new growth of bushes planted as late as February.

De Rouen aims for her garden to reach peak bloom on her daughter's birthday, April 14. Some years she's cut roses as late as Christmas, but her fertilization program is aimed at blossoms only through late October.

While De Rouen blesses her climate for the near absence of powdery mildew, she curses its propensity for blackspot so infective and invasive that it can actually kill mature rosebushes. Although she bows to the use of chemicals to control fungus on modern hybrids, she resists them as treatment for insects. Since she doesn't spray her old garden roses, De Rouen plants them in groups, as she does her chemically dependent Hybrid Teas.

The Baton Rouge Rose Society recommends that roses be fertilized with a balanced fertilizer every four to six weeks throughout their growing season. Rosarians in search of more blossoms and more perfectly formed ones better this feed by applying alfalfa meal, cottonseed meal, and Epsom salts immediately after spring pruning and again during the first weeks of June and September. If soil tests indicate a need for trace elements, they are applied in soluble form.

An additional source of nutrients comes in the many forms of mulch materials available in Louisiana, including bagasse, the natural by-product from sugarcane harvests.

USDA ZONE 9A: TUCSON, ARIZONA (25° TO 20°F)

Les Hayt of Tucson, Arizona, says it isn't average winter lows (usually about 22°F) that worry his roses, it's summer's inevitable heat (for between 60 and 95 days annually it's over 100°F). Because of such scorching weather, when even average nightly lows during July and August are between 80° and 85°F, nearby rosarians make do with two magnificent flushes of bloom each year—one between April 15 and May 30 and a second between October 15 and frost (plus or minus ten days from November 25). Depending on how hot it gets, there may be roses in between, but they, too, suffer from heat.

Not only is no winter protection required, bushes may be pruned early—according to Hayt, between January and February 10.

Planting also commences early, beginning December 15 (or as soon as bareroot plants are available). Because of pending heat, new plants should be in the ground by the first week of February.

April 5 is the target bloom date for roses in Tucson and is on the mark plus or minus ten days each year. As already mentioned, blooms are intermittent (with a tedious summer lull) through Thanksgiving.

Hayt subscribes to a monthly feeding program from February 15 to November 15. Alternately, he feeds with a balanced fertilizer (preferably, 20-20-20) and one concentrated in nitrogen, such as 16-8-4. In addition, he swears by Epsom salts and feeds mature bushes ½ cup every other month from February 15 to October 15.

Powdery mildew is a problem in Arizona, but mostly only in spring. Thrips, on the other hand, are mighty for most of the growing season, especially when temperatures soar. When infestations are heavy, Hayt sprays.

Despite the unfortunate summer highs, roses per-

form beautifully in Tucson. The local rose society publishes a list of regional star performers. Reading it is
like reviewing local rose talent in at least five other
USDA zones, proving once again that fine roses perform well regardless of where they grow. It's simply
that because of Tucson's unrelenting summer heat,
roses strut their stuff only twice each year. Still, that's
enough.

USDA ZONE 9B: SANTA BARBARA, CALIFORNIA (30° TO 25°F)

The minimum winter temperatures in Dan Bifano's
Santa Barbara garden are precisely where the USDA
says they should be — most frequently at 28°F.

With such a temperate climate (average winter and
summer temperatures vary by only 15 degrees F),
Bifano recommends that pruning commence the second week of January and conclude before February 1.
Concurrently, bareroot bushes budded onto 'Dr. Huey'
rootstock are planted and mounded with mulch as
soon as they're available, usually by the first week of
the year. No other winter protection is required.

Having once exhibited his roses, Bifano is familiar
with more than one approach to pruning. He refers to
his current technique as traditional since he prunes
canes to 20- to 30-inch lengths. Shorter canes would,
of course, result in larger (albeit fewer) blooms.

Admitting that he doesn't like to dwell on each
bush, Bifano uses a general approach that calls for cutting out all but three to five of the freshest, strongest,

best-directed canes. Because his technique results in good landscape display, he betters it a step further by pruning canes on each bush at various levels, thereby achieving a more pleasing display of blossoms.

Fertilization begins on March 1, when bushes are unmounded and shallow trenches are raked around drip lines to accommodate a per-bush meal of 5 ounces Osmocote (9-month formula), ½ cup Epsom salts, and ½ cup Vim. These materials encircling each bush are then covered with three to four shovelfuls of a blend consisting of 50 percent the best bulk compost available, 25 percent aged chicken manure, and the balance fish meal and alfalfa meal.

The entire affair is watered in well, after which bushes are left alone until blossoming begins — intermittently at first, but there's usually a flush by April 1.

For the next five months, Bifano suggests feeding each bush on the following schedule:

Week 1 — 2 ounces Epsom salts.

Week 2 — 1 gallon diluted fish emulsion.

Week 3 — 1 gallon diluted Peters 20-20-20.

Week 4 — rest.

On September 1, new basins are raked around bush drip lines to accommodate, per bush, ½ cup Bandini rose food, ½ cup Epsom salts, and ¼ cup Vim.

This mixture is blanketed, per bush, with 2 cups alfalfa meal and a shovelful of aged chicken manure.

From September 1 until October 15, weekly feedings are given alternately with fish emulsion and Peters 20-20-20.

No fertilizers are applied between October 15 and December 1, at which time each bush receives a dose of 0-10-10.

Harvesting of blossoms continues from April well into winter — until Christmas if no hips are desired (if they are, blossoms aren't cut after November, allowing plants time to set seed).

Although his rose society doesn't publish a list of top rose performers for the area, Bifano took an informal survey of 30 of Santa Barbara's finest rosarians. The results read like my list of "Immortal Roses" in *The Rose Bible*. Among Hybrid Teas, star performers include 'Color Magic', 'Pristine', 'Peace', 'Double Delight', 'Just Joey', and 'Honor'. High scores for Floribundas went to 'Iceberg', 'Playboy', 'Europeana', and 'Sexy Rexy'. Predictably, 'Gold Medal' was the favored Grandiflora, 'Graham Thomas' the pick of the Austin English roses, and 'Sally Holmes' the Climber of choice.

On one hand, Bifano's survey tells me that Santa Barbara and Petaluma have something more in common than their adjoining USDA zone — that the same roses perform well for us. On the other hand, I'm not so certain our identical USDA zone rating has as much to do with the matter as do stellar roses that simply transcend locale.

USDA ZONE 10: LOS ANGELES, CALIFORNIA (35° TO 30°F)

Besides its immense size, Los Angeles is also a wonder of climates. Depending on how near which side of a mountain range a garden is, how much cement is nearby, and whether cooling breezes blow, L.A. gardens lie somewhere within USDA Zone 10. Whether a particular area is actually subcategorized 10a or 10b is of little consequence. Except for some winters so mild that plants never truly go dormant, southern California is a haven for roses. Few know or prove that so conclusively as Tommy Cairns and Luis Desamero, who share a garden in Studio City.

With a Ph.D. in analytical chemistry and a D.S.C. in toxicology, Cairns is a font of information regarding fertilizers and their absolute effects on roses and which chemicals keep diseases and pests at bay. With their combined love of roses and talents for exhibiting them well, Cairns and Desamero are formidable at the rose show table; they've won scads of ribbons, trophies, awards, and sweepstakes at local, regional, and national rose shows. Desamero was twice named Exhibitor of the Year by the American Rose Society, and Cairns has exhibited (and won) at international rose competitions in England and New Zealand. Their garden includes 300 Hybrid Teas, 50 Floribundas, 20 old garden roses, and 500 Miniatures (grown in 7-gallon black plastic pots).

Although the thermometer has dipped to 22°F in the past decade, the coldest nights of the year (hovering around 30°F) usually produce only ground frost, which is gone the moment sunlight finds it.

Cairns begins pruning his roses anytime after Christmas and finishes the job in ten days. When asked by nearby gardeners when their rosebushes *must* be pruned, Cairns says before February. For his friends in Altadena (only 18 miles away), Cairns suggests that gardeners begin pruning two weeks later than he does. The rule of thumb in L.A. is that the farther away from the ocean you are, the later you should prune (not past Valentine's Day, however). Planting is early, too — immediately after Thanksgiving or whenever bareroot plants are first available. No winter protection is required.

First blooms are expected the last week of March or the first week of April. Flowering thereafter is constant, often until Christmas.

Being blessed with ideal growing conditions for roses unfortunately doesn't mean freedom from diseases and pests. Because of the usual diseases, primarily powdery mildew, and common pests, including thrips and spider mites, Cairns follows a weekly spraying routine.

The "Cairns-Desamero" fertilizer program is well known to rosarians in the Pacific Southwest District of the American Rose Society; it's been widely published in their quarterly journal *Thorn Scratchings*. Before reviewing what is surely the most aggressive feeding program of all the rosarians in this chapter, it's important for you to understand their approach to growing roses.

Above all else, Cairns and Desamero are exhibitors, formidable ones at that. They know well what a rose needs to win a ribbon, or, better yet, a trophy, and once you have that picture in your mind's eye of what rose perfection is all about, it's impossible to erase it. I, for instance, stopped exhibiting 15 years ago, but the roses that still give me the shivers are those I'd happily place on a show bench for judges to consider.

In any case, the Cairns-Desamero fertilizing diet is touted for both "garden display and exhibition." The program is suggested for each mature rosebush (downscaled for smaller bushes and Miniatures) from mid-March through October 30 on a weekly basis.

Week 1 — Grow More, 2 diluted gallons per mature rosebush (1 tablespoon per gallon).

Week 2 — Epsom salts, ½ cup per mature rosebush.

Week 3 — fish emulsion, 2 diluted gallons per mature rosebush (1 tablespoon per gallon).

Week 4 — Grow-Vite, 2 diluted gallons per mature rosebush (1 tablespoon per gallon).

Local rosarians who follow this diet swear they've never before seen such results. If I lived there, I'd try it, too.

USDA ZONE 11: HAWAII (ABOVE 40°F)

USDA Zone 11 was established for those areas where minimum winter temperatures stay above 40°F. Minimum temperatures in Gilbert Wyckoff's garden never even get close — to 55°F at most, more usually only to 58°F.

In such a tropical climate, when to prune is an arbitrary decision. For Wyckoff, that's January, the first week of February at the latest.

Again because of climate, planting is conducted whenever bareroot bushes are available. Roses in containers, of course, can be transplanted anytime as long as they are kept well watered, which is generally not a problem (annual rainfall averages over 100 inches).

According to Wyckoff, if properly fed immediately after pruning, bushes will begin to blossom five weeks later. With correct fertilization, flowering persists until the following year's arbitrary pruning date. To achieve such results, Wyckoff suggests:

Immediately after pruning, per bush—2 cups dolomitic limestone, $\frac{2}{3}$ to $\frac{3}{4}$ cup 16-16-16, and $1\frac{1}{2}$ to 2 tablespoons ammonium nitrate.

5 weeks later, per bush—$\frac{1}{2}$ to $\frac{2}{3}$ cup 16-16-16 and 1 tablespoon ammonium nitrate.

March 15–20, per bush—$\frac{2}{3}$ to $\frac{3}{4}$ cup Sierra Blend (17-6-10).

After the late-March feeding, Wyckoff repeats applications of $\frac{1}{2}$ to $\frac{2}{3}$ cup of 16-16-16 every six weeks.

The reason Wyckoff and nearby rose growers have chosen the Sierra fertilizer is that it's purportedly formulated to release its contents over an eight- to nine-month period. Still, Hawaiian rosarians report, heavy rainfalls leach fertilizers from the soil, requiring that additional ones be applied.

Those same downpours lead to fungal problems, namely, blackspot and powdery mildew. Insects are the usuals, including thrips, but also some semiexotic ones such as Chinese leaf beetles, which feed only at night and only on the undersides of leaves, and large green grasshoppers that relish blossoms as well as foliage. The use of chemical fungicides and insecticides seems integral to successful rose growing in the Hawaiian Islands.

Although I know gardeners in Hawaii who treat rosebushes as annuals, Wyckoff and his fellow rosarians claim that, with proper care, rosebushes can indeed enjoy a reasonably long life. Grown commercially, for cut flowers, bushes have a floriferous life expectancy of seven to eight years, after which they are rendered effete for bloom production. Grown for general garden purposes, bushes are expected to have a substantially longer life (to at least 15 years).

Afterword

I LEARNED SO MUCH FROM MY ZONAL GURUS — NOT JUST
that I wouldn't care to live where some of them do (and
envy others), but also that there's more than one good
way to grow a rose.

Bill Radler, growing roses in shivering Wisconsin,
must tip his bushes during winter — a lot of trouble. On
the other hand, he doesn't have to live in constant fear
of an attack of downy mildew, as must many of us in
temperate climates. Jan Shivers of chilly Indianapolis
frets about planting roses as early as late March, while
Gilbert Wyckoff, gardening in tropical Hawaii, can
plant rosebushes any month of the year he pleases.
Windy Chicago's Steve Rulo doesn't believe in mulch,
whereas tranquil Santa Barbara's Dan Bifano swears by
it. Louie Chestnut fertilizes her roses in Wichita modestly, while L.A.'s formidable rosarian Tommy Cairns
feeds his aggressively. In short, we rosarians do what

we must to grow roses well wherever we've chosen to grow them.

Above all else, I've learned that there's no use doubting the sound reasoning behind making the rose America's national flower; it lovingly flourishes from coast to coast. I just wonder why it took until 1986 for legislators who decide such matters to make up their minds. In any case, I applaud the choice.

Glossary

Alba roses developed from a natural cross between the Damask rose *R. damascena bifera* and *R. canina,* a species native to Europe. Once called tree roses because they often grow taller than 6 feet, they are also extremely hardy and tolerant of considerable shade. Most blossom white or near white and carry a strong perfume.

Anther. The pollen-bearing part of the stamen.

Balanced fertilizer contains a balance of the essential elements — nitrogen (N), phosphorus (P), and potassium (K).

Balling. The refusal of rose blossoms to open fully because petals are damp and stuck together.

Bareroot roses are winter-dormant plants sold with no soil around them. Bareroot bushes are graded according to specific standards of number of canes of specific height.

Basal break. A major new growth emanating from rosebushes at or just above the bud union.

Blind growth develops foliage but no new flowers.

Boss. A bunch of stamens in the center of a blossom.

Bourbon roses developed on the Île de Bourbon from a natural cross of *R. chinensis* and *R. damascena.* Because of their graceful vigor, Bourbon roses make fine Climbers and grow well on fences; they are also the first family of old garden roses for whom precise parentage was recorded. Blossoms vary in color from pure white to deep red; most are powerfully fragrant. Although no subsequent bloom flush ever rivals the first, many Bourbon roses flower sporadically throughout summer and modestly in fall.

Break. Any new cane or lateral growth originating from a bud eye.

Bud. An immature flower.

Budded roses are varieties of roses that have been grafted onto rootstock.

Bud eye. The "eye" on the node of a stem; the red or green spot from which all new rose growth originates.

Bud union. The bulbous landmark that develops after a hybrid rose is grafted onto rootstock.

Budwood. Fresh woody growth from a specific variety, intended for budding onto rootstock.

Bush roses are those bushes with upright, often rigid growth habits that are praised for their remontancy rather than for their contribution to the landscape.

Button eye. A dense collection of aborted modified leaves at the center of a flower that gives the impression of a (usually green) button.

Calyx. The protective cover over rosebuds that later divides into five sepals.

Candelabra. An especially large (sometimes unmanageable as cut flowers) cluster of blossoms on a strong stem (often from a basal break).

Cane. A major stem on a rose plant from which lateral stems grow.

Centifolia roses are the result of complicated hybridity between at least four distinct species roses. Although it is uncertain how the original *R. centifolia* came into being, its family was developed extensively by the Dutch during the seventeenth century. Bushes of Centifolia roses are often lanky, and blossoms are globular, softly colored, heavily petaled, and richly perfumed.

China roses are distinguished among old garden roses primarily because of their ability to blossom recurrently each year. Blossoms of China roses have whimsical naive charm, and the bushes on which they occur have airy growth habits and sparse foliage. Because China roses are diploid, their chromosome structure made it difficult to mate them with other roses of the late 18th century.

Climbers are climbing roses that blossom repeatedly each year.

Consulting rosarian. A person so devoted to roses that he or she is deemed qualified to offer advice. A good consulting rosarian is worth his or her price in gold; nitpickers give roses a bad name.

Cultivar. A *culti*vated *vari*ety with unique characteristics.

Damask roses are believed to originate from a natural cross between an unidentified Gallica rose and *R. phoenicea*, a species. Damask roses are lofty growers (often to heights greater than 5 feet), and foliage is generally gray-green, elongated, and downy. Blossoms are usually clear pink and powerfully fragrant.

Deadheading. The removal of spent blossoms.

Decorative blossoms. Those with informal, not showy, shape.

Dieback. The progressive dying back of rose wood. Classically, dieback occurs when any rose wood is cut at the wrong place, after which stems start to die in a downward direction until the spot is reached where a proper cut should have been made. Rose wood need not always die in a downward direction, however; there is also dieup.

Diploid. A plant with two sets of chromosomes.

Disbudding. The early removal of buds to ensure that mature blossoms reach their greatest stage of beauty. For roses that look best one-to-a-stem, disbudding requires the removal of one or two small side buds. For roses best grown as sprays, disbudding requires the removal of the centermost, largest bud.

Double roses have more than 21 petals per bloom.

English roses are those hybridized by David Austin, a rose breeder in Albrighton, England, whose dream it was to unite the best qualities of heirloom roses (old rose form and fragrance) with those of their modern offspring (disease resistance and remontancy). He has succeeded.

Floribunda roses are hardy, disease resistant, and free-flowering modern roses that blossom in clusters rather than one-to-a-stem. Although generally praised for their contribution to the landscape, many Floribundas also produce blossoms as shapely as those of any modern rose.

Flush. An intense period of blooming.

Gallica roses, highly developed between the mid-17th and 19th centuries, are the oldest distinct family of garden roses. The majority of Gallica roses blossom in strong colors, although often with subtle combinations of colors or distinct stripes; almost all are fragrant.

Grandiflora roses began in 1954 with the variety 'Queen Elizabeth', a cross between 'Charlotte Armstrong' (a Hybrid Tea) and 'Floradora' (a Floribunda). Grandiflora roses occur in sprays, as do Floribundas, but individual blossoms should be formed similarly to the Hybrid Tea.

Ground-cover roses grow prostrate along the ground, either hugging it or matting to 2-foot heights.

Heirloom roses are the same as antique or old garden roses — those introduced before 1867.

Hybrid roses result from mating two separate rose species or varieties.

Hybrid Musk roses began when a German nurseryman mated *R. multiflora* and 'Rêve d'Or', a Noisette. The majority of Hybrid Musk roses mature into 5- to 6-foot shrubs that bloom profusely in early summer and modestly in autumn. Hybrid Musk roses have little to do with the true Musk rose except for their vague lineage via Noisette roses and a fragrance that embraces a musky quality in an otherwise sophisticated bouquet.

Hybrid Perpetual roses were hybridized during the mid-19th century, when rose shows became popular. At the risk of clumsy plants, Hybrid Perpetual roses were bred for the elegant appearance of their buds and partly opened blossoms. Although thousands were introduced into commerce, only a fraction remain. Most varieties of Hybrid Perpetual roses repeat-flower each year, but nowhere near so often as their modern offspring.

Hybrid Tea roses began with the introduction of 'La France' in 1867. Although there is wide variation in color and bloom form, buds are tall, high-centered, and shapely. The "Hybrid" portion of the name refers to hybridizers' efforts to mix rose lineage and come up with something new. "Tea" refers to the fact that these roses are descended from the Tea rose, which originated in China. Also, their fragrance is thought to be similar to that of tea leaves (more accurately, the wooden crate in which bags of tea were stored). Although many Hybrid Teas flower in clusters, most gardeners think of them as one-to-a-stem. All bloom throughout summer.

Imbricated petals are piled one on top of another. Rose blossoms with this many individual petals usually divide their bloom into quarters before they finish aging, at which point button eyes become conspicuous.

Inflorescence. A cluster of one or more sprays of florets.

Miniature roses are diminutive versions of other varieties. Once, the plants of "minis" were supposed to fit under a teacup. Now they grow on shrubs, too.

Modern roses are hybrid roses, introduced after 1867.

Moss roses resulted from a sport of a Centifolia rose. Although Moss roses appeared as early as the late 17th century, they weren't developed until the second half of the 19th century, when they were bred extensively from multiple parentage. The sizes of their bushes vary widely, as do the colors of blossoms. "Mossing" results from the formation of conspicuous glandular mosslike growth on stems, calyxes, sepals, and even foliage.

Node. The point of attachment of leaves to stems.

Noisette roses were begun by John Champney, a rice farmer in South Carolina, probably from a cross between one of the original China stud rose and an unidentified Musk rose. Later the Noisette brothers improved the family by introducing Tea roses as parents. Eventually, Noisette roses became known for their fragrant, softly colored, silky blossoms, albeit on tender bushes. Most varieties of Noisettes are most famous as climbers rather than as shrubs.

Old Rose blossoms are those that are cupped or shaped like a rosette rather than with a high-pointed center. They are sometimes separated from modern roses by a date — 1867 — the year in which 'La France', the first Hybrid Tea rose, was hybridized. Old roses are also called "heirloom" and "old garden roses."

Own-root roses are those grown from cuttings rather than budded onto rootstock.

pH. The number on a 14-point scale that indicates the relative acidity or alkalinity of a soil sample. A pH of 7.0 is neutral; higher numbers are for alkaline soil, lower for acidic. The ideal pH for roses is near 6.5 (slightly acidic).

Pistil. The female organ of a flower, including the stigma, style, and ovary.

Pollen parent. The male parent of a hybridized rose.

Polyantha roses originally resulted from a cross between the species *R. multiflora* and the China stud rose 'Old Blush'. Subsequent crosses produced roses with clusters of fragile blossoms on tough-growing, short bushes. Although resented for their lack of fragrance, they're praised for their trouble-free, free-blooming bushes.

Portland roses emerged after the Duchess of Portland sent a rose imported from Italy that bloomed all summer to the hybridizing staff at Malmaison. French breeders developed a family that is characterized by upright, mid-height shrubs that produce dense foliage and shapely, short-stemmed blossoms.

Ramblers are climbing roses that bloom once each year.

Remontant. The ability to blossom continuously throughout a season. The term "remontancy" is used interchangeably with "repeat flowering," "recurrent flowering," and "perpetual flowering."

Rootstock. The rose variety onto which other rose varieties are budded. Hopefully, the rootstock remains underground, and only the hybrid grows above ground.

Rugosa roses are descendants from *R. rugosa,* a particularly hardy species rose that flourished in northern China, Korea, and Japan more than 3,000 years ago. Although recent Rugosa hybrids are modest growers, like their ancestor, most possess unusually sturdy growth habits and flourish in poor soil even when neglected. Some varieties require little or no pruning; many are intensely fragrant; most produce hefty crops of hips.

Seedling roses grow from seeds harvested from a rose hip, whether naturally crossed or hybridized.

Semidouble roses have 10 to 20 petals per bloom.

Sepal. One of five divisions of the calyx, resembling bracket-shaped, individual leaves that lend architectural support to the bloom held above them.

Shrub roses differ from rosebushes in gracefulness. Whereas most modern bushes are bred for their ability to repeat-flower, Shrubs are for the garden at large. They are easy to grow, and many varieties grow gracefully naturally. Although the majority of Shrub roses in commerce bloom throughout summer, some blossom only once.

Single roses have between 5 and 12 petals per bloom.

Species roses are wild roses.

Sport. A spontaneous rose mutation that results in new colors or growth habits of an existing variety with no assist from mankind. A rosebush with white blossoms, for instance, may suddenly bloom deep red along one stem. Or a rose that supposedly grows only as a shrub suddenly starts to climb.

Stamen. The male organ of a flower, composed of the pollen-producing anther and filament.

Stigma. The tip of the pistil.

Sucker growth grows from rootstock rather than from the hybrid budded above. Blossoms of rootstock are rarely pretty, although roses such as *R. chinensis* produce nice flowers. Sucker growth should be eliminated from plants as soon as it's indisputably recognized.

Systemic fertilizers, insecticides, and miticides are absorbed directly into plants through foliage or roots.

Tea roses originated from crosses of Bourbon and Noisette roses with two of the original stud roses from China. Their bushes lack vigor and hardiness, but their lovely blossoms can handily compensate for such deterrents.

Tetraploid. A plant with four sets of chromosomes.

Upright rosebushes are those that grow sternly vertically.

Sources

UNITED STATES

Antique Rose Emporium
Rt. 5, Box 143
Brenham, TX 77833
409-936-9051
800-441-0002
Heirloom and Shrub roses.

Edmund's Roses
6235 S.W. Kahle Rd.
Wilsonville, OR 97070
503-682-1476
Fax: 503-682-1275
Modern roses.

Garden Valley Ranch Nursery
498 Pepper Rd.
Petaluma, CA 94952
707-795-0919
Fax: 707-792-0349
http://www.gardenvalley.com
Wide selection.

Greenmantle Nursery
3010 Ettersburg Rd.
Garberville, CA 95440
707-986-7504
Heirloom roses.

Heirloom Old Garden Roses
24062 Riverside Dr. N.E.
St. Paul, OR 97137
503-538-1576
Own-root roses.

High Country Rosarium
1717 Downing at Park Ave.
Denver, CO 80218
303-832-4026
Winter-hardy roses.

Jackson & Perkins
1 Rose Lane
Medford, OR 97501-0701
800-292-4769
Wide selection of varieties growing on virus-free rootstock.

Lowe's Own Root Rose
  Nursery
6 Sheffield Rd.
Nashua, NH 03062
603-888-2214
Own-root roses.

NorEast Miniature Roses
P.O. Box 307
58 Hammond St.
Rowley, MA 01969
508-948-7964
800-426-6485
Fax: 508-948-5487
or
P.O. Box 473
Ontario, CA 91762
714-984-2223
800-426-6485
Fax: 714-986-9875

Sources

Roses of Yesterday and Today
802 Brown's Valley Rd.
Watsonville, CA 95076
408-724-2755
Fax: 408-724-1408
Heirloom roses.

Sequoia Nursery
2519 E. Noble Ave.
Visalia, CA 93277
209-732-0190
Minis and Ralph Moore varieties.

Tiny Petals Nursery
489 Milnot Ave.
Chula Vista, CA 91910
619-422-0385
Miniature roses.

Wayside Gardens
1 Garden Lane
Hodges, SC 29695
800-845-1124
Generalists.

CANADA
Hortico, Inc.
Robson Rd., R.R. 1
Waterdown
Ontario, Canada L0R 2H1
416-689-6984
Fax: 416-689-6566

Pickering Nurseries, Inc.
670 Kingston Rd., Hwy. 2
Pickering
Ontario, Canada L1V 1A6
416-839-2111

ENGLAND
David Austin Roses
Bowling Green Lane
Albrighton
Wolverhampton WV7 3HB
England

Peter Beales Roses
Attleborough
Norfolk NR17 1AY
England

AUSTRALIA
The Perfumed Garden Pty
  Ltd.
47 Rendelsham Ave.
Mt. Eliza 3930
Australia

NEW ZEALAND
Trevor Griffiths & Sons Ltd.
No. 3 R.D.
Timaru
New Zealand

SOUTH AFRICA
Ludwigs Roses C.C.
P.O. Box 28165
Sunnyside
Pretoria 0132
South Africa

Index

SONGS, ROARS, AND RITUALS

LESLEY J. ROGERS

AND

GISELA KAPLAN

Songs, Roars, and Rituals

COMMUNICATION IN BIRDS,

MAMMALS, AND OTHER ANIMALS

HARVARD UNIVERSITY PRESS · CAMBRIDGE, MASSACHUSETTS · 2000

An earlier version of this book was published in 1998 by Allen & Unwin as
Not Only Roars and Rituals: Communication in Animals

Drawings by Tina Wilson

Library of Congress Cataloging-in-Publication Data

Rogers, Lesley J.
    Songs, roars, and rituals : communication in birds, mammals, and other animals /
Lesley J. Rogers and Gisela Kaplan.
        p. cm.
    Rev. ed. of: Not only roars and rituals. 1998.
    Includes bibliographical references (p.).
    ISBN 0-674-00058-7 (hard : alk. paper)
    1. Animal communication.   I. Kaplan, Gisela.   II. Rogers, Lesley J. Not only
roars and rituals.   III. Title.
QL776 .R64 2000
591.59—dc21   00-025602

*To the memory of Tipsy,
a dog special to us among all animals*

CONTENTS

It is reasonable to ask at the beginning of this book why communication in animals interests us. What can knowledge of animal communication achieve, both in terms of understanding our own environment and in terms of our ethical position toward the natural world?

Researching animal behavior is a humbling experience. It shows how little we know about the hundreds of thousands of species that inhabit the globe and how little we know of the ways in which they communicate within and between species. How exciting it is when we think that perhaps we may have cracked another part of a code in this enormously large world of secret codes.

We are constantly discovering more about the complex capabilities of animals. No one can help being impressed by the wealth of social subtleties and complexities that individual species display. In the songs, roars, and rituals they perform, we begin to see meaning. Here is our personal wonder, pleasure, and excitement in studying animal communication. These are qualities that ultimately sustain the most enduring inquiries.

We also know only too well that new knowledge of animal behavior is needed urgently. Many species are tumbling into extinction because of direct human intervention and human mistreatment of the precious legacy of the natural world. In some cases, we do not even know why. In others, we know why, but have found few acceptable ways of coexisting with other species. Instead, we have deprived them of habitat and conditions they need to survive. Some of that mistreatment, exploitation, or coercive control may in part be based on ignorance. As the social philosopher Hannah Arendt once said, most people who "do evil do not intend to do evil." The rate of extinction of species shows that we are doing evil and, ironically, in so many instances we are doing this while actually proclaiming our liking for animals. We harm them even by assuming that they must like, react to, and be comfortable with the same things that satisfy us. This is often far from the case. Only in the twentieth century have we humans truly begun to understand that the existence of animals and their well-being is tied to ours. In turn, our well-being, at least partly, is dependent on their being allowed to maintain their lives.

In this introduction to animal communication, we attempt to provide a sympathetic but scientifically well-founded argument about a set of complex behaviors in animals. We have considered a broad range of communicative patterns in mammals and birds, and even in frogs and other species. One focus in this book is on learning to communicate so as to suggest to the reader, and to remind ourselves, that we still need to free our thinking from the legacy of Descartes and his view that the capacities of animals are purely mechanistic. One of the aims of this book, then, is to suggest that many animals are sensitive to what they do and to what we may do to them. Many may suffer at our hands and many are doomed to slide into extinction unless we can learn to respect animals in ways that leave them unfettered space to lead their lives. Although this is an introductory book on the broad issues of communication in animals, we hope very much that it is a book to be enjoyed as much by the general reader as by the student of ethology and by colleagues in the field, offering some special morsels and giving a portrait of animals consistent with our view that animals matter a great deal.

Many of the ideas that form the backbone of this book were refined in valuable discussions with our colleagues and friends, Professors Michael Cullen, Judith Blackshaw, Richard Andrew, Peter Slater, Jeannette Ward, Dietmar Todt, Allen and the late Beatrix Gardner, and also Drs. Christopher Evans, Patrice Adret, Michelle Hook-Costigan, and Jim Scanlan. We are also most grateful to our anonymous reader for Harvard University Press for excellent suggestions and to our editors Michael Fisher and Nancy Clemente.

SONGS,

ROARS, AND

RITUALS

Chapter One

A large flock of galahs, Australian cockatoos, is feeding on grain scattered on newly plowed soil. Hundreds of white crests, though flattened, are distinctly visible against the birds' bright pink breasts and the background. Each bird maintains a characteristic social distance from the others and the hundreds of bowed yet bobbing heads suggest complete attention to feeding—until, catching sight of an approaching farmer, one bird raises its crest and screeches. At this signal of alarm the flock takes to the air as if the decision to do so were instantaneous. A signal has been sent and its meaning interpreted reliably by each member of the flock. Communication has occurred.

An enormous elephant seal lumbers up the beach, head raised, snorting as he threatens a rival. The animals make aggressive lunges at each other, blood is drawn, and, with growling sounds, a truce is reached. One seal bows his head and moves away. Victor and loser have communicated on a matter of disputed territory and partner ownership has been decided.

These are grand spectacles of communication, but intimate and close-range contact has its own forms of more subtle communication. A mother orangutan cradles her baby of seven days on her chest as she hangs by all four limbs. She smiles, as a human might do, and the infant glances up at her. A bond has formed between mother and infant and is maintained by communication.

As these examples show, communication in animals can take many forms, and before we explore such, it is important to have a working definition of what we mean by communication in a more general sense. There are many different definitions of communication and they vary with the field in which the researcher is working. When referring to communication in humans, psychologists often restrict the concept to acts that we perform with the *intention* of altering the behavior of another person. Linguists, however, are prepared to use a broader definition of communication to include the gestures and facial expressions that we make quite unintentionally while speaking. Since the person receiving these signals perceives and interprets both the intentional and unintentional signals, they feel it is important to include both types of signaling in discussions of communication in humans.

There is no question that a large amount of communication among humans is intentional, but much unintentional signaling takes place as well. For example, in many cultures, someone giving a friendly greeting to another person raises his or her eyebrows for a moment. This facial gesture is called "eyebrow flashing." Unless we make a conscious effort to think about it, we are not aware of having performed an eyebrow flash. Even the receiver may not be aware of having seen the eyebrow flash, despite the fact that it is a very important aspect of the greeting and alters the receiver's interpretation of the words spoken at the time. As Irenaus Eibl-Eibesfeldt (1972) has demonstrated, greetings made without the eyebrow flash are interpreted as less friendly even when the spoken words are identical. People in some cultures do not eyebrow flash (most Japanese people, for instance do not do so and, as Eibel-Eibesfeldt found, they even think it is indecent), and this can create unintentional difficulties in intercultural communication. There are many other examples of what is called nonverbal communication in humans, most of which are both signaled and received unintentionally.

We can always find out what aspects of signaling by humans are intentional by asking senders exactly what message they meant to communicate and what aspects of the signal they are aware of performing. This is not possible when we are studying communication in animals. Even if an animal is sending a signal intentionally, it is very difficult for us to prove that this is so. The question of intentional versus unintentional signaling in animals is a hotly debated topic and one of major significance for the way in which we view and treat animals, but it is very difficult to study.

We must now decide on a definition of communication that will be useful in the study of communication in animals. Communication requires one individual to send a signal of some description and another individual to receive that signal and interpret its meaning (Figure 1.1).

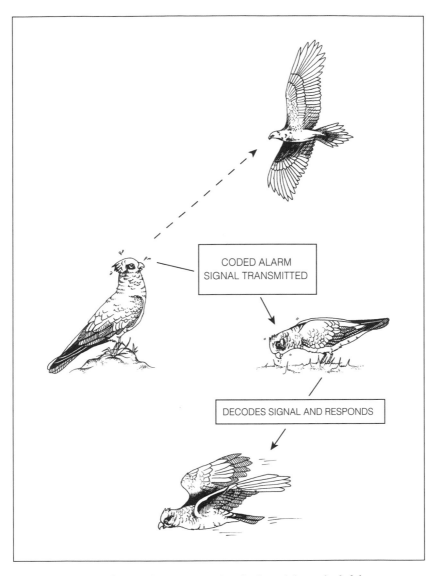

FIGURE 1.1 Sending and receiving a signal. The galah on the left has seen an eagle flying overhead and sends a coded alarm signal. This signal is transmitted through the air and detected by the galah on the right. The latter must discriminate and decode the message, which it does very rapidly, and then it responds by flying off. Note that the predator too may receive the message and respond by attacking the sender. Drawing attention to oneself is a risk of issuing a warning signal.

Biologists specify how the signal must be detected and processed by the receiver: the signal must be perceived by the receiver through one or more of the sensory systems—usually by the sense of vision, hearing, smell, or touch. In broad terms, we can say that an animal has signaled when it changes its behavior, and that communication has occurred when that signal is perceived and interpreted by at least one other animal. Of course, there are many ways in which a signal can be transmitted and many ways in which it can be received.

Communication is often seen as a way of changing another's behavior without physical force or any large expenditure of energy. In a paper published in 1972, Michael Cullen illustrated this point. He said that the command "Go jump in the lake" is a signal, whereas the push that might be delivered with it is not. The push may, in fact, convey very important information to the receiver, but the biologist views the push as physical force rather than true communication (Cullen, 1972). In this example, the verbal command is perceived by the sense of hearing, probably in conjunction with an angry facial expression perceived by the visual system; the verbal signal may change the receiver's behavior, although in this case the receiver is likely to take up a defensive posture rather than do what is commanded. The receiver might also choose to ignore the verbal signal, but could not ignore the physical force that follows the command.

The example of the alarm signal given by the galah is energy-efficient because a relatively small effort on the part of the galah that issues the alarm call leads to a large energy response: the whole flock takes flight. This signal is also time-efficient because the whole flock takes off almost instantaneously. It would be very inefficient in terms of energy and time if the signaler had to go around and physically push each member of its flock into taking off. There are, however, instances of signaling that are less efficient in energy and time. The loud roaring of red deer stags is one.

The broadest definition of a signal considers that communication occurs if any aspect of one animal's presence or behavior leads to a change in another animal. Any change in posture or other aspect of the sender is considered to be a signal. The signal, according to this definition, does not have to be specific or precisely tailored to the situation. It might merely involve a change in body posture or a slight movement of the mouth or eyes.

A somewhat narrower definition of a signal, as used by John Krebs and Nick Davies (1993), specifies that the sender (or actor) must use a specially adapted signal: a signal that has evolved to be used for communication. This is basically the same definition of signaling stated earlier by Edward O. Wilson (1975). Wilson said that communication is an action by one organism that alters the behavior pattern of another organism in a fashion that is adaptive to either one or both of the participants. The word "adaptive" is important here. Wilson said that by "adaptive" he meant that the signaling or the response, or both, have been genetically programmed by natural selection. Hence this definition confines communication to signaling and receiving that have become part of the genetic characteristics of the species. Means of communication that are learned during the individual's lifetime, and may be passed on from one generation to the next by cultural transmission, are not included in Wilson's definition of communication. Of course, genes always play some role in behavior—for example, genes determine whether we have hands or wings and that determination influences what kinds of signals we can send. But that is not what Wilson means by adaptive signaling; he means that the behavior of signaling, or the behavior of the response itself, is to a large extent controlled by genes.

STUDYING COMMUNICATION

As observers, we can tell that the signal has been perceived and interpreted only if the receiver changes its behavior in response to the signal. Therefore, to determine whether communication has taken place we may look for a change in the sender's behavior followed by a change in the receiver's behavior. Sometimes, however, the receiver of the signal may not respond. Nonresponse to a signal presents a problem to human observers of animal behavior because we have no way of knowing that communication has occurred unless the receiver responds overtly to the signal. Thus scientists who study the behavior of animals are forced to ignore signaling that the receiver ignores; they say that communication has occurred only when the behavior of the receiver is observed to change as a consequence of receiving the signal. Although we recognize that this approach means that we will overlook some of the signals that pass between animals, it is not a serious problem at present—we still have much to learn about signals between animals that do, in fact, change the behavior of the receiver. It is also likely that most signals given by animals in their natural environments cause the receiver to respond in one way or another.

Among the scientists interested in communication between animals are behavioral ecologists, who focus on special signals that have evolved to ensure the survival of the individual animal. The warning call of the galah and its ability to trigger flight is an example of this kind of communication. So too are courtship rituals that have evolved to form and maintain bonds between individuals and to ensure that mating behavior is confined to members of the same species. Many of these signals involve elaborate choreography performed in a highly stylized, stereotyped, or ritualized manner. These signals are performed with little variation between individuals and are patterns of behavior that are quite distinctive to the species. They are called displays. Displays are the same as signals, at least the most obvious ones, although usually we use the term "displays" to refer to visual signals only, not to vocal signals or signals conveyed by any of the other senses.

In 1914 Julian Huxley described the extraordinary and complex mating display of the great crested grebe *(Podiceps cristatus)*. The courting pair perform a complex ritual of precision swimming, beginning with synchronized skimming across the surface of a lake, then diving at the same time and rising together with weeds in their beaks and assuming an upright posture by treading water while they face each other. Another courting display is the male riflebird's *(Ptiloris* spp.) rhythmic opening and closing of one wing after the other; he stretches each wing over his head and bobs his head as he does so. This visual display is accompanied by sharp, explosive sounds, produced each time a wing is opened. The combined auditory and visual performance attracts the female and she responds by becoming sexually receptive. Elaborate courtship displays are performed by many species, from insects to humans.

Ethologists, who study the behavior of animals, are interested in courtship and other displays such as these but also in somewhat less ritualized signaling that could be part of any aspect of social behavior, unrelated to survival in any obvious way.

To study communication in animals we watch for changes in behavior, first by the sender (or actor) of the message and then by the receiver, sometimes referred to as the "perceiver" or the "reactor." Without the signal, there would be no change in the behavior of the receiver. But observing communication is a little more complicated than simply looking for a change in the behavior of the sender followed by a change in the behavior of the receiver because sometimes signals can actually *prevent* a change in the receiver's behavior. The receiver may, for instance, go on performing the same behavior as long as it is receiving a signal but switch to another behavior only when the signal is no longer given. The female riflebird may continue to show sexual responses as long as the male continues his courtship display but cease to do so if he stops displaying. In this case, the continued presence of the signal maintains the receiver's state of readiness.

Hence the receiver's behavior can change during the time when the sender is signaling of after the signaling ceases. We can put these two types of response by the receiver together and simply say that communication has occurred when the behavior of the receiver changes either after the signaling begins or after it stops.

Some signals are sent and received very rapidly and they cause immediate responses—the warning call is a dramatic example. Other signals act more slowly because they are not immediately detected by the receiver, especially signals that use odors. For example, marmosets, which are small monkeys of the South American rainforest, deposit scented secretions on branches; these signals are detected by other marmosets when they contact the same branches, even some time after the marmoset that deposited the message has moved away. Both short-delay and longer-delay signaling represent communication.

There is another form of longer-delay signaling in which the signal is received and processed but the receiver's behavior does not change until after a long period of delay. For example, a female wild dog, or a wolf, may signal that she is coming into estrus both by her behavior (she mounts other dogs more often) and by her odor (of secretions from the vagina and in her urine). Although these signals are received by the alpha male in the pack, he may not respond by mating until she has reached the peak of her estrus and is most likely to conceive. Delayed forms of responding to signals, such as this one, are difficult to study because it is not easy to link the sending of the signal to the receiver's change in behavior. But such signal-response delays are common among animals that attend to odors and are important aspects of communication that we humans tend to forget—compared to many species of animals, we are less aware of odors, even though they do influence our behavior.

The variations in delay time from sending the signal to changing the behavior of the receiver and in the intensity of the signal (from subtle to very obvious) mean that any definition of communication has to be quite broad. In addition, we prefer a broader definition of communication to include signaling and responding that is largely learned, and we do so for two reasons. First, learned communication can be as an important as adaptive (genetically programmed) communication. Second, in most cases of signaling in vertebrates, there is no empirical evidence to say whether or not a form of communication is largely programmed in the genes or largely learned.

CONSPICUOUS AND SUBTLE SIGNALS

Some forms of roaring or bellowing by animals require considerable energy expenditure and rather large amounts of time to signal information. The same is true of some elaborate visual displays, often used in courtship. Signaling that requires such large amounts of effort is said to be "honest signaling" because it lets the receiver know something important about the signaler, his size or physical health and strength, for example. Amotz Zahavi (1975) argues that receivers should not respond to signals unless they are honest. This would mean that honest signaling would be selected by the receivers, and so the receivers would be in control of the evolutionary process. The end result of this process of selection would be the evolution of signals that are very costly to produce; Zahavi called these "handicaps" (Zahavi and Zahavi, 1997).

The peacock's tail, used in sexual signaling, is the prime example of a handicap. It is a handicap in everyday activities, but, Zahavi says, it is precisely because the male's tail is a handicap that females prefer it to be as long and cumbersome as possible. The tail demonstrates a male's ability to survive despite the handicap, which means that he must be healthy and have other qualities that are essential for day-to-day survival. Males with longer, and more colorful, tails are likely to have "good" genes, and females will choose to mate with them. Marion Petrie, Tim Halliday, and

Carolyn Sanders (1991) have shown that peahens prefer to mate with peacocks with the largest number of eyespots on their trains. This result may explain why the apparently oversized, ornate train is likely to have evolved despite the handicap it causes the male in moving around and fleeing predators. Females prefer to mate with males that signal honestly.

The deep croaks of many species of toads are another example of honest signaling because the larger the toad the deeper the croak it can produce. The frequency of the fundamental (lowest) tone of the toad's call, therefore, signals honestly about his size and thus his potential to win in a contest (Davies and Halliday, 1978). The same can be said of the roaring of red deer stags; this vocalization requires great muscular effort and is produced most effectively by males in a good condition to fight (Clutton-Brock and Albon, 1979; also described in Bradbury and Vehrenkamp, 1998).

Some signals, however, are "dishonest," meaning that they lie about the sender's physical condition. Many signals conceal the physical state (strength or, especially, weakness) or state of health of the sender. These dishonest signals are used when the sender wants to withhold information in order to bluff another or to deceive another (this is summarized in Bradbury and Vehrencamp, 1998). The threat display of the mantis shrimp *(Gonodactylus bredini)* is a classic example of bluffing. These shrimps live in solitary burrows in coral reefs. They make use of holes in the coral, but the holes are in short supply and the shrimps compete for them. A shrimp that possesses a burrow must defend it vigorously from would-be occupiers. The resident will attack intruders that are not too much larger than itself but will flee from intruders that are much larger. There is one stage of development when the resident is very vulnerable and would be unable to defend itself should a fight ensue, and that is for the first three days after it has molted. Molting involves shedding the shell (exoskeleton) to expose a new shell underneath. This new exoskeleton is very soft and would provide no protection in a fight. The shrimp, therefore, is not in a position to attack while its new shell is soft, but it still performs the threat display to intruders as if it were able to attack. The signal is dishonest and may bluff the intruder (Adams and Caldwell, 1990).

We have discussed a number of signals that require much effort to produce. Other signals require very little effort and so cost little to produce.

Among animals we can find various degrees of economy of effort, as well as a range of signals from the very obvious to the very subtle. Conspicuous signals are more costly than less conspicuous ones. It has been suggested that the amount of conflict between the signaler and the receiver determines how conspicuous a signal will be (this is summarized in Dawkins, 1993). When both the sender and the receiver benefit from the communication taking place, inconspicuous signals should evolve. This would lead to "conspiratorial whispers" and, for example, subtle signals by which one member of a group warns the others that a predator is nearby. When there is conflict between the sender and the receiver, large and loud signals will evolve, as is the case in disputes over territory or sexual partners. In other words, a kind of coevolutionary arms race takes place; such signals become louder and louder or more and more conspicuous. The honesty of these signals is said to be ensured by their cost to the sender. There is, however, little evidence to support this idea as a general principle.

In fact, the size, strength, and duration of a signal may have little to do with sender-receiver costs and benefits and may instead be determined by the type of environment in which the signal must be sent. As we discuss further in Chapter 2, some environments cause the signal to attenuate rapidly and so demand the expenditure of large amounts of energy to send the signal in such a way that it can be detected by the receiver. The need to adapt signals to the physical environment is a most important factor in their evolution, but social factors also have an influence. The sensory systems used by the receiver to detect the signal must also evolve according to environmental requirements. They need to be attuned to detecting signals in particular environments. To overstate the case, it is no use specializing in the ability to detect high-frequency sounds in an environment in which such frequencies are not transmitted effectively.

The animal's ability to process the information that it receives and to remember the signals may also influence communication. Some signals may be designed to ensure that they are remembered. There may even be some simple formulas that assist memory and apply to a wide range of species. This might explain why a surprising number of poisonous species, from insects to toads and snakes, are colored black and yellow or black and red. Perhaps these color combinations are remembered easily by their predators. The "aim" of a species that is poisonous to eat is to signal this fact to any species that might possibly consider preying on it and to ensure that predators remember and stay away.

COMMUNICATION BETWEEN SPECIES

Most communication occurs between members of the same species (intraspecies communication), but there are occasions, as we have already seen, when one species signals to another or when one species responds to the signals of another species (interspecies communication). Communication about being poisonous to a potential predator is an example of communication between different species. Indeed, most known examples of interspecies communication involve predator-prey relationships. The potential prey signals to the predator in an attempt to deflect its attack. When cornered by a predator, the last resort of the potential prey is to try to scare off the predator by looking as big as possible, showing bright colors, or making a terrifying sound. Toads adopt a threat posture in which they puff up with air and stand high on their limbs, thereby making themselves look as large as they can.

Other strategies can be used by animals that are cornered. The sudden flash of a brightly colored signal may confuse the predator just long enough for the potential prey to get away. This tactic is used by some lizards, such as *Anolis* species, which perform push-ups and flash the dewlap when they encounter a predator such as a snake (Leal and Rodriguez, 1997). The Australian frill-necked lizard has an even more impressive display to communicate with a predator: it raises the large ruff around its neck so that, from the front, it looks many times larger; it opens its mouth to reveal the brightly colored tongue and lining of the mouth and then hisses. This striking display is usually followed by a rapid retreat, the lizard running on its hind limbs, ruff still raised. If the predator has been thrown momentarily off guard by the display, the lizard may have a slight advantage as it beats its retreat.

Another form of interspecies signaling by prey to predator is aimed at deflecting the attack to a less vulnerable part of the prey's body. The eyespots (ocelli) on the wings of some moths and butterflies may be used in this way, as was first demonstrated by David Blest (1957). When a bird is poised to attack, the moth or butterfly opens its wings to reveal the ocelli. Since birds are very interested in eyes, they tend to peck at the ocelli instead of the body of the moth or butterfly. Alternatively, revealing the ocelli may startle the bird and give the potential prey time to escape. This form of interspecies communication is so important for survival that some species have stylized the display by employing different ways of flashing the ocelli, either rhythmically or in a more static fashion.

Plovers feign injury to deflect the attention of the predator away from their offspring in the nest on the ground. As the predator approaches, the mother plover moves away from the nest in a manner that would signal she has a broken wing. This is a dramatic form of interspecies signaling. Another form of prey-to-predator signaling has been called pursuit-deterrent signaling. Tim Caro has used the term "pursuit-deterrent signalling" for communication in which the potential prey signals that it has seen the predator or that it is able to escape (Caro, 1995). The effect of the signal appears to be to stop the predator from attacking. For example, on seeing a predator, the Thomson's gazelle performs stotting (high leaps from all fours with the tail up displaying the white rump), bannertail kangaroo rats drum their feet, and swamp wrens flick their tails.

The stotting of Thomson's gazelles is an example of honest signaling, using high-energy expenditure to advertise the sender's physical prowess to the predator. It is costly both in terms of energy and in terms of the loss of valuable time for escape. A number of researchers have puzzled over this seeming contradiction. It was first thought that this was a visual signal to warn other gazelles in the herd to flee. But Zahavi (1979) suggested that stotting is, instead, directed at the predator, signaling the gazelle's physical fitness and therefore its ability to escape. C. D. Fitzgibbon and J. H. Fanshaw (1988) have provided some evidence in support of this idea. They found that a predator is more likely to attack a gazelle that stots at a low rate than one that is in better physical condition and can stot at a high rate. Stotting in the presence of a predator may thus save the life of an individual gazelle. It is therefore an "honest" signal, showing the predator what the gazelle can actually do, rather than being a form of manipulation.

The rich variety of signals between prey and predator is a manifestation of the importance of communication in survival. Communication between species may be of mutual benefit or may be aimed at enhancing the survival of the signaler over that of the receiver. Usually the outcome of signaling benefits the sender exclusively, not the receiver, but sometimes the receiver may benefit in ways that are not immediately obvious. Even though prey–predator signaling may lead the predator to abandon its pursuit, abandonment may be in the predator's interest because success is more likely to be achieved by stalking a prey that has not seen the predator, or one that is weaker and can be caught more easily.

Other forms of interspecies communication involve detection of predators but not direct signaling to the predator itself. The best example of this form of signaling is the response of vervet monkeys to the eagle alarm call of starlings living in the same area. The monkeys heed the starling's alarm signal and take cover. It is most unlikely that the starling is directing its signal to the vervet monkeys; it is trying to warn other members of its own species. The monkeys are simply able to "tune in" to the starlings' signals and exploit them.

HOW COMMUNICATION PATTERNS COME ABOUT

Many of the ritualized displays performed by animals look so bizarre to us that we wonder how they came about—and no doubt many human displays look equally bizarre to animals. Most of the various forms of signaling that are used by different species of animals have not arisen afresh in each separate species. As one species evolves into another, particular forms of signaling may be passed on, owing to the effects of both genes and learning or experience. Some signals have significance across many species, and so remain much the same over generations and in a number of species. But many signals, as they are passed from generation to generation by whatever means, go through changes that make them either more elaborate or simply different. If we examine closely related species, we can often see slight variations in a particular display and we can piece together an explanation for the spread of the display across species. Some very elaborate displays may have begun as simpler versions of the same behavioral pattern that became more elaborate as they developed and were passed on from generation to generation.

But how might signals or displays have come about in the first place? Some displays appear to have developed from movements made when the animal is getting ready to perform a particular behavior. These are known as "intention movements." Other signals may have come about when particular parts of a behavior pattern are elaborated on. Sometimes the part of the behavior pattern that is elaborated on appears to be irrelevant to the situation in which it occurs. For this reason, it has been called a "displacement" activity, although it is now debated whether the activity is really displaced or outside of context, and that is why we will use the term "displacement" within quotation marks. For example, two cocks threatening to fight may sometimes break off their aggressive displays, directed at each other, and peck at the ground with the beak closed. This "titbitting" behavior has been considered to be a "displacement" activity because it is not obviously relevant to the display of aggression. But those who came to this conclusion might merely have been unable to interpret the animals' behavior accurately enough to know what it really means. It could be relevant and observers simply cannot see that this is so, as Marian Dawkins said in her book *Unravelling Animal Behaviour,* published in 1986.

Another kind of behavior that has been referred to as "displacement" behavior in many contexts is grooming or preening. A cat that is eager to be fed but cannot persuade its owner to open the refrigerator may suddenly stop meowing and rubbing its owner's legs and switch to licking itself; or a bird that is unsure whether to eat a prey animal that it has not seen before may switch its attention away from the prey and preen itself briefly. In both these examples, the act of grooming or preening appears to be irrelevant to the main theme of the behavior pattern in which it occurs, but we may see it as irrelevant behavior only because we are ignorant of its function or purpose. It may therefore be better to refer to such examples as "redirected" behavior rather than "displacement" behavior. The performance of such redirected behavior may be observed and interpreted by another animal, in which case it serves as a signal.

Both intention movements and redirected behavior may be modified to signal to other animals. In addition, the physical and behavioral adjustments that animals make to regulate their physiological functions— to maintain body temperature within the correct range, for example— may be used to signal. We will discuss each of these in more detail later on. The point to stress here is that many elaborate displays appear to have evolved from simple behaviors that animals perform in their everyday life. These simple behaviors may also signal in subtle ways, but they become signals that are more obvious to the human observer when they have been exaggerated and so have become ritualized. Although the examples we consider are mostly the more exaggerated signals, we recognize that the less obvious signals may be just as important.

INTENTION MOVEMENTS

First we must distinguish between intention movements, which we are discussing in this chapter, and intentional signaling. In Chapter 3 we will discuss whether animals merely emit information that signals their emotional state or deliver planned communication in which signals are sent after the animal has made a decision about the context and other factors important at the time. In such cases, we use the term "intentional" to refer to the state of mind of the signaler, or at least to the cognitive processes involved in signaling. In this chapter, we use the term "intention movements" as ethologists do, to refer to those behaviors performed in preparation for an activity. Such behaviors signal what the animal is about to do next but they do not, in themselves, tell us anything about whether the animal thinks about performing them as opposed to performing them uncontrollably and without any form of thought. It is possible that the more ritualized these behaviors become—and so the more obvious they are as signals—the more likely it is that they will be performed with at least some of the intentionality we refer to in Chapter 3, but there has been virtually no research on this topic.

The first example of an intention movement that we will consider is the preparation for flight in birds. Before they take off into flight, many birds crouch, raise the tail, and withdraw the head (Figure 1.2A) and then stretch the body in the direction of the intended flight (Figure 1.2B). A bird may adopt this posture several times before it takes off, and thereby it signals to other members of the flock that it is about to fly. It has been observed that a pigeon does not usually disturb the other members of its flock if it performs flight-intention movements before taking off but that, if it flies off suddenly without these intention movements, the whole of the flock is likely to take to the air. In short, flight-intention movements signal that the individual is about to fly but should not be followed by the rest of the flock, whereas taking flight without prior flight-intention movements signals alarm and the whole flock takes off.

Richard Andrew (1956) studied in detail the flight-intention move-

FIGURE 1.2 Flight-intention postures and displays. A and B: Flight-intention movements. Crouching and raising the tail (A) is followed by lowering the tail and stretching the head and neck in the intended direction of flight (B), and these movements may be repeated several times before the bird takes off. C and D: Displays of the green heron *(Butorides virescens)* that incorporate aspects of flight-intention movements. C shows the forward threat display adopted in territorial defense, and D shows the stretch display performed as a prelude to mating. E: The head and tail-up posture of the kookaburra *(Dacelo gigas)* adopted when the bird is making its territorial laughing call. (After McFarland, 1985, and Smith, 1977.)

ments of certain species of birds and the involvement of head bobbing and tail flicking in many social displays. These aspects of the flight-intention movements have been incorporated into signaling patterns (displays). In some cases the meaning of the signal appears to be quite removed from the original intention movement. For example, the American green heron signals pair formation and courtship by adopting a posture in which the head is withdrawn, the beak held in the air, and the feathers on the head sleeked down (Figure 1.2D). This appears to be a modified flight-intention movement, and it contrasts with the species' aggressive display in which the beak is pointed forward, the feathers are ruffled, and the tail is vibrated (Figure 1.2C). The aggressive display also has elements of flight-intention movements but it includes aiming of the bird's weapon (the beak) at its opponent. There are even elements of modified flight-intention movement in the posture of the kookaburra *(Dacelo gigas)* when it makes its territorial call, which sounds like laughing.

Similarly, a gull about to attack stretches its neck out horizontally and directs its beak at its opponent, as Niko Tinbergen (1960, 1965) so clearly described for herring gulls. Tinbergen also described the upright threat posture of the herring gull, in which the neck is stretched upward and the head pointed downward (Figure 1.3A). Having adopted this posture, the gull struts toward its opponent. The positioning of the head and neck is exactly the posture that a gull adopts in circumstances in which it actually pecks its opponent. When the bird uses this posture as a threat display, but without actually pecking, it is a strong signal that the gull is about to attack. In this case, the intention movement of pecking has been used as a signal to display aggression.

Displaying of weapons is also characteristic of aggressive or threat displays in mammals. When a dog is about to attack, for example, it bares its teeth in preparation for biting. Bared teeth have become a display that signals aggression in many mammals. But we must add that the bared-teeth display is accompanied by changes in the eyes, ears, and body posture of the dog. Only by taking all these features into account can we accurately interpret the meaning of the bared-teeth display (see Andrew, 1965). A dog with its teeth bared, eyes open wide, ears erect, and tail up in a confident posture is threatening (Figure 1.3B), but one with teeth bared, eyes almost closed, ears flattened, and tail down between its legs is

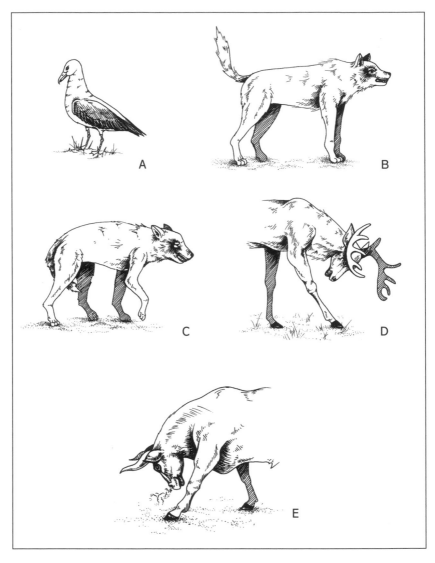

FIGURE 1.3 Threat postures. A: A herring gull adopting an upright threat posture (drawn from a photograph by Tinbergen, 1960). B: A dog with teeth bared, eyes open wide, ears forward, and tail up in a confident threat posture. C: A dog with teeth bared, eyes almost closed, ears flattened, and tail lowered in a defensive threat posture, indicating a high level of fear. D: A deer threatening to attack by displaying its weapons. E: A bull threatening in the same way.

afraid (Figure 1.3C), and will flee unless it is cornered, when it will attack. The latter display indicates that the dog is feeling a mixture of aggression and fear.

There are many other examples in which the showing of weapons signals that the animal is about to attack. A deer (Figure 1.3D) or a bull (Figure 1.3E) about to attack lowers its head and orients its horns at the object of aggression. These are all postures adopted in preparation for an actual attack, but in the display itself they do not actually lead to an attack on the opponent. Instead they are examples of intention movements being used to signal the possibility of aggression. Most such displays of aggression end with one animal backing off, thereby avoiding serious injury.

"DISPLACEMENT," OR REDIRECTED BEHAVIOR

We gave the example of titbitting in cocks as "displacement" behavior, on the grounds that when it interrupts aggressive displaying, it appears to be unrelated to the main purpose of the display. The cock pecks at small objects on the ground without picking them up, and thus the behavior does not appear to be related to the goal of feeding either. It may, however, have a function in relieving tension briefly and thus reducing the chance that an actual attack will occur. Cocks often threaten each other at the borders of their territories, and in such cases each animal experiences a conflict between approaching (and being attacked) and fleeing. "Displacement," or redirected, activities are often engaged in when an animal experiences conflict. Titbitting is one example, and by observing this behavior, another animal might recognize the position of the border of the territory. In other words, the "displacement" behavior might become a signal. Of course, once it has become a signal it can no longer be called a "displacement" activity because it has a genuine function related to the context in which it occurs. Taken together with our earlier point about the so-called irrelevance of "displacement" behaviors being merely a matter of our inability to understand them, this consideration makes the term "displacement" behavior very problematic indeed. Nevertheless, despite objections to the term, these *apparently* irrelevant behaviors do exist and elaboration upon them does appear to explain some forms of signaling.

"Displacement" preening is one of the most often cited cases. When such preening or grooming occurs, it may signal that the animal is in a state of conflict. We mentioned the cat that grooms itself when prevented from obtaining food. This is a form of approach-withdrawal conflict. The cat decides to lick itself instead of either approaching or withdrawing. Courtship behavior often involves conflict about whether to approach or withdraw, and this might explain why preening or grooming often occurs in courtship displays. In 1941 the Austrian ethologist Konrad Lorenz described preening as a feature of courtship displays in ducks (see also Lorenz, 1965). Shelducks *(Tadorna tadorna)* turn their heads to preen feathers on the back or wings during courtship. This is considered to be a displacement activity. The mallard duck *(Anas platyrhynchos)* does likewise but restricts its preening to brightly colored feathers on the wing. Preening reveals the feathers that have been specialized as part of the display. In the mallard the preening has become stylized, or ritualized. In the garganey duck *(Anas querquedula)* the ritualization is even greater; this species rubs its beak on specialized blue feathers on the outside of the wings in a way that mimics preening, although preening does not actually take place. The courtship display of the mandarin duck *(Aix galericulata)* has the greatest degree of ritualization of all these species of ducks. The mandarin duck does not actually preen but mimics the preening of two specialized secondary feathers that project up from its wings by touching them once only with the beak. The ritualization of the preening motion, and also the specialized feathers themselves, are an elaboration that appears to have evolved from the simple act of preening. The display is enhanced by the enlargement of the feathers that the duck touches with its beak and their rust-red color, which makes them stand out from the other feathers. The duck also raises a crest on the back of the head, increasing the ritualization of the behavior. In other words, the mandarin duck performs an exaggerated and highly specific display.

Differences between species in courtship displays may help to isolate closely related species from one another in situations where they live in overlapping territories. Through the use of different courtship signals, cross-breeding may be prevented. No confusion between species occurs as long as the signals indicating a willingness to mate are different for each species. In cases where species-specific mating signals occur, there is an intimate relationship between the evolution of a species and its communication signals.

In time, what might have begun as "displacement" (or redirected) preening has become a more specific signal employed in courtship displays. The example of courtship preening in ducks shows how signals might evolve, although it remains possible that learning has an essential role in establishing the final pattern of the display. Many other examples of ritualization of displacement behaviors have been described. Feeding of the female by the male is an aspect of courtship in many species, from budgerigars to gulls. The female begs for food much as the young do. When the male feeds the female during courtship, his provision of food is considered to be "displacement" behavior because it is not his goal at the time—his goal is to mate with her. In some species of birds, the behavior is ritualized by the giving of gifts in courtship. Like preening during courtship, feeding is part of the signaling process, indicating the strength of bonding and that the male will provide food for the female and offspring. Gift giving and feeding are of course also rituals in the courtship behavior of humans.

AUTONOMIC RESPONSES USED AS SIGNALS
Some of the behavioral and physical adjustments that animals must make to maintain their physiological state are also used to signal. These are known as autonomic responses because they are controlled by the autonomic nervous system. In humans, we know that these responses occur automatically, without conscious control. For example, in cases of extreme fear, the hair on our bodies is raised in preparation for cooling, necessary if we need to flee. Other autonomic responses occur also, but here we are interested in this particular one because raising of the hair is also common in other mammals. This fluffing of the hair, called piloerection, functions as a signal of fear in some species. In marmosets (*Callithrix* sp.) and tamarins (*Saguinus* sp.) piloerection in the form of fluffing of the tail signals fear and indicates that the monkey is more likely to flee than approach.

Richard Andrew (1972) was the first to point out the importance of autonomic responses in displays. He also noted that the raising and lowering of the feathers for autonomic control of body temperature has become a feature of many avian displays. Feather raising is quite difficult to interpret because slight raising (fluffing) of the feathers encloses air around the body and provides insulation for heat loss, whereas further raising causes ruffling of the feathers so that their tips no longer touch each other and consequently heat is lost because air is no longer trapped around the body. Ruffling often occurs in aggressive displays, when cooling might be needed, and fluffing often occurs when a bird is quiet and submissive. Laughing gulls, for example, perform an aggressive display in which they lower the head and jerk it rhythmically while making a deep call and ruffling the feathers. Galahs also indicate threat or aggression by ruffling the feathers (Figure 1.4).

Sleeking of the feathers is another way by which birds increase heat loss because it also reduces the amount of air trapped around the body. Feather sleeking occurs in the aggressive displays of some species. It appears commonly in states of high arousal, and it has also become incorporated into the camouflage posture of tawny frogmouths when a predator is near (see Figure 4.1). Whether feather sleeking is used as a signal between tawny frogmouths is unknown.

Urination and defecation are other autonomic responses that occur in a state of high arousal, evoked by very frightening stimuli. Not surprisingly, therefore, urination and defecation are used by some animals as part of fear or threat displays. Tawny frogmouths often turn and spray their extremely pungent feces at a predator approaching from below. When bushbabies (galagos, lower primates) mob a predator they frequently urinate on their hands and rub the urine on their bodies while emitting warning vocalizations and adopting threatening postures. The autonomic responses have become incorporated into the threat display.

The autonomic nervous system also controls the constriction and dilation of the pupils in the eyes, as we will discuss in Chapter 3. Pupil size may change according to the emotional state of the individual. The individual is not conscious of the change of pupil size but the observers, although not usually doing so consciously, assess and use this information. This is an aspect of autonomic function that is used involuntarily in communication in humans as well as in other species. In humans, dilated pupils give the face a more seductive appearance, and women used to put drops of the antimuscarinic drug belladonna in their eyes to dilate the

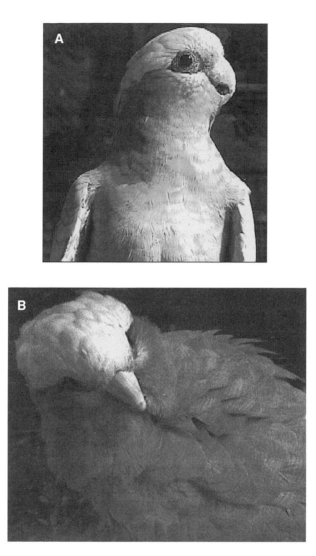

FIGURE 1.4   Feather ruffling in a galah *(Cacatua roseicapilla)*. A: Sleek posture. B: Feathers ruffled in an aggressive-threat posture. Both photographs are of the same individual. Note that in B the body feathers are raised and the feathers on the cheeks are elevated to an almost horizontal position, making the bird appear much larger than it is. (Photographs by G. Kaplan.)

pupils. They did this at the expense of being able to see clearly—the drug also paralyzes the muscle that controls the focus of the lens in the eye. In this case, signaling must have been seen as more important than receiving signals.

WHY SIGNALS BECOME RITUALIZED

A ritualized signal is one that is exaggerated, stereotyped, and usually repeated over and over. Quite obviously, a stereotyped signal states its point clearly and ritualization ensures that the signal is not easily confused with any other signal. This may be advantageous in itself, but there may be another reason why signals become stereotyped. As Desmond Morris suggested in 1957, ritualized signals are so stylized that they give away less information about the internal state of the sender than signals that are simpler intention movements, "displacement" behaviors, or autonomic responses. The last three types of signal convey information about the emotional state of the sender or indicate whether the sender is uncertain whether to attack or flee. Ritualized signals tend to conceal information about the sender's emotional state. In a sense, ritualization involves a loss of detailed information about the sender. As Morris suggests, ritualization may have come about precisely because it conceals this kind of information. Ritualization may be the signal-senders' way of manipulating the receiver without giving away too much information about themselves.

If it is the case that the sender is attempting to manipulate the receiver, the receiver might attempt to ignore the sender. The result might be increased ritualization by the sender, then increased ignoring by the receiver, and so on. This hypothesis is called the "arms race" explanation for ritualization. It differs from another hypothesis holding that ritualization came about to avoid signal confusion. The arms race hypothesis is, in fact, a far more beguiling view of animal communication than the one postulating avoidance of signal confusion. It seems to appeal to people accustomed to a pervasive advertising culture manipulating us all. Despite this appeal, there is no proof as to which hypothesis, if either, is correct. We note that, so far, researchers have been concerned with studying the conspicuous, ritualized signals that animals send. More attention to the subtle, quieter, and less exaggerated signals may change our views on the reasons for, and the evolution of, all signals.

CONCLUSION

The terms "communication" and "signaling" are quite interchangeable. Animals indulge in a great deal of communication about a wide range of matters. Their social life depends on communication. Communication occurs in even the simplest organisms that interact with each other, even if it is only for mating. In more complex organisms, a rich variety of communication occurs, making use of all the sensory systems and ranging from simple signals to complex ritualized displays. Some of these displays may be to a large extent the result of natural selection but even these signals may involve some learning. Other signals may be acquired largely by learning and be passed on from generation to generation as a form of culture. In some social situations and in certain environments "conspiratorial whispers" are the most effective form of communication, but in other social situations and environments the most effective communication involves the expenditure of a great deal of energy. The variety of signals, as well as responses, is enormous and fascinating.

Chapter Two

SIGNALS AND SENSORY PERCEPTION

Animals have a number of different senses and they make use of them all when they communicate. As humans, we are aware of the senses of vision, hearing (audition), touch (tactile sensation), taste (gustation), and smell (olfaction). We receive signals in all these sensory modalities but we are most aware of the visual and auditory ones. Language uses sound and is processed by the auditory system, but in most circumstances it is accompanied by visual signals and sometimes tactile signals as well. We are less aware of olfactory signals, and gustatory signals rarely reach our consciousness. Other species exploit these senses to a far greater extent.

The fact that we are less conscious of communication by odors or taste than by audition and vision does not mean that this form of communication is absent in humans. In his book *The Scented Ape* Michael Stoddart suggests that humans may be specialists in odor communication and that it influences our behavior much more than we think (Stoddart, 1990). Like most other mammals, we have specialized glands for releasing scents, and although we are far less able to detect very low concentrations of odors than members of many other species, such as dogs, we are quite good at discriminating between odors. We may use this ability to communicate among ourselves, but if we do, much of that communication goes on unintentionally and without our conscious awareness.

CHEMOSIGNALS

Marmosets deposit scents on trees and do so by rubbing the branches with the secretory glands on their chests or around their genitals. These odor, or olfactory, messages are called chemosignals. Some chemosignals indicate the general whereabouts of a species even when the individual who deposited the scent mark is not in the immediate vicinity. Other scent marks can signal the identity of the species, the identity of the individual, or its sex and social position. Marmosets deposit different odors that signal each of these very important social markers. All this complex information is communicated as smells, to be detected by the olfactory system.

Lemurs *(Lemur catta)* make use of the scent glands on their wrists, which they rub on their long, striped tails for olfactory communication. Alison Jolly has described "stink fights" in which a number of animals gather together on the ground with their tails raised and "throw" odors at each other by moving around and waving their tails back and forth over their heads (Jolly, 1966).

The sense of olfaction is one of the major senses of many aquatic species. Eels are extremely sensitive to very low concentrations of chemicals in the water, and it is thought that they use their sense of smell to return to the stream of their birth from miles away at sea. They may also use this sense to communicate with each other. A number of species of fish (minnows, catfish, sucker fish, and darters, for instance) release into the water an alarm substance from specialized cells in the skin whenever they incur even minor damage. Other members of the same species detect the alarm substance using their sense of smell and respond with typical fright reactions. Schooling fish, such as minnows, aggregate and swim away from the source of the alarm substance. Other more solitary fish sink to the bottom of the water and remain motionless; yet others swim to the surface and may even jump out of the water. In these species the sense of olfaction is critical for survival and plays a greater role than it does in humans.

ELECTRICAL SIGNALS

Some species have sensory abilities that humans lack, or do not use to any known degree. The ability to sense weak electrical fields is one of these. Electric fish (Gymnotidae and Mormyridae) have organs in their tails that send out pulses of electricity (up to 300 pulses per second) and these are used for navigation and detecting prey as well as for social signaling (Bullock and Heiligenberg, 1986). In some species, male and female fish pulse at different frequencies. The frequency of electrical pulses can indicate the sex of the fish and also its dominance in the social structure. Some species can vary the pulse rate to communicate. If there is a meeting between two fish sending out electrical signals at similar frequencies, either one or both will change the frequency of pulsing to avoid jamming the other's signals. Because the fish also use the electrical pulses for navigation, there would be confusion if they could not distinguish their own pulses from those of others. Dominant fish do not shift their frequency of pulsing to avoid jamming the transmission of another fish—that is up to the subordinate ones.

The Australian platypus *(Ornithorhynchos anatinus)* can detect electrical signals and uses this ability to locate its prey under water. The sensory organs used for this are located around the tip of the bill and enable the platypus to detect the electrical waves produced by the contracting muscles of its prey. As far as we know, however, the platypus has no specialized organ by which it can produce electrical signals itself, and so it is unlikely that it uses electrical signaling as a means of communicating with other members of its own species. Nevertheless, it is possible that a platypus can detect the electrical discharges generated when another platypus contracts its muscles during movement and can exploit this as a means of communication. This has yet to be studied.

TASTE

Taste is another sense that is used for communication, particularly by animals living in water. It is also used by many species of mammals, often in conjunction with olfaction. Cats, for example, deposit urine to mark territory. Other cats will approach the deposit of urine and sniff it, or even lick it or touch it with the upper lip and then lick the urine from the lip. Once on the tongue the urine can be tasted by means of receptors on the tongue and roof of the mouth. The urine contains substances characteristic of the cat from which they came, and the decay of these substances also indicates how long ago the animal was in the area. By smelling and tasting the urine the receiver can also tell whether the cat is ready to mate. In other words, the taste and odor convey information about the hormonal condition of the depositing cat, and this is possible because modified products of estrogen and testosterone are secreted into the urine.

Sheep and goats acquire similar information about the hormonal condition of the female, but they taste and smell the urine by licking it from the anogenital region (the area around the anus and genitals).

AUDITION

Animals also communicate by using a rich variety of auditory signals. Bird vocalizations are astounding in their variety, and most are within the hearing range of humans. Likewise, most mammals produce vocalizations that humans can hear, but some species also make ultrasonic calls. Although the calls of rats and mice are partially audible to us, most of their vocalizations are too high pitched for us to hear. If you walk into a laboratory full of rats in cages, you will hear a range of squeals and snorts, but the actual sounds are far more intense than you can perceive. This cacophony of vocalizations can be made audible to the human ear by recording them on a tape recorder capable of picking up ultrasound and then playing back the tape at a much slower speed so that the sounds are pitched at lower frequencies within our range of hearing.

Most rodents use ultrasounds to communicate. Mothers recognize their pups by the ultrasound that the pups produce, and they will retrieve their pups when they make ultrasonic distress calls. Adults also communicate with each other by ultrasounds. Some primates, such as marmosets, are able to vocalize in ultrasound, and bats specialize in it.

Certain communication sounds made by animals are quite pure in tonal quality, particularly those in the songs of birds. The two most beautiful examples of the musical songs of birds are perhaps the songs of the European nightingale *(Luscinia megarhynchos)* and the Australian magpie *(Gymnorhina tibicen)*. By transcribing the sound into a visual pattern, called a sonogram or sound spectrogram, we can see what these songs look like and study them in detail (see Figure 2.1). The sound pitch, or frequency, is plotted on the vertical axis (Y axis) and time is plotted along the horizontal axis (X axis). The loudness, or intensity, of each part of the sound is indicated by the darkness of the marks plotted. A pure tone is a single frequency at any one time, although this frequency may change. Other tones have a fundamental (lowest frequency) with harmonic overtones that appear as stripes above the fundamental. The absence of overtones gives the song a characteristic pure, whistle-like quality, as illustrated by the song of the Australian pied butcherbird *(Cracticus nigrogularis),* and harmonic overtones make the song sound rich and musical (Figure 2.1). Compare these song structures with the broad band structure of rasping calls, in which the sound energy is spread across the frequencies, and referred to as "noise" (Figure 2.2).

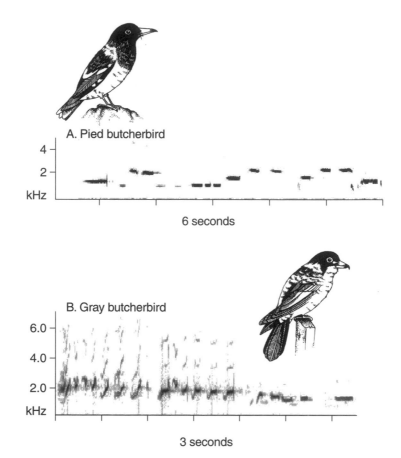

FIGURE 2.1 Sound spectrograms of butcherbird songs. A: The song of the pied butcherbird *(Cracticus nigrogularis)*. Note the pure tones. B: The song of the gray butcherbird *(Cracticus torquatus)*. Note the beginning of the song, where the syllables have loud fundamental frequencies (the dark marks at the bottom, approximately 200 kHz). Note also, above the fundamentals, the overtones (represented by marks at approximately 308 and 505 kHZ in the second section of the song). The last third of the song consists of pure tones much like those of the pied butcherbird. (Sound spectrograms produced by G. Kaplan.)

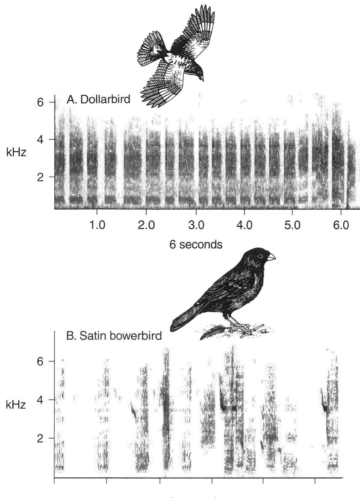

FIGURE 2.2 The sound spectrograms of noisy calls. A: The distress call of a dollarbird *(Eurystomus orientalis)*. Note that there are some overtones but that there is also a broad spread of frequencies across the range up to 5 kHz, called noise. B: Rasps made by a satin bowerbird *(Ptilonorhynchus violaceus)*. These calls have mostly a broad band of frequencies but there are some loud tones (black marks). In addition to the vocalizations presented here, the satin bowerbird produces a song that is very musical. (Sound spectrograms produced by G. Kaplan.)

Despite the fact that noisy birds do exist and that even songbirds produce some noisy calls, many birdsongs have tonality (musical sounds). By
comparison, many vocalizations produced by mammals are noisy, although there are many exceptions, such as the calls of gibbons and certain calls made by squirrel monkeys, macaque monkeys, and even chimpanzees. We give further examples in the chapters that follow.

VISION

Communication using the sense of vision is widespread among animal
species. These signals are made by moving limbs in certain ways (gestur-
ing), by adopting certain body postures, or by creating facial expressions.
The baboon that bares its teeth is not smiling but signaling its anger. A
dog indicates submission by arching its back and lowering its tail, sometimes wrapping the tail between its hind legs (Figure 1.3). A lizard that
bobs its head up and down is either signaling ownership of territory or
performing a courtship ritual. There are many examples of visual signaling in animals and we mention more later on. On some occasions visual
signals are used alone, but at other times they occur in conjunction with
vocalizations or communication signals involving the other senses. Combined signaling with more than one sense may ensure that the receiver
gets the right message.

THE BEST SIGNAL

To make sure that a signal can be detected by the receiver it is important
to choose the best form of signaling for the environment. Next we will
discuss how signaling in a particular sensory system has to be adapted
to the habitat in which the animal lives, and we will do that by discussing each sensory system separately, but first we should say that most signals use more than one sensory system at the same time. They are thus
multimodal (Partan and Marler, 1999). By stimulating more than one
sensory system at once, the sender captures the attention of the receiver,
and this seems to be true for humans, primates, birds, and insects as well.
The begging signals of nestling reed warblers *(Acrocephalus sciraceus),* for
example, are both visual and vocal. The nestlings open their beaks wide
to reveal the brighly colored skin inside and simultaneously they produce
vocalizations. The parents respond to the combined effects of stimulation
in these two sensory modalities by adjusting the rates at which they pro-

vide food. The two signals together provide more accurate information about the nestling's state of hunger than either of the signals does separately. In fact, the common cuckoo nestling tunes into this parent-offspring communication and exploits it to obtain food from the reed warbler parents (Kilner, Noble, and Davies, 1999).

Over a Noisy Background

When the famous musician Paganini played with an orchestra he made sure that the sounds of his violin would be heard above the orchestra by tuning it a quarter of a tone higher than the other instruments. This sharpening of pitch was not enough for his playing to sound out of tune but it did allow his notes to penetrate above the background harmony of the orchestra. This technique is exploited by some animals that need to signal over loud background noise. There is an insect in the rainforests of southeast Asia that we call "the chainsaw insect" because its penetrating whine is heard above the cacophony of other insects as a sharp, higher frequency.

Being seen as well as heard is a special problem in forests because only certain visual signals can be seen easily in the dappled and varying light of dense forest and against the background of complex patterns formed by vines, trunks, and leaves. If you wanted to send a visual signal in a "noisy" visual environment, it would be pointless to display stripes or patches of black and white. Zebras are actually camouflaged by their black and white stripes when they stand still in dappled light beside or under bushes. Black and white patterning makes effective camouflage, and the receiver would be unlikely to detect a signal that depended on the use of such patterns unless it involved movements that made the patterns more visible. It is not surprising therefore that many species of the forest are brightly colored on those parts of their bodies that are used to send visual signals.

At Dawn and Dusk

At dawn and dusk the light is purplish, and animals that forage for their food at these times are better able to avoid predators if their coloration blends in with a background illuminated by purplish light, made up of the longer (red) wavelengths together with the shorter (blue and violet) wavelengths. The middle-of-the-range wavelengths (yellow and green) are missing in purple light, and so animals with these colors would appear dark in such light. This means that the best way to signal in these conditions would be to use blue, red, or purple for brightness and yellow or green for contrast. Galahs are most active at dawn and dusk, and at these times, when they tend to feed on the ground, their grey backs camouflage them from aerial predators. Flocks of galahs are also quite difficult to see against the evening or dawn sky until the flock turns suddenly and there is a bright flash of the rose-colored breasts, a sight never forgotten. This quick turn may be some form of social signal related to group cohesion, but there is no proof that this is so.

In the Rainforest

The daytime quality of light in forests varies with the density of the vegetation, the angle of the sun, and the amount of cloud in the sky, as shown in detail by John Endler (1993). Both animals and plants have different appearances in these various lighting conditions. A color or pattern that is relatively indistinct in one kind of light may be quite conspicuous in another.

In the varied and constantly changing light environment of the forest, an animal must be able to send visual signals to members of its own species and at the same time avoid being detected by predators. An animal can hide from predators by choosing the light environment in which its pattern is least visible. This may require moving to different parts of the forest at different times of the day or under different weather conditions, or it may be achieved by changing color according to the changing light conditions. Many species of amphibians (frogs and toads) and reptiles (lizards and snakes) are able to change their color patterns to camouflage themselves. Some also signal by changing color. The chameleon lizard has the most striking ability to do this. Some chameleon species can change from a rather dull appearance to a full riot of carnival colors in seconds. By this means they signal their level of aggression or readiness to mate.

Other species take into account the changing conditions of light by performing their visual displays only when the light is favorable. A male bird of paradise may put himself in the limelight by displaying his spectacular plumage in the best stage-setting to attract a female. Certain butterflies move into spots of sunlight that have penetrated to the forest floor and display by opening and closing their beautifully patterned wings in the bright spotlights. They also compete with each other for the best spot of sunlight.

Very little light filters through the canopy of leaves and branches in a rainforest to reach ground level, or close to the ground, and at those levels the yellow to green wavelengths predominate. A signal might be most easily seen if it is maximally bright. In the green to yellow lighting conditions of the lowest levels of the forest, yellow and green would be the brightest colors, but when an animal is signaling, these colors would not be very visible if the animal were sitting on a yellowish to greenish background. As John Endler explains, the best signal depends not only on its brightness but also on how well it contrasts with the background against which it must be seen (Endler, 1993). The green tree frogs that inhabit Australia's rainforests (15 different species of *Litoria*) are colored in shades of green on their backs and bright yellow or white on the undersurfaces of their bodies and on the limbs. These colors may provide camouflage in the lower levels of the rainforest. Colors close to, but not identical to, yellow and green are best for signaling in this locale because they are bright and can also be distinguished from the background. In this part of the forest, therefore, red and orange are the best colors for signaling, and they are the colors used in signals by the ground-walking Australian brush turkey *(Alectura lathami)*. This species, which lives in the rainforests and scrub lands of the east coast of Australia, has a brown to black plumage with bare bright red skin on the head and neck and a neck collar of orange-yellow, loosely hanging skin. During courtship and aggressive displays, the turkey enlarges its colored neck collar by inflating sacs in the neck region, and then flings about a pendulous part of the colored signaling apparatus as it utters calls designed to attract or repel. This impressive display is clearly visible in the light spectrum illuminating the forest floor.

In higher zones of the forest or in more open areas where trees have been felled, blue-gray illumination is predominant, and there blue or blue-green coloration is the brightest and red or orange again provides the best contrast. The blue-green and red combination of colors is exploited by the swift parrot *(Lathamus discolor)*, which inhabits open forest in southeastern Australia, and the eclectus parrot *(Eclectus roratorus)*, which lives in the upper levels of tropical rainforests and the adjacent eucalyptus woodlands of the most northerly tip of Queensland. Interestingly, the best signal colors are sported differently by the male and female eclectus parrots. The male is bright green with scarlet red flanks under the wings and a large orange-red beak, while the female is bright blue and scarlet with a black beak. The male has blue feathers in the wings but these are displayed only in flight.

Species that seek out small gaps in the canopy, where reddish light predominates, should signal with red, orange, or yellow for maximum brightness and use purple or blue for contrast. The male Australian rainbow lorikeet *(Trichoglossus haematodus)* uses this combination of colors in a clownish fashion: he has a blue to purplish head and underbelly, a bright red beak, and an orange and red breast, together with a green back and green upper wing surfaces. The green upper surface provides camouflage despite the conspicuous colors used for signaling because it disrupts the outline of the bird's shape; in particular, the green upper surface conceals the bird from aerial predators such as falcons or hawks. This species is a striking example of the outcome of evolutionary processes that have selected a balance between colors that will conceal and colors that can be used to signal.

Less colorful birds and other animals that inhabit the rainforest tend to rely on forms of signaling other than the visual, particularly over long distances. The piercing cries of the rhinoceros hornbill characterize the southeast Asian rainforest, as do the unmistakable calls of the gibbons. There is also the long, rather terrifying call of the male orangutan, which carries over considerable distances to advertise his presence. In densely wooded environments, sound is the best means of communication over distance because, in comparison with light, it travels with little impediment from trees and other vegetation. In forests, visual signals can be seen only at short distances, where they are not obstructed by trees. The male riflebird exploits both these modes of signaling simultaneously in his courtship display. The sounds made as each wing is opened carry extremely well over distance and advertise his presence widely. The ritualized visual display communicates in close quarters when the female has approached.

Under the Sea

Under the sea, too, light conditions are varied and constantly changing. As snorkelers know, shallow areas of the sea have ever-changing patterns of light of different wavelengths and intensity. The ability to change color, which many sea creatures posess, is a distinct advantage under the sea—it can be used to avoid being seen by predators. In this environment, too, social signaling commonly involves changing color. The cuttlefish not only changes color to camouflage itself against the background but also flashes color messages to other members of its own species, sometimes changing color only on the side of the body that its conspecifics (members of same species) will see as they swim past. The other side retains its camouflage pattern. This is an extreme case of directing the signal in precisely the desired direction, at the same time avoiding detection by other cuttlefish and predators.

As we have seen, sound signals also must be chosen according to the auditory environment. Sound can be heard over greater distances in certain conditions. For example, sound travels well in water and this is why whales use sound to signal over many miles. Sound is attenuated by vegetation and the surface of the sea floor. In general, high-pitched sounds are attenuated more than deep, low-pitched ones. So calls that need to advertise the presence of the sender over long distances should be both loud and deep, like the long-distance calls used by whales. The same principles apply to sounds transmitted in air, and thus the long call of the orangutan and the bellow of the elephant are both loud and low-pitched. High-pitched ultrasound is also used by some aquatic mammals (dolphins, for example) to navigate and find prey in murky or dark waters (Stebbins, 1983).

We have seen that olfaction is an important sense in fish communication. Although fish use visual and auditory signals as well, chemicals released into the water can be carried by currents over very long distances. They are ideal for long-distance communication underwater, although the direction of current flow limits the signal to downstream receivers. The males of some species of fish signal their presence to females by releasing chemicals into the water. When females detect the chemical signal, using their olfactory sense, they swim upstream toward the male.

Once the male comes into sight, visual signals play an additional role in beckoning the female.

In the Dark

Visual signals are ineffective in dark environments such as caves or burrows. Thus species living in these environments communicate by sounds or smells. Bats use ultrasound, sound of such high frequency (or pitch) that it is outside the hearing range of humans. They use ultrasound both to navigate in the dark and to communicate with each other. Cave-dwelling oilbirds *(Steatornis caripensis)* and swiftlets *(Collocalia* sp.) also use ultrasound to navigate and communicate when they are inside the dark caves where they nest, although they use vision outside the cave.

In their underground burrows, moles and rats may communicate by sound. In fact, vision is so unimportant in this environment that one burrowing species, the mole-rat *(Spadix ehrenbergi),* has effectively no eyes. Through the course of time and the process of evolution, the eyes have become minuscule and the skin and fur have grown over them. Even the external ears are not detectible. The mole-rat has become a cylindrical-shaped animal with short legs and tail, the perfect design for moving along tunnels only just big enough for it. These animals communicate with each other by tapping their snouts on the walls of the burrow. The vibrations are seismic signals that can be detected by a mole-rat in another tunnel of the burrow even if it is quite a distance away. At closer quarters the mole-rats communicate by vocalizing rather than tapping, and they also use odors. A study by Uri Shanas and Joseph Terkel (1997) has demonstrated that mole-rats release an odorous secretion from a gland in the orbit of the eye when they groom themselves. The secretion runs down a duct and out through the nostrils. By grooming, the mole-rats spread the secretion over their bodies and it serves to decrease aggression between males. In effect, the odor signals, "Don't fight".

Communication by seismic vibrations is also common in nocturnal desert rodents. North American kangaroo rats *(Dipodomys)* and African gerbils (types of rat, including *Gerbillus* and other genera) strike their feet against the ground to produce drumrolls that characterize the individual's species. Jan Randall has shown that kangaroo rats have individual signature rhythms that communicate the animal's identity and lower the risk of disputes over territory among neighbors (Randall, 1997).

The white-lipped frog of Puerto Rico *(Leptodactylus albilabris)* is believed to have the greatest sensitivity to seismic stimuli of all known species. The male embeds himself in mud and produces advertisement chirps or aggressive chuckles; as he expands his vocal sac in order to make the chirp call, the sac strikes against the muddy substrate to produce a seismic "thump" that is detected by other members of his species in the vicinity. These signals may be used by nearby males to synchronize their calls when singing in chorus and to maintain separation between individual frogs (Narins, 1990).

In addition to sound and odor, animals may use electrical signals to communicate in the dark. Electrical signals are an effective mode of communication in the murky waters of streams, and they are used by the electric fish of South and Central America to navigate and communicate with each other. We have already seen the way in which electric fish communicate their sex and dominance.

MEASURING COMMUNICATION IN ANIMALS

It is not always simple to prove that communication has occurred in animals, and it is even more difficult to decipher exactly what has been communicated. First we need to know a lot about the behavior of the species we are investigating, and then we have to use certain techniques to determine whether a signal has been sent and received. We may detect that communication has occurred by observing behavior to see whether a particular activity performed by one animal consistently leads to a change in the behavior of another animal, or animals. This requires very careful scrutiny, and observations must be repeated many times. Once the initial observations have been made, they can be followed up by experiments designed to determine the exact nature of the communication. There are several clever ways of proceeding.

Audio Playback Experiments

One of the main ways to study communication in animals is to record the signal of interest and then play it back to the animals and see whether they respond in a predictable way. For example, many songbirds sing to advertise their territory. These territorial songs can be recorded on audio-tape and then played back over and over again through a loudspeaker placed in an unoccupied territory. If males of the species stay out of the area where the loudspeaker is located, it may be concluded that the song is indeed a territorial vocalization. Of course, it is not as simple as this because we need to have an experimental control. We need to know how rapidly males would move into an unoccupied territory without a loudspeaker broadcasting the song.

Experiments of this type have demonstrated that the European great tit *(Parus major)* produces a specific territorial song. John Krebs removed pairs of great tits from their territories in a forest and then placed a loudspeaker broadcasting the song of the great tits in some of the territories and left other territories empty. He found that the territories without loudspeakers were reoccupied far sooner than those with the loudspeakers broadcasting the song (Krebs, 1977). This experiment shows that the song does advertise that a given territory is taken and warns other males of the species to stay out of it. But the fact that the territories with loudspeakers were eventually occupied suggests that continued maintenance of a territory requires more than simply singing in one spot. It might require that the birds move around in the territory and use visual displays to accompany the song.

Even though this particular experimental procedure can demonstrate that a song advertises territory and signals to other males to keep out, it is important to go a step further to see how specific the song has to be in order to communicate this signal effectively. This can be done by playing another song, or a modified version of the original song, through loudspeakers placed in unoccupied territories to see whether these sounds also inhibit males of the species from moving in to occupy the territory. If these songs do not keep males out of the territory, or if they are clearly less effective in doing so than the original song, we can conclude that there is some specificity in the song. If, however, sounds other than the song also keep males out of the area around the speaker, there is no such specificity, and we would be unable to conclude that the song itself was communicating territory ownership.

With this technique, it is possible to determine exactly what aspects of the song convey the important information about territory ownership. This can be done by modifying the recorded song in various ways. Parts of it might be left out, or the song could be played backward. Alternatively, the order or sequence of the syllables (parts of the song; see Figure 2.1) may be changed. There are many ways of modifying the song. The effect of playing back the modified song can then be compared with the effect of playing back the unmodified song. In this manner, it is possible to single out the essential aspects of the song that warn other males to keep out of the territory.

John Krebs followed up his first experiment by playing back modified songs. In fact, he noticed that the great tit has a repertoire of several songs. One male may sing up to eight different types of song. Since individual birds vary in how many song types they sing, he was interested to see whether the size of the repertoire would alter the signal, making it more or less effective. To do this, he located loudspeakers that played back only one song in some unoccupied territories and speakers that played back a repertoire of up to eight songs in other territories. The territories in which the larger repertoire was broadcast were reoccupied after a much longer delay than those in which the smaller repertoire was played (Krebs, Ashcroft, and Webber, 1978). This experiment demonstrated that singing more song types together in a repertoire is a more effective signal than singing only one song type. Hence males with more elaborate songs can maintain their territory more effectively than those with less elaborate ones.

The fact that variations of a song produce different results raises another issue about the design of playback experiments, as Donald Kroodsma (1990) first realized. It is important to select many different songs to play back. In some of the early playback experiments, only one song, or very few songs, were played through the loudspeaker, and this lack of of variety could have seriously limited the results. In fact, many avian species learn to recognize the territorial songs of other members of their species holding territories next to their own and respond differently to the territorial calls of their immediate neighbors than to those of birds from more distant territories.

Emma Brindleym has investigated the responses of European robins (*Erithacus rubecula*) to the songs of neighbors and strangers (1991). Despite the large and complex song repertoire of European robins, they were able to discriminate between the songs of neighbors and strangers. When they heard a tape recording of a stranger, they began to sing sooner, sang more songs, and overlapped their songs with the playback more often than they did on hearing a neighbor's song. As Brindley suggests, the overlapping of song may be an aggressive response. However, this difference in responding to neighbor versus stranger occurred only when the neighbor's song was played by a loudspeaker placed at the boundary between that neighbor's territory and the territory of the bird being tested. If the same neighbor's song was played at another boundary, one separating the territory of the test subject from another neighbor, it was treated as the call of a stranger. Not only does this result demonstrate that the robins associate locality with familiar songs, but it also shows that the choice of songs used in playback experiments is highly important.

The playback technique can be used to study the territorial vocalizations of other species, and it can also be used to study other kinds of auditory signals. For example, Jan Randall determined the meaning of the drumrolls made by kangaroo rats by playing back foot-drumming recordings of three different species to wild populations of each species. Two of the species (*Dipodomys spectabilis* and *D. ingens*) responded to hearing the playback by drumming and the other species (*D. desertii*) approached the loudspeaker. These responses to the playback are typical of each species: *D. desertii* chases intruders away and only rarely drums the feet, whereas the other two species engage in drumming exchanges. Thus each species responds to hearing the playback of sounds used in communicating about identity and territory in ways typical of the species (Randall, 1994, 1997).

The playback technique can be used to investigate other forms of communication, not just those about territory. For example, playing the songs of male canaries to female canaries stimulates them to build nests. Alternatively, playing the warning call of a species stimulates appropriate evasive action. Christopher Evans and Peter Marler (1993) found that the alarm call of cockerels differs depending on whether they see a predator on the ground or in the air. When they see a hawk, or even a hawklike image, moving overhead, they emit a long screech (Figure 2.3A), which is entirely different from the call given when they see a predator on the ground, such as a dog or raccoon (Figure 2.3B). The latter is a repeated pattern of short pulses ending with a little flourish. It should be noted that the warning call signaling the presence of an aerial predator is a thin high-pitched sound, as is the warning call of the galah and many other species. The source of such calls is difficult to locate, and hence the caller is less likely to be detected by an aerial predator.

Having recorded these two calls made by the cockerels, Evans and Marler used the playback technique to assess whether the calls signaled anything specific to other chickens. They tested each chicken individually

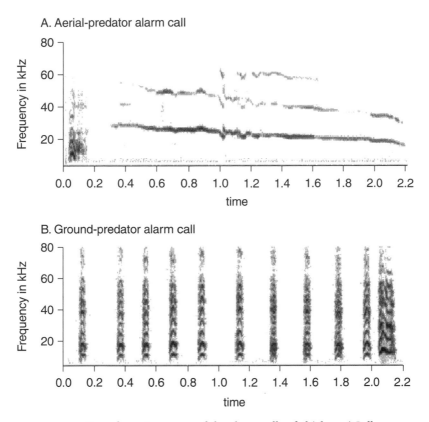

FIGURE 2.3 Sound spectrograms of the alarm calls of chickens (*Gallus gallus*). Chickens produce different calls to signal the presence of predators on the ground and predators in the air. A: The alarm call given when an aerial predator (hawk) is seen flying overhead. B: The alarm call given when a ground predator (dog or raccoon) is seen. (Adaptations of recordings made by C. S. Evans and P. Marler; sound spectrograms courtesy of C. S. Evans.)

in a cage in the laboratory, where it could not see any predators and was not exposed to any other changing visual stimulus that might cause it to vocalize. They then played the two kinds of alarm signals through a loud-speaker. When the aerial alarm call was played back, a chicken hearing it would crouch and look up as if trying to catch sight of the predator in the air. When the ground-predator alarm call was played, the chicken hearing it would run for cover or strut while calling in a way that might drive the predator away. Thus the two alarm calls have specificity and signal to the receiver to take appropriate measures to avoid being caught.

Vervet monkeys *(Cercopithecus aethiops)* also produce different vocal-izations for different predators. Males make a deep barking call for a leopard and females make short, high-pitched chirps in the same circum-stance. A chutter-like call is made for a snake and a single cough-like call for an eagle. Dorothy Cheney and Robert Seyfarth carried out playback experiments at a field site in Africa. They found that the vervet monkeys took the appropriate evasive action for the predator indicated by the call (Cheney and Seyfarth, 1990; Seyfarth, Cheney, and Marler, 1980). When the leopard call was played, they dashed to the nearest tree and climbed it. On hearing the snake call, the monkeys stood up on their hind limbs and peered into the grass. When the eagle call was played, they looked up and took cover, behavior not dissimilar to the evasive action taken by the chicken on hearing its own species' aerial alarm call.

Living in the same territory as the vervet monkeys are superb starlings, and these birds also make different calls for eagles and terrestrial preda-tors. Cheney and Seyfarth discovered that the vervet monkeys knew the meaning of the predator calls made by the starlings as well as their own species-specific calls. When the starling's eagle alarm call was played over a loudspeaker, the monkeys looked up; when the starling's ground-predator alarm call was played, most of the monkeys ran to the trees. No response was given when the starling's song was played back, and that was a control for the experiment because the song does not indicate the presence of any predator. Apparently the monkeys have learned to interpret the alarm signals of the starling. In this way different species living in the same area may make use of each other's communication signals.

Video Playback Experiments

Auditory signals have so far been the main focus of attention in the playback technique, but recent advances in video imaging have made the technique applicable to visual signals. It is now possible to make video recordings easily and, through digital manipulation, to change the recorded image for playback. Thus the behavior thought to be a visual signal can be recorded on video and played back to another member of the species in a controlled setting to see whether it elicits a reliable response in the receiver. Then, just as for the playback of altered songs, components of the video image can be eliminated or modified to determine exactly what aspects of the image are essential for the signal.

Of course, this technique is successful only if the species being studied pays attention to video images, which are two-dimensional and flicker. Humans cannot see flicker when it is very fast but some animals can see flicker at frequencies that we cannot detect. Fluorescent lights flicker on and off at so fast a rate that we perceive the light as being on continuously. But some birds may be able to see the flicker, and it would appear to them as a strobe light does to us. Video playback may also be seen to flicker by some species, and this would make it far from suitable for testing those species.

Nevertheless, Evans and Marler found that chickens do attend to video images in experiments where they used the video image of a chicken as a companion to a rooster stimulated to give alarm calls. First, they found that a rooster is much more likely to emit an alarm call on seeing an aerial predator when another live chicken is present in an adjoining cage. Next, they were able to show that replay of a video image of a chicken, with an accompanying soundtrack, would have the same effect as a live chicken of enhancing alarm calling by the rooster. Then they played a video image of another species, a bobwhite quail, and found it to be less effective than the video image of the rooster's own species (Evans and Marler, 1991).

Video imaging has also been used to study the visual signals made by male lizards in courtship and aggressive encounters. Joseph Macedonia, Christopher Evans, and Jonathan Losos used video playback to investigate head-bobbing and pulsing of the dewlap, the skin under the chin that can be extended and contracted, performed by two species of *Anolis* when males encounter each other. These are aggressive visual displays. The researchers found that video images of head-bobbing and dewlap displays elicited similar displays by the live lizards watching them, and that seeing a video of a member of the same species was more effective in eliciting the aggressive display than seeing a video of another species. This illustrates at least some degree of species specificity in visual signals of aggression (Macedonia, Evans, and Losos, 1994).

Video recording and playback can also be used to study communication by facial expression in animals. The image can be varied by changing the eyes, nose, mouth, or other features, either by distorting its contribution to the total facial expression or by eliminating each feature in turn from the expression. In this manner, the relative importance of the various features in any particular facial expression can be determined. For example, orangutans, and many other primates, perform one kind of play-threat display by opening the mouth, puffing up the lips, showing the teeth, and raising the eyebrows (Figure 2.4). It is not known which (if not all) of these features signals to another orangutan, but now it would be possible to find out by using video playback of manipulated images.

Playing video images to animals to study signaling has the advantage of being able to repeat exactly the same sequence of videotaped recordings as many times as the experimenter wishes. Exactly the same sequence can be presented to different animals, or again and again to the same animal, to test the reliability of the signal.

CONCLUSION

When communicating, different species use their different sensory systems to varying extents, depending on where they live and the most effective way to send a signal. We may say that communication is entirely context-dependent, meaning that what is communicated and when communication occurs depends on the environmental context surrounding the animal.

As observers of animals, we must first establish whether communication has actually occurred by determining whether a signal sent by one animal changes the behavior of the animal receiving it. Then we must determine exactly what has been signaled. Most communication between animals must depend on the use of specific signals that are not ambiguous, but there are examples of the same signal being used in entirely different contexts and causing quite different responses by the receiver. These signals would seem to be less specific, unless the same signal means something different when it is given in a different context, or the signals are, in fact, different in subtle ways that have eluded us. By using the playback technique and modifying the calls played back, we should eventually be able to distinguish between these alternatives.

FIGURE 2.4   Open-mouth play-threat display of an orangutan. Note the puffed area around the mouth, the bared teeth, and the raised eyebrows. This signal was directed toward another orangutan and it was followed by a play attack on that orangutan. (Photograph by G. Kaplan.)

Chapter Three

IS SIGNALING INTENTIONAL OR UNINTENTIONAL?

We humans do not always communicate verbally. Sometimes we communicate vocally, using sounds that are not words, and sometimes we communicate by touching another person. And almost always, whether we are speaking or not, we create facial expressions. These forms of communication are all nonverbal. Nonverbal communication may be intentional or unintentional. But a large amount of the communicating that we do by nonverbal utterances or facial expressions is unintentional, signaling something about our internal (emotional) state.

The fact that there are many different vocalizations that humans emit without any intention of communicating raises the possibility that all or most vocalizations made by animals are also unintentional utterances. Those who believe that signaling by animals is unintentional make an absolute division between animals and humans, reserving intentional communication for humans alone. They believe that animals simply emit vocalizations, and other signals, unthinkingly. They assume that the vocalizations and other signals produced by animals are involuntary, that they cannot be controlled consciously and are simply generated as automatic expressions of the animals' internal states.

Those who hold this view say that a chick peeps when it is cold and twitters when it finds a warm place as if it were a little machine, not because it actually wants to communicate that it feels distress or pleasure. In fact, the divide between animals and humans is widened even further by those who assume that animals may not be aware of feeling distress, pleasure, or any other internal state. The animal is seen as a robot without feelings or the ability to think, let alone communicate intentionally.

This view of animals has an equally mechanistic explanation of the animal that receives and responds to the signal. The hen might respond to the chick's distress calls by leading it to food but she does so without

thinking, not knowing what she has heard or even that she is responding. The interaction between the chick and the hen is interpreted as simply one little robot making a sound that causes a slightly larger robot to change its behavior.

To refute this attitude about animals we would need to consider whether animals are capable of thinking for themselves and whether they can actually feel things that they communicate to others. It is not our intention here to explore the broad topic of thinking and awareness in animals (see *Minds of Their Own* by Lesley Rogers, 1997b), but we will consider those aspects of communication that tell us something about whether or not animals communicate intentionally.

The fact that a signal is sent by one animal and that it leads to a change in the behavior of another animal is not, in itself, evidence that the sender intended to communicate or that the receiver intended to respond. It is very difficult to prove that the animal sending the signal intends to communicate, but there is new evidence showing that animals communicate specific information in specific circumstances. These findings work against the notion that animals emit signals simply as a reflection of their emotional state and in an uncontrolled and random way. Emotions certainly play a role in signaling by animals, as they do in humans, but communication in animals is not simply an automatic expression of the emotions, as we discuss below (see also Marler and Evans, 1996).

THE EFFECT OF HAVING AN AUDIENCE

If an animal communicates its internal, emotional state unintentionally, it might be expected to signal in exactly the same way whether it is alone or in the company of other animals; if it communicates intentionally, we might expect it to confine its signaling to occasions when it has an audience.

Warning calls are a special case for considering the presence or absence of an audience. Let us consider the case of a chicken *(Gallus gallus)* that emits a warning call when it catches sight of a hawk flying overhead. In Chapter 2, we saw that cockerels make one warning call for a predator seen flying overhead and a different call for one approaching on the ground (the aerial-predator versus the ground-predator alarm call: Figure 2.3). Thus a cockerel makes a specific screeching call when he sees the

aerial predator but, by doing so, he draws attention to himself and increases the chance that he will be taken by the predator. By issuing the warning call, the individual may save the group but risks his own life.

There has been much debate about whether this is a genuinely altruistic act on the part of the caller or whether it is not particularly altruistic because the individual shares some of his genes with other members of the flock and, therefore, by calling he increases the chance of survival of those genes. We will consider whether the individual issuing the warning call does so intentionally or simply emits the vocalization when his internal state is changed by seeing the predator.

Obviously, the bird that sees the predator feels fear. The call issued could simply be an expression of that internal state of fear—an automatic, unintentional signal of the chicken's emotional state. The first piece of evidence to indicate that this is not the case is the fact that the chicken gives different calls for aerial and ground predators although both predators induce a state of fear. It could, however, be suggested that an aerial predator elicits more fear than a ground predator (or vice versa) and that the different calls are merely a reflection of the amount of fear that the individual feels. Switching from one call to another completely different call as the internal state of fear increases does appear to occur in some species, as we will see later in this chapter. In other species, however, increasing states of arousal (fear) are accompanied by the same call being issued more often or more loudly.

The second piece of evidence against the idea that the two different alarm calls are emitted unintentionally is the fact that the presence or absence of an audience influences whether calling occurs or not. If the cockerel happened to be alone when he saw the predator, there would be no advantage in making a warning call. In fact, to issue a warning in this circumstance would be nothing less than disadvantageous. But if the cockerel cannot control his vocalizations and merely emits the warning call as a reflection of his particular internal state at the time, he will call irrespective of whether he is alone or in the presence of other members of his species. In contrast, if the cockerel can control his vocalizations and raises the alarm only when he has the intention of warning other chickens, he should not call when alone.

The latter is the case, as Peter Marler and his colleagues have shown.

They measured the alarm calls made by a cockerel in a cage with a video monitor placed overhead. When an image of a hawk in flight, or an approximation of one, was presented on the video monitor the cockerel made aerial-predator alarm calls, but only when there was a male or female of his own species in a nearby cage (Karakashian, Gyger, and Marler, 1988). He rarely uttered an alarm call when the same cage was empty or when it contained a bird from a related but different species (they used a bobwhite quail). An audience of the cockerel's own species had to be present for normal levels of alarm calling to occur. As we saw in Chapter 2, Marler and Evans were later able to show that a video image of a hen of the same species, instead of a live hen, would also serve as an audience.

The need for an audience before aerial-predator alarm calling will occur shows that the cockerel is not a simple robot emitting alarm calls when he is triggered by the appropriate stimulus (the predator). The social environment is taken into account before calling occurs. It could be said that the cockerel does not call when alone because he does not become sufficiently aroused by seeing the hawk unless another chicken is present. This could mean that he does not call intentionally but requires two conditions to be met before he will call automatically. Such an explanation will suit those who wish to make an absolute distinction between the communication systems of animals and humans. However, it does not seem to be correct, because the cockerels showed the same amount of looking overhead, crouching, immobility, scuttling away, and sleeking down of their feathers with and without an audience. Apart from the absence of alarm calling, the cockerels when alone reacted to the hawk to the same extent, irrespective of the presence or absence of the hen (Marler and Evans, 1996). This shows that they were, in fact, just as afraid when alone as when they had an audience. We may therefore conclude that the cockerel actively suppresses alarm calling when alone. We think the most likely interpretation of these findings is that the cockerel makes the warning call only when there is a reason for doing so and that, when he does call, he does so with the intention of warning other members of his own species, most likely kin. More experiments will be necessary before we can be sure of this explanation.

As we saw in Chapter 2, vervet monkeys give different alarm calls for different predators. The presence of an audience also determines whether

they give alarm calls. Solitary vervet monkeys have been observed to escape from an approaching leopard in total silence (Cheney and Seyfarth, 1990). Apparently, the absence of other vervet monkeys negated the need to call and alarm calling was suppressed, just as with the cockerel.

Cheney and Seyfarth (1985, 1990) also conducted experiments on captive vervet monkeys, demonstrating that adult females give more alarm calls when their offspring are present. Despite this effect of audience, however, Cheney and Seyfarth concluded that vervet monkeys do not know anything about the mind-state of their audience—whether their audience knows or does not know that a predator is nearby. The researchers based this conclusion on the fact that the monkeys go on making alarm calls long after every other monkey in the group has seen the predator; and in the presence of their offspring, mothers call no more often, or differently, for predators that offer great threat to their offspring than for those that pose a lesser threat.

Although these observations suggest that the signaler does not differentiate its own vulnerability from that of its audience, more information is needed before a firm conclusion can be reached about the ability of the monkeys to modulate calling according to the state of knowledge of group members. But it is clear that they can vary alarm calling according to the presence or absence of an audience. They do not signal impulsively and involuntarily but decide whether to signal or not and what signal they will use in a given context.

The presence of an audience also increases the calls that cockerels produce in the presence of food (Evans and Marler, 1994). There is a typical food call, consisting of repeated pulses of sound, that the cockerel produces when he sees food, or another stimulus that he associates with food, and this call attracts hens. The hens run to the male and the male drops the food, allowing the hens to eat it. This behavior is often followed by courting and mating. In fact, food calling is enhanced by the presence of a hen.

Evans and Marler (1994) were able to show that the enhancement of calling in the presence of the hen is not just a general effect on the motivation (or arousal) of the cockerel to feed, because the presence of the hen increases the food calling but not the pecking at the food. In other words, the presence of the hen had a specific effect on signaling about

food but did not have any effect on behavior not used for signaling. It would seem, therefore, that the cockerel signals with the intention of alerting the hen to the presence of food and does not simply emit calls automatically when he sees food.

In addition, Evans (1997) has now shown that the hen looks for food on the ground when she hears the food call. Evans observed the behavior of a hen when she was played the food call through a loudspeaker. On hearing the call, she put her head close to the floor and walked around as if looking for food, even though there were no grains of food on the bottom of the cage in which she was tested. Thus her searching for food was triggered by hearing the food call specifically and not by her having caught sight of any grains of food. The receiver of the signal responded in a specific manner.

It is most important to note that either a male or female conspecific is an effective audience for a cockerel to signal the presence of an aerial predator, whereas only a female is an effective audience for the food call. This demonstrates even more specificity of the situation in which the cockerel will produce calls, and this specificity is also necessary for the survival of the species. Both males and females can benefit by being alerted to the presence of an aerial predator, but food calling is used by males to attract females as a prelude to courtship. In other words, the effect of the audience is not simply a matter of its presence or absence; the audience has specific relevance to the particular social context and, it would seem, to the intent of the signaler.

In the examples given so far, calling is enhanced by the presence of an audience, but this is not the case for all types of calling. The presence of an audience has no effect on the amount of calling the cockerel gives when he sees a predator on the ground. Marler and Evans (1996) reasoned that this is so because the ground-predator alarm call is used not only to alert other members of the species to the presence of a predator but also to confront the predator itself, and to try to drive it away. This contrasts with the aerial-predator alarm call, which is associated with behavior that would hide the bird from the predator. The aerial-predator alarm call is a thin sound that fades in and out, making its source very difficult to locate, whereas the ground-predator alarm call is conspicuous, abrupt, repeated, and easy to locate. It appears to be designed to capture the ground predator's attention and is accompanied by behavior that might make the predator decide to look elsewhere for a meal.

Drawing attention to itself would appear to be the best strategy for a bird to adopt when confronted by a predator on the ground. Chickens can fly far enough to get away and they can run fast too, but the strutting and calling display directed at the predator might be a less energetically costly way of signaling to the predator that the bird could escape if approached. This maneuver may resemble the stotting of Thomson's gazelles when faced with predators. The stotting signals how fit the gazelles are and thus how they could escape, as we saw in Chapter 1.

Fleeing would be the only alternative available to the chicken approached by a predator on the ground. This strategy might follow the strutting and alarm calling at a moment when the bird's calling and strutting activity has put the predator off guard. Whatever the reason for the bird's strutting around when confronted by a predator on the ground, there is as much reason to strut around and make the ground-predator alarm call when an audience is present as when it is not. This might explain why having an audience has no effect on ground-predator alarm calling.

The difference of the audience effect on aerial-predator alarm calling versus ground-predator alarm calling illustrates that calling is very specific to the context in which it occurs, and that there is no single, simple set of rules that the bird follows to control its vocalizations. Although this does not prove beyond all doubt that birds communicate intentionally, it certainly indicates that they may do so. Also, there is further evidence to suggest that chickens can control when and what they communicate, and this finding concerns the use of calls to deceive another individual, as we will discuss next.

DECEPTION

The use of signals to deceive another is perhaps the most sophisticated form of signaling. In the most developed form of deception, the deceiver may know the usual context of the signal and then use it in an unusual context with the intent of deceiving another animal. It appears that animals sometimes communicate deceptively, but it is very difficult to prove beyond doubt that they have done so intentionally. Nevertheless, there is some evidence indicating that animals do engage in deception with intent, as outlined by Rogers (1997b).

Marcel Gyger and Peter Marler (1988) have observed that cockerels sometimes make food calls when no food is present. They appear to do this only when the hen is far enough away that she cannot see whether food is actually present where the cockerel is located. On hearing the call, the hen approaches the cockerel, presumably to search for food in his vicinity. Thus, by issuing the food call when no food is present, the cockerel can deceive the hen into approaching provided she is so far away that she cannot see that he is cheating. According to Gyger and Marler, the cockerel does not use food calls deceptively when the hen is close enough to see that he is signaling deceptively.

These are interesting observations, but more experiments need to be carried out to decide whether the calls are indeed being used deceptively. It is possible, for instance, that the cockerel emits food calls to attract the hen only when she is farther away because he is more motivated to obtain her company when she is at a greater distance, rather than because he has figured out that he can deceive her only when she is farther away. Nevertheless, studies like Gyger and Marler's are important and interesting approaches that attempt to unravel the difficult problem of intentionality in animal communication, and they lay the groundwork for more research in the area (see the 1997 paper by Christopher Evans for more discussion).

Other examples of deception have been reported by ethologists studying the behavior of animals in their natural environment. We will not list them all here, but we do draw attention to one form of deception that has been observed in many different species: issuing a warning call or behaving as if a predator were nearby when there is no evidence that that is the case. We refer to this behavior as "crying wolf," after the story of the boy who cried "Wolf!" too often and so was ignored when he really needed help—an excellent example of habituation in the receivers.

Predator-warning behavior appears to be used in many species to distract the attention of the receiver who is eating a favored food; after diverting the receiver's attention, the deceiver moves in to grab the food for itself. The Arctic fox has been observed to use warning calls in this manner, and so have domestic dogs and certain species of birds (described in detail in Rogers' *Minds of Their Own*, 1997b). In *The Thinking Ape*, Richard Byrne (1995) describes many observations of deception in primates. One incident involved the pretense that a predator was nearby: a baboon being chased by another baboon was observed to stop and look around as if there were a lion or other predator in the near distance, and when it did so, its pursuer stopped and looked around too, giving the pursued baboon time to escape. Seeing no evidence of a predator in the area, Byrne interpreted this behavior as deception. The pursued individual had manipulated the pursuer by signaling incorrect information.

Deception is perhaps the most complex form of communication. It can occur only when a communication system is firmly in place and usually functions in a consistent and reliable (referred to as "honest") fashion. Individuals who are detected signaling dishonestly are punished or their signals are ignored. Deception is a risky form of communication. Its existence suggests the intentionality of communication.

Mimicry is a form of deception. Wolfgang Wickler (1968) has described the way in which certain nonpoisonous butterflies mimic the appearance of poisonous ones to gain protection from avian predators that have learned to avoid the poisonous butterflies. In this case, the deception is definitely unintentional. Other forms of mimicry may, however, be intentional. We do not yet know for certain, but some forms of vocal mimicry in birds may be used to deceive predators and such behavior may well be intentional. By mimicking the vocalizations of their predators, some avian species may signal that the territory is occupied by another member of the predator's species and so prevent the predator from moving in. There is some evidence that this occurs, but much more research is needed before we can say anything conclusive about the behavior. We will discuss mimicry in more detail later.

ALARM CALLS THAT REFER TO PREDATORS

We have discussed the different calls produced by chickens and vervet monkeys to warn other members of their species of specific classes of predators. These signals are called referential signals because they appear to be analogous to human words used to refer to animals, objects, or events. A number of other species also use different calls to refer to different types of predators (see Macedonia and Evans, 1993).

In a refinement of this behavior, prairie dogs *(Cynomys gunnisoni)* can actually signal the details of a predator in their alarm calls. Con Slobodchikoff and his colleagues (1991) recorded the alarm calls that prairie dogs made as humans approached at a walking pace. Since this species has been preyed on by humans for more than a hundred years, the experiment was relatively natural, or at least relevant to the species. The human "predators" wore different clothes in different tests, white laboratory coats or colored shirts, and different people were involved. By recording the calls made by the prairie dogs and then analyzing different detailed features of the calls, the researchers were able to show that the prairie dogs may be able to distinguish one human being from another and that they may incorporate information about the physical features of individual predators into their alarm calls. This is an interesting result, but it needs to be supported by tests showing that the prairie dogs actually use this information when they hear the different signals. If so, these animals not only are perceiving much more detail than we might have thought but also are signaling this information to each other. By using playback experiments it should be possible to see whether the prairie dogs actually use the detailed information encoded in the alarm signals.

Ring-tailed lemurs *(Lemur catta)* produce differentiated alarm calls to alert their group members to an aerial or a ground predator, but they also have a general call, a relatively soft "glup" sound, that they produce when they first catch sight of any predator or, indeed, when they perceive any startling visual or auditory stimulus. This seems to be a general alert signal to the group. If an aerial predator has been detected, they follow the "glup" with loud calls, first rasps and then shrieks when the predator is within attack range. If the predator is a carnivore (ground predator), the "glup" is followed by "clicks" and "yaps." Thus the lemurs signal information about aerial versus ground predators and also about the proximity of the predator.

The ground squirrels of California *(Spermophilus beecheyi)* produce "chatter" calls when they see a predator on the ground and "whistles" when an eagle or hawk flies overhead, but their calls are not as specific as the alarm calls of chickens or the eagle and snake alarm calls of vervet monkeys. Sometimes they chatter when they see a hawk in the distance or whistle when they are being chased by a carnivore. These apparent errors in reference to specific predators may, in fact, be conveying more detail about the situation in general. These calls may communicate the urgency of the situation and so convey information about potential versus imminent danger rather than simply indicating that the predator is a hawk or a dog. Thus while some species have specific calls to refer to different predators, just as we use different words for different animals, others may signal the urgency of the situation instead.

THE ROLE OF EMOTION

We have presented evidence showing that animals do not simply vocalize in an uncontrolled manner as a way of expressing their emotions. Nevertheless, their emotional state does affect their signaling, just as emotions affect speech and other forms of communication in humans. The variation in calls made by ground squirrels may, as mentioned above, indicate the urgency of the situation, conveying the proximity of the predator and perhaps also the behavior of the predator. The emotional state of the signaler may be the factor that determines these variations in signaling. When the squirrel is very afraid it may whistle, and when it is only mildly afraid it may chatter. In general, hawks may be a greater threat than ground predators and thus more likely to elicit high levels of fear and therefore whistle calls, but when a hawk is far away instead of nearby it elicits only a chatter. By contrast, being chased by a carnivore is a highly fear-inducing situation and the squirrels whistle when they are so threatened.

Similar systems of calling have been reported for other species: for example, the black-winged stilt (*Himantopus himantopus*), a wading bird, has two types of alarm signal, depending on the distance of the predator from the bird's location. Again, increasing fear may lead to a switch from one call type to another. Similarly, as mentioned above, ring-tailed lemurs give rasping calls when an aerial predator is far away and shrieks when it is closer.

Other species vary the rate of calling as the risk of being caught by a predator increases, as has been documented for yellow-bellied marmots (*Marmota flaviventris*). At field sites in Colorado and Utah, Daniel Blumstein and Kenneth Armitage (1997) studied the alarm calls the marmots gave on the approach of a trained dog, a model badger, a radio-controlled badger, and a walking person. The marmots made three different alarm calls, but the calls did not appear to be specifically related to any particular type of predator, possibly because all the "predators" used in the study were artificial ones. But the marmots' rate of calling increased as the predator came closer. Calling rate is therefore an indication of the level of fear. By playing back one of these calls at various rates, the researchers were able to show that the rate of calling did, in fact, signal the degree of risk to other marmots. Thus the receiver could interpret the meaning of the call from the calling rate.

Emotional state can be influenced by hormones and this can be reflected in signaling. The amount of aerial-predator alarm calling by cockerels is influenced by the level of testosterone circulating in the bloodstream, possibly because the hormone changes the bird's emotional state and the way it attends to the predator.

In humans we can tell the level of emotion by the intensity and quality of the voice. This may also be the case in animals, but the topic has not been studied to any great extent. We do, however, know that calling is more frequent and louder when animals are more aroused. The more distressed a young chick feels, the more often it peeps and the louder it peeps. A similar pattern of responses accompanies increased distress in a wide range of species, including humans. Emotional aspects of signaling may also be conveyed by other methods of communication accompanying vocalizations. Humans signal their emotional state when speaking by body posture and facial expression. A twitch of muscles in the face or a wringing of the hands can be more informative than the actual words being spoken. Animals too accompany their vocalizations with other signals that may indicate emotional state. Cockatoos, for example, raise their crests while they vocalize when they are alarmed.

In some cases, the behavior accompanying a particular vocalization is quite obviously another direct response to the stimulus that elicited the vocalization. Ground squirrels scurry into their burrows while giving their whistle calls. Vervet monkeys stand on their hind limbs and look down into the grass at the same time as they give the snake alarm call, look up and take to cover when giving the eagle call, and scamper up a tree when giving the leopard call. These characteristic actions accompanying each alarm call add to the power of its meaning, and the speed or vigor with which they are performed may indicate the amount of fear that the signaler is feeling, although this has not yet been studied.

More subtle behavioral changes may also accompany vocalizations. As Eckard Hess (1965) showed three decades ago, in humans, the size of the pupils in the eyes varies with emotional state and attitude. Also, humans assess the pupil size of other people with whom they are interacting, although they do so quite unconsciously. A greeting accompanied by dilation of the pupils is rated positively, whereas one with constriction of the pupils is rated negatively and viewed with distrust.

Pupil size may be an important aspect of communication in animals also. We know that it varies with the state of arousal or emotion. Some years ago Richard Gregory and Prue Hopkins (1974) reported that the pupil size of a parrot constricted whenever she produced learned words and also while she was listening to familiar words. There has been no research to test whether other parrots respond to the changes in pupil size, but it is potentially possible that they do.

Other emotional responses such as the erection of hair or feathers may also accompany vocalizations and signal emotional content. We have already mentioned raising of the crest in cockatoos. Most readers will be familiar with the way dogs raise the hair on their backs during aggressive encounters. Unfortunately, most studies of communication in animals focus on only one aspect of signaling and ignore the complete picture, so there is little detailed information on these added aspects of signaling.

THE ROLE OF COGNITION

Despite the contribution of emotions to signaling in animals, we must emphasize that animal signaling is not purely the expression of emotions, which are controlled at lower levels of brain function. Some signaling involves more complex cognitive processes in addition to those used to express emotions. By cognitive processes we mean higher levels of brain function, those that involve decision making, memory, and assessment of the environment. It is possible that some signals given by some species are purely emotional, emitted without cognition. But it is likely that most vocalizations involve both emotional and cognitive processes, although the emotional contribution may be greater in some signals and the cognitive contribution higher in others. The balance between emotion and cognition will vary with the function of the signal and the context in which it is given. This is likely to be as true for the vocalizations of animals as it is for those of humans.

The emotional content of human speech holds our interest and adds to the meaning of the communication, as is clearly demonstrated by the contrast between computer-generated speech and human speech. Computer-generated speech is monotonous, conveying less meaning than human speech, and our attention wanders when we hear it. Most animal vocalizations depend on varying contributions of emotions and cognition. The food calls given by many species (such as chimpanzees, macaque monkeys, and chickens) are not monotonous and it is not the case that identical vocalizations are produced every time food is found. Instead, they vary according to how much food there is and the quality of that food. Chickens, for example, produce food calls at higher rates when the food is of the preferred kind, but other aspects of the call are varied in other species. The information about quantity and quality may be generated by the emotional state of the chicken that is producing the calls, since both more food and food of better quality may increase the bird's excitement.

At the same time as they express the emotions, signals can be referential (which requires one form of cognition), and they can be emitted or suppressed depending on the presence or absence of an audience, or on other external factors. The relative importance of emotional versus referential processes varies with the particular call. For example, the leopard alarm call of vervet monkeys appears to have more emotional content than either the eagle alarm call or the snake alarm call—the leopard alarm call has been observed to occur occasionally in aggressive social interactions and sometimes when a raptor swoops down at the monkey, whereas the eagle and snake alarm calls have never been heard unless the specific predator to which they refer is present. Each of the latter two calls, therefore, has a unitary meaning, whereas the leopard alarm call appears to have more than one meaning.

Joseph Macedonia and Christopher Evans (1993) have, however, reasoned that the leopard alarm call does not simply signal the monkey's level of excitement or fear, as in the case of the whistle calls of ground squirrels, because the same leopard call is produced whenever the monkeys see a leopard regardless of what degree of threat it actually poses—whether the leopard is asleep, hunting, attacking, moving away, or approaching. It could, of course, be argued that a leopard causes maximum levels of fear irrespective of what it is doing, and that may be why there is no variation in calling.

So far, most research on the referential use of vocalizations in animals has focused on signaling about the presence of predators or food, but much of the communication in animals must be concerned with social relationships. Although survival depends on alerting conspecifics to predators and food, social interactions are an equally important aspect of an animal's life. It follows that a considerable amount of communication must occur about social situations, but virtually nothing is known about these forms of communication. Certainly, Cheney and Seyfarth (1985, 1990) have shown that vervet monkeys are aware of the social relationship between a mother and her offspring: when an infant vocalizes in distress, other monkeys turn to look at the mother of the infant rather than going to its assistance themselves. This is an example of active suppression of a response to a signal by monkeys who are not related to the infant. It shows that social signaling depends on the social context.

There are many other ways in which vervet monkeys, and other species, may communicate about social situations in an active manner, but unfortunately we know nothing about this potentially rich field of communication. As Sue Savage-Rumbaugh has said, apes may be less interested in communicating about objects than are humans and more interested in communicating about social matters (Savage-Rumbaugh and Lewin, 1994).

We are far from understanding communication at the social level, but it is reasonable to say that, although emotional states may be an aspect of social communication in animals, communication may also be generated by cognitive processes.

ANIMALS THAT UNDERSTAND HUMAN LANGUAGE

It would help us to find out for certain whether animals communicate intentionally if we could ask them what they intended to communicate and they could reply using communication signals that we could understand. There are two potential ways of achieving this two-way communication:

either we could learn to use the communication signals of the animal species we wished to study or we could teach the animal to use some form of human language. Since we have not yet been successful in understanding more than rudimentary aspects of animal communication signals, the latter has presented itself as the best option. Apes have been taught to communicate with humans using American sign language or by pointing to symbols that represent words. They have not been taught verbal communication using spoken English, for example, because the vocal apparatus of apes is very different from that of humans and does not allow them to make the same range of vocalizations that we do. This does not mean that apes' vocal abilities are limited—they can and do use a range of complex calls, with a vocal range extending to very high frequencies. Birds can produce the same range of sounds as humans, and they can be taught to communicate with humans using vocal signals, as was a parrot called Alex.

We will discuss intentional communication in apes first. Allen and Beatrix Gardner trained several chimpanzees to communicate with humans using American sign language, beginning in 1966 with one called Washoe (see Gardner, Garner, and van Canfort, 1989). The chimpanzees learned to use signs to refer to objects and individuals, and all of them acquired vocabularies that allowed them to express requests, such as "Icecream, hurry gimme" (to use the Gardners' translation), "You tickle me Washoe," "Please flower," "Please blanket out" (requesting a change in location of a blanket then in the cupboard), "You me out" (a request for the human observer and chimpanzee to go outside), and "Open help" (requesting assistance in opening a lock or a bottle). By the chimpanzees' frustrated behavior when these requests were not honored, compared with when they were, it was clear that these were intentional forms of communication. The chimpanzees also announced when the next activity in the daily routine should occur with statements such as "Time vacuum," "Time toothbrush," and "Time Dar out" (Dar being the name of one of the chimpanzees). This announcement of a pending event is an aspect of awareness of the future that indicates intentionality. Emotion entered into the signing—more emotive events evoked more signing—but cognition was obviously a major aspect of their communication.

To convince critics that the chimpanzees were expressing genuine requests and were coming up with answers to questions by use of their own powers of cognition, it was necessary for the Gardners to prove that the chimpanzees were not using subtle cues given inadvertently by the humans caring for them. By responding to cues produced by the humans in their presence, the apes could appear to be communicating intelligently and intentionally but would merely be performing some sort of clever mimicry. In other words, they might be similar to Clever Hans, the horse that was once thought to be able to read numbers written on a board and to count them out by tapping his foot on the ground. Later it was found that the horse used subtle cues that his owner supplied unknowingly, such as the blink of an eyelid when the horse tapped the required number of times. Clever Hans could not perform the task when his owner was not present.

To test whether a similar use of cues might be occurring with the chimpanzees, the Gardners designed an experiment in which the chimpanzees had to name objects shown to them on a video monitor. Their responses were recorded by a human who could not see the screen and did not know what the chimpanzees were observing. There was no human who knew what was on the television screen present in the room with the chimpanzee. In this controlled experiment, the chimpanzees were able to name objects accurately. Therefore, their use of sign language was self-generated and not some form of mimicry or associative learning.

The chimpanzees also used the sign language they had learned to tell humans things they did not already know. For example, when very young, Washoe dropped one of her toys into a hole in the inside wall of the caravan in which she lived. That night, when Allen Gardner visited her, she attracted his attention to a part of the wall below the hole and signed "Open, open" many times over. From this communication Allen deduced what had happened and retrieved the toy. Washoe had used sign language to communicate something really new to a human. This shows genuine communication with intention. Again, there is no question of the chimpanzee's having communicated merely by reading subtle cues given by a human. Although this was claimed rather vehemently by several researchers in the field at one time, a complete analysis of the data accumulated by the Gardners shows that this narrow interpretation is most unlikely to be correct. Moreover, more recent findings by other researchers who have trained apes to use language support the conclusion that apes can learn to communicate with humans intentionally, creatively, and intelligently.

Sue Savage-Rumbaugh has trained chimpanzees and a bonobo (a rare species of chimpanzee, *Pan paniscus,* also known as a pygmy chimpanzee) to communicate with humans by pointing to symbols on a board (lexigram symbols) (see Savage-Rumbaugh and Lewin, 1994). She has said that while the sign-language–trained chimpanzees used their acquired language mainly to manipulate humans, the symbol-trained chimpanzees seemed to have more of a two-way communication with humans. This claim needs to be proven, but if it is correct, manipulation by the signing chimpanzees might stem from the fact that they were trained by being given small food rewards when they signed correctly, and thus they would associate signing with getting a food reward from humans. The other factor that might be important is that humans communicated with the symbol-trained apes using spoken language, not sign language, which is generally used to communicate with chimpanzees trained to use sign language. The combined use of speech by humans and symbols by the apes might have facilitated the human–animal exchange because humans could speak to the apes directly using their natural form of communication. Whatever the reason, the symbol-trained apes have impressive two-way communication with humans, and they are able to use that communication to refer to events that have occurred in the past or to talk about other individuals not present at the time the conversation takes place. This is clear referential use of communication.

Not only is meaning—referential use of symbols—important to these apes, but so is syntax, the grammatical word order in sentences. This was discovered by Savage-Rumbaugh in her work with the bonobo Kanzi (Savage-Rumbaugh and Lewin, 1994). Kanzi learned to communicate, by pointing to symbols, by being present at an early age when his mother was being taught to use them. He learned to use the symbols to generate language in much the same way that a human child acquires language. He also acquired the ability to understand spoken English. In a sense he is now trilingual, because he is able to understand spoken English, to use symbolic language, and, most likely, to use his own "chimpanzee" mode of communication. This is more than we expect of the average human child.

Kanzi also learned to understand the syntax of English, as Savage-Rumbaugh was able to show in the following experiment. Kanzi was given instructions via headphones by a person in another room who could not see him. In the same room as Kanzi was another person who did not know what instruction Kanzi had received and who recorded his behavior. Kanzi was instructed to perform a task in pidgin English ("Go get orange testing room") or in syntactically correct English ("Go and get the orange from the testing room"), and the rapidity of his responses was recorded. The results demonstrated that he responded more rapidly and more effectively when the syntactically correct instruction was given than when pidgin English was used. Therefore he has acquired understanding of not only the meaning of words (semantics) but also the structure (syntax) of English language. The symbolic language by which he has learned to communicate with humans does not permit this expression of syntax, but he does process and respond to syntax. In fact, Kanzi can understand numerous sentences in spoken English.

This remarkable demonstration of Kanzi's ability to understand human language shows that apes possess the ability to process language and that they may use this ability in their own vocalizations or other forms of communication. It even raises the possibility that other species that live in close contact with humans understand what humans are saying even though they cannot themselves speak. In his work with dolphins at the University of Hawaii, Louis Herman and his colleagues recognized this possibility of comprehension in the absence of audible or visible production of signals, although in this case he was considering the dolphins' ability to understand the gestural "language" of humans rather than speech (Herman, Pack, and Palmer, 1993). Dolphins can follow complex commands presented to them as gestures asking them to perform various acts in sequence, even though they have not been trained to produce vocal or other communication that can be understood by humans. In saying this, we must not overlook the dolphins' own complex vocal and other forms of communication, which might also share aspects of human language.

It is possible that many species that live in close contact with humans acquire some comprehension of both the semantics and syntax of human language even though they cannot produce it. We all know that dogs, for example, understand simple commands, but we might also speculate that they understand much more of the conversations we have in their presence, and the same may be true of pet birds. In fact, a study by Millicent Ficken, Elizabeth Hailman, and Jack Hailman has shown that chickadees (*Parus sclateri,* an avian species in Mexico) sequence their different calls in particular ways according to rules and the context in which the calls are given. They thus use a simple form of syntax, as the researchers state (Ficken, Hailman, and Hailman, 1994). It is probable that many other examples of syntax will be found in the communication systems of animals, and it need not be found only in vocal communication.

Of all the species that could have been chosen for the research on teaching human language to animals, apes were not a surprising choice. Apes are closest to humans genetically and in terms of evolution; so it was considered they would be more likely to be able to learn to communicate using language than any other species. Irene Pepperberg, however, saw potential in training a species far removed from humans—the Grey parrot *(Psittacus erithacus).* Parrots have an advantage over apes because they can mimic human speech vocally and might be able to communicate directly without the need for an interface of signs or symbols.

In her laboratory Pepperberg (1990a, 1990b) began by training a parrot called Alex. The training had to differ from the usual way in which parrots are taught to mimic speech. Instead of mindlessly repeating words or phrases over and over to the bird quite out of context and therefore without particular meaning to the bird, she and her students engaged in simple but meaningful interactions in front of Alex. For example, one person would ask, "Where is the key?" and another would hold the key up with a reply such as "Here is the key." The first person would then ask, "What color is the key?" and the other person would state the color, and so on with objects of different colors, shapes, and textures. When Alex began to use words, he was given the objects that he asked for, and the humans also rewarded him by telling him he was a good bird.

With this training, Alex has learned to name up to 100 objects and to answer questions correctly about their shape, color, and texture. He can also count, and when presented with an array of objects of various shapes and colors on a tray, he can say how many of the objects are, for example, green triangles or blue four-corners (by which he means cubes). Alex also expresses desires, such as "I want peanut" or "Come here." In all aspects of his communication, he performs as well as the language-trained apes, a fact that supports our suggestion that many species may be capable of understanding aspects of human language. This comment aside, the relevant point about the research with Alex is that he uses his acquired vocabulary to communicate intelligently with humans. He is not simply emitting signals mindlessly, out of context or unintentionally.

CONCLUSION

In 1975, the primatologist David Premack asserted that whereas humans have both affective and symbolic communication, all other species, except those tutored by humans, have only affective communication (Premack, 1975). By affective communication he meant communication about emotions in an uncontrolled way. At the time he wrote, apes had already been taught to communicate using sign language (Premack himself had been part of the research program), and their abilities to communicate symbolically were known. Instead of extrapolating this knowledge to communication by species using their own species-specific patterns of communication, Premack saw the language-trained apes as exceptions that had acquired something extra as a result of their contact with humans. The more recent research of Marler, Evans, and colleagues on vocalizations in chickens discounts Premack's claim. They have shown that alarm and food calls are not simply produced automatically without control (Marler and Evans, 1996). We might therefore conclude that the apes who have been taught to communicate using signed or symbolic forms that humans can understand tell us something important about their species and, in that respect at least, are not exceptions.

The research on Kanzi and his ability to comprehend the syntax of spoken English has led us to suggest that many other species may have similar abilities despite the fact that they cannot speak to us or communicate by signing or using symbols. We would go a step further and suggest that the ability to understand the syntax of spoken English indicates that bonobos, at least, must communicate using their own species-specific signals (vocal and gestural) in ways similar to the ways humans use language. We base this statement on the fact that a species that can comprehend human language is also likely to have similar processing capabilities that are used for its own forms of communication; in turn, this means that the species must produce language-like communication. The fact that language-like production of communication has not yet been found in animals tells us only that far too little research on natural communication has so far taken place—it does not tell us that it does not exist.

In fact, detailed examination of the vocalizations of different species frequently reveals that humans are unable to distinguish between calls that actually differ from each other. In other words, we may not hear differences that the animals hear. Many years ago, this was found to be the case for the most common call of Japanese macaque monkeys *(Macaca fuscata)*, known as the "coo" call. The monkeys make "coos" in a variety of social situations, and although these all sound the same to human listeners, detailed analysis revealed that the calls differed in each situation. More recently, the same has been found for the trill calls of spider monkeys *(Ateles geoffroyi):* although all trills sound the same to us, spider monkeys can tell exactly which individual made the call. These examples should indicate to us that there is much more in the vocal communication of animals than we hear or understand.

Chapter Four

Birds have inspired human imagination. To fly like a bird is a dream as old as Greek mythology and the desire of Icarus to fly away from Crete on wings made of wax. The white dove has come to symbolize peace; birds also symbolize freedom. Bird feathers have been used to signal special powers or to confer a special status on the human wearer. Birds feature in many human dances—many cultures have prided themselves on being able to mimic birdsong and bird displays. Human fascination with birds may also arise from having something in common with birds—humans and birds share a strong investment in communication by vocalization. In fact, the complexity of song and communication systems developed by birds and by humans has no equal among vertebrates, except for whales and dolphins.

Birdsong had been studied and described long before scientists took a scholarly interest in it. Today, the study of birdsong is a substantial field in its own right. It is studied for the sake of learning about its communicative value, but also because it is aesthetically pleasing. It may be described in terms of its structure as well as its function. Researchers may be interested in the acquisition of song or in how and where song is produced. Ethologists are interested in birdsong in relation to questions of territory or reproductive strategies.

In evolutionary terms different species of birds may be as far apart from each other as ungulates are from humans. The first bird evolved in the Jurassic period, although most ancient bird species evolved later, in the Cretaceous period. Millions of years separate the appearance of the various species (Feduccia, 1996). For instance, the first known occurrence of some flightless birds, including species of game birds and waterfowl, may have been close to 100 million years ago, separated from the appearance of parrots by about 10 million years. Owls evolved about 60 million years ago, about 30 to 50 million years earlier than songbirds.

Songbirds and most other birds of prey were among the "newcomers," appearing in the Tertiary period as recently as a mere 5 to 30 million years ago. Albatrosses, frigatebirds, penguins, and petrels evolved earlier. Thus, when humans began to evolve about 4 million years ago, the air, the ground, and the waters were already occupied by winged and beaked species.

Some people have thought that all animals that have wings and lay eggs are the same kind of creature, but birds' evolutionary distance from one another and their differences in behavior make this as absurd as saying that mice and tigers are similar. But it is not just for reasons of appearance that birds have been seen as a unitary set of species; the history of ideas has also played a role. Descartes's notion that only humans are "complete" beings by virtue of their ability to think had particularly bad repercussions for birds. A false impression was created that birds are essentially like mechanistic toys. Likenesses of birds have been used as colorful decorations in living rooms or as self-propelled music boxes on mantlepieces, just to adorn human dwellings, with little thought of the live birds.

Some birds have evoked a negative image of evil or death. Think of the crow on the witch's back. Vultures are a symbol of death, and any haunted house worth its reputation has birds flying from it, dark and menacing with their sharp beaks and claws. Such associations gave rise to the links between birds and bats and prehistoric monsters. This negative imagery of birds contrasts with the positive association with their flight and songs.

But even positive images of birds have not led to the abandonment of the view that birds are less capable of higher cognition than mammals. The prevalence of this view has a number of consequences for studies of communication in birds. It influences what we prejudge as being the capability of birds and affects what we discern as human observers. In certain avian species, basic vocal signals may be innate and automatic. But in more complex avian species, such as the psittacine group (parrots, cockatoos, budgerigars), corvids (crows, ravens, jays), and the Cracticidae (Australian magpies, currawongs, butcherbirds), studies have shown that many of the vocalization skills are learned behaviors. Mastery of these skills is partly responsible for success in finding a partner, breeding, and acquiring and holding on to territory. There is nothing automatic about the production of vocalizations even in chickens *(Gallus gallus)*, even though their vocalizations are simple compared with those of songbirds. Hence in studies of communication in birds we may often be dealing with learned, complex vocalizations and very complex social interactions.

We are only just beginning to understand the complexity of bird communication. Researchers who have shown that a variety of birds are capable of complex communication have fought traditional views. Irene Pepperberg's (1990a, 1990b) research on communication by her Grey parrot Alex is one example. Alex communicates with the researcher using English words. He can count and discriminate shapes, colors, and objects. He can understand commands and express wishes. Pepperberg's research suggests that Alex has learned to use English words to communicate in a comprehensive way, not simply by mindless association of certain words with certain events. These capabilities appear to be the result of thinking (or consciousness) rather than automatic responses. Alex the parrot may well be on a par with the great apes in his abilities to communicate and reason. Many other avian species may have abilities similar to those of Alex. One famous Australian corella, a particularly argumentative species of cockatoo, has learned to argue with and even shout at its owner in human language (BBC, 1996). The studies by Konrad Lorenz (1966) on corvids (European ravens) and Kaplan's recent studies on the Australian magpie (1996, 1999) show similar complexity of communication.

METHODS OF COMMUNICATING

When we speak of communication in birds, it is customary to look at the relative importance of visual, auditory, and olfactory communication for individuals of a given species. In some classic studies it was found that, in relation to other means of communication, acoustic signals are of prime importance. Many years ago this was shown to be the case in the domestic hen's recognition of her chick. When a transparent bell was placed over a small chicken, preventing the hen from hearing its calls, the hen paid no attention to the distressed chick. A turkey deprived of auditory cues also failed to recognize her own offspring, and consequently attacked and even killed them, as she would any intruder. Hence, in some contexts and in some avian species, acoustic signaling is dominant over visual signaling, but most communication in birds makes use of more than one sense simultaneously, especially the visual and auditory senses. Many species of birds perform visual displays while vocalizing.

Recognition of individuals need not involve sophisticated vocalization patterns but may require excellent hearing. The acute hearing of many birds may also be used to find food. For instance, the Australian magpie *(Gymnorhina tibicen)* locates its food largely by sound. Its hearing is so good that it can locate scarab larvae moving in the soil several inches under the surface. The Australian tawny frogmouth *(Podargus strigoides)* could theoretically find its food if blindfolded. It can hear the rustle of beetles and cockroaches in the undergrowth from the height of a tree branch. We might expect acoustic signals to bear characteristics relevant to the bird's social and ecological environment, and also to its hearing capacity, but this is not necessarily so. Australian magpies have very intense, high-amplitude calls and songs, which seems extravagant given their exceptional hearing. By contrast, the tawny frogmouth uses low-amplitude and low-frequency sounds to communicate. Tawny frogmouths, unlike magpies, are nocturnal. In the stillness of an Australian bush night, the repetitious hoot of the tawny frogmouth can be heard for miles.

Visual Signals

Although birds use vocalizations extensively for communicative purposes, they are by no means their only way of communicating. Visual communication is used widely by birds, requiring suitable eyesight to perceive the visual signals. A study by Patrice Adret has shown that visual stimuli (in the form of video images) have reinforcing properties in zebra finches *(Taeniopygia guttata),* although the study allowed auditory cues as well (Adret, 1997). Merely showing the head of another male zebra finch on screen roused the experimental bird to song. Bengalese finches *(Lonchura striata domestica),* investigated by Shigeru Watanabe, were found to rely predominantly on visual cues for discriminative behavior. The auditory signals in his experiments provided purposely ambiguous information and in those cases the bird's attention switched to visual signals that were not ambiguous (Watanabe, 1993). Australian magpies and tawny frogmouths are now also known to use visual signals to communicate. This was established in an experiment by Kaplan. For thirty days Kaplan wore the same clothes while she fed the birds. On the thirty-first day, she exchanged the feeding clothes for others with different colors and designs. Even though the auditory cues remained the same, birds of both species showed fear responses. On day 32, Kaplan carried the regular feeding clothes into the aviary and changed from the new to the regular feeding clothes in front of the birds. The fear responses disappeared in both birds on completion of the change. Interestingly, however, the magpies adapted to allow any form of clothing from then on, but the tawny frogmouths continued to show fear responses even with slight variations in the clothing. Of course, a change of clothing may be perceptually difficult to accommodate, because birds rarely change plumage color and patterns other than when they mature from nestling to adult or, in some species, when they change plumage with the seasons, as do the partridge in Europe and the male superb fairy wren in Australia.

It is difficult to speak about visual perception in birds in general terms. There is a tremendous diversity in optical designs and retinal structures across avian species. Some species even have infrared or ultraviolet vision. Owls and a variety of other nocturnal species (such as owlet nightjars) can see at very low intensities of light. Diurnal birds of prey have probably the best long-distance sight and visual acuity of any species. Most bird species have limited movement of the eyeball but this is compensated for by great flexibility in head movements. The eye of the barn owl, for instance, is fixed rather firmly in its socket, but the head can move 270 degrees, both vertically and horizontally. There are only two bird species so far investigated that show extensive movement of the eyeball. One is the bittern, which in its "freezing" position (head and beak up, neck stretched) can turn the eyes forward and downward to see below its beak and straight ahead in binocular vision. Another is the snipe, which can turn its eyes upward to watch a bird overhead without moving its head at all.

The eyes of birds are often at the side of the head, and therefore a good deal of visual information is obtained in monocular vision. This provides a large visual field, including areas above and, in some species, behind the head of the bird. This kind of vision is of great advantage for survival, but it is not clear whether it serves any communicative function. Certainly, birds perform lateral (or broadside) displays that may require use of the lateral field of vision.

Like mammals, avian species have a wide range of body postures available for signaling a message by visual means. Head bobbing, arching of the neck, extending of the wings outward, and certain sorts of running, stomping, and crouching postures may be used in both agonistic (threat) and courtship behaviors: the same posture can have embedded in it the potential for both flight and attraction. Many courtship rituals rely on rapid changes in body posture.

One of the best known and most dramatic courtship rituals that relies largely on motion and body posture is performed by the grebes (*Podiceps* spp.) as a dance on water. The sequence is rather complex: In horned grebes *(Podiceps auritus)* the male "bounces" forward and dives several times: then both male and female rise to full height by treading water, facing each other in what is sometimes referred to as a "penguin" display; they continue to dance in that posture until finally they swim apart. The village weaver male *(Ploceus cucullatus)* uses a wing- and head-pointing display to attract a female's attention not only to himself but to the nest he has built. There are many bird species that use dance or ritualized movement as a component of their courtship display. Lyrebirds (*Menuridae* spp.) are famous for their dancing as well as their vocal displays (see Robinson and Curtis, 1996).

Plumage Signals

Feathers are often used for signaling. Although plumage color is not a universal factor in recognition of the sex of a bird, it plays this role in a large number of species. Males of many species use it to attract a mate. Recognition of sex, in some species, may occur exclusively through visual cues—plumage color or eye color, as Glenn-Peter Saetre and Tore Slagsvold from Oslo found in experiments with caged pied flycatchers *(Ficedula hypoleuca)*. When they painted a pied flycatcher female in the colors of the male, all other males treated the bird as if it were male. A male painted as a female was treated by the others as a female. This identification was maintained even when the song of the male was played in conjunction with presentation of the male bird painted as a female (Saetre and Slagsvold, 1992). It is worth noting here that some male pied flycatchers naturally have plumage coloration that is closer to that of the female. In free-ranging birds, males treat such birds as if they were female and may even engage in courtship rituals for their benefit. Males equipped with a plumage color that mimics that of a female can accrue territorial advantages. They may invade a territory without encountering the aggression of a competing male and may succeed in staying.

Apart from sexual recognition, plumage color and patterns may signal such things as individual identification, dominance status, and mating readiness. Plumage may also provide a sign stimulus (Konrad Lorenz's term) that can lead to attack. For instance, the red breast of the male European robin functions as such a sign stimulus that leads to attack by other males. Even stuffed models placed on a branch provoked attack when the breast was red, but not when the red was missing.

While sexual recognition and individual identification as a result of plumage are passive, pregiven signals that are genetically determined, dominance status and mating readiness require some additional, active social communication to get their meanings across. Birds of paradise, for instance, go to extraordinary lengths to display their plumage. As mentioned earlier, the male Victoria's riflebird *(Ptiloris victoriae)* will choose a sunny, exposed part of the rainforest and rhythmically display tail or wing feathers, performing a fascinating dance, with colors flashing in the sun, that will attract a female to come close for inspection. The male will then proceed with his display, but this time he half folds his wings around the female (without touching her) in quick succession, first the left and then the right, in such a way that the female becomes almost a captive in the courtship ritual.

Perhaps the most spectacular use of feathers in signaling is shown by the peacock with tail feathers fanned out like a wheel, shimmering with each new turn of the body. As well as its iridescent green and blue colors, the peacock's tail has hundreds of eyespots, patterns that mimic eyes, all appearing to be looking inward toward the body of the peacock. In Chapter 1, we saw that eye-like patterns (ocelli) are used by some moths and butterflies to direct the attention of predatory birds away from the body and to the less vulnerable wings, or even to startle the bird long enough to escape. The peacock uses the eye-like patterns for intraspecies communication to attract a female during courtship.

An eye-like pattern is used for the same purpose by males in one of the 43 species of the birds of paradise, the bluebird. The pattern is hidden at the abdomen and surrounded by magnificent long bright blue feathers. Only during courtship do these blue feathers with their eye-like markings (black and shiny bright red) come into full display. For this to happen, the bird needs to hang upside down on a branch and fan out all the blue feathers to expose the eye-like pattern. These then hang over the chest. He swings them rapidly to and fro while emitting rasping, rhythmic, and mesmerizing percussion sounds in quick succession.

A most unusual and complex form of visual display occurs in bowerbirds (*Chlamydera* spp.). Here the display of feathers has been replaced by decorations external to the bird. We could almost speak of tool use. Instead of, or in addition to, parading bright or striking plumage to a prospective female, males build a bower. The bower may be decorated with all manner of objects of similar colors, depending on the species' preferences. During courtship, the male displays plumage and may vocalize and even dance, but there is always the additional element of a stage, uniquely constructed specifically for the purpose of attracting a female. Like the lyrebirds, male bowerbirds clear an area on the forest floor for dancing. In addition, the males of most bowerbird species build a structure that is of no use for raising young but is an integral part of their courtship display. Mating success is linked to the bower and the entire display, including vocalizations, dancing, and construction of the site. For the best performers, the enormous effort pays off by giving them access to many females.

Signals issued by feather posture alone have rarely been studied systematically, yet they may be quite important ways of communicating visually. Many birds fluff their feathers in a certain way when they are ill but they may also raise their feathers as a warning signal. Tawny frogmouths can raise all their body feathers simultaneously to make themselves look menacingly larger than they are. This display is not necessarily accompanied by a vocalization, but it always precedes an attack and appears to be used in territorial disputes among conspecifics. In interspecies interactions, tawny frogmouths seem to shrink their body size by sleeking their feathers down as close as possible to the body and by stretching their necks. The bird then gives the appearance of a branch, a camouflage that works well against a gum tree (see Figure 4.1).

Facial Expressions

It is equally possible to attribute communicative importance to the facial expressions of birds. The idea that birds have "facial expressions" is quite foreign to many people and there has been no systematic work done on this aspect of avian communication. The concept that a bird has a "face" may seem strange, but that is largely because humans have linguistically claimed the "face" as something uniquely human, a feature that bestows individuality. (There are now a few select mammalian species to whom we grant individuality and thus a face). Although it is recognized that many avian species express individuality in their vocalizations, it is usually not accepted that birds do so in their appearance. But individual birds do "look" different, and they look different in different

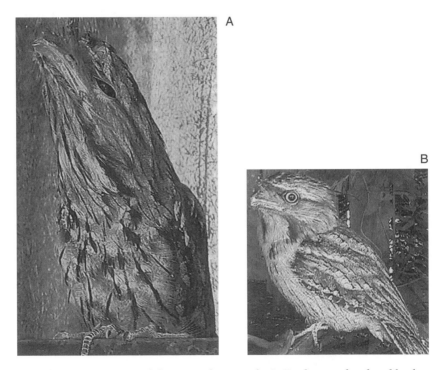

FIGURE 4.1   Postures of the tawny frogmouth. A: Feathers on head and back sleeked down and neck and body extended in a camouflage posture. B: Neutral posture adopted by the same bird. (Photographs by G. Kaplan.)

contexts. Facial expression is achieved either by movements of the beak or by independent positioning of feathers on the chin or above the beak, on the ear coverts, on top of the head (the crown), at the nape of the neck, and in some species also by the bird's moving the feathers above the eyes independently of the other feathers.

Like primates, birds have open-mouth displays, really open-beak displays, which, together with other body signals, can be used in fear or threat displays. Many species use a variety of open-beak displays; in the tawny frogmouth, the open beak displays the inside lining of the large oral cavity, which is a striking light-green color. This effectively emphasizes the enormous size of the beak and makes it look more ominous than it actually is. Several species of birds open their beaks as a threat, usually without vocalizing but sometimes augmenting this display with hissing or breathing sounds. Galahs and many other psittacine (parrot) species use open-beak displays accompanied by shrieks, hisses, or exhaling-air sounds. The barn owl (*Tyto alba*), for instance, a bird that is rarely heard, emits an exhaling-air sound in warning while the beak is half open and then sharply claps the upper and lower parts of the beak together several times, often without the slightest change in body posture or feather composition.

In galahs and other crested cockatoos, movement of head feathers is very easy to detect, even from some distance. The crest goes up not just in alarm but in states of friendly arousal. The feathers that flank the beak (the ear coverts) can be ruffled to express anger and possible attack. Lowering or flattening of feathers is usually associated with fear, but such a display commonly involves the whole body rather than just the head. Birds often show "cuddly" and babyish behavior by fluffing the feathers above and below the beak, a phenomenon readily observable in Australian magpies. For close, conspecific interactions, these facial expressions are powerful signals emitted with a minimum expenditure of energy.

Smell and Touch

Compared with auditory and visual communication, relatively little is known about communication by smell and touch in birds. We know that many bird species preen each other, usually as an exercise in bonding and reassurance. For some avian species, particularly parrots, preening and tactile responses are very important in social interactions. In some species, such as the red wattlebird *(Anthochaera carunculata)* and the Australian magpie, newly hatched nestlings that have not yet opened their eyes will not defecate until they feel the vibration at the nest indicating the presence of a parent. They then lift their cloacal region toward the edge of the nest and the parent takes the firm feces into its beak and carries the waste out of the nest. Although this is not exactly a form of tactile communication, the tactile signal of the parent elicits the response. Later in the development of magpies, the parent may actually prompt defecation by tapping its beak directly on the offspring's cloacal region (observed by Kaplan).

Olfaction in birds is less well developed than the other senses but it is not absent. Olfactory cues have been shown to play a role in food selection in a number of species (as has been summarized by Malakoff, 1999), but the studies in this field are limited and it is not known whether odors are used to communicate between individuals. The sense of olfaction is unusually well developed in the New Zealand kiwi *(Apteryx australis)*, which locates its food by sensing odors (Wenzel, 1972), so it is probable that olfaction is also used for communication in this species. The same may be true of other species of birds that are known to locate food by its odor. These include the turkey vulture, *Cathartes aura* (Stager, 1967), a number of shearwaters and petrels (Grubb, 1972), the common raven, *Corvus corax* (Harriman and Berger, 1986) and the starling, *Sturnus vulgaris* (Clark and Mason, 1987).

The tawny frogmouth defecates as a deterrent when feeling threatened, as in cases of mobbing attempts by other avian species. The bird will fly close to the animal to be deterred and deliberately spray large quantities of its extremely pungent excrement over or near it. Tawnies are the skunks of the air, and their warning scent, if dropped on fur or skin, is difficult to eliminate. Usually, this warning signal is reserved purely for other species, and it is not clear whether tawny frogmouths themselves can actually smell their own droppings or perceive the intensity of the odor of their excrement.

Even if auditory and visual cues are likely to be the most important signals in avian communication, it can at least be said that no single sense functions entirely in isolation. Courtship displays in birds are a good ex-

ample. Auditory messages are usually accompanied by visual displays that can be very elaborate, involving motion and even "dance." Some tactile contact may also be part of the ritual (neck touching, beak fencing, or, more indirectly, the exchange of gifts).

HOW VOCALIZATIONS ARE PRODUCED

Vocalization depends on appropriate centers in the central nervous system. In birds, there are a number of specific, so-called sound-emission sites, some of which are conspicuously different from those of other vertebrates (mammals, including humans, reptiles, and fish). The chief sound-producing vocal organ of a bird is the syrinx. Although avian species also have a larynx, like humans, Rod Suthers (1990) and others have thought that the larynx plays no significant role in sound production. However, researchers are still debating whether supersyringeal structures, such as the trachea, larynx, tongue, and even the upper and lower mandibles, play a role in modifying sounds. The tongue may be important in psittacine species. Recent work by Dianne Patterson and Irene Pepperberg (1996) on American English vowel production in the Grey parrot has shown that this parrot can produce vowels of striking similarity to human vowels despite the very different anatomy of the psittacine vocal apparatus (lack of teeth and lips, for instance). Indeed, many parrots can produce such vowels, as a sonogram of galah "speech" shows (Figure 4.2).

There are several important differences between the avian and the human vocal apparatus. The most obvious one is the location of the main sound-producing organ. The human larynx is situated in the neck, and hence is close to the mouth. The avian syrinx, by contrast, is located well within the body of the bird. It sits at that part of the trachea (windpipe) where the bronchial branches split and go to the lung on one or the other side of the body. Thus a bird has two airstreams impinging on its vocal organ rather than one, as in humans. The onset and termination of vocalization (called phonation) is usually controlled by the syringeal muscles that open or close the lumen (airway) on each side of the syrinx.

The syrinx is an organ that varies in complexity from species to species. Although the precise mechanisms of sound production are not fully known, it is thought that voiced or whistled song originates from vibra-

tion of the medial tympaniform membrane. The syrinx has internal medial tympaniform membranes that are housed within the interclavicular sac, an air sac in the pleural cavity. In that location the membranes are sensitive to the air passing through from the lungs, and they are controlled by the syringeal muscles and by air pressure surrounding the membranes. The elasticity and complexity of the membranes may determine the quality of sounds.

Songbirds have a very complex syringeal system, in which the syringeal muscles and the internal membranes interact to produce nearly pure tones (single-frequency tones, similar to human whistles) and also, as in the lyrebird, parallel notes, seemingly played on two instruments at once. The latter sounds are produced from both sides of the syrinx at once, as we will discuss below.

In the Australian kookaburra, with its loud and raucous call, the syringeal muscles are barely developed. By contrast, the syringeal muscles of the Australian magpie are very noticeable. It is possible to trace the development of song in an Australian magpie in relation to the development of the syringeal muscles. Full song is produced only when the syringeal muscles are fully grown.

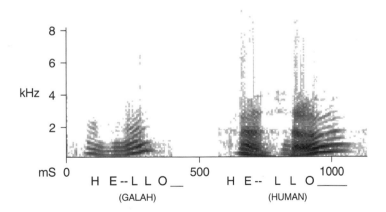

FIGURE 4.2 Mimicry of human speech by a galah *(Cacatua roseicapilla)*. Time on the Y axis is in milliseconds. Although the "hello" produced by the galah is of shorter duration than that spoken by the human, the patterns of the two vocalizations are almost identical. The fundamental notes and the overtones are very similar. (Sound spectrograms produced by G. Kaplan.)

It is possible for a songbird to produce sounds from different sources at the same time—to use both sides of the syrinx simultaneously or independently. Suthers confirmed this in 1990 for the brown thrashers *(Toxostoma rufum)* and gray catbirds *(Dumetella carolinensis)*. He found that in both species the frequency range of sound contributed by the right syrinx was higher than that of the left syrinx, and that phonation was frequently switched from one side to the other, not just in between syllables but within a single syllable. Simultaneous use of both sides, at least in the species they examined, resulted in syllables that are "two voiced," syllables that are not harmonically related and are of different amplitude modulation. This means that one side of the syrinx is not dominant, as is the case with canaries. In addition, some birds utilize air reservoirs in the chest as resonance chambers for the production of sound. These may be used in conjunction with the syrinx, or even in the absence of a syrinx, as for instance in bustards, emus, and cranes, which have clavicular and cervical air sacs. The sounds these air sacs produce are hollow and of low frequency, like the sound of a drum being struck under water.

The sound repertoire is not exhausted at this point. Some species use beak clapping to communicate. Beak clapping in storks, some owls, in the three frogmouth species, in noisy miners *(Manorina melanocephala)*, and in Australian magpies is used as a strong and aggressive warning signal to other species. Some species also generate auditory signals by pecking an object, such as a tree, to indicate territoriality, and woodpeckers use such signals for sexual communication. The male musk duck in eastern Australia *(Biziura lobata)* produces as part of his courtship ritual an odd "plonking" sound of his feet in the water.

Wing flapping and wing beating, as in wood pigeons and crested pigeons, may function as warning signals. The sound of wing beating by a crested pigeon *(Geophaps lophotes)* is a high trill that can be heard some distance away, and since not every flight motion produces this shrill sound, we suspect that wing beating in crested pigeons is used for communicative purposes. William Thorpe and Donald Griffin (1962) found that the flight sounds of some small birds contain ultrasound. They are therefore not audible to the human ear and probably also not to birds such as owls that prey on these small birds, but they are certainly audible to bats and other vertebrates with ultrasonic abilities. A large number of

songbird species, nearly all tits (*Parus* spp.) for example, show a behavior called "wing quiver," which is said to have communicative function. The wing quiver is caused by a vibratory movement of the wings, mainly the wingtips, at a sound frequency of about 15 Hz. In the black-capped chickadees *(Parus atricapillus),* wing quivering usually occurs in front of the nest hole before the bird enters the nest, and Marcel Lambrechts and his colleagues concluded from their observations that wing quivering functions as a request or invitation to the mate (Lambrechts, Clemmons, and Hailman, 1993).

A most unusual way to produce sound, for a bird, is tool use. The male palm cockatoo *(Probosciger aterrimus),* found only at the very tip of Australia's tropical north and in New Guinea, fashions a stick to a manageable length. He then holds it in one foot and drums the stick on a tree while emitting very high-pitched but not very loud shrieks, dancing at the same time and swaying his head. With this triple activity—swaying of the body, vocalization, and drumming—the palm cockatoo advertises his territory.

THE MESSAGE IN VOCALIZATION

Many researchers still distinguish beween calls and song. The assumption behind this distinction has been that calls are short and simple and are produced by both sexes throughout the year, while song has at times been thought of as a special category of vocalizations reserved for male vocalizations during the breeding season. This distinction is no longer considered very useful, partly because of overlap (when does a call finish and a song begin?) and partly because not all song occurs only in the breeding season. In many songbirds, but by no means all, only the males sing and they are said to do so to attract a female. Other species, however, do not confine singing to the breeding season. In the tropics, many females sing. Also, in moderate climate zones, there are some species, such as the Australian magpie, in which males and females alike sing all year round. Some birds also have a song type that could easily be regarded as consisting of a few specialized calls.

From an evolutionary perspective it could be argued that patterns of vocalization may have become more common and more complex over time—that the most recently evolved species have the most complex vo-

calizations. The most recently evolved birds are the passerines, or song-birds, with about 56 families worldwide (from finches to scrub birds, swallows to pittas, starlings to flycatchers, pardalotes to crows, wrens to lyrebirds, warblers to currawongs—a very diverse group). Within this or-der we distinguish suboscines and oscines. Suboscines are birds suppos-edly equipped with a syringeal anatomy more primitive than that of "true" songbirds, the oscines. To the human observer complex song may be aesthetically more pleasing. However, suboscines' song may well have become more complex over evolutionary time. It would be easy to sur-mise that syntax or meaning is implied in the concept of complexity. But neither the complexity nor the beauty of the song is in itself an indicator of content. The actual communicative value of a long, beautiful, and complex song (such as that of the nightingale or of the lyrebird) may not be greater than that of shorter or less melodious vocalizations.

The frequencies of bird vocalizations commonly range between 2 and 10 kHz, frequencies that humans can easily hear and that are therefore easy to record and measure. Only a few avian species are known to pro-duce infrasounds, such as the pigeon (sound levels down to 0.5 Hz), and a few species produce vocalizations in the ultrasonic range (above about 20 kHz). As noted in Chapter 2, the experimental technique of playback is the standard way of investigating the meaning of vocalizations. Play-back involves recording the vocalizations of a bird and then playing them back to another bird or group of birds and observing the results.

Sending a vocal message can of course take many different forms, as we pointed out in earlier chapters. For birds (and many insects), which have such a high investment in communication by acoustic means, it is impor-tant to be aware that effective sending of messages may be impaired by factors in the environment in a number of ways.

We speak of auditory saturation, for instance, for sounds that are im-possible to transmit over a long distance. Background noises such as wind, waves, rain, or the movement of leaves in a forest may cause wave reflections and bring about a lowering of signal intelligibility and a dimi-nution in the carrying power of the signal. The background noise of other species, such as insects and frogs, may also interfere with transmis-sion of the vocal signal. Then there is aggregate noise produced by the same species living communally in a colony, in large family groups, or in a bachelor flock, and even background noise created by the movement of wings. Hundreds of birds taking to the air at once can create a substantial noise even without vocalization. All these factors may impede communication of a message by sound.

The receiver must therefore be capable of extracting the relevant information from random background noise and have the capacity to detect information-carrying signals of an intensity even below that of the background noise. Who cannot be impressed when watching a penguin, for example, enter its colony of perhaps tens of thousands of other raucous birds and identify its young by sound alone. A message, at its most basic level, reveals the species identity of the sender. The study of birdsong makes it clear that each species has its species-specific vocalizations, although there may be individual variations, and even dialects according to region. Any vocalization therefore at the very least conveys the meaning: "I am here and I am a great tit" (or a starling, or a nightingale, or any other species).

We distinguish broadly between the syntax and the semantics of a message. Syntax refers to the structure of the song or call. Semantics refers to the content or meaning of the message. The two can be intertwined. It is conceivable that most vocalizations are intended to impart meaning. The exceptions are some vocalizations of a few cave-dwelling species such as the cave swiftlet *(Aerodramus vanikorensis)*, which uses clicking sounds for echolocation just as bats do.

A bird's vocalization may be simple or complex. But it is often misleading to claim that a vocalization is "simple," because our fleeting observations of one species may not represent that species' entire repertoire and because we, as casual human observers, may not always be able to detect the finer distinctions in a vocalization. For instance, it is now known that the allegedly "simple song" of a finch has 13 themes and 187 variations. The entirety of vocalization variations in birds is called a repertoire, just as in a human singer, and the number of different song types available to one species is referred to as the repertoire size. Repertoire size has been examined in quite a number of songbirds. From available information, it seems that the brown thrasher holds the record in repertoire size, as Clive Catchpole and Peter Slater (1995) point out. The brown thrasher has an estimated repertoire size of between 1500 and 1900 song types. Improvisation and new learning may result in further changes and increases in the repertoire size. For instance, as John Kirn and his colleagues discovered in 1989, the red-winged blackbird adds to its repertoire each year.

But repertoire size, by itself, is not an indication of an increase in meaning. Meaning is far more difficult to assess than repertoire size. We use the term "vocabulary" to refer to the semantics—the actual meaning of the calls. Passerines may have a vocabulary of about 20 different calls, whereas gulls and other non-songbirds may have half that. However, ongoing research is constantly discovering more and more variation in avian vocabulary. Given that individual differences are very marked in vocalizations of complex songbirds, we may expect a good deal of variation and with that variation may come complexity of meaning.

The understanding of meaning in avian vocalization is in its infancy. Traditional ethology tended to describe animal behavior in terms of four main motivational systems: aggression, fear, feeding, and sex. These categories were related to physiological processes underlying the behavior. In 1953 Niko Tinbergen argued that behavior was due to relatively invariant and immediate responses to internal and external stimuli. This approach was an important first step in studying vocal and other behaviors systematically. Since his ground-breaking work, much research has been undertaken to investigate the development of vocal behavior in conjunction with physiological and even anatomical development. More recent studies have shown that vocal behavior in birds does not always conform to Tinbergen's simplified model. It is now known that learning plays a part in the development of song in all true songbirds so far studied. There is a period of vocal plasticity—a period during the development of the young bird when it is able to extend its vocabulary and learn its song. Even in those avian species with simple calls some learning may be involved. Fernando Nottebohm and his colleagues (1990) showed, for instance, that learning is enhanced or decreased by the acoustic context. Zebra finches that were asked to solve the problem of a missing harmonic in an experiment learned the operant response in a fraction of the time when the specific problem was embedded in a whole song (Nottebohm et al., 1990). The period for learning may vary widely between species. In some species of sparrow, learning is restricted to the first two months of life, while in others it may go on much longer. Peter Slater showed that the young chaffinch is able to learn new songs as late as 10 months after birth (Slater, 1989). The vocalizations of Australian magpies remain highly plastic throughout the first year of life at least. There is evidence from hand-raised magpies of learning of new sounds and new (human) words throughout this period (Kaplan, 1996). More details about learning to vocalize are given in Chapter 6. Here we want to emphasize that avian vocal behavior is extremely complex and certainly not automatic or based simply on underlying physiological factors.

WHAT IS SONG FOR?

The functions that have been established for birdsong can be summarized as territorial defense and sexual attraction. Donald Kroodsma (1996) has argued that sedentary species may develop elaborate songs, whereas migratory birds may use song to a lesser degree for the purpose of advertising their nesting or transient territories. During the breeding season, the growth of male sexual organs may be accompanied by changes in plumage (as in the superb blue fairy wren, for example) or by the onset of elaborate song for the purpose of attracting a female. Vocalizing to defend territory is generally regarded as a more efficient way of communicating than physical confrontation. Less energy is expended in the process and injuries may also be minimized. Many bird species first issue warning calls to an invader but then follow the calls by direct flight at the invading individual if the vocal warnings were not sufficient to deter the invader. Neighboring birds know their territorial borders, and a form of truce, even if a watchful one, may exist between neighbors. This is illustrated by the behavior of the white-throated sparrow *(Zonotrichia albicollis),* which sings far less energetically when a neighboring bird approaches its territory than when a stranger approaches.

The connection between song and breeding is equally strong. There is ample evidence today that many males sing to attract a female just as some choose plumage to achieve the same result, and males of some species do both. Song requires energy, and one of the arguments put forward is that prolonged and strenuous singing advertises the good health and fitness of a male, just as a shiny and colorful plumage may. A study of the great reed warbler *(Acrocephalus arundinaceus)* has shown that females select males with larger song repertoires and that the survival of offspring is increased by such a choice (Hasselquist, Bensch, and von Schantz, 1996), and the same is known to be true of other species (Catchpole, Dittami, and Leisler, 1984). Apart from its possible physiological function across a variety of songbirds, the communicative value of the song may be: "Take me because I am healthy." Further, the song may say, "I am experienced and will therefore make a good partner." The singing male may convey an honest signal because an accomplished song is a mark of a mature adult, a bird that has had plenty of exposure to his species-specific calls. The male great reed warbler, for example, increases his repertoire with age and this expansion is a mark of his proven ability to survive.

Research done in the 1960s has shown that auditory stimulation has a direct effect on the secretion of hormones that stimulate growth of the sexual organs, which, in turn, stimulates the secretion of sex hormones. The secretion is induced by sound and, in some species, triggers the female to become ready for mating. A classic study by Daniel Lehrman (1965) showed that the cooing of the male dove triggers reproductive changes in the female.

Singing Together

Duetting has been an important subfield of song study and it occurs in a wide range of avian species. It is now recognized that duetting plays an important role in the vocal communication system of birds, especially those that live in the tropics. When talking about music sung by humans, we tend to use the term "duetting" for two voices singing not just simultaneously but in some agreed and orderly fashion that produces harmonies or contrasts in sound structure. Duetting in birds refers to the process of B starting to sing when A has stopped singing and A continuing where B left off. Calls made by duetting birds may overlap but usually the calls of two birds follow each other so closely and so precisely that they sound like the vocalizations of one bird, a phenomenon called antiphonal song (see Figure 4.3). In short, a duet is an agreed-upon sequence of calls that fit together owing to the choice of frequency, rhythm, and even overtones (harmonics). Duetting is now thought to be a specific form of communication, a way of retaining auditory contact especially in densely forested environments, which make maintenance of visual contact difficult.

Although duetting may play a part in synchronizing the gonadal state

of the pair (to prepare for breeding), its functions also include communication when visual contact is lost or at risk of being lost. This is particularly true in wooded areas and dense rainforests (hence the prevalence of
duetting in tropical regions) or during winter flocking and migration.
Duetting may also serve to synchronize defense of a territory or, more
commonly, to reinforce a pair bond. Duetting seems to occur more frequently in pairs with a prolonged monogamous bond. Australian magpie larks *(Grallina cyanoleuca)* duet regularly (Figure 4.3), as do Australian magpies, the black-faced cuckoo shrike *(Coracina novaehollandiae),*
and the bar-headed goose *(Anser indicus),* but the contexts in which these
species duet seem entirely different. Studies by Charles Blaich and his
colleagues (1996) found that pair-bonded zebra finches engage in con-
tact-call duets far more frequently than unpaired finches, and in a non-
random fashion. Duets are not necessarily initiated by the male. In the
bar-headed goose and the bay wren *(Thryothorus nigricapillus),* for instance, it is the female who calls first, answered by the male.

Further types of singing together are choruses and caroling. In the
chorus, a whole group of birds sings at the same time, sometimes eliciting countersinging by neighboring and competing birds or by unrelated
groups. There is a form of chorus that we call caroling, which occurs
when members of a family group or communal breeders reconfirm their
bond and, together, announce their possession of their territory. Austra-

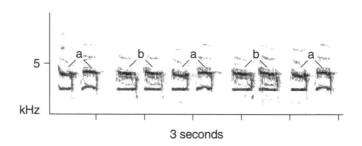

5 —

kHz

3 seconds

FIGURE 4.3   The antiphonal song of two Australian magpie larks *(Grallina
cyanoleuca).* The vocalizations produced by the two individuals (a and b) as they
duet are indicated. The marked similarity of the vocalizations by the two birds
and the precision of timing make it appear as if the vocalizations were made by
just one bird. (Sound spectrograms produced by G. Kaplan.)

lian magpies and kookaburras (also called laughing jackasses) use carol-ing and countersinging to test the strength of a neighboring group. As in individual calls, in caroling and chorus singing there may also be some status signaling involved. The parent bird starts to sing and then is joined by its mate and offspring or helpers at the nest. In kookaburras (laughing and blue-winged), the offspring may supply a form of percussion sup-port while the parent birds burst into full staccato calls ("laughing").

Variations and Richness

The loudness of a vocalization (amplitude) can make a substantial dif-ference to a message. Many bird species, as Richard Andrew has found, have loud-faint pairs of song display (Andrew, 1961). The loud vocaliza-tion may be for territorial display and can mean that the caller would at-tack if the territory borders were infringed. For instance, Carolina chicka-dees and Australian magpies have a vocalization that is uttered only when they are ready to attack. A fainter call signaled to mates and offspring may indicate that the communicator is ready to interact but not to attack.

Thus even if we consider only those vocalizations used to communi-cate messages about breeding and territoriality, the variations and rich-ness of the message can be substantial. Some species of gulls even have specific copulation calls. Among weaverbirds (songbirds of the subfamily *Ploceinae*), John Crook found that, in at least four species, females have specific vocalizations they use to solicit copulation (Crook, 1969). In Australian magpies, females and males use the full song repertoire all year round. Bird vocalizations can also signal information about food; they can express anxiety or alarm, rivalry, interest, or defense readiness; they can tell others to fly away (follow me) and convey similar short instruc-tions. None of these may be specific to the sex of a bird. Male and females alike will utter calls when predators approach and in many other situa-tions.

Attributing specific functions to birdsong is useful in ascertaining the meaning of the vocalization and what evolutionary advantages might flow from one activity (song) over a host of possible others. But this approach may overlook or underplay other aspects of song. To con-sider song only in terms of territory defense may underplay how it is learned. Simply establishing a relationship between song type and territory may lead one to overlook, as J. M. Williams and Peter Slater (1990) have pointed out, that both repertoire size and numbers of neighbors are likely to have strong influences on the distribution of song types in a population. They conclude that geographical variation of song may be an epiphenomenon of vocal learning and that one need not propose purposes for geographical variation in song or for song dialect boundaries.

Straightforward functional explanations of song may also be unable to account for a whole range of other vocalizations. For instance, one of the magpies that Kaplan raised spent an average of 2 hours per day vocalizing, presenting elaborate variations of a long repertoire, for no apparent reason. The vocal pattern was rearranged every time and seemed to record the auditory events of the day, embellished perhaps, but recognizable as auditory events that had occurred within the bird's earshot. Over 20 percent of these vocalizations, recorded over an entire year, consisted of mimicry of sounds of sympatric species (those living in the same area)—kookaburras, peachface parrots, dogs, and humans. Free-ranging Australian magpies show the same behavior at the height of summer, well before their breeding season and just after the worst pressures of feeding their young from the previous season have abated and the food supply is plentiful. These examples provide some evidence to suggest that singing may increase as the pressures to defend territory and/or the young decrease (quite opposite to the claim that singing increases purely for the purposes of breeding and defense).

There may be "cultural" aspects involved in singing at this time. For instance, magpie females may sing to their offspring while feeding them. This vocalization may include not just the individual song of the mother but also mimicked sequences. In one recording made by Robert Carrick, Norman Robinson, and Bruce Falls in the mid-1960s in Canberra, a magpie mother "sang" something that sounded like a horse's neigh to her offspring just before feeding them (original tapes acquired by courtesy of Emeritus Professor Bruce Falls); and we now have a number of examples of similar mimicry across Australia (see below). These mimicked vocalizations might be cultural and have no direct survival function, unless it can be argued that conveying the information that horses were in the territory was vital knowledge for survival. Alternatively, this vocalization could have been a by-product of another form of mimicry that was vital for survival.

Meaning

Research on any aspect of semantics in the last 50 years or so differs from earlier studies in one exciting way. It is now known, and still being discovered in more bird species, that birds are capable of referring to objects outside themselves (called external referents) and can communicate this knowledge to others (through "referential signaling"). Studies in the 1950s, for instance, showed that some bird species signaled to conspecifics that they had found a particular food source. This was observed in herring gulls *(Larus argentatus)* by Hubert and Maple Frings (1956), and shown in a study by H. Friedmann of the African honeyguide *(Indicator indicator)*, which leads conspecifics to nests of wild honey bees (Friedman, 1955).

The most common area of investigation of external referents concerns alarm calls. It has been shown for a number of bird species that the alarm calls for aerial predators are different from those for ground predators (see Chapter 2). In fact, Peter Marler (1981) noted some years ago that warning calls about aerial predators have similar acoustic qualities among very different species of birds. Whether uttered by a chaffinch, a blue tit, a blackbird, or a reed bunting (all European birds), the warning call is delivered with approximately similar intensity and at about the same pitch, 7 kHz.

The source of the warning call is not easily located. To explain this, we have to digress briefly into the physics of sound. Hearing and locating a source are usually achieved by both ears (a binaural function); the ears assess and compare crucial elements of the message such as phase, intensity, and time difference, thereby decoding the message and the location of the sender. Phase differences (the differences in time between when a sound wave reaches one ear and when it reaches the other) can be detected more effectively at low frequencies. At higher frequencies, the wavelength of sound decreases, rendering phase difference more difficult to detect, depending on the size of the listener's head, and hence the source more difficult to locate. In fact, depending on how far apart the listener's ears are (and therefore how large the listener's head is), there is in each individual case one frequency of sound whose source is impossible for the listener to detect by using the difference in time between the sound's arrival at each ear. If a bird used this frequency as the frequency of its alarm call, its predator would be completely unable to use timing to locate its potential prey.

Identifying the location of the sound source is further aided by the so-called sound-shadow intensity effect. If, for example, the sound source is to the listener's right, the left ear will be in the "sound shadow" of the listener's head. An intensity difference thereby occurs between ears, and this disparity can help establish the direction from which the sound comes. If a bird wants to avoid detection, it should pitch the call at a frequency that makes phase difference ambivalent and minimizes the sound-shadow intensity effect. By doing so, the bird can prevent clear identification of the direction of the call and hence can call to warn of the presence of a predator without running an immediate risk of being caught and eaten.

Peter Marler (1955, 1981) showed that a call of about 7 kHz does exactly that, and then showed that several species of birds use that frequency for alarm calling. This research suggests that certain sets of alarm calls may become common to many species because of their physical properties. Discovery of such rules of communication also make it more understandable why communication between very different species is possible. Marler found that alarm signals in some Corvidae and sparrows have similar structures and therefore induce interspecific reactions. In other words, the alarm call of one species may benefit a variety of other species, as we saw in Chapter 2.

Many other signals used by avian species have not been fully investigated, but some of them are certainly known to pet owners and those who rehabilitate wild animals. Among them are signals that indicate emotions. For instance, dogs have been known to cry for their owners. Birds shake in fear while they utter species-specific (often barely audible) high-frequency vocalizations. Animals communicate their emotions and desires to humans, and pets have also been observed to communicate with other species. Robert Leslie (1985) described a case of deception based on interspecies communication between two birds, a parakeet and a blue jay. The visiting parakeet, perched on the outside of the jay's cage, seemingly hungry, indicated by eye position and other cues that it wanted

the chopped spinach in the cage. The blue jay moved the chopped spinach close to the edge of its cage, but on the inside, and when the parakeet reached for the spinach the blue jay attacked the parakeet's head
with its beak.

Attachment may be expressed by a combination of preening behavior
and low gutteral sounds. For instance, low-frequency gutteral sounds are
emitted by Australian magpies when they preen a partner or offspring or
the human who cares for them. Galahs emit a specific short "approval"
call in conjunction with the response of another galah (or human), and
during preening the preened bird purrs much like a cat.

It is interesting to note here that similar patterns of intonation occur
across human cultures. Anne Fernald, for instance, has shown that in humans melodious speaking signals approval; sharp, staccato bursts express
disapproval or denial; and low legato murmurs are meant to comfort—
and these patterns are common to different cultures (Fernald, 1992).
These patterns may apply not only to humans but to animal species as
well. Sharp calls are usually interpreted as repudiating calls while low
legato murmurs/purrs are associated with comforting: there is cross-species similarity, as Marler (1981) described for alarm calling.

Mimicry

Birds have another set of vocalizations not equaled by any other group
in the animal world: mimicry. Mimicry is extremely widespread and
highly developed among Australian bird species but is found also
throughout the rest of the world. The Australian species best known for
mimicry in the wild are both species of lyrebirds (Robinson, 1991), Australian magpies, and bowerbirds (several species). In contact with humans, even if remaining free, they can also mimic human speech. Among
European birds, the starling is the star of mimicry (Hausberger, Jenkins,
and Keene, 1991). We know that parrots and budgerigars are excellent
mimics in captivity, but the first examples of mimicry in the wild have
been found only recently, for example in the Grey parrot (Cruickshank,
Gautier, and Chappuis, 1993). European marsh warblers (*Acrocephalus
palustris*) copy the calls of over 70 different species that they hear in both
Africa and Europe, between which continents they migrate (Dowsett-
Lemaire, 1979). It is from such mimicry that young birds of this species

are thought to learn their songs; they cannot learn them from their fathers because their fathers cease to sing before the chicks hatch.

The question remains: what is mimicry for? Why would birds deliberately transgress their species-specific sounds and move into the vocal territory of other species? We know that insects can mimic appearance, smells, and even noxious taste signals, and that dolphins and seals may use some vocal mimicry, but as far as we know today only birds mimic other species extensively in their vocalizations. Purists argue that such mimicry by birds is not "true" mimicry; they define "true" mimicry as having deceptive purposes useful for survival.

According to the models derived from studies of the insect world, true mimicry involves three parties: the mimicked one, say butterfly A, the mimicker, called butterfly B, and the predator that is fooled by butterfly B—the predator will not eat B because it looks like the unpalatable butterfly A. There has been no unambiguous evidence to date that birds mimic to avoid predation. However, it is possible that a bird may mimic another to safeguard a territory. Although this is not mimicry to avoid predation, it clearly functions to aid survival, either by safeguarding a territory from a rival or by repelling a predator who may prey on the young in the nest. In considering mimicry, we must also take into account differences between intentional and unintentional vocalizations, as we did in Chapter 3 for signaling in general (see the 1997 review by Christopher Evans for more detailed discussion).

A second reason for mimicry, and the one most commonly cited, has to do with the breeding season. Lyrebirds, for instance, adorn their songs during the breeding season with all sorts of sounds, taken from the sound repertoire available to the male. These added sounds typically include mimicry of the sounds made by other birds, the most distinctive being currawongs, kookaburras, yellow-tailed black cockatoos, and catbirds (mostly species that mimic others themselves). Lyrebirds may also include sounds of barking dogs, car horns, creaking door hinges, and even chainsaws (Robinson and Curtis, 1996). Male lyrebirds sing their long sequences of mimicked calls to attract a female. It is as if they "wear" the song component like medals—the more elaborate and extensive the collection, the more the female may be impressed.

But the function of vocal mimicry may extend even further, at least in the case of the Australian magpie. Mimicry in magpies has now been recorded from all over Australia, and preliminary data have shown that sounds are mimicked very selectively (Kaplan, 1996, 1999). Extensive exposure to some sounds resulted in no mimicry, while very short exposure to others immediately produced mimicry. The conclusions drawn so far are that mimicry occurred only in species that shared the same territory. Visitors, transient species, seemed systematically excluded.

In this case it seems possible to argue that territorial knowledge is very important for a species that is highly territorial, and is incorporated into the magpie's own repertoire. The sonogram in Figure 4.4 shows that the mimicry of the kookaburra is more melodious than the original, but the

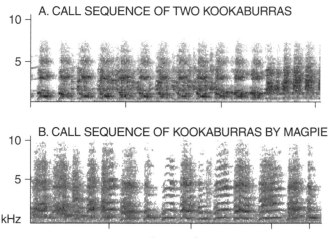

3 seconds

FIGURE 4.4 Mimicry of a kookaburra by a magpie. A: A sound spectrogram of two kookaburras *(Dacelo gigas)* laughing jointly. B: Mimicry of the kookaburra's laughing by an Australian magpie *(Gymnorhina tibicen)*. Note the matching rhythmic pattern. The fundamental notes match also but most of the overtones do not. The magpie's rendition of "kookaburra" is rhythmically very precise, but it is a little more melodious than the original, demonstrating the vocal differences between songbirds (passerines) and non-songbirds (nonpasserines).

magpie has attempted to follow the rhythmic patterns of the "laugh" rather precisely, mimicking not just one kookaburra but the joint calls of two birds.

The quality and complexity of bird vocalizations has also raised the issue of whether some bird species may be capable of communication that approximates aspects of language. First, it needs to be noted that "communication" and "language" are two different concepts. We have already seen that effective communication is possible by means other than sounds and language. Second, there is the issue of how we define language. Well-known contemporary linguists such as Steven Pinker (*The Language Instinct,* 1994) and Derek Bickerton (*Language and Species* 1990) have made a strong case for the species-specificity of human language, arguing that human languages are qualitatively different in structure from systems of animal communication. We have no problem with defining human language as "species-specific"—saying that human language has attributes found exclusively in humans—since other, nonhuman, species also have unique attributes. However, what is occasionally asserted, and often only implied, is not just the uniqueness of human language but the uniqueness of the processes required to achieve language— that is, intelligence.

There have now been several studies that have challenged the view that language is unique to humans. For instance, a study of Japanese quails undertaken by Keith Kluender and others (1987) showed that quails can learn phonetic categories. These results challenge theories of speech sounds that posit uniquely human capacities. Irene Pepperberg has demonstrated that her parrot Alex understands commands and concepts and can communicate them. There is then some evidence, both phonetic and semantic, that not all processes associated with the acquisition of human language are unique to humans.

CONCLUSION

Avian species have certainly developed great virtuosity in both vocal and visual communication. For this reason alone human fascination with birds will continue to be strong. It is clear from research so far that some, if not all, of the signals made by birds are not merely emitted reflexively, but involve learning and quite complex decision making, depending on the social context. Some of the astounding vocal abilities that certain bird species share with mammals are almost certainly the outcome of convergent evolution, meaning that these abilities evolved separately in the avian and mammalian lines of evolution. Other special features of bird communication probably existed in vertebrates long before mammals evolved and used them. But whatever their evolutionary origins, the vocalizations of birds follow principles or rules that are relevant to other species. As Nosumu Saito and Masao Maekawa (1993) and many other researchers have pointed out, comparing avian vocal communication with human vocal communication can be most instructive.

Chapter Five

COMMUNICATION IN MAMMALS

There has been less well-controlled experimental research on the communication systems of mammals than on those of birds. Most recent research on mammals has found that their communication systems are more complex than was once thought, and that many of these signals vary according to the context. As in other species (see Chapter 3), some signals are sent unintentionally and reveal something of which the sender is not aware, whereas others appear to be sent intentionally.

VISUAL MESSAGES

The visual signals used by mammals are diverse and complex, but there are basic signals that strongly resemble each other across many mammalian species, including humans, and some of them appear to have been used over long stretches of evolutionary time. Visual signaling in mammals is usually confined to changes in body posture, such as stretching, jumping, arching the back, and moving the limbs. Tool use purely for visual signaling does occur in mammals, but it is relatively uncommon.

In our discussion of the male bowerbird's use of his bower in courtship displays, we noted that visual displays may involve objects other than the body. Such use of objects in visual displays is of importance in avian communication, and there are even examples of fish, amphibian, and reptilian species using objects for display. It is therefore significant that mammals do not often use objects to enhance visual displays. One of the few examples cited in the literature is object use by wild orangutans, observed by John MacKinnon (1974). When MacKinnon kept following them through the rainforest, they looked down from the trees and started to throw sticks. Some of these "weapons" barely missed him, and in a few cases stick throwing became more intense when he continued to follow the orangutans. MacKinnon rightly read this behavior as a warning signal that he should stay away. Another exception may be the gibbon's branch shaking, which some researchers, such as Peter Marler and Richard Tenaza (1977), have regarded as a visual rather than an auditory signal. We also know that baboons throw stones at predators.

Visual displays may be categorized according to which part of the body is used. The body as a whole, including its posture and movement, can function as a signal. Locomotion itself is a form of communication. A particular gait and the corresponding body postures may well determine how another animal will respond. Limb movement is a separate aspect of visual display. For mammalian species with tails, the tail may be used extensively to accentuate the meaning of the animal's emotions or intent, or it may even constitute a signal on its own. In many ungulates (hoofed mammals) and carnivores the tail is used in greeting, threats, and courtship, each with its characteristic postures and speed of movement. Monkeys also use the tail extensively in friendly and aggressive displays (see Figure 5.1, which includes tail and genital display), as Richard Andrew (1972) has shown. In Chapter 2 we discussed the use of tails by lemurs in "stink fights": raising of the tails and waving them so that odor is wafted toward the other animals. We did not mention the visual aspects of this display: the long tail of *Lemur catta* is dramatically striped in black and white. In moonlight this striping would be visible and it may constitute part of the signal. In many species, the movement of the tail mirrors the movement of the head in several displays. For instance, holding the head and tail high signals high arousal and/or dominance. Lowering of the head and tail signals submission and even fear. Familiar body movements in our own human signaling system are shared with many other mammalian species—waving, head shaking, jumping, raising the arms, and so on.

Another region of the body from which signals can emanate is the face (Figures 5.2 and 5.3). Most of the research on faces has been carried out on primates and this is a very large field of investigation. Facial expressions and nonverbal communication in primates have been of interest partly because a primate's face is similar in anatomy to the human face and partly because Darwin singled out the face as an important site for the expression of emotions (see Chevalier-Skolnikoff, 1973, or Ekman, 1974, for details).

Early work by Jan van Hooff (1967) showed that there are possible primate homologues of both human laughter and smiling. The nearly silent bared-teeth display has been described as phylogenetically one of the oldest facial expressions, shared as it is not just by primates and humans but by many other mammals as well. Usually this gesture is associated with a threat or strongly aversive stimulation. A silent bared-teeth display is a sign of fear and submission, found in many higher primates. Our human smiling may have arisen from this facial expression, although, if so, it would have had to undergo a change in meaning from its agonistic origin to become an expression of attachment. Or the human smile could have

FIGURE 5.1   Genital display of a marmoset. The marmoset on the right is displaying its genital region to the human taking the photograph. The marmoset on the left is looking at the display and is probably receiving an odor released from scent glands in the anogenital region of the displaying marmoset. (Photograph by the University of New England Media Unit.)

its origins in the play face (see Figure 2.4), and some consider this more likely. Van Hooff believes that human laughter and human smiling have different phylogenetic roots; he thinks laughter arose from displays of fearful submission. Laughter is associated with breathing and breathing technique—that is, a vocal activity—but smiling is solely a movement of facial muscles. Chimpanzee laughter is closely coupled with breathing, but Robert Provine (1996a) found that unlike humans, who exhale continuously when laughing, chimpanzees produce one laugh sound per expiration and inspiration. Signe Preuschoft's study of Barbary macaques *(Macaca sylvanus)* further confirmed the phylogenetic difference between the smile and laughter made by van Hooff 25 years earlier (Preuschoft, 1992).

Another facial expression found in many mammals as well as in humans is the yawn. Yawning is probably more widespread than the descriptions in the literature indicate. When humans yawn, they are usually indicating that they are tired or bored, as a detailed study by Robert Provine confirmed (Provine, 1996b). Yawning is thought to be "contagious," like laughter, and a yawn can also be sent as a signal to express disapproval. In mammals, yawning may mean a variety of things. In baboon parlance, a yawn by itself either signals uncertainty or expresses fear; in the latter case, the yawn can become part of a signal of aggression when other body movements are added. By contrast, dogs may yawn when they have been praised, or yawning may express frustration.

Other facial expressions that we share with primates are grimacing, tongue movement, staring, certain eye movements, and expressions of sadness. The eyes play an especially large role in facial expressions that humans share with primates. Often in concert with other facial expressions, the eyes can express fearfulness, anger, curiosity, and real or feigned indifference. The stare, as Jean-Pierre and Anne Gautier (1977) have pointed out, conveys several meanings for Old World monkeys. One is a threat. Another is a reprimand. A male gorilla will use a stare if grunts are unsuccessful in settling squabbles between females or juveniles. In dogs, a stare can also express a wish or demand. Dogs often stare when they beg from humans or each other.

Juichi Yamagiwa (1992) pointed out that the role of stares in primates is rather complex and may have different context functions among bonobos than among rhesus macaques or gorillas. Bonobos and chimpanzees may use mutual staring as a form of positive contact with each other, while the stare of the gorilla without any subsequent physical contact may be used in conflict resolutions. In the late 1950s Niko Tinbergen suggested that displays of any kind can be conveniently divided into those that are distance-increasing and those that are distance-decreasing. Peter Marler (1968) extended this classification by suggesting that pri-

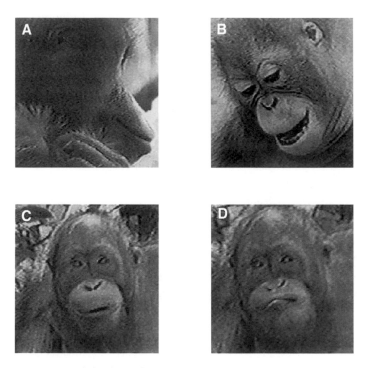

FIGURE 5.2   Facial displays of orangutans. These are Bornean orangutans *(Pongo pygmaeus)*, which we filmed in Sabah, East Malaysia. A: Jessica is holding her 1-week-old baby and smiling, just as a human might. B: A play face. The lips are puffed, the mouth is partly open, and the lower teeth are just barely showing (compare the play-threat display in Figure 2.4, where the mouth is opened wide and both the upper and lower teeth are displayed). C and D: Two frames from a videotape taken in close succession. This young male is expressing mild anger first by parting the lips to grunt (C) and then by protruding the lips into a pout (D). (Videotapes by G. Kaplan.)

mate communication functions to achieve either aggregation or dispersal. Moreover, as has been observed in bonobos, a direct stare may be a means of seeking a sexual encounter or it may be a reprimand or an assertion of dominance.

Eye stares in primates are often accompanied by lowering of the eyelids. The eyelids then become exposed, and in some primates these can be quite spectacular. In various macaques they are white and in some baboon species a silvery color. If the eyelids remain exposed or are rapidly opened and closed, the signal is made more threatening or at least more conspicuous. The human habit of painting the eyelids for accentuation is an interesting custom in view of primate signaling with the eyelids.

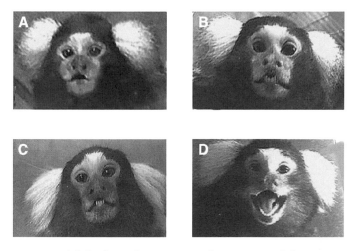

FIGURE 5.3 Facial displays of marmosets. These images of the common marmoset *(Callithrix jacchus)* are taken from videotapes. A: The facial expression that accompanies the twitter call, given to initiate social contact (see Figure 5.4). B: A face expressing apprehension or mild fear and threat. Note that the mouth is drawn back and the lower front teeth are displayed. When a human makes a facial expression like this in the presence of marmosets, they become very agitated. C: Expression of a level of fear higher than that shown in B. The mouth is similar to that in B but the ear tufts are lowered. D: The highest level of fear/threat is expressed and the marmoset is making the mobbing call, a rapidly repeated tsik sound). The mouth is open wide to display all the lower teeth and the incisors of the upper jaw. The ear tufts are pulled back. (Video images courtesy of M. Hook-Costigan.)

Raising the eyebrows either by retraction of the scalp or independent eye-brow movement further reveals the eyelids. Jean-Pierre and Anne Gautier (1977) point out that in various mangabeys and baboon species scalp movement is accentuated by side whiskers or the raising or flattening of tufts of hair on the top of the head.

There is also a furtive expression used by humans and orangutans when they want to look at something they ought not to. An extension of this kind of eye movement is the flirt. Our own work on eye movements in orangutans has shown that eye movement is employed more often than head movement. We have also observed "flirting" orangutans who edged closer and closer to each other and only occasionally looked at each other from the corner of their eyes. These eye movements were so brief that they were not detectable by the naked eye, but had to be discov-ered in frame-by-frame analysis of videos (Kaplan and Rogers, 1996). Additional signals that humans, as a species, have largely lost, such as lip smacking, ear flattening, eyelid flashing, and hair bristling, are com-mon in most primates. Tragically for monkeys and apes, their very physi-cal expressiveness has made them desired "objects" for display in circuses, clubs, and other entertainment centers. Group living, which is partly re-sponsible for an extensive range of physical signals, makes them interest-ing animals to observe, and their signals, even if often misunderstood, look familiar to the human species.

The reason for the perceived similarity among humans, monkeys, and apes of visual signals given by the body and especially by the face lies not only in the morphology of the face but in associated brain mechanisms. In humans, the left side of the face is dominant in emotional expression. In Marc Hauser's study of the facial expressions of rhesus monkeys and the human response to their expressions, he found that facial expressions in rhesus monkeys begin earlier on the left side of the face and involve larger movements of the facial features than on the right side of the face (Hauser, 1993). Thus the left side of the face is more expressive. This has to do with the control of such expressions by the brain. The right hemi-sphere of the brain controls the left side of the face and the right hemi-sphere is involved with emotional expression in a range of species. By contrast, the left hemisphere of primates and other species processes species-specific calls. In fact, human and nonhuman primates have the same pattern of brain asymmetry for sending and receiving vocal signals. Alan Fridlund (1994) has recently warned, however, that we should not jump to the conclusion that commonalities necessarily mean a shared genetic heritage. Nevertheless, since other mammals and even birds and amphibians appear to have a similar asymmetry, it now seems likely that these characteristics do reflect a shared genetic heritage (Bradshaw and Rogers, 1993).

SOUND SIGNALS

Mammals frequently use sound for communication, sometimes sound within the hearing range of humans but also outside it. The range of frequencies used outside human hearing may be below (infrasound) or above (ultrasound) the thresholds of human auditory perception.

Echolocation

Use of ultrasound by animals was discovered in the twentieth century, largely through the work of H. Hartridge and G. W. Pierce. Hartridge worked on bats and concluded that they were able to avoid objects in flight by listening to the echo of their own sounds in the ultrasonic range. Research on echolocation was expanded significantly by the work of Donald Griffin (see Griffin, 1958). Pierce took up entomology as a hobby and later wrote about ultrasonic sound in crickets.

This discovery of the use of ultrasonic sound for navigation and communication was more important than we might think today. It opened our minds to the possibility that our own senses may not suffice for a full understanding of animal communication. Human audition ranges from about 0.02 kHz (20 cycles per second) to a maximum of about 20 kHz (20,000 cycles per second). The most sensitive and comfortable hearing for humans lies at frequencies around 2 kHz. As we have seen already, this frequency range is also commonly used by birds. We now know that, as well as a range of insects—from moths to grasshoppers, crickets, and locusts—there are rodents, whales, dolphins, seals, sea lions, and certain primates whose vocalizing and hearing range extends well above that of the human species. John Altringham (1996) showed that some bats of the Megachiroptera family use echolocation and that all bats from the suborder Microchiroptera, which includes hundreds of species in Old and New World areas, use echolocation, whether they are omnivorous, insectivorous, or carnivorous.

Some species of bats use echolocation not just to detect objects (to be avoided in flight) or potential prey but also to locate conspecifics. For instance, between birth and weaning the pups of the Mexican free-tailed bat *(Tadarida brasiliensis mexicana)* live in segregated colonies, or crèches, of about 4,000 pups per square meter. Each female has a single offspring and needs to locate it, usually twice in a 24-hour period. Gary McCracken (1993) established that a mother finds her pup largely by locational cues derived from echolocation.

The discovery of echolocation in sea-dwelling mammals, such as dolphins and whales (cetaceans), was made as late as the 1950s (by A. F. McBride for one) and later reported by Winthrop Kellogg (Kellogg, 1961). These two researchers found that the echo-ranging signals (clicks) are highly directional and extremely varied. The sonar characteristics of sea mammals differ, and each species has its own structures and frequency ranges. Transient killer whales, for instance, use short and irregular echolocation "trains" composed of clicks that appear to be structurally variable and low in intensity. Even within the same species of killer whales (*Orcinus orca*), there are substantial differences in the echolocation pulses. Whales that are resident in a region use regular sequences, while transient killer whales employ irregular sequences. As Lance Barrett-Lennard (1996) and his colleagues argue, sequences of short-duration sounds that are irregular in timing and frequency more closely resemble random noise than do sequences of more structured sounds and thus are less likely to be detected by marine mammals (the prey of killer whales) against background noise. By using these "noisier" sounds to locate their prey, transient killer whales can detect and approach marine mammals without their knowledge.

Signals as reliable as those used in echolocation can also serve a communicatory function. In the Microchiroptera there is evidence for a continuum between the use of ultrasound for echolocation and for communication. It has been shown by Brock Fenton (1994) and many others that the echolocation calls of one individual can be used simultaneously by other animals, both conspecifics and other species. For example, "feeding buzzes," which are echolocation calls with high repetition rates produced by bats when they attack airborne targets, indicate that prey is available and are often exploited by conspecific bats to identify vulnerable prey. Some moths also use "feeding buzzes" to detect the presence of predatory bats.

Yet echolocation does not necessarily give the killer whale a substantial advantage in catching prey, as Lance Barrett-Lennard and his colleagues found (1996). Although most fish species have auditory sensitivity in the low-frequency range of around 3 kHz and are thus unlikely to detect killer whale clicks, the typical prey of the killer whales can in fact hear the clicks. The pinnipeds (seals) and cetaceans (dolphins, whales) that are the prey of transient killer whales have acute hearing up to frequencies beyond 30 kHz, well within the range of killer whale sonar clicks. Porpoises swim away from killer whales at high speeds on erratic courses. Dolphins and gray whales move into shallow water when killer whales are nearby. Some prey have also adapted by emitting their own echolocation signals outside the range of killer whale hearing. For instance, killer whales cannot hear the echolocation pulses of Dall's porpoises, which center on frequencies of 135–149 kHz, because killer whales can sense frequencies only up to about 105 kHz. However, killer whales can hear the sounds generated when porpoises surface and breathe, and so they may find these prey animals without the aid of echolocation signals. Transient killer whales often search for prey in waters close to the shore, where there is camouflaging noise from waves striking the shore.

From Whistles to Roars

Other sounds that sea mammals make cannot be catalogued here—there are too many. Like those of birds, their vocalizations are species-specific, and often each individual has a characteristic pattern of vocalization. In the last 40 years there has been a great expansion of our knowledge of vocalizations in sea mammals. By the 1960s, considerable knowledge of the complexities of vocalizations of sea mammals had been acquired, and Roger Payne had described the vocalizations of humpback whales as song; there was even a record called *The Songs of the Humpback Whales*.

We now know that dolphins, for example, emit richly diversified whistles, usually at low frequencies. And we also know that their vocalizations, like those of birds, contain acoustic signatures of individuals and many sounds with precise meaning. M. C. and D. K. Caldwell (1965) first reported that bottle-nosed dolphins *(Tursiops truncatus)* had individually specific signature whistles. And a study by Vincent Janik, Guido Dehnhardt, and Dietmar Todt (1994) found that, beyond individual identities, the whistles also contain context-related information. Like birds, dolphins give different alarm calls in response to different predatory species, such as sharks, human beings, and killer whales. Perhaps the most spectacular dolphin behavior is the response to distress whistles made by other dolphins. A distress call by a sick or injured dolphin will bring other dolphins to its rescue. William Stebbins (1983) has reported that a dolphin having difficulty in rising to the surface to breathe air will be assisted by other dolphins and literally lifted up to the surface. Agonistic behaviors are expressed by jaw clapping or arching of the back. The tail flukes, the flippers, and the tail itself may be employed in such displays, and when accompanied by rising and falling whistles, they may indicate strong threats.

Seals have long been used in circuses because of their playfulness and ability to learn tricks. Seals, sea lions, and walruses (all pinnipeds) were, until recently, thought to command only a very limited range of vocalizations and to produce them only on land. It has been known since the 1980s that seals may mimic, but they usually do so when they are on land. A study in 1984 by Evelyn Hanggi and Ronald Schusterman of harbor seals *(Phoca vitulina)* found that they also vocalize under water during the breeding season. The vocalizations are different for each individual. Some vocalizations produced during the breeding season, such as the roar, are combined with visual aquatic displays. It has been suggested that such vocalization either plays a part in male-male competition or is a way of attracting females. Male walruses produce bell-like sounds that they use in combination with visual displays to attract females. However, it is perhaps a little premature to draw conclusions on the function and meaning of these display behaviors and the roars of seals.

Reproductive Strategies

During different seasons of the year, in accord with the reproductive cycle, mammals use different classes of vocalizations specific to communication about mating readiness and breeding. Many mammalian species have developed elaborate strategies surrounding the time of reproduction. Vocal, visual, or chemical signaling during the ovulatory period, the period of breeding readiness of the female, occurs in most mammalian species.

These signals function in a social context where it might be prudent for the female to advertise her reproductive condition or, alternatively, to hide the onset of the ovulatory period. Females may exploit their readiness for mating to entice males to fight on their behalf, or to ensure that they mate with the best possible male. In elephant seals *(Mirounga angustirostris)* the female gives a copulation call that incites aggressive competition between males. She witnesses the fight and the winner mates with her.

The mating strategies used in baboon societies are very different. The threat of infanticide is very real in baboon troops, and it occurs particularly in troops where only one male is present. An outsider male who successfully challenges the position of the troop male will attempt to kill offspring that are not his. Groups with several males are thought to be safer, partly because of the mating strategies employed by the female. The baboon female calls during mating, and as Sanjida O'Connell and Guy Cowlishaw suggested (1994), these calls may invite several males to mate with her, thereby creating uncertainty about paternity. This uncertainty might well protect her offspring. Baboon females also signal their estrous period by the reddened skin of the buttocks, which they display to males.

We know from other mammals that vocalizations may stimulate ovulation by the female. For instance, the roars of male red deer *(Cervus elaphus)* are said to trigger copulation readiness, if not ovulation, in females. Red deer males roar loudly and repeatedly during the breeding season (Clutton-Brock and Albon, 1979). Karen McComb (1991) found that the roaring rate was positively associated with reproductive success and fighting ability. The intensity, duration, and rate of the call may serve to advertise fitness in males. Although roars often precede fights with competing males, McComb found that male deer roar in the same way whether competitors are present or not and go on roaring at a rate of two roars per minute throughout a 24-hour period. These vocal displays are accompanied by other displays, such as waving of horns and broadside body movements showing off physical attributes. She found that females preferred males with a high roaring rate whether the males fought or not.

Primate Vocalizations

After the diverse group of mammals using ultrasonic sound (sea mammals and bats), the largest group of mammals in which vocalization has been examined and analyzed in great detail is the primates. Humans and most anthropoid primates have sacrificed high-frequency sensitivity for improved auditory discrimination within a restricted frequency range. In this lower frequency range, they have finer discriminatory powers in all three parameters of vocalization: frequency, intensity, and timing (temporal disparity). In addition, some mammals—marmosets and tamarins—are known to hear ultrasonic frequencies as well as frequencies audible to humans. Figure 5.4 shows vocalizations of marmosets within the human auditory range.

The fact that most primates are gregarious has led researchers to argue that the communication systems of such species are relatively complex, in accord with the complexity of their social organization. The Costa Rican squirrel monkey *(Saimiri oerstedi)* has become the most common laboratory model for studies of primate vocalizations over the past 20 years, especially calls expressing emotions and isolation. Most of these studies have been conducted in the artificial setting of a laboratory, supplemented only occasionally by studies in the natural environment. Laboratory work is important for controlled studies, but field work is needed to confirm what is found in the laboratory. One of the few field studies was undertaken by Sue Boinski in 1991. She found that, in the squirrel monkeys' natural environment, the duration of peep vocalizations (contact calls) is positively correlated with spatial separation, confirming that the duration of their peep calls provides information about the distance of the caller.

Some of the long-range vocalizations of primates are specialized calls that primates use when they discover food. Call characteristics are influenced by the quality of the food, its quantity, and its divisibility, as is also the case in birds. Marc Hauser (1993) and his colleagues found that chimpanzees emit a vocalization, which the researchers called a "rough grunt," when they find large amounts of food. Such vocalizations show

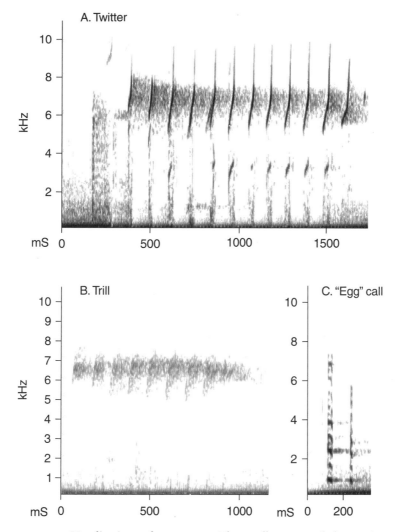

FIGURE 5.4 Vocalizations of marmosets. These calls were made by captive common marmosets *(Callithrix jacchus)* in our colony at the University of New England in New South Wales, Australia. A: Twitter calls, which are given to initiate social contact (see Figure 5.3 for the accompanying facial expression). Note the steep change in frequency. These calls extend into the ultrasonic range but the high frequencies are not represented in the figure. B: The trill call, given when the marmoset is slightly aroused. C: The crackle or "egg" call, which indicates mild alarm. These are just some of the vocalizations produced by marmosets. For more details see Epple, 1968. (Recordings by M. Hook-Costigan.)

that an individual is capable of making several decisions before vocalizing, such as "Is there more food than I need?" and "Can this food be divided among others without a fight?"

The acoustics of the habitat influences the structure of vocal signals by primates, as it does in all species. Charles Brown (1995) and his colleagues found that the rainforest is less favorable for high-fidelity sound propagation than open spaces but that, nevertheless, species that live in the rainforest have developed vocalizations with high-fidelity transmission by using the appropriate frequency and other acoustic qualities. Tropical rainforests, in particular, pose several problems for effective communication that do not occcur in savannas and open woodlands. The forest is an environment with high background noise, largely caused by insects, and high reflection of sounds from trunks and leaves. Foliage, temperature gradients, and ground effects can also contribute to fast degradation of the structure of a signal. Moreover, visual methods of long-distance communication are not readily available (trees and leaves also obstruct visual contact), and so forest-dwelling species have to use vocalizations for contact calling. Brown and his colleagues have shown that selection for vocalizations with a reduced chance of distortion has influenced the form of the vocal repertoire of two rainforest species (the blue monkeys, *Cercopithecus mitis*, and gray-cheeked mangabeys, *Cercocebus albigena*) more strongly than those of two savanna species (vervet monkeys, *Cercopithecus aethiops*, and yellow baboons, *Papio cynocephalus*). The forest environment leads to adaptations that overcome problems of distortion and thus influence the form of signal repertoires.

In rainforests individual primates lose sight of each other and must rely on acoustic signals to stay in touch, whereas on savannas they can usually retain visual contact with each other. This difference might explain other aspects of the evolution of vocal repertoires with different physical characteristics in primates living in rainforests and on savannas. Mangabeys and baboons vocalize in choruses, just like birds, enlisting the participation of many individuals. They scream, and although their vocalizations are very similar, the distortion scores are lower for the forest-dwelling mangabeys than for the savanna-based baboons.

The habitat of the New World squirrel monkeys is also densely foliaged, so in this species, too, there is a real possibility of the separation of members of the troop. Boinski (1991) noted that the female vocal exchange among squirrel monkeys acts as an "auditory beacon" to monitor the position of females and hence of the troop. To verify this, common marmosets were experimentally tested for responses to loss of visual contact. An experiment that deprived common marmosets (also arboreal monkeys of the South American rainforests) of visual contact showed that they immediately modulated their calls in duration, peak frequency, frequency range, and median frequency. Lars Schrader and Dietmar Todt (1993) found that modulation increased with decreasing sensory information about mates. Also, the amplitude of the mammals' calls increased as much as 8 decibels during the experiment, an escalation that improves transmission of the calls. Schrader and Todt concluded that modification of specific call parameters can protect information encoded in the calls against possible signal disturbances caused by the environment. Thus call modulation is found to be linked to spacing.

Most of the auditory signals of the forest species studied so far have been classified as messages related to the integration of the whole group, such as alarm calls or contact solicitations, but such calls, of course, are not limited to forest dwellers. Alarm calls may even be specific enought to relay information about the type of threat that is imminent—signal what kind of predator is approaching. The semantic content of vervet monkey alarm calls was shown in important work by Robert Seyfarth and Dorothy Cheney (1980). Their experiments revealed that the vervet monkeys classify and "read" the message purely on the basis of its acoustic structure, even when they are deprived of any visual clues. They found that vervet monkeys achieve major changes in signal function by changing frequency peak: calls with an early peak serve an integrative or cohesive function for the group; calls with a late peak indicate a state of arousal (sexual or agonistic).

Larger forest-dwelling primates have succeeded in exploiting vocalization over long distances, despite the severe constraints imposed by a forest environment. Mangabeys in the Kibale Forest in western Uganda can be heard (by the human listener) from a distance of 500–600 meters through dense forests and, at certain times, even from as far away as 1,200 meters. The loud calls of chimpanzees, known as "pant-hoots," are also audible for more than 900 meters, as Peter and Mary Waser (1977) have reported. The "long call" made by orangutan males, a spine-chilling roar, is audible for at least 1 kilometer. These calls may advertise presence but may also convey specific information on local dialects, as Andrew Marshal, Richard Wrangham, and Adam Arcadi have recently found. Although they studied captive chimpanzee populations it was clear that the pant-hoots varied from one group to another and that learning occurred in order to communicate (Marshal, Wrangham, and Arcadi, 1999).

Gibbons (*Hylobates* spp.), also forest dwellers, are among the most conspicuous vocalizers of all primates. They are territorial and monogamous. Not unlike some bird species, they sing duets in which the female usually takes the lead. These are extensive vocalizations and the skill involved in producing them lies mainly in the coordination of the "song" in the duet. The song of gibbons also tells of the length of the pair relationship—inexperienced pairs usually have problems with their duetting coordination and may not finish their song. The sounds of these duets can be heard for miles across the rainforests of southeast Asia. In the case of gibbons, the song is less concerned with maintaining contact with individuals than with protecting territory—advertising their presence in a patch of forest.

Nonvocal Sounds

Sound signals are not confined to vocalizations. Mammals may be better equipped to make sounds with their limbs than birds. And there is plenty of evidence that the limbs are used extensively in a large variety of contexts, such as territorial defense, courtship, and identity marking. For instance, banner-tailed kangaroo rats *(Dipodomys spectabilis)* use individually distinct foot-drumming signatures to communicate their identity to territorial neighbors. They can also discriminate between the foot-drumming signatures of neighbors and strangers. Jan Randall (1994) thought that familiarity among neighbors promotes a stable social organization in this solitary, nocturnal rodent. Foot drumming is also used in the threat displays of nocturnal lower primates (prosimians). Gibbons shake branches, break them off, and drop them in what has been called a brachiation display. It is a stunning and very noisy affair, achieved solely by using branches. Alpha male chimpanzees (the dominant males) like to make noise too when they display, breaking branches and bashing them as they run. Presumably the noise reinforces perception of their physical strength. Gorillas use chest beating, first documented in detail by George Schaller in 1963. Lip smacking is another nonvocal sound that plays an important role in some apes and monkey species during allogrooming (grooming other individuals). It is used by an approaching monkey to indicate its peaceful intention and then maintained during the process of allogrooming.

Early research on primates attempted to catalogue primate vocalizations, particularly those of the great apes (chimpanzees, gorillas, and orangutans). The vocalizations of orangutans have not been studied systematically, but studies on chimpanzees and gorillas have had some interesting results. When Peter Marler and Richard Tenaza compared the vocalizations of gorillas and chimpanzees in 1977, they found that "the most striking conclusion to be drawn from the data is the surprising degree of correspondence between the two species in the rank order of use of corresponding calls." By this they mean that there were important similarities between the species in the order of most-used to least-used vocalizations. This is an important point because the social organization of chimpanzees is not at all like that of gorillas. These similarities may indicate the animals' common evolutionary origins, cultural transmission by learning, or the fact that both species are subject to similar environmental constraints on vocal transmission. Almost certainly all three factors exert an influence.

SCENT DEPOSITS AND OLFACTORY MARKERS

Chemical communication is a widespread form of communication among mammals. It has been recorded in rodents (mice, hamsters, rats, voles), marsupials (koalas, sugar gliders, opossums), ungulates (horses, deer), dogs, primates (Old and New World monkeys), and even elephants. Chemical communication is much older than mammalian existence. Fishes, amphibians, and reptiles also use chemical communication, in alarm signals and in courtship, in kin recognition and territorial defense. Members of the most ancient marsupial family, the Didelphidae (such as the gray opossum), show extensive scent-marking behavior. They also show estrous synchrony, caused by odors known as pheromones, and estrous activation, also triggered by pheromones (Fadem,

1985). A pheromone is a chemical, or mixture of chemicals, released into the environment by one animal that causes a specific behavioral or physiological response in another animal. As well as the species named above, many insects use pheromones. Olfactory communication has a long evolutionary history.

The scent-releasing glands of many species are larger in the male than in the female, and in both sexes are more highly developed during the breeding season. Species with well-developed scent glands tend to be polygynous, and territorial males tend to scent-mark more than non-territorial males. We have seen that communication tends to become more complex with the complexity of the group, and territoriality is another variable that adds to the range of communicative needs. Territoriality needs to be communicated, and hence scent marking becomes a constant activity in the effort to maintain a territory.

Chemical signals seem to occur most frequently among species that are subject to predation and have a limited home range. In primates, at least, it is known that the most developed system of chemical signaling and communication is found in those species most subject to predation, especially those that are nocturnal and/or arboreal. Such arboreal species include New World monkeys, such as marmosets and tamarins, as well as Old World nocturnal species, such as prosimians. All these species rub their scent glands on objects in their environment, marking them with their scent. Prosimians also mark themselves with urine: they urinate onto their hands and rub the urine into the fur.

Primate species that are largely terrestrial (living on the ground) and diurnal (active during the day) tend to rely on chemical signals to a lesser degree. For instance, apes do not have well-developed olfactory lobes (located in the brain) and do not rely on scent marking. Apes are large and/ or live in strong groups and generally have few predators. They are mobile and may forage over large areas. All these characteristics have led to the belief that intense reliance on olfactory signals occurred in ancient primate species and that use of olfactory signals has been largely superseded over time to include other senses considered to be more suitable for communication. However, apes do rely on olfaction to signal reproductive conditions and olfaction may play a greater role in other aspects of their social behavior than we currently realize.

The line between intentional and unintentional communication by odors may be fluid. For instance, individual A (female) of a species may give off scents that will entice individual B (male) to mate with her. Individual A may not have produced the olfactory signal intentionally, it being merely a result of her changed hormonal state. Individual B has learned to interpret the signal correctly. But let us say that individual B has the choice of several females that are emitting signals similar to those of individual A. Individual B can therefore choose according to the quality and type of smell. Whether the choice is made intentionally or unintentionally is likely to vary with the species. Males of many species, avian and mammalian alike, have developed very elaborate strategies to ensure that they will succeed in getting a mate. Olfactory, visual, and vocal communication is used to achieve this end. Moreover, mate choice is not confined to males. In the great majority of species, females do the choosing and the male the displaying and competing (see McFarland, 1985).

Scent may be used to make territorial claims and to defend the territory, and odor signals require more than merely releasing a specific odor from the animal's body. There is a good deal of work involved in scent-marking a territory. Gisela Epple found in the 1970s that olfactory signals have a complex set of communicative functions in the life of the common marmoset. Marmosets have several glands that release different odors, under the chin, on the chest and in the anogenital region. First, there is intragroup communication, including sexual communication, regulating social relationships among adults and infant-adult relationships. Second, olfactory signals are important in intergroup communication concerned with territorial defense and the formation of new groups. Third, olfactory signals help to maintain orientation in the environment. Further studies by Epple (1988) and her colleagues on saddleback tamarins *(Saguinus fuscicollis)* and cotton-top tamarins *(Saguinus oedipus oedipus)* have shown that their olfactory communication may fulfill a range of communicatory functions similar to the range seen in the marmoset.

While olfactory signals in the urine play an important but balanced role in some monkey species, other mammals depend on olfactory cues almost exclusively. For instance, interactions between house mice depend to a significant extent on olfactory communication. An experiment conducted by Jane Hurst (1993) and her colleagues showed that male house mice remain tolerant toward subordinate males largely because the subordinates leave urine deposits in spots and streaks across the entire territory (substrate odor deposits). Resident male mice, both dominant and subordinate, behave aggressively toward subordinate males that do not deposit fresh odors in the group's home territory. It is obviously important to be known in an olfactory capacity to dominant males. The quality of urine in subordinate males is different from that of dominant males. Hurst and her colleagues suggest that regular urine markings by subordinate males is an efficient system, allowing territorial males to concentrate their defense on intruders. It appears that mice and quite a number of other mammalian species need to supplement their visual displays with cues from other sensory modalities, in this case smell. The substrate marking by a subordinate male reassures the dominant male that no attack is planned on his status and territory.

In the European rabbit (*Oryctolagus* spp.), chin marking is one of the most conspicuous forms of olfactory communication. Robyn Hudson and Thomas Vodermayer (1992) found that secretions from the chin gland were used by females as a sexual advertisement but also served nonsexual functions. Female rabbits are able to discriminate between chin marks from different animals on the basis of the donor's hormonal state. The researchers conclude that chin marking may also play a role in the establishment and maintenance of group identity. Group stability and territorial stability may thus be served by extensive use of olfactory signals. Michael Stoddart (1992) has found a similar use of odors in the social behavior of marsupial sugar gliders *(Petaurus briceps).*

We have not yet raised the possibility that signals may get lost, misread, or overlooked. The issues of selective attention and selective memory may be of great importance in communication and constitute a study in their own right. Suffice it to say here that a recent study on golden hamsters (*Mesocricetus auratus*) by Robert Johnston (1995) and his colleagues has drawn our attention to the fact that not all messages have a recipient and that, for some species, this seems to have evolved by design. The researchers tested hamsters for their responses to the partially overlapping scents of two individuals to see whether the hamsters would be able to identify both individuals. They found that the hamsters remembered only the scent mark on top—the one deposited most recently—even if the other scent had been identified before in a separate test. If scents are "read" only selectively, we would have to adjust our thinking about communication to include as part of the process selective detection and selective perception. We would have to realize that individuals may be able to focus their attention on a particular odor relevant at a particular time and in a particular context, neglecting other odors that are present.

TACTILE SIGNALS

A good deal of communication can also happen by touch. Grooming in mammals is an important gesture of intimacy and closeness. It reinforces pair bonding, as it does in birds, and in certain primate groups, such as rhesus monkeys and baboons, grooming is associated with status within the group. Dominant members of the group are groomed by subordinate ones. Sometimes, there are lines of animals each grooming the next one in the row. Tactile communication in baboons and bonobos is often used to signal appeasement, reassurance, and loyalty. An animal's intention to groom usually has to be advertised so that the individual being approached is assured of the peaceful purpose. In baboon groups, the approaching individual smacks its lips loudly and then continues the lip smacking throughout the grooming process.

Another form of body contact is embracing. Obviously this form of tactile contact relies on the existence of limbs that can do the embracing. We find this form of communication largely in monkeys and apes, although it does occur in mating frogs and toads. Hugging, cuddling, and cradling are activities not confined to mother-infant interactions; they are found among nonrelated animals, even of those of adult age. Bonobos may be unusual, even among apes, in that they use "loving" tactile contact (all sorts of tactile activities, including sexual ones) for settling conflicts within the group. Notably, as Frans de Waal and Frans Lanting (1997) point out, it is mostly the females who maintain peace by means of physical contact with each other. Lip touching of two conspecifics—kissing—may be simply a friendly greeting or it may be an overture to sexual advances.

Orangutans, too, use touching extensively in certain social contents. Mother-infant relationships, which are very intense and long-lasting, are established by close physical contact (as we describe in detail in our book *The Orang-utans*, 1999). Juveniles and even adults (usually females) continue to use touch as a form of communication, often without eye contact. Juveniles often walk along holding hands. Although orangutans are largely solitary, rather than living in groups like the other apes, the sense of touch in personal relationships continues to play a role through adult life. It obviously features in sexual behaviour.

Elephants use their trunks extensively to communicate with each other. They have very sensitive skin and the trunk needs only to glide gently over the body, or touch the trunk of another, for a message to be conveyed. The trunk is used to help baby elephants stand up and walk when the herd is moving to new feeding grounds, and also for reassurance and many other subtle communications.

Dolphins and whales use touch as a form of communication for many of the same reasons (as far as we know) that touching is used in other species. They nuzzle each other with the snout or swim alongside each other, brushing along the skin.

Many mammalian species use licking as a form of reassurance, as an expression of bonding, or as a signal of status. Dogs and related canids, for instance, use licking extensively and in a variety of social contexts, as Michael Fox (1971) showed in his book on canid behavior. Dogs go through extensive daily rituals of reassuring each other and of reconfirming the status of the lead bitch. They may do this by touching the other dog's nose or licking the other's snout. Conflict resolution is usually swift, whether it is fierce or friendly. In extreme cases, a dog may be expelled from the pack or even killed (depending on the species), but dogs usually resolve conflicts in a conciliatory manner. In conflict resolution, licking is directed behind the ear, on the neck, and, if allowed, in the anogenital region. Small bites, shoves, and pushes are all part of a gentle and friendly communication.

RECOGNITION OF INDIVIDUALS

Can animals recognize conspecifics as individuals? Do they relate to individuals in a specific way? Or do they just respond to key markers of categories, such as plumage color, a particular scent, or a specific vocalization, that are sufficient to trigger "familiarity" or "stranger" status? And are such questions meaningfully applied to all animals or only to some? Those who hold a mechanistic view of animals would certainly regard mere reaction to specific markers as sufficient for survival and would say that animals' abilities stop there. But many people think at least some animals have more extensive abilities. Stanley Cohen (1994), for instance, draws attention to the intelligence and capabilities of pet dogs (see also Fox, 1971). Most pet owners are convinced that their pets can identify them as individuals. This recognition of the owner is part of the close relationship that is formed between owners and pets (see Chapter 8). But to what extent does this recognition of individuals apply in the wild, and how exactly do animals recognize each other? It is not always easy to determine scientifically what signals animals might use to achieve recognition of individuals.

For animals to recognize individual conspecifics as unique entities, most researchers assume, they need to have a memory of each individual, a representation composed of a variety of key markers, or "integrated, multi-factor representations." This assumption was tested in golden hamsters *(Mesocricetus auratus)* by Robert Johnston and Paula Jernigan, who showed that golden hamsters respond to individually distinctive signals on the basis of the meaning (or the referent) of the signal. In their experiments, male golden hamsters were exposed repeatedly to the scents of females in estrus, and the males clearly could distinguish between a familiar female (an individual) and a strange one, and also could distinguish between two odors of the same female while still attributing them to the same individual. Johnston and Jernigan suggest that this result indicates the importance of higher-order, cognitive processing in the social behavior and communication of hamsters because the animals categorized stimuli according to their significance and not strictly by their sensory characteristics (Johnston and Jernigan, 1994).

Recognition of the alarm calls of different conspecifics also seems to be important factor in the recognition of individuals, because some individuals signal the presence of predators more reliably than others. Unreliable signalers that "cry wolf" too often can be ignored if they are recognized. Some recent research on the ground squirrel *(Spermophilus richardsonii)* has shown that this may be the case. James Hare (1998) recorded the alarm calls of different squirrels and then played them back to selected individuals in their natural environment. He found that a squirrel no longer attended to hearing the same individual's alarm call after it had been played back four times. Habituation had occurred. Then he played back either another alarm call by the same individual or the alarm call of another individual. The squirrel became more vigilant after hearing the call of the new individual but not after hearing another call by the first individual. It was able to distinguish one individual's call from another's.

The ability to make distinctions between individuals would also help group-living animals observe rules in established social hierarchies and in other social relationships. For example, individual recognition in rhesus monkeys has been shown to be very sophisticated. Vocalizations by a dominant member of a group may require a different response than vocalizations by a subordinate. The maintenance of group structure and (in the case of alarm calls) even survival may depend on the ability to distinguish the vocalizations of dominants and subordinates. Habituation to alarm calls by trusted/senior individuals of a group could threaten survival.

Not only do receivers of calls distinguish individuals but they also respond to the calls according to the caller's relationship to themselves. In a social system in which the mother's relatives (the matrilineal line) play a significant role, categorization of other animals' calls by lineage might be important. Playback experiments using calls of unrelated and related individuals have been conducted by Drew Rendall and his colleagues (1996). They have shown that female rhesus monkeys *(Macaca mulatta)* respond significantly faster and longer to contact calls of matrilineal relatives than to calls from other relatives and from nonrelatives. Their study demonstrates that rhesus monkeys are able to distinguish unrelated individuals from kin. But even after such experiments have been conducted under controlled conditions, it is not certain whether true recognition of individuals has occurred because other cues (such as the location of the individual) may assist in identification. The researchers point out, however, that the capacity to recognize vocalizations of individuals and kin represents an important adaptation in long-living primates, who have complex social relationships between individuals.

In large social groups, individual conspecifics may need to be known to each other. The question is whether individuals in a group would at once recognize an intruder and whether they could do so by visual information alone. According to recent studies (for example, Parr and de Wall, 1999), chimpanzees can perceive similarities in the faces of conspecifics who are related to individuals they know but are unfamiliar to them. They can recognize kin by facial features (Parr and de Waal, 1999). This ability was discovered when researchers showed pairs of photographs of conspecifics to the chimpanzees. The chimpanzees were able to recognize relationships between mothers and sons but not relationships between mothers and daughters, a fact that is likely to have social implications for chimpanzee society.

As we have seen before in the discussion by Janik, Dehnhardt, and Todt (1994), dolphins use signature whistles that identify individuals. There seems little doubt that mammals recognize each other individually, but determining exactly how they do so in each species requires much more research.

HUMAN COMMUNICATION WITH NONHUMAN PRIMATES

The effort to communicate effectively with nonhuman primates via language or a system of symbols has generated much innovative research. The phylogenetic affinity of the great apes to humans seems to make it possible to devise ways of bridging the gap between animals and humans. If real communication with the great apes could be achieved, we would gain much information about their personalities: their thoughts, memories, wishes, fears, and a host of other things that cannot be deduced from observation alone or that are not unambiguously measurable. Some notable researchers have tried to create that bridge by including apes in their personal lives, raising chimpanzees and gorillas as if they were their own children. Others have moved into the natural environment of the apes, staying in close proximity to them until they were finally tolerated or even accepted by the group. These pioneering research efforts led to a sense that some real communication had taken place, based on trust and mutual respect. Many new insights were gained in the process, and if we can speak today of awareness and consciousness in animals, we can do so largely because of the research on communication undertaken with great apes.

However, researchers have gone down a number of blind alleys. For instance, many studies of vocal abilities in primates were driven by the wish to understand the origin of human language rather than the workings of animal communication. Roger Lewin (1991), for example, argued that chimpanzees may hold the only key to the origin of human language. These studies assume the superiority of vocal communication. But vocal communication may not be a superior form of communication; it may simply be the one we understand best and one that has served the evolution of human primates extremely well. Also, it is often assumed that species close to humans—primates—should show more evidence of vocal learning (higher plasticity in their development) than species that are more distant from us in evolutionary terms. This is not the case. The development of vocalization and vocal learning have been shown to exist in songbirds, as we noted earlier and as we will discuss further in Chapter 6. In fact, overall, less is known about vocal development in primates than in birds, even though we now have some very detailed knowledge of the vocal communication systems of the great apes. Although, as we have shown, there have been very successful attempts to teach birds to speak, attempts to teach apes to speak have failed, because the vocal apparatus of apes is not constructed to produce human speech sounds. Apes can communicate with humans by using sign language or symbols.

ETHICAL QUESTIONS IN COMMUNICATION RESEARCH

Investigations of animal learning, adaptation, and communication have often ignored the animal as a whole organism, especially when only one aspect of the animal's behavior was being studied. Meredith West and her colleagues (1997) have recently raised ethical questions about experiments on vocal learning in birds and primates. They argue that in the past researchers, in their desire to establish the parameters of learning, often used methods of testing that would now be considered unacceptable. In some early experiments, for instance, monkeys were kept in very small chambers for an entire year with no physical access to other animals. Similar ethical issues have arisen in studies of birdsong, where some birds are often kept in prolonged isolation in order to control the experiment.

Although conditions for animals have improved greatly over the past 20 years, living conditions for experimental animals inevitably involve deprivations. Most experimental species are kept in sterile environments and confined to cages where they have little to do. These problems, ethical and experimental, have of course been recognized, and many studies have attempted to remedy the situation by improving the physical environment of captive animals or by complementing laboratory studies with field studies. The problem is that there is no perfect system of studying animal communication that is completely noninvasive, involves no deprivation, and is scientifically unassailable. In the natural environment, controls are more difficult to establish and hence results may be more unreliable. The laboratory setting, by contrast, allows the establishment of controls, but may distort results by its very artificiality. West and her colleagues found that differences in social and physical settings in cage and aviary tests could lead to the display of different levels of competence (or the lack thereof) in social and communicative skills.

CONCLUSION

The topic of learning and communicative competence invites further comment, and we will explore it further in the next chapter. Suffice it to say here that there appear to be many aspects of communication with a long evolutionary history which we share with birds and mammals alike, whether these be body postures and displays, facial expressions, or vocalizations expressing alarm, reassurance, and anger. It is these that researchers have tended to recognize most readily and that are being catalogued. The challenge is to recognize and study the complexities of species-specific forms of communication which we humans do not share or do not share fully.

Chapter Six

LEARNING TO COMMUNICATE

In earlier chapters we discussed some of the varied patterns of communication used by different species. In most cases we focused on the communication patterns of adults; very often these patterns are not present in the behavioral repertoire of infants or juveniles but develop as the animals grow up. This development is partly due to maturation as the animal gets older, a process dependent on the unfolding of its genetic program (which is read out from the genes passed on through generations), and partly due to experience and learning. These two processes are often regarded as separate, but they are not. At every stage of development, maturation, experience, and learning interact.

Let us consider a familiar example that is very relevant to communication. The maturation of the reproductive organs and the consequent release of sex hormones has a major impact on vocal communication in many species because the hormones affect the growth of certain parts of the brain and the vocal apparatus—the larynx in mammals and the syrinx in birds. In the human male, changes in the larynx cause the voice to deepen. In birds, syrinx growth often coincides with the emergence of new vocalizations. For example, roosters start to crow when they approach sexual maturity because that is the time when their sex hormone levels rise. If the sex hormone, testosterone, is injected into young chicks, they will crow, but they will sound like very squeaky roosters because the syrinx has not yet developed enough to make a full crowing sound.

In songbirds, it is known that the sex hormones affect the development of certain structures in the brain that are used to control singing. As Fernando Nottebohm (1989) has shown in his research on the canary *(Serinus canarius)*, certain regions of the forebrain enlarge as the amount of testosterone circulating in the blood increases. The genetic program for development plays a part in determining this sexual maturation process but experience also contributes.

To continue with the songbird as an example, the season of the year provides the trigger for the development of the sexual glands. As spring approaches days grow longer, and this increase in daylight is the stimulus that causes enlargement of the sex glands and increased release of sex hormones into the bloodstream. In males, these changes in turn cause the regions in the brain that are used for singing to enlarge. Once this has occurred, the bird is able to sing the songs special to the breeding season.

In establishing the canaries' songs, learning is also involved. Male canaries elaborate on their songs each year; they learn from hearing themselves and other canaries, and they remember their own songs from year to year. Thus the song that each bird produces has been determined by the interactive effects of its genetic program, the experience of increased day length, the level of the sex hormone testosterone, and learning. The genes and the environment interact to determine the song of each canary, and as might be expected, each individual sings a different song. We discuss this interaction in more detail in Chapter 7. Here we note that there are differences between avian species in when birds sing and whether only males sing. As we mentioned earlier, both male and female Australian magpies sing and they do so all year round. So far, there has been little research on species that sing all year round and in which both sexes sing.

Not only must a bird know how to sing, but it must also know in exactly what place and at what time of day it is advisable to sing (singing in another bird's territory would provoke attack). The bird must also know which individual to direct its singing toward. Similar criteria apply to all animal species and also to other forms of communication. Since communication is social behavior, it is not surprising that there are many different aspects of communication that have to be learned. First, we discuss learning to produce vocalizations and then we consider the importance of learning when, where, and how often to communicate.

SONG DEVELOPMENT IN BIRDS

There has been much interest in the study of song development in birds. Three kinds of evidence indicate that a vocalization is learned. The first kind of evidence is the development of abnormal vocalizations in birds that are raised in isolation from conspecifics, so that they never hear the vocalizations of their own species. The second is the abnormal development of vocalizations in individual birds that have been rendered deaf early in life. This is not a procedure that would be approved for experiments conducted nowadays, but it was used three decades ago and we report the results because they contain valuable information that should not be lost. The third kind of evidence is that of vocal imitation or mimicry of the vocalizations of other species and of sounds in the environment.

There is no evidence that vocal learning occurs in the Galliformes (chickens, turkeys, quails, pheasants) or the Columbiformes (pigeons), but it does occur in the Passeriformes (in the large number of different species of songbirds known as oscines, but not in all the Passerines), Apodiformes (hummingbirds), and Psittaciformes (parrots). There are, of course, numerous species in each of these categories. The ability of parrots to imitate human speech, and sounds such as the creaking of doors and the noise of a bottle being opened, is well known (see our discussion of the parrot Alex in Chapters 2 and 3 and also see a 1975 paper by Dietmar Todt). Many songbirds also mimic sounds in their environment and, when hand-reared, will mimic human speech. We discussed this special kind of learning in detail earlier; here, we are more concerned with the first and second kinds of evidence showing that avian vocalizations are learnt.

Learning of vocalizations is characteristic of those oscines that have complex songs as well as those with local dialects (variations in their vocalizations from one region to another). One of the latter species is the chaffinch (Fringilla coelebs). Some time ago, William Thorpe conducted some very important experiments in which he hand-reared male chaffinches in isolation from other members of their species and then studied their song development. In this species only the males sing. When the chaffinches became adults, the songs of the hand-reared males were very different from the songs of wild, adult chaffinches, although they were of roughly the same length, covered roughly the same range of frequencies (pitches), and were subdivided into packets of sound in somewhat the same way. It was as if the males reared in isolation retained a template for the song but, lacking social experience with their own kind, were unable to learn the species-specific song (Thorpe, 1961).

As confirmation of the importance of learning, it was found that, if the male chaffinches are played a tape recording of a chaffinch song as they grow up, they learn that song and produce a song that is almost identical. The same has been shown in other species, such as the song sparrow *(Melospiza melodia)*. Other species show a similar dependence on hearing another bird singing early in life but, unlike the chaffinch, they need to interact with a living bird—simply hearing a tape recording of the sound is not sufficient. The Australian zebra finch *(Taeniopygia guttata)* is an example, as we discuss further below.

Even establishment of the template of the song requires some learning, but in this case the bird learns by hearing itself. This was first demonstrated in the song sparrow by rendering birds deaf early in life. The deafened birds developed songs that were entirely different from the songs of adults in the wild. They exhibited either no evidence of a template of the species-specific song or a very crude template, much less structured than the template that develops in isolated, hand-reared song sparrows. Their songs were even more abnormal than those of hand-reared members of their species. The same result was found in deafened chaffinches and other songbirds.

Birds learn to sing very early in life. Certain vocalizations are learned more readily than others: each species selects particular vocal patterns to memorize. Genes seem to determine this initial selection of the first types of song to be memorized (see Marler, 1991 and 1997, for more detail). Later learning shapes further selection of songs to memorize.

There are several distinct phases in the development of song, which we will illustrate by discussing the chaffinch. Soon after hatching, young chaffinches produce begging calls to which the parents respond by supplying them with food. By the time of fledging (at about the age of 5 weeks), these calls have been replaced by rambling, soft vocalizations, referred to as "subsong." Subsong is often produced when the birds are dozing or perching quietly. The bird runs through a whole series of different notes and the sequence can be very long. Subsong occurs in many species and, as Peter Marler (1970) has pointed out, it is remarkably similar to the babbling sounds that human infants make when they are acquiring speech. Both the subsong of birds and the babbling of humans provide auditory feedback—the individual hears the sounds that it is making—and so self-learning is probably occurring. The equivalent of subsong also occurs in parrots during a stage of life when they are practicing their learned vocalizations. Irene Pepperberg (1991) has reported on what she calls "solitary sound play" by the parrot Alex when he was being taught new vocalizations. At these times, Alex produced sounds that were similar to, but not exactly the same as, the new words that he was learning.

The subsong of the chaffinches comes to imitate parts of the parents' song, although not precisely. This imitative song is called plastic song because it is still variable and has not yet developed into adult song. The bird's song practice subsides during the winter. The next spring singing begins again, and this time it is subsong interspersed with plastic song. One month later, the song crystallizes into "full song." The same pattern occurs in many other species of songbird, including song sparrows, cardinals, and buntings. The Australian magpie does not follow this linear pattern of song development to crystallized song, although it does have a plastic song.

As mentioned above, chaffinches exposed to an adult's song during their early development learn that particular song and produce a copy of it when they themselves become adults. A short exposure to the adult's song during the first few weeks of life is sufficient; the bird will then reproduce that song in adulthood even without further exposure to it for many months. This shows that there is a sensitive period in the chaffinch's early life during which song learning occurs. Chaffinches, and many other songbirds including zebra finches, learn song early in life, and when they become adults, they do not change their song. Canaries also learn their songs early in life, but they are able to change their songs from season to season when they are adults. It appears that they go on learning throughout their lives.

Learning in adulthood is not limited to canaries: some parrots have been reported to learn new sounds when very old. We have seen a parrot (a galah) more than 60 years old learning new words after moving into our household. These words were the names of two of our dogs. Not only did the galah learn to imitate the words but he uses them only when the dogs are missing or expressing aggression to each other—he has never used the words out of context and he does not use them very often. This ability to change vocalizations in later life also appears to apply to the natural vocalizations of parrots.

The same ability has been shown in budgerigars by Susan Farabaugh and her colleagues. These researchers found that individual caged budgerigars *(Melopsittacus undulatus)* changed their contact calls so that they resembled more closely those of another budgerigar caged alongside. The budgerigars showed mutual learning of each other's calls. By imitating each other, they converged their calls so that they became more alike (Farabaugh, Linzenbold, and Dooling, 1994).

The ability to continue to learn in adult life does not, however, lessen the importance of the sensitive period for vocal learning in early life. There appears to be a window that opens in early life and allows the bird to learn a wider variety of songs than it can learn either before or after that sensitive period. This was demonstrated clearly by experiments conducted by Donald Kroodsma in the late 1970s (Kroodsma, 1978). He exposed long-billed marsh wrens to a large number of different songs, a few songs every 3 days. The period of exposure began soon after hatching and continued until about 85 days of age. The wrens learned very few of the songs they heard before about 25 days of age, although the number they learned increased from 10 days of age on. The best period for acquiring a variety of songs was 25–55 days after hatching, but there was a period of less learning around 40–45 days; from 55 to 80 days there was a decline in the number of songs learned, although the exposure to different songs was just as various throughout this entire period of time. The results show clearly that there is a sensitive period during which the marsh wren learns new songs (see Figure 6.1).

The ending of the sensitive period may depend on changing hormone levels; an injection of testosterone into zebra finches before the normal end of the sensitive period has been shown to curtail the learning of new songs. This effect contrasts with the onset of song production in the next spring season, when testosterone levels rise and the zebra finch sings the songs it learned earlier during the sensitive period. It would appear that high levels of the hormone testosterone crystallize the song so that no new learning will occur. The same hormonal condition also stimulates the singing of the songs that have already been learned. In adults the seasonally fluctuating levels of testosterone also affect song: a recent study by Troy Smith, John Wingfield, and their colleagues has found that male song sparrows sing songs that are more variable in the autumn, when their testosterone levels are low, than in spring, when the levels are high, although the same repertoire of songs is sung in both seasons (Smith et al., 1997).

Sensitive periods for learning are not restricted to song learning or to avian species. There are sensitive periods for learning other behaviors, such as the sensitive period for forming social attachments by the process of imprinting. There may also be a sensitive period for learning language in humans, as isolated examples indicate but do not prove. There is the documented case of Genie, a human child who was denied any form of normal social or linguistic experience for the first 13 years of her life (re-

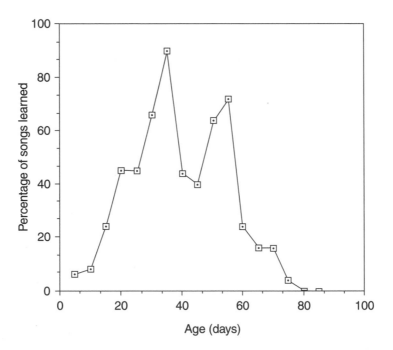

FIGURE 6.1   The sensitive period for song learning. This graph shows the percentage of songs learned by long-billed marsh wrens *(Cistothorus palustris)* at different ages after hatching. The birds were exposed to a large number of song types during this period but not all at once. Over each sequence of 3 days they were exposed to only a few of the songs.They copied more of the songs heard between days 25 and 55 than at other times, although fewer songs were learned between days 40 and 45. (Calculated from the data of D. Kroodsma in Slater and Jones, 1997).

ported by Curtiss et al., 1974). Genie never acquired full speech capacity, and the abnormality of her first 13 years, and indeed the years that followed, may have contributed to this failure of recovery. There have been similar cases with comparable results, but all these cases of isolated humans have had highly abnormal aspects that confound the conclusions that can be drawn from them. This might also be said of the birds that were reared in isolation. It is not possible simply to take something away—in this case, the bird's normal experience of hearing song and experiencing other social interactions—without causing unexpected effects on behavior in general. Development is not a simple process from which one can extract a single aspect without causing unpredictable effects.

The inability to learn song or language after an early life of social deprivation might be an aberrant outcome not directly related to the simple subtraction of a normal aspect of social experience. There is a well-known example that may help to illustrate this, and that is the experiments performed by John Paul Scott (see Scott and Fuller, 1965), in which he raised dogs in isolation from the time of their birth. When they were brought into contact with people later in life, they behaved in very abnormal ways, one of which was to rush and bite at the flame of a cigarette lighter. Being raised in isolation led not just to an absence of some patterns of behavior but to the emergence of behaviors never seen before. These results alert us to be cautious in interpreting experiments in which animals are raised in social isolation, as in the studies of the songbirds.

SINGING TUTORS

As we have said, chaffinches and marsh wrens will learn songs from tape recordings played to them during the sensitive period. But zebra finches and some other species cannot learn from tapes. They need to see and interact with another bird of their own species at the same time that they hear it singing. Even if the other bird sings within their earshot but is hidden from their view behind a screen, they will not learn their species-specific song. It is some aspect of interaction with the singing bird that counts, as was shown by Patrice Adret (1993). He was able to train zebra finches to sing by allowing each bird, caged alone, to peck at a key to turn on a tape recording of a zebra finch's song. By turning on the tape recorder the birds were able to interact with the artificial "tutor." The birds trained in this way pecked at the key many times in a day in order to hear a small segment of song (only 15 seconds in duration), and they often flew up and down in front of the loudspeaker as the tape recording was playing. They learned to sing the same song as the tutor and produced it when they became adults. Control birds exposed to the same tape record-ing of song but in a passive way (they could not turn it on themselves) did not copy the recorded song. This research shows that some form of interaction with the tutor is essential for learning to occur, no matter how unusual that interaction is.

Peter Slater and his colleagues have shown that a zebra finch may pre-fer to learn the song of its own father, but this is not at all a straightfor-ward process (Mann and Slater, 1994). Male zebra finches usually learn their songs in the second month of life. In the experiments conducted by Slater, the young zebra finches were housed with their parents until they were 35 days old, and so each could hear its father's song over this period, which precedes the sensitive period for song learning. Then each young bird was caged separately in the central part of a cage with three parti-tions (Figure 6.2). From day 35 to day 100 of life each bird was exposed to singing birds placed in the compartments on either side. In the first ex-periment, an adult male was housed alone on one side and an established pair of birds on the other side. Neither male was the parent of the young bird in the central cage. The young birds learned to copy the song of ei-ther the single or the paired male, but they preferred to learn the paired male's song rather than the single male's song.

In another experiment, Slater and his colleagues exposed a young ze-bra finch to his father caged alone on one side and his mother caged with an unfamiliar and unrelated male on the other side. Of the 13 birds tested in this way, 10 copied the song of the unfamiliar male housed with the mother, 2 learned their father's song, and 1 learned equally from both tu-tors. Thus the preferred tutor is the male paired with the bird's mother, not the actual father, even though the father's song had been heard for the first 35 days of the young bird's life.

The final experiment gave the young zebra finch a choice of learning from his father housed with an unfamiliar female on one side or from an unfamiliar male housed with his mother on the other side. Of the 16 birds tested, 10 learned to copy their fathers and 6 copied the unrelated

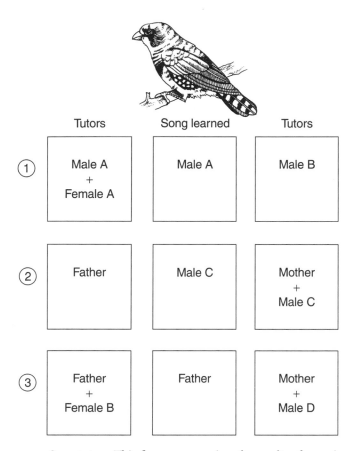

Tutors	Song learned	Tutors
(1) Male A + Female A	Male A	Male B
(2) Father	Male C	Mother + Male C
(3) Father + Female B	Father	Mother + Male D

FIGURE 6.2 Song tutors. This figure summarizes the results of experiments on zebra finches by Nigel Mann and Peter Slater (1994). Each young male zebra finch was placed in a central cage with potential song tutors on either side. The song copied by the learner is indicated in the central box. Males A to D and females A and B are unrelated and unknown to the young male who is learning his song. Note that the young bird prefers to learn the song of a male paired with a female and also to learn the song of his father if the father is paired. But the young bird prefers to learn the song of an unfamiliar, unrelated paired male rather than his father's if the father is not paired.

tutor. In this case the birds showed a preference for the father's song. This preference could have been established by the young bird's exposure to its father's song from hatching until day 35. However, the preference for the father's song after exposure during the sensitive period for song learning is not straightforward, because it occurs only when the father has a partner. If he is unpaired, the mother's partner is preferred over the father. Hence both the mother and the father influence the young bird's selection of a tutor.

Preference for a particular singing tutor is not, as these experiments show, a simple matter. Another experiment found that tutors that are more aggressive and interact with the young zebra finch by pecking and chasing him are copied more than less aggressive ones (Weary and Krebs, 1987). We assume this happens because even aggression increases the interaction between the tutor and the young bird that is learning, but it is surprising that a somewhat punitive interaction would be effective. This is an area that deserves further investigation.

The bond between female and male is not unimportant in the learning of song. Research by Meredith West and Andrew King (1988) on the North American cowbird *(Molothrus ater)* shows that the female can be most important in shaping the song of young males in this species. Since this species is parasitic—it lays its eggs in the nests of other species, as cuckoos do—the young are raised without hearing the calls of their own species. Instead, after fledging, they form flocks in which singing by the males is shaped by the young females. The female performs a display of "wing stroking" when she is attracted by the song of a young male. This apparently reinforces the male because he is more likely to sing the same song again if the female has performed this display. Therefore, in time, the songs of the males become matched to the preferences of the females. The females train the males to sing the correct song even though they do not sing themselves. If the males are put into a flock with females of a different group of cowbirds, they learn, also in response to wing stroking by females, to sing the song of that group instead of their own.

THE CULTURAL TRANSMISSION OF SONG

The transmission of song from one generation of an avian species to the next by the process of learning has been viewed by ethologists as cultural transmission. In fact, several researchers in the field (e.g., Slater and Ince, 1986; Trainer, 1989) refer to the changes in song that result over time as the song is passed from generation to generation as "cultural evolution," as distinct from genetic evolution. It is thought, however, that the changes that occur as song is passed on are due to errors in copying (the bird does not produce an exact copy of the song that he heard) rather than being innovations on the part of the singer or some new form of adaptive behavior. Inevitably, small errors will creep into the copied song over time, but nevertheless copying is surprisingly accurate. In addition to this source of change in the song over time, variations also result because each bird may copy elements of songs from more than one individual.

The amount of change in the song from generation to generation varies with each species of bird. White-crowned sparrows *(Zonotrichia leucophrys)* copy their species-specific song dialects extremely precisely (Baptista, 1975; DeWolfe and Baptista, 1995), whereas indigo buntings *(Passerina cyanea)* modify their song type slightly with each generation (Payne, 1996). Peter Slater and his colleagues (1980) have estimated that the chaffinch copies with an accuracy of 85 percent. In other species only the most common songs are sung from one year to the next. In some cases, what appear to be simple copying errors may occur because the songs heard are distorted by other noises in the bird's environment. L. Lehtonen (1983), who studied the songs of great tits *(Parus major)* in Finland, believes their songs have become simpler over recent decades because the environment has become more noisy. If environmental noises do affect song, we might well contemplate a world in which the songs of birds are degraded to their simplest form. A comparison of the urban members of a species with their conspecifics living in remote, wild environments might be an interesting way to test this hypothesis, but we would have to consider the potential influence of other factors that could also cause a difference in the songs sung by the two populations.

In fact, we know there is regional variation in the songs sung by birds of the same species. Birds living in one region may sing songs that are slightly different from those sung in a nearby region (see, e.g., Slater, 1986, 1989). The most common pattern is for the songs to change gradually as the distance between populations increases. This spatial variation in the song could be the result of a bird's copying different songs of more than one of its neighbors. Thus both time and spatial separation could contribute to changes in the songs. An alternative explanation, by B. B. DeWolfe and Luis Baptista (summarized in Bradbury and Vehrencamp, 1998), relates regional variation to migration; species that migrate and return to territories that may be some distance removed from the home range in which they learned their dialect might have to adjust their dialect to the new location. Sedentary species would have no need to do this and so would retain relatively stable dialects.

Great emphasis has been placed on the cultural transmission of vocalizations, but signaling in other sensory modalities may also be transmitted by learning. It now seems that birds may be able to learn visual signals as well as vocal signals. This would mean that both visual and vocal signaling could be passed on by cultural transmission.

Some patterns of signaling may also be used as a means to pass on information from one generation to the next—to assist cultural transmission. For example, European blackbirds use mobbing calls not only to attempt to drive a predator away but also to teach naive conspecifics that the predator is a threat to their survival (Curio, Ernst, and Vieth, 1978). In this way, young birds learn about predators from adults and the information is passed from one generation to the next.

VOCAL LEARNING IN NONPRIMATE MAMMALS

Compared with the many studies of vocalization in birds, there has been very little research investigating vocal learning in mammals (but see Janik and Slater, 1997). In particular, there have been fewer studies in which mammals have been experimented on by rearing them in isolation, compared to such studies in birds. This is probably because researchers have been much more aware of the ethical implications of raising mammals in conditions in which they are deprived of social contact than of raising birds in isolation, although this is an artificial distinction because birds are just as dependent on social relations as mammals. The hand-rearing experiments discussed above show that this is true.

To find evidence of vocal learning in mammals in the wild, we can first look to see whether any of them mimic sounds in their environment. Perhaps the best known example of a mammal doing so is that of Hoover, a harbor seal *(Phoca vitulina)* kept in the New England Aquarium in Boston. He learned to mimic human speech, including the phrases "Hello there" and "Come over here." Sound spectrograms of the seal saying these words and a human saying the same thing have been published by Katherine Ralls and her colleagues (1985) from the Smithsonian Institution (see Figure 6.3). The similarities between these spectrograms are

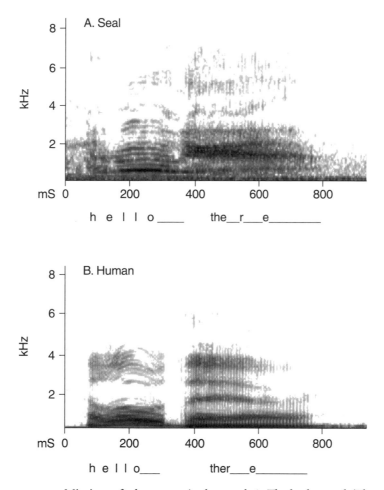

FIGURE 6.3 Mimicry of a human voice by a seal. A: The harbor seal (*Phoca vitulina*) called Hoover says "Hello there" with an American accent. B: The same words spoken by a human. (These sound spectrograms were made from an audiotape generously provided by Katherine Ralls, via James Scanlon. Other examples can be seen in Ralls, Fiorelli, and Gish, 1985.)

remarkable. Hoover also says, "Get out of there" and "Hey," which he strings into sequences with other sayings, and then ends with mimicry of human laughter. To the naked ear Hoover sounds like a human with an unnerving slur in the voice and a Boston accent. Another male seal in the same aquarium learned to say "Hello," showing that Hoover was not a unique case. Seals can learn human speech sounds when they are in circumstances that favor this type of learning. Hoover was reared without contact with his own species in early life.

It seems that vocal learning may not be uncommon in seals living in their natural environment. There is considerable variation in the vocalizations of members of the same species of seal living in different localities. Although there may be other reasons for spatial variations in vocalizations, these differences indicate that seals may learn their natural calls. It is possible that adult males mimic the calls of males in neighboring territories, as do some male songbirds.

There are several species of seals for which geographical variation in vocalizations has been reported, but perhaps the best example is that of Weddell seals *(Leptonychotes weddelli)*. Separate colonies of Weddell seals living in different fjords in the Vestfold Hills of Antarctica, only 20 kilometers apart, were found to share only 5 out of a total of 44 different vocalizations (Morrice, Burton, and Green, 1994). Even the shared calls were not absolutely identical. A much earlier study of elephant seals *(Mirounga angustirostris)* inhabiting islands off the west coast of North America, carried out by Burney Le Boeuf and Richard Petersen (1969), found that threat vocalizations made by males vary from one island's population to the next and that these local dialects have persisted from generation to generation. This variation occurred despite the fact that there was some movement of males between islands; the researchers suggested that young males that move to a new island copy the threat calls of the established male population on that island.

Whales in captivity have been found to imitate human speech, as was first reported by John Lilly (1965). Bottlenose dolphins *(Tursiops truncatis)* mimic their species-specific whistles and will also learn to mimic whistles that are used in training them to perform tricks. It appears that the dolphins' own whistles can be modified by experience. Diana Reiss and Brenda McCowan (1993) found that bottlenose dolphins mimicked computer-generated whistles and that they also learned to produce particular whistles in association with certain interactive behaviors, such as playing with rings or balls. There is no question that all the behavior of dolphins is highly plastic and creative, including their communication behavior. As far as we know, whales and seals are the most versatile vocal learners of all mammals.

VOCAL LEARNING IN PRIMATES

The other mammalian species in which vocal learning has been investigated to some degree are the primates. We have discussed the remarkable capacities of the great apes to learn sign language and symbolic forms of communication by which they can communicate with humans. This is ample evidence that they can learn complicated forms of communication. But do they learn their own vocalizations? Unfortunately, there have been surprisingly few studies of the learning of the species-typical calls of any of the apes. John Mitani (1994) and his colleagues have reported differences in the pant-hoot vocalizations (loud calls) of chimpanzees in two different localities in Africa, and they have some suggestive evidence that male chimpanzees calling at the same time match their pant-hoot sounds. This indicates that chimpanzee vocalizations can be shaped by learning, but more detailed investigations are needed. We summarize what is known of vocalizations made by orangutans in our book *The Orang-utans* (Kaplan and Rogers, 1999), but these data are patchy and no reliable developmental work has been done.

A study of contact calls in pygmy marmosets *(Cebuella pygmaea)* by Margaret Elowson and Charles Snowdon (1994) found that these monkeys modify their trill calls when their social environment is changed so that they can hear the calls of previously unfamiliar members of their own species. They modified both the frequency band width and the peak frequency of their trill calls, and these changes occurred in monkeys of all ages, from infants to adults. Thus the trill call, at least, of the pygmy marmoset is plastic, able to change, even in adults. Learning influences the call. Note the similarity to changes in birdsong. The ability to change vocalizations when the social environment changes may be essential to social cohesion in avian and mammalian species.

There is an important study by Robert Seyfarth and Dorothy Cheney

(1986) on vervet monkeys (*Cercopithecus aethiops*). They managed to record eagle alarm calls made by 24 infants, 53 juveniles, and 55 adults (see Chapters 2 and 3) in the wild. They also noted the aerial species to which the eagle call was applied. Infants used the call to refer to birds flying overhead, but they did not call to all species of eagle and they often called when they caught sight of non-raptor, innocuous species, such as bee-eaters. Compared with the infants, juveniles showed a much greater awareness of different species of eagles, although non-raptor and innocuous species, such as storks, still incorrectly evoked their alarm calls. Adults, by contrast, gave the eagle alarm calls to refer to six different species of raptors, including the goshawk and the owl, and the only non-raptor that evoked their alarm calls was the vulture. However, the call for the vulture was observed to occur in fewer than five cases. The results show that infants use the eagle alarm call rather nonspecifically to refer to a wide range of aerial predators, whereas adults have learned to use the call specifically to refer to raptors. It took nearly 2 years to collect these data. They show very well that learning the meaning of a call must take place during growth from infancy to adulthood and that the monkeys may have particular images in mind when they produce this alarm call.

Marc Hauser (1988) has discovered that infant vervet monkeys also learn to recognize the alarm calls given by starlings. We have already discussed the vervet monkeys' attention to the alarm calls made by starlings that live in the same locality. The adult monkeys are able to exploit those calls to detect the presence of a predator in the air or on the ground. Given the interspecies nature of this form of signaling, it is not surprising that the vervet monkeys have to learn the meaning of the starlings' calls. Hauser conducted his research by playing back tape recordings of not only the starlings' ground-predator alarm calls but also their songs. Infant monkeys less than 3 months old were able to distinguish between the starlings' alarm calls and their songs, but they did not interpret the alarm calls as indicating danger. They simply looked at the loudspeaker when it was broadcasting a starling's alarm call but not when it was broadcasting the bird's song. By the time they were 3 to 4 months old, they had learned the meaning of the starlings' ground-predator alarm call—they responded to it by scampering up the nearest tree. Moreover, infants that had been exposed to more examples of the starlings' alarm call learned sooner than those exposed less often. These results need confirmation by research with more subjects, but they demonstrate interspecies learning of vocalizations. This is a very special case of learning.

Learning seems to occur for at least one other call made by vervet monkeys. Hauser (1989) studied the age-related changes in the *wrr* call that they make when they encounter another troop of vervet monkeys. He found that infants less than 3 months old produce a *wrr*-like call when they are distressed by being lost and that it is even more like the *wrr* call of adults than that of older infants. Although infants 10–18 months old produce *wrr* calls during encounters with other groups of monkeys, their calls are not acoustically identical to those of adults. In summary, very young infants (up to 3 months of age) make *wrr* calls when they are lost and at other times when they seek contact; then there is a period from 3 to 10 months of age when no *wrr* calls are made, followed by a period from 10 months to 3 or 4 years when *wrr* calls are made that are not the same as the adults' calls; and finally, the adult *wrr* is made after the monkey is 4 years old. This timetable for development of the calls was speeded up in infants belonging to groups that experienced more encounters with other groups of monkeys, a finding which suggests that learning plays a role in the development of the adult call used in a specific context. However, maturation of the vocal apparatus may also contribute to the development of calls. These transitions in the call that occur with age and/or experience are most interesting and deserve further study. Hauser noted that the period when *wrrs* were not produced (3 to 10 months of age) is also the period when other types of vocalizations are being acquired, and this other learning process might distract the young monkey from making the *wrr* call (see Figure 6.4). When it begins to make the call again, the structure of the call may have been degraded and that may be why it has to be learned again. Similar transitions have been reported in the development of language in human children.

Hauser (1994) has also shown, in a study of rhesus monkeys *(Macaca mulatta)*, that the characteristic dominant role of the left hemisphere in processing the species-specific vocalizations is not present in infants. It develops with increasing age. Hauser determined which hemisphere was dominant by scoring which ear the monkeys used to listen to a loudspeaker playing back their calls. Adults favored the right ear, and this means that most of the processing is occurring in the left hemisphere, because the auditory input goes mostly to the hemisphere on the side opposite the ear. Infants showed no preference for one ear over the other. These results do not tell us whether this developmental change in the processing of the vocalizations is influenced by experience, learning, or simply maturation, but it is possible that all these processes are involved. We know that experience influences the development of brain asymmetry in birds and learning can affect it, too, as the research of Lesley Rogers (1997a) has shown.

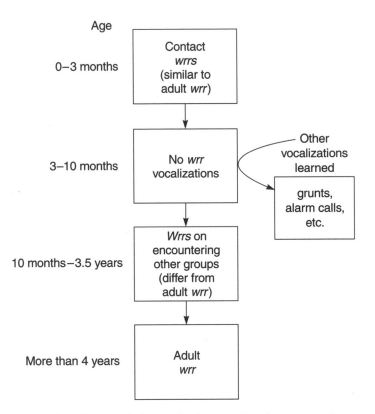

FIGURE 6.4 Developmental changes in the *wrr* calls of vervet monkeys. Adults produce the *wrr* call, a trilled call, during aggressive encounters between neighboring groups. Infants make a similar call when they become separated from their mothers. Note the period when no *wrr* calls are made, a stage when other calls are being learned. (After Hauser, 1989.)

Some studies on primates have found less evidence of vocal learning. The calls of the squirrel monkey *(Saimiri sciureus)* have been studied in some detail. Research carried out in the early 1980s by Anna Lieblich and her colleagues (1980) and by John Newman and David Symmes (1982) showed that there was little age-dependent change in the calls of squirrel monkeys, and also that the calls were not greatly affected when the monkeys were reared in social isolation from other members of their species. This result suggested that the calls of this species were strongly determined by inheritance—by the genes. However, more recent studies have indicated that this conclusion was incorrect. Maxine Biben and Deborah Bernhards (1995), of the National Institutes of Health in Maryland, have shown that the *chuck* calls of young females are more similar to those of members of their own social group than to those of members of other groups, a finding which suggests that learning is involved. Also there are marked differences in the types of calls that the monkeys make at different ages. Although this does not prove that learning occurs, it does show that there is flexibility in their vocalizations. There appears to be learning of the specificity of when and where these calls should be used.

Overall, it can be said that the present state of knowledge shows that marmosets, tamarins, squirrel monkeys, and many other primate species change their vocalizations with development, as John Newman (1995) of the National Institutes of Health has pointed out. In addition, we would like to return to a point that we made earlier: almost all the primate calls that have been studied are the more obvious calls, used to indicate alarm, distress, or contact with other members of the animal's social group; the more intimate and softer social calls have been ignored. It would be of great interest to compare the development of these calls with that of the more obvious calls.

CONCLUSION

From extensive research on song learning in birds, we can conclude that learning plays a major role during a sensitive period in early life. In some species, no new songs are learned in adulthood. In other species, such as the canary, adult song remains plastic, although seasonal changes in hormone levels determine when singing will occur.

It is simply too early to reach any firm conclusions about the learning of vocal communication in primates, or other mammals, but developmental changes do occur and at least some of these are known to be affected by experience and learning. There are some similarities between species of primates in the way the structure of their vocalizations changes with age. In addition, primates share with birds and humans the stage of vocal development referred to as babbling. Infant primates are very vocal compared with adults, and the highly varied subsong of songbirds is similar to the babbling of human babies. This would appear to be a stage when the young animal is practicing the structure of the vocalizations.

Not only must the structure of calls and song be learned but so too must the meaning of each call. The studies by Hauser were a step forward because they took into account the meaning of the call and did not just document the changes in the structure of the vocalizations with increasing age. There is enormous scope for more work along these lines.

It should also be noted that there is some evidence that different groups of monkeys belonging to the same species have different dialects (as Steven Green (1975) has shown to be true of Japanese macaques living in three different locations), and this too may indicate that learning of vocalizations occurs, as we explained for birdsong. With the vervet monkeys, where it is known that the meaning of calls is learned, it would now be interesting to know whether this type of learning forms a cultural tradition. In fact, we wonder whether the vervet monkeys of Barbados, taken there from Africa many years ago, have retained the same use of alarm calls and use them with the same specificity to refer to predators as do the vervet monkeys in Africa. Even if one generation teaches the calls to the next, the meaning may have changed to some extent with the presence of different predators in the new environment. Some information from the chimpanzees that have learned sign language shows that signs may be passed on from one generation to the next. Roger Fouts and his colleagues (1989) observed Washoe actively teaching her son, Loulis, how to sign: she was seen to mold his hands into the correct sign. This indicates that, in chimpanzees, the mechanisms for an active cultural tradition are in place.

Ryo Oda and Nobuo Masataka (1996) have studied the responses of two populations of ring-tailed lemurs *(Lemur catta)* to the different alarm calls that sifakas *(Propithecus verreauxi)*—another type of lemur—

give to aerial and ground predators. One population of the lemurs consisted of free-ranging groups living in the same area as sifakas, in Madagascar, and the other population was captive and had no contact with sifakas. The free-ranging group responded appropriately to the sifaka's calls, but the captive group was unable to tell the difference between the two calls. Thus experience with the sifaka's calls is important and learning must take place, but it is not known whether each individual learns the meaning of the two calls afresh in each generation or cultural transmission assists this process. The results of these studies show, however, that cultural transmission alone, without any relevant experience, does not suffice, because the captive group would have retained the ability to interpret the calls had that ability been passed down from previous generations.

Although most of the research on learning to communicate has focused on vocalizations, it should be remembered that primates, as well as other mammals, also communicate by scent marking, visual displays, and various forms of touch. It is important to investigate whether learning occurs in these other forms of communication. Is there, for example, a stage in development when visual displays are plastic, as there is in the development of song? It is not unreasonable to suggest that animals might show "babbling" in visual displays, as they do for vocalizations. In fact, Laura Petitto and Paula Marentette (1991) have shown that babbling in humans is not confined to vocal production: deaf children exposed to sign language from birth display manual babbling in which they run through the various hand positions used in signing, just as hearing children do by trying out sounds vocally. Thus an early phase of development when practice occurs is quite probably related to communication but is not necessarily confined to vocal communication. And since vocal babbling is not unique to humans, other forms of babbling may be found in animals too. As far as birds are concerned, we know much more about their vocal learning than we do about learning in any other group of animals, but we know virtually nothing of how they develop their visual displays, in all their complexity and variety.

Chapter Seven

THE EVOLUTION OF COMMUNICATION

In this chapter, we examine aspects of signaling and receiving that may be passed from generation to generation by a program encoded in the genes. Many important aspects of signaling are learned by each animal during the course of its life, particularly during its early life. But learning is not the only factor involved. All the behavior patterns that are used in communication depend on the interaction between genetic factors and experience or learning. Signals can be learned and passed on from generation to generation, as we saw in the discussion of the cultural transmission of song.

GENES AND LEARNING

In insects, some forms of simple behavior are programmed entirely by the genes, but the same is not true of the more complex behaviors used by vertebrates for communication. Almost all the forms of communication discussed in this book depend to various degrees on learning. But this does not mean that they have no genetic component. It is difficult, if not impossible, to look at the behavior of the signaler or the receiver and say how much of that behavior is determined by genes and how much depends on learning because the two interact and also because there is great variation from one animal to another. On this point we may differ from those biologists who consider genes to have a direct causal, and often overriding, influence on both signaling behavior and the processes involved in receiving and remembering signals. This genetic determinist view is encapsulated in those definitions of communication that require a signal to be adaptive, meaning genetically programmed. This is the definition of signaling formulated by Edward O. Wilson (1975) and held by John Krebs and Nick Davies (1993), as well as many other behavioral ecologists and also ethologists. Because they focus on the genetic program, they tend to be less interested in questions about learning and the development of communication behavior.

As we discussed in Chapter 6, songbirds reared in isolation sing abnormal songs but retain a template of the song. At first this result was interpreted to mean that genes determined the template and then learning elaborated upon that template to give the full song. In other words, each bird was said to inherit a foundation for its song, on which it builds by the process of learning that occurs when the young bird hears other birds singing. However, the experiments in which birds were rendered deaf early in life showed that even the template of the song is not present if the bird cannot hear itself sing. The results of such experiments, however offensive their methodology, do indicate that the earlier notion that genes alone determine the template for song may be incorrect, unless the effect of hearing no sound led to degradation of an existing template.

Nevertheless, genes do specify some broad aspects of the sensory systems that a particular species will have available to perceive signals—such as a sensory system for seeing certain wavelengths of light; ultrasound detection; the ability to detect electrical fields. This genetic endowment determines the nature of the signals that will be most effective for the species. Genes may also specify aspects of the structures that will be used to produce signals, such as the colors and sizes of feathers or the structure of the syrinx. In these cases, we may regard the genetic factors as constraints on the development of the structures and behaviors used for signaling, or as constraints on the development of sensory organs and the other processes that are used to detect, discriminate, and interpret the meaning of the signal. The amount of influence such genetic constraints exert on the development of the behavior of a species varies from species to species and from one form of communication to another, but in every case the genetic program provides only broad constraints. It does not determine the exact details of the behavior patterns used in communication.

Often, learning is not merely an elaboration, or fine-tuning, of a basic template that has been specified by the genes. In many cases, experience can so completely change behavior that the original genetic blueprint is no longer recognizable. The sensory capabilities of an animal depend on experience, as was clearly shown in experiments with kittens conducted by Colin Blakemore and Grahame Cooper. They discovered that a kitten that has been allowed to see only vertical black and white stripes for a short period after it first opens its eyes is unable to see horizontal stripes for the rest of its life (Blakemore and Cooper, 1970). The early experience so modifies the way the kitten processes visual information that, from then on, it does not respond to an object that is waved back and forth horizontally, whereas it runs to play with one that is moved up and down. The cells in the visual cortex that would normally respond to horizontal lines shift their preference and now respond to vertical lines. The opposite is true of a kitten exposed to horizontal stripes instead of vertical ones.

At first, this research might seem to indicate that genes make absolutely no contribution to the kitten's ability to see. However, a kitten that is kept in the dark over the same period of time as the others were exposed to the stripes is able to see both vertical and horizontal stripes, and indeed stripes at any angle. Therefore, the ability of the kitten to see stripes at any angle when it first opens its eyes appears to be determined genetically, unless another form of environmental stimulation acting before the eyes open also exerts some influence. Visual experience immediately after the eyes open has a critical effect in changing the way the visual system is wired, and it determines what the kitten will be able to see from that time on, what signals it will perceive. In the normal environment, a kitten would see lines at all angles and thus the early visual experience would reinforce the genetic plan. Only by putting the kitten in an abnormal visual environment can the importance of learning be shown.

We use this example of early experience in the kitten to illustrate the interaction of genes and early experience and, in this case, to demonstrate the overriding role of experience during a sensitive period of life. A similar effect of early experience has been shown by one of the authors (Rogers, 1995, 1996) to affect the development of the nerve connections that are used to process visual inputs in the chicken. Exposure of the chick embryo to light just before hatching stimulates the development of nerve cells that project from the chick's midbrain to its forebrain. In fact, because the embryo is oriented in the egg so that its head is turned with the left side against its body, only the right eye is stimulated by the light, which can pass through the eggshell and membranes that surround the embryo. Only the connections in the midbrain that receive input from the right eye are stimulated to grow. The connections on the other side of the brain that receive input from the left eye do not develop to the same extent because the left eye is not exposed to light. Therefore, an asymmetry develops in the visual pathways as a result of exposure to light before hatching. If chicks are hatched from eggs that have been incubated in the dark, no such asymmetry develops and there are fewer connections from both sides of the midbrain to the forebrain.

The visual behavior of the chick is also altered in ways that we would expect given the differences in the visual connections caused by light exposure or incubation in the dark. Chicks exposed to light before hatching can find and peck at grains of food scattered on a background of small pebbles when they are tested with a patch over the left eye but not when the patch is over the right eye. The chicks with a patch over the right eye display attack responses, whereas those with a patch over the left eye do so only rarely. Chicks hatched from eggs incubated in the dark do not show these asymmetries. They perform the same with both eyes. After incubation in the dark, chicks peck at grains and pebbles randomly. It is even possible to reverse the asymmetry by allowing the embryo's left eye to be exposed to light instead of the right eye. This is done by easing the embryo's head out of the egg just before hatching and putting a patch on the right eye. The left eye can then be stimulated by light. After this procedure has been carried out, the chicks hatch normally but have reversed asymmetry (Rogers, 1990).

The exposure of the developing embryo to light has these long-lasting effects on the visual connections to the forebrain and on the chick's behavior provided that the experience occurs just before hatching, when the visual connections are first becoming functional. In other words, there is a sensitive period during which light exposure has this effect. Exposure to light earlier during incubation or after hatching has no influence on the development of asymmetry in the visual connections or in behavior. This is a clear example of the way in which a specific kind of experience in early life can alter brain development and the way that information is perceived and processed subsequently. In fact, the asymmetry caused by light may also affect some aspects of social behavior and communication in the chick, since the eye used to look at another chick may signal whether it is likely to attack or not (left eye for attacking and right eye for not attacking).

Like this early visual experience, everything else an animal learns in early life can radically modify its subsequent behavior. The examples of song learning discussed previously illustrate this point. There are critical ages at which animals must be exposed to certain stimuli or at which they must learn certain things, and if these things do not happen, they will not develop in a way that is typical for the species. This principle applies to the behaviors used in communication as much as to any other behavior. Perhaps the most important thing to say here is that social learning in early life has many and various effects on the communication abilities and patterns that an animal develops.

It is, of course, essential for communication between members of the same species that all individuals share the same communication system, although there may be regional variations and also seasonal and age variations. Each individual's use of the common communication system can be established by social learning. It does not have to be programmed by genes, although sometimes it is assumed that the commonality of a particular signaling system implies that it is entirely genetically determined. Such a view may have its roots in considering animals as mechanistic and behavior as fixed action patterns. It denies the fact that behavior patterns can be learned consistently and well, with little variation between individuals or from one generation to the next.

We find it necessary to stress the role of learning because researchers interested in the evolution of displays and other forms of communication often tend to give it only passing recognition and then proceed to discuss evolution without any further mention of learning. We ask the reader to keep this in mind as we discuss the commonality of communication systems within and between species. When we speak of evolution, we are referring to the process of genetic selection. We do not deny that this process occurs and that it is particularly relevant to the physical structures that are used in signaling, such as feathers, organs used for sound production, and skin or eye color, but the signaling behavior itself may also be passed from generation to generation by learning and these two processes are intertwined, not separate. Unless the genetic and experiential contributions to a particular behavior pattern have been studied in detail, we will not follow the all-too-common practice of assuming that genes have the overriding role in determining the behavior pattern. We note that few evolutionary biologists would think that the entirety of the signaling behavior is determined by genes, but, in our view, they often place far too much emphasis on the genetic determinants at the expense of experience and learning. Genetic explanations for the complex behaviors that animals use to communicate tend to trivialize the processes of development.

THE EVOLUTION OF FEATURES
TO ENHANCE SIGNALING

We have mentioned the specialized wing feathers that ducks preen during courtship displays. The behavior pattern of ritualized preening evolved along with the specialized structure of the feathers. The behavioral act of ritualized preening draws attention to these specialized feathers and the feathers, in turn, enhance the behavioral act itself.

The most striking example of feathers used for the purpose of display is the male peacock's train. The train has evolved to be so large that it is a considerable handicap to the bird in its day-to-day life, as we discussed in Chapter1. Yet this disadvantage is balanced by the train's effectiveness as a courtship signal. Raising the tail and bowing the head is a feature of courtship displays in other species of the pheasant family (including chickens and pheasants) and fanning of the tail accompanies these acts in other related species. The peacock courtship display is thought to have evolved from these simpler displays through exaggeration of the structure of the train in both its size and its visual attractiveness. The hundreds of eyespots visible when the male displays are attractive to humans as well as peahens.

There are other features that enhance displays. A colored beak makes displays with the beak more obvious, and a contrasting color in the skin, feathers, or fur around the eyes enhances any display using the eyes. Contrasting coloration around the eyes occurs quite commonly in birds and mammals. The color of the iris may also enhance displays in which the eyes are featured. The size of the pupil of the eye is more obvious if the iris is a light color. In fact, a dark-colored iris may be used to conceal the size of the pupil. It is interesting to note that the only way that humans can distinguish the sex of galahs *(Catacua roseicapella)* is by the color of the iris, males having a dark-brown iris and females a pink iris. The sex difference in the color of the iris means that males can detect the size of the female's pupil but females cannot so easily do likewise for the male's pupil. Signaling of an emotional state by pupil size might, therefore, in this species, be a female-to-male signal but not vice versa.

SEXUAL SELECTION

Since peahens select to mate with peacocks with more spots on the train of the tail, they may be the ones that have caused the evolution of the peacock's tail (Chapter 1). Whether they are really choosing on the basis of the number of eyes on the tail and not overall size or some other associated feature, such as brightness or color contrast, we cannot say, but they are selecting males with the biggest handicap. In so doing they may be choosing to mate with the healthiest peacocks and the ones with the best genes. Thus, female choice may lead to the evolution of bigger, larger, and brighter ornaments, such as the tail. This is known as the "good genes" hypothesis for explaining the evolution of physical characteristics that are used to signal. The hypothesis can be applied also to vocal signals in cases where females choose to mate with males that call more loudly and at faster rates. In some species of songbirds, larger song repertoires may be favored by females, and so the complexity of the singing patterns would increase (Nottebohm, 1972). Competition between males for territory and for priority access to females also leads to elaboration of songs and louder calling. This is considered to be an aspect of sexual selection since it depends on mating success.

Of course, any tendency to call more loudly or to have brighter and larger ornaments makes the male more conspicuous to predators, and a balance must be reached between attracting females and not becoming too conspicuous to predators (Ryan and Keddy-Hector, 1992). This is where the habitat of the species becomes important. In certain habitats the balance between sending the most conspicuous signal and remaining concealed from predators will be achieved in one way and in other habitats it will be achieved in another way, as we discussed earlier. As John Endler (1992) has said, a signal evolves as a local balance between the relative strengths of sexual selection and predation. If predation is the main factor influencing survival, color patterns have to be cryptic and vocalizations not easily detected or located. If there are few predation pressures, color patterns become more obvious, even garish, and vocalizations become louder and more easily located.

THE EVOLUTION OF SENSORY SYSTEMS AND PROCESSES USED TO PERCEIVE SIGNALS

Communication requires not only a signaler but also a receiver; evolutionary changes may occur on the receiver side of the dyad as well as on the sender side, as Tim Guilford and Marian Dawkins (1991) have pointed out. They discuss evolutionary changes in the sensory receptors used for detecting the signal as well as in the processes that are used to discriminate one signal from another and to decode or interpret the message that has been transmitted.

We have said that sexual selection depends on males advertising that they are physically fit or in good health, and that this requirement leads to the evolution of conspicuous ornaments and attractive calls. These signals might also be designed to stimulate the female's sensory system as much as possible. This idea is referred to as the "sensory exploitation" hypothesis. According to this hypothesis, the female's sensory system is driving evolution and the male adapts his signaling to fit her ability to perceive and respond to his signals.

It is possible that the female's sensory system is specialized to perform a function other than receiving the male's signals and that the male takes advantage of this specialization by adapting his signals to match this aspect of the female's perception. For example, if the sensory system of the female is designed for catching prey, the male will adapt his signaling to appeal to her way of finding prey (Ryan and Keddy-Hector, 1992). If the prey, such as an insect, is moving, the male may perform courtship displays that involve movement. If the prey is detected by color patterns, the male may use similar patterns in courtship displaying, and so on.

Research on the mating calls of túngara frogs belonging to the genus *Physalaemus* by Michael Ryan and his colleagues supports the hypothesis of sensory exploitation. The ability of the female frogs to perceive certain sound frequencies appears to be the process that drives the evolution of the calls by the male (Ryan et al., 1990; Ryan and Keddy-Hector, 1992). Males of the species *Physalaemus pustulosus* produce a whine-like call finished off by a "chuck" sound. The female's auditory system is designed to respond preferentially to the chuck part of the call. The females of a related species, *Physalaemus coloradorum*, prefer male calls with the added chuck sound over ones that are just a whine, even though males of their own species do not add the chuck to their call. This preference by the female can be determined by placing her in the center of an acoustic chamber and playing the male calls through speakers on opposite walls of the chamber. When one speaker plays a whine without the chuck and the other a whine with the chuck, the female approaches the speaker playing the whine with the added chuck.

Females of both species of frog have a preference for calls with the added chuck sound, but only the males of one of those species has managed to exploit that preference. This could mean that *Physalaemus coloradorum* males will eventually adapt their calling pattern to exploit their females' preference. Certainly, were these males to use the chuck, they would be preferred as mates over ones that do not use it. It is likely that males of a species ancestral to *P. pustulosus* and *P. coloradorum* did not add chucks to their calls and only *P. pustulosus* males evolved the ability to stimulate the female's sensory system to the best advantage. In other words, the female's sensory system appears to have had a preexisting bias that has been exploited by *P. pustulosus* males (Ryan and Rand, 1999). Such exploitation of the female's preference may come about by learning and cultural transmission within groups or populations, or by genetic selection. It is usually assumed that the signals of the male frogs are determined solely by genetic selection, but, so far, no experiments have been designed to see whether learning is involved.

REMEMBERING SIGNALS

Guilford and Dawkins (1991) postulated that the ability to make memories may evolve and so may be important in the evolution of signaling. The receiver often has to remember which animal sent the signal, whether the signal had been sent previously, and in what context it had been sent. Therefore, different capacities for memory could affect signaling. But could genetic selection improve the capacity for processing and remembering a specific signal? As we saw from the example of the kitten exposed to stripes, experience can have profound effects on sensory perception. Experience also affects signal interpretation and the memory processes involved in communication. Recognition of these radical effects of experience and learning leads us to believe that any hypothesis which considers only genetic selection of these abilities is likely to be too simplistic. We can speak of the evolution of the structure of the eye, for example, and consider how it changed over evolutionary time from one species to the next. But it is problematic to apply the concept of genetic evolution to the changes that might have taken place in the processing of visual memory, interpretation, and attention, since these are so malleable by experience. The same applies to other forms of sensory perception.

Of course, as the brain evolved, its capacity to process information and to store memories increased overall, but even a very simple brain can process, detect, decode, and remember quite complex signals. A more highly evolved brain may process and remember a greater number and range of signals because of its increased capacity, but it might not be able to process and remember any single signal better than a simple brain. This is another reason why we think that talking about genetic selection for an increased ability to process and memorize a single type of signal is problematic.

Discussions of genetic selection might better be confined to tangible elements of the sensory receptors that are used to detect the signal and perform some of the initial aspects of discriminating the signal from the background, and not be applied to memory processes. In the case of sensory receptors, single genes may influence a single factor, such as the presence of a particular visual pigment (so affecting color vision, which we discuss next). In such cases, it is not so difficult to make a link between genes and function. In vertebrates, at least, the more complex processes of decoding the signal and remembering that go on at higher levels of cognition are certainly not dependent on a single gene. Since these processes are heavily influenced by learning and experience, it would be an oversimplification to say that they are determined by genes in any unitary way.

Making memories depends on the expression of genes (for example, the "early" genes, known as c-fos and c-jun), changes in the connections between nerve cells, and changes in chemical and electrical transmission between nerve cells (Rose, 1992), but the making of any specific memory is not dependent on any single genetic characteristic. It is possible to block certain key processes in nerve cells and so affect an animal's ability to form memories. This can be done by injecting the animal with certain drugs that interfere with the specific cellular process being studied or by using genetic technology to target certain genes that make particular enzymes and so prevent them from being expressed. In fact, it is possible to "knock out" genes in specific regions of the brain, and the type of memory impaired by doing so can be determined. For example, mice with a genetic mutation that prevents formation of a particular enzyme (alpha-calcium-calmodulin kinase II) in the part of the brain known as the hippocampus have impaired spatial ability (Silva et al., 1992; Mayford et al., 1996). This enzyme, present in nerve cells, is essential for the electrical changes that occur in the hippocampus when spatial memories are formed. Manipulating the gene that enables the cells to make this enzyme has an effect on spatial memory. This result shows that genes are involved in memory formation and some of them have important roles. But although the mice may appear to have a rather specific form of memory loss when they are tested on one or two tasks in the laboratory, this is most unlikely to be the case if they were in their natural environment. An inability to remember spatial locations or use multiple spatial cues would affect a wide range of abilities essential for survival in the natural environment. Laboratory tests now use sophisticated molecular genetic techniques, but at the behavioral level the same tests may be often very basic. The methodology is therefore insufficient to prove that it is possible to genetically select animals that will have specialized abilities to make specific memories, such as memories that would be used in a particular form of species-specific communication.

When a memory is formed as a result of a learning experience, a cascade of cellular changes takes place (Rose, 1992). The activation of genes is part of this cascade, but the specificity of the cellular events and the memory itself have nothing to do with a single gene, or even a subset of genes, that are specifically related to forming that type of memory alone. Furthermore, experience and even the forming of memories itself affect the subsequent activation of genes. There are certainly genetic mutations that have an effect on learning and memory, but these are very nonspecific in their effects and so do not add empirical support to the hypothesis of Guilford and Dawkins about the selection of genes for making memories of specific signals. Perhaps, specific genes for specific memories will be found to exist in some forms of communication in invertebrates, but this is unlikely to happen in communication in vertebrates for the reasons we have outlined. But of course genetic selection may affect very broad capacities to learn and remember.

EYES AND EVOLUTION

There are also broad evolutionary contributions to the receiving of signals. Let us consider specializations of the eye in a few species of vertebrates. The eye of the frog is specialized to detect certain stimuli: there are cells in the retina that respond specifically to small spots, each about the size of a fly, as long as these spots are, or have been, moving. The retinal cells are called "bug detectors" (see the summary in McFarland, 1985). They have an obvious role in the feeding behavior of frogs and they may also be important in signaling behavior. It is as if the eye of the frog is a filter that allows the frog to attend to certain stimuli in preference to others. The same filter could be used for prey catching and signaling. Hence visual signals used by frogs would be attended to more actively if they involved the movement of small stimuli. In fact, two species of frog (*Staurois parvus* of Brunei and *Taudactylus eugellenis* of Australia) have been observed to signal during courtship by holding up an opened front hand, or foot, and waving it. Each of the frog's digits with their rounded ends would make a spot-like image on the receiver's retina and the waving would provide movement. This visual stimulus is very likely to stimulate the "bug detectors" in the retina. The visual signal has been matched to the perceptual capabilities of the frog, just as the vocalizations of the male túngara frog have been matched to the females' auditory system.

The retina of a bird's eye contains oil droplets of different colors located next to the cells that respond to stimulation by light, the photoreceptors. The oil droplets act as a kind of filter allowing the bird to attend more to some colored stimuli than to others. Exactly which color will be more attractive depends to some extent on the color, or colors, of the oil droplets a species has and also the visual pigments present in the photoreceptors. Chicks of domestic fowl *(Gallus gallus)* have pink oil droplets and they prefer to peck at red and yellow food grains. In addition to the filter in the retina, other processes in the brain may be involved in determining the red and yellow preference, but the oil droplets are thought to play a role. The preference for pecking at small red and yellow objects might have evolved because most of the grains that chickens eat in the wild are red to yellow in color. Once this color preference had evolved, it could have been applied to signaling behavior. Later in life, adult chickens develop red combs that signal their sex, state of health, and hormonal status. A preference for "seeing red" would enhance the signaling capacity of the comb. Thus the specialization of sensory perception, which might have evolved first for feeding, could be exploited for sexual and aggressive displays.

For further examples of the relationship between visual perception and visual signaling, let us consider color vision in more detail. An animal's ability to see color depends on the presence of color pigments in the receptor cells of the retina, and the presence of these is determined by genes. Humans have three such pigments (red, green, and blue) and they allow us to see the wavelengths of light spanning from red to violet. Because of these three pigments we are said to have trichromatic vision. Many other species of mammals have trichromatic vision also, but there are some that have only two color pigments and they are called dichromates. Interestingly, the marmoset *(Callithrix jacchus)*, the tamarin *(Saguinus fuscicollis)*, and the squirrel monkey *(Saimiri sciureus)*, all South American monkeys (called platyrrhine monkeys), are special cases in which all the males are dichromates together with some of the females, while the rest of the females are trichromates (see Jacobs, 1993). The reason for this sex difference in color vision is that some of the genes determining the pigments are carried on the X chromosome, the same chromosome that also determines an individual's sex.

The trichromatic females can see a greater range of colors than either the males or the dichromatic females, and consequently they probably have a better chance of finding ripe fruit in the dappled and changing light of the rainforest. But if trichromatic color vision is an advantage in finding fruit, why has it not conferred such a selective advantage on the trichromates that they have completely replaced the dichromates? Why have the dichromates not disappeared from existing populations of platyrrhine monkeys? It is possible that this evolutionary process is still in progress and that eventually the dichromates will be replaced by trichromates, but it is perhaps more likely that being a dichromate provides an individual with some other advantage that a trichromate lacks. Dichromates may be able to penetrate certain forms of camouflage and so detect prey that trichromates cannot. They may also be able to detect movement through foliage better than trichromates can. These abilities may be useful for finding foods other than ripe, colorful fruits, such as insects and nuts, which these monkeys also eat. Thus a mixed population of dichromates and trichromates would have a combined searching strategy superior to that of a single population of trichromates, and since these monkeys alert each other to the food they find, the combined knowledge would be shared.

The dichromatic and trichromatic forms of color vision may also confer different advantages in detecting different kinds of signaling. Marmosets, for example, use their tails as well as their faces in visual signaling. Their long tails have dark and light stripes that may be seen easily against a dappled background by dichromates, whereas the face has yellowish skin that changes hue in different states of arousal or sexual condition. This color change should be seen more clearly by trichromates. Thus groups of marmosets may consist of two types of individuals who pay different amounts of attention to different signals. This idea has yet to be tested.

Color vision is present in a large number of species. Most species of birds can see color better than we can, and they make full use of their color vision in displays using feathers in a rich variety of colors. Many avian species have four visual pigments in the retina: they are tetrachromates. It is known that several species of birds (pigeons, starlings, and zebra finches, for example) can see ultraviolet light—they can see shorter wavelengths of light than humans can. Indeed, it is likely that perception of ultraviolet light is widespread in birds, and Andrew Bennett and his colleagues have recently shown (1997) that the ultraviolet colors in the plumage of starlings and zebra finches are used in mating displays.

The only reptiles that we know to have been tested for color vision are two species of turtle, and they both have excellent color vision. It is more than likely that other reptiles can see color also, and we have already noted the use of color changes in displays by such reptiles as chameleon lizards. In fact, color vision evolved much earlier than reptiles, as a visit to a tropical coral reef makes eminently clear: there the fish are brightly colored and they use these colors in their displays. Bees also have color vision. Examination of those species that have color vision and those that do not has led researchers to conclude that color vision evolved separately several times over in different branches of evolution (Neumeyer, 1990). These separate appearances testify to the selective advantage that color vision confers on a species, although of course it is only an advantage in environments where color can be discriminated.

As we have already discussed, many rainforest birds are brightly colored and they use these colors to signal. The scarlet macaw *(Ara macao)* of the South American rainforest and the various birds-of-paradise that inhabit the rainforests of New Guinea, with their spectacular plumage, are the most striking examples of vibrant color in birds. In contrast to the wide variety of colors of the forest-dwelling birds, the colors of seabirds are more uniform, mainly black or brown and white. The reason is that the sea is a much more uniform environment than a forest and it is also very glary. Color is not easily distinguished against the glare of the sea or sky, and the ability to see color would not be highly advantageous in this environment. Seabirds may, however, find color a useful means of signaling at close range and where the amount of reflection is low. An excellent example is the yellow beak of the herring gull with its bright red spot, at which the gull chick pecks when the adult returns to the nest with a crop full of fish. The peck by the chick triggers the adult to regurgitate the fish and feed the chick.

Color vision is not useful to nocturnal species, so it was lost in nocturnal species. The earliest primates, the prosimians, are nocturnal and they have either very limited color vision or are completely color-blind, even though they evolved from species that, it appears, were able to see color. The primates that evolved later in evolutionary time may have "rediscovered" the color vision that their ancestors had lost, and they did so when they became diurnal and could benefit from having color vision (Mollon, 1990; Neumeyer, 1990). Alternatively, it could be argued that the extinct ancestor of both the prosimians and the higher primates was not, in fact, color-blind and that the loss of color vision in present-day prosimians is a more recent development.

Since the color vision of the diurnal primates of the Old World is trichromatic, it is thought to have evolved together with a food preference for colored fruits. Once it had evolved, color vision could be used for displays in primates. The displays of many diurnal primates depend on colors, whereas those of the nocturnal ones do not. The prosimians are mostly dull in color or have black and white stripes, as does the ring-tailed lemur *(Lemur catta)* on its tail. Among the later-evolving, diurnal species, the mandrill *(Mandrillus sphinx)* is the most striking exploiter of color, with a red and white striped snout and pink to blue skin on and around the genital area. Other diurnal primates, such as baboons and some macaque monkeys, have red, hairless skin on the buttocks that they present to other members of their troop as an appeasement display. The buttocks area of the female becomes redder when she is in estrus. This visual display, together with a change in the odor that she releases as a vaginal secretion, attracts the male and stimulates sexual behavior.

THE EVOLUTION OF VOCAL COMMUNICATION

So far, we have presented examples of evolutionary processes that may have been involved in visual displays, but apart from the discussion of the calls of the túngara frog, we have made only passing reference to the evolution of vocal communication and its relationship to auditory perception. We must emphasize that vocal signals are usually accompanied by visual signals, which are sometimes quite elaborate and are sometimes the postures that animals must adopt in order to produce the vocalization. In evolutionary terms, these two aspects of signaling are intimately linked. Unfortunately, researchers studying communication tend to concentrate on only one aspect of the signal pattern (usually either visual or vocal), and this inattention to other aspects limits our understanding of the entire signaling "package." This is particularly so in the study of vocal communication—the vocal signals have been described in great detail, but very little attention has been paid to the accompanying visual signals. We suggest two reasons for this. The first reason is related to the type of technology available for studying communication in the past: whereas it was relatively easy to take high-quality sound equipment into the field to record the vocalizations of animals, video records of animal postures in the field were, until recently, difficult to obtain because of cumbersome recording equipment and often impossible to obtain because researchers were unable to move the equipment to a place where they had direct sight of the subject.

The other reason for the focus on vocalizations has been the drive to understand the vocal communication of animals, particularly primates, in order to understand the evolution of human language. This focus on language has led many researchers to ignore anything other than the sounds made. If there has been any broader perspective than this, it has been to consider the gestures that primates make with their hands, and on the basis of such studies some researchers (e.g., Hewes, 1973) have considered the possibility that human language evolved from the gestures of primates. Communication by voice and communication by hands are human forms of communication. Little attention, however, has been paid to communication in primates by eye movements, body postures, odors, breathing patterns, or ear movements, any of which—alone or in combination—could have laid a basis for the evolution of human language.

It is not our aim to cover the evolution of human language here, but we remind the reader of the apes taught to use sign and symbolic language to communicate with humans and, in particular, of Kanzi's ability to understand the syntax of English. There are other characteristics of animals' ability to process sounds that are shared with humans and considered to be essential for language. These include the ability to control vocalizations and to use them referentially and the ability to perceive sounds categorically, as we discuss next.

Categorical perception is the ability to perceive sounds in categories that are discrete from one another, even though the variation in sound is actually continuous. The receiver picks parcels of auditory information out of this stream of variation and puts them into categories. Consider this example: Humans can hear the difference between "da" and "ta" sounds without any difficulty. If we use a computer to generate a range of sounds from "da" to "ta" so that there is a continuous gradation from one to the other and then play this range back to human subjects, they will say that they heard a collection of "das" and "tas" but not a continuum. Our perception creates a boundary between the two sounds that makes us believe there is a far more abrupt transition from "da" to "ta" than there actually is. We categorize the sounds, and this is said to be an important ability for understanding speech sounds. Not surprisingly, it was long thought that the ability to categorize sounds was uniquely human. We now know that that is not so. Brad May, David Moody, and William Stebbins (1989) have shown that Japanese macaque monkeys *(Macaca fuscata)* have categorical perception. The researchers selected two calls that the monkeys make when they want to establish contact with each other, one with a peak in frequency (pitch) early in the call and the other with a peak later in the call. From these they synthesized a range of calls, grading one into the other, and tested the monkeys with them to see whether they could distinguish one call from the other. The researchers found that although the monkeys were presented with a continuous gradation of calls, they perceived them as falling into two distinct categories, showing that the monkeys have categorical perception.

Categorical perception has also been demonstrated in chinchillas, which were tested with speech sounds; moreover, the boundary between one category and another found in chinchillas was the same as that in humans. Even Japanese quail categorize speech sounds, and a range of avian and primate species hear their own species calls categorically. There is now no question that this aspect of perception is shared by animals and humans (Kuhl, 1988).

The same is true of another aspect of vocal processing once thought to be unique to humans—lateralization, the processing of speech sounds and the production of speech by the left, not the right, hemisphere of the brain. For many years it had been thought that the specialization of the left hemisphere for speech and language processing was a characteristic unique to humans and a mark of our superiority to all other species. As John Bradshaw and Lesley Rogers (1993) have pointed out, there is now conclusive evidence that many species, including monkeys, mice, birds, and frogs, process or produce the vocalizations of their own species using only the left side of the brain. This attribute of the brain also evolved very early, contrary to beliefs once held.

Despite these similarities in auditory processing across many different species, there are, of course, differences between species in auditory perception and vocal production. These differences are determined by auditory experience, learning, and evolutionary processes. We will discuss some of these evolutionary differences briefly. We have seen already that bats can hear sounds that we do not and that they use these ultrasounds both to communicate and to signal. As in the case of vision, the hearing ranges of species vary and each species has evolved to match the transmission properties of the environment in which it lives.

A question often asked about the evolution of birds is, why have their songs become so complex? We discussed earlier the experiments in which John Krebs played back songs of European great tits in the field and found that the larger the song repertoire he played through the loud-speaker the more effectively birds were kept out of the area surrounding the speaker. The more complex the song, the better it is at advertising that the bird holds a territory. This is a plausible reason why more complex songs evolved. There is also some evidence that females prefer to mate with males with more complex songs, and this too would provide a reason for song complexity to evolve. It also provides a reason why the learning required to perform complex songs takes place.

Dialects of birdsong, regional variations among the members of one species, have been a source of speculation in regard to the evolution of song, but, so far, evidence is lacking that there is any link between song dialects and genetic differences. We will avoid further speculation on this topic and simply refer the reader to the book on birdsong by Clive Catchpole and Peter Slater (1995).

CONCLUSION

The evolution of communication is a topic that has attracted the attention of ethologists and anthropologists. There has been much speculation and some testable hypotheses. But at present, it is not a field in which we can establish many facts. This is partly due to the intangibility of evolutionary processes and the consequent difficulties they present for direct experimentation. We cannot go back in time to sample the potential effects of the genes of extinct species and, more particularly, we cannot observe the behavior of extinct species. Behavior does not leave a fossil record, but we can attempt to piece together the jigsaw of the evolution of communication by observing the signals and displays of existing species and design experiments to test hypotheses about these species. There are a multitude of exciting experiments lying ahead in this area of the study of communication, but we urge caution when researchers consider hypotheses that tie complex behavior and brain functions to unitary genetic causes, no matter how neat such links may appear to be.

Chapter Eight

HUMAN-ANIMAL CONTACTS

Human-animal communication occurs in many different contexts and takes a variety of forms. Without question, our attitude toward animals plays a significant role in the way we communicate with them, in the freedom we accord them, and in the manner in which we are willing to learn about their worlds and lives. Now, more than ever, we need to learn more about animals and more about our attitudes to animals. Our attitudes will ultimately decide how many species will have a future. Many human–animal encounters are not favorable for animals. Indeed, some contact with animals exists solely for the purpose of mass-producing them for consumption.

There is another side, however, the only one in which communication really plays a role, and that is contact between humans and animals as partners in work or as companions. These relationships can become very significant for us and possibly also for the animal. The dog, in particular, has been of great importance to humans for at least 12,000 years (Serpell, 1995). Animals bond with humans and many humans bond with their pets. Two to three thousand years ago, such a bond might have lasted for the best part of human life. In the days of the Roman Empire the human lifespan was about 24 years. Today, of course, humans live so much longer that pet owners tend to have serial relationships with dogs and cats. Domestication extended to goats and sheep about 9,000 years ago, followed by cattle and pigs and, in some areas, the horse (about 5,000 years ago).

The sheer passage of time makes us wonder how far domesticated species have changed as a result of becoming captives of human society and how this relationship might have affected their patterns of communication. The amount of change is likely to differ from species to species, partly because human contact varies among domesticated species and partly because, as Jonica Newby (1997) pointed out, most domesticated animals have never attained the status of closeness that dogs and cats have. Human-animal relationships have not remained static through the ages, yet their history remains largely unwritten. There are some notable exceptions, for instance the portraits of changing perspectives presented in works published by James Serpell (1995, 1996) and by Aubrey Manning and James Serpell (1994).

MYTHOLOGY AND FAIRY TALES

We begin with an unusual perspective on the human-animal relationship—namely, with fairy tales and popular mythology. Why raise them in a book on animal communication? First, fairy tales and myths about animals abound in all cultures and we might well read from them what a society desires or fears. In *Biophilia* (1984), for instance, Edward O. Wilson writes at length about the serpent as a mythical being that is feared in practice but held in awe in cultures around the globe. Yet other species are "poetic," as Wilson called them, because they arouse our curiosity. Second, in fairy tales, musicals, and fables, humans have always expressed their desire, if not their yearning, to understand what animals say and mean. Dr. Dolittle, for instance, thinks of animal communication as language that we have simply failed to learn but that we could learn. Third, animal communication is firmly embedded in the customs, folklore, and writings of many cultures. Finally, how fairy tales and mythology deal with animals—and herein lies our interest—may well mold the attitudes of young humans to animals and influence the kind of relationship with animals they will develop.

In contrast to the study of animal communication, which is fraught with difficulties in attributing reasonable explanations to acts of animal signaling, in the wonderful world of fairy tales stories unfold effortlessly and are clearly understandable. Animals of course feature in most fairy tales, but not always in the role of communicators. There are some stories, however, that focus our attention on animal communication. We cannot do more here than give just one example from a very rich field.

One of the most interesting stories we know in which human and animal worlds overlap is a fairy tale by Wilhelm Hauff called "Mutabor," written in the early nineteenth century. Hauff's tales are set in the era of Haroun-al-Raschid, the legendary ruler of Baghdad in the late eighth and early ninth centuries. We relate this story in some detail because it illustrates the assumptions of it makes about animals when speaking of animal communication.

In Hauff's book, a traveling group of businessmen tell each other stories as they slowly make their way on camel back through the desert. The story "Mutabor" is one of the most famous. In it, an evil magician wishes to get the sultan out of the way and, via a trader, offers the sultan a powder in a box with a Latin inscription. The inscription says that anyone sniffing this powder will turn into the animal he sees when turning toward Mecca and speaking the word "Mutabor." The sultan and his adviser promptly try this and turn into storks, since there are some storks in sight. Both men can now understand what the storks are saying. The inscription also says that one condition for their return to human form is that they must never laugh while they are in animal form. If they do, they will forget the word "Mutabor" and remain animals forever. However, on understanding what the storks are saying, both men are promptly very amused by a young female stork who is practicing a dance performance. They laugh heartily at what they perceive to be a clumsy attempt at dancing. They are now caught in stork form and find it difficult to adjust, particularly to the food, although they like their new ability to fly.

Eventually, the story leads us to a sad owl, shedding tears in a distant palace. She is actually a princess who was turned into an owl when she refused the hand of the evil magician's son. She can only be freed if someone proposes marriage to her while she is still an owl. The sultan/stork, a bachelor for many years, offers his hand in marriage, and she, still an owl, leads him and his adviser to the place where the magician always meets his supporters. There they hear the word "Mutabor" and can now change back into human form. The owl is transformed into a beautiful young girl and the sultan returns to his rightful place in society as a just and celebrated man.

There are several aspects of this story worth noting. First, natural curiosity drove the sultan and his adviser to sniff the powder despite the risks involved. We can assume that they were interested in knowing what animals had to say to each other. Second, they thoroughly enjoyed understanding the society of the stork. Third, we can assume that "stork language" translates into that of another animal species (here the owl), and that the sultan is a better man as a result of his experiences as an animal.

He has certainly been enriched, and the wife he could not find in human form he did find when he was an animal. On the other hand, capturing someone in animal form is obviously meant to be a punishment. The owl/girl cried because of the loneliness and the night she had to endure. The pivotal point of the story is how and when the owl and the storks would rediscover the magic word that would return them to human form. It was also made clear that the characters retained their identities as sultan and adviser, even as storks. Only the bodies had changed, not the minds.

One of the most telling parts of the story, and this is why we have related it here in detail, is that the evil magician predicted very accurately that both the sultan and his adviser would laugh once they were turned into animals. And of course the reader is equally caught up in the plot. Would we think that it is easy not to laugh? Or would we think, like the magician, that animal behavior is ridiculous or amusing and therefore that it would inevitably make us laugh? The story works only if it is assumed that laughter is inevitable.

The story also portrays the sultan and the adviser as acting in some ways like ethologists. Neither man actually enters the society of storks; they both just eavesdrop on their conversation. But, interestingly, by changing form they become "bilingual." They can still understand human language but they also understand the animals. By extrapolation this might also mean that animals can understand us even though we cannot understand them.

Respect for animals is probably a precondition for good communication with animals. In some human cultures respect for (some) animals is inbuilt as, for instance, in the Hindu religion, which considers cows sacred. In Australian Aboriginal cultures the conception of a new child is thought to be linked to an animal or a tree or a rock in situ. It is the presence of a lizard during conception that will give the child a lizard spirit. No doubt, such spiritual links can significantly alter the perception of animals by people holding beliefs of this kind.

HISTORIES OF HUMAN-ANIMAL RELATIONSHIPS
There are anecdotal stories and myths about animals that are alleged to have reared humans. Occasionally, we hear of so-called feral children

who are supposed to have been reared by wild animals. If these children ever existed, they presumably learned to communicate with their foster families. These stories range from pure fiction to supposedly "real" cases. There is, for instance, the myth of Romulus and Remus, the founders of Rome, who were allegedly nourished by a shewolf. Then there is the story of a boy, Tarzan, who was described as growing up with apes. Other famous stories of feral children include that of Kaspar Hauser, that of the Wild Boy of Aveyron and, more recently, that of the Indian children Kamala and Amala, said to have been raised by a wolf (Maclean, 1977). There was also a boy reared by deer, who is said to have used his hands to imitate the movement of ears for communicative purposes. Douglas Candland's book on feral children (1993) provides fascinating examples.

Unfortunately, in modern cases in which children were thought to have been raised by animals, the reason for that assumption was that the human child or juvenile showed no mastery of human speech. The public interest these cases created was focused on documenting the development of the human capacity for speech rather than the communication and actual experiences of the person growing up in isolation from humans. But we may not have lost a golden opportunity. Steven Pinker (1994) from the Massachusetts Institute of Technology is right in suggesting that most of the stories are myths. In reality, these children were probably locked away in rooms by humans who deprived them of speech and communication, not reared by animals. (We mentioned the documented case of Genie in Chapter 6.) These cases, therefore, tell us little about animal-human contacts and communication.

Animal-human attitudes and communication stem from the history of specific animal relationships with human societies. Domestication is the most obvious case. Domestication has been defined by Juliet Clutton-Brock (1994) as a process by which an animal is bred in captivity for purposes of subsistence or profit, and lives in a human community that maintains complete control over its breeding, territory, and food supply. Clutton-Brock and other researchers in the field distinguish "domestication" from "taming," and this is a useful distinction in that taming may involve companionship. Taming may involve both humans and animals in work or leisure but may well exclude the final elements of domestication—targeting animals for slaughter. In both processes, the domestic or tamed animal is rightly regarded as a cultural artifact of human society. This is a very recent phenomenon in natural history.

In social histories, the domestication of animals has been treated as a watershed in human progress. Tim Ingold (1994) demonstrates that in many accounts the domestication of animals is perceived as signaling nothing less than the beginnings of "civilisedness." Perceptions of human progress are thus intrinsically tied to the subjugation of animals. Ingold argues that, from the nineteenth century until quite recently, only those who produced their own food were regarded as fully human. Hunting and gathering, or foraging, was considered not much better a way of life than the way of life of an animal, because hunting and gathering is precisely what animals do. The superiority and inferiority of human and animal societies could therefore be decided on methods of gathering food. Subsistence was inferior and surplus superior.

However, our views of hunter-gatherers have changed markedly in the last two to three decades, because more objective studies have revealed that hunter-gatherer societies were not "primitive." Nor are (or were) they wretched people at the point of starvation and lawlessness, as Charles Darwin thought. Indeed, some influential papers of the early 1970s showed that tribal societies were often affluent societies, without disease or immediate survival pressures. Moreover, the hunter-gatherers' knowledge of the behavior of animals, their sounds and their habits, was intimate. Only in this way could they hunt them successfully.

Domestication also required not only detailed knowledge of the species but a commitment, and often also resulted in an attachment. Pets are one example of such attachment, but people may even bond closely with working animals. For instance, cormorants are still used in some southeast Asian countries, chiefly Indonesia and Japan, to help their owners catch fish. Monkeys are used to pick coconuts, dogs for hunting game and foxes, and pigeons for relaying messages. In Mongolia to this day, deer are the most cherished (and often the only) possession of humans, and the people's relationship to the deer is embedded in mythology to the point that they associate their deer with their gods. Very often these ancient working relationships have been positive one-to-one relationships between humans and animals. The owners not only worked with the animals but slept with them. They shared food and their family life with them, often even allowing the animals to be unrestrained.

To get animals to do our work, there must be at least a degree of training and communication. Why else would animals, especially those that are much larger and stronger than humans, obey the whims of their owner or caretaker? In the last century in Thailand, elephants were taken into battle with neighboring countries, and today some elephants still work in the timber industry transporting logs. Mainly in Thailand, but also in Malaysia and India, there are still training schools for elephants. Each trainer spends a good deal of time with his elephant, and each elephant is teamed up with an older and more experienced elephant. Training may take up to 2 years. In that time the elephants learn to respond to verbal commands and requests. It is possible to achieve a level of cooperation that requires no threats of punishment and not even food rewards. In the forests of southern and southeast Asia, rider and elephant are often on their own. Trainer and trainee learn to trust each other through experience, consistency, and, not least, effective communication. Such communication cannot go just one way, from trainer to trainee. Some of it must also go the other way. The trainer must understand the ways of an elephant and must be able to read the elephant's signals appropriately. A trainer who does not understand when an elephant expresses anger or resentment may have a very short life.

The water buffalo plows the fields in Asia, still linked with its human master by the plow. Most of the peoples in the Middle East rely on the camel for personal transport and the transport of goods; they tend to care for them very well because ultimately their own lives are linked with those of their animals.

We do not want to romanticize relationships with animals that are built on their removal from a life of freedom with their own kind and that are, at times, subject to outright exploitation. What needs to be said, however, is that in these intimate forms of work relationships, the level of communication with the animal is often as good as or even better than that between pet and pet owner. Mutual reliance can occur only with good communication.

WAR ON ANIMALS

The Industrial Revolution in Europe probably did more to change our thinking about the nonhuman environment than any other single set of events. Production could be driven to new heights, and industrialization was based on the ideas of specialization and overproduction— the manufacture of surplus for profit. These attitudes were transferred to the nonhuman environment. Taking from nature whatever was thought necessary for sustaining a never-satisfied desire turned our relationship with the natural environment into one of indifference and alienation. Hunters may well have admired the strength, shape, or intelligence of animals they pursued, but people's attitudes toward animals changed with the development of industries that raised animals on a mass scale for the purpose of consuming them. Knowledge about animals and their behavior was no longer considered relevant unless it affected production. Nor was respect for animals and their world at all necessary in this kind of relationship between humans and animals. Such fundamental changes in attitudes can be traced readily in the imagery of travelogues, movies, and popular accounts over the last 150 years. It is noticeable, as we found when we researched the imagery of orangutans in such source materials, that modern attitudes vacillated between fear and indifference, but rarely included respect (Kaplan and Rogers, 1995). The Industrial Revolution bequeathed a remarkable legacy. Not only do goods and services carry a price tag in human society, but the natural world does too. Every plot of land, every tree, every ecosystem, every animal has been assigned a price at one time or another in the twentieth century. And once nature was "priced" in this fashion, it has been difficult to maintain a balance between greed and sustainability. The extinction of species of both flora and fauna is now a daily event and the number of species lost if growing exponentially.

In the second half of the twentieth century, we have encountered additional ethical problems as genetic engineering pushed arguments about the rights of animals to new limits, as Colin Tudge (1993) pointed out a few years ago. Do animals have the right to remain untampered with genetically? "Designer" animals are bred to provide "spare parts" of living tissue for humans. The image of the mouse carrying an unfurred human-shaped ear on its back may be bizarre, but it symbolizes a new, and this time grotesquely visible, peak in animal exploitation. Cloned animals are now also a reality. Needless to say, historically these new activities represent the lowest point in human–animal relationships—and also the lowest point in human-animal communication.

Simultaneously, however, there have been strong counterforces, concerned with the ethical issues of raising animals for profit on the one hand and the conservation issues of wildlife on the other. Even mainstream thinking in Western societies had to admit that our management of the natural world has led to an impoverishment of our understanding of the natural world (Nelson, 1987; Kellert, 1994). Now there are conservation societies, wildlife protection societies, ethics committees, animal liberation societies, and a myriad other projects spawned by alarm at the treatment of nature and animals. The Great Ape Project, for instance, advocates the rights of apes as our closest evolutionary relatives. Animal protection societies and societies for the prevention of cruelty to animals have impressively large numbers of members and they are very numerous.

Yet for many species, the slide toward extinction continues. This is partly so because certain species offer "products" for which some people will pay high prices, such as the ivory of elephants, the skin and teeth of tigers, the horn of rhinoceroses, the live bodies of apes for pets, zoos, and circuses, the whale meat for speciality restaurants and many other species, such as birds, for our amusement. Other species, such as the orangutan, could be marked to vanish from this earth because of the space for agriculture, mining, forest timber, and even habitation that we humans take from their natural habitat. The national parks and wildlife reserves that have been steadily created throughout the twentieth century have often been isolated areas. They usually occupy less than 1 percent of the area within the political boundary of a nation, too small in the long run to sustain diversity and too small to sustain healthy populations. Many species, such as bald eagles, peregrine falcons, ospreys, and some owls, have been severely damaged by pesticides, and only the banning of DDT and other dramatic interventions brought some species back from the brink of extinction. Australia, like many other countries in the world, is at risk of losing almost all its owl species (in Australia, owls are all on the vulnerable or endangered list).

Only a few species have genuinely benefited from expanding human habitation, and these are mostly species that are not popular, such as invertebrates (especially cockroaches), rodents (mice and rats), and opossums and squirrels. Among bird species, there are the sparrows, the crows, and the pigeons. Many of these are treated as vermin. In cities, especially in industrialized countries, human tolerance for animals, including insects, in close proximity has often dramatically declined. Humans routinely buy household sprays and rodent poisons. Pesticide spraying is often higher in cities than in rural areas. In homes, gardens, streets, and public spaces, the human inhabitants have declared war on all the remnants of living things. The very same people may then keep pets. This seems only to be a contradiction. What it indicates is that in modern urban areas, in particular, humans expect to have total control over animals and to make decisions about what species can coexist with them at any time. Part of the history of human-animal relationships is the dismal story of the destruction of human-animal coexistence. Inevitably, such developments in human history have brought with them highly selective perceptions of animals and attitudes toward their welfare, let alone attitudes toward communicating with them.

POSITIVE BONDS AND THE BENEFITS OF ANIMALS

Despite the bleak picture of ecological crises that can be drawn at the beginning of the twenty-first century, there remain attempts to try to coexist with and to see value in animals beyond profit or other selfish uses. In laboratories, in research stations, and on some farms, there are attempts to provide animals with better living conditions. Some people have started to acknowledge that animals have preferences, interests, and needs beyond physical survival. Marian Dawkins (1993) argues for giving animals choices in the selection of their environment. Why not ask them, she proposed? Of course, doing this entails not only respect for animals, but also the realization that animals can tell us something—that they can effectively communicate with us.

Many people keep pets and here communication between human and animal may work relatively well because of the species selected as pets. First, we tend to choose species with communication systems that operate largely within our own range of perception. We may not hear as well as dogs or see as well as cats in the dark, and we do not have the same color perception as birds, but we can hear them, see them, touch them, and speak to them. And, second, when we do get close to our pets, we usually claim to understand them. Our pets train us as much as we are supposed to train them. We learn to respond to their wishes to leave the house. We seem to be perfectly aware when they want to be near us, want affection, attention, or simply their food. We can understand some of their signals and they understand ours.

Beyond humans' desire to share their private lives with pets, many industrial societies have now also designed programs in which animals are used for more benign purposes than in the past. Boris Levinson (1969) discovered the great advantages of companion animals in clinical psychology and medicine. Research has since been done showing that animals can reduce stress in humans, that companion animals can increase self-esteem, and, even more dramatically, that they can lower levels of accepted risk factors for cardiovascular disease (Blackshaw, 1996).

Interestingly, these "uses" of animals are often related to communication and the senses. This is a relatively new field. A recent study showed that dogs can identify matching human body scents 80 percent of the time. A dog's olfactory sensitivity, selectivity, and memory, as well as its capacity for odor pattern recognition, is used in criminal investigations and security operations. Ray Settle and his colleagues (1994) predict that these skills are unlikely to be challenged by any artificial sensor in the foreseeable future.

The literature today also refers to a "human–companion animal bond." There are now programs in place throughout the Western world that have placed the human-animal bond on a new footing. Pet Facilitated Psychotherapy is one such program. Better known are the Pets as Therapy programs and Seeing Eye Dogs for the Blind. There are also Hearing Dogs for the Deaf. A study by G. Guttman, M. Pedrovic, and M. Zemanek in 1985 found that children who have pets not only have greater self-esteem than those without pets but are also better in nonverbal communication. Lynette and Benjamin Hart and B. Bergin (1987) argue that people in wheelchairs who participate in any of the health programs with pets tend to smile more, are greeted more often, and engage in conversation to a much greater extent than wheelchaired people without pets. Pets are thus regarded as great facilitators in communication among humans, and there are clear benefits for humans in keeping pets, whether for services they perform (cats killing vermin or dogs protecting the home) or companionship they provide.

Relatively little has been written about the actual communication between animals and humans, or the quality of life that animals are afforded by humans. In an industrial society that overall appears anti-animal, it is often difficult for people to develop attitudes that give primacy to the interests of animals, let alone develop the willingness to communicate with animals—close and specific domestic bonds excepted. On many occasions, humans seeking contact with animals may not be aware that this is not welcomed by the animals and that not all animals feel privileged to be singled out for human attention. In today's world, most wild animals are afraid of humans. They have cause to be. For those of us who rehabilitate wildlife there is a further lesson, sometimes quite shocking, to be learned: Most of the time, those animals do not need or want us at all. The best service we can do the ones remaining in the wild is to leave them alone and let them remain in a habitat in which they can thrive, if we can still do that. Arnold Arluke (1994) describes these issues as the modern contradictions in the relationship between animals and humans, who shower some animals with affection while simultaneously maltreating and killing other animals. Ironically, at the very time in history when we have probably the most widespread association with pets, and loving or romantic bonds with some animals are at a new historical peak, countless species in the wild are slipping quietly into extinction.

CONCLUSION

Darwin, and other authors in the twentieth century, have bequeathed to us several substantial problems in our relationship with animals, by telling us that animals in some way or another are our evolutionary ancestors. This notion compelled many to fight hard against the idea of continuity with animals. At the same time the Darwinian theory of evolution has remained a plausible scientific explanation for the development of life on earth. Within that theory, however, there continued to be an emphasis on upholding the uniquenesses of human beings as the pinnacle of creation. This distinction between humans and other animals has begun to be broken down by studies showing that nonhumans have brain asymmetry, the ability to use tools, the capacity to solve problems, sensory perception, the ability to learn, and a host of other capacities that were previously considered restricted to humans.

The communication system is one of the chief systems considered to distinguish humans from animals. Controversy has raged throughout the twentieth century about the possibility that animals have a language-like system of communication, and about the possibility that animals can communicate effectively with humans in human language terms. Herbert Roitblat, Heidi Harley, and David Helweg (1993) rightly point out that little work in psychology has engendered as much emotional involvement and heated argument as research into animal "language."

Throughout this book we have referred to research that has put its energy into training dolphins, apes, and birds to acquire sufficient communication skills (either as vocalizations or as symbols or sign language) to communicate across the species divide. In this effort, researchers have tried to learn more about the possibility of consciousness in animals, their ability to make use of past events or ponder future events and choices. These training and communication efforts have shown extreme dedication on the part of individual humans. They have often involved a lifetime of work, and a gracious indulgence on the part of the trained animal, which, after all, was entirely deprived of any of its natural life alternatives and often also of same-species companionship. Together humans and animals have lived and grown to explore the possibilities of meaningful communication across human/animal borders and to answer perhaps some of the questions about the extent of similarities and differences between humans and some animals. Humans' interest in such work has many sources and probably many intellectual justifications. One of the most relevant is the desire to learn more about the evolution of linguistic competencies. We cannot study this from fossil records because communication, for all its vitality and importance, leaves no trace in fossils.

We have referred equally in this book to studies that have placed animals in close proximity to humans (the laboratory or even the home) and to those that have studied animal communication in the natural setting. Charles Snowdon (1993) has called ethologists "cross-species anthropologists." It is only in the natural environment that answers to a number of questions concerned with communication will be forthcoming. For instance, as Snowdon says, ethologists may do studies in the field designed to answer questions about the evolutionary precursors of various linguistic phenomena: What are the environmental conditions that might have led to symbolic communication? What are the circumstances that lead to syntactic structures? What developmental influences affect the acquisition of phonology, comprehension, or usage?

It needs to be asked whether an emphasis on vocal and hence linguistic development is adequate. As we have seen, communication systems are complex and may involve several senses at once, some of which the human observer is capable of studying only by developing technological aids for their detection. Equipped with the naked eye or ear and our sense of smell alone, we would never have discovered the diversity and complexity of animal communication that we now know about, and surely much remains to be discovered.

Researchers from very different fields and with very different agendas might well agree that the study of animal communication, and the consequent discovery of commonalities of some aspects of communication across species, raise the possibility of viewing human language as one of several alternative systems of communication. Never before in human history has there been such intense engagement with animals in a scientific manner to try to understand how they communicate with each other and how they may communicate with humans. Never before has there been such an urgent need to undertake such studies.

REFERENCES

INDEX

Adams, E. S., and Caldwell, R. L. 1990. Deceptive communication in asymmetric fights of the stomatopod crustacean *Gonadodactylus bredini*. *Animal Behaviour*, 39, 706–717.

Adret, P. 1993. Operant conditioning, song learning, and imprinting to taped song in the zebra finch. *Animal Behaviour*, 46, 149–159.

———. 1997. Discrimination of video images by zebra finches *(Taeniopygia guttata)*: direct evidence from song performance. *Journal of Comparative Psychology*, 111(2), 115–125.

Altringham, J. D. 1996. *Bats: Biology and Behaviour*. Oxford University Press, Oxford.

Andrew, R. J. 1956. Some remarks on behaviour in conflict situations, with special reference to *Emberiza* spp. *British Journal of Animal Behaviour*, 4, 41–45.

———. 1961. The displays given by passerines in courtship and reproductive fighting: a review. *Ibis*, 103, 549–579.

———. 1965. The origins of facial expressions. *Scientific American*, October, 88–94.

———. 1972. The information potentially available in mammal displays. In R. A. Hinde (ed.), *Non-verbal Communication*. Cambridge University Press, Cambridge.

Arluke, A. 1994. Managing emotions in an animal shelter. In A. Manning and J. Serpell (eds.), *Animals and Human Society: Changing Perspectives*, pp. 145–165. Routledge, London.

Baptista, L. F. 1975. Song dialects and demes in sedentary populations of White-crowned Sparrow *(Zonotrichia leucophrys nuttalli)*. *University of California Publications in Zoology*, 105, 1–52.

Barrett-Lennard, L. G., Ford, J. K. B., and Heise, K. A. 1996. The mixed blessing of echolocation: differences in sonar use by fish-eating and mammal-eating killer whales. *Animal Behaviour*, 51(3), 553–565.

BBC Worldwide. 1996. *Parrots: Look Who's Talking*. Video. Natural History Unit, London

Bennett, A. T. D., Cuthill, I. C., Partridge, J. C., and Lunau, K. 1997. Ultraviolet plumage colors predict mate preferences in starlings. *Proceedings of the National Academy of Sciences*, 94, 8618–8621.

Biben, M., and Bernhards, D. 1995. Vocal ontogeny of the squirrel monkey, *Saimiri boliviensis peruviensis*. In E. Zimmermen, J. D. Newman, and U. Jürgens (eds.),

Current Topics in Primate Vocal Communication, pp. 99–140. Plenum Press, New York.

Blackshaw, J. K. 1996 Developments in the study of human-animal relationships. *Applied Animal Behaviour Science*, 47 (special issue on human-animal relationships), 1–6.

Blaich, C., Steury, K. R., Pettengill, P., Mahoney, K. T., and Guha, A. 1996. Temporal patterns of contact call interactions in paired and unpaired domestic zebra finches *(Taeniopygia guttata)*. Paper delivered at the International Society for Comparative Psychology Meeting, Montreal.

Blakemore, C., and Cooper, G. F. 1970. Development of the brain depends on the visual environment. *Nature*, 228, 477–478.

Blest, A. D. 1957. The function of eyespot patterns in the lepidoptera. *Behaviour*, 11, 209–256.

Blumstein, D. T., and Armitage, K. B. 1997. Alarm calling in yellow-bellied marmots: I. The meaning of situationally variable alarm calls. *Animal Behaviour*, 53, 143–171.

Boinski, S. 1991. The coordination of spatial position: a field study of the vocal behaviour of adult female squirrel monkeys. *Animal Behaviour*, 41(1), 89–102.

Borgia, G. 1995. Complex male display and female choice in the spotted bowerbird: specialized functions for different bower decorations. *Animal Behaviour*, 49(5), 1291–1301.

Bradbury, J. W., and Vehrencamp, S. L. 1998. *Principles of Animal Communication*. Sinauer, Sutherland, Mass.

Bradshaw, J. L., and Rogers, L. J. 1993. *The Evolution of Lateral Asymmetries: Language, Tool Use, and Intellect*. Academic Press, San Diego.

Brindley, E. L. 1991. Response of European robins to playback of song: neighbour recognition and overlapping. *Animal Behaviour*, 41, 503–512.

Brown, C., Gomez, R., and Waser, P. M. 1995. Old World monkey vocalizations: adaptation to the local habitat? *Animal Behaviour*, 50(4), 945–961.

Bullock, T. H., and Heiligenberg, W. 1986. *Electroreception*. Wiley & Sons, New York.

Busnel, R.-G. 1977. Acoustic communication. In T. A. Sebeok (ed.), *How Animals Communicate*, pp. 233–252. Indiana University Press, Bloomington.

Byrne, R. 1995. *The Thinking Ape: The Evolutionary Origins of Intelligence*. Oxford University Press, Oxford.

Caldwell, M. C., and Caldwell, D. K. 1965. Individualized whistle contours in bottlenosed dolphins *(Tursiops truncatus)*. *Nature*, 207, 434–435.

Candland, D. K. 1993. *Feral Children and Clever Animals: Reflections on Human Nature*. Oxford University Press, New York.

Caro, T. M. 1995. Pursuit-deterrence revisited. *Trends in Ecology and Evolution*, 10, 500–503.

Catchpole, C. K., and Slater, P. J. B. 1995. *Bird Song: Biological Themes and Variations*. Cambridge University Press, Cambridge.

Catchpole, C. K., Dittami, J., and Leisler, B. 1984. Differential responses to male song repertoires in female song birds implanted with oestradiol. *Nature, 312,* 563–564.

Cheney, D. L., and Seyfarth, R. M. 1985. Vervet monkey alarm calls: manipulation through shared information? *Behaviour, 94,* 150–166.

———. 1990. *How Monkeys See the World: Inside the Mind of Another Species.* University of Chicago Press, Chicago.

Chevalier-Skolnikoff, S. 1973. Facial expression of emotion in nonhuman primates. In P. Ekman (ed.), *Darwin and Facial Expression,* pp. 11–90. Academic Press, New York.

Clark, L. and Mason, J. R. 1987. Olfactory discrimination of plant volatiles by the European starling. *Animal Behaviour, 35,* 227–235.

Clutton-Brock, J. 1994. The unnatural world: behavioural aspects of humans and animals in the process of domestication. In A. Manning and J. Serpell (eds.), *Animals and Human Society: Changing Perspectives,* pp. 23–35. Routledge, London.

Clutton-Brock, T. H. and Albon, S. D. 1979. The roaring of red deer and the evolution of honest advertisement. *Behaviour, 69,* 145–170.

Cohen, S. 1994. *The Intelligence of Dogs. Canine Consciousness and Capabilities.* Free Press/Macmillan, Toronto.

Crook, J. H. 1969. Function and ecological aspects of vocalisation in weaver birds. In R. A. Hinde (ed.), *Bird Vocalisations,* pp. 265–289. Cambridge University Press, Cambridge.

Cruickshank, A. J., Gautier, J.-P., and Chappuis, C. 1993. Vocal mimicry in wild African Grey Parrots *Psittacus erithacus. Ibis,* 135, 293–299.

Cullen, J. M. 1972. Some principles of animal communication. In R. A. Hinde (ed.), *Non-verbal Communication,* pp. 101–122. Cambridge University Press, Cambridge.

Curio, E., Ernst, U., and Vieth, W. 1978. The adaptive significance of avian mobbing. II. Cultural transmission of enemy recognition in blackbirds: Effectiveness and some constraints. *Zeitschrift für Tierpsychologie,* 48, 184–202.

Curtiss, S., Fromkin, V., Krashen, S., Rigler, D., and Rigler, M. 1974. The linguistic development of Genie. *Language,* 50, 528–554.

Davies, N. B., and Halliday, T. R. 1978. Deep croaks and fighting assessment in toads *Bufo bufo. Nature,* 274, 683–685.

Dawkins, M. S. 1986. *Unravelling Animal Behaviour.* Longman, Harlow, U.K. (2nd ed., 1995.)

———. 1993a. Are there general principles of signal design? *Philosophical Transactions of the Royal Society of London B,* 340, 251–255.

1993b. *Through Our Eyes Only? The Search for Animal Consciousness.* W. H. Freeman Spektrum, Oxford.

de Luce, J., and Wilder, H. T. (eds.). 1983. *Language in Primates: Perspectives and Implications.* Springer-Verlag, New York.

Dowsett-Lemaire, F. 1979. The imitative range of the song of the marsh warbler

Acrocephalus palustris, with special reference to imitations of African birds. *Ibis,* 121, 453–468.

Eibl-Eibesfeldt, I. 1972. Similarities and differences between cultures in expressive movements. In R. A. Hinde (ed.), *Non-verbal Communication,* pp. 297–314. Cambridge University Press, Cambridge.

Ekman, P. (ed.). 1974. *Darwin and Facial Expression.* Academic Press, New York.

Elowson, A. M., and Snowdon, C. T. 1994. Pygmy marmosets, *Cebuella pygmaea,* modify vocal structure in response to changed social environment. *Animal Behaviour,* 47, 1267–1277.

Endler, J. A. 1992. Signals, signal conditions, and the direction of evolution. *The American Naturalist,* 139, S125–S153.

———. 1993. The color of light in forests and its implications. *Ecological Monographs,* 63(1), 1–27.

Epple, G. 1968. Comparative studies on vocalization in marmoset monkeys *(Hapalidae). Folia Primatologica,* 8, 1–40.

———. 1975. The behavior of marmoset monkeys *(Callithricidae).* In L. A. Rosenblum (ed.), *Primate Behavior: Developments in Field and Laboratory Research,* pp. 195–239. Academic Press, New York.

Epple, G., Küderling, I., and Belcher, A. 1988. Some communicatory functions of scent marking in the cotton-top tamarin *(Saguinus oedipus oedipus). Journal of Chemical Ecology,* 14(2), 503–515.

Evans, C. S. 1997. Referential signals. *Perspectives in Ethology,* 12, 99–143.

Evans, C. S., and Marler, P. 1991. On the use of video images as social stimuli in birds: audience effects on alarm calling. *Animal Behaviour,* 41, 17–26.

———. 1994. Food calling and audience effects in male chickens, *Gallus gallus:* their relationships to food availability, courtship and social facilitation. *Animal Behaviour,* 47, 1159–1170.

Evans, C. S., Evans, L., and Marler, P. 1993. On the meaning of alarm calls: functional reference in an avian vocal system. *Animal Behaviour,* 46, 23–38.

Fadem, B. H. 1985. Chemical communication in gray short-tailed opossums *(Monodelphis domestica)* with comparisons to other marsupials and with reference to monotremes. In D. Duvall, D. Müller-Schwarze, and R. M. Silberstein (eds.), *Chemical Signals in Vertebrates,* vol. 4: *Ecology, Evolution, and Comparative Biology,* pp. 587–607. Plenum Press, New York.

Farabaugh, S. M., Linzenbold, A., and Dooling, R. J. 1994. Vocal plasticity in budgerigars *(Melopsittacus undulatus):* evidence for social factors in the learning of contact calls. *Journal of Comparative Psychology,* 108, 81–92.

Feduccia, A. 1996. *The Origin and Evolution of Birds.* Yale University Press, New Haven.

Fenton, M. B. 1994. Assessing signal variability and reliability: "to thine ownself be true." *Animal Behaviour,* 47(4), 757–764.

Fernald, A. 1992. Human maternal vocalizations to infants as biologically relevant signals: an evolutionary perspective. In J. H. Barkow, L. Cosmides, and J. Tooby (eds.), *The Adapted Mind: Evolutionary Psychology and the Generation of Culture,* pp. 391–428. Oxford University Press, New York.

Ficken, M. S., Hailman, E. D., and Hailman, J. P. 1994. The chick-a-dee call system of the Mexican chickadee. *The Condor,* 96, 70–82.

Fitzgibbon, C. D., and Fanshaw, J. H. 1988. Stotting in Thomson's gazelles: an honest signal of condition. *Behavioral Ecology and Sociobiology,* 23, 69–74.

Fouts, R. S., Fouts, D. H., and van Cantfort, T. E. 1989. The infant Loulis learns signs from cross-fostered chimpanzees. In R. A. Gardner, B. T. Gardner, and T. E. van Cantfort (eds.), *Teaching Sign Language to Chimpanzees,* pp. 280–292. State University of New York Press, Albany.

Fox, M. W. 1971. *Behaviour of Wolves, Dogs, and Related Canids.* Jonathan Cape, London.

Fridlund, A. J. 1994. *Human Facial Expression: An Evolutionary View.* Academic Press, San Diego.

Friedmann, H. 1955. The honey guides. *U.S. National Museum Bulletin,* 208, 1–279.

Frings, H., and Frings, M. 1956. Auditory and visual mechanisms in food-finding behaviour of the herring gull. *Wilson Bulletin,* 67, 155–170.

Gardner, R. A., Chiarelli, A. B., Gardner, B. T., and Plooij, F. X. (eds.). 1994. *The Ethological Roots of Culture.* Kluwer Academic Press, Norwell, Mass.

Gardner, R. A., Gardner, B. T., and van Cantfort, T. E. (eds.). 1989. *Teaching Sign Language to Chimpanzees.* State University of New York Press, Albany.

Gautier, J.-P., and Gautier, A. 1977. Communication in Old World monkeys. In T. A. Sebeok (ed.), *How Animals Communicate,* pp. 890–964. Indiana University Press, Bloomington.

Green, S. 1975. Dialects in Japanese monkeys: vocal learning and cultural transmission of locale-specific vocal behaviour. *Zeitschrift für Tierpsychologie,* 38, 304–314.

Greenewalt, C. 1968. *Bird song: Physiology and Acoustics.* Smithonian Institution Press, Washington, D.C.

Gregory, R., and Hopkins, P. 1974. Pupils of a talking parrot. *Nature,* 252, 637–638.

Griffin, D. R. 1958. *Listening in the Dark.* Yale University Press, New Haven.

Grubb, T. C. 1972. Smell and foraging in shearwaters and petrels. *Nature,* 237, 404–405.

Guilford, T., and Dawkins, M. S. 1991. Receiver psychology and the evolution of animal signals. *Animal Behaviour,* 42, 1–14.

Guttmann, G., Predovic, M., and Zemanek, M. 1985. The influence of pet ownership on non-verbal communication and social competence in children. In *Proceedings of the International Symposium on Human-Pet Relationships,* pp. 58–63. IEMT, Vienna.

Gyger, M., and Marler, P. 1988. Food calling in the domestic fowl, *Gallus gallus:* the role of external referents and deception. *Animal Behaviour,* 36, 358–365.

Hanggi, E. B., and Schusterman, R. J. 1994. Underwater acoustic displays and individual variation in male harbour seals, *Phoca vitulina. Animal Behaviour,* 48(6), 1275–1283.

Hare, J. F. 1998. Juvenile Richardson's ground squirrels, *Spermophilus richardsonii*, discriminate among individual alarm callers. *Animal Behaviour*, 55, 451–460.

Harriman, A. E., and Berger, R. H. 1986. Olfactory acuity in the common raven *(Corvus corax)*. *Physiology and Behavior*, 36, 257–262.

Hart, L. A., Hart, B., and Bergin, B. 1987. Socializing effects of service dogs for people with disabilities. *Anthrozoös*, 1, 41.

Hasselquist, D., Bensch, S., and von Schantz, T. 1996. Correlation between male song repertoire, extra-pair paternity, and offspring survival in the great reed warbler. *Nature*, 381, 229–232.

Hausberger, M., Jenkins, P. F., and Keene, J. 1991. Species-specificity and mimicry in bird song: are they paradoxes? A reevaluation of song mimicry in the European starling. *Behaviour*, 117, 53–81.

Hauser, M. D. 1988. How infant vervet monkeys learn to recognise starling alarm calls: the role of experience. *Behaviour*, 105, 187–201.

———. 1989. Ontogenetic changes in the comprehension and production of vervet monkey *(Cercopithecus aethiops)* vocalisations. *Journal of Comparative Psychology*, 103, 149–158.

———. 1993. Right hemisphere dominance for the production of facial expression in monkeys. *Science*, 261(23 July), 475–477.

———. 1996. *The Evolution of Communication*. MIT Press, Cambridge, Mass.

Hauser, M. D., and Andersson, K. 1994. Left hemisphere dominance for processing vocalizations in adult, but not infant, rhesus monkeys: Field experiments. *Proceedings of the National Academy of Sciences*, 91, 3946–3948.

Hauser, M. D., Teixidor, P., Fields, L., and Flaherty, R. 1993. Food-elicited calls in chimpanzees: effects of food quantity and divisibility. *Animal Behaviour*, 45(4), 817–819.

Herman, L. M., Pack, A. A., and Palmer, M-S. 1993. Representational and conceptual skills of dolphins. In H. L. Roitblat, L. M. Herman, and P. E. Nachtigall (eds.), *Language and Communication: Comparative Perspectives*, pp. 403–442. Lawrence Erlbaum, Hillsdale, N.J.

Hess, E. H. 1965. Attitude and pupil size. *Scientific American*, April, 46–54.

Hewes, G. W. 1973. Primate communication and the gestural origin of language. *Current Anthropology*, 14, 5–24.

Hinde, R. A. (ed.). 1969. *Bird Vocalizations: Their Relations to Current Problems in Biology and Psychology*. Cambridge University Press, Cambridge.

Hodun, A., Snowdon, C. T., and Soini, P. 1981. Subspecific variation in the long calls of the tamarin, *Saguinus fuscicollis. Zeitschrift für Tierpsychologie*, 57, 97–110.

Hudson, R., and Vodermayer, T. 1992. Spontaneous and odour-induced chin marking in domestic female rabbits. *Animal Behaviour*, 43(2), 329–336.

Hurst, J. L., Fang, J., and Barnard, C. J. 1993. The role of substrate odours in maintaining social tolerance between male house mice, *Mus musculus domesticus. Animal Behaviour*, 45(5), 997–1006.

Huxley, J. S. 1914. The courtship habits of the great crested grebe *(Podiceps cristatus)*; with an addition on the theory of sexual selection. *Proceedings of the Zoological Society of London,* 35, 491–562.

Ingold, T. 1994. From trust to domination: an alternative history of human-animal relations. In A. Manning and J. Serpell (eds.), *Animals and Human Society,* pp. 1–22. Routledge, London.

Jacobs, G. H. 1993. The distribution and nature of colour vision among the mammals. *Biological Reviews,* 68, 413–471.

Janik, V. M., and Slater, P. J. B. 1997. Vocal learning in mammals. *Advances in the Study of Behavior,* 26, 59–99.

Janik, V. M., Dehnhardt, G., and Todt, D. 1994. Signature whistle variations in a bottlenosed dolphin, *Tursiops truncatus. Behavioural Ecology and Sociobiology,* 35, 243–248.

Johnston, R. E., and Jernigan, P. 1994. Golden hamsters recognize individuals, not just individual scents. *Animal Behaviour,* 48(1), 129–136.

Johnston, R. E., Munver, R., and Tung, C. 1995. Scent counter marks: selective memory for the top scent by golden hamsters. *Animal Behaviour,* 49(6), 1435–1442.

Jolly, A. 1966. *Lemur Behavior.* University of Chicago Press, Chicago.

Kaplan, G. 1996. Selective learning and retention: song development and mimicry in the Australian magpie. *International Journal of Psychology. Abstracts of the Twenty-Sixth International Congress of Psychology, Montreal, Canada, 16–21 August 1996,* vol. 31, nos.3 and 4 ("Animal cognition and perception"), p. 233.

————. 1999. Song structure and function of mimicry in the Australian magpie *(Gymnorhina tibicen)* and the lyrebird *(Menura). Advances in Ethology,* vol. 34, ed. Shakunthala Sridhara, supplement b, p. 22.

Kaplan, G., and Rogers, L. J. 1995. Of human fear and indifference: the plight of the orang-utan. In R. D. Nader, B. Galdikas, L. Sheehan, and N. Rosen (eds.), *The Neglected Ape,* pp. 3–12. Plenum Press, New York.

————. 1996. Gaze direction and visual attention in orang-utans. Paper delivered at the Sixteenth Congress of the International Primatological Society, Madison, Wisc.

————. 1999. The *Orang-utans.* Allen and Unwin, Sydney. Also available in 2000 from Perseus Press, Boston.

Karakashian, S. J., Gyger, M., and Marler, P. 1988. Audience effects on alarm calling in chickens *(Gallus gallus). Journal of Comparative Psychology,* 102, 129–135.

Kellert, S. R. 1994. Attitudes, knowledge, and behaviour toward wildlife among the industrial superpowers—the United States, Japan, and Germany. In A. Manning and J. Serpell (eds.), *Animals and Human Society,* pp. 166–187. Routledge, London.

Kellogg, W. N. 1961. *Porpoises and Sonar.* University of Chicago Press, Chicago.

Kilner, R. M., Noble, D. G., and Davies, N. B. 1999. Signals of need in parent-offspring communication and their exploitation by the common cuckoo. *Nature,* 397, 667–672.

Kirn, J. R., Clower, R. P., Kroodsma, D. E., and De Voogd, T. J. 1989. Song-related brain regions in the red-winged blackbird are affected by sex and season but not repertoire size. *Journal of Neurobiology*, 20, 139–163.

Kluender, K. R., Diehl, R. L., and Killeen, P. R. 1987. Japanese quail can learn phonetic categories. *Science*, September, 1195–1197.

Krebs, J. R. 1977. Song and territory in the great tit *Parus major*. In B. Stonehouse and C. Perrins (eds.), *Evolutionary Ecology*, pp. 47–62. Macmillan, London.

Krebs, J. R., and Davies, N. B. 1993. *An Introduction to Behavioural Ecology*. Blackwell Science, Oxford.

Krebs, J. R., Ashcroft, R., and Webber, M. 1978. Song repertoires and territory defence in the great tit. *Nature*, 271, 539–542.

Kroodsma, D. E. 1978. Aspects of learning in the ontogeny of bird song. In G. M. Burghardt and M. Bekoff (eds.), *The Development of Behavior: Comparative and Evolutionary Aspects*, pp. 215–230. Garland, New York.

———. 1990. Using appropriate experimental designs for intended hypotheses in "song" playbacks, with examples of testing effects of song repertoire sizes. *Animal Behaviour*, 40, 1138–1150.

———. 1996. Ecology of passerine song development. In D. E. Kroodsma and E. H. Miller (eds.), *Ecology and Evolution of Acoustic Communication in Birds*, pp. 3–19. Cornell University Press, Ithaca and London,

Kroodsma, D. E., and Parker, L. D. 1977. Vocal virtuosity in the brown thrasher. *Auk*, 94, 783–784.

Kuhl, P. K. 1988. Auditory perception and the evolution of speech. *Human Evolution*, 3, 19–43.

Lambrechts, M. M., Clemmons, J. R., and Hailman, J. P. 1993. Wing quivering of black-capped chickadees with nestlings: invitation or appeasement? *Animal Behaviour*, 46(2), 397–399.

Leal, M., and Rodriguez, J. A. 1997. Signalling displays during predator-prey interactions in a Puerto Rican anole, *Anolis cristatellus*. *Animal Behaviour*, 54, 1147–1154.

Le Boeuf, B., and Peterson, R. S. 1969. Dialects in elephant seals. *Science*, 166, 1654–1656.

Lehrman, D. S. 1965. Interaction between hormonal and external environments in the regulation of the reproductive cycle of the ring dove. In F. A. Beach (ed.), *Sex and Behaviour*. Wiley and Sons, New York.

Lehtonen, L. 1983. The changing song patterns of the great tit, *Parus major*. *Ornis Fennica*, 60, 16–21.

Leslie, R. F. 1985. *Lorenzo the Magnificent: The Story of an Orphaned Blue Jay*. John Curley & Associates, South Yarmouth, Mass.

Levinson, B. M. 1969. *Pet-oriented Child Psychotherapy*. Charles C. Thomas, Springfield, Ill.

Lewin, R. 1991, Look who's talking now. Do apes hold the key to the origin of human language? Ape-language studies with one chimpanzee suggest they just might. *New Scientist*, April 27, 39–42.

Lieblich, A. K., Symmes, D., Newman, J. D., and Shapiro, M. 1980. Development of the isolation peep in laboratory-bred squirrel monkeys. *Animal Behaviour,* 28, 1–9.

Lilly, J. C. 1965. Vocal mimicry in *Tursiops:* ability to match numbers and durations of human vocal bursts. *Science,* 147, 300–301.

Lorenz, K. 1941. Vergleichende Bewegungsstudien an Anatiden. *Supplement of the Journal of Ornithology,* 89, 194–294.

———. 1965. *Evolution and Modification of Behavior.* University of Chicago Press, Chicago.

———. 1966. *King Solomon's Ring.* Methuen, London.

Macedonia, J. M., and Evans, C. S. 1993. Variation among mammalian alarm call systems and the problem of meaning in animal signals. *Ethology,* 93, 177–197.

Macedonia, J. M., Evans, C. S., and Losos, J. B. 1994. Male *Anolis* lizards discriminate video-recorded conspecific and heterospecific displays. *Animal Behaviour,* 47, 1220–1223.

MacKinnon, J. 1974. *In Search of the Red Ape.* William Collins, London.

Maclean, C. 1977. *The Wolf Children.* Allen Lane, London.

Malakoff, D. 1999. Following the scent of avian olfaction. *Science,* 286, 704–705.

Mann, N. I., and Slater, P. J. B. 1994. What causes young male zebra finches, *Taeniopygia guttata,* to choose their father as song tutor? *Animal Behaviour,* 47, 671–677.

Manning, A., and Serpell, J. 1994. *Animals and Human Society: Changing Perspectives.* Routledge, London.

Marler, P. 1955, Characteristics of some animal calls. *Nature,* 176, 6–8.

———. 1968. Aggregation and dispersal: two functions in primate communication. In P. C. Jay (ed.), *Primates: Studies in Adaptation and Variability,* pp. 420–438. Holt, Rinehart & Winston, New York.

———. 1970. Bird song and speech development: could there be parallels? *American Science,* 58, 669–673.

———. 1981. Bird song: the acquisition of a learned motor skill. *Trends in Neuroscience,* 4, 88–94.

1991. Differences in behavioural development in closely related species: birdsong. In P. Bateson (ed.), *The Development and Integration of Behaviour,* pp. 41–70. Cambridge University Press, Cambridge.

———. 1997. Three models of song learning: evidence from behaviour. *Journal of Neurobiology,* 33, 501–516.

Marler, P., and Evans, C. 1996. Bird calls: just emotional displays or something more? *Ibis,* 138, 26–33.

Marler, P., and Tamura, M. 1964. Culturally transmitted patterns of vocal behavior in sparrows. *Science,* 146(3650), 1483–1486.

Marler, P., and Tenaza, R. 1977. Signaling behavior of apes with special reference to vocalizations. In T. A. Sebeok (ed.), *How Animals Communicate,* pp. 965–1033. Indiana University Press, Bloomington.

Marshall, A. J., Wrangham, R., Arcadi, A. C. 1999. Does learning affect the structure of vocalizations in chimpanzees? *Animal Behaviour*, 58, 825–830.

May, B., Moody, D. B., and Stebbins, W. C. 1989. Categorical perception of conspecific communication sounds by Japanese macaques, *Macaca fuscata*. *Journal of the Acoustic Society of America*, 85, 837–847.

Mayford, M., Bach, M. E., Huang, Y-Y, Wang, L., Hawkins, R. D. and Kandel, E. R. 1996. Control of memory formation through regulated expression of a CaMKII transgene. *Science*, 274, 1678–1683.

McComb, K. E. 1991. Female choice for high roaring rates in red deer, *Cervus elaphus*. *Animal Behaviour*, 41(1), 79–88.

McCracken, G. F. 1993. Locational memory and female-pup reunions in Mexican free-tailed bat maternity colonies. *Animal Behaviour*, 45(4), 811–813.

McFarland, D. 1985. *Animal Behaviour: Psychobiology, Ethology, and Evolution*. Pitman, London.

Mitani, J. C., and Brandt, K. L. 1994. Social factors influence the acoustic variability in the long-distance calls of male chimpanzees. *Ethology*, 96, 233–252.

Mollon, J. D. 1990. Uses and evolutionary origins of primate colour vision. In J. R. Cronly-Dillon and R. L. Gregory (eds.), *Evolution of the Eye and Visual System*, pp. 306–319. Macmillan, New York.

Morrice, M. G., Burton, H. R., and Green, K. 1994. Microgeographic variation and songs in the underwater vocalization repertoire of the Weddell seal *(Leptonychotes weddellii)* from the Vestfold Hills, Antarctica. *Polar Biology*, 14, 441–446.

Morris, D. 1957. Typical intensity and its relation to the problem of ritualisation. *Behaviour*, 11, 1–12.

Narins, P. M. 1990. Seismic communication in anuran amphibians. *BioScience*, 40, 268–274.

Nelsen, A. 1987. *History of German Forestry: Implications for American Wildlife Management*. Yale School of Forestry and Environmental Studies, New Haven.

Neumeyer, C. 1990. The evolution of colour vision. In J. R. Cronly-Dillon and R. L. Gregory (eds.), *Evolution of the Eye and Visual System*, pp. 284–305. Macmillan, New York.

Newby, J. 1997. *The Pact for Survival: Humans and Their Animal Companions*. Australian Broadcasting Corporation, Sydney.

Newman, J. D. 1985. Squirrel monkey communication. In L. A. Rosenblum and C. L. Coe (eds.), *Handbook of Squirrel Monkey Research*, pp. 99–126. Plenum Press, New York.

————. 1995. Vocal ontogeny in macaques and marmosets: convergent and divergent lines of development. In E. Zimmermen, J. D. Newman, and U. Jürgens (eds.), *Current Topics in Primate Vocal Communication*, pp. 73–97. Plenum Press, New York,

Newman, J. D., and Symmes, D. 1982. Inheritance and experience in the acquisition of primate acoustic behavior. In C. T. Snowdon, C. H. Brown, and M. R. Petersen (eds.), *Primate Communication*, pp. 259–278. Cambridge University Press, Cambridge.

Nottebohm, F. 1989. From bird song to neurogenesis. *Scientific American*, February, 55–61.

———. 1992. The origins of vocal learning. *The American Naturalist*, 106, 116–140.

Nottebohm, F., Alvarez-Buylla, A., Cynx, J., Kirn, J., Ling, C.-Y., Nottebohm, M., Suter, R., Tolles, A., and Williams, H. 1990. Song learning in birds: the relation between perception and production *Philosophical Transactions of the Royal Society of London*, 390, 115–124.

O'Connell, S., and Cowlishaw, G. 1994. Infanticide avoidance, sperm competition, and mate choice: the function of copulation calls in female baboons. *Animal Behaviour*, 48(3), 687–694.

Oda, R., and Masataka, N. 1996. Interspecies responses of ringtailed lemurs to playback of antipredator alarm calls given by Verreaux sifakas. *Ethology*, 102, 441–453.

Parr, L. A., and de Waal, F. B. M. 1999. Visual kin recognition in chimpanzees. *Nature*, 399, 647–648.

Partan, S., and Marler, P. 1999. Communication goes multimodal. *Science*, 283, 1272–1273.

Patterson, D. K., and Pepperberg, I. M. 1996. A comparative study of human and parrot phonation: acoustic and articulatory correlates of vowels. *Journal of the Acoustical Society of America*, 96, 634–648.

Payne, R. 1995. *Among Whales*. Scribner, London.

Pepperberg, I. M. 1990a. Cognition in an African Gray parrot *(Psittacus erithacus)*: further evidence for comprehension of categories and labels. *Journal of Comparative Psychology*, 104, 41–52.

———. 1990b. Some cognitive capacities of an African Grey parrot *(Psittacus erithacus)*. *Advances in the Study of Behavior*, 19, 357–409.

Pepperberg, I. M., Brese, K. J., and Harris, B. J. 1991. Solitary sound play during acquisition of English vocalisations by an African Grey parrot *(Psittacus erithacus)*: possible parallels with children's monologue speech. *Applied Psycholinguistics*, 12, 1151–1178.

Petitto, L. A., and Marentette, P. F. 1991. Babbling in the manual mode: evidence for the ontogeny of language. *Science*, 251, 1493–1496.

Petrie, M., Halliday, T., and Sanders, C. 1991. Peahens prefer peacocks with elaborate trains. *Animal Behaviour*, 41, 323–331.

Pinker, S. 1994. *The Language Instinct*. Penguin Books, London.

Premack, D. 1975. On the origins of language. In M. S. Gazzaniga and C. Blakemore (eds.), *Handbook of Psychobiology*, pp. 591–605. Academic Press, New York.

Preuschoft, S. 1992. Laughter and "smile" in Barbary macaques *(Macaca sylvanus)*. *Ethology*, 91, 220–236.

Provine, R. R. 1996a. Laughter: the study of laughter provides a novel approach to the mechanisms and evolution of vocal production, perception, and social behavior. *American Scientist*, 84 (January/February), 38–45.

———. 1996b. Contagious yawning and laughter: significance for sensory feature detection, motor patterns generation, imitation, and the evolution of social behavior. In C. M. Heyes and B. G. Galef (eds.), *Social Learning in Animals: The Roots of Culture*, pp. 179–208. Academic Press.London.

Putney, R. T. 1985. Do wilful apes know what they are aiming at? *The Psychological Record*, 35, 49–62.

Ralls, K., Fiorelli, P., and Gish, S. 1985. Vocalizations and vocal mimicry in captive harbor seals, *Phoca vitulina*. *Canadian Journal of Zoology*, 63, 1050–1056.

Randall, J. A. 1994. Discrimination of foot-drumming signatures by kangaroo rats, *Dipodomys spectabilis*. *Animal Behaviour*, 47(1), 45–54.

———. 1997. Species-specific foot-drumming in kangaroo rats: *Dipodomys ingens, D. desertii, D. spectabilis*. *Animal Behaviour*, 54, 1167–1175.

Reiss, D., and McCowan, B. M. 1993. Spontaneous vocal mimicry and production by bottlenose dolphins *(Tursiops truncatus)*: evidence for vocal learning. *Journal of Comparative Psychology*, 107, 301–312.

Rendall, D., Rodman, P. S., and Edmond, R. E. 1996. Vocal recognition of individuals and kin in free-ranging rhesus monkeys. *Animal Behaviour*, 51(5), 1007–1015.

Robinson, F. N. 1991. Phatic communication in bird song. *Emu*, 91, 61–63.

Robinson, F. N., and Curtis, H. S. 1996. The vocal displays of the lyrebirds *(Menuridae)*. *Emu*, 96, 258–275.

Robinson, F. N., and Robinson, A. 1970. Regional variation in the visual and acoustic signals of the male musk duck *(Biziura lobata)*. *CSIRO Wildlife Research*, 15, 73–78.

Rogers, L. J. 1990. Light input and reversal of functional lateralization in the chicken brain. *Behavioural Brain Research*, 38, 211–221.

———. 1995. *The Development of Brain and Behaviour in the Chicken*. CAB International, Wallingford, U.K.

———. 1996, Behavioral, structural, and neurochemical asymmetries in the avian brain: a model system for studying visual development and processing. *Neuroscience and Biobehavioral Reviews*, 20, 487–503.

———. 1997a. Early experiential effects on laterality: research on chicks has relevance to other species. *Laterality*, 2, 199–219.

———. 1997b. *Minds of Their Own: Thinking and Awareness in Animals*. Allen & Unwin, Sydney, and Westview Press, Boulder.

Roitblat, H. L., Harley, H. E., and Helwig, D. A. 1993. Cognitive processing in artificial language research. In H. L. Roitblat, L. M. Herman, and P. E. Nachtigall (eds.), *Language and Communication: Comparative Perspectives*, pp. 1–23. Lawrence Erlbaum, Hillsdale, N.J.

Roitblat, H. L., Herman, L. M., and Nachtigall, P. E. (eds.). 1993. *Language and Communication: Comparative Perspectives*. Lawrence Erlbaum, Hillsdale, N.J.

Rose, S. 1992. *The Making of Memory*. Bantam, London.

Rumbaugh, D. 1995. Primate language and cognition: common ground. *Social Research,* 62, 711–730.

Ryan, M. J., and Keddy-Hector, A. 1992. Directional patterns of female mate choice and the role of sensory biases. *The American Naturalist,* 139, S4-S35.

Ryan, M. J., and Rand, A. S. 1999. Phylogenetic influence on mating call preferences in female túngara frogs, *Physalaemus pustulosus. Animal Behaviour,* 57, 945–956.

Ryan, M. J., Fox, J. H., Wilczynski, W., and Rand, A. S. 1990. Sexual selection for sensory exploitation in the frog *Physalaemus pustulosus. Nature,* 343, 66–67.

Saetre, G.-P., and Slagsvold, T. 1992. Evidence of sex recognition from plumage colour by the pied flycatcher, *Ficedula hypoleuca. Animal Behaviour,* 44(2), 293–299.

Saito, N., and Maekawa, M. 1993. Birdsong: the interface with human language. *Brain and Development,* 15, 31–40.

Savage-Rumbaugh, S., and Lewin, R. 1994. *Kanzi: The Ape at the Brink of the Human Mind.* Wiley & Sons, New York.

Schaller, G. B. (1963. *The Mountain Gorilla.* University of Chicago Press, Chicago.

Schrader, L., and Todt, D. 1993. Contact call parameters covary with social context in common marmosets, *Callithrix j. jacchus. Animal Behaviour,* 46(5), 1026–1028.

Scott, J. P., and Fuller, J. L. 1965. *Genetics and the Social Behavior of the Dog.* University of Chicago Press, Chicago.

Sebeok, T. A., and Umiker-Sebeok, J. (eds.). 1980. *Speaking of Apes: A Critical Anthology of Two-way Communication with Man.* Plenum Press, New York.

Serpell, J. A. (ed.). 1995. *The Domestic Dog: Its Evolution, Behaviour, and Interactions with People.* Cambridge University Press, Cambridge.

Serpell, J. A. 1996. *In the Company of Animals: A Study of Human-Animal Relationships.* Cambridge University Press, Cambridge.

Settle, R. H., Sommerville, B. A. , McCormick, J., and Broom, D. M. 1994. Human scent matching using specially trained dogs. *Animal Behaviour,* 48(6), 1443–1448.

Seyfarth, R. L., and Cheney, D. M. 1986. Vocal development in vervet monkeys. *Animal Behaviour,* 34, 1640–1658.

Seyfarth, R. M., Cheney, D. L., and Marler, P. 1980. Vervet monkey alarm calls: semantic communication in a free-ranging primate. *Animal Behaviour,* 28, 1070–1094.

Shanas, U., and Terkel, J. 1997. Mole-rat harderian gland secretions inhibit aggression. *Animal Behaviour,* 54, 1255–1263.

Silva, A. J., Paylor, R., Wehner, J. M., and Tonegawa, S. 1992. Impaired spatial learning in alpha-calcium-calmodulin kinase II mutant mice. *Science,* 257, 206–211.

Slater, P. J. B. 1986. The cultural transmission of bird song. *Trends in Ecology and Evolution,* 1, 94–97.

———. 1989. Bird song learning: causes and consequences. *Ethology, Ecology, and Evolution,* 1, 19–46.

Slater, P. J. B., and Ince, S. A. 1979. Cultural evolution in chaffinch song. *Behaviour,* 71, 146–166.

Slater, P. J. B., and Jones, A. E. 1997. Lessons in bird song. *Biologist,* 44, 301–303.

Slater, P. J. B., Ince, S. A., and Colgan, P. W. 1980. Chaffinch song types: their frequencies in the population and distribution between the repertoires of different individuals. *Behaviour,* 75, 207–218.

Slobodchikoff, C. N., Kiriazis, J., Fischer, C., and Creef, E. 1991. Semantic information distinguishing individual predators in the alarm calls of Gunnison's prairie dogs. *Animal Behaviour,* 42, 713–719.

Smith, G. T., Brenowitz, E. A., Beecher, M. D., and Wingfield, J. C. 1997. Seasonal changes in testosterone, neural attributes of song control nuclei, and song structure in wild songbirds. *Journal of Neuroscience,* 17, 6001–6010.

Smith, W. J. 1977. *The Behavior of Communicating: An Ethological Approach.* Harvard University Press, Cambridge, Mass.

Snowdon, C. T. 1993. Linguistic phenomena in the natural communication of animals. In H. L. Roitblat, L. M. Herman, and P. E. Nachtigall (eds.), *Language and Communication: Comparative Perspectives,* pp. 175–194. Lawrence Erlbaum, Hillsdale, N.J.

Stager, K. E. 1967. Avian olfaction. *American Zoologist,* 7, 415–420.

Stebbins, W. C. 1983. *The Acoustic Sense of Animals.* Harvard University Press, Cambridge, Mass.

Stoddart, D. M. 1990. *The Scented Ape.* Cambridge University Press, Cambridge.

Stoddart, D. M., Bradley, A. J., and Hynes, K. L. 1992. Olfactory biology of the marsupial sugar glider—a preliminary study. In R.L. Doty and D. Müller-Schwarze (eds.), *Chemical Signals in Vertebrates,* vol. 6, pp. 523–528. Plenum Press, New York.

Suthers, R. A. 1990. Contributions to birdsong from the left and right sides of the intact syrinx. *Nature,* 347, 473–477.

Thorpe, W. H. 1961. *Bird Song.* Cambridge University Press, Cambridge.

Thorpe, W. H., and Griffin, D. R. 1962, Lack of ultrasonic components in the flight noise of owls. *Nature,* 193, 594–595.

Tinbergen, N. 1953. *Social Behaviour in Animals.* Methuen, London.

———. 1960. *The Herring Gull's World.* Basic Books, New York.

———. 1965. *The Study of Instinct.* Clarendon Press, Oxford.

Todt, D. 1975. Social learning of vocal patterns and modes of their application in grey parrots *(Psittacus erithacus). Zeitschrift für Tierpsychologie,* 39, 178–188.

Todt, D., Goedeking, P., and Symmes, D. (eds.). 1988. *Primate Vocal Communication.* Springer, Berlin.

Trainer, J. M. 1989. Cultural evolution in song dialects of yellow-rumped caciques in Panama. *Ethology,* 80, 190–204.

Tudge, C. 1993. *The Engineer in the Garden: Genes and Genetics from the Idea of Heredity to the Creation of Life.* Jonathan Cape, London.

van Hooff, J. A. 1967. The facial expressions of the catarrhine monkeys and apes. In D. Morris (ed.), *Primate Ethology.* Weidenfeld & Nicolson, London.

Waal, F. de, and Lanting, F. 1997. *Bonobo: The Forgotten Ape.* University of California Press, Berkeley.

Waser, P. M., and Waser, M. S. 1977. Experimental studies of primate vocalization: specializations for long-distance propagation. *Zeitschrift für Tierpsychologie,* 43, 239–263.

Watanabe, S. 1993. Visual and auditory cues in conspecific discrimination learning in Bengalese finches. *Journal of Ethology,* 11, 111–116.

Weary, D., and Krebs, J. 1987. Birds learn song from aggressive tutors. *Nature,* 329, 485.

Wenzel, B. M. 1972. Olfactory sensation in the kiwi and other birds. *Annals of the New York Academy of Sciences,* 188, 183–193.

West, M. J., and King, A. P. 1988. Female visual displays affect the development of male song in the cowbird. *Nature,* 334, 244–246.

West, M. J., King, A. P., and Freeburg, T. M. 1997. Building a social agenda for the study of bird song. In C. T. Snowdon and M. Hausberger (eds.), *Social Influences on Vocal Development,* pp. 41–56. Cambridge University Press, Cambridge.

Wickler, W. 1968. *Mimicry in Plants and Animals.* Weidenfeld & Nicolson, London.

Williams, J. M. and Slater, P. J. B. 1990. Modelling bird song dialects: the influence of repertoire size and numbers of neighbours. *Journal of Theoretical Biology,* 145, 487–496.

Wilson, Edward O. 1975. *Sociobiology: The New Synthesis.* 1975. Harvard University Press, Cambridge, Mass.

———. 1984. *Biophilia.* Harvard University Press, Cambridge, Mass.

Yamagiwa, J. 1992. Functional analysis of social staring behavior in an all-male group of mountain gorillas. *Primates,* 33(4), 523–544.

Zahavi, A. 1975. Mate selection: a selection for a handicap. *Journal of Theoretical Biology,* 53, 205–214.

———. 1979. Ritualisation and the evolution of movement signals. *Behaviour,* 72, 77–81.

Zahavi, A., and Zahavi, A. 1997. *The Handicap Principle.* Oxford University Press, Oxford.

Zann, R. 1990. Song and call learning in wild zebra finches in south-east Australia. *Animal Behaviour,* 40, 811–828.

Zuberbühler, K., Cheney, D. L., and Seyfarth, R. M. 1999. Conceptual semantics in a nonhuman primate. *Journal of Comparative Psychology,* 113(1), 33–42.